HOME WORLD

BONNIE MILANI

PROMONTORY PRESS

HOME WORLD

Copyright © 2013 by Bonnie Milani
www.homeworld-the-novel.com

All rights reserved. No part of this publication may be reproduced, stored in a retrieval system, or transmitted, in any form or by any means, electronic, mechanical, photocopying, recording, or otherwise, without the written prior permission of the publisher.

PROMONTORY PRESS
www.promontorypress.com
ISBN: 978-1-927559-24-6
First Edition: August 2013
Cover by Dawn Austin

Typeset at SpicaBookDesign in Caslon

Printed in the United States
0 9 8 7 6 5 4 3 2 1

Every writer has his own Muse.
I've been blessed with a troop of angels to whom I give thanks
here with all my heart and all my soul:

My Angels of the bloody editorial knives:
Angelle Haney Gullett and Craig Sabin

My Inspiration Angels:
E.M. Havens, author of Fate War: Alliance
Annelie Wendeberg, professor extraordinaire and
author of *The Devil's Grin*

And my Mentor Angel:
Author Mary Rosenblum, who believed I had talent when
I didn't believe it myself.

I

The Protector's shuttle dropped into atmosphere above the North American mainland. It raced its sonic boom west across the steel blue waters of the Pacific until the green ridges of the Hawaiian Islands rose from the horizon like broken dragon teeth. Within the quiet luxury of the Protector's private cabin, Jezekiah Van Buren leaned forward for a better view. Even this far out, he recognized the misty outlines of Maui and Kauai to the north of the island chain. To the south, he made out the Big Island, Hawaii itself. And Oahu, dead ahead, its outline etched in his heart.

Home. After three years of living the myth out on the galactic rim, he'd almost convinced himself that Home World was all a fantasy. Now, the beauty of the reality surprised him. Though not half as much, as the thrill he felt just in being here. The shuttle banked north, following the island chain to the space port up on Niihau. Jezekiah twisted in his seat to keep Oahu in sight as long as possible. Foolish to welcome the sight of home. There was nothing for him on Earth: no hope, no freedom – just Mother's duty and Letticia's hatred. He did not want to be here. Yet his body felt the islands' call and his soul sang with joy. Sensors woven into the fabric of the seat picked up the telltale changes in his body's chem signals that betrayed his eagerness and fed them to ShipMind. The shuttle upped screen magnification instantly. Squinting, he glimpsed the sunlit sparkle on Pearl Harbor before it vanished behind the gray-green coast.

"You *sure* your sister ain't going to knife me, Milord?" The worried voice of the pretty boy wearing Jezekiah's clothes broke his reverie.

Milord. The very title sounded like a death knell. He'd managed to forget, these past couple of years, that he was condemned to be the future Lord High Protector of Earth. Jezekiah rose, put on a smile to disguise the loathing in the thought. "Quite. Unless you open your mouth and let her hear that accent." Simple cosmetics let the crewman fake the fiery red hair and impossibly blue eyes of the Great Family Van Buren, but the sweat sheening his skin was real fear. Admirable bravery, nonetheless, for a Sprite. SpriteType was gene coded for beauty, not courage. He pulled the boy's collar straighter, smoothed the silken drape of his double's blouse to show the flame-orchid crest emblazoned on it to better effect. No point telling the boy now that little sister Letticia was not really the reason they were trading places. "Just do the smile and nod. That's all anybody's expecting."

Which was as well, since their disguises consisted of nothing more than hair dye and contact lenses. He could have had the ship's surgeon do a thorough job, of course, But that would have made the switch official. Made it part of the ship's records, got it posted to NetMind. Odds were too great Letticia would be monitoring ship's records, looking for any hint he was planning something exotic. He had no desire to gift dear little Letticia a heads up on this switch. He was too eager to reach the Manor alive.

Jezekiah circled his stand-in, checking for any glaring flaws. The resemblance wouldn't pass more than a casual glance: the boy was a bit younger than his own twenty-three years, a bit narrower in the shoulders. Still, the lad bore himself well, and had a SpriteType's instinctive flair. He swept his jittering doppelganger a formal salaam. "You are perfection personified, Milord."

"Yuh-huh. Scuttlebutt's putting odds on blood, it is. 'T'ain't bettin' in my favor, neither, they ain't."

"The bet's on my blood, not yours."

"Yuh-huh. Less'n your sister gets eager." Pretty Boy's eyes searched his, seeking reassurance. "So why's she want to kill you anyway?"

It was a better question than the boy should be asking. The engineered characteristics that went into the SpriteType gene pack were designed to produce happy-go-lucky personalities in exquisitely beautiful bodies, not deep thinkers. But Type coding only guaranteed looks and talents, not luck. A Sprite who'd been forced to live by his wits the way this one had learned to think about things like surviving the night. He knew how that felt. Rather too well. But those were not memories he could afford at the moment. Or ever, if he had a choice.

"Wish I knew," was all he said. It was the simple, wholehearted truth. Letticia didn't want the Ring. Never had. Nor was she supposed to know anything about her part in the treaty he had worked out. Of course, with Letticia 'wasn't supposed to' didn't mean much. He pretended his sudden shudder was due to the cool air. Still, Kip Marsden would have alerted him had Letticia pried into his node too far; even Lush – no, better learn to think of his baby sister as Letticia – had never outwitted Kip. Yet. So Letticia shouldn't have any reason to want to kill him. Yet she had most certainly spent a goodly part of the past few months trying. That was one of the main reasons he was coming home in such a hurry – he wanted this treaty ratified before that damned assassin of hers got lucky. The other reason was on Den Lupus, preparing his alternatives. If this treaty failed, Strongarm would take the Van Buren Commonwealth down with it.

He couldn't afford to worry that possibility right now. Jezekiah straightened the Sprite's shoulders, tugged the trousers to a sharper crease. "Doesn't matter for you, in any case. *You* will be under the protection of the Protector's own Sec chief. No one is going to risk attacking you." He hoped.

He stood back, considered the effect. Not bad at all, for a joy toy who'd been gracing a petty officer's bed this morning. It would do for distance work, and Kip Marsden would make sure the KnowNet cams kept their distance. Past that – Mother was clued. And on Earth that was all that mattered.

Which bent the odds of making it to the Manor alive in his favor. Assuming, of course, that Letticia hadn't got clever while he'd been gone. Assuming that she hadn't clued her assassin to anticipate precisely such a diversion. He forced the odds on that out of mind. Still, if the last few attempts were any indication, her hired killer would get quite close enough to recognize the substitution. Ideally, just not in time to find Jezekiah in the crew line.

Jezekiah dropped back onto the shuttle's seat. The tendril of ShipMind woven into the soft leather read his measure, molded the cushions to him. He'd lost the habit of luxury these past two years; now, he allowed himself a moment simply to luxuriate in its enveloping comfort. He'd lost his edge in the Family games, too, though. That was the real worry. The little voice at the back of his mind recognized the bitter tinge in the thought. He hadn't *lost* his edge, it murmured. He'd blunted it, deliberately and with enthusiasm. The thought of what Mother would say if he were fool enough to share that particular truth made him grin.

"'T'ain't funny from my end, it ain't." Pretty Boy jammed hands on hips and scowled. "I still got time to back out of this, I do."

Not really, Jezekiah thought, but there was no point in telling the boy so. Maybe he should drug the poor sot after all. Would not do at all if the fellow ran screaming for shelter when he met Letticia's hatred at face range. He decided against it. Mother was clued; terror and Kip Marsden would handle the rest.

"Sorry." He put his working smile on, watched the lad relax at its false re-assurance. "I was just thinking what a lucky sot you are. You will be my personal guest, remember. You get to sleep VIP, eat VIP, even screw VIP if you want. It struck me funny that you should worry."

There, that put the dreamy look back in the lad's eyes. He really was a lucky sot; his dreams were simple. Jezekiah felt a sudden pulse in the energy field encircling his Ring finger and tamped the jealousy down. He'd need to find gloves. Thick ones: the energy field that was the Heir's Ring lit its yellow diamond shell from within. The result wrapped a cold, golden star around his finger. In a crewman's line, it would stand out like a system buoy. Or an assassin's beacon, in this case.

So, then. One more item on the to-do list. For these last few minutes, though, he was still free. If he played his hand right, he'd be back off Earth in a week. Without the Ring this time. Without the threat of the Protectorship hanging over his head. Free, once and for all and forever.

He upped the screens' magnification again, shifted focus to Oahu. The tiny colored flecks he'd seen before bloomed into sails where windsurfers rode the breakers. Beyond them, Diamond Head's blunt cone loomed over the curve of white sand that was Waikiki. The familiar blackened skeletons of ancient towers broke the jungle along the shoreline, a long, dark thread binding the Manor to his Family's history.

"*Scrat me,*" said an awestruck whisper at his shoulder. "Those Home World stories really are true, they are." Pretty Boy had peered out with him, sham dignity forgotten. "Always thought the legends were sawyered, I did." The boy's lips and eyes formed matching o's of wonder. Decidedly not an acceptable Van Buren expression.

"Some of them are. But not Hawaii. There's no need to lie about Hawaii." Which tidbit was itself a lie. Still… no point ruining the lad's fantasy. He'd make a fine bit of free PR once he was back out on the rim. And Makers knew – he corrected the Lupan expression – *God* knew 'free' was all Earth could afford these days.

The shuttle banked lightly, angling toward the great public port on tiny Niihau. *Docking at three minutes, Milord,* ShipMind announced. After two years holding his own on the rim, the title jarred. *The reception party is assembled.*

The muscles between his own shoulder blades tightened with the words. Jezekiah rose, shook his crewman's coverall loose. He touched knuckles to forehead, crewman style, pinched color into the lad's cheek. "Smile. You're on."

He felt the old, cold calculations settle in behind his eyes. His pulse steadied, the old half-smile formed of itself. So, then. He was home.

Earlier Van Buren Protectors had carved Earth's deep space port out of Niihau's broken volcano. Port facilities were carved into the inside curve of the mountain itself, creating a stone pueblo that overlooked the magnificent bay. Shambling along in the sweating crew line, Jezekiah risked a casual check back at the shuttle. Mother's personal ship nestled on the Protector's private landing pad, sleek and slim as a baroque pearl against the sapphire sea. Beyond it, a TransitLine cruise ship was freshly docked at the tip of the curve. The line of disembarking tourists snagged where it snaked behind the glittering dignitaries swarming Mother's dock. Fathers from the full dozen worlds of the Van Buren Commonwealth worlds lifted children onto their shoulders to catch a live-eye glimpse of a Van Buren prince. The children, less concerned with princes than pleasure, squealed in delight and played catch-as-catch-can with the KnowNet cams whisking past.

Nice touch, that cruise ship. Gave him a flood of tourists to blend into. Had to be Mother's work: it would take Van Buren level clearance to permit a *hoi polloi* liner to dock while one of the Family was on the field. Odd though, for Mother – she hadn't allowed the rank and file within weapon range since the Tong rebellion.

"Aw, damn me, they *lied*, they did!" The woman ahead of Jezekiah wobbled to a stop. She had the massive build and albino complexion of the deep space mining clans. Explanation enough for her troubles. In a pinch, a ship-bred miner could survive a good fifteen minutes in full vacuum. In *weather* they were defenseless. Already her skin was reddening in the Hawaiian sun.

And yet… there was wonder in her eyes. Glancing down the queue Jezekiah saw that wonder reflected in a hundred faces. He'd seen it in a thousand tourist vids, some of them his own propaganda. The difference was that this time he felt it himself. This time he, too, felt every cell in his body thrill to the feel of Earth. He felt the pull, the sense that *this place* was right, that this was where he *belonged*. Genetic manipulation had adapted humanity to survive the physical demands of other worlds. But even the most radically engineered Types, even polymorphic LupanType, were still fundamentally human. Earth was *home world*, and every cell in every body on that dock knew it.

The wonder still shone in the miner's eyes when her knees gave out. She dropped straight, nearly taking Jezekiah with her.

"Where you popper?" Jezekiah asked, using crew pidgin. Clansmen normally packed small, pop-up umbrellas to protect their skins from planetside suns. The umbrellas also prevented ship bred miners from attacks of psychotic agoraphobia at the sight of open sky, but no one with a sense of self-preservation reminded them of that.

"No thought t'need it. It's Paradise they said." She breathed deep, nearly choked on air wet and heavy with the scents of ocean salt and metal tang. "It's *lie*, they did."

"No lie. Just summer." Jezekiah looked up as an airborne Sec cam buzzed the line. It slowed as it reached him, and he felt his skin tingle as it ran bioscan check on him.

"No screens, either – *scrat* that thing!" The miner woman swung her duffle bag wide off her shoulder, making the Sec cam bounce in its wake.

"Good shot." The cam zoomed off, apparently satisfied. Still, he'd been spotted, no question. So, then. He could expect to find Kip Marsden waiting for him the other side of customs. Which couldn't be soon enough. *Damn*, it was hot out here. "Need hand?" he asked as the miner doubled over her duffle, wheezing.

"It's no groundhog dainty can be carryin' me." Her words were stronger than her voice.

"Lender, only," Jezekiah said. He offered her his free arm, bracing himself so the weight she put on it wouldn't stagger him. Truth was, it felt good to simply be himself, do simple, honest work. Good to be able to speak from his heart, for himself. Likely the last time he'd dare such honesty, he thought, and his little voice chided him for the resentment.

Besides, he'd forgotten himself just how sticky hot Hawaii's weather really was. The crew's customs line snaked along the unshielded section of the dock, leaving the off-world hands to either exult or fry in the Hawaiian sun while they inched toward the bureaucrats manning the crew customs booths.

A hundred feet or so ahead a trio of towering pylons flanked Niihau Port's customs terminal. Open scanner booths filled the space between the pylons' stone bases. Tourist scans, those. Their section of the dock was weather shielded. *Paying* visitors were sheltered from the unpleasant inconvenience of real weather. Mother wasn't about to disappoint the chow line. For once, Jezekiah caught himself resenting the fact.

"Damme, worse'n scrattin' Streiker, it is." The miner wheezed, leaned on him hard.

"T'ain't, either." Jezekiah drew breath to chuckle at the defensiveness in his tone, wound up choking on a gush of hot, wet air instead. "Chance, at least, on Home World."

"*Fuh*. Maybe." On Streiker, parents careless enough to birth a natural were sterilized. The baby itself was simply thrown out onto the blue Streikern ice.

She eyed him speculatively, suddenly curious. "You Home World local, I bet. Maker, maybe, I bet."

"Half true." Alone of all the worlds of the Commonwealth, only Earth still produced true, genetically unmodified human beings. Only on Earth, on Home World, could one still find completely *natural* humans, those astonishingly unpredictable people untouched by genetic engineering whose looks and talents and traits were determined by luck rather than a pre-packaged Type code. Only Home World still housed Makers. Made for improbable FunNet romances on the rim and unenviable living conditions on Earth. Among the Lupans, Makers ranked one step below God Himself.

"Got hard body check coming, you do, yeah?" The miner's voice called Jezekiah's attention back to the line.

"Yeah." Dark memories tried to well up. He shoved them down. Not in time.

The miner straightened, though the motion cost her, and laid a kindly hand on his shoulder. "Give for take – tell 'em you miner clan, you want. Jump you in my own self, you want." She managed a leer in compliment and gold-capped teeth flashed in the sun.

"Thanks, but can't." It was no mean offer. She might be nothing more than hired crew on Earth, but she had the rank to grant him status within her own clan. He pried her fingers from his shoulder enough to kiss their tips. "Got family waiting other side." That half of said family was trying to kill him wasn't her worry.

"Your call." She wheezed in earnest. Bad sign; humidity out here would rot her lungs if she stayed unsheltered too long.

Craning to see past the curve of the line, Jezekiah ran his gaze past the dark uniforms of the crew and customs folk, looking for Kip Marsden's broad figure. He caught the recurrent flash of reflected sunlight from the transit shuttle station at the terminal exit. But no sign of Kip Marsden. A flicker of fresh worry tickled his gut. That Sec cam had already registered his biopat. Plugged into NetMind as he was, Kip would have pinpointed his location on the instant. Ought to be a whole Sec team strolling the dock by now. So where was he?

Damn and damn again. He had a whole new problem, if Kip didn't show. Crew customs might not be as comfortable as the tourists', but its scanners were just as efficient. He almost wished for a moment he truly was an Earth-born natural. Then he could stride through bioscan with impunity – without a Type's genetic ID code, the man-made interstellar brain that was NetMind could not 'see' him. As it was, even the most cursory scan would spot his biopat in a heartbeat. At which point bureaucratic hell would break lose. Which was precisely the kind of ruckus his would-be killer would be looking for.

Something pale near the booth's pylon caught his eye. A man in a light suit, broad-brimmed hat pushed back on his white-blond hair, shouldered through the in-coming queue. He was tall enough to seem slender, but his lazy sneer made a burly deckhand change his mind about shoving back.

Aryans. Jezekiah let the miner's weight bow him a bit lower. Trouble by definition. *Ugly* trouble if Mother had the Aryans looking for him instead of Kip Marsden. AryanType was hard-coded suspicious, and Mother's interrogators were trained to indulge the trait. The Aryan ran his cold, blue gaze across the nearest crew folk without interest, then settled his back against a pylon, pulling his broad-brimmed hat low against the sun. Watching.

Interesting, his little voice murmured. The Aryan carried no scanner. Despite the heat Jezekiah shivered. The fellow looked vaguely familiar, though he couldn't put a name to the face. Could only mean he was attached to the

Manor staff. It also meant the fellow would know him. He'd certainly be easy enough to spot. Even an eyeball scrutiny would recognize him under the hair dye and contacts, if someone knew who to look for. The Aryan was obviously looking. Looking eyeball only, keeping it out of Net. Easy enough to vanish him, too, out of Net.

So, then. Little sister Letticia had learned to hedge her bets. Be easy enough to spin a tale for the Aryans, send them looking for an imposter. Might not even have needed a cover story. A simple order would suffice; Aryans would carry out any Van Buren order that didn't directly threaten Mother. Letticia could have him picked off out here and cry *ooops* later. Quite a nice idea, actually, his little voice noted. Warranted remembering. Assuming, of course, he survived it.

For a moment, he considered simply pulling off his gloves. Let the Heir's Ring proclaim his identity. That was the easy way out, the path of perks and privileges. The path he'd vowed to escape. He left the gloves on.

Beside him, the miner doubled over, gasping, her face a dangerous shade of red. Jezekiah wrapped her arm over his shoulder, half-dragged her to the shade of the port wall. Helped that the move put the crew queue between himself and the Aryan.

Jezekiah lowered her to a squat, eased her head down to her knees. No question that she needed a medic. Stretching, he spotted the medics' Helping Hand sign just beyond the crew customs booth and nearly whooped with delight. The medics' booth ran straight through the mountain wall to open out on the terminal passage. Once inside he could simply catch a tour car to the Manor.

He squeezed the miner's shoulder gently. "Stay put. I'm going to send help." Head down, he eased toward the customs booth, trailing a hand along the rock face like a spacer who'd yet to find his groundhog legs. Keeping the queue between himself and the Aryan, Jezekiah stumbled toward the 'authorized staff' door at the back of the customs booth.

"Good try, monk. Get back in line." A customs agent blocked his way with a scrawny arm. The man's features had the humorless set of a NumbersType whose parents were either too poor or too cheap to pay for anything more than the most basic gene pack.

"Need water," Jezekiah croaked. Hot as it was he didn't even have to fake it.

"Yeah, sure. You and every other monkey trying to dodge scan." The agent moved to shove him back.

Jezekiah locked the agent's hand on his shoulder. He leaned forward and put heart and soul into preliminary retching noises.

"Gobbing monkey! Get over there!" The agent dodged aside, shoved him hard and fast toward the Helping Hand counter. "Just make sure you check yourself through here afterward!"

Hand clamped over his mouth, Jezekiah waved a bleary assent.

It was already crowded inside the station, and raucous. Crew folk provided the crowd, jump suited men and women huddled arms-on-knees in the chairs lining the walls. The ruckus came from a group of bejeweled Pandari merchants whose retainers were demanding personal heaters at the top of their collective and impressive lungs.

The humans who had settled Pandar world had been gene-coded to survive the mummifying aridity and UV radiation of Pandar's blue-white sun. Even within the protection of the terminal's weather screens, this lot needed breathing filters to survive Hawaii's humid air. They huddled together in a brilliant clump, embroidered collars pulled up around their ears, nictating membranes flickering in distress across their eyes. The metallic threads on their robes raised rainbow reflections on their blue-black skin that matched the enameled patterns of their breathing filters.

A harried medic shoved a teardrop container of water into Jezekiah's hand in passing, and Jezekiah let himself sag against the wall, cradling its moist coolness against his face. The coolness revived the cold little voice at the back of his mind, reminded him he needed to get out of here.

After he kept his promise. He was past the Aryan's line of sight here. Already ID'd, too: every doorway in every public building had bioscanners built into it. The medical staff might be too busy to monitor scan, but SecNet would have fed his reading straight into Kip Marsden's link. Even if not – he could slip his hand into any sync link in the terminal, and the resources of the planet were his. He didn't need to run any more. At least, not yet.

Jezekiah worked his way over to an open bin of water teardrops behind the staff counter near the terminal side door. He filched an armload of teardrops from the bin, eyeballed the terminal passage for his escape route while he shoved them into a Helping Hand carryall. Fifty feet beyond the station, the terminal arched open onto a fern studded stone plaza. Through the exit arch, he could see the sunlit flash of departing transit cars. He hoisted the carryall higher on his shoulder. All he needed now was to collar a medic and he'd be on one of those cars.

Odd, though. Still no sign of Kip. He ran a quick scan down the terminal passage as he turned back toward the dockside of the station. No Kip – but he glimpsed a different figure lounging against a comm kiosk, watching the other tourists trudge past with professional indifference. He'd half-seen that figure on half a dozen worlds between here and Den Lupus, felt that presence in his gut.

So, then. So much for keeping his word. No hope of keeping his promise now, nor time to mourn the loss. He closed his eyes against the upswell of shame. *No choice*, his little voice urged. He needed to be out of here before the assassin spotted him. Dead, he was no good to anyone.

Jezekiah bumped into one of the Pandari retainers. He used a bowed apology to put the woman's voluminous robes between himself and the assassin's line of sight. Realized with a shock of relief that the jeweled pattern of her robes marked her as a medic. Stifling a grin, he shocked her to silence with a hand clamped around her shoulders. He had her steered half-way to the dockside door before her nictating membranes stopped flickering enough for her to actually take note of him.

"No questions." Jezekiah used his formal voice, tone calculated to demand obedience. "A Van Buren operative needs your aid. You'll find her squatting against the wall by the crew line. Treat her well." Jezekiah shoved the carryall of water into the medic's hands. He clasped the retainer's shoulder, added a meaningful smile. "The Protector will reward you. Now go."

Eyes still flickering, the medic swung the carryall over her bejeweled shoulder and strode outside.

So, then. He'd kept the dirt out of his soul a few minutes longer. Elbowing his way back to the water bin, Jezekiah filled another carryall. He swung it over his shoulder and strode out of the Helping Hand booth's terminal door and into the trudging mass of tourists. With luck, the assassin would take him for one of the station hands assigned to keep newcomers lubricated until their transportation arrived.

Only his luck didn't hold. He made the mistake of looking back just before he reached the exit. Down the corridor, the assassin looked up, looked his way. And smiled a feline, predatory smile.

Damn! Jezekiah's mouth went dry. Only chance now was to reach the next transit car before the assassin got within range. There were a couple of still-empty cars at the stop. Around him, the crowd of tourists slowed as they hit the hot, humid wall of Hawaiian air. He shifted the carryall higher on his shoulder and picked up his pace. If he beat the tourists, he could commandeer the car before the assassin caught up.

Something hard hit him hard in the chest. Jezekiah slammed the carryall around into it, his pulse jumping.

"*Hei*, you!" A short young woman in a red sarong glared up at him from beneath a skewed plumeria wreath. She took in his crewman's coverall and changed the glare to a smile of patently false welcome.

Joy toys, he thought. "Sorry," he muttered, and moved to skip past.

"You wan' gul? Show you good time, eh?" She was barely shoulder height on him, but she shifted with him to block his path.

"*Later*."

Her smile widened, though not enough to touch her eyes. Clearly this was a girl who did not enjoy her work. Odd, then, that her stable master hadn't used Seed on her – but no, not odd, not on Earth. Grandfather Ho didn't distribute

Venus Seed on Earth. Mother'd seen to that. He brushed past her and kept walking.

"Eh, wha' kine spacer no wan' gul?" She back tracked with him. "You stay come. Give good time, eh?" She was a tasty little piece, some primal section of his mind noted. Buxom but willow-hipped and lithe. With clear brown skin that bespoke fresh air and sunshine rather than a Seed sot's haggard, driven lust.

"No money." He said it sharper this time, and louder. He put his free hand out, palm up in peace sign, and brushed past her again. Behind him, he could hear a flock of tourists gaining ground, aiming for the nearest transit car.

"No hu-hu. You pay later." She skipped ahead to block him again, giving him a view down her cleavage that tickled his groin.

Damned determined little piece. Or desperate. He refused to let himself consider the kind of penalty she must face for failure. "Later." He didn't need to fake the desperation in his own voice. He lengthened his stride to jogging pace.

The joy toy jogged backward with him. She wasn't even sweating, he noticed with envy. "*Heia*, you don' like gul?" Her gaze took on a narrow-eyed assessment – tinged, he noted, with relief. "You wan' boy, eh? You come. Got lots pretty boy."

"No!"

She skipped into his path, nearly tripping him. Sidelong, he saw her throw a glance past his shoulder. He followed her line of sight to a trio of groundskeepers with the boulder builds of Samoans. Even in this sun, only one of them – an ambulatory mountain with a gleaming, black mole at the corner of his jaw – wore a broad rimmed straw hat. They were watching the exchange with interest. And ambling closer.

Damn and damn again! The exchange had cost him precious moments. The tourists flocked past to engulf the transit car. Jezekiah swore softly. The only other empty car sat at the end of the plaza, far enough off to discourage most travelers. He shifted the carryall to the other shoulder, forcing the girl to skip out of its way.

Behind him the Samoans had spread out across the path. Their broad figures blocked his view of the terminal. Which was as well, since they also blocked the assassin's sight of him. He'd have been relieved, had mole face not been grinning so broadly. The sight stirred memories that he refused to awake.

It took him two steps before the realization struck home. He glanced back again, mouth suddenly dry. *Not* a mole on that Samoan. It was a tracker stud, one of a pair that would be embedded in temple and jaw. The mark of a Registered killer. That explained the hat.

So, then. He was being herded.

He lengthened his stride abruptly. Swearing, the joy toy grabbed his arm. No invite this time. Her grip was hard as a man's. Whirling, Jezekiah swung the carryall hard at the girl's head.

She dodged, stepped in under it to jab her fingers into Jezekiah's wrist. His arm went numb. She yanked the sack out of his hand, smacked the carryall into his midriff hard enough to double him around it. He heard the water slosh near his ears. Then her knee caught him between the eyes and the world went black.

II

Jezekiah came to amid a jumble of voices. He kept still, shamming unconsciousness while he tried to assess his situation. He was stretched out on what felt like a couch, one that smelled surprisingly clean despite the musty dampness of the air. There was light beyond the ember of pain that sulked between his eyes, and a murmur of voices.

Cautiously, he flexed the muscles in his arms, noted with relief that the feeling was back. Odd, though: they hadn't tied him. Or gagged him, for that matter. He ran a mental scan down his body, feeling for bindings. Nothing. Wherever he was, his kidnappers were obviously not worried about keeping him. He forced down a surge of fear at the implication there. He willed himself still, let his little voice quick-calc probabilities.

So, then. They weren't being nasty, yet. That was a trick, most likely, but it just might suggest they were willing to be bought. If so, he was in luck. If not, it gave him a probing point, a lead to his captors' weakness. One way or the other, he'd have to work quickly. He had to reach Mother before Strongarm arrived. The stakes were too high to fail now.

Somewhere nearby, a chair creaked. "Stop worrying," a woman's voice said, and Jezekiah felt his breath catch. It was a young voice, the tone part dismissive, part defensive. *Letticia?* He thought, and his pulse shot ice. No – the tone lacked his little sister's sneer. Still, some distant part of his mind recognized the speaker. "Ask him yourself," she added. "He's been eavesdropping a while now."

"How you feeling, your Lordship?" A man's voice, husky and warm, spoke near Jezekiah's ear.

The shock of that voice popped Jezekiah's eyes open, wide, making the ember of pain behind his eyes flare to life. "Kip?"

"Yuh-huh." Rudyard Kipling Marsden grinned at him from eye level. The worry lines creasing his dark forehead had deepened these past two years. More gray streaked the tight curls above his chocolate face, so the silver arc of the command link embedded in his skull above one ear stood out a little less brightly. Yet even hunched on a chair, elbows on knees, he was unmistakably SecType: long legs hinting at height designed to intimidate, broad shoulders and muscled forearms bespeaking the strength to overpower. It was the laugh lines crinkling at the corner of his eyes that made him utterly and uniquely Kip. "How you feelin', your lordship?" he asked again. "Mote here says she didn't break anything. She didn't, did she?" There was a shadow of doubt in his voice this time.

"Just my head." Jezekiah pushed himself up on an elbow. Mistake. The pain between his eyes ratcheted higher. He closed his eyes again, tried to will himself to ignore it.

"Here, let me –" That was the woman's voice.

He felt her breath on his cheek, recognized the plumeria's honeyed scent. Jezekiah jerked back by instinct when her hands touched his face. She held him still, while her fingers worked magic along his temples.

"Okay, try that," she said. Much too soon.

Jezekiah realized he was holding his breath. He let it out cautiously and inched his eyes open. The pain was gone.

"Feel better, your lordship?"

Damn if Kip didn't sound like a proud father. Jezekiah swiveled his head cautiously. "As a matter of fact, yes." This Mote had definite possibilities. Even the tension knotting his neck was gone.

"Told you I didn't hurt him, Captain," the girl Mote said. She ignored the grunt of disagreement from Jezekiah and started to rise.

He caught her hand to stop her. "Would you mind telling me –" he forgot the rest. Her hand felt more like pumice stone than flesh. He frowned down at it, took in the outsized ridge of her scarred knuckles, felt the calluses edging her palm. Samurai hands. He lifted the frown to her face, got a wary scowl in return.

Close-up, she was younger than he'd thought, not more than eighteen. Definitely a natural. She had a Samurai's square face under decidedly unSamurai black curls. Her eyes had an islander's happy lilt that seemed to smile despite her scowl. His little voice snapped at him that he had no business smiling back.

"My *name*," she said, and there was no smile in her voice, "is Keiko Yakamoto. That's 'cake-o' to you. Call me a piece of cake at your own –" She cut that off at Kip's warning cough, jerked her chin up to a defiant jut.

"Mote here's Admiral Yakamoto's daughter," Kip added.

"Ah." Jezekiah suppressed a shiver of sympathy. "Well, that certainly answers most of my questions. I take it your father trained you–" He felt his jaw drop. "Yakamoto's daughter. Working with Samoans? With *Tong* ops?"

"Captain said you had an assassin after you." She folded her arms across her breasts, tucked her chin in, dark eyes inviting challenge. Would have been more effective had the plumeria wreath not slid down over one eye. She yanked it off, jammed it under her arm. "He said to get you out of Niihau, and make it look natural." She recognized the inadvertent pun, realized she'd left herself open. Jezekiah watched her lips tense, knew she was waiting for him to make a cruel joke out of it.

He didn't. He had experience enough, now, to understand just how much it would hurt.

His silence took some of the fight out of her posture. "If he'd told me you only like boys, I wouldn't have-"

"I prefer girls, actually." Which was true, when he had a choice. "But – *Samoans?*"

"Oh, them. They're no hu-hu."

"Indeed. After what your father did to the Tong during the Rebellion, any one of those Samoans should have killed you on sight."

"Told you no hu-hu. Grandfather loaned them to me." She shuffled, shifted attention to Kip. "You don't need me anymore, do you, Captain?"

"Yes, he does."

It came out sharp enough to put a flash in those lilting eyes. Keiko snapped the wreath off at Jezekiah as if it were a Tong throwing star. He caught it, touched flowers to his lips to hide his grin and put on an answering scowl of his own. Considering the implications in that name it was harder to do than it should have been. He lifted a questioning brow at Kip. "Grandfather?"

"Yuh-huh." Kip Marsden shuffled unhappily.

"Grandfather *Ho?*" Jezekiah blinked disbelief at Kip, blinked again at Kip's nod. Good thing he was already seated. The confirmation would have sat him down anyway. "*Himself?*"

"Old man Ho's got a soft spot for the kid. Mote – Keiko's – mother was islander." Interesting. A sudden shadow of sorrow flickered across Kip's face. A sorrow he clearly did not want this Keiko to see. He wrapped his hand around the girl's ear and pulled her into a fatherly head lock.

"Don't you go getting bright ideas about it, either, eh?" She ducked out of Kip's hand, fists coming up clenched. "I am *not* like her! I do *not* go whoring."

"I didn't think you had. Quite the contrary." He watched her blush, stifled a satisfied grin at the confirmation of his expectations. So, then. She was still a virgin. The thought pleased him more than it should. His little voice reminded him he had more important business on the table, and precious little time to attend it. And yet... "Does your father know about the Samoans?"

That stopped her. Jezekiah watched her blush drain to white. He frowned a question at Kip, got a head shake for answer. So, then. Working with Sec was the least of the things this Keiko Yakamoto was hiding from her father. Definitely a girl with promise. "So why did Grandfather Ho lend you those enforcers?"

"What you want to hear, Van Buren? I told Grandfather I was going to be covering you and he told me to take the homies along for back up. *Pau.* Finish. Nothing else to tell."

Jezekiah glanced at Kip. "The Samoans were *Grandfather's* idea?"

"Yuh-huh." He let the implications hang unspoken.

Interesting indeed. Grandfather Ho had put his own ops at risk to protect the Van Buren Heir. Which meant he wanted something, something only the Heir could provide. The thought re-knotted the muscles in his neck. Grandfather Ho's spies were at least as good as Mother's. The Tong chief would certainly know about the treaty he'd worked out with Strongarm. He could only hope the old man hadn't found out what was in it. "You're quite sure he didn't give you a message?"

"*Haoles.*" Keiko put enough contempt into the islander term for non-natives to earn a poke from Kip. She shrugged an apology – to Kip, he noticed, not himself. "You don't believe me, go ask him yourself, eh?"

"I think I shall have to." Old, red memories welled up. He rose, slapped at his coveralls, wishing he could slap the memories down. "At the moment, however, I need to report to Mother."

"I got to go now, too. Admiral start wondering if I don't turn up soon."

Kip shot Jezekiah an inquiring glance, waited till Jezekiah nodded. "Yeah, Mote, you're good to go."

Her bare toes scuffed at the stone floor in her eagerness to leave, but her eyes pleaded with the big man. "You won't tell the Admiral, eh? He finds out –" She darted a sidelong glance at Jezekiah, questioned Kip with her eyes. He noted with satisfaction that Kip shook his head in reassurance.

"You know me better than that, Mote."

"Yeah, well…" She shrugged in Jezekiah's direction, as much apology as he was going to get. "I've got Type trial coming up. I just don't want to give the Admiral a reason to make it any harder than it's going to be already." Keiko turned on her bare heel and slipped out though the cabin door.

He watched her close it behind herself. His little voice tutted he had no reason to hope she'd at least glance back at him. Or feel disappointed she didn't.

Yet disappointment wasn't the reason his eyes lingered on the door. He lifted a brow at Kip. "That's a manual door. Don't think I've ever seen a door you had to close by hand."

"Won't see 'em anyplace but Earth, neither. It's a natural's cabin. Real thing.

No sync access at all." Kip stretched, making the handle of a heavy caliber pacifier bulge beneath the arm of his loose cotton jacket. "No scanners, neither."

So, then. Letticia wasn't the only one keeping his whereabouts out of Net. Except that even on Earth there was only one group of true, genetically untouched naturals left. He quick-calc'd the implications there, felt the muscles in his neck knot up. "A Tong cabin."

"Yeah, well, technically it's a gardener's hut. Works out the same." Kip drew his pacifier, grinned reassurance at Jezekiah before he checked the pistol's power light. "Sure as hell couldn't have those Samoans deliver you to the Manor. So we needed a safe house. One that wouldn't tip the little bi- uh, your little sister to your whereabouts. Mote suggested this one."

"How far are we from the Manor?"

"Already on the grounds, your lordship." Kip re-holstered the pacifier, strode to the door. He twisted the handle, stepped back to usher Jezekiah out. "We can walk over to Madam's office in ten minutes."

Outside, the air was scented with ginger and gardenia. And only a hint of moisture, Jezekiah noted with relief. He allowed himself a moment to give thanks to whatever past genius had invented weather shielding before he stepped out into the courtyard to survey the area. The cabin was a converted storefront, last in a row of identical chambers forming a semi-circle around a courtyard of red-brown flagstones. Beside the cabin, an ancient wall towered a full story above his head, its stone gone mossy green beneath a flowering trumpeter vine. Fallen blossoms dusted the shadows red.

It all felt vaguely familiar. Jezekiah ran a fingertip down one bell horn flower while he tried to place the feeling. The tickle of memory vanished in the sudden challenge of an outraged hummingbird. He conceded territory with upraised hands, turned to see if Kip was ready. And saw the scorch marks marring the far side curve of the storefront row.

Memories flooded back then: a sunlit picnic day, the sun glare on Mother's white blouse. Remembered the scrape of his shoes as he raced Letticia across this courtyard. Then the whistle in the air, the sudden red spatter of his father's blood across this wall. The day happiness ended.

"Sorry 'bout I hadda bring you here, your lordship."

"No problem. It's the price of the Protectorship." He managed a tight smile for Kip, strode out to where the plaza opened onto a vista of the great Pacific.

Beyond, the earth sloped away toward Waikiki and its dark, wild ruins, death masks of the old NorthAm empire. From here, he could make out the brilliant rainbow mosaic still clinging to one shattered tower. He let the salt air wash out the memories.

Lupan work, those ruins. Strongarm's ancestors, not Ho Tong. That thought triggered a shiver. Dangerous as the old man was, at least Grandfather Ho was human-only. The Lupans –

Too bad, he told himself, and felt his heart clench. The Lupans were his ticket out of the Protectorship. He'd play them as hard as he needed. Only they would do worse to Earth this time, if he failed.

He heard Kip step up behind him. Jezekiah turned his back on the sea to join him. "So why the change in plan?"

"Tell you while we walk." Kip started toward the courtyard's inland exit. He stopped, grimaced, then marched back to close the cabin door by hand.

They left the plaza, turned inland at the end of the wall onto the landscaped promenade of old Kalakaua Avenue. The big man set a pace worthy of Strongarm's hunting lope. Jezekiah had to stretch to keep up. The SecType ran scan as they walked. His gaze swept their path, head cocked, eyes flicking from spot to spot in short, precise motions. Targeting.

Gravel crunched under their boots while Jezekiah calc'd out the unhappy implications. "I take it that assassin managed to dodge your folk." He switched position to walk on Kip's left, leaving the big man's gun arm free.

"Yuh-huh." Kip slowed his pace, eyes targeting the flowering oleander lining the walk. Then threw Jezekiah face down and whirled, laser pistol out and ready.

"*Heia*, no hu-hu, eh?"

"Damn it, Mote! When you gonna learn to announce yourself?" Kip holstered the gun. "I could'a shot you!"

"I'd have ducked."

From his serpentine vantage point, Jezekiah watched a pair of hard calloused feet skip past. He resisted the impulse to steal a glance up the sarong skirt above them and simply scrambled to his feet. He most certainly did not want Kip to haul him up like a helpless pup in front of Keiko Yakamoto.

She grinned up into Kip's scowl. "Teufelsman's tracking you."

"Yeah, I know." Kip cocked his head, looking inward to check scan feed. "His log says he's 'escorting the Heir'." He snorted in disgust, but Jezekiah noted the worry beneath it.

Evidently, Keiko did as well. "I get him gone right quick. Borrow a spec sack?"

"Huh." Kip pulled in a breath long in patience, then snapped a stasis pouch out of a jacket pocket. "I do *not* want another complaint filed with the Admiral, hear?"

"No hu-hu. Makes two of us, eh?" She winked conspiratorially at Jezekiah, then vanished back into the shrubs lining the gravel path. It took Jezekiah several determinedly calming breaths to realize she'd made no sound at all.

"Teufelsman?" The AryanType name clicked into place with the face. "I saw him on the dock, eyeballing the crew line. He didn't spot me. So how did he know I was here?"

"Ask your little sister. I sure as hell didn't request him."

Somewhere deeper in the bushes a man yelped. The yelp morphed into venomous German. An oleander bush twitched and Keiko skipped back onto the path. The bulging stasis pouch dangled from the waist folds of her sarong. "You mind if I tag along with you two, Captain?" Keiko rocked on the balls of her feet, regarding Kip with exaggerated innocence.

"Yeah, think you better." Kip shook himself, reminding Jezekiah unexpectedly of Strongarm. At his nod Keiko danced ahead, leaving Jezekiah and Kip to bring up the rear.

Watching hers, Jezekiah decided it was a very attractive rear. "So why use Keiko as a diversion?"

"She wasn't the diversion, your lordship. I was." Kip tapped the silver crescent above his ear. "I'm permanently sync'd into Net, so I'm real easy to track. I figured the little bi- uh, Young Mistress Letticia would be expecting me to escort you off the shuttle. So I did." He grinned suddenly, a startling flash of white teeth in his dark face. "Sure wish you coulda seen your sister's face when I brought up that doppelganger. If looks could cook, that boy'd be soup."

"You didn't leave him with her?" The thought triggered a horrified chill.

"Nah, your lordship. The boy's sittin' pretty with a couple of like-minded Sec ops. I'll send him home paid and happy once I've got you safe'n sound."

"Good. Give him a VIP tour before he goes. Surviving a face-to-face with Letticia merits recognition. By the way -" Up ahead, Keiko paused to let a butterfly rest on a finger and he forgot the rest of the sentence.

"*Way*, Your lordship?" No mistaking the way Kip's targeting gaze suddenly focused on him. Or the tingle of scan, checking his biopat for telltales.

He didn't like what the answers would show, either. Jezekiah willed his pulse to a properly disinterested rate. He still earned himself a disapproving grunt. "By the way... You'll be hearing from a Pandari medic looking for a reward for services rendered. Make sure she's paid; she's telling the truth."

"Huh. First time for everything, I guess." Kip tilted his head slightly, eyes focused inward on the Sec grid his comm implant flashed him. "Speakin' of first times, your lordship-"

"I shall keep my paws off Mistress Yakamoto." Jezekiah salaamed with sincerity. The man was right. Keiko Yakamoto was decidedly not an evening's entertainment. More like a lifetime's investment. And that was time he did not have, not on Earth.

Ahead, Keiko pirouetted to check a low archway. Smoky glass shafts of ancient escalators still tied this section of Kalakaua Avenue to memories of the old NorthAm shopping centers that used to line this area. A matched set of metal stairs dropped away into underground caverns here, where ancient Americans had parked their cars and Ho Tong their bomb squads.

She caught Kip's unspoken command and danced back to join them. "Don't feel anybody down there." Her tone was pure business, cool and professional. "Want me to go down and check?"

"Not hardly. That goddamned assassin's not showing in Net anywhere. If he's down there – " Kip started to say something, decided against it. But his expression went grim.

Easy enough to guess what it was. There were only two ways that assassin could have got off the dock undetected: either he lacked a Type code altogether, or he'd found a way to disguise it. Either way the implications chilled Jezekiah's gut.

"No hu-hu." Keiko pulled the stasis pouch from her sarong's folds, held it up. "If he's there, he'll be near the base of the stairs. Find out easy enough."

She opened the pouch gingerly, twirled it at her side as she jogged back to the archway. The breeze washed a familiar, unpleasant odor back to Jezekiah. She snapped off its contents as she passed the opening and dove.

Silence.

"All clear." Keiko rose, dusted herself primly.

"I'm obviously missing something here." Jezekiah followed Kip's nod to join her. "What makes you so sure?"

"You hear anybody yelping?" Her chin lifted in challenge.

"That hardly-"

"You catch dog shit in the face, Van Buren, you yelp." She wiggled the brown-smeared pouch at him at fingertip length. "Ask Teufelsman."

Kip threw his hands up in exasperation. "God damn it, Mote, I told you I don't want-"

"He called me a Tong whore." This time the chin set bespoke danger.

She thought she'd kept her shame private. But Mother had selected Jezekiah's gene pack with diplomacy in mind, then honed talents to skill. He recognized the shame of honor too hard won and too often doubted. Recognized it and felt it echo deep in the hidden dungeons of his soul. For a moment he almost regretted – he cut the thought off. There was no future in it.

"I rather doubt Teufelsman will risk a complaint." He allowed himself to visualize the image that suggested and found himself grinning like a Lupan.

"Yuh-huh." Kip's shoulders shook with suppressed laughter. "Mote, why don't you take point? And get that damned pouch outta my nose."

Keiko dropped the pungent stasis pouch in a nearby litter bin then skipped ahead. Jezekiah felt his groin answer the smile she flashed at Kip.

He tried to cling to the good cheer. His little voice refused. *Kip Marsden couldn't find that assassin in Net.* Kip, who was Mother's personal sync meister, whose very essence was literally entwined in NetMind. Kip, who had access to every detail of every living human on every human world in and out of the Van Buren Commonwealth except the Protectors themselves. And he was good enough to sawyer his way into those if Mother needed him to. All he required was that the human have a Net entry.

He quick-calc'd odds on the Assassin's Guild breeding a true, genetically random natural. The odds came back at dismissive infinitesimals. Genuine un-Typed naturals were rare even on Earth. With good reason: the genetic markers that defined each Type were more than mere talent predictors, more by far than simple determinants of the physical characteristics necessary to match citizen to his world's environment. Most importantly of all, every gene pack spliced into every embryonic life carried a sync-D, its owner's unique personal ID embedded within the Type code. That ID self-registered with NetMind the instant a baby left the womb. That ID granted its owner lifelong, immediate access to the universal, ubiquitous web of daily existence that was Net. With a Type code you always knew what you'd be good at. Net access ensured life was comfortable, careers satisfying, entertainment a sync link away, and partners compatible. Without it, doors quite literally did not open.

Yet Kip Marsden couldn't find his would-be killer in Net. Which meant the assassin was either a Ho Tong natural, or -

"Think Letticia's hiding his Net entry?" He made it sound nonchalant.

"I damn sure hope not. Even she shouldn't be able to pull that one off. Though-" Kip rethought it, started over. "Better ask your lady mother that one. Or Yakamoto."

"*Keiko?*" Jezekiah tried not to notice the sudden spike in his pulse.

"The Admiral." Kip left it there, but his lips thinned to a grim line.

"Ah." So, then. Jezekiah felt a swell of sympathy, tamped it down. Letticia had never trusted sympathy; it only made her suspicious. "She must have pulled one stellar stunt to earn Admiral Yakamoto's personal attention. Just what did she do?"

"Tried to sawyer Madam's node guards."

"She tried to break into *Mother's* node?" The implications stopped his breath for a moment. So, then, indeed. NetMind set no limits to the power of a Van Buren Protector; that was one of the reasons the Family took so Darwinian an approach to its offspring. The thought of Letticia worming her way into that kind of power made even his toes curl. Worse, such an attempt meant a charge of high treason if Mother decided to make an issue of it. A few years back he'd have made sure she did. Now – he needed Letticia alive, if not happy.

Still, Mother had obviously decided to give Letticia another chance. This latest escapade might actually play him the cards he needed. Certainly

Letticia must understand by now that she'd reduced her choices to cooperation or death. Ideally, she would willing to cooperate. He might even be able to get her to call off that damned assassin. Or at least find out why the hell she'd hired him in the first place.

He felt the Heir's ring pulse with his heart. Knew even before they rounded the last fern tree that they'd reached the Manor.

He was home. Now the games began in earnest.

III

On the inside, SecNet looked like a rain-speckled spider web. For one entire second, Letticia Van Buren pulled the data drop that held her personal essence out of its energy stream to simply revel in the glory of NetMind. Uncountable billions of droplets flashed past her tiny node, each droplet carrying uncountable billions of databytes. All of it just a single strand in the omnipotent, omniscient, omni-present neural cloud that was NetMind. *This* was real power! If only she could make Mother see .... But Mother couldn't, any more than the rest of them. To Mother, NetMind was just an invisible tool. Like herself.

The injustice of it all spiked her droplet's energy output. She nulled the outbound ripple before it could attract one of SecNet's viral guards. Carefully – oh, so carefully! – Letticia reinserted her dewdrop essence into the data stream, rode it to her nest. She'd mimed SecNet's own antigens to build her place here, tricked its defenses into accepting her little nest as part of themselves. Now the immaterial essence of her personal web hung suspended from the synapse nub of an afferent neuron, giving her a safe harbor within SecNet's very core. It was a trick no other syncmeister in the Commonwealth could match, not even Marsden. And she didn't even dare let them know she could do it!

It was a risky business, even for her. SecNet's neural tracers sent crash-and-burn feed directly into the motor centers of an intruder's body. But they didn't kill. Kip Marsden wasn't as merciful as Mother, either. Marsden's defenses left their victims alive. Gave the Aryans' interrogators something to play with.

No choice, though – right now she needed speed and SecNet tied into *everything*: Demo, Comm, Med, Finance, KnowNet. Even Mother's personally secured files resided here, though the lock on those was biospecific to Mother. She couldn't risk touching that one, not for a while. Marsden was just *waiting* for her to repeat that last mistake and Mother might not forgive her a second time.

Still, she was glad now she'd risked it. It'd got her a bargaining chip.

Letticia sub-linked into CommNet, felt the caress of a viral guard shiver through her synapse link. It let her pass, and she found the outbound Jumpline she sought. The Jumpline's owner sync'd in on schedule twenty centoseconds later and Letticia piggybacked her message to his. She had no time to linger in Net after that. The answer to that message would not be long in coming.

She came out of download disoriented. It took her a moment to recognize the feel of her*self*, pinpoint the places where her body touched link pad and chair. Too long. She raised one hand by force of will, pinched her other arm savagely. The pain helped clear her head. She blinked, searching for something physical to focus on.

Her trophies caught her attention. Scholastic awards in math and finance and cyberbioneurology – shoddy little plaques she kept there to please Mother – didn't matter. It was the ugly, hulking statue against the far wall that gave her focus. That was her victory totem – some ancient Hawaiian piece Jezekiah had found and coveted. She had got to it first. She kept it there to remind herself he *could* lose.

She was herself again when her comm unit squawked a few moments later.

"I'll thank you to remember you are no longer acting Heir, Grand-Niece." Johann Petrovich Van Buren's familiar snarl soured the air even before the dark cloud beside her chair morphed into his shape.

"I'm hardly in need of the reminder, Uncle. But I note you answered the call."

The cloud lengthened, solidified, and Letticia made herself smile up into the caricature glare of the Streikern Protector: the Family's trademark too-blue eyes set in his world's characteristic snow white skin. He wore the Family's red-gold hair in the standing Mohawk of Streiker's warrior class though his had long since gone white along its base. Dense white body hair poked up above the collar of that silly black uniform and out of the sleeves. Combined with that beak of a nose it made him look like a fat, indignant rooster.

Still, he was *here* and that was what mattered. She smiled up at him slyly. "I have something for you."

"One would hope. I was not pleased to discover your invitation packeted with my ambassador's report." JP turned on his heel to pace her chamber. The glow from the display cases along her walls matched the holo's glow, making his presence seem uncomfortably real.

Safe behind his back, Letticia rolled her eyes in silent suffering. She made sure she looked innocent again before JP reached the dark totem and turned. "First, I need a ride off Earth."

Miserable son of a bitch. He actually *barked* he laughed so hard! "Name one reason I should not simply inform your mother Muriel that you've extended your pernicious snooping into my confidential diplomatic communications."

"Would proof Jezekiah's sold Streiker out to the Lupans do?" She kept the smile sweet with effort. Even a syncmeister of Marsden's caliber couldn't prove she'd piggybacked that message. But if it came to JP's word against hers, she'd be zit anyway. JP didn't have the imagination to make up that kind of lie, and Mother knew it. Her only hope was that she'd learned enough to scare him. "Of course, I *could* just tell Grandfather Ho."

Oh, that wiped the sneer off, didn't it? For once she was almost grateful to Jezekiah. She'd never have guessed what JP was up if he hadn't sent Mother such lovely reports.

"Be careful, Niece." Those too-blue eyes narrowed – but he was being thoughtful about it now. "Your mother could regard any attempt on your part to contact Ho Tong as treason."

"You're forgetting that it goes for both of us. And you know I'd have to tell her all about that stockpile of Venus Seed you've been accumulating if she caught me, wouldn't I?"

"Are you actually attempting to threaten me, you malevolent little chit?"

"It's not a threat, it's a promise!"

JP's hand snapped up before he remembered he couldn't hit her in holo. He converted the gesture to a check on some control outside holo range.

Oh, God, what would she do if he cut her off? "You *know* Mother would never let you get away with undercutting her distribution deal with Grandfather Ho!" She said it fast, before he could shut her off.

"For what it's worth: your mother is quite aware of my dealings with Ho Tong."

"Nonsense! Mother would never–"

"She would and does. She has precious few options. Earth has virtually no off-world income sources save a few exports and tourism. She can't afford to lose the revenue stream." He paused to sneer down that beak of a nose. "Or am I to believe you to be as utterly ignorant of Home World's finances as you are of its politics?"

"I *know* we're poor! You don't need to rub my nose in it!" As if she'd have wasted time talking to him otherwise! She'd have had a ship of her own if Mother had any money to spare. "That has nothing to do with you distributing Venus Seed for Grandfather Ho."

"Then allow me, Niece, to set what passes for your mind at ease – or your mother's, on the off chance you actually have the wit to report this conversation to her. I have quite a different purpose in mind for Ho Tong's Venus Seed."

"What?" This conversation was not going the way she'd expected. Letticia scratched memory for some means of pulling JP back to her. "Do you expect me to believe *Mother* knows you're using Pandar's merchant ships to sneak Venus Seed onto your stockpile bases? Without it appearing on any of Octavian's cargo manifests." So, *there*! She'd show him! "According to his financials Pandar's losing an average of five ships a year due to Venus Seed addiction. That's a projected loss of five hundred billion creds per annum. Bet Cousin Octavian would sure like to know -"

"- That you've managed to infiltrate his trade codes? I'm quite sure he would." JP managed to make his sneer look smug.

"Won't stop him from charging *you*, though." She hoped he couldn't see how hard she suddenly found it to swallow. Letticia clenched her fists on the arm rests, felt cold disgusting sweat seep between her fingers. "Now, do I get that ride?"

JP reached the totem, turned back to look down that beakish nose of his. "Possibly. If you can prove that ludicrous charge of yours."

"What, that Jezekiah sold you out to the Lupans? Of course he did. Why do you think he was on Den Lupus?"

"Don't lie to *me*, Niece!"

"Oh, but I'm not lying, JP. I don't have to. I've already told my lies. To your spies. The ones you had tracking Jezekiah."

Oh, *that* made him think, didn't it? She felt the first real thrill of power. Like the rest of them, he couldn't even imagine the degree to which she could comp NetMind.

JP paced back to his spot opposite her chair and stopped, one black booted toe still tapping. "Why?"

For heaven's sake how could he be so stupid? "Because Jezekiah's going to kill me, that's why!"

"Your capacity for narcissism never fails to astound me." He pinched the bridge of his nose, reminding her for an instant of Mother. Maybe nose-pinching was some gene-coded trait that just triggered when somebody became Protector. "Why-" he said it slower this time, like she was some kind of idiot – "should I believe you? My people thoroughly documented your brother's trade mission. And I assure you my ops are competent."

"You have a diplomatic shuttle scheduled outbound in half an hour. Do I get a ride on it or not?"

He reached for some control, already ready to forget her.

"All right!" Letticia clamped her arms to her sides so JP wouldn't see her wipe the sweat off her palms. Oh, Mother would scrag her for zitting out their dirty little secret. But, then, Jezekiah was going to kill her anyway, so it didn't really matter. Besides, she was on *her* strong ground now. She could always cover her tracks. And it was way past time somebody in the Family saw what *she* could do.

She leaned back, realized with a flush of pleasure that her palms had dried. "When was the last time one of your spies actually slept with my dear brother?"

"I fail to see what-" She lifted her brows archly and he reconsidered. "On Bogue Dast Station." For a moment, he looked like he'd enjoyed the report, too.

"Uh-huh. But once he left Bogue Dast he started taking up with local girls, didn't he?"

"I am not concerned with your brother's penchant for improving the local breeding stock. What mattered is that he remained-"

"- In Commonwealth territory. You're catching on, JP." It was her turn to sneer now. Letticia made sure he saw it, too. "Only he didn't. Because Bogue Dast station is the jump-off point to the Lupan Dominion. Because after Bogue Dast, all your ops saw of Jezekiah was a holo. My *brother* was working his way out to Den Lupus."

"Impossible. My people made physical contact with him at every function. *And* ran scan on him. His biopat matched."

"Of course it did. I layered Jezekiah's biopat into the holo feed, embedded pressure sensors-"

"I do not need a lecture on NetMind mechanics!"

"Oh, but you do." Why did nobody ever want to hear the fun stuff? Letticia chewed on a fingernail, watched JP above it. "See, it's the pressure sensors that do the trick. They let the holo read the hard world contact and feed the sensory impression right back to the source. So a handshake given feels like a handshake returned. Only it's really tough on complicated contact like sex, so Jezekiah had to-"

"That's quite enough!" At least the old berg was thinking, to judge from the red flush working up his face.

"No, it's not. Because the piece that really matters was his reports." She resisted the urge to smirk, kept her tone just as casual as it could be. "That was the *really* hard part. Jezekiah had to report in every week. And *I* had to make sure it looked like he was sync'ing in from wherever he was supposed to be."

"Naturally you eavesdropped on his reports."

"Naturally. So? Do I get on that shuttle?"

"Possibly."

Letticia shot upright in outrage. "But you said-"

"That I would consider it. So I am." He locked hands behind his back, paced away again. "Assuming you can prove your charge. So far, you have only offered conjecture and innuendo. Even assuming Jezekiah intended to betray Streiker, why should the Lupans listen? Anything the dogs wanted from Earth they took with them six hundred years ago."

Oh, damn. Jezekiah had never put a 'why' in his reports, the miserable brat. Heavens, she could barely hear herself think, her heart was pounding so hard. Gob it all! Jezekiah would never sell out Streiker, not unless he could show a profit worth the risk. If only she could sync in – but she couldn't, not with JP. Still, Jezekiah *had* been on Den Lupus, and he *had* got a treaty out of the dogs' Parliament. So he'd obviously found something to offer.

She scrounged personal memory seeking tidbits. Except for its military, Streiker was *nothing*. It'd only been colonized after the Schism, and then only as a buffer against the Lupans, to make sure the damned dogs never did to the other worlds what they'd done to Earth. World was a damned ice ball – even its oceans lay under a mile of primeval ice.

Wait…now there was a connection. JP had to import just about everything: any minerals or whatnot the planet had were buried under miles of ice so hard and deep it was cheaper to ship raw ore in from other worlds than drill down. Only Streiker's star didn't have any other planets, so the Streikern had been stuck mining asteroids…. JP would give his eyeballs to get his hands on a wandering mother lode of a planet. Which was precisely what Jezekiah's reports said some fool of a Lupan had found – "Why? Because of Rogue, why else?"

"Nonsense. Rogue is no longer in Lupan territory." But he stopped pacing to listen.

"Not quite." The connections were falling into place nicely, now. "Even fast as that ball of rock is traveling, its trajectory won't carry it into Streiker's official space for a lot of years yet. By which time the mining colonies the Lupans have dug in there will have pretty much scraped it clean, won't they?"

"Make your point, Niece!"

She noticed her palms were dry again and smiled up at JP. "The point is this: Rogue is the reason the Lupans would listen to Jezekiah. My dear brother has made a treaty with some Lupan warlord called Strongarm." She had no clue what Jess'd promised the dog, but she must've hit close to home: JP went red-white-red. He started pacing again. Letticia rose, paced over to place herself at his side, equal's footing. "Now just clear me out to-"

"No."

"What do you mean, 'no'?" Suddenly her whole body felt cold and wet. "You *promised*!"

"I have done no such thing. I said I would consider your request." JP met her eyes a moment then took a deliberate step away. "You have made a public spectacle of your incompetence rather too often, Niece. Worse, you have betrayed your Protector merely to save your own worthless life-"

"I did not! I'd never betray Mother!" She heard her stupid body sobbing, but couldn't stop it. "Only Jezekiah-"

"Do you think for one instant, your brother would risk approaching the *Lupans* without your mother's knowledge and consent?" He whirled on her, fists up and clenched. "You have indeed given me cause for action, Niece. In exchange, I shall not inform your mother of your betrayal. I shall give you that chance of avoiding execution. I shall not, however, help you add cowardice to your list of failures."

He turned on his heel, already refocusing his attention to whatever it was in his own office. "Good evening, Niece. Should you survive Jezekiah's reprisal, perhaps we shall speak again." An instant later, he was gone.

It took a good thirty seconds for the enormity of his rejection to fully register on her. After that, all she could do was throw herself down and scream.

IV

Kip Marsden turned Jezekiah over to Mother's chief of staff at the Manor entrance. The woman gave him time to shower out the hair dye and change clothes, then shooed him off to report to Mother herself.

He took a service corridor to Mother's office for expediency's sake. His presence annoyed hell out of the spidery servo-bots that had to scuttle tools, trays, and equipment around him, but it was a necessary evil. The public sections of the Manor bustled with politicos in pursuit of advancement, every one of whom would feel duty-bound to chat him up en route. Happily, the up-and-coming members of Mother's staff considered the service corridors beneath their dignity. It was an attitude he and Mother both encouraged.

By habit, Jezekiah gave himself a quick dust-down when he stepped out into the hallway of Mother's office. He'd put on muscle working crew so the shirt his major domo had laid out for him refused to seal across the chest, making the shirt gape open like some joy toy rig. Nothing he could do about it now, though, except hope Mother accepted the seeming informality. It was going to take all the good will he could cadge to convince Mother to at least consider the one un-negotiable demand Strongarm had imposed on the treaty. He ran through his argument one last time, then tugged the shirt as close to closed as he could and marched up to present himself to the wary red eye of Mother's major domo.

Welcome home, Milord. The major domo's disembodied baritone put a hearty welcome into the words. But the carved *tiki* wood doors stayed closed. Jezekiah shivered as the prickle of a bioscan worked its way down his body. Nothing personal: Mother's guards simply did not make exceptions.

The prickling ended. *Your Lady Mother will see you now, Milord.* He could have sworn the major domo's red eye winked at him before it swung the massive doors open.

The pale yellow walls of Mother's office curved away in a gentle oval. Sunlit shafts from the tall windows lining the wall behind her desk raised bright reflections on the dark wood floor, shimmered the silk trim on the Persian carpets scattered across it. Some early Van Buren had looted the office of the NorthAm Empire's president before old DeeCee sank back into its swamp. Subsequent ancestors had kept the office intact when they built the Manor, giving the Family one more visible tie to old Earth and the Original Species. It was still a gracious, simple room. Only the windows were no longer glass, the brocaded walls fronted battle shields, and the intruder defense system was set to agony.

Mother was seated behind the dark wood desk, scowling at one of her comm displays. The massive cored diamond of the Protector's Ring sparked with every move. The diamond itself was nothing, of course, merely a casing for the power band that was the actual Ring. That band drew its radiance from her, its field sync'd to the pulse of her heart. It was the only jewelry she wore, the only adornment she needed: the symbol of her power. And her enslavement.

Jezekiah felt bitterness sour his throat, willed it down. It was his brain he needed to follow right now, not his heart. Besides he was, he realized, truly happy to see Mother again.

She was dressed as he remembered, a simple cotton shirt chosen for comfort rather than show, hair pulled up in a simple twist. One red-gold curl dangled loose at the corner of one impossibly blue eye, sign she'd been in a hurry as usual. She hooked it impatiently behind her ear, and Jezekiah stifled a grin at the familiar habit.

Yet something was off. Jezekiah slowed his pace crossing the room, quickcalcs triggering. She looked trim as ever. Only her slenderness had a haggard feel to it that hadn't been there when he left. She looked older, too, than she should for a mere forty-three. Wasn't age, though: the fine lines shadowing her mouth and eyes had the look of worry rather than years. So, then. There was more trouble at home than her messages had ever admitted. *His* trouble, if he failed to escape the Ring. His stomach knotted on the thought.

He managed to keep his courtier's smile in place when Mother finally looked up. He gave it up when her face lit with a joy so pure it tightened his heart. The Protectorship be damned – it was Mother he loved.

She shot out of her chair, started around the desk. A shaft of sunlight caught the Protector's Ring. Rainbows spun around the massive, cored diamond encircling her finger, splashed ruby reflections across the pale walls. Mother jerked back at the sight as if the Ring had shoved her.

Jezekiah found his eyes burning as he watched her slowly back into her chair, force her emotions back behind the working mask of impersonal disinterest. Watched her push herself back into the golden cage of duty.

That was the trap of the damned Ring: duty first, last, always, only. Duty to the exclusion of all human decency. That was the living death he had spent his life training to endure. He'd accepted it as a given when he left. Been secretly proud of it, in fact. Now... He'd be damned, now, if he was going to enslave himself to the Ring. He'd seen what freedom meant.

Jezekiah stopped five paces shy of the winged leather chairs facing Mother's desk as protocol dictated. He bowed, held it five seconds as protocol demanded. Their eyes met as he straightened. It wasn't Mother who acknowledged him now. It was Madam Muriel Van Buren, Lord High Protector of Earth.

Jezekiah waited till she nodded. He kissed fingers to her properly, then settled into one of the chairs — and snapped erect as a warning thrill ran through his back and fingertips. Damn and damn again. He knew Mother's furniture was rigged for bioscan. But he hadn't expected she would feel the need to run scan on him. The sensors in this chair would flash any telltale change in his chem signals to her display, alerting her instantly to any conscious falsehood. What the feedback did to him depended on the usefulness of the lie. Fortunately, he'd never been in the habit of lying to Mother.

Mother dropped back in her own chair. "I just had a most interesting call. It seems JP is not happy with you."

"Why?" There was a tidbit he hadn't expected. The fact he hadn't anticipated it worried him more than the fact itself.

"I don't know. Your great-uncle should have no reason to suspect you." She lifted one red-gold brow in question. "Have you given him one?"

"You've seen my reports. You know perfectly well I haven't."

"I know perfectly well what you've committed to comm. The question is what you've done in private." Mother's eyes flicked to her comm display.

This time, the tingle was sharply unpleasant, a pricking at every point the chair touched his body. Jezekiah kept the smile in place, though he had to grit his teeth to manage it. The chair decided he was honest at last and the tingle faded. He made a point of settling deeper into the cushions. It helped that the leather rustle hid his sigh of relief.

The comm chimed, drawing Mother's scowl back to itself. *Milord Johann Petrovich Van Buren,* the major domo intoned and her lips tightened. *Protector of Streiker, Lord High Master of the Van Buren Council, Ruler of –*

"I know who he is," Mother took a breath, held it. "You can tell Johann Petrovich to –" she let the breath out. "To wait. I'll accept his call shortly."

Yes, Milady. The comm fell silent.

"Now precisely what is in that treaty of yours that's *not* in your reports?"

Jezekiah winced through the scan's full-body bite then leaned forward, letting his eagerness show. "It's more than just a treaty. It's an alliance."

"With the *Lupans*?" Mother slapped palms on the desk, leaned forward over them. "Are you out of your mind? I was willing to consider trade-"

"Just hear me out, would you?" Jezekiah realized he'd shot to his feet as well, was leaning over the desk to match her eye to eye. He felt the dismay hit his expression, saw his shock mirrored in Mother's expression. Feeling like an errant nine-year-old, he sank back into the damned chair. And hoped fervently Mother would decide not to take offense.

"My, you have changed, Jess." Mother lowered herself into her chair, leaned back into the cushions herself.

"I shouldn't have-" ducked his head in apology. "I forgot my place. I'm sorry."

"Don't be." She started to smile, rethought it. "I sent you out there to help you grow up. I'm hardly in position to complain that you have." This time she did smile. There was a sadness in it that wrenched his heart. "Now, then. Tell me why I should consider a Lupan alliance."

"They've got long jumpers."

That brought Mother up sharp and straight. "How? They have no tech but what the Commonwealth sells them. They're not smart enough to design their own."

"Or so they've led us onlies to believe." He saw her question and allowed himself a smile. "That's what the Lupans call the rest of the species: onlies. As in 'human only'."

"As opposed to-" Mother left the rest to her shudder.

"Exactly. Though they're not half bad once you get used to the fangs." At least not in daylight. Jezekiah remembered the first time he'd seen Strongarm go feral and suppressed a shudder of his own.

She lifted her chin, studied him through lidded eyes. "Octavian has spent fortunes trying to develop a jump drive that could travel farther than a megaparsec in a single shot. Are you suggesting his techs sold their work to the Lupans?"

"Not at all. The Lupans developed it on their own."

"How? The Type was designed for combat, not brains."

"They're still fundamentally human. They've been intermarrying with the miner clans and free world folk for centuries. Someplace along the line they've developed one damned fine strain of engineers. I know. I've been on one of Strongarm's ships." He gave that a beat, let her work through the implications before continuing. "Think what it means. The alliance terms give us exclusive access to that jump drive. It will make Earth rich again. Make us a power again."

"And what do the dogs-" Mother grimaced at the vulgarity. "The *Lupans* demand in return?"

The desk comm squawked to life again, flashing red. *Milord Johann Petrovich Van Buren.* The major domo sounded nervous.

"Later." Mother nodded for Jezekiah to continue.

"Best case-"

Beside Jezekiah's chair a patch of air pearlesced. The pearl darkened, taking on substance as it lengthened to man size. It solidified abruptly leaving only a faint glow at its edges to hint that the red-headed bear of a man glaring down at them was not physically present.

Age had swept snow up into the base of Johann Petrovich Van Buren's crest of red-gold hair, but it left the glacial cold in his impossibly blue eyes untouched. On his pale hand, the Protector's ring glittered like blue ice. "I told your major domo I wanted to speak with you, Muriel."

"And I told you to wait, Uncle." Mother had to lift her head to see him, but her eyes drooped to a dangerous angle.

"I waited. Now I want an explanation."

Jezekiah quelled the impulse to scoot out of range. He angled his chair toward his uncle's holo instead and put on an expression of unimpeachable innocence. "I should think I am the one who should be demanding an explanation, don't you? After all, I suffered an inordinate amount of stress and pain dodging your assassin."

"Nonsense and you know it. *My* assassins are competent. I use Ta'an." JP almost preened. "I'm not afraid of Guild prices for the best."

"Uncle-" Mother drew JP's glare back to herself. "If you have a complaint to make, then make it. Otherwise, have the courtesy to allow me to finish debriefing my son."

"Make it I shall." Johann Petrovich leaned forward across the desk at Mother, pushing illusory hands through the comm display. "I want to know just what that boy of yours was up to on Den Lupus."

Jezekiah kept the spike of dread out of his expression. Only one way JP could even suspect he'd been on Den Lupus. He shot a glance at Mother behind JP's holo'd back, saw the subtle tightening around her eyes that said she'd drawn the same conclusion.

Bad sign, that, on all scores. It'd be more than his freedom he forfeited if Letticia had told JP too much for him to spin it. If JP knew enough to scream treason he'd forfeit his life. But it was Mother who would pay the greater penalty: JP would make sure the Council cut off Commonwealth trade. That would starve the Van Buren communities all across Earth. Cut Mother's financial lifeline. But not Ho Tong's. After that, it was just a matter of time before Grandfather Ho raised another rebellion. And he'd be successful next time.

Mother lifted her head, managing to look down her nose at JP even as she looked up. "Has it occurred to you, Uncle, that just possibly I am trying to find out myself? An endeavor your presence does nothing to facilitate."

"If you'll allow me?" Jezekiah locked a smile in place. "I do believe I can answer both your questions quite simply."

From the corner of his eye, Jezekiah saw Mother glance at her comm. The leather armrest tingled gentle warning where his fingers touched it. His breath caught in dread, but the tingle stopped at warning. He hid the relieved sigh. "It is ancient history that the Schism cost Earth her industrial base along with the bulk of her population. Or that the Family's subsequent elevation of Earth's off-world colonies to Commonwealth status marginalized us."

"Do not presume to teach your elders their history, boy." JP snapped around to glower at him.

"Simply placing a point in context, Uncle. Because with both our tech and industrial bases gone, Earth survived only on the tourist trade of off-worlders making pilgrimage to Home World."

"We're all aware of your context, boy. Make your point." JP didn't bother to hide the sneer.

"My point is that it's no secret the rebellion cost Earth the bulk of her tourist trade."

"Using tourists for target practice can have that effect." JP almost smiled at his own wit.

"It cost us six hundred thousand of our own people's lives, Uncle. Most of them right here in the islands." He sensed more than saw Mother's shudder. Reminder enough, had he needed it, that those memories still stalked her nightmares. "It also effectively destroyed our export industries. The only revenue Earth has left is from the tithes Ho Tong pays us on its Venus Seed trade."

"A fact which every world in the Commonwealth has cause to lament." JP lifted a lip at Mother. "You should have killed off Ho Tong when you had the chance, Muriel. Taken over Venus Seed production yourself. That would at least -"

"-Have cut into the profits you've turned running escort for some of those Seed shipments," Jezekiah cut in. "As it is, both you and Cousin Octavian on Pandar have profited handsomely from our economic strains. So you can hardly claim surprise that I was assigned to rebuild our tourist trade. It was the *only* mission I had. I concluded it and returned home. That is all I did."

"Liar!"

"I happen to find that term singularly offensive of late, Uncle." The sudden steel in his own voice surprised both of them. He leaned forward to meet JP's glare and hold it. "My assignment was to rebuild Home World's tourist trade. That is what I did. End of story."

"Prove it!"

Jezekiah lifted an inquiring brow at the sync link built into Mother's desk. At her nod, he slipped his fingers into the link. A lifetime's habit let him blink off the dizzy flash as the link sync'd his body's biopat into the vast neural network of NetMind, let him ignore the uncountable billions of data feeds streaming past to focus on the key sequence that accessed the biochip files containing the folder he wanted. He waited till Mother's link confirmed the transfer, then broke sync and sat back. He hadn't been fool enough to spend his *entire* tour on Den Lupus. He kept his face properly disinterested while he watched Mother absorb the size of the profits in the treaties he'd teased out of the rim worlds' negotiators.

Had he known her less well, he'd have thought Mother was gloating in earnest when she finally released a summary of the treaties to JP's link. "Are you satisfied now, Uncle? You've seen the reports delivered for yourself, and witnessed that I've had no chance to modify them."

"Assuming they're true." JP took an ostentatious minute to crosscheck the honesty of the names involved.

"Oh, for-" Mother slapped a palm on the desk. The Ring shot rainbows across the ceiling as it struck the wood. "To quote yourself, that's nonsense and you know it. Now be so good as to leave us. Or I may feel obliged to suggest that the Council investigate the source of Streiker's recent 'discovery' of new ore deposits."

"Don't attempt to threaten me, Muriel. You give away too much." JP stepped backward through the empty chair to sneer down at Jezekiah. "At least I know now what you were up to in the dogs' lair."

"If so, then you seem uncommonly ungrateful for it." Jezekiah kept the smile sweet with difficulty. "Because what I did was save your snowy white -" He caught himself a word shy of suicide – "hide."

"Save your fairy tales for your mother, boy. I deal in facts."

Jezekiah dropped the smile. He pushed himself out of the chair to meet JP's blue glare eye to eye. "*Fact*, then: Streiker warships have been hijacking Lupan ore barges all along the Commonwealth rim for the past several years. *Fact*: some of those barges belonged to an up-and-coming young war lord named Strongarm. *Fact*: prior to my intervention, said Strongarm was preparing to give Streiker a taste of your own medicine."

"What I do in free space is none of Earth's damned business, boy! Much less yours."

"On the contrary, a Lupan war is very much Earth's business. Which makes it mine. Not to mention the Council's."

Had JP been present in body, his backhand would have knocked Jezekiah sprawling. As it was, his knuckles only passed through Jezekiah's cheeks.

"Enough!" Mother leaned across the desk, the Ring raising brilliant reflections off the polished wood. "I remind you where you are, Johann Petrovich. I suggest you take the warning to heart."

JP inclined in acknowledgement. He stepped sideways, passing his image through the chair and visibly resisting the urge to kick it out of his way. He paced the length of the Persian carpet before he spoke. Even then it was over his shoulder. "Those are serious charges, boy."

"True. But the escalation in hostilities is documentable." Jezekiah pulled in a calming breath, held his tone level. "Witness: for the past few months your scout ships have been disappearing."

"Things like that happen in deep space." JP stopped at the far end of the rug to stare out a window at Pearl Harbor in the distance.

"Occasionally. Only the disappearances are no longer occasional, are they? Your real concern now is that the last scout returned to Streiker. With its crew dead."

"Butchered, is more like it. With Lobo clan pins stuck through their throats." JP ran a pale hand across his eyes, as if he were trying to wipe the image away.

"Precisely." Strongarm had made sure Jezekiah saw that crew. The memory still turned his stomach. "That's Strongarm's warning, Uncle. A tiny taste of what his troops will do to Streiker unless you back off." He waited, but JP did not turn around. "That's what I was up to on Den Lupus. "Buying us all a chance to avoid a Lupan war."

"So this is what Earth has come to." JP stepped closer to the window. Jezekiah caught himself listening for the click of boot heels against the wood. The holo'd silence jarred. "Home World's Heir serves as the dogs' messenger boy."

"I didn't come back merely for your convenience." Jezekiah felt his fists ball. Wrong move; he could not afford a show of anger, not now. He shook himself to ease the tension, recognized Strongarm in the gesture. "Nonetheless I've given you fair warning. As Mother says, I suggest you take it to heart. Because I assure you, I will make certain you do not drag Earth or the Commonwealth after you into another war."

"So, then. I have my answer at last." JP turned enough to let Jezekiah see his contempt. Only this time, he focused the sneer on Mother. "You've cast Earth's lot with the dogs, haven't you, Muriel? Perhaps you should re-think your loyalties."

Jezekiah realized he'd cleared Mother's desk only when he felt her grip on his arm. She yanked him back, rose to meet JP's sneer with blue fire. "It is not *my* loyalty that has been suborned, Uncle. Nor my son's." She slapped her palm down on a comm control and JP's image evaporated.

For a moment, Jezekiah simply leaned on his knuckles, willing his pulse back to a rational level. Mother leaned on the desk beside him, shoulders hunched. He watched the pulsing play of light across her Ring, noted that its pulse outpaced his own. Mother straightened, then, and he blinked in surprise at the naked wretchedness in her expression.

She realized her mistake. Hugging herself, she jerked away from him to face the window. When she looked back, her eyes were taut with misery. "Did you authorize Letticia to discuss her part in your tour?"

"No."

Mother nodded. "Then I cannot postpone it any longer."

Damn, he did not like the sound of that. "Postpone what?"

"Letticia's execution. I'd hoped -" She looked away, her knuckles a white border to the Ring. "That will be all for now, Jess."

"She was only bragging, Mother. You know that."

"That will be *all*, Jezekiah!"

Damn, and damn again. He'd lose it all – *Earth* would lose it all – if Mother killed Letticia now. He risked waiting, pushed luck further by laying a hand on Mother's arm. She jerked in surprise. Thankfully, she did not pull away. "Give Lush another chance. You know she never intended treason. All she's ever wanted was your attention."

"I wish I could believe that was all she wanted." She pulled away. But she didn't dismiss him.

So, then. She was leaving him an opening. Hoping he'd find her another excuse to avoid that hideous order. He only wished he dared tell her just how desperately Earth needed Letticia alive. But it was still too soon for that particular truth. "Look, telling JP about faking my presence on the tour was an indiscretion, no question. But we both know he'd have figured it out shortly in any case. This way, we know what he knows, and how he learned it. We'll be able to control any spin he tries to put on the story. It was a stupid stunt, I grant you. But the consequences don't warrant execution."

"If JP were her only ... indiscretion I would agree. Unfortunately it's not." She broke off to pace away, shoulders hunching again.

The sight of it twisted a vise so hard around his heart he gasped for breath. Made him start to step after her. Almost. But Mother could not afford to indulge weakness here, not even the weakness of a mother's love for her daughter. Instead, he locked his arms across his chest, hid his love for her behind his working mask. "Tell me what she's done. Maybe I can help. She did keep JP off my trail, after all."

"Not through any desire of her own, I assure you."

"Agreed. But she kept JP from assigning one of his own ops to killing me. I doubt I'd have been as successful dodging one of *his* assassins."

"True." Mother managed a wan smile. "Unfortunately, it's not enough of a mitigating circumstance." The smile faded. "In order to create a sim for you Letticia needed access to your personal node. I granted it. She then used the access to your node as a jump-off point to try to infiltrate mine."

"Kip told me. Still-"

"Did he also tell you I did not authorize that TransitLiner to dock beside your shuttle this morning?"

"No. But what's that -" Oh, damn. Damn and damn again. "She faked your ID."

"Precisely. She usurped the authority of the Protector. Which is high treason." Mother turned, head up, eyes down. "I'm sorry you had to come back to this. I wish-" She cut the sentence off, stepped back to her desk and reached for the comm. "Get me Admiral Yakamoto."

Jezekiah dove across the desk, slapped his hand across the comm. "Belay that."

Madam? The major domo's baritone went neutral. But comm spat a neural lock across his hand, its disruptive field trapping him in place while it bit into every cell of his body. Jezekiah tried to meet Mother's eyes, found even that tiny movement denied him. He could only wait until her blue fury faded.

"Enough."

The field evaporated. Jezekiah collapsed with it. He cracked his chin on the polished wood and tried unsuccessfully to stop his teeth from chattering.

Mother leaned forward on her knuckles. The Ring created a sun bright flare beneath her hand. "Do not presume on your welcome, Jess." She said it slowly, each word an effort. "I cannot afford to be in a forgiving mood right now."

"I'm not asking you to forgive me. Only to give Lush another chance." He managed to twist around enough to face her.

"Letticia has had too many second chances. I'm out of excuses." Yet she did not repeat the call command, did not summon the one man she would allow to execute a Van Buren. Telling him without words how desperately she wanted not to make that call.

"I'm not offering excuses." Jezekiah managed, finally, to push himself up from the desk. He reached for her hand. She twitched away and he dropped the attempt. "I'm offering hope. Lush can be the key to breaking our dependence on Seed income."

"How?" Mother straightened with a snort. Only he could have heard the sob it hid.

"That'll depend on how far she's willing to cooperate." It was also as much as he dared say until he knew how far that would be. "The Lupan Parliament still hasn't ratified that treaty. But the whole point of setting up that treaty was to give us a new, permanent revenue source. One that would finally free you from having to turn a blind eye to Ho Tong's Seed. If I can get Lush to cooperate, Strongarm has guaranteed their Parliament will approve the treaty. Without her-" he shrugged, making it look philosophical "the odds turn against us. I think that's worth a try, don't you?"

Head still down, Mother paced over to the warmth of a tall window. Sunlit particles danced red-gold across her hair, raised a bright halo off her pale shirt and slacks.

Admiral Yakamoto is here, Madam.

"Send him in." Jezekiah's heart dropped as Mother turned to face him. The Ring's flare dimmed the sunlight to shadow.

"I regret you still find the Admiral necessary." He let his breath out, feeling his dreams drain out with it.

"We may all regret it, I fear." She inclined her head, working mask firmly in place. "Coordinate interviewing Letticia with the Admiral. After that, I will see."

Jezekiah bowed, quickly, to hide the flood of relief.

He waited through the Admiral's arrangements, strode out behind the man when Mother dismissed them.

He managed not to shiver until after he heard the doors swish shut behind him.

V

Deep in sync, Letticia Van Buren uncoiled one fine tendril of her mind. The living synapses of NetMind's thoughts flashed past her spy nest in glittering clusters of pure energy that swelled, sparked, merged, then shot apart again. She extruded a feeder, caught a passing neuron, felt her essence sync to NetMind's pulse. Felt the power of that pulse throb in her own veins as she melded herself to the glory that was NetMind. Oh, *why* couldn't she just lose herself in Net? Why'd she have to be stuck with her stupid, hard world body all the time? It was her body that was going to catch it when Jezekiah found her, her body that was going to *hurt*. She didn't mind the idea of dying. Rather liked the idea, in a way – it would free her from this worthless, lumpy piece of flesh. But death would take away NetMind, dump her essence into *nothing*ness. She heard her body cry aloud at the thought. Her horror rippled outward through Net, forcing her to scramble to block it. She absolutely could not afford to attract any of Marsden's viral guards. Not now. Right now she had to get that idiotic assassin into safe keeping before Sec found him. And get herself out of here before Jezekiah found *her*.

She'd be dead for sure otherwise. Mother's precious golden boy wasn't nearly as merciful as Mother herself. Jezekiah would be after her blood this time. Two years she'd spent guarding his back, maintaining his precious cover – but he wouldn't remember that, would he? Oh, no, all *he'd* think about was one silly, incompetent little assassin. It just wasn't fair! She quashed the jealous sting. God *damn* that stupid assassin to hell! What a waste of good money! Left her scrambling to cover his tracks. Again. Now she was stuck relying on the locals. It'd make things infinitely worse if Mother ever found out about that one.

Well, now *that* certainly took her mind off Net's glory. Letticia snapped her essence onto a new energy strand a microsecond before a guard cell flashed past. The cell shot by without noticing her and she retraced the data string anchor she'd laid down on her last foray. She'd hidden all the *really* dangerous stuff in her spider hole, using NetMind itself to protect it. She called up the doppelganger'd sync-D she'd created to cocoon her assassin's identity. Only … his reading was gone.

Fighting the flash of terror, she traced the thread of his false ID through the fabric of NetMind's demographic files. Nothing. No breaks, no frays – and no assassin. She curled her data strands back into herself, considered risking a hard world call. Decided against it. Too likely that bastard Marsden would have some SecType monitoring her comm lines. Or worse, that damned Admiral Yakamoto.

Too late to fix it now. She had to get herself out of the Manor, and fast. She scuttled back to her spider hole, feeling the fear of Jezekiah blossom like a synapse zit. She ran feelers across the delicate strands of her web, forced herself to take time. She *had* to make sure she'd left no trail for Marsden to track. Oh, why did Jezekiah have to be so nasty? The treasonous underpart of her mind threw up childhood memories while she checked for signs of intrusion: Jezekiah trying to fix a doll she'd broken, Jezekiah sneaking her chocolate behind their tutor's back. He'd always claimed chocolate could fix anything shy of a broken heart….

Something didn't feel right – oh, damn, her eyes were burning. Stupid body! Stupidstupidstupidstupid… Why was she crying about all that *now*? Jezekiah didn't care about her any more. He'd stopped caring, stopped understanding, once Mother made him Heir.

Even his memory betrayed her. A viral cell appeared from nowhere. Too late her defenses screamed. A dark cell sparked to life, duped itself instantly. She had no chance to comp it – the vile thing mutated even as it replicated. The new guard hooked an acid tentacle onto her probe. In a rush of terror, her body tried to jerk free of sync. Letticia willed it still, even as fire screamed down her veins.

She could get past this, if she didn't resist. The fire was only a test. She locked onto that thought, hugged it tight. That hook wouldn't kill her, she reminded herself. It'd just make her wish it would. She willed herself to go null -

The guard released its hook. The fire in her veins faded, but her damned body was left drained, shivering with ghost-pain. She floated helplessly in sync, listening to her body pant.

"Mistress Van Buren," a voice said.

Jezekiah? Pure terror shot her body upright. She felt the snap as sync broke, blinked physical sight frantically back into blurred eyes.

"Mistress Van Buren," the voice said again.

It took her a full second to realize she *heard* it. Damn him, he'd been *watching* – She dragged a suddenly damp palm across her eyes, trying to focus, twisted around in the chair.

Admiral Matsuo Yakamoto stared back from her doorway. He was not even as tall as herself, and the dark blue of his StelFleet uniform made him look thinner, though he managed to make 'thin' look taut as tempered steel. He stood at that Samurai "try me" version of attention, those silly paired swords dangling at his side.

"If the young mistress would honor her servant with a reply?" The admiral's tone dripped patience.

"What?" Only a SamuraiType dared talk to a member of the Family that way. A SecType couldn't even imagine using that tone, and an Aryan would have better sense. But then, it was theoretically possible to buy-off a SecType or Aryan. The Family's gene-techs had made sure SamuraiType was hard-coded loyal.

"I will inspect your quarters now," the Admiral said.

Impudent bastard. "What for?"

He stepped into her room, and Letticia's heart spiked despite herself. Behind him, the air in the doorway shivered as a sec screen formed.

"There's nothing left to see." *Vile* son of a bitch! He'd blocked her escape. Left her no choice but to put on a good show. At least nothing *he* could find. Samurai or not, Yakamoto was just Mother's tame watchdog, not a SecType syncmeister like that bastard Marsden.

She had her muscles under control now. She dropped back into her lounge seat, covering her relief with indifference. Maybe, just maybe, she could get him out of here before Jezekiah finished his report to Mother. Just maybe she could still get out. "Why are you checking my quarters?"

"Your lady mother ordered it." He was already strolling past her, eyes sweeping the room with impersonal attention. His very lack of interest intensified the fear-throb at her temples.

"*Why* did she order it?" Heavens, it was worse than talking to a trained monkey.

"One does not question. One obeys." He was so predictable her lips formed the words with him.

Predictable, predictable…that gave her a lead, maybe even a way to drive him out of here. She shoved out of the chair. He *should* have bowed when she rose. Instead, Yakamoto paced on toward the totem. Arrogant, *gobbing* bastard. He was going to make her pursue him like some common, store-bought NumbersType.

She caught up to him and stopped, forcing him to stop to face her. "Or maybe you're looking for something other than evidence, *dear* Admiral Yakamoto. Maybe it's my person you *really* want to search?" If there was anything that ever made the great Admiral Yakamoto squirm, it was any suggestion of sex. She just hoped he squirmed his way back out her door. She put her hands on her hips, rolled them suggestively, ran the tip of her tongue across her lips. Disgusting sensation.

Yakamoto's breath hissed between his teeth. For an astounded instant, Letticia thought he was actually going to hit her. But he turned on his heel instead, put his back to her once more. Only the flare of rage she'd seen in his eyes lingered in her vision, left her knees feeling like water.

She managed to walk back to her chair with dignity, dropped back into its safe embrace. She reached for the sync-link. And found herself grasping Yakamoto's calloused knuckles.

"You will permit me, Mistress." He flicked her hand off his as if she were something dirty. "I must read your link."

"What?" Suddenly her heart seemed to block her words. "You can't read my link," she got out and her confidence returned. "It's privatized to me, and me alone."

"Captain Marsden of Sec has been good enough to prepare this for me." He reached into a tunic pocket to pull out a fine mesh glove. The tip of its index finger sported a tiny, portable link.

"Marsden wouldn't —" she re-thought that in a hurry and her mouth went dry. He *couldn't* dare, she thought frantically. Even so, she leaned on the arm of the chair, trying to block the Admiral.

"Will you move aside, Mistress?" There was no more expression in Yakamoto's dark eyes than in his voice.

She locked her fingers around the chair arm. Terror lent strength to her fury. "I'll tell Mother!"

"Do so. Let us hope your sync will not have even more to tell." He waited, implacable.

"You won't find anything, you nasty old man!"

"That is to be hoped." The Admiral looked down at her without expression. Somehow, he made the very air around her go cold.

"I haven't done anything! There's nothing in my sync!"

"Good." He slipped the link-glove on, snapped the slender metal strap around his wrist.

"You can't!" Letticia screamed. "It's mine! It's *me*!" She clamped her hand across her chair's sync link patch, threw her body's weight on top of it.

She felt Yakamoto's fingers press into her neck, just below the back of her jaws. It *hurt*, damn him. She had an instant's surprise. Then her body failed her.

Letticia had only the dimmest sense of 'later' when she heard the whisper of his metal-sheathed hand sliding out of her link. She felt the sound between her legs, like a physical violation.

"The numbness will wear off in a few minutes," Yakamoto said somewhere above her head. He sounded utterly unconcerned. Of course. *Her* life didn't matter. Not to him. Not to any of them. All they cared about was Jezekiah.

She wanted to lunge at him, claw his eyes out for violating her so. But her worthless body just hung over the chair, ignoring her. Useless, worthless, stupid, damned thing. She hated it, hated it. She managed to get her teeth around her bottom lip and bit, hard. The pain forced some life back into her mouth. "God damn you."

The Admiral was still standing by her chair. "You will feel weak for some minutes. That is normal. You will find your records intact when you recover."

"Then what?" Oh God, she was *croaking*. Goddamn him…

"That your lady mother will decide." She hear his boots click toward the door. "And your brother."

A surge of fear gave her strength. Letticia pushed herself upright on a trembling elbow. "Listen –" Her elbow collapsed. Letticia cracked her chin against the arm of the chair, slid past it onto the floor.

Yakamoto didn't even bother himself to help her up. She tasted blood in her mouth, spat it at the Admiral's polished boots. Then watched his boots turn, sharply, precisely, and stride out of her field of vision. She heard her door hiss open, heard the boots scuffle as the Admiral paused.

"The suite is secured." Her stomach tightened at the sudden respect in his tone. "Do you wish me to attend you?"

"Thank you, but no."

Only the physical lack of strength blocked a scream of pure terror. Letticia listened to the click of Yakamoto's boots fade, swallowed a whimper at the soft thud of lighter shoes cross the floor toward her after the door hissed shut.

She found strength, finally, to pull herself up onto the chair. And meet Jezekiah's eyes.

VI

Jezekiah ambled into her quarters as if he owned them. Frantic, Letticia tried to scramble to her feet. Meet death with her head up, the way a Van Buren was supposed to. Only her stupid knees wouldn't hold. They gave way beneath her, leaving her to collapse with a humiliating grunt. Helpless, she could only cling to the chair, eyes burning with suppressed tears of terror and watch Jezekiah stroll toward her.

He nodded dismissal to Yakamoto as he passed. The Admiral actually snapped to attention, then turned on his heel and left.

The sec screen rippled to life behind him. Letticia clawed at the arm rests, tried to at least get off her knees. Her shoes just scrabbled uselessly against the granite floor, left her draped across the seat like some cheap joy toy. Left her trapped, while Jezekiah circled her chair like some red-headed vulture.

Gob him, he was going to make her *wallow* in it, too. She glared up, let him see her hatred. "If you think I'm going to beg, you're wrong. So get it over with, dammit. Save me from looking at your ugly face."

"You'll look at uglier ones before we're through. And like it, if you know what's good for you." Jezekiah stopped at her side, leaving her a view of the Family crest embroidered atop his cream-colored slippers. How weird. He wasn't acting threatening at all. Of course, with Jezekiah that didn't mean a whole lot.

She cringed despite her intentions. But he only hauled her up by the arm and thumped her into the chair. Yakamoto's nerve pinch was obviously wearing off. Her elbow *hurt* where it clipped the arm rest.

"Damn it, Lush, don't you ever bathe?" He stepped back to let her see him wrinkle his nose.

"Don't be stupid. Of course, I do." Whenever Mother reminded her. "And don't call me Lush. I'm not a baby anymore."

"Physically, at least." He lifted a brow at her major domo's nearest eye. "Draw my sister a bath. See to it she gets in it. And that she makes it to the welcome reception."

Yes, Milord. A whoosh of water from the bathroom underscored the answer.

"Why? So you can drown me?" Horrible thought. Her mouth went dry even as she felt fear-sweat break out on her forehead.

"So I can draw breath in your presence without choking. Also, because you will have to attend my welcome reception tonight." He strolled away, making a point of waving a hand in front of his nose. "I'd rather not have our guests wondering whether we've poisoned the air."

"Don't worry. I'll smell worse three days into the grave." She focused her hatred into the kill-spot between his shoulder blades, wishing she had a knife. Or the strength to strangle him. But trying would only make her look like a fool. She didn't want her last sight to be Jezekiah laughing at her.

She locked shaking hands around her ribs. If he dragged this out any longer she really would beg. She would *not* give him that satisfaction. She just couldn't. She summoned the will to force the words out. "Look, if you're going to kill me, do it and get it over with."

He circled her other sync chair, tracing its edge with a finger. Watching her. Odd. From her angle he didn't look angry or nasty. He just looked…sad. Didn't sound it, though. "You're not listening, Lush. If I wanted you dead, you would be."

It could even be true. Jezekiah was nothing if not efficient. Relief cut power on her strength. Suddenly, even her bones felt limp.

Across the room Jezekiah dropped into the sync chair, stretched those long, fine legs of his out like he owned the place. The Heir's ring gleamed like soft fire on his hand. "Fortunately for you, I have no desire-" He made a show of re-thinking that – "no intention of killing you just now. Matter of fact, I've just saved your life. Twice over. In less than an hour, too. Think that's a record even for you."

He smiled that maddening half-smile of his. Oh, he was definitely up to something – she knew that smile from old. But at least it wasn't her death. "Well, then, what *are* you after?"

"Your cooperation." He leaned back to study her down the length of his nose, just like Mother. Miserable bastard. "For which you should be truly grateful. If I hadn't spoken up for you, the Admiral's visit would have been shorter and infinitely more painful."

"Liar! Mother wouldn't execute me!" She couldn't. Mother kept her *safe*. That's what mothers did.

"Cross-check with the Admiral if you're fool enough to believe so. He's right outside the door." That nasty little half-smile widened. Somehow, it didn't look at all pleasant.

"That won't prove anything. He'll just parrot whatever you've told him to say. I know a better way-" Letticia reached for her sync.

"Don't!"

To her own surprise, Letticia's hand froze above the link. She blinked at it, then him.

"You cannot afford to go spying again. Not now. Not for one very, very long time. If you do, even I won't be able to save you." He leaned forward, the smile gone. "Listen to me, little sister. And listen well, because more than just your life depends on it." Heavens, he looked positively *earnest*. "When you sawyered your way into Mother's node you committed high treason. That is a capital crime, even for us. Are you capable of understanding that, Lush? What's worse is you usurped her authority in order to sneak an assassin onto Earth. What in hell did you expect her to think except that you're aiming for her?"

"Nonsense! Mother knows I would never do anything against her! That assassin's after -" Almost she stepped into the trap. Letticia snapped her jaws shut defiantly.

"Me. I noticed. Given that the fool has taken potshots at me on three worlds and one trade station, I'm even inclined to believe you." He cocked his head, as if he were only curious. "Incidentally – just why *do* you want to kill me? You never wanted the Ring."

"Because-" Gob it all, why'd he have to ask such a stupid question *now*? "Because if you were out of the way, we'd have the perfect excuse to take over the Venus Seed trade."

"How?" For once he actually looked puzzled.

The idea she had managed to surprise him lent her strength. Letticia wormed her way higher on the chair, feeling the old excitement rekindle. "Because I was monitoring JP's reactions to your mission. He's been pissed as hell since you reached the free worlds. And he didn't even know for sure you *were* on Den Lupus! So I figured if an assassin got you out on the rim, Mother and everyone else would blame him."

Well, that was a disappointment. Jezekiah just cocked his head at her like she was some kind of fool. "Forgive me for being dense, Lush, but I miss the point. If the aim was to kill me on the rim why-"

"Of course that wasn't the aim! I didn't want to *kill* you, stupid!" Letticia leaned forward, feeling the hot energy flooding her cheeks. "I just needed an excuse for the assassin to track you back here. Then, once he was on Earth, I'd catch him and blame Grandfather Ho for trying to take out Mother's golden boy! Then Mother would finally have a reason she couldn't ignore to arrest the old man and execute him the way he deserves. And we could take over Venus Seed distribution entirely instead of just getting a cut of the profits." She sat back, reveling in the perfection of his surprise. "It would have been perfect if you hadn't gone and made such a fuss about it at Niihau."

For a whole glorious set of seconds Jezekiah just blinked at her. Then he bit his lips, ran a hand across his face as if he were hiding... what? What on Earth did *he* have to be upset about? "Did it ever occur to you that any such act would give Grandfather Ho precisely the excuse he's been trying to find to call up another rebellion? Even if we survived it this time whatever's left of our economy would be in shambles."

Oh, that was bad. She'd forgotten about all those stupid monkeys Ho Tong had. They never showed up in Net. Heavens, hiring that assassin hadn't even been her idea! She'd got the idea from the old man himself, though he'd only wanted to kill Jezekiah. Well, she could hardly tell Jezekiah that now.

He put that damned politician face on, his expression going neutral like she was some kind of enemy. "Tell you what: just turn your assassin in and I'll keep that line of reasoning between ourselves."

Odd. He seemed almost understanding. At the moment she couldn't be sure whether that was good or not. "Well, it doesn't matter. Because I don't *have* any assassin now." Which was only too true.

"You'd best call him off, in any case. Because the only thing standing between you and the Admiral's swords right now is me."

That was a lie. It had to be. But Mother had certainly been scrummed this last time. It really was a good idea not to push her luck just yet. At least, not in front of Jezekiah. Which left her at his mercy. A waft of steam from the bathroom reminded her the water was still running. She twisted in her seat to glare at the major domo. "Shut that damned thing off!"

Milord? The traitorous damned thing waited till Jezekiah nodded before it stopped the water.

The fact did not improve her mood. "Either tell me what you want or get out. I'm tired."

"This won't take long. We have guests coming."

"So? What's that got to do with me?" She didn't even try to hide her annoyance. "Mother never lets me near her stupid diplomats."

"This isn't a diplomat. It's a suitor." He crossed legs, the smile dangerous again. "You, dear sister, are going to get married."

So it was revenge after all. Letticia felt all the blood had drain down her body to pool in her toes. So that was why he didn't kill her. He wanted her to *suffer*. Force her to let some man rub his disgusting hands all over her. And worse. Hideous, horrible thought. She pulled herself up, forced the words out. "No. I'd rather die."

"That would certainly please Admiral Yakamoto. Shall I call him back in?" He lifted a brow, waited.

Letticia tried to say yes. But her lips refused to form the word.

"Good. That's more like it." He stretched lazily.

Only... looking closer he didn't really look lazy, at least not the way he used to. He'd acquired a definitely feline grace, all right. But he reminded her suddenly of a cat watching a mouse. The way that stupid assassin should have been watching him. She made a mental note to research feline methods of torture. That fool assassin was going to regret his incompetence when she got her hands on him. In the interim, she was the mouse. "Who?" It didn't help her mood any to hear herself squeak.

"You'll find the arrangement can be quite pleasant, if you make the effort."

"*Who*, dammit?"

"One very rich, very powerful, and actually very gentle man. From your perspective, though – try to focus on the profit potential."

"Gob you, *who* – what profit?" Letticia sat up, interest vying with suspicion. "You're not talking about Streiker, are you?"

"You're quite safe on that score. You're not going anywhere. He's coming here."

Letticia settled a bit. It would be nice to be *really* rich. To really *feel* safe again. Only nobody really rich would marry into a backwater like Earth. Except maybe – "*Pandar*? You know damned good and well a Pandari can't survive on Earth! They- oh." She brightened, felt the hope spike fade at his expression.

"No, the man won't die from the climate." Jezekiah massaged the bridge of his nose and breathed deep. As if it were *his* patience being tested! "Aside from the dubious fortune of being stuck with you, he should actually enjoy it on Earth."

"Well, who, then?"

"His official name is Myrra's Cub. But he goes by his battle name. Strongarm."

Well that was no help. She stretched a yearning hand toward sync, gave it up at Jezekiah's warning cough. "Who?"

"You've certainly heard of him while you've been spying for JP. Lord Strongarm. Son of the Lupan Speaker for Parliament. Alpha war lord of the Lupan Dominion." The half-smile went dangerously crooked. "The one giving JP nightmares."

"Lu-". The horrible, awful image behind the name clicked home finally. "Goddamn you!" Words just were not adequate. She snatched off a shoe and fired it at him.

Jezekiah caught the slipper without so much as a sideward glance. She yanked the other one off, raised it.

"I wouldn't, if I were you." He raised the slipper he'd caught in warning.

Gob it, he always had been a better shot than she was. Letticia threw the shoe down. She pulled her chilling toes up under her, tried to fight back the images of mangled women, of gloating Lupan males – her whole body went cold. She shook herself, clinging to disbelief. "You're lying. Mother wouldn't let you do that to me."

"Mother doesn't know."

"Why, you lying, miserable-" Letticia shot out of the chair with a strength she hadn't known she possessed. She launched herself at him, fingers clawing for his eyes.

Jezekiah tossed her shoe aside, rose smoothly to trap her arms at her sides. He hauled her kicking across the floor to the bathroom and threw her into the tub. She was still screaming when he dunked her head under the water.

He lifted her by the neck, gave her a moment to gag out water and gasp in air. "Are you ready to listen now, or shall we continue the swimming lesson?"

"Gob you-"

He shoved her under again, held her down until she thrashed for air. Lifted her back up and raised a questioning brow.

"All right!" He released her neck and Letticia shoved herself as far away as the tub allowed. "You won't think you're so big when I tell Mother what you said. She won't let you sawyer *her* that way."

He settled one haunch on the flat edge of the tub, leaned his back against the wall, arms folded. "I'm not trying to trick either of you. I'm simply sealing a treaty."

"Well, then, marry the stupid son of a bitch yourself!"

"I would, if it would work. However Strongarm wants a woman. Unfortunately for him, you're the only eligible candidate."

"That's why you didn't put it in your reports-" Ooops. She cut the sentence off with a wince.

"Precisely." She wished he looked as amused as he sounded. "It's the main reason Mother will sign off on the marriage with enthusiasm. It gives her a new excuse not to execute you. The other reason is that it also opens up an income stream that will finally free her from relying on Ho Tong's tithes on their damned Seed trade. Make Earth less of a pariah among the Commonwealth worlds."

"So? It's still death for me. Just a nastier one. I've *seen* the history vids. I know what Lupan males do to women."

"You've only seen what our founding patriarchs wanted their people to see. Truth be told, Lupan men are rather prized as husbands out on the rim."

"Well, of course. The deep space breeds aren't much better than dogs themselves."

"As a matter of fact, I expect you'll enjoy your wedding night immensely if you give Strongarm half a chance." To her surprise his smile softened. Went... the only word she could think of was 'real'. "I am offering you something better, Lush. Something precious beyond price."

"What? Hair balls?"

"Hardly." The smile faded, but it left a rare happy-ish glow behind. "What I'm offering you is safety, little sister. One of the deadliest warriors in all the branches of humanity for your own, personal protection. A man who will belong to you alone, heart and soul, always and forever. Who'll love *you*, not for your title or what you can do for him." For the first time she could remember, he dropped the working mask and looked like his old, bubbly self. Like he had before Mother named him Heir. "Can you imagine what that's like, Lush? Having someone you can trust? Someone you don't have to play games with?"

Well, she certainly wasn't fool enough to trust *him*. "What if I *want* to play games?"

"You won't. Not if you give Strongarm a chance." He shifted for comfort, his voice going gentle. "He can stop the nightmares, little sister. Make you forget Father's death. He can keep you really and truly *safe*."

Safe! If only – Letticia sat up feeling the joy light her eyes. Realized too late how her face had betrayed her, how she'd let him see the hope. She jerked back with a splash, hating her body for betraying her.

For once, Jezekiah didn't seem to care. "That's what I'm gifting you, Lush. A chance not just to *be* loved, but to know it. To know to the very core of your soul that one person in this universe loves you more than life itself. I'm giving you something I would give up the Ring to give myself."

Give up the Ring? Oh, he couldn't be telling the truth! The Ring made you sacrosanct. Made you *truly* safe, even from the other Protectors. And yet, there was an eagerness in his expression she hadn't seen in years. "Why?

He came back to his usual sarcastic self in an eye blink. The little half-smile of his working mask snapped back into place. "Why what?"

Games. He was trying to throw her off with word games. But her heart had finally stopped trying to punch its way out of her rib cage. She was starting to *think* again. "Why should I? If I gob your goddamned dog, *you* get your treaty, Earth gets rich, Mother gets to dump Ho Tong. All I get is gobbed."

"You get to live."

"That's not enough. Sweeten the offer, Jezekiah. Give me a *reason* to live."

"What do you want?" He said it as if he didn't know.

Well, she could run a test of her own. "The Heir's ring."

His working mask flickered, showed her ... well, if it'd been anybody else, she'd have said 'satisfaction'. For an instant Letticia thought she'd walked into a trap. Only she was already *in* his trap, so that couldn't be it. But *something* was going on behind those big blue eyes. Something he'd found out on Den Lupus, something big enough, *rich* enough to make him consider trading the Heir's ring for it. She rubbed goosebumps off her arms. This time the wet chill had nothing to do with them. "So? Do we have agreement?"

"Tentatively." The mask was firmly back in place now so there was no telling at all what he was really plotting. "Subject to two conditions."

"What-"

He stopped her with an itemizing finger. "One, no trade until after the marriage is consummated."

"Oh, for heaven's sake!" But there was no getting around that one. "Agreed."

"Two: you will call off that damned assassin. Now."

"What assass-?" She yelped as he lifted her by the blouse front.

"*Don't* play the fool with me!" He dropped her hard enough to crack her head against the tiled wall.

"All right. I'll call off any hired killer I might have under contract." When she found him. She pulled in a long breath, resisted the urge to rub the back of her head. "But there's one term *I* get to add: once I have the ring, *you* leave Earth. Permanently. Otherwise I just might get my theoretical money's worth out of that theoretical killer." She lifted an eyebrow at him, letting him taste his own medicine. "Agreed?"

"Agreed." Jezekiah didn't even nod. He just rose and strode out her door. Not even a backward glance.

Gob it, somehow he'd sawyered her again. Letticia beat the water in frustration. Stupidstupidstupid... *How* did he always manage that? She gave the water a final slap, leaned back to play the interview over in her head. Jezekiah had agreed to give up the Ring *and* leave Earth without even a hiccup. Obviously, then, that was what he'd wanted all along. Equally obviously, that something was out on Den Lupus. Which meant the dogs had something fabulous, something he couldn't get any other way.

Well, that was easy enough: Rogue. Jezekiah's reports weren't the only ones that had dwelled lovingly on the raw wealth of that wandering planet. Streiker wanted it, too: JP had been bribing judges all along the rim for the past few years trying to lay claim to it. Only some silly dog kept getting in his way -

Strongarm! That was the name of the dog who held claim to Rogue! At least it sounded right. She could check in sync easy enough. Give her a chance to locate that gobbing assassin, too. She started to heave herself out of the tub, rethought it even before the twin bursts of compressed air that were the major domo's 'hands' pushed her back in.

No, sync wasn't the answer, not where Jezekiah was concerned. He'd expect her to try to probe his node, have a trap waiting. For once, Letticia stood still in the tub while the major domo's ethereal hands stripped off her dress. She shrugged out of her underwear herself then slid back into the water and wrapped arms around her knees to let the major domo scrub her back.

It wasn't at all gentle about it. The rock hard scrubbing made her wonder if that was how it would feel when Jezekiah's dog rubbed its paws across her. Unthinkable humiliation! Well, she still had time to find a way around that one. And she still had one useful tool. She stretched up an arm for a scrubbing. "Major domo: fetch me Lt. Teufelsman."

VII

He had laid hands on a woman in anger. Six hours, two showers, and a nap later Jezekiah still felt dirty when his major domo's invisible hands blew him out of his quarters to face his welcome home reception. Not an issue here, his little voice reminded him. Yet the Lupan attitude still haunted him. A Lupan man who touched a woman in anger forfeited his claim to manhood, end of story. End of life, too, generally – Lupans had precious little use for a man who couldn't control himself. *Damn*, he wanted to be back there! Wanted to feel whole again, *clean* again.

Kip Marsden waited for him on the public side of the Sec post guarding the Family wing. He was in full dress uniform, the broad swath of his black jacket breast glittering with service medals, his black knee-high boots polished to a mirror shine. Against the rose-veined marble of the walls he looked like an inverted wedge of night cut into the stone. Until he grinned. "How's the head, your lordship?" Scan tingle underscored the question.

"Still in place." Jezekiah did not need to fake the answering smile. Kip had to be here on his own idea; protocols did not require the Heir have a Sec escort at Manor events. Better yet, his presence would deter the myriad well-wishers eager to bask in the Heir's reflected glory. Still – "Why the escort? Afraid that assassin will try for me here?"

"Better safe'n sorry." Kip fell into step beside Jezekiah. "Still haven't found that sonuvabitch."

"I believe you can stop worrying about the killer. I've just had a conversation with Letticia on that subject."

"Yuh-huh." Kip cocked his head, listening to his Net feed. The hall light traced a silver arc along the comm implant in his graying curls. "No offense, your lordship, but I ain't half so worried about your little sister as I am about old man Ho."

"Why so?"

"'Cause that goddamned sonuvabitch ain't *nowhere* in Net, that's why."

"Grandfather Ho?"

"Funny, your lordship, real funny." Kip scowled off another eager admin op. "If that old *mahe* had been willin' to let his people be gene-coded back when Madam Muriel offered, we wouldn't've had the rebellion in the first place."

"Yes, we would. Grandfather Ho would simply have found another excuse." And another. And another, had Mother not finally ceded him the right to ship Venus Seed off-world rather than commit full-scale genocide. From Grandfather Ho's perspective, the rebellion was simply a trade war.

"Think maybe you been out on the rim too long, your lordship." The glare Kip gave the next well-wishing wannabe made the fellow positively skip out of the way. "Think you forgot what Matsuo Yakamoto and his Samurai did to the Tong villages along the pali coast."

"I haven't forgotten. Any more than I'm likely to forget seeing my father splattered across the garden wall." Or the horror of digging through Father's shattered body to drag Letticia out of the gory rubble beneath.

"Sorry for bringin' it up." Kip seemed to pick up on the thought. "But I can't see that sonuvabitchin' assassin. And the only place on this whole damned planet I *can't* see is Ho Tong's HQ."

"You realize, of course, he could simply be a natural." They passed an exec senior enough to warrant recognition. Jezekiah returned the woman's salaam in passing. "Without a Type code NetMind wouldn't register him." He lifted a brow at Kip. "Like your Mote."

"Nah, Mote's-" Kip re-thought whatever it was. "I mean, that assassin's a haole natural. All the off-world haoles carry the Type codes that adapt 'em to their worlds. Even the mixed Types. He should'a shown up."

"Unless-" Somebody's *very* nubile joy toy fluttered past, eyes flashing an invitation. Jezekiah kissed fingers to her and made a mental note to find out who the somebody was. "Unless he was coming home, too."

"Yeah. That's what's scarin' me."

They reached the ballroom entrance. There were enough jewels bedecking the crowd within to make the overhead lights seem like an afterthought.

"Milord Jezekiah Van Buren, Heir Designate of Earth!" the major domo's voice boomed as he stepped into the spicy sweet mist of a hundred perfumes. The romantic refrain that was the Heir's anthem swelled, silencing the chatter within.

Around the curving sweep of the hall, glitterati turned in unison. The arched walls opened out onto weather screened balconies and the blue-black Pacific beyond. A full moon splashed silver across the waves along Waikiki, its gleam reflected in the pale outlines of foolhardy windriders skimming the waves out beyond the breakers. Within, floating chandeliers sent crystal reflections dancing across the edges of the merged halos.

The music ended, allowing the attendees to re-assemble into their various conversational knots. Jezekiah bowed to the degree protocol required, swept his working gaze across the sea of professional smiles, automatically sorting allies from enemies. He recognized the old habit, felt his self-loathing creep up another notch. *Damn*, he missed Strongarm! You *knew* who your friends were at Strongarm's affairs. Here – only one of the smiles facing him was genuine. Jezekiah grinned back at the round-eyed wonder of his doppelganger, noted that the boy's arm was wrapped happily around the waist of a bemedalled SecType.

"You said give him the VIP tour, your lordship," Kip murmured from his place at Jezekiah's back. "Figured the boy earned a fancy treat. Frank there will keep him out of trouble."

"Good. Make sure he's set up with a decent annuity when he leaves, too." At least he could give the boy a *choice* about whoring. The thought eased some of self-loathing. Jezekiah re-focused on the crowd. "So, then. How many warms have we got?"

Kip cocked his head, scanning. "All the ambassadors and aides are physical. Got their joy toys here, too. Other'n that it's just Madam's admin folk. Rest of 'em are holo'd." He clucked softly. "'Cept for your sister and her gobbin' Aryans."

Jezekiah's stomach clenched. Damn, he'd forgotten to warn Letticia away from Teufelsman. Another thread dropped. Another sign he'd lost his edge. Still, he could not afford to address the issue in public. Any more than he dared crane his neck looking for her. "Where?"

"Far right corner, near the kitchen entrance."

Jezekiah angled his greetings to follow Kip's direction. Letticia was impossible to miss once he got her in line of sight. She wore a stiffly full-skirted gown of yellow satin, the sleeves puffed into peaks to anchor the chains of pearls suspended between them. She should have been making her own rounds of the guests. Instead, she had her hand buried in a pocket hidden by the flaming orchid crest brocaded into the cloth of the skirt. She was giggling like a tweener schoolgirl, her eyes focused on nowhere. A trio of Aryans in white formal dress kept would-be fawners at bay.

"Find out what she's giggling about when you get a chance." Swallowing annoyance Jezekiah turned the smile on 'high' and stepped into the crowd. He accepted eye contact from the off-world cousins he'd need to court, nodded benignly at others.

"Incoming'," Kip muttered in his ear.

"Saw them." Impossible to miss the lithe young women closing in on him like ribboned torpedoes. The courtesans winnowed out the lesser lords effortlessly. Trailing wakes of disappointment, they targeted him. Already their eyes were making promises.

There were piranha minds behind those enticing eyes. No matter which of them he chose for the night, he'd be in dangerous waters. Jezekiah swept his smile across them, keeping it impersonal. Useful range of sponsors, though. He recognized Pandar's crest in the artful strands of firestones masquerading as a gown on one spectacular ebony toy. The woman was a full head taller than the white-blonde AryanType edging in beside her. That promised some entertaining fireworks later in the evening; the Aryan's ice blue gown bore the silver scythe of Streiker. Maybe he'd take them both, Jezekiah thought. At the very least, they would distract each other.

Jezekiah kept Kip's broad back between himself and the toys while he smarmed the crowd. Holo'd they might be, but the images were convincing enough to fool the human mind. Ethereal toes skipped back at the threat of Kip's solid boots.

"The Lord High Protector of Earth!" the major domo boomed. "Madam Muriel Van Buren!"

Abruptly the crowd swept back in unison, and he turned to face Mother. Even in full dress gear, she kept it simple. She'd added a pearl and ruby comb to the French twist of her hair, a matching pin to the breast of her cream silk gown. She was holo'd herself, of course – Mother never risked having all three of them together in public. Which was as well, actually. He'd have hugged her otherwise, and scandalized the Commonwealth.

"Madam." Jezekiah bowed – deeply, this time.

"Jezekiah." She extended her hand, and he went through the pantomime of kissing it. He watched her eyes flick away from him as he straightened, followed her line of sight to Letticia's corner.

The little idiot should have joined him to greet Mother; showed the rest of the Family a united front. Behind him Jezekiah felt the ripple of movement as the diplomatic gossip mongers posted notice of the snub. By morning, the outer worlds would be abuzz with rumors that would have their cousins jumping to dangerously wrong conclusions if Mother signed the treaty. Training kept him from scowling while he quick calc'd odds that Letticia had intended such trouble. Not, he decided. She lacked the foresight. "Want me to bring her over?" he asked softly.

"No. Leave them guessing. I want to see who tests the bait first." Mother smiled her rounds, motioned him to join her as she swept into the crowd. Kip fell into place between their backs.

"I've gone through that treaty of yours." Mother hooked Jezekiah's arm through hers, warned the Streikern ambassador off with a smile.

"Excellent – ouch!" Neural needles bit into his arm beneath her holo'd fingers. "When did you have feedback capacity built into your holo? Is that another of Letticia's refinements?"

"It was Lt. Teufelsman's suggestion, actually." Mother's smile stayed fond; she put the warning in her eyes.

So, then. Jezekiah put his smile on lock down. He was going to need the cover if she intended to test him here. "So what have I done to warrant the demonstration?"

"I've gone through the background terms you neglected to mention. Such as Lupan marriage pacts. Just whose marriage did you have in mind, O Heir of mine?"

"Don't worry, you're safe-" This time the needles found a nerve. Jezekiah nodded to an off-world cousin through the stars popping novas around his eyes. *Damn and damn again.* Woman didn't need a chair to inflict torture.

"So I gathered. Am I to assume you propose to marry Letticia to this Lord Strongarm?"

"Yes." Good thing, his little voice murmured, he could say so with such fervent honesty.

"Mind telling me why you didn't include that particular tidbit in your report?"

"No point announcing it till I was sure I could get her to cooperate."

"Don't you think you should have got my agreement first?" Warning pinch, this time. They reached a reigning cousin, and diplomats twittered as Mother paused to trade salaams.

"I'm afraid I took that as a given. The marriage solves-" This time the pain made him gasp.

"When did you begin making those decisions?" Mother stopped too sharply, leaving Jezekiah's arm wrapped around air. She reclaimed his hand, raised it. Music swelled on cue and the assembly twittered applause.

Through pain-starred eyesight, Jezekiah swept her the opening bow, then led her into the waltz. Two jabs later he remembered that Mother preferred to lead. He was pain-shocked enough that it took him a full circle of the dance to realize she'd actually, *physically* poked him. Took him a third circle to get his voice to work. "Nice trick."

"Wondered how long it would take you to notice." Mother swung him through the next circle. "Kip Marsden picked it up from Letticia."

"See? Told you she's good for something."

"Do I detect a hint of sarcasm in that?"

"Not at this range."

"Smartass." Jezekiah's shoulder muscles winced in anticipation, but she let it pass. Let him see, for a moment, just how much the suspicion pained her. "It was a good idea, Jess. Or it would have been, under other circumstances. As it is-" Mother let the implications hang.

"As it is, Strongarm's probably the only man in the universe who has a chance to save Lush from herself." He forestalled Mother's retort by swinging her off her feet. "Strongarm will be good to her, Mother. Hard as it is to believe, he just might actually make her happy."

"Don't make this any harder on me, Jess." Mother's working smile held steady, but her eyes went dangerous.

"Not my intent, I assure you."

"Indeed? Then kindly tell me how you intend to explain such an alliance to JP and the Council? Our cousins will certainly see it as a threat to Commonwealth security."

"JP is the only real obstacle. Octavian will come around once he sees the trade opportunities. Omar's entertainment moguls will drool at the prospect of a fresh Lupan market, so he won't object. Rest of the Family will follow their lead." Mother went silent, running quick-calcs of her own. Jezekiah risked a smile. "With luck, we can isolate JP politically. Even JP can't start a war all by himself."

"Don't bet on it." Still, she left his muscles in peace.

Under the circumstances, that was a good sign.

He let her think until the music began its final swell. "So, then. Are we agreed?"

Mother leaned back enough to smile at him. It was her formal, public smile. He felt it like a gut punch. "No."

"Why-" Too sharp. Jezekiah smoothed tone and expression into proper form. "Reason?"

"Strongarm. Lupan society is a matriarchy. By his own standards, this Strongarm will expect to be subordinate to his wife."

"That should hardly be a problem here – ouch!" He rolled his shoulder to ease the spasm.

"Strongarm is a *war* lord. The most powerful one of the Lupan Dominion. Give Letticia control of him and by extension you give her control of his battle fleet. At that point there will be no controlling Letticia." Mother's smile did not waver; her voice did. "I'm willing to let you try to rehab Letticia. But we cannot take such a chance. Pursue your treaty. But you will have to find another bride."

The music swelled to its finale. Jezekiah swung Mother off her feet in a final swirl, sending the crowd into twittering spasms of applause. He stepped back, dropped Mother the final bow. Applause thundered when she raised him to kiss him on the cheek. "Now," she murmured in his ear, "I suggest you get to work."

With a final nod, Mother swept off to make her guest rounds. Numbly, Jezekiah finished his own round of greetings. He'd just kissed fingers to a Pandari concubine when he felt Kip's presence at his ear.

"Better check this, your lordship." Kip shifted eyes toward Letticia. She was still in her corner, still surrounded by her Aryans. And clearly sync'd in.

Jezekiah gave the concubine a deeper bow than her status warranted, making the nictating membranes across her eyes flicker counterpoint to her fluttering lashes. That was going to be feed for the gossip mill, but his major domo could handle rumors. It was quite adept at fielding nervous inquiries from lesser lovers.

Even with Kip clearing a path, it took a seeming eternity to reach Letticia's corner. She was too lost in sync to see him coming, though the Aryans certainly did. One of them tried to nudge her back to reality. He gave it up a breath before Kip's shoulder knocked the breath out of him.

Jezekiah stepped up to Letticia's other side. Smiling benignly, he wrapped a hand around Letticia's wrist and yanked her hand out of its pocket. He was close enough to hear the satin tear as the portable link she'd had sewn in it ripped loose. She'd been so deep in sync the break in her link made her sway. Jezekiah held her upright while he pried her fingers free of the link. She sported pearl ear cuffs, the pale jewels carved to fit the curve of her ear. This close, he saw that she'd neglected to wash behind them.

He cradled her head against his shoulder like a loving brother for the benefit of the curious trying to peer around Kip's protective back. Using Letticia's arm for cover he passed the link to Kip. "Cover me," he mouthed, and shot the Aryans a look that ensured they'd cooperate.

Smile on lock-down, he edged Letticia through the opaque shield that separated the kitchen from the ballroom. Spidery servobots chittered frantically and scuttled out of the way, gyroscopic arms weaving to keep trays of glasses and goodies upright. The chittering followed him even after he'd pulled Letticia out of the traffic path. Fair bet, Jezekiah's little voice noted, he'd just proven bots really could swear.

"Uhhh?" Slowly, Letticia blinked focus back into her eyes. They narrowed to a viper's stare when she recognized him. "Gob you, Jezekiah-"

"Shut it." He jerked his arm around her waist hard enough to ensure she did. "If you are so goddamned determined to die, why the hell didn't you let the Admiral take care of it this morning?"

"Huh?" She was already paling from lack of breath. Fear drained what color was left. "What are you talking about?"

"What is so damned funny it's worth snubbing Mother?"

"I did *not*!"

"Hell you didn't." He kept the smile in place, though the effort made his muscles ache. "Listen, Lush, you've used up all the room for error you've got. Whatever else you're playing at, stop it. *Now*. Mother has your death warrant ready to *sign* you little idiot."

"She wouldn't!" Letticia jerked away enough to glare up at him. "You *promised*—"

"I intend to keep that promise. I've got you a stay of execution. But even I can't override Mother once she gives the order. Which she will do, unless you pretend to be one very good, very contrite little girl for the next few weeks. Do you understand me?"

She started to protest. Caught the fury in his eyes and shut it. "Is Mother really angry?"

"Be grateful you're in public. Now I suggest you waltz on out there, find Mother, and apologize. *Nicely*."

"But what'll I *say*?"

"Try the truth. You were in sync—"

"Oh, I *can't*!" Spoken wide-eyed and honest for a change. So, then. She'd been spying again already. He must have let the realization show because Letticia changed tack. "I'll just tell her how much I want to meet your doggy war lord."

"No!" That idea conjured an image he did not even want to imagine. Jezekiah ran a mental ten-count, got his voice under control. "Just tell her you were busy finding a way to sawyer Octavian's TransitLine stock."

"Oh, but I've *never* screwed with Pandar!"

Except her guilty start said she had. "Then you're overdue to try it. Which is why Mother will believe you." He'd have to warn Octavian to enhance his code guards. Better warn Kip as well; Cousin Octavian was a firm believer in *quid pro quo*. Jezekiah let her break free, scattering the procession of servobots with her skirt. Instantly her hand reached for her pocket. "I've got your link, Lush."

She clutched at her skirt pocket, eyes horrified as a mother who'd found her baby's crib empty. "Give it back!"

"Can't, Lush." It surprised him how much he wanted to, just to make her pain go away. He watched her plea morph to hate. He felt that to the core of his soul and shoved the hurt into the crowded dungeon at the back of his mind. One more old habit come back to life. "But I won't give it to Mother, either. Provided you tell me what the hell you were laughing at." He hoped with every fiber in his body it wasn't treasonous.

"Watching out for you, stupid!" She tried to jerk her wrist free, gave up with a wince. "Teufelsman caught a Tong enforcer outside. A *registered* one. He's making the monkey dance to get him to talk. It just looks really funny—"

"Scrat it!" Jezekiah yanked Letticia around with a force that made her yip and the dodging servobots chitter. She was still gasping as he shoved her through the screen.

Kip Marsden slipped through the doorway the instant Letticia passed it. "She tell you what they been doin'?" His frown said he already knew.

"Is there a back door to the kitchen?"

"Yuh-huh. But you let me handle this, your lordship. Don't want you outside unshielded till we got that assassin in wraps."

"The assassin shouldn't be a problem anymore. Ho Tong will be, if that registree is who I think." Jezekiah glared around the kitchen, trying to guess the location of the back entrance.

"Huh." Kip's scowl deepened, but he tilted his head. A servobot detached itself from the re-formed conga line of servers, passed its tray of dainties to a replacement, then scuttled down an open aisle. Kip nodded at Jezekiah to follow. "But you stay by me. And you *run* if I say go."

Minutes later they jogged out of the servants' entrance into the darkness of a delivery platform. Kip cocked his head, then nudged Jezekiah toward the roadway beyond. The moon lit the road for them, silver glow darkening the midnight shadows. *Hunting light*, Strongarm called it. Memory flashed Jezekiah the image of the Lupan on a night hunt. They were still within the weather screens, but the thought raised a shiver.

He heard a moaning scuffle when they reached the corner of the Manor. They were at the working side of the complex, here. A road cut through the hill sloping up behind the Manor, allowing TransitNet's drone trucks access to the delivery dock. Kip held Jezekiah on the safe side of the building wall. In the darkness beyond, the scuffle stopped.

"You gobbing little monkey," a vaguely familiar man's voice snarled. "I'll put *you* down there!"

"Eh, so *lack* you!" Keiko Yakamoto's voice shot back. "Told you, he's working with me. Let him go and we got no hu-hu, eh?"

"What the hell is she doing here?" Jezekiah hissed into Kip's blocking shoulder. The back of his mind noted incongruously that Kip had surprisingly dainty taste in cologne.

"Perimeter guard," Kip whispered over his shoulder. "There's an assassin loose around here, remember?"

In the darkness beyond, the moan deepened. It ended with a thud. Followed by a yelp, quickly stifled.

Jezekiah caught the white flash of Kip's grin. Dodging the SecType's warning hand, he craned around the building to see for himself.

Halfway down the building a knot of Aryans formed a semi-circle around a man's huddled figure. Keiko stood between the lead Aryan and his victim, her back to Jezekiah. She was still wearing the red sarong, but her hands were up and at the ready. The lead Aryan – Teufelsman, as he'd expected – was doubled over, clutching his arm, his glare fixed on Keiko.

He'd forgotten how ugly thwarted desire could look. Any woman with common sense would recognize it and either give in or get out. Keiko's stance said she wasn't about to do either. He had no business, Jezekiah's little voice snapped, feeling proud of her for it. It wasn't going to do either of them any good.

Behind Keiko, the victim pushed himself to his knees. Even kneeling, he matched her height. Jezekiah swore under his breath. *Damn and damn again.* He'd been right. Moonlight glistened the sheen of sweat on the Samoan's bare shoulders, the dark wetness running down his lips and chin. Against the sheen of his skin the registree's studs embedded in his temple and jaw stood out darkly. Unmistakably the mole-faced Samoan who'd grinned at him on the dock. Unmistakably Ho Tong.

One of the Aryans on the side of the half circle pointed a dark teardrop at the fellow. The Samoan arched backward, his body convulsing.

"Stop it!" The anguish in Keiko's voice caught Jezekiah's breath. "I wen tell you he's working Sec!"

"You wen tell me he's working Sec," Teufelsman mimicked. He rubbed his arm, then spat. "Run back to your father while you can, monkey. I will get the truth out of this one for myself."

"You wen got the truth! Leave him go!"

Behind Keiko, a second Aryan pointed his teardrop at the convulsing Samoan. He jerked the control upward with a flick of his wrist. The victim's legs straightened as if some unseen hand had yanked him upright. Blood spurted where he bit his lip to stop the scream.

Keiko kicked out and the Aryan dropped, teardrop control rolling free. Behind her, the Samoan collapsed. His wheezing gasps added a ragged edge to the night's whispers.

Teufelsman jabbed his uninjured hand at Keiko's back. Moonlight gleamed on the slender wand in his fist. A second Aryan darted forward, jabbed his wand into Keiko's side. Her body spasmed. She jerked away, fell backward over the huddled Samoan.

"God *damned* sonuvabitch!" Kip's whisper mirrored the cold fury that knotted Jezekiah's gut. "Stay close, your lordship." Kip stepped silently out. Except for the moonlight running like liquid silver along the comm implant in his skull he could have been simply another shade of the night.

Jezekiah fell in behind. He most certainly intended to stay close. Very close, given the way Kip shrugged the safety off the laser pistol.

Cradling her side, Keiko rose to a lopsided fighter's crouch before they reached the open end of the half circle. She kept herself between the Samoan and Teufelsman.

Jezekiah stayed behind Kip, using the big man's broad back to keep his own bright clothes out of sight. Close enough, too, to abort Kip's draw if need be.

"I have been wondering how to prove you are one of Ho Tong's monkeys."

There was a vicious satisfaction in Teufelsman's voice. "I owe your lover thanks for giving it to me. I think I shall let him die quickly. As a gesture of appreciation. Because after this, you're *mine*." He raked his eyes down Keiko with an air of ownership that turned the fury behind Jezekiah's eyes red.

"I rather doubt that." Jezekiah stepped around Kip. All eyes snapped up to him as moonlight flared off the creamy silk of his suit. He strolled into the opening of the Aryans' half circle to come up behind Keiko. She twisted round to face him. Fighting stance still. Saying without words that she trusted him no more than Teufelsman. The thought hurt. It also reminded Jezekiah to stay out of kicking range.

"On what grounds," he asked Teufelsman, "do you interfere with my Sec ops?"

"Milord?" Teufelsman straightened, pale face going pearly white in the moonlight.

"It's quite all right." Jezekiah told Keiko. He kept the tone deliberately offhand. "Continue your rounds. I shall explain the situation to Lt. Teufelsman." Even if Teufelsman somehow had some incriminating tidbit on Keiko he didn't care. Guilty or not, he wanted her away from Teufelsman's lust.

Keiko sidled closer instead. "I'm not leaving." Her hands stayed at the ready, chin jutting stubbornly.

He certainly couldn't argue with her about it here. Jezekiah locked hands behind his back, thwarting the impulse to strangle her. "Yakamoto-"

"I gave him my *word*!" The moon's silver light let him see the misery behind her defiance. Her gaze slid past him, looked up to Kip. Pleading. Opening her soul to him without even acknowledging his existence.

Mistake, to let his own heart open in response. A hideous mistake, and he knew it. Only he knew the way her throat would be tightened, knew the fear-shame behind the plea. He felt her simple, blind honesty pour into the emptiness in the core of his being. And realized an instant too late that he'd given himself in return.

He had to do something. He rocked back on the balls of his feet, focused on keeping his working mask in place. Kept the surge of utter despair private.

"You see, Milord?" Predictably, Teufelsman misread the movement, tried automatically to press his illusory advantage. "Clearly, she takes her orders only from Ho Tong."

"Like hell she does, you gobbin' snowball!" Kip edged clear of Jezekiah, a solid, threatening shadow. "Mote's out here on *my* orders. Which you'd know if you'd bothered to check!"

"But I did check, my dear captain. Why do you think the little monkey is still on her feet?" Teufelsman's voice was sweetly venomous. "The question is whether Van Buren Sec now also gives orders to Ho Tong enforcers."

Kip's silence lasted a beat too long. So, then. Kip had known about the enforcer. No chance of keeping that quiet now, not unless he wanted to leave a stack of white-blond corpses on Mother's back door. Nothing for it but to make the girl official. Which just might be useful on several levels, come to think of it. Jezekiah turned his smile cold and watched the Aryan wilt. "Captain Marsden acts on my authority. Or are you questioning that as well?"

"My most humble apologies, Milord. My error." Teufelsman bowed with what grace he could manage. He made a point of clutching his arm as he straightened. "The Yakamoto monkey is certainly free to go. However-" he salaamed Kip with open malice – "In Sec's own interests, I feel it my duty to examine the motivations of this Tong killer more closely."

"He's here because I asked him to come." Keiko had edged closer to Kip, giving the Samoan room to crawl out of the Aryans' wand range. "That's the only reason he's here, and you know it. You're just torturing him for fun, you -"

"Clams, Mote." Kip hauled her back before she took a flying leap at the Aryan.

Amazingly, she shut up. She was tiny enough, Jezekiah noted, that Kip's palm covered her entire shoulder. A part of his heart found pride in Kip's protectiveness. The rest of it twanged jealously. He tamped the foolishness down hard. Keiko was too innocent by far for the Aryans' kind of dirt. That was what mattered. He inclined his head, letting the Aryan know he was dismissed. "Should I find an interrogation necessary," he told Teufelsman, "Captain Marsden will notify you. Until then-"

"Milord." Teufelsman was already backing away. His henchmen fell in behind him, white suits fading into the night like dimming lights. They retreated in a group toward the Manor's main entrance.

Kip let Keiko go once the Aryans were out of range. She dropped to her knees beside the Samoan, cradling him while his body shuddered.

Unwise to let himself watch her. He felt too much of her rage and shame already. No point making it worse. Jezekiah forced himself to watch the Aryans' retreat instead. The shadowy figures disappeared around the building's edge. Only Teufelsman looked back. Jezekiah felt it in his gut when the Aryan locked eyes on Keiko.

Keiko snapped erect as Teufelsman's eyes found her. She twisted to face the Aryan's direction, one hand going to the back of her neck.

Kip must have felt it, too. With a grunt, the big SecType angled his targeting gaze on Teufelsman. The Aryans would surely encounter an uncommon number of SecTypes on various odd duties as they made their rounds tonight. Fair bet, more than one of those encounters would involve a painful accident for Teufelsman. The thought gave Jezekiah an inordinate amount of satisfaction.

Beside him, Kip knelt to pat Keiko's shoulder. "Easy, Mote. You know that sonuvabitch can't touch you while I'm around."

"Admiral figures he already has." The Samoan convulsed. She clutched him tighter, her cheek against his head, rocking with him. "Admiral figures I wen go wi' every man I see."

"Then I shall set his mind at ease, come morning." Jezekiah kept the tone impersonal with effort. "For now, let's get him out of here." Together he and Kip anchored the Samoan's arms around their shoulders, lifted him to his feet.

Pain-blind as he was, the fellow still fought them. It was Keiko who calmed him. She reached up to take the Samoan's face in her hands, murmured something in Hawaiian. The man went limp.

The drag of his weight made Jezekiah almost wish he'd kept up the struggle. But Keiko Yakamoto was looking at *him*, now, and with an interest that reminded him he was a man. Suddenly, the Samoan's weight no longer mattered. He caught himself straightening. And very grateful for the night's shadows.

VIII

Keiko helped Captain Marsden and the Van Buren boy lower Kamehameha No Name on to a stone bench by the moon gate near the Admin wing. She could sit a while with Kameh here, least till she was sure he could walk on his own. The moon gate opened on to the Manor's public gardens. It was a place where the people could mingle with proper Types. Haole tourists *expected* to see the people here, expected to gape at the human monkeys in their natural habitat. No haole around tonight, though, except for the Captain and Van Buren. And the half dozen SecTypes trying to sneak along on the perim. To her Samurai trained ears, each snapped twig and rustled branch pinpointed a guard's bulk and weight and location. For SecTypes, though, they were *nui* quiet.

The Captain and Van Buren were both sweating by the time they straightened up. In the moonlight tiny sweat beads glittered Van Buren's forehead like a crystal version of a Maori tattoo. To her surprise, he didn't seem upset about it.

"You can't take long, Mote." Captain Marsden bent to rest his hands on his knees, breathing deep. Even so, his head was cocked, eyes less on her than on whatever it was he saw on that permanent grid his comm implant gave him.

"No hu-hu. Be back soon as he can walk again." The thought of such a good man enslaved to a machine twinged her heart. Keiko stretched up, put her love and gratitude into a hug. Kissed his cheek for good measure.

Past the Captain, Van Buren cleared his throat. A sidelong glance caught him doing a quick breath-check. Keiko felt the insult in her gut. Well, he'd wait a damned long time for the kind of kiss he was expecting. She heard the Captain grunt and realized her fist had clenched, too. She let go and gave him an extra kiss for apology. Then braced herself and turned to thank Van Buren.

She'd expected one of those chest-to-groin smirks. Instead – Sweet Madam Pele, *mahe* looked innocent as a puppy dog waiting for a treat. Impossible to stay angry at the fool. Much to her annoyance, Keiko caught herself grinning back. After all, the man really had helped, even sweated up a shirt that probably cost more than the Admiral'd earn in a month – and was the dream-fuck of every haole woman in the Commonwealth, according to the people's gossip. Keiko straightened the smile and gave him a proper Samurai bow – keeping her eyes up on him and a hand across her chest. The courtesy obviously disappointed him.

Huh. That was a new one. He looked hurt as a new puppy, too. She tried – unsuccessfully – to keep her eyes off Van Buren's retreating back as Captain Marsden led him and their invisible escort back to the Manor. *Not* her business to let daydreams wander that way. Prince Handsome he might be, but only for haole princesses. He'd never be *her* Prince Handsome. Even so, the idea that she'd really hurt his feelings lurked under her heart.

The sense of sneaking guilt was still there when Keiko tucked Kameh into the back of the island hopper waiting for him down on Waikiki. Even under torture, she couldn't have said why it still lingered long past midnight when the party broke up and she waved Captain Marsden goodnight. Yet instead of heading home she found herself doubling back to study the Manor's residential wing from the leafy privacy of a fat banyan tree.

She'd never actually been *in* the Manor – monkeys and other animals weren't allowed through those fine doors, not since the rebellion. But she knew from a lifetime's daydreaming in this tree where Jezekiah Van Buren was housed. She shut the dream-memory down: the *reality* was he'd never see her as anything more than another joy toy, something to play with and discard when the newness wore off. Still, it couldn't hurt to say thank you more politely than she'd done. Looked like his reading lights were on, so she wouldn't be waking him up. She'd just need to get out of there before he got other ideas.

The farthest branches of the banyan nearly brushed the Manor's weather screens. Smoothing her mind, Keiko stepped off the tip of the last branch let herself fall spread eagled onto the screen itself. Trick to screen crawling was thinking 'cloud', fooling the body into denying its weight. Of course, it still felt like hugging a fire ant nest but that was just physical pain. Admiral'd made sure she'd learned how to ignore things like pain long time back.

She reached Jezekiah's balcony, dropped through the screen to land silently on the pale stone floor. She tugged her sarong back into shape and stepped into the room.

Jezekiah was awake. But he most certainly wasn't alone.

It was the Streikern toy who recognized the gasp first. Of course, she had the advantage of being on her knees. Jezekiah's own view was limited to the white-blonde thatch between her legs. His hips were wrapped in the muscled vise of her Pandari counterpart and rocking in rhythm to her thrusts. The tiny, cold section of his mind that was watching these two for a weapon thrust resented the necessity. Until he heard the sharp gasp near the balcony.

Jezekiah shoved the Streikern away and rolled clear. He hit the floor on his back, saw silver flash past overhead. He heard the knife smack into something hard. Tracked its trajectory to the balcony. And the astonishing sight of Keiko Yakamoto in a red sarong, starlight haloing her hair, the Streikern's stiletto dangling from her fingers. What little was left of Jezekiah's erection died at the comically wide-eyed horror in her face.

The Streikern op stepped off the bed, silken hair tumbling across pearly shoulders. Her Pandari counterpart slid up beside Jezekiah, eyes flickering at Keiko. She reached up to pull a jeweled comb from her coif, freeing her hair to puff out in an ebony sphere. She snapped the comb's teeth free with a flick of the wrist. What was left was a gem-studded needler.

"I wouldn't, if I were you." Jezekiah caught the Pandari's wrist, earning himself a warning flicker of white across her dark eyes.

"She's an assassin!" That was the Streikern, head down, targeting Keiko. In profile she reminded him of a Lupan hunting dog.

"If that were the case, we would not still be standing here. Instead, I rather think the young lady has a message for me." He covered the dread of what that message was likely to be with an arm sweep toward the door. "Ladies, if you'll be so good?"

"Milord, you are in danger." The Pandari oozed herself off the bed, putting herself between him and Keiko. She kept the needler hidden behind her back.

"True, but not from this young lady." Jezekiah captured the dainty gun, used his free hand to lift the Pandari to her feet when he rose.

He hadn't thought it possible for Keiko's eyes to widen further, but she managed. It was her sudden, ceiling-fixated misery that reminded him he was naked.

Decidedly inappropriate that the sight of her embarrassment should cheer him. Particularly since it was entirely possible she'd been sent to kill him. Yet Jezekiah tucked the needler under his arm and tugged a sheet off the bed. He dismissed the toys with the lift of a brow while he wound the sheet into a toga. He stowed the needler in the top fold where he could reach it fast.

"The monkey still has my knife." The Streikern had gone stiff, as if the loss were a matter of personal honor. Being Streikern, it likely was.

"Keik?" Silver flashed between himself and the Streikern. The stiletto poinged into the sandalwood wall near her nose.

The Streikern bared teeth, but yanked the slender blade free. She slipped on her shoes, swung her gown over a pale shoulder and stalked toward the door. Behind her, the Pandari's eyes flickered thoughtfully past Jezekiah's shoulder. "I beg you to reconsider, Milord. There are no doors near the balcony. How did she get in here?"

"Allow me some secrets, if you will." Damn and damn again, he hadn't even thought to wonder that. Jezekiah covered the gaffe with a smile that implied he knew perfectly well, then shooed her out. He made no attempt to return her gun. Pointedly, she did not ask for it.

The major domo shut the door behind the two women. Jezekiah leaned his back against it, kept the smile in place while he ran frantic calcs behind it. Still, if she'd been sent as an assassin, she was uncommonly ineffective at it. The thought triggered an entirely inappropriate flash of delight. Maybe, just maybe, the girl was simply here to see him. He felt the hope touch his groin, hoped she'd recognize it. "So, then, Mistress Yakamoto: care to answer the question?"

"What question?" With the women gone, Keiko stepped in to drink in the room. No embarrassment, now; just straight out wonder. The only thing that *didn't* interest her seemed to be himself.

His burst of cheerfulness shrank. "Two of them, actually: first, how in hell did you get in here?"

"Crawled down the weather screens." His gasp finally earned him her attention. "Well, I couldn't very well walk in the front door, could I? Monkeys aren't allowed in the Manor. Or you forget that, Van Buren?"

As a matter of fact he had. It was one of several important things he'd forgotten the moment he saw her. "Did it occur to you that you could get yourself killed with a stunt like that?" His little voice hissed that *her* death was not the one he should be worried about. Yet the way his gut twisted had nothing to do with fear for himself.

Keiko only shrugged. "Die now, die later. Life's a death sentence either way. So?"

"So NetMind-"

"Can't see me." She'd wandered as far as the bookshelf along the wall by the door. She stroked the shielded spines of the ancient volumes in wonder, her fingers calloused enough she likely didn't even feel the buzz of their protective shield. Either way, she seemed to forget Jezekiah entirely.

Which was as well, because at the moment he was quite sure he looked like a suffocating fish. It took him several attempts before he got the words out. "You can get in anywhere, then."

"Sure. Long's it's not battle screened. Those things'll fry anything that touches them. Otherwise, I'm just invisible-" She straightened slowly, turning at last toward him. He watched her face register the implications.

So, then. "How many other Ho Tong ops know the trick?" Beneath the sheet, he thumbed the safety off the needler.

"Nobody. Yet." Her chin set in a stubborn line. If she'd been Lupan, her ears would have gone flat.

Odd that anyone so tiny should remind him so powerfully of Strongarm. But the honest outrage in every stubborn line of her body proclaimed did it. Told him more surely than any scan that any danger from this girl would come face to face. From the heart. He felt his knees sag in relief. Fortunately his sync chair was close enough to let him drop into it before they jellified completely. "But it was Grandfather Ho who sent you?"

"Nobody sends me anywhere, Van Buren." Keiko backed slowly toward the balcony, hands up now, her expression wary. "I came on my own."

"Then why?"

"Because I wanted to say 'thank you'. Your lights were still on, so I thought – " She remembered visibly why the lights had been on. Damned if the girl didn't blush even now.

"Thank me for what?"

"Saving Kameh. That *paka* Teufelsman would've killed him for sure tonight if you and the Captain hadn't stepped in."

"You're welcome. You're sure there was no other reason?" Idiocy compounded – he'd allowed his eyes to follow his desires.

"You want to go to bed in one piece you better believe it's just that." She tugged her sarong higher. Her hands came back up defensively.

"Do you truly expect me to believe you risked life and liberty simply to thank me on behalf of a friend?"

"You can't believe, then you never been a friend." Her eyes drooped, answering insult with challenge. "Kameh wanted to say *mahalo* himself. Only he can't, being registered. So I've said it for him. You want to try for anything else, you better use that needler you got under that sheet." She turned and strode for the balcony.

"Wait!" He couldn't even tell himself why he called her back. Or why he shot out of the chair to run after her. She already had one strong leg up on the railing, but she braced for combat nonetheless.

Jezekiah skidded to a stop just shy of a black eye. Close up, her skin smelled of rain-wind and jasmine. Made it a fresh challenge to keep his line of sight decent. "Take a message to Grandfather Ho for me." He saw her chin jut and raised a hand in peace. "As a favor, nothing else."

She agreed, warily. Listened to the message, then nodded once and stepped off into the night.

Heart thumping, Jezekiah grabbed after her. The weather screen buzzed his fingertips. But Keiko was already gone.

He backed into the room. Odd, how hollow the place felt of a sudden, how chill. He tried to tell himself it was only the wee hours weighing in. Himself told him he was a fool.

Jezekiah dropped into the sync chair, winced as the needler's sharp nose poked his ribs. He set the jeweled gun on the arm rest, thumbed the safety back on. Ran his finger across the sparkling stones while he tried to sort emotion from sense. Tried to shelter his heart from kind of hurt Keiko Yakamoto could inflict. He had nothing to offer the girl that would not shame her. Not on Earth.

He stared down at the pulsing gleam of the Heir's ring, wishing he could tear the damned thing off. One day back in the political swill and he was plotting to betray the only woman who saw him just for himself. The thought left him feeling slimy. Sensors in the chair picked up the chem signals; he heard the major domo start a bath for him. With a moue of disgust Jezekiah pushed himself out of the chair and slunk toward bathroom.

He almost hoped Grandfather Ho would refuse his message. Otherwise, Keiko Yakamoto was likely to have reasons of her own to want him dead. And he knew already that he would hesitate for that one fatal second before he could make himself pull the trigger on her.

Morning, Milord. Jezekiah's major domo whipped the covers off his body, yanked the pillow off his head with a flourish. *You want to get up.*

Like hell he did. Damn. He knew he had to get up early. He just hadn't thought early would come so soon. Eyes closed, Jezekiah groped air for his pillow. His major domo chose to interpret the move as an invitation. It latched an airy hand around his and hauled him ungracefully upright.

Jezekiah pried one eyelid open, winced it closed at the sunlight streaming in across the balcony. Still, nothing for it except hope the rest of the world was in worse mettle than himself. He dragged his chin off his chest, got both eyes open. Kept them open this time.

"Hear you had an interesting night, Jess." Mother regarded him from the sync chair nearest his bed. She was wearing a simple wrap dress and sandals he remembered as her old favorites, her hair pulled back in a red-gold ponytail. Still, a stray curl managed to dangle free over one eye. The eye was not amused. "Juggling Streiker and Pandar both. I'm impressed."

"Only necessary, I'm afraid." The first shock of her presence was wearing off, leaving questions for its aftermath. Mother was clearly off-duty. Equally clearly, she was here for business, not catch up. His little voice reminded him he shouldn't let the fact hurt so much. But he'd learned out on the rim how it felt to have someone care about him. He'd thought, for one fleeting heartbeat, Mother had come because she cared about *him*. He should have known better, and he knew it. He wrapped himself in sheeted modesty and swung his legs off the edge of the bed. "What's impressive is getting both Pandar and Streiker's ops to report to you. Mind if I ask how you managed it?"

"I didn't. JP hauled me out of bed this morning to complain about it."

"Ouch." He refused to let his mind conjure the image of just how colorful that conversation must have been.

"Followed, in very short order, by Octavian." Mother lifted a brow at the ceiling. "Shower for him. Kona for me. Double strength." A rush of water within the bathroom answered at once. Mother waited till the chair's dispenser lifted a cup of steaming coffee into her hand, then turned the brow on him. "At least neither of them can accuse me of having bred boring children. We can continue our chat while you clean up."

"With your permission?" Fortunately the sheet was already loose so he could toga it around his torso without an embarrassing struggle. He salaamed Mother with a flourish, then startled her by planting a kiss on the top of her head as he passed. At kissing range, he noticed the strands of silver now stretched past her temples. He started to pat her shoulder. Remembered in time Mother would not accept sympathy, not even from him. Especially not from him. He settled for speaking over his shoulder, keeping his tone light-hearted. "Do tell me JP wasn't complaining about my performance in bed."

"He's more concerned about the company you've attracted." Mother swiveled her chair to track him. The major domo piped her voice into the shower for him. "Keiko Yakamoto does not belong in the Manor, much less your quarters."

Damn and damn again. Jezekiah frowned his question back out the bathroom door.

"The off-world ops didn't have a name for your visitor, but they certainly provided a professional grade description. Kip Marsden gave me the name. I got him out of bed an hour ago." A pause, while Mother sipped coffee and Jezekiah stifled a groan. "What was she doing here, Jess?"

"Kip and I saved one of Keiko's friends from Teufelsman last night. She came to say thank you." He stepped into the jet of hot water, hoping Mother'd let the shower noise buy him a minute's thinking time.

She didn't. The major domo simply fed her voice into the shower stall. "In a threesome?"

"With *words*, Mother!" He hoped the damned stall didn't have viz as well. "And while you're wondering, she got in here by climbing the weather screens. Which turns out to be a Samurai trick, not Ho Tong!" Which tidbit was quite likely a lie, but his shower didn't have biofeedback capacity. He hoped.

"I know. Admiral Yakamoto told me. He also wishes you a good morning, by the way."

She let him wince through the implications on that one while the shower rinsed him off and ran him through its dry cycle. The buffeting was hard enough to make him wonder whether maybe it did have feedback capacity. Airy hands tried to slip underwear on for him as soon as he stepped out. Jezekiah grabbed his shorts from the major domo's invisible grip and finished dressing himself. He ignored the unit's disapproving sniff, set his working mask in place before he stepped back into his quarters. "So where is the problem, then? Surely Kip and the Admiral have both told you Keiko is no Ho Tong op."

"You haven't done your homework, Jess. The girl's connections to Ho Tong go far deeper than that. Kona?" Mother lifted her cup questioningly.

"I think I'll settle for just water, thank you." Jezekiah started for his suite's kitchenette. A servobot scuttled out of a wall niche to intercept him. It raced up the nearest chair on four spidery legs, a silver serving platter balanced neatly atop a separate set of silver grips. The little unit planted a dewy glass of cold water in his hands, slapped a fresh napkin across his wrist. It paused to regard him with what felt amazingly like annoyance then scuttled back down into its niche. Jezekiah stared after it, wondering if he were only imagining that it was glowering at him.

Cradling the glass against his nose, Jezekiah settled into a chair facing Mother. "You know, I could build a trade empire just on this?" He held the glass up so sunlight sparkled off the dew on its sides. "It's worth whatever you choose to charge for it on the rim."

"Water? How? Every world has its own water, even Pandar." It was a sign of how desperate finances had become that Mother allowed him to distract her.

"But not *Home World* water." He drank, genuinely savoring the clean rain-water taste. "No other world's water ever tastes quite right. On the Miner clan ships they distill water from their own urine." He drained the glass, held it out for a refill. "You do not even want to think about what goes into the meatloaf."

"Thank you for that bit of enlightenment." Mother looked at her coffee, set the cup aside with a shiver.

"So, what's the problem, Mother? I must be more jump-lagged than I thought, because I don't see it."

"It may be more a solution than a problem." Mother sipped, studying him. There was a speculation he did not like at all underlying it. "Keiko Yakamoto just may save you the trouble of finding a backup to Letticia."

"How?" Jezekiah sat up fast enough the glass almost slipped out of his fingers. The Ring pulsed suddenly on Mother's hand, a solar flare off a white ceramic cup. Belatedly he realized he'd just provided Mother precisely the reaction she had not wanted.

She noticed the light pulse, visibly willed herself to calm. "I know how engaging Mistress Yakamoto can be. Believe me, I have cause to know. But you cannot allow yourself to become emotionally entangled with the girl. You can't afford it. *We* can't afford it. Even if she were acceptable mistress material, there's only heart-break at the other end of that kind of liaison."

"Then what's this visit all about?" He drained the glass, held it out. The chair's dispenser refilled it for him. "If you're worried about my starting a love affair with Keiko, allow me to set your mind at ease. Even were I so inclined-" which he was, distressingly so – "Keiko Yakamoto is not." *Yet.* He chose a wryly resigned smile, plastered it on his working mask. "In any case, the girl isn't mistress material. She's the marrying type."

"So I'm told. By all accounts she is a brave, loyal, resourceful innocent." Mother's eyes drooped, adding a frisson of danger to the speculation. "Kip Marsden positively dotes on the girl. Which leads me to suspect your Lupan warlord may find her appealing as well." She sipped, studied. "In case he has the good sense to run screaming from Letticia."

"Keiko still won't do." Amazing. His whole body shook with outrage. Definitely not a reasonable response by any measure.

"And why not? She's young, nubile, rather entirely too appealing, and – with a bit of spin – from excellent family."

"Status. The Lupan Parliament will only ratify the treaty if our marriage candidate matches theirs in status. Afraid that leaves us with Letticia." He didn't have to fake a show of thinking hard. "Or we find a fancy title for whichever of your senior ops has a suitable daughter. Create a nobility-"

"And the royal ambitions that go with it. You know better than that." Mother positively harrumphed. She finished her coffee, slapped the cup down and waved off the chair's offer of a refill. "By contrast, the Admiral tells me Mistress Yakamoto stands for the Samurai Type trial in the next day or so. Once she's passed-"

"*If* she passes." It surprised himself how much the possibility that she wouldn't frightened him.

"Agreed. *If* she passes." To her credit, Mother did not suggest that Keiko's survival would be arranged. At least Keiko would not go through life wondering whether she could really make the grade on her own. If Mother recognized his discomfort with the idea she chose not to comment. "Assuming she survives, then, she will be SamuraiType coded. She will also take the Samurai loyalty oath." She leaned back, lifted a brow. "I do hope I don't need to point out the advantages, O Heir of mine."

"Of having the alpha warlord of the Lupan Dominion subordinate to a SamuraiType oath-bound to you?" It really should not have taken such an effort to pretend amusement, Jezekiah's little voice murmured. But then, he should not have had to pretend in the first place. "My apologies, Ma'am. I should have seen the obvious."

"We won't explore the reasons why you didn't. What matters is that you accept the necessity of doing what's right for your world."

"Of course." He lifted his hand to stare at the glowing diamond band of the Heir's ring. Realized only when he felt Mother beside him what he'd allowed his face to betray. He had to catch himself from flinching, instinct expecting a blow.

Instead Mother only stroked his hair. "It's the price of the Protectorship, Jess. You do what's right for your world. Always. No matter what the personal cost."

"Even when it's wrong for you?"

"Especially when it's wrong for you." The sorrow in the way she said it made him wonder for the first time how many such decisions she must have made. He knew already one of them.

"Take the Heir's ring back, Mother. I don't want it."

"You'd be unworthy of it if you did." She rose, fingers lingering on his hair. Offering him as much of a sign of a mother's love as she dared. Even that sign was fleeting. Comm chimed, her own major domo calling for her attention. Mother ruffled his hair, then rose. Old habit tucked the errant curl into place without success. "I want you to handle this, Jess. Talk to the Admiral. And have a corresponding conversation with your Lord Strongarm."

She started for the door, turned before it opened. "One other thing. For your own peace of mind, Jess: do your homework on Keiko Yakamoto. You might feel better about forgetting her."

The door swished shut behind her. Jezekiah stretched his legs out, fingers drumming pace to the calcs running in the back of his mind. She was right and he knew it. There was no reason his heart should refuse to accept it.

He slipped his fingers into the chair's link, felt the dizzying sensation of the neural feed melding his biopat to Net. Within sync he felt like a droplet within the infinite starry cloud that was NetMind. *Major domo –* He felt the lobe of NetMind that was his major domo as if it were his own thought, merely a corresponding element of a shared universe. *Open a jumpline. To Lord Strongarm. Coordinates are keyed under my biopat.*

That will take some time, Milord.

So much the better. *Alert me when the link is ready. In the interim, where's Letticia?*

Breakfasting, Milord. In the guest wing. The major domo sounded vindictively smug about it.

Damn. So Lush was hiding rather than trying to make amends with Mother. Well, maybe that was for the better. Because he was about to start doing what was right for himself. His world was on its own.

He found Letticia in the guest wing kitchen. Off-world digestive tracts being what they were, Mother's guests generally brought their own chefs, so this kitchen was more human-reliant than the family's. At that, the room was strictly efficient: a wide central isle flanked by polished steel cupboards and sink, floor and counters in silver-flecked granite. The only warmth in the place came from the red plastic cushions on the work table chairs and the pale wood of the butcher block that divided the central isle.

Letticia had pulled one red chair up to the butcher's block. The drawer where she'd hidden a portable sync link was still open. She had one hand buried in the link, her eyes focused on whatever it was Lush saw in Net. The cropped mess of her hair was still wet, so at least she'd bathed. She was wrapped in a bathrobe she'd outgrown years ago, though she'd gone so thin it kept her decent. Hunched there, without the cover of her usual sneer, she looked lost and lonely and scared. He felt her loneliness to the core of his soul. Almost – almost – he reached out to hug her, tell her she was safe. Jezekiah fought down the urge; she'd neither believe nor appreciate the sympathy. Letticia had buried trust along with their father.

Her cup of coffee was still steaming. Beside it a plate of thick-sliced toast looked untouched. Jezekiah's stomach rumbled appreciatively. The sugary aroma of the Hawaiian sweet bread reminded him he hadn't eaten yet himself. He pulled in a long, tantalized breath, then gently pulled Letticia's hand out of sync. He caught her before she fell off the chair, held her till her eyes focused.

"Unhh…" Letticia jerked her hand free. The sharp movement drained what color she had, forcing her to grab the edge of the block for support.

"Drink this." He wrapped her fingers around the coffee cup.

"Gob you! No!" She slammed the cup down, swore as hot coffee sloshed over her hand.

"Then eat the toast. If you don't, I will." That worked. Letticia shoved a thick yellow slice into her mouth so fast butter oozed out between the corners of her lips.

She glared at him above squirrel cheeks, mumbled through them. "Now what do you want?"

"To keep you out of trouble." Damn, he really *was* hungry. He turned to scrounge for a cup, crew habit returning. A server popped out of a bot hole in the counter top. It shoved a steaming cup into his hand with an emphasis that bespoke rebuke. He lifted his cup to it in salute, turned back to find Letticia slinking her hand into the link. He used the opportunity to grab the remaining slice of toast off her plate.

"That's mine!" Letticia grabbed for the toast, sync temporarily forgotten.

"Order another." Jezekiah leaned back against the counter to savor a bite of the sweet, chewy bread. "Now do tell me that you were working on an assignment for Mother."

Letticia snatched up her coffee. The cup handle slipped on her butterslick fingers. Hot coffee splashed across her plate, bounded in a brown rivulet over the block's edge. Swearing, she scooted away from the butcher block but managed to grab the cup.

Jezekiah popped the last bite of her toast into his mouth. He ducked out of missile range an instant before black coffee and white china spattered against the wall where he'd been. "I take it that's a 'no'." He took a moment to lick butter off his fingers while the servobots cleared away the mess on the floor and counter. "Then you had damned well better not be spying again."

"I wasn't." Letticia wiped her hands on the moist novelette the major domo offered. "I was tracking your latest foul up. So, there." She folded her arms and pouted for emphasis.

"Just how have I fouled up, pray?"

"Your pet dog is in trouble. With JP."

"More likely JP's in trouble with Strongarm." Jezekiah kept the tone skeptical, but his heart lurched. Damn, could she have infiltrated his node already? She'd have him and the whole damned Commonwealth at her mercy, if so. He sipped coffee to hide the shudder. It tasted bitter. "How so?"

"So it's *your* fault, not mine. It's your precious trade treaty that started it all." Letticia snapped her fingers. A servobot slipped a fresh cup of coffee into her outstretched hand. "Want to know how?"

"I suspect I'll find out soon enough." Jezekiah faked a yawn and finished his coffee. It was the surest way of getting the truth out of Letticia. She never could resist indifference. "Assuming you're telling the truth."

"Oh, I am. I never lie when the truth will do." Letticia settled back to gloat. "That Lupan trade route you set up skirts Streikern space. So JP filed a protest with the free world assembly."

"Which the free worlds ignored. Tell me something I don't know."

"Because they think the Lupans will give them a better profit. So JP's teaching them both a lesson. He's confiscated a whole Lupan caravan of ore barges headed for free world markets." Letticia lifted her cup to smirk at him. "A Lobo Clan caravan."

Strongarm's clan. Strongarm's caravan, that meant. God *damn* JP! By habit Jezekiah reached for the spigot to wash his cup. This time the servobot did slap his hand. He surrendered the cup without argument, rubbed at the sting while he calc'd out consequences. Strongarm would have to retaliate – a loss of face that size demanded it. Certainly that was what JP was counting on. Gave him the chance to spin the incident to his own ends. Unless – "How much did Strongarm lose?"

"If you're thinking of making good on Strongarm's losses, forget it. Net loss on that cargo exceeds Mother's operating budget for the year." He could hear the smirk in Letticia's voice. "Looks like your little doggie is either going to the poor doggie kennel or get himself blown out of space."

Damn and damn again. It was only Mother's training that kept him from slamming a fist into a cabinet. "Does Mother know?"

"Not yet." Letticia's smirk expanded to a gloat. "Maybe *you* want to rescue your puppy? I'd love to watch you manage that one."

"If I have to, I will. There's more than one way to spin this…" For more than just himself, too. "Link us into FiNet, Lush. I want to track that caravan's cargo."

"Why? Don't you believe me?"

"Just do it."

Pouting, Letticia sync'd in. She put the feed on viz so he could see it with her. A rainbow market chart coalesced in front of the fridge, contracted to tight focus. The astonishing spike in Streiker's silver trade marker made Letticia whistle. She had Den Lupus' chart up before Jezekiah even thought to check. Its navy blue marker showed a corresponding valley.

Strongarm had just bought back his own cargo.

The chart vanished. For once, Letticia unsync'd herself. She frowned up at Jezekiah, clearly running calcs. "Just how rich is that dog, anyway?"

"Rich enough to turn JP green with envy." Jezekiah stifled a grin at her new-found interest. If that greedy gleam in Lush's eyes was any indication, JP just might have done him a good turn after all. "Rich enough to buy his wife anything she can imagine and indulgent enough to let her do it."

"He certainly doesn't know how to handle money!" Letticia sniffed, but tapped her plate. A servobot slid a fresh plate of hot toast in front of her. She settled back, munching while she thought. "Why didn't he wait? JP would've dumped that ore quick enough. The volume alone would've depressed prices all along the rim. If your doggie friend wanted to waste his money on a beau geste he should have waited till JP bailed. Then he could have got his cargo back cheap-"

"Well, then, it looks like Strongarm could use a good money manager. Maybe he needs you more than he realizes." Jezekiah kept the tone offhanded. No point pushing it further; Letticia was already eyeing her link, already calc'ing possibilities.

He kissed fingers to her in farewell and strode out the door. So, then. That would keep Letticia in the competition. At least until little sister thought to pull up Strongarm's viz….

In the interim, he had an unhappy chore of his own to pursue.

Just north of Waimanalo beach the road split in two, just before the main haole road started the climb up to the Koolau watershed. The dawning sun turned the haole road into a gleaming gold ribbon that ran straight uphill till it disappeared into the lush darkness of the Koolau mountains. The branch off – Tinker Road – was more a memory than a real road, so broken and overgrown that the proper Types dashing past in their skimmers probably never even saw it. Jogging toward the split, Keiko Yakamoto traced the path the Admiral had set for her morning's training run and felt her heart drop with the road's rise. Had to be her imagination, but she could swear that damned haole road had got steeper since last time she'd run it. Old Tinker road dropped invitingly away downslope, to the long smooth stretch of beach about eight klicks below. Down where the rising sun sparkled the waves rolling into shore and put a cherry tinge to the white sand. Out beyond the breakers a shiny red dot left its own trail of white foam parallel to the shore. Somebody, Keiko noted jealously, was lucky enough to be out racing a hover ski.

No. Arms pumping, Keiko locked eyes grimly forward and listened to the slap of her bare feet on the road. A proper Samurai would never give into lazy temptation. She had *orders*. A proper Samurai never questioned orders. A proper Samurai just obeyed, no matter what the cost. Especially on a punishment detail. Only that damned haole road just went straight up. And up. And up… And she was *so* tired…

No! She caught her pace dragging, forced her knees to lift higher. That was a monkey's weakness. She would *not* give in. She'd prove to the Admiral she was worthy. Prove she was just as Samurai as he was. Not like her mother at all. With wrenching effort Keiko pulled her mind back to the rising road ahead, let her thoughts flow in the pumping rhythm of the run. Road'd level out…In another fifteen klicks …On top of the mountains…

A long tour-type skimmer buzzed past, its backwash flapping her khaki shirt around her ribs. Keiko set her jaw and tried to ignore the pebbles its repulse field spat at her. This batch must be fresh off the ship to be out so early. She caught a glimpse of eager faces and jabbing fingers through its clear bubble screens. Swearing, Keiko slowed her pace. She invested a breath in a prayer to the goddess Pele that this batch of tourists wouldn't want to stop to take vids of the local wildlife. Last time she'd got ambushed that way, she'd flashed Tong signs at their cams just to get even. She still didn't know how the Admiral had found out, but she'd been on punishment detail for a month after that one.

No luck. The skimmer was already slowing down. It came to a full stop just beyond the Tinker branch-off. Through its weather screens she saw tourists diving for their cams eagerly enough to make the skimmer bounce on its field as it pulled to the side. With the fat old men in the lead, too. That kind always wanted a free feelie when they posed with the monkey. Mood she was in this morning, that could mean dead haole on the highway. The thought lifted her spirits. In that case, she wouldn't be giving into temptation at all. She'd be averting an 'incident' – beating a tactical retreat. With a silent thanks to Tutu Pele, Keiko picked up speed and darted down Tinker Road. Behind her she heard the tourists shouting for her to come back. She resisted the urge to flip them the universal finger over her shoulder.

After the thirty klick run from Diamond Head, Tinker was still a challenge. It didn't lead anywhere, not since the Admiral's Samurai had wiped out Waimanalo town during the Rebellion. The Van Burens didn't let the tourists near those burned out relics. They didn't maintain the homie roads, either. What the wind and brush and sprouting kiawe trees had left of the asphalt was cracked and crumbling, making footing treacherous. A couple of klicks before the beach the ground leveled off in a thick stand of ironwood trees the homies called Sherwood Forest. Even after the hop, skip, and jump down Tinker, she was still a good twenty klicks short of her assigned distance. She ought to finish her run along the shore. That's what a proper Samurai would do, especially because running on the sand would be so much more exhausting.

She really did try. She practiced broken field running through the trees till she reached the beach, shadow boxing the gray trunks on the way. Worked, until she reached the shoreline. Beyond the trees, white sand and sea wind swept her good intentions away. A hundred feet out that hover ski rider was still bouncing across the waves like some manic ping pong. Whoever it was, he was having a fine time for himself; his joyous whoops rode the wind. The happy sound of his voice brightened her own mood. Looking south, the beach ended in the dark hulk of the Koolau. Tracing the curve of the pali cliffs she made out the misty outline of Makapuu Point and Manana Island beyond. It was almost magically peaceful.

Or would have been, if the fool riding that hover ski hadn't noticed her and decided to head in to try his luck. Damn, now that he had the hover ski pointed straight at her she could put him in perspective. He was one *big* mahe. The man made the hover ski look like a baby's bike. Sportsy type, too: he was sun-browned as any homie. So much for trying to finish her run on the beach, then. Damned fool would probably think she was trying to play coy and give chase. That one was too big to take chances with. Snorting in disgust, Keiko shook the stiffness out of her legs and started back toward the trees. Why did men always think running *away* meant 'come here'? Maybe NetMind had an answer, but she'd never find out if she didn't earn her Samurai Type code. Mad as the Admiral'd been last night he was likely to pull her out of the Type trial altogether if she got into a smack down now. Make her stay a monkey for life…

"Heai!" The mahe on the ski managed to outshout the wind and waves. It was his voice she finally recognized.

"Kameh?" Keiko paused to scowl back at the shore. That was Kamehameha No Name, all right. He'd reached the shore and kept on coming. Above the water line the ski's field blew the soft sand up into a fine white mist. The ocean wind turned it into a stinging cloud and spat it at the forest. Keiko ducked behind the gray trunk of an ironwood tree and let the cloud blow past. She waited till the engine's roar scaled back to a growl before poking her head around the tree.

Kameh stood straddling the ski, feet planted like brown tree trunks in the sand. Sunlight gleamed on the dark registree's studs embedded in his temple and jaw. Below the studs his face was bruised and swollen from the beating Teufelsman had given him last night. But he was still grinning like he'd just raided somebody's stash. "Heia, gul, you want a ride?"

"Whose ride?" She *really* ought to make excuses and get back to her run. Kameh attracted trouble even faster than she did. Worse kind of trouble, too. But she owed him respect for what he'd endured last night. Besides, he was a *friend*, the real thing. Keiko grinned back and swung around the tree. "Where you get one hover ski, eh?"

"Not mines." He shrugged, unconcerned. "*Faha* Samoa."

Faha Samoa, the Samoan way. Which meant whoever Kameh had borrowed that hover ski from was probably thinking about now just how nice a wave hop would be and wondering where in hell his hover ski had gone. Kameh would return it, of course, once he'd finished his joy ride – that was a matter of honor – but all hell could break loose between times if he'd borrowed from the wrong person. "You didn't borrow from a haole, did you?"

"Nah." Kameh leaned forward to flick sand off the shiny hood. The back of the ski tilted up with him. "Belongs one cousin up Kaneohe way. Want a ride? This one fast machine."

"Can't. I got to make it up to the watershed and back 'fore noon lessons."

"What for?" Kameh sounded almost equally puzzled and outraged. "Admiral trying kill you or what?"

"Nah, he's just trying to train me up for Type trial." She couldn't whine about a punishment detail, not to Kameh. Being Registered made his whole life a punishment. Keiko ambled over to run her fingers across the ski hood in admiration. "Sure is one pretty ski, eh?"

Kameh trapped her hand in his. "Get you one just like it, you want."

"No can do, brah." She pulled her hand free, though she didn't let him go. Against the outsized ridges of her knuckles his great paw didn't seem quite so massive. "Type trial's live or die. If I screw up, I don't come back."

This time it was Kameh who pulled his hand away. "So why you go try, eh?" He slapped the engine's control patch and the ski shuddered as its hover field died. The absence of its underlying growl made the waves suddenly sound louder. Kameh folded his arms and scowled while the machine settled onto the sand beneath him. "What you want be Samurai for anyway? That Samurai stuff all guano, eh? Why you want to leave the people?"

"I don't!" She *really* ought to head out. Only she recognized the dread in

Kameh's eyes and knew his fear for her own. Keiko rested her butt against the hood of the ski instead, let herself just feel the warming sand sliding up between her toes. "I just want to be a *person*, you know? I want to be *somebody*. Not a -" She cut the sentence off before she said 'a whore like my mother'. Kameh's mother had gone whoring, too. Hadn't a choice, once the Venus Seed addiction took her. Maybe, Keiko thought, she'd been lucky her mother'd run off after all. She hadn't had to grow up watching how Seed destroyed a person. If her mother had stayed, maybe she would have killed the haole trick who'd beat her to death, too.

Didn't matter. Kameh knew her well enough to know what she was thinking. He swung one tree trunk leg over the ski. The machine slid a good fifty centimeters when he leaned against it beside her. It was a sign of just how serious he was that he didn't try to rest an elbow on her head. He just folded his arms and frowned down at her. "That what you doing in Van Buren's bedroom last night? Makin' yourself a somebody?"

"Oh, Sweet Tutu Pele!" Keiko threw her hands up and started to stalk off toward the trees. She got half a step before Kameh hauled her back with a hand on top of her head. He turned her around to face him with a twist of the wrist. Proved just how well he knew her by holding her at arm's length, keeping his body beyond her kicking range. "I just went up there to say thank you. Nothing happened. Trust me – he already had all the company he wanted." The memory of just what kind of company she'd interrupted flooded back and burned up her cheeks.

"Musta been one big nothin', eh?" Kameh tilted her head back gently, obliging her to face up to him The way he pursed his lips just made her blush harder.

"Yeah, well, Van Buren musta thought it was a big kind of nothing. 'Cause somebody wen tell the Admiral about it. Got me another damn punishment detail." She tried wriggling to see if she could break his grip on her skull. Definite no go. She settled for funneling her exasperation into her scowl. "So how'd you know, anyway? Van Buren tell the whole damned island I was there?"

"Don't know about the Heir. Grandfather one who told me." Kameh finally took the hint and let her go. He looked down at his hands as if he suddenly didn't know what to do with them.

"Uh-huh. And how'd he know?" Yet Grandfather *had* known or Kameh wouldn't be here. Not so comfortably, anyway. The fact niggled at her memory and made her wonder if Grandfather already knew she'd promised Van Buren to get him a talk time. Maybe that was another reason Kameh was here, so she could pass the message on. Be like Grandfather to make it easy on her.

"Maybe he got ears in the Manor," Kameh was saying. His shrug added that he didn't care either way. "One thing sure: he got eyes and ears both on you, gul. Old man love you like he don't love nobody else. He know where you are, twenty-four seven." He decided, finally, to just fold his arms again, his broad, brown face turning sorrowful. "He don't want you get killed in that lolo Type trial."

"Makes two of us, eh?" Made three of them, judging from how miserable Kameh looked. Keiko reached up to lay a hand on his forearm. She couldn't love him the way he wanted her to, but she loved him nonetheless, and honored him for accepting it. "But that's not why you're out here this hour, brah. *Ke ha pilikia*? What's the trouble?"

"You know Grandfather got one big hate for the Samurai."

"Really? You wen stay up all night just to tell me that?" She arched her brows in exaggerated surprise, hoping to make him smile. Didn't work. "Yeah, well, the Admiral's not exactly in love with him, either." Story of her life. Two main people she loved in the whole world and they had to hate each other. "So why you out here, eh? Grandfather send you looking for me?"

"Maybe." Kameh tried for a smile, but he only managed worried. "Grandfather got plans for you, gul. You get yourself killed, going break his heart." He grunted in some kind of private amusement. "Bad times around here, then. 'Cause you 'bout the only heart that old man got."

This was getting just too depressing. Keiko smacked Kameh's arm – open palm, for noise rather than hurt. Against his muscled arm the blow sounded like a cracking branch.

"Ow! Why you go hit me, huh?" He rubbed at the fading white imprint of her knuckles.

"I hate to surprise you all, but you know I just might make it. Admiral doesn't *want* to kill me." She hoped.

"Don't matter. You live, you be Samurai." He rubbed at the red spot she'd raised. "Way Grandfather see it, you dead either way."

"Oh, that's just talk. Grandfather knows I love him."

"Yeah, he know -" Kameh cut the sentence off with a wince. He lifted a hand toward the Registree's stud embedded in his temple. Rethought it and rolled his head instead.

"Hurt?" The sight of his pain tightened Keiko's throat. She stroked his shoulder, wishing she could rub out all the pains he endured.

"Always." He swung his head side to side like a puzzled bull. He tried to hide the pain when he stopped, but it still showed in the pinched set of his eyes. "You listen, gul. Grandfather don't want you standing Type trial."

"But, *why*? I'll still be me. I'll just be a *person*, is all."

"Don't know. All I know is he's got somethin' big planned. Whatever it is, he wants you with the people for it. You go Samurai on him and he kill you same as he would your father. Faster, maybe."

"But he wouldn't-"

"Yeah, he would!" The sorrow in Kameh's face underscore the truth of it. "Then he got to kill me, too, and he know it. 'Cause he know I always going come if you call, Keik. Even he send me off-world, I come back if you call."

"So what he want me do?" She felt tears trying to burn up her throat, and gulped them down. "Flunk? That's just another way to die." That wasn't it, and she knew it. But she couldn't think past the idea Grandfather would ever hate her. It just hurt too much. She'd never thought Grandfather wouldn't understand.

"He don't want you hurt, gul. That why he sent me watch for you." Kameh looked away, embarrassed. Admitting silently Grandfather knew he'd have been out here watching anyway.

"He wants you come home. To your own people."

"But I can't leave the Admiral! "

"Why not?"

"'Cause it's *wrong*, for one thing!" The enormity of such a betrayal blanked her mind, denied her the words to explain what she felt.

"Why?" Kameh clasped her hands, earnest and urgent. "What your father ever done for you 'cept try and make you mean like himself? When he ever be good with you, eh?"

"I owe him, brah. He didn't have to raise me." The shock of the idea was wearing off. The amount of indignation swelling up behind it surprised her. "He could've just left me wherever my worthless mother dropped me. Nobody would've questioned it – I'd just be another joy toy's kid. Probably be Seed sick myself by now." She'd never thought before about just how hard it must've been for the Admiral to take her in. Just how much of *his* life he'd invested in training her. Giving her the only kind of chance she could ever have to prove she was a real person. If she ran from Type trial now, she'd betray herself as much as the Admiral.

She jammed hands on hips, feeling her strength grow in her answer. "You tell Grandfather I'll always love him. But I've got to stand Type trial. For the Admiral almost as much as for myself."

"Old man not going to like it." He cut himself off with a grimace.

"You okay?"

"Yeah. Somebody running scan on me. Always make these things hurt worse." He rubbed his neck, shoulders hunching. "Must be one Sec patrol nearby. Better I go 'fore they get here, eh? Don't want to make you trouble." He swung back onto the hover ski.

"Hey, Kameh?" She caught his arm before he could back the ski up. "Take Grandfather a message for me? Tell him Van Buren wants to talk to him. They can work the timing out themselves."

"Yeah, I tell him." Kameh slapped the engine patch and the ski roared back to life. "Only you think quick, eh? You let Grandfather know."

He was gone in a roaring swirl of white sand and sea foam just before the Sec skimmer thudded over the tree tops south of them.

From the skimmer's elevated vantage point, Waimanalo Beach stretched northward like a flat cotton ribbon. The early sun put a silken sheen on the wet sand along the water line. The shine made the expanse of forest above the shore seem even darker, but it brightened the khaki shirt and shorts of the young woman on the beach. Against his expectations, Jezekiah Van Buren caught himself leaning forward in the passenger's seat, eager for a better glimpse of Keiko Yakamoto. Not a good sign, that eagerness. Not good at all. After that little conversation with Mother this morning, he thought he'd put his foolish reaction to Keiko in perspective: an aftermath to jump lag and crew habit, nothing more. He couldn't afford to allow Keiko to become a personal distraction in any case. If he wanted to escape the Ring he had to keep Letticia from getting herself executed for treason long enough to marry Strongarm. She'd settle down, once she had Strongarm's level head and honest heart to guide her. Make a damn fine Protector, too. Mother would see that, and the advantages to making Letticia her Heir instead. Then he'd be free. Then he could think about other options for Keiko Yakamoto. She'd have her Samurai Type code, and Mother's gratitude to go with it. The girl would be able to write any ticket she wanted with that kind of status-bump. Maybe even a ticket out to the free worlds. Yes, he could definitely find options...

"Now you wanta tell me again just why we're haulin' our sorry asses out here this hour of the morning?" Kip Marsden scowled across the skimmer's cockpit at Jezekiah. Kip held the master's seat, so the early morning sun glared off his comm implant when he turned his head. The glare wasn't enough to hide the disapproval in the scowl.

Damn, he'd let his guards down again. Clearly Kip had caught the telltale spike of speculation in his biopat. "Just obeying Mother's orders. Honest." Jezekiah squinted past Kip's personal sun flare to watch Keiko on the beach below. She'd certainly noticed their approach; the skimmer's heavy repulse fields made even the ironwood trees below bob like manic courtiers. Yet she'd turned her back to them, focused her attention instead on a red hover ski bouncing away across the waves. He didn't need to up magnification to guess the identity of the massive homie manhandling the ski. He also didn't need the jealous upsurge that followed recognition.

"Think you better stay in the skimmer, your lordship." The words were polite enough, but there was no mistaking the warning in Kip's tone. "What with an assassin on the loose and all that."

"Point taken." Jezekiah lifted hands in surrender. "Unfortunately, Mother made it quite specific that I speak to Mistress Yakamoto myself." Luckily that particular lie was close enough to the truth he could make himself believe it, at least long enough to pass Kip's scan. "What's she doing down here anyway? Thought you said the Admiral had sent her on a training run up to the Pali Highway."

"That's what he said." Kip paused while the skimmer settled itself on the sand. "Be a cold day in hell 'fore Mote ever does only and exactly what her father tells her, though." The beach disappeared as a mist of white sand wrapped itself around the skimmer's shields. The sand slid off when the skimmer shut its engines down and the world drained back into view.

So did Keiko Yakamoto. She'd strolled up the beach to meet them, stood hands on hips, feet apart now, reminding Jezekiah of a ship's captain waiting to dress down an errant crewman. Did not help his peace of mind that he remembered how it felt to be the crewman. He heard Kip's grunt and stifled a grin. Anyone who didn't know Kip would have thought his disapproval was aimed at Keiko.

"Listen, your lordship." Kip stopped the skimmer from opening its doors with a gesture. "I don't want you getting' the wrong idea, here. Mote's a good kid. Honest, too. Way too honest for her own good, you get my drift. You ask her a question, you gonna hear what she really thinks." He bit his lip, all too visibly searching for some politically correct phrasing.

"In other words, she's likely to tell me to gob off." Odd how the prospect cheered him. Even after only a day back in the political swill he welcomed the prospect of any kind of honesty.

"Yeah, well, don't say I didn't warn you." Kip told the skimmer to keep perimeter watch, then popped the doors. Motioning Jezekiah to stay put he stepped out first, lifted a hand in greeting to Keiko while he ran a three-sixty scan of his own.

The precaution was both sensible and necessary and Jezekiah knew it. Yet in front of Keiko Yakamoto, it made him feel less of a man. Jaw set, he slid out of the skimmer without waiting for Kip's signal. That earned him a sharp scowl from Kip, but it made Keiko look at *him*. To his disappointment, she didn't look particularly happy to see him. She didn't quite turn her nose up at him. Judging from the way her lips set, she was simply mad at him. Jezekiah's little voice murmured he really should not try so hard to figure out why.

She waited respectfully for Kip to finish his scan before she spoke. "Heia, Captain. How you find me, eh?"

"Kameh." Kip shot Jezekiah a final moue of annoyance before he trudged across the sand to meet her, leaving Jezekiah to follow. "Any time you're not where the Admiral thinks you are, all I gotta do is run scan on Kamehameha No Name. Boy follows you 'round like a damn puppy dog." He reached her side, laid a fatherly hand on her cheek. "You want to watch how much time you spend with that boy, Mote. Those studs make him a beacon for trouble in every lobe NetMind's got."

"I know." Keiko scuffed a brown toe through the sand before she shrugged the warning off. "But he's *ohana*, Captain. Family."

"Perhaps I can help, then." Jezekiah stepped up beside Kip. Keiko didn't really snub him, he decided. She simply opted to ignore his existence. Didn't help his ego at all to hear Kip choke down a snicker. It put a sharper edge to his words than he'd intended. "At very least I can offer you a job that will keep you too busy to get into trouble."

"Yeah, I know exactly what kind job you got in mind!" Keiko turned on him with such ferocity that Jezekiah dropped back a step. "What'd you do, put out some kind of broadcast I stopped by your room last night? Whole damned island knows I was there last night. And they all think they know why, too!"

"That's hardly surprising, is it?" Oh, damn, that came out wrong. Jezekiah saw her lips go white and kicked himself mentally. What was wrong with him? He hadn't stuck his foot in his mouth that thoroughly since he was twelve.

Too late to fix it now. Keiko advanced on him, jaw out, fists balled. He realized, suddenly, just how hard and calloused her fists were.

"Uh, Mote-" Kip blocked her advance with an outstretched hand.

"That's all right, Kip. Let her pass." Jezekiah pulled himself up to meet Keiko's anger face on. If he was going to take a beating from a woman, at least he could take it like a man. "I *meant*, Mistress Yakamoto, that I did not mention your visit last night to anyone."

"Yuh-huh" She stopped short of punching him, though she settled into a fighting stance to glare. "Admiral just thought it up for himself. That's why he gave me punishment detail again." She jabbed a finger in the general direction of the mountains. "He send me clear up to the watershed and back."

Ouch. That was a full marathon run. No wonder she was angry, especially with the rigors of the Samurai Type trial coming up. On the other hand- "In which case, Mistress, may I observe that you are somewhat off-course?"

She looked so startled he'd noticed that Jezekiah almost laughed aloud. He remembered in time that he was still in punching range and stifled it.

"Give it up, Mote." Kip had his head cocked again, listening to scan while he watched them. "I can vouch for his lordship. He didn't rat you out."

"Huh." Some of the anger went out of her, leaving suspicion in its wake. "So if da kine here-" she jerked a thumb at Jezekiah – "keep shut, who wen told the Admiral, eh?"

"I'm afraid that was my lady mother." Despite the risk, he grinned at the way her eyes went wide. "I really must congratulate you, Mistress. You have managed to haul, let's see-" He made a show of counting them off on his fingers. "Three Van Buren Protectors, one Home World Sec Chief, one retired StelFleet Admiral, and one very tired Van Buren Heir all out of bed in a single morning." He finished by lifting a brow to match. "I do think you just set a new record."

"Yeah, well, don't you take credit. If you're tired, it's your own fault." She frowned, puzzlement growing as the names on his list registered. "What's your family got to do with last night, anyway, eh?"

"It may surprise you to know that what you interrupted last night was actually a diplomatic negotiation." There was a large enough grain of truth in that one to let him say it with a straight face.

"Oh, yeah, I could tell"- She slapped hands over her mouth, eyes going horrified above them. "You mean your family was *watching*?"

"I sincerely hope not." From the corner of his eye Jezekiah saw Kip turn away to pretend it was a cough that made his shoulders shake so hard.

"Then what're they so upset about?"

"I believe the job I mentioned will answer that question. If you'll allow me?" Jezekiah started to wrap an arm around her shoulders. Converted it to hands up and off when her dismay morphed back into a glare. "Why don't we take a walk while I explain?"

"No ya don't, your lordship." Kip clamped a hand on Jezekiah's shoulder. "You just lean that royal ass of yours against the skimmer. ShipMind'll up shields anybody starts shootin'."

He swept his gaze across the trees, seemed satisfied with whatever his built in scan showed him. "You want some privacy, I'll be right down the beach." He waited till Jezekiah dutifully parked his back against the skimmer's bulk then ambled off, head swiveling in short, sharp motions.

"So what kind of job do you have in mind, Milord?" Keiko took up the Samurai's loose-limbed style of attention just beyond arm's reach.

Something that had been niggling at the back of his mind finally coalesced. "You do have the most erratic accent, Mistress Yakamoto."

"I can talk haole when I have to." That got her out of the attention stance, if only to put her into jaw-up defensiveness. "I can *read*, too. Samurai *wei* and *shotai* scripts, Commonwealth Standard." Her jaw came up. "I can even read old Eng a bit. Better'n you can, I bet."

"Quite likely on that last one. I'm impressed." He meant it, too. Amazing how much he wanted her to speak to him with the same easy trust she had for Kip. Only he did not deserve her trust the way Kip did. He never would, as long as he was trapped by the Ring.

"Yeah, well, don't be. Us Naturals don't have a choice, do we?" Shame flickered across her expression, hidden quickly under old habit. "No Type code, no NetMind entry. No NetMind entry, and you just don't exist. Period. So the Admiral's had to teach me everything the hard way." The way her expression closed bespoke just how hard some of those lessons had been.

"You might be surprised to learn that on Den Lupus they teach everything the hard way, too."

"Den Lu- you mean the *Lupans*?" For an instant, her face lit with delight. But only for an instant. The suspicion came back, harder and colder. "Nice, but you didn't have the Captain track me down out here to talk about Lupan language lessons. Milord."

"Actually, I did." This was absolutely ludicrous. Why was he so damned *happy* just talking with her? Worse, why did he so want her to be happy with him?

"Listen, Milord." Keiko cast a pointed glance up at the highway. "I've got a long run ahead of me, and you're not helping me get through it. So why don't you just tell me what the Lupans got to do with last night?"

"Can you keep a secret?" He knew the answer, of course, even before her expression went guilty.

She scuffed a toe in the sand, annoyance vying with curiosity. The curiosity won. "Why?"

"Because even your father doesn't yet know what I'm about to tell you." He watched her blink through the implications. "The alpha war lord of the Lupan Dominion is coming to Earth in two months."

"Are we at *war?*"

"Not yet. Not at all if I can help it." Damn, the girl was transparent as a weather screen. A man could build a good life with a woman like that. Never have to wonder where her loyalties lay. Or what schemes she was hatching behind his back. A man would always know where he stood with Keiko Yakamoto – He realized suddenly he'd found the answer to his 'happy' question. "Lord Strongarm is coming as my guest. He's going to marry my sister."

He leaned back against the skimmer, rested a foot against the metal side for comfort. And ignored the whisper at the back of his mind that he was allowing himself to indulge some fairly treasonous ideas of his own. "He'll need a local guide. Someone we can trust. Someone who can show him the islands without needing a heavy Sec presence." He indicated Kip's watchful figure with a nod. "According to Kip Marsden, you are the one person on the planet who fits the bill." He gave that a beat, gave himself the chance to enjoy watching her decide to believe him. "Interested?"

"Showing him *how?*" Her chin came up again.

"Just the *scenery*, Yakamoto! Without Ho Tong using the man for target practice."

"Nothing else? You sure?"

"Nothing else. I promise." He meant it, too, he realized. He most certainly did not want Keiko Yakamoto getting too close to Strongarm, at least not until after the man was safely married to Letticia. He'd had it right last night when he felt his soul swell in answer to this girl. It wasn't crew habit or jump lag that fluttered his guts when Keiko turned those lilting eyes up at him. It was something infinitely worse, something he'd been on his guard against half his life. He'd let himself fall in love. He tried to clamp the knowledge down, shove it into the dungeon at the back of his mind. Mother was right: love was a vulnerability no Van Buren could afford. Giving into it now would only set him up for a choice of treasons: betraying Earth or betraying himself.

"Heia, Van Buren. You all right?"

He blinked Keiko back into focus, smiled as he realized she was waving calloused knuckles under his nose. It was a sorry excuse for his usual grin, but it was real. "I'm fine. Just thinking."

"You sure the sun's not getting to you? The Captain always stashes a medi-kit in his skimmers-"

"No, I'm fine. Really." It was the puzzled worry in her frown that decided him, the fact she saw him simply for himself. No matter what Mother wanted, no matter what Earth needed or what he'd intended, he wanted – no, he *needed* – Keiko Yakamoto for himself. All he had to do was convince her to love him back before Strongarm arrived. The decision made him feel as if his heart had suddenly burst its chains. Made him feel free again for the first time since he'd come back. He felt his smile widen, let it reach his eyes. "So – are you interested?"

"Shaka. A chance to meet a real, flesh'n blood Lupan and live to talk about it? Who wouldn't be?"

Letticia, for one. "I'd rather not think about that answer, if you don't mind." Jezekiah put his smile on lock down, lifted a brow. "So, shall we tell your father?"

IX

The sun was working on hot by the time Marsden lowered their skimmer onto the patch of rusty earth landside of Kalima dock. He wished it were only the trade winds battering Oahu's north shore that made ShipMind up screens before it popped the locks. But the winds weren't that bad. It was Kalima itself made ShipMind nervous. Kalima dock was pure local. Pure Ho Tong.

Marsden swore under his breath as Jess Van Buren clambered out into the settling cloud of red dust before Marsden had both feet on the ground. Shit on a shell, that boy knew goddamned well he was supposed to wait till his escort got around to cover his back. Still – Marsden noted with grudging approval that Jess stayed within the screens. Kept one foot on the skimmer threshhold while he did his own careful eyeball of the area. Well, good. Somebody out on the rim had taught that boy fighter's habits.

"Looks clear to me." Jess leaned an elbow atop the skimmer. He asked Kip's opinion with an eyebrow.

"Got a Streikern biopat out there." He cross-checked, found the ID. "Shipping agent, attached to the Streikern embassy. Name's-"

"Irrelevant. He's only JP's tool. I'd expected-" He shrugged the comment off. "Anything else?"

Yeah, there was: a fuzzed reading out on the edge of the dock. It winked out the instant he focused on it. He re-scanned, got nothing. But the fleeting impression he'd got gave him shivers. He sure as hell was going to research it when they got out of here. If they got out. For now – "Just mules and mech. No weapons."

Which meant squat. Marsden cross-checked the fuzzed reading against the mules' pats. The mixed-Type laborers known as mules generated weird readings sometimes. He wanted to be sure with this lot. The mules might not be Ho Tong, but they still took orders from Grandfather Ho. And a pick could kill you just as sure as a laser. Or that goddamned assassin. Marsden upped magnification on the permanent grid behind his eyes, ran viz sweep. Display showed him a barefoot boy footing it down the dock. "We definitely been spotted. Runner's announcin' us now."

"In which case, you might as well speak your mind now. If I'm wrong on this, neither of us may have another chance." Jess said it friendly, but coming from his lordship it wasn't a request.

"What you want to hear, your lordship? You knew goin' in I don't like this."

"That's not what's bothering you."

"Yuh-huh." Marsden ran a murphy check on the laser pistol holstered under his arm. Gave him an excuse to avoid those blue Van Buren eyes. "I fixed that blind spot on the weather screens you told me about. Re-set the master domo to test weights for human norms." Marsden focused on setting the laser beam to broad band just in case. "Think you should know Mote told me about last night 'fore Madam did. Child musta been up all night."

Jess didn't look surprised. But, then, wasn't much about people that ever did surprise Jess Van Buren. For an instant, Marsden almost pitied the boy.

"Did Keiko also suggest the fix?" Both brows went up this time. Boy was definitely too interested.

"No. Mote pulls that stunt again, she's gonna get blown right off." Marsden felt his jaw harden and knew Jess recognized the suspicion behind it. "And I didn't tell her about it, neither, in case you're wondering."

"I wasn't." Jess leaned an elbow against the skimmer door, watching. "That's still not what's bothering you."

Ah, well. Jess never had been one to let go easy. "Think you shoulda left Mote outta this, your lordship. Admiral ever gets the idea the girl's sided with Grandfather Ho, he'll kill her himself." Dark ugly memories tried to well up. He shut them down, shoved the gun back in its holster. Thought again and unsnapped the holster lock. "Wouldn't be the first time that man's killed a good woman."

"Rest assured I've informed him that Keiko contacted Grandfather Ho on my instructions. If this doesn't work, she's covered."

"Yeah, but-"

Anger sparked Jess' biopat. It vanished before Marsden was even sure he'd spotted it. "I know what Admiral Yakamoto did during the rebellion. Executing one's children, however, is a Van Buren habit, not Samurai." Jess' biopat smoothed into his working pattern, no emotions registering at all despite that maddening little half-grin. "Shall we?"

"Yeah." Wasn't any point pushing matters now. Marsden told the skimmer to stay awake and ready, then nodded Jess toward the long concrete staircase leading up to the quay.

It was a long climb to the dock platform. Had to be – Kalima dock was built high and heavy to withstand the onslaught of the north shore's monster waves. This time of year the pipeline was quiet, so the surf rolled in five stories below. Come winter, the trade winds would curl those waves right around the dock floor. Even now, the wind wrapped them in thunder soon as they stepped through the skimmer's screens. Beyond the staircase the dock ran a quarter klick out into the ocean. Loading cranes towered at hundred foot intervals along both sides, all of them nice and bright with red and yellow paint.

Marsden pulled his civvie jacket close around him, locked his elbow over his side to keep the pistol more or less out of sight. Beside him, Jess' fine shirt billowed out like a windsurfer's sail. Boy had his head back, lips parted like he was breathing his last breath. Which they both just might be. If Grandfather Ho decided to nix them out here, wouldn't be much he could do about it except shove Jess off the pier and hope the boy could dive like he could talk. Marsden pulled in a deep breath, too, and trudged on.

Past the beach, the wind took on a metallic undertone of machine oils and exhaust. Squinting into the distance, Marsden could just make out the misty bulk of a heavy skimmer passing the tip of Kalima Point, its repulse fields steaming the ocean beneath it. Headed north – toward Niihau. Officially, Kalima was where Madam's ops off-shipped the islands' few remaining luxuries. Little junks like chocolate and macadamias that cost more'n houses out on the rim. In reality, the Van Burens' stuff only provided cover for the real cash crop: Grandfather Ho's Venus Seed.

For a second Marsden thought about alerting his guys at the deep space port to check that cargo out. He wrote the idea off. Been one helluva lot of chatter on SecNet lately. Most of it involving Streiker and Den Lupus. Might be a good idea to avoid sending his off-world Sec brethren any more headaches for a while. Ho Tong was going to ship its damned Seed off world no matter what he did. Let Commonwealth Sec worry about it – they had the budget to afford it. Made him wonder –

"Hey, your lordship?" Scan fed him the telltale green blip in his biopat. "Scuttlebutt says Seed'll even put a boner on a dog- ah, Lupan. That true?"

"It is." Jess' blip darkened to fury so fast Marsden swallowed a whistle. Leveled out just as fast, too. "It also kills them."

"Ouch. That could put a hitch in your trade treaty." The implications put an abrupt hitch in Marsden's stride. "Uh, you ain't thinking of offin' Ho Tong's Seed trade, are you? 'Cause if you are, we might just as well jump now."

"My goals do not include suicide." Scary, how Jess' pattern went red-black. Scarier still that not a hint of that bitter rage showed in his expression. "Mother would kill me herself if I tried such a stunt. We can't afford to lose our cut of the profits. At least not until I have that treaty ratified."

Marsden started breathing again. Good. Still didn't mean they'd get off here alive, but at least the boy wasn't planning on death. Farther up the quay, a group of bare-chested men squatted in a half-circle around a stack of cargo crates, contentedly watching a wizened old homie talk contract with the Streikern shipping agent.

Scan still showed no weapons. Marsden tried to be grateful. He might've managed it if it hadn't been for the Samoans. A pair of those ambulatory one-tons ambled away from the main group as soon as he and Jess set foot on the dock. They took up watcher stations halfway between Grandfather and the landside entrance. Marsden snorted softly. So much for easy retreat. If things went sour, they were both going to dive for it.

Marsden found them a spot in the shade of one of the towering cranes lining the quay. The Samoans moved up into blocking positions a couple of pylons to landside. Nice'n mellow, and grinning with their teeth. Just waiting for the signal.

"What you want to do about that Streikern?" Marsden ran a murphy scan on the agent, came up clean.

"Nothing. We'll wait it out here. If Grandfather Ho accepts JP's deal, we're going to have to jump for it." So he'd noticed the Samoans, too, even with his eyes on Grandfather Ho. Boy *had* learned a thing or two out there on the rim. "In which case, I do hope you can summon your skimmer before we hit water."

"Yuh-huh." Made two of them. He linked into the skimmer and told it to keep the engines running.

"Relax." Jess smiled, though there wasn't any humor in it. "They'll have orders to leave us alone. At least until Grandfather Ho makes his decision."

"Yuh-huh." Skimmer reported no prob so far, so he had nothing to do but wait. Marsden made a show of looking comfy and grinned back at the Samoans.

Out on the dock, Grandfather Ho lounged on top of the stack of crates. Wily bastard looked like any other skinny old homie. He wore a pair of baggy shorts ancient as his hide, was bare chested and barefoot and brown as a macadamia – except for that gleaming red-and-yellow dragon tattoo. The dragon coiled around his right arm so its gaping mouth spit fire across his palm. That dragon marked him as *zhu* – the luck and leader and lord of Ho Tong. Local legend said he could make the dragon spit fire. If he could, he didn't need to. Old man was pushing eighty, but he could still take out any three of those youngsters *mano a mano* and they all knew it.

The Streikern agent did not. He towered over the old man, his pale skin shining with sweat despite the oversize parasol he carried. His suit looked like pure silk the way it gleamed, and blue Streikern diamonds flashed every time he jabbed a finger toward the old man's nose. Lucky for him, Grandfather Ho was taking it with the kind of sorry patience folk of real power reserved for the young and hopeless. The fool Streikern did not know just how lucky that was.

"So, then." Jess had one foot braced against the white concrete. He'd been watching the chat up ahead like it was just a FunNet show. It was only now, when he let out a long, soft sigh, that Marsden realized the boy'd been holding his breath. "Grandfather's not going to deal."

"That good or bad?"

"Well, it means we don't have to jump." He turned enough to grin at Marsden. "Yet."

Abruptly, the rep turned his back on Grandfather Ho and stalked back toward the entrance. Damn fool was buried so deep in that parasol he sashayed past Marsden and the Samoans without even seeing them. Marsden felt a quick pulse of hope as the big men looked back at Grandfather. It faded when they settled back into grinning. He'd kinda hoped they'd follow the agent. He'd a damn sight sooner find the haoli's carcass in the ocean than his own.

Beyond them, Grandfather Ho nodded to the mules. One by one, the men at his feet began hauling crates off Grandfather's stack and lugging them up the dock to wait for the next transport.

"All right, let's go." Jess said when the last man ambled off to take his place in the conga line.

Marsden shot a last grin at the Samoans and took up shotgun position at Jezekiah's side. The prayer he kept to himself.

Jess stopped just short of Grandfather's crate. Damned if that boy didn't actually salaam to the old man. Damned and again if the old man didn't give it right back to him, like they were equals. Which, truth be told, they were, out here.

"It seems your Streikern uncle is not the only one unhappy with you, young Lord Van Buren." Grandfather Ho made it sound like the news'd hurt his feelings.

If Jess found that strange he didn't show it. "It does seem my fate to annoy people. Why do you suppose that is?"

"Perhaps it is because you make a habit of giving away that which is not yours. Or perhaps it is simply the company you keep." Grandfather Ho shifted haunches. "Van Buren Heirs do not usually play with dogs."

"Alas, the duties of a Van Buren Heir allow us no room to play at all." Jess smiled up at the old man like they were talking weather. "Especially not with Lupans."

"Ah, then the rumors one hears about a certain trade treaty may be true?"

"Possibly. It depends on whose rumors you've heard."

"Ah. The rumors I heard mentioned an alliance between Home World and the Lupan Dominion." Grandfather Ho settled into a more comfortable angle on his crates. The shift in position put his dragon arm into the sun. Tattooed scales shone where the light touched them. "An alliance sealed by a marriage contract. To your sister Letticia, no less."

"Are you shittin' me?" Oops. That slip got Marsden two matched sets of eyebrows. "Sorry, your lordship." Marsden shuffled an apology and tried to pretend he wasn't there.

Oh, shit on a shell. No wonder Streiker was up in arms. Marsden set local scan to auto, ran a quick check on Lupan power players. The answer came back nasty. Wasn't but one Lupan warlord could swing a treaty for the whole damned doggie Dominion and the run-down on that one jellied his knees. Why the *hell* would Jess Van Buren want to risk gifting power like that to a dumbass little bitch like Letticia?

"My compliments to your informants," Jess was saying.

"I shall forward your praise." The old *zhu* gave Jess a snake-eyed smile that made Marsden's fingers itch for his gun. "Yet I somehow doubt you came merely to praise my children."

"Quite true. I came to extend my appreciation for the aid of your Samoans yesterday."

On Marsden's grid Jess' biopat went black. The sight of it wrenched Marsden's heart. With anybody else, that kind of reading would've meant blood on the sidewalk. Only Jess Van Buren stood there smiling up at his father's killer and holding it all inside.

"It is rare for one of your Family to acknowledge a service." Grandfather Ho sat back, easy as an orca watching a shark. Along his arm, light rippled down the dragon's belly.

"Rarer still for Ho Tong to provide the service. You will forgive me if I suspect the service anticipates reciprocation."

Only somebody watching scan could tell how hard it was for the boy to say that. A good part of Marsden wished he wasn't the one watching. The rest of him wished he could tell what Grandfather felt. Far as Net feed was concerned, old man wasn't even there. Damned monkey.

"What greater reward could a mere natural ask then seeing a Van Buren acknowledge a debt of honor?"

"Perhaps an increase in Ho Tong's own 'little junks' exports when new trade routes open up? It would certainly increase your profits."

"As well as your Van Buren tithes and taxes."

"A mutually beneficial outcome, no?" Jess smiled up at Grandfather just as sweet as sugar cane. But his biopat stayed black.

"Possibly." Grandfather Ho smiled back. It was the way his eyes drooped that made Marsden's trigger finger twitch. "However, we are not greedy. Our request is much smaller than that."

"Namely?"

"Merely permission to ship our little junks directly to Den Lupus. Assuming these new trade routes you mention do indeed open up."

"You will forgive me if I find that an odd request. It is no secret that Venus Seed is fatal to Lupans. What advantage would you have to destroying your market?"

"As you have so wisely pointed out: increased profits. While the market lasts."

Red flickered along the edges of Jess' biopat, morphed into cold, calculating blue. "Not to mention an empty, habitable world with full civilized infrastructure already in place when the Lupans are dead."

Marsden heard his own breath hiss between his teeth. A planet-sized base for Tong operations. Shit on a shell! Good thing Jess Van Buren was here. 'Cause he'd'a shot the old bastard just to play safe otherwise, and been happy to die doing it.

Jess only smiled that crooked little half-smile of his. "Then I fear I must disappoint you. Much as I desire to extend my appreciation, I will not be party to sending Venus Seed to Den Lupus. Not directly, not through middlemen, not by proxy. No exceptions."

"Is it possible that the future lord of Earth does not trust his humble servant?"

Marsden did chortle at that one. Regretted it, too, when Grandfather angled to face him. Old man was looking at him with the smile of a saint. Sight gave Marsden shivers.

"Have we not already earned trust, Captain? Did my children give you cause for complaint on Niihau Port?"

"No complaints." Marsden let it go at that.

Grandfather didn't change expression. But beneath his dragon arm, the crate took on a red gleam. "Yet last night one of my *keiki* gave his service in good faith. *His* reward was torture."

Oh, shit. Didn't need scan to see where that one was going. Around them, the atmosphere on the dock went taut. Suddenly, even the wind went quiet.

"His lordship saved your boy from a full-fledged Aryan interrogation last night. Him and me carried your boy to safety together. Mote can vouch for that." Knowing Mote, she already had. Knowing Grandfather, it didn't matter.

Beyond the stack of crates, men casually picked up makeshift weapons. Broad range scan flashed Marsden the image of three spear-length *tiki* sticks apparently floating toward his back. He tightened focus, got a close up of the sticks' sharpened metal tips. The Samoans were closing in.

Marsden had the pistol out and locked between Grandfather's eyes before they took the next step. The spike in his own biopat triggered SecNet. Sync upped his field range, checking to see if any hot weapons had come on line. It saw enough to flash Manor Sec a scramble command.

"Leave it." Jess gripped Marsden's gun arm. Not hard enough to spoil his aim, but enough to earn attention.

"Yuh-huh." Marsden relaxed his trigger finger just enough to avoid a fatal twitch.

Jess folded his arms, cocked his head at Grandfather. Anybody judging from eyesight alone woulda thought he was just admiring the scenery. "Why the show of force, *Zhu* Ho? We are here to talk thanks. It would hardly be gracious of you to murder us in exchange. It would also be decidedly unprofitable. If you will forgive me the reminder, Admiral Yakamoto would be only too happy to turn his Samurai loose again."

"True. We have unfinished business between us, he and I." Grandfather looked past him. Around them the tension eased.

Damn if the wind didn't whip back up, flapping Marsden's jacket. Behind his eyes, scan grid showed the *tiki* sticks floating back toward the Samoans' watch posts. For now, anyway. No promise they wouldn't pick the gripe up when it was time to leave, but the old man was usually good as his word. Reluctantly, Marsden nulled the scramble command and re-holstered his pistol.

"You face death well." Grandfather looked satisfied about it, too, miserable old sonuvabitch.

"You obliged me to learn early." Damned if Jess didn't smile at the old man. It was the way the black core of his biopat swelled up under that cold, blue surface that made Marsden catch his breath. Damned and for sure he never wanted to see that little half-smile aimed at him.

"Allow me, then, to offer you a small gift in admiration."

Grandfather Ho rested his elbows atop the crates flanking him, brown arms dangling. "Know this: you have made us all an enemy within the Lupan camp."

Ouch. That one struck home. A yellow pinprick of surprise blossomed in Jess' biopat, vanished just as quick. Not that it showed in his face.

"Your generosity embarrasses me. Would you happen to know the enemy's name?"

"Alas, at the moment this old memory fails me."

"Another time, then." Jezekiah gave Grandfather the full, from-the-waist salaam, then turned on his heel to leave.

"There is perhaps one small matter."

Jezekiah froze mid-step. Even in profile, Marsden recognized the danger in the way those blue eyes narrowed. But the boy had them wide and innocent again before he finished turning back. "Namely?"

Grandfather sat up to rest his back on the crate behind him. He turned his dragon arm palm up, stroked a finger along the dragon's tattooed belly. In the shadows the yellow scales along its belly seemed to ripple. "You will not aid us. But perhaps you would not mind aiding our *keiki*."

"He means Mote," Marsden whispered when Jess frowned.

"Ah. I assure you, I have made sure Mistress Yakamoto will encounter no difficulty with either the Aryans or her father."

"Then perhaps you would not mind one further tiny favor."

Old man sounded too silky for good health all of a sudden.

"How?" The underside of that cold, blue border of his biopat took on the crimson tinge of desire. Not a good sign. Leastways, not for Mote.

"My *keiki* is enduring the Samurai Type trial tomorrow. I would have you assist her."

"Do you want me to waive the trial?"

"I would not insult my *keiki's* honor by interfering in the Samurai's trial. She will survive or not as her will and her skill dictate. I merely ask that you stop her father from recording her Type code in Net."

"Hey, now wait just a minute!" The absolute injustice of it drove the words out before Marsden had time to think. "You know goddamned good'n well that little girl's trained her whole goddamned life to earn a Type coding. What you want to go and sawyer her for? You're gonna take away the only chance she'll ever have to be a person!"

Well, that wasn't the brightest thing he'd ever done: both men were scowling at him like he'd just spat in their soup. Oh, shit. Both of 'em. Well, nothing to do now but finish it like a man. "You got no cause to harm her, old man. It wasn't that child who hurt you."

Damned and for sure old man Ho didn't like that reminder. Yellow light brightened the dragon's scales. Above his arm, heat-shimmer wavered the air above his arm. Beside him, Jess' biopat went flat black. Marsden swallowed, hard. He'd be lucky to live the day out if he pissed these two off together. But, hell. At least he'd had a life. That was more'n than Mote would have if she had to stay natural. He set his jaw and answered Grandfather glare for glare.

"Indeed." Jess was looking too thoughtful by far. He took his time about answering, that little half-smile slowly taking shape. "I'll have a word with the Samurai Council. I expect they'll manage to handle the matter without unduly distressing the Admiral."

"Excellent." Goddamned old sonuvabitch almost purred. "Your kindness has improved my memory. It seems the name of the enemy is Kaitin ibn Bengal."

"My gratitude." Jezekiah kissed fingers then strode landward. It was only scan that showed that name mattered.

Well there was another name that mattered a helluva lot more right now.

Marsden fell in behind Jess. He kept his mouth shut till they reached the skimmer.

"Goddammit, your Lordship, you can't do Mote that way." Jess didn't like it, but Marsden forged on. "You ain't seen what that girl's gone through last couple'a years. Child spends three-quarters' her wakin' life trainin' and the rest dodgin' the damned Aryans."

The skimmer raised the shotgun door for Jess. He leaned an elbow on the roof and lifted a brow pointedly. "Shall we continue this conversation en route?"

"Beggin' your pardon, your lordship, but I seen your reaction on scan." Marsden ducked around the master's door, leaned over the skimmer's roof to face Jess down. "Mote ain't nobody's bed wench, your lordship. She's not like the pros you're used to. She goes with you, she's gonna be yours heart and soul."

"She made that point rather sharply last night."

"Yeah, well, never knew you to back away from a challenge, you take my meaning. Sooner or later you're gonna charm her into your bed. Only Mote'll believe you mean it. You let her get Type-coded, she'll have a chance to get over it. But you make her stay natural and use her that way, you gonna damage her for life."

Marsden had expected Jess to ride out the rant; boy always was a listener. What he hadn't expected was the to-the-bone sorrow that flooded Jess' biopat. Looked like the boy'd just lost his papa all over again. Bitter as the thought was, Marsden felt his spirits lift in hope.

"I can't promise you she won't get hurt, Kip. But I promise you I will not break her heart. Will you trust me on this?"

Devil himself would've trusted those big blue eyes when Jess Van Buren wanted him to. But so long as the boy was asking, Marsden crosschecked the words for honesty against his biopat. To his surprise, they matched.

What jarred was the satisfaction that washed the boy's reading. Like a piece of a puzzle had just fallen into place.

X

Battle sense screamed down the back of her neck. Keiko Yakamoto dove beneath an umbrella plant. Her fingers loosened the twin *tanto* knives in their sleeve scabbards while she searched the dawn underbrush for the danger. She found it at the forest edge: a shadow scowling at her in the graying light. The shape melted into the ferns before she even recognized the shadow as a man. But the back of her neck pounded warning.

Keiko forced down a surge of fear. She eased her back closer to the tree, tried to fit this new danger into the pattern of the trial. A second hunter? She wondered. Shouldn't be. Samurai code said Type trial was to be one on one combat, even odds, and the Admiral was code fanatic to the core. In all her eighteen years, she'd never known her father to break a rule. Unlike her unworthy self.

Made no sense. It was her father who hunted her. Over on Oahu the Admiral was sitting in a sync chair at Samurai HQ, linked into the living machine that hunted her. A matching link embedded in the mech hunter's biogel brain melded the Admiral's mind to the hunter's body. She reached out with her *ki*, that essence of psychic energy the Samurai trained into battle sense. The shadow was still there, at the edge of her senses. She felt the Admiral's cold presence, too. His biomech hunter was still behind her, but closer. Either way, she felt death.

Two hunters it was, then. So much for even odds. She felt a jolt of surprise that the betrayal should surprise her. Maybe it was even the point – maybe the Admiral'd rigged the odds on purpose, just to make her prove she was *better* than real, Type-coded Samurai. Be just like him. Maybe, just maybe, he was giving her the chance to make him proud. The idea gave her a tickle of hope. Be worth dying, if she could see pride in his eyes once before she went, if she could prove to him once and for all she wasn't a whore like her mother. That she was a *real* Samurai.

Except a real Samurai wouldn't've got herself in this spot in the first place.

Scowling, Keiko studied the shore line. The forest flat-lined at the sand's edge, the foliage gray-green in the fading night. Beyond the earth sloped downward, turned to obsidian sand where Hawaii met the Pacific. Nothing moved there except an old sea turtle inching out of a tidal pool. No man-sounds, either, just the white hiss of the wavelets across the ebony sand. And her heart, pounding loudly against her ribs.

She scanned the shore westward, *ewa*-side. There, gray light gleamed on the long, ropy fingers of *pahoehoe* lava reaching out into deep water. It was a living flow, the lava still oozing into the sea beneath the crust. Waves whispered where they washed across the lava's black fingertips, clouding the ocean mist into steam. Deep, too: its outer edge formed a black wall waist high to a man. Even from here, Keiko could smell the lava's hot sulfur through the salt breeze.

Had to be another route. She closed her eyes, reached out with battle sense – Something cold and lethal answered.

Keiko hurtled forward. She heard steel hiss where her head had been. She hit the ground in a curl. Black sand slithered down the collar of her loose blouse as she rolled down the slope. She glimpsed a black shape overhead. Heard sand crunch half a meter beyond. The biomech had already hit the beach. It would cut her down before she reached her feet –

She hurled one of the tanto knives as she snapped out of the roll, letting battle sense guide her aim.

Her knife caught the biomech above the heart. Physically, it was SamuraiType man – short for a CombatType and wiry, designed for stamina rather than brute strength. The blow spun him back against the lava wall. He thudded against it, his black swathing nearly invisible against the rock. The smaller of his two swords fell onto the sand. The first rays of the rising sun lit the orchid and fist insignia along its blade. He pushed himself upright on the lava, leaned panting against it. He was as good as dead, and they both knew it.

The black hunting mask hid his face. But through it, his eyes locked on hers. He still clenched his other sword, the meter-long *katana*, in one fist. He would still kill her first, if he could. They both knew that, too.

Behind her – Battle sense screamed warning.

Keiko whirled. She felt the shadow-man closing in. There was a feline intensity in his *ki*. A death-intent so strong it made her gasp. She'd have no chance at all against that one. Not here.

She edged toward the lava wall, staying well clear of the biomech's strike range. Mortally wounded or not, the hunter would be lethal as long as the Admiral could will it to move. Keiko kept a part of her *ki* on it as she hoisted herself up onto the lava flow. She picked her way across the shining lava coils, heading for the deadly center of the flow, her remaining *tanto* blade at the ready.

And – nothing. The shadow-man's touch was gone. Fighting terror, Keiko reached out with battle sense, seeking his chill, feline touch. Nothing –

The back of her neck pounded warning.

Keiko leaped. The biomech's sword whistled beneath her feet. The sword hissed again as she bounded off the hardened *pahoehoe* lava. She did not feel the blade's strike, only the sudden wetness along her back and neck. The biomech fired her own *tanto* knife at her. Blood spun off the blade in an arc of brilliant red. She twisted away, fired her remaining blade as she turned. His sword still streaked her thigh.

Fire shot up her leg and Keiko felt her knee buckle. She threw herself sideward, twisted mid-air to come in under the biomech's guard.

The hunter was doubled over the hilt of her *tanto* knife. Its fingers clutched the handle, as if it had driven the blade into its gut itself. Its breath hissed between its teeth in agony. The sight of it nearly dropped her to her knees in horror. Sweet Madam Pele. She'd never thought it could *hurt*.

Behind the mask its eyes found hers. "Finish it." Even now, it was a command, not a plea.

"Toss me your sword, then." It could still finish *her* if she got in range of the *katana*.

"Never!" The biomech tugged off its mask, looked up to face her. Face her with her father's face, with the tiny white scar above one eye. With her knife buried redly in his gut.

"Strike." It spoke with her father's voice, contemptuous of the blood reddening its hands, glistening its pants.

"Then give me your sword! Don't make me hurt you worse!"

"*Life* is pain," he hissed back. "Now *strike*, damn you."

Choking back a sob, Keiko edged forward, hands at the ready. The biomech let the *katana* droop at its side, leaving her an opening. She lunged with stiffened fingers for the biomech's throat. Saw death gleam in her father's eyes – and froze.

"Coward. Worthless as your mother." The biomech yanked her blade out with its free hand, leaving a wet, red bulge in his black clothing.

"You're my father," she screamed at him.

The biomech answered with his sword – *iai* draw, eye-blurring and lethal.

Keiko dropped flat ahead of the blow and rolled. Metal sang in her ear as the *katana* struck rock a hair's breadth from her head. Keiko flipped onto her feet and ran. She streaked toward the heart of the flow, the back of the lava hand where black crust was thinnest. She felt rather than heard the whistle of the tanto blade behind her. She dropped, snapped flat. Heard the knife flash past above her back. Keiko flipped onto her feet. And ran.

The ground was dangerously hot here. Steam vents shot sulfur fumes into the air beside her, burning her throat and eyes. Ocean spray whipped the steam into serpentine coils, stained her khakis with sulfur dew. No thinking now. She focused her very essence on *air*, skittered across the lava light as a bird.

She raced for a dullish patch, battle sense raging. She felt the hunter's eyes burning into her back, now, felt her death in its mind. Sensed rather than saw the sword slicing toward her back. But she dared think of nothing beyond wind and air—

Metal shrieked.

Keiko whirled. Behind her, the biomech's leg erupted in flames. He tried to jerk back. But the metal skeleton beneath his synskin was already fused to the molten rock seething at his feet. Around him, sea mist hissed into scalding steam in the searing heat. The biomech tried to twist away. He tottered a moment, eyes reflecting the lava's brilliant red-orange blaze. Then the crust shattered. He pitched forward, arms flung wide, grasping at air.

His scream ended abruptly.

Keiko forced herself to circle the broken crust. The *katana* sword overhung the oozing red lava. Already the steel blade glowed white-hot. It melted into the lava as she watched. But the emblem of Admiral Matsuo Yakamoto burned behind her eyes.

She had "killed" her father. That, at least, ought to please him.

It was near noon by the time Keiko staggered up the slope of the old Kaneeleele *heiau*. She couldn't remember just now all the stories Grandfather Ho had told her of the Before Time, when the shrine had first been built. She tried to dredge some of the old stories up, to keep her mind focused, keep exhaustion at bay. All she could remember was that the *heiau* was a holy place, wrapped in taboos that were ancient when the old NorthAm empire was born. And that Grandfather had promised someone would wait for her there.

Keiko pulled herself up the last hillock on the feathery branches of a fern tree. Fifty feet away, the *heiau* stood like an old sentinel. The carved totems guarding the shrine's stockade were grayed from salt wind and sun, the shell facings worn smooth. But the wood was still solid, the doorway to the shrine within bright with flower leis. The people took care of this place like they took care of each other.

An old woman sitting cross-legged on one of the flat rocks in front of the *heiau* looked up as Keiko lurched out of the ferns. She waved, smiling, then swept the pile of bright red ginger she had been weaving into leis off her lap.

Keiko lifted a hand to wave back. Only her arm wouldn't work. She hit the sand on both knees. She had a moment to feel vaguely grateful she'd picked a sandy spot to collapse on as she pitched forward on her face...

The old woman was smiling down at her when Keiko regained consciousness. Behind her, canvas roofing blocked the sun. Engines thrummed underfoot, deep bass counterpoint to the *whisk-whisk* of the white foam flashing past the rail. She was in a boat, she thought dimly, and wondered at the relief she felt. The cushion under her head smelled of salt air and old age. But it was softer than the wood planking she usually got, even if it did shudder a bit. Maybe the Admiral would let her nap a bit longer. It was getting dark anyway. Keiko smiled back at the old woman, felt her eyelids drift downward – *dark*! She jerked upright, came fully awake as the synskin bandages melding to the wounds in her back and thigh spasmed.

"*Ho'o manawanui, keiki*," the woman said. "Take it easy, child." She clipped a medi-pac back into place at her belt, then wrapped a careful arm around Keiko's shoulders. "You wen hit da sand hard, eh?"

Keiko tried a nod. Even that hurt enough to make her rethink it.

"*Heia*, we get one hour more, we come Oahu." Keiko almost sobbed at the gentle touch of the old fingers on her hair. "Come stay, we talk story, eh? No hu-hu, get you home quick like, you see."

Keiko scrunched her eyes closed and buried her face in the woman's shoulder, pressed her thanks into her flesh. With any luck, the Admiral wouldn't mind her getting in late tonight. She'd had enough of a beating for one day.

It was full dark by the time Keiko managed to shower and wince into a simple kimono. The Admiral was in his study, same as always at this hour. Meaning she was supposed to bring him tea. Same as always. This one night – she flattened the swell of resentment. She was weak-willed, that was all. Like her mother. Keiko let the fury grow this time, found strength in it. She'd proven she wasn't like that today. Proven she was worthy. The thought lent her resolution. A true Samurai put duty ahead of everything. That was why the Admiral was ignoring her. He was treating her like a real Samurai. Feeling better she hauled herself into the kitchen and prepared the Admiral's tea.

Her hands shook too hard to even think of carrying the tea tray down the hall. Keiko nudged the tray carefully along the hallway floor with one foot instead. She shouldered herself along the wall with it, using her dreams to fund her will power. She was real, finally. Nobody could hold her mother's whoring over her any more. She'd passed Type trial. Taken the best the Admiral could throw at her and walked away alive. He'd have to be proud of her now. The idea cheered her so much she didn't even swear when she bumped her nose into a doorpost.

She reached the Admiral's door and slid down the wall onto her knees beside the tray. She felt her head droop, snapped upright hard enough to jar the synskin bandages along her back. It'd tick the Admiral *nui* off if she showed any eagerness. A *Samurai* kept emotions private. She wiped the anticipatory sweat off her palms on the floor before she knocked. She waited till she heard the Admiral's grunt of permission to slide the door open and push the tea tray through. She pushed herself through on her knees after it –

Battle sense screamed down the back of her neck. Keiko dove past the tea set, kicked the kimono flap aside to come up in a fighting crouch.

Nothing. Just the Admiral sitting at his desk, pretending to work on his haiku. But she felt his rage in the back of her neck.

Oh, damn, was he *still* testing her? Maybe this was still part of the trial. Maybe he was just testing her self-control. Or her housekeeping. She sidled back to the tea set, battle sense probing for attack. She kept her eyes on him, tried to feel out some other source of danger. Got nothing.

The study was as cold and mean as the Admiral. Even daytime, with sunlight bounding off the pale stones and plumeria of the courtyard outside its weather screens, she always felt cold in this room. Tonight it felt like even the suits of ancient Samurai armor guarding the courtyard entrance were shivering.

Keiko pulled in a long breath, then picked up the tea tray and rose. She held it steady more by force of will than strength, forced herself to focus on the Admiral's great swords – the meter-long *katana* and smaller *wakizashi* – mounted on the wall behind him, on the scrolls of his own *haiku* beside them. Anything except the Admiral himself.

She dropped to her knees again – too hard – in front of his desk, but managed to set down the tray with its old brown teapot and single cup without spilling the tea. The desk itself held only a simple link unit in one corner, opposite a live *tanto* blade mounted on a stand in easy reaching distance from the Admiral's hand. The pale scroll of parchment he was pretending to work on held the center, with a traditional ink well flanking it. He looked like he'd been sitting in that position for the past hour. A drop of ink had dried in a black tear on the pen's tip.

Neck throbbing, Keiko poured his tea. She replaced the pot, then scooted back a pace, head up, hands on thighs. And waited.

"What have you done?" It was a sign of his anger that the Admiral used his formal voice: calm, neutral, betraying neither *tatemae* nor *honne* – neither his public feelings nor his true ones.

"I lived?" What the hell else did he *think* she'd done? Keiko lowered her gaze from the ceiling to meet his. She made sure to keep both the bewilderment and resentment out of her expression.

"What else?" The quietness of his anger scared her.

What else was there? Maybe she'd said it wrong? "I survived Type trial?" *Sweet Madam Pele*, please *don't let that sound sarcastic!*

"You fought Ho Tong style. Why?"

Oh, praise the goddess and ancestors, it really was just a test after all. "'Victory is achieved by ascertaining the rhythm of the opponent and attacking in a rhythm the opponent has not anticipated'," she quoted, taking refuge in 'The Book of Five Rings'. "The hunter let himself get sawyered" – *wrong, remember it was the Admiral guiding that hunter* – "uh, became absorbed in the rhythm of the chase. He failed to anticipate the rhythm of the lava." She could only hope that made sense.

"I did not ask 'how' you killed the biomech. I asked why you used Ho Tong tactics."

Keiko pretended not to see the danger in the question. "You taught me that all weapons must be as one. I tried to apply your teaching to my strategy. During the Rebellion, Ho Tong successfully used the islands themselves as their weapon. With my personal weapons gone, I used the Ho Tong tactic and made the lava my weapon."

"Enough." Her father drew in a deep breath, eyelids drooping. "Reasoned like a Samurai. Spoken like a Samurai." For a moment, he looked gray with exhaustion, like he was as tired as she was. Then he opened his eyes and the tiredness vanished in cold fury. "*Then what have you done to warrant denial?*"

"Sir?" She'd heard that wrong. It had to be wrong. But it turned her blood to ice.

"The Council of Elders denied you Type status." The Admiral was almost hissing now. "I have argued the originality of your tactics. Cited your work with Van Buren Sec as proof of your good faith. *Offered my life as warrant of your loyalty.* And still the Elders denied you Type status."

"They've got no right!" Keiko shot to her feet. Cringed back at the black rage in her father's face.

"Denied it at the request of Milord Jezekiah Van Buren himself." The pen snapped between his fingers. He flipped the pieces aside without a glance, leaned over the desk on scarred and calloused knuckles. "I want to know what you have done. Now."

"Nothing! Sir!"

"Liar!" His knuckles cracked against the desk. The Admiral rose, paced away from the desk to stare out at the garden, leaving her to plead with his back.

"Please, sir." She felt melted inside, like somebody'd set fire to her insides.

She twisted on her knees, choking on the words. "I've only met the Heir once, when he landed a couple of days ago. You know that! If you don't believe me, ask Captain Marsden. He'll vouch for me."

"Were you working with Sec in Milord Jezekiah's bedroom last night?"

"Who told you-" Oh, shit.

He whirled to face her. "Milord Jezekiah!"

Any hope she'd had of lying died. The Admiral had already seen the truth in her face. Wouldn't matter now that it wasn't the truth he'd expect. Keiko hid the despair, locked her expression into Samurai neutrality. "If he told you I bedded him, he was lying."

"So you admit it."

"I went there to thank him-"

"And how did you get into his quarters?"

"I crawled down the weather screens." The links finally started to connect. "You mean he's upset about *that*? But I *told* him-"

"Where did you learn that tactic?" The Admiral's hands came up, knuckles white as his face. The threat in his *ki* was so powerful it almost drowned the sound of his voice. "From the Tong rebel?"

"No! I taught myself." Sweet Madam Pele, why didn't he just kill her and get it over with? It would have hurt less. She held herself straight, preparing herself to die properly. "You leave the gate locked sometimes and the major domo can't see me. So I had to figure a way to get into the house ..." She realized she was swaying, willed herself steady. "It's just a matter of weight distribution. You just keep balanced until you reach the drop point, then focus weight in your feet. Probably wouldn't work with a real person..." She heard her voice trail off.

"In short, a technique that can be used exclusively by Ho Tong's assassins." He closed his eyes, leaving Keiko to gape at the mix of shame and pride and sorrow in his face.

"I'm not Ho Tong! Sweet Madam Pele, you know that! I *told* Van Buren that!"

"Perhaps Milord Van Buren did not believe your words." He opened his eyes and his expression hardened into the old, familiar contempt. "Or perhaps you gave him reason to forgive you the transgression."

"I told you, I didn't do anything wrong! Why can't you believe me? Just this once?"

"Because, while you were dawdling on a beach, instead of returning directly to duty, the Heir contacted Master Takagawa. He 'suggested' you could be of greater use to him as a natural than as a decent, honorable human being."

The horror of what that meant silenced her. For a moment, Keiko thought he would hit her. But the Admiral simply stepped around the desk, bent to retrieve the broken pieces of his pen. He lowered himself into his chair, laid the reed pieces too carefully beside the parchment. He lifted the inkwell with exaggerated care.

It felt, suddenly, like even her bones had melted. Keiko sank back on her knees, head down, finally, totally hopeless. Felt his eyes boring into the top of her head.

The ink well cracked. She looked up to see the Admiral staring at the reddening ink seeping through his fingers, his eyes blind with a misery that ripped straight into Keiko's heart. "You disgust me," he said tonelessly. "Get out."

Choking on sobs she could not utter, Keiko crept back out of her father's office. She crawled backward all the way down the hall, back to her own room. And crouched beside her bed, face buried in the side of the bed, numb with fear and rage and sorrow. Sweet Madam Pele, *why*? She didn't count for anything. How could Van Buren hate her so much? For what?

She couldn't think any more, could hardly even breathe. There was only one person who really cared about her. Only Grandfather Ho would understand.

Silently, she opened a window and slipped out into the night.

XI

Wake up, brother dear. The voice was feminine and sweetly poisonous.

Damn, that sounded like Letticia. The thought snapped Jezekiah out of the last mellow stage of sleep. By instinct he grabbed the jeweled needler he'd stashed under his pillow. Eyes still closed, he sniffed for the telltale scent of unwashed sister. Got nothing. Relieved, Jezekiah rolled over and pulled a pillow over his head.

Brutal hands jerked him off the bed. He hit the floor in a roll, came up with the needler live and ready.

He was alone.

Heart pounding, he spun to cover the balcony. Nothing.

Poor little baby. The disembodied voice was definitely Letticia's. *Did he hurt his little knees-ies?*

Jezekiah willed his pulse rate down as he rose. The needler he kept up. "Major Domo! What the hell kind of stunt is this?"

No stunt, Letticia's voice dropped the fakery, reverted to its normal snappishness. *I hibernated your Major Domo.*

"You *what*? How?" The question came out on its own. His conscious mind was still engaged in trying to believe his ears.

You couldn't understand if I told you. Her smirk was audible.

"All right, you've got my attention. For what?" Jezekiah made a show of thumbing the safety back on the needler.

For this!

And suddenly Strongarm was *there*, bloodied fangs bared and lunging for his throat.

Almost, almost he fell for the illusion. As it was, the holo made Jezekiah pull a tight butt-pucker as the Lupan's image charged through him. He held his ground until the holo evaporated. "I see you've been doing your homework." Managed a shadow of a smile at the major domo's nearest 'eye'. "I do hope that wasn't *you* Strongarm was angry at."

Gob you, Jess! An airy whirlpool knocked Jezekiah sprawling. Across the room knick-knacks swung off the shelves and launched themselves at him.

He swatted a vase away from his head. He heard it shatter against a wall as he dove for his sync chair. It felt suddenly as if the very air was being sucked into vortex. Head swimming, he braced himself against the chair's arm, shoved his Ring hand into the link. The info stream felt dissonant this time, hostile, as if NetMind itself was trying to push him away. With a rush of horror he realized he was actually feeling Letticia's presence in NetMind.

Major Domo! Attend me! He focused every fiber of his being on the Ring, concentrated on the hierarchy embedded in NetMind's core code to override Letticia's command. His feed wavered. Gradually the crushing hostility faded. The frenzied air stilled, allowing him to gulp air back into his lungs. The knick-knacks that hadn't embedded themselves in the walls crashed to the floor.

Milord, forgive me. It was his major domo's own voice this time. Its rich baritone quavered in distress. *The young mistress –*

"Overrode you. I realized." Jezekiah let himself drop back against the cushions, content to simply be breathing. "How long has she been able to do that?"

This was the first, Milord.

"That's a relief. Make sure it's the last. File this: Heir's command, irrevocable; alert Mother's Major Domo to a possible incursion. If Letticia attempts to override you again in any respect, burn her feed. Permanently."

Yes, Milord. Order secured and transmitted, Milord.

"Good. Now get Letticia in here bodily. Immediately."

Yes, Milord. With pleasure, Milord. There was no doubting the satisfaction in the major domo's tone.

Letticia's quarters were only on the other side of the Family's wing. Jezekiah barely had time to pull on a shirt and pants before the door slid open. Invisible hands shoved Letticia through hard enough to send her stumbling into the foot of his bed. She hit the sandalwood bedstead with an oof and slid down it onto the floor. This time Jezekiah did not offer her a hand up.

If Letticia noticed the change in his attitude, she hid it well. She was wearing a sack of a dress that looked like it had once been white. It had definitely been slept in far longer than was good for either it or her. Her eyes and nose were red and swollen. Fear masquerading as fury.

Oh, gods, how he knew that fear: of consequences, of him, of life itself. Her expression conjured memory of the shivering little girl he'd dug out of the rubble beneath Father's body. He remembered her terror, and felt it with her. His brother's heart forgave her instantly. For a moment he wanted nothing more than to clasp her to him and soothe away the demons that haunted her. The way he used to do, before Mother named him Heir. Before he was enslaved to the Ring.

Now – he could no longer help her by caring. Jezekiah dropped back into the sync chair, locked his working mask in place. "Care to tell me what that suicidal bit of foolishness was all about?" Anguish made the words sound harsh.

"It was self-defense!" Letticia elbowed herself onto the edge of his bed. "You and all your talk about how 'gentle' your dog is! Well, I checked him out! I've seen what he's really like!"

Exactly what vid she must have found clicked home. "Great gods, Lush, you picked up a challenge vid! The man was fighting for his life!" He allowed himself a chuckle. "As a matter of fact, he was fighting to defend his sister."

"What's it matter? That's how he fights, isn't it?" She broke off with a shudder, fighting tears.

So, then. She had been giving the marriage serious thought. Given Letticia's penchant for pigheaded contrariness her terror implied a definite personal interest. Jezekiah felt some of the tension ease out of his shoulders. "Not with women." He leaned forward, softened his tone. "Now listen to me, Lush, and listen carefully. A Lupan man will not – cannot – harm his wife. For two reasons."

"Don't try to feed me any of your fairy tales!" Letticia snapped off the bed, took a step toward the door.

At Jezekiah's gesture, the major domo's invisible hands shoved her back down. Significantly harder, he noted, than was really necessary. She landed with her face buried in the sheets, feet kicking.

"It's the truth, Lush." Jezekiah waited till she rolled back to glare at him before continuing. "Reason number one: when the old NorthAm genetechs were designing LupanType eyes, they spliced in eagle and owl genes for vision. One of the by-products was that LupanType picked up the avian trait of impression. Only the trait came out gender-specific, male only. So when a Lupan man mates, it's for life."

"So?"

"So, my dear little sister, for a Lupan man there's only one woman in his life. Period. Permanently. They don't even have a word for infidelity."

"Spare me the language lesson. What's that got to do with anything?"

Only Letticia could have missed the implications. "With luck, reason number two will help you understand. To wit: somewhere along the line, LupanType managed to develop a mutation of its own. They call it the Touch. It's a kind of psychic bond that joins the mating pair."

"But I *saw*!" She was crying in earnest now, tears and nose running unchecked. "I saw what those claws can do –" She hugged herself, biting her lips to stop the quivering.

"You saw a challenge fight." He refused to let himself think just now of how many sec codes she must have broken to find that vid.

"What's it matter? It shows you what he's like!"

"As a matter of fact, it matters a great deal. Because that vid shows Strongarm defending his sister from a forced marriage." He sighed inwardly at her surprised flutter. Leave it to Letticia to never wonder *why*. "That should give you an idea of what the man will do to anyone who tries to hurt you. Assuming, of course, he doesn't run screaming in terror from you himself."

"Oh, that's just mean!"

"Why, does the truth hurt?" He leaned forward, making sure she honed her focus on him. "Learn this: when a Lupan man uses the Touch, he binds his soul to his woman. The upside of that is the most intense orgasm in the entire human pantheon." This time the sigh was for himself, pure jealousy. "The downside is that the man has to find the woman appealing enough to trigger the Touch in the first place."

"Don't be stupid. Of course he'll want me. I'm a Van Buren!" She blinked, thought. "And I've been bathing."

Jezekiah pulled in a breath, caught himself rubbing a finger along the bridge of his nose in unconscious imitation of Mother. "I'm afraid that won't quite do. You're going to have to make the man *like* you."

"Demean myself to a dog? I most certainly will not!"

"Or die. It's your choice."

"Oh, for heaven's sake!" Fuming, Letticia snapped off his bed and started for the door.

"By the way-" Jezekiah waited till she stopped, half-turned toward him.

"If you try overriding my major domo again, you'll do a crash and burn. Just thought you should know."

"Don't worry. I won't. I've done all I needed in your node." Letticia added a sneer and flounced out.

Jezekiah let himself sag in the chair. So, then. He'd got her thinking, at least. Which left him free, finally, to tackle the challenge he feared. He told the major domo to check itself for sabotage, then called up Kip. He was going to need the SecType's help on more than one level when he found Keiko Yakamoto.

XII

Keiko drifted up out of sleep. Gradually daytime sounds and aromas pulled her away from the dream-arms of a red-headed prince. Dreamscape lovers' murmurs vanished in the muffled sound of a spoon scraping a cooking pot. She came awake rejoicing in the warm, sensuous caress of a heavy silk coverlet.

Only wakefulness carried memory. The horrific scope of her failure crashed over her. She screwed her eyes shut, tried to dodge the image of her father's shame, erase the awful slander she'd seen in his face. But the memory rekindled her outrage at the injustice of it all. She had to find a way to prove she was worthy. Had to make him see she wasn't like her mother.

Only she'd never manage it without a clear head. She opened her *ki*, tried to allow the sense of safety in Grandfather's compound ease her spirit. Sought peace – and sensed a watcher.

She feigned sleep while her *ki* absorbed the watcher's feel. Recognizing it, she rolled onto her side to smile at the bare-chested young man squatting by the curtained door. "Heia, Kameh."

"Heia." Even squatting on his haunches Kamehameha No-Name had to look down at her. The twin black studs embedded in his temple and jaw gleamed in the room's soft light when he lifted his head to rest it against the stone wall. But she felt his peace radiate through the room.

"Feels late. Thought you'd be working." His presence reminded her she didn't remember falling into bed. Didn't remember much of anything after one of Grandfather's trucks had dropped her off here. Keiko gave herself a quick pat-down under the covers to make sure she wasn't naked. Breathed relief to find somebody had loaned her a muumuu.

"Yeah." He shrugged, a true islander's easy approach to time. "*Tutukane* say you wen get nui hu-hu."

"Grandfather say you stand guard, too?"

"No, he did not." Beside Kameh Grandfather Ho pushed open the heavy curtain, allowing the scent and sound of the kitchen to enter with him. Over his shoulder Keiko caught a glimpse of steam rising from the stove in his kitchen. Free of the curtain, both the old woman's song and the aroma from her cooking pot gained strength. "Grandfather told this young warrior to go about his business. It seems he and I have different ideas about what that is."

Kameh was already on his feet. He towered over Grandfather, shoulders broader than the old man's body by half. Yet Keiko caught the sudden tinge of fear in Kameh's *ki*.

Grandfather must have sensed it, too. If he did, it didn't surprise him. That was odd; she couldn't imagine why Grandfather would expect his people to fear him. But then Grandfather gave her a smile that soothed the ache in her heart and she forgot to wonder about it. She tugged her borrowed muumuu down to a decent length, then slid off the bed to hug him.

Grandfather stroked her hair gently before holding her out at arm's length. "*Pehea oe, keiki*? How are you, child?"

"*Maika'i no, Tutukane*. I'm fine, Grandfather." He let her go and Keiko twirled, arms outstretched, to prove it.

The back of her neck throbbed warning.

Keiko whirled, hands ready. Found nothing. Just Grandfather, looking amused. And an empty spot beside the door. "Where'd Kameh go, *Tutukane*?"

"About his business."

"He must have been *really* late." Her fault, again. "Please don't be angry with him. It was my fault."

"Our choices are our own. Let us hope his future choices are more wise." Grandfather rubbed hands against the small of his back. "Stay away from that one, *keiki*. His path is not yours. He has nothing to offer you."

"He *cares*, Grandfather. That's an awful lot in my book." Battle sense tingled again. This time the throb faded instantly. Weirder and weirder. Keiko rolled her neck, trying to puzzle it out.

"We have only just opened your book, as you call it. You have a glorious future. If you choose to accept it." He stretched, looking like it hurt him.

Keiko forgot the whisper of doubt. She was at his side instantly, worried hands on his arm.

He smiled down at her, and her worry eased. "These old bones grow weary. Pull out that chair for me, *keiki*."

She whipped the white wicker chair away from its desk, slid it gently behind Grandfather's knees.

"This old heart rejoices to have you with us." He lowered himself into the chair with a sigh, his worn red and yellow shorts bright against its white paint. He turned his dragon arm upward, tattooed scales gleaming against his leathery skin.

Sweet Madam Pele, he was upset with her, too. Keiko felt her neck tighten.

She knelt beside him, head down. "I'm sorry, Grandfather. I shouldn't have come. Forgive me."

"You ask a great deal, *keiki*." She flinched when he laid a hand on her head, but he only stroked her hair gently. "How am I to forgive you for finally coming home? Better, I think, I should ask whether this time you will stay."

The inevitable question drained the joy out of her body. She had no answer for it; never would until she'd proved to the Admiral she was worthy. Probably never could, now. All she could do was hang her head.

"Your silence answers for you."

She felt his hand leave her head, felt its absence in her soul. She looked up, pleading. "Forgive me, Grandfather. You know I love you-"

"Your lips say so. Your actions say otherwise."

"It's not a lie!" Why couldn't – She refused to let her mind follow her heart back to the old regret. "I passed Type trial, Grandfather. I didn't fail this time, I really didn't. But the Samurai Council blocked my Type code anyway."

"Why do you suppose that was?"

"I don't know! Admiral says it was because Jezekiah Van Buren told them to." The memory lit new anger. She felt her chin set in defiance. "So of course he thinks I slept with the fool-"

"Did you?" Grandfather smoothed the defiance out of her chin with a fingertip.

"You know I didn't!"

"Then perhaps that is why. Perhaps the denial is your young lord Van Buren's revenge. Perhaps this is his way of drawing you to him."

"You think so?" The flash of delight only triggered a fresh swell of anger. "Well, he picked one damned stupid way of doing it! Of all the mean, nasty ways-"

"'Want' does not mean 'love', *keiki*. Not for a Van Buren. Would a man who loved you cause you such pain?"

She had no answer for that question, either. Grandfather was right, of course. How could a prince ever see anything more than a bed wench in her? She realized her fists had balled, forced them open before she hit something.

Grandfather chuckled, making her blink up at him. "Perhaps the Van Buren has done us both a favor, *keiki*. You could not have come back to us if you were Samurai."

She'd never thought of that. "But I'm one of the people. You always said-"

"A Samurai cannot be one of the people, *keiki*. Not after what your father did to us." He slipped a leathery finger back under her chin, lifted her face to his. "Why do you pursue his course? Have you ever seen him happy?"

"No, but- well, that's 'cause he's stuck with me."

"No, child. It is because he is Samurai. They live only for death." Grandfather lifted his palm to her face and Keiko rested her cheek against it. "You are not cut out for such a travesty of life, *keiki*. Join us. Come home to your true family."

"I can't! Not yet!" She felt the warning burn that threatened tears. She bit her lips till the burn faded. "Not till I show the Admiral I'm not like my mother. I'm not a whore."

Grandfather's fingers clenched. Battle sense throbbed the back of her neck in response. "You forget, *keiki*, your mother was one of the people."

"I know, but-" The implication struck home. Had it not been for Grandfather's hand, her jaw would have dropped. "You knew her." Of course he had. It was obvious, once he said it. "Why did you never tell me? What was she like? Was she really as bad-"

"You must decide who you are before you can understand who she was." Grandfather's smile faded, leaving his lips set in a stern line. Above his arm, heat shimmered the air. "Are you ready to make that decision?"

"I have to prove I'm honorable." She clutched at his hand, pleading. Dropped it at the bite of the dragon's breath. "Please, Grandfather. Let me prove myself. Let me have a *choice*."

"A wise answer. Your path must be of your own choosing." He breathed deep, eyes drooping. The dragon's glow ebbed and he patted her hand, his expression gentle again. "I will ask you again on the coming memory night. In the interim, I think our young Van Buren lord is about to endure some interesting times. Will you allow me to make a suggestion?"

XIII

His major domo patched Kip in on audio while Jezekiah rammed through a shower. He'd expected the anger in Kip's voice, as he'd expected that the big man would be looking for Keiko on his own. He had not expected that Kip would fail to find her. Or that the sound of worry in Kip's voice would trigger such a lump in his own gut. Damn and damn again. There was no political reason he should care at all. Yet the fear she would believe he'd betrayed her overrode even his growing concern over Strongarm's disquieting silence.

He tried to reassure himself the problem was simply that she was invisible in Net. Jezekiah paused, one foot raised above a pant leg. Something was naggingly wrong in that thought. He pulled his pants on, puzzling at it.

Your lady mother wishes to see you, Milord. No mistaking that silken basso. That was *Mother's* major domo speaking.

"Tell Mother I'll be along as soon as I've-"

Madam wishes to see you now, *Milord.*

End of argument. Invisible hands tucked him into his clothes and marched him out the door.

The reason for the summons came clear the moment the doors to Mother's office swung open. The major domo released its grip in time to let him stride through under his own power. Would have been nice had it also warned him he'd be walking into the triumvirate glare of Mother, JP, and cousin Octavian.

Certainly explained Mother's summons. Jezekiah converted the glitch in his step into a sweeping salaam to his reigning relatives. So, then. *Something* had got Octavian listening to JP enough to make a joint show. Which meant hunting for Keiko would have to wait. If he skipped out now, he'd be gifting JP the opportunity to swing Octavian – and with him the Commonwealth Council – over to support of his attempt to hijack Rogue. And the Commonwealth would die.

Which meant in turn he needed to one-up whatever profit JP had offered Octavian to get him here. His little voice hoped the profit wasn't Earth itself. Expression on neutral, Jezekiah kissed fingers to Mother properly while he quick-calc'd odds on what JP's carrot had been. He had the answers short listed by the time he reached his position at the apex of their triangle and raised a questioning eyebrow at Mother.

"It seems Johann Petrovich suspects us of coordinating your friend Strongarm's response to Streiker's ... attachment of his caravan." Behind her usual reserve Mother looked drawn.

Jezekiah held his breath, but she did not order him into one of her damned chairs. He kept the relief private, turned the brow on JP. "I'm flattered, Uncle. I hadn't realized we'd graduated to puppet master status."

"Hardly the time to be modest, Cousin." Octavian's holo'd figure lounged in his private nook within the captain's quarters of his personal jump ship. The pinprick lights above his table drew answering glints from the jewels hemming his robes, deepened the pink shadows within his table's feathery centerpiece. Behind Octavian's red-gold top knot, crystal stemware filled a mirrored case, turning the pinpricks into myriad rainbows. The rest of the cabin was hidden in the shadows of the ship's night. "The question's rather whether you pulled the Lupan's strings yourself. Or whether Madam Muriel pulled them with you."

So that was the charge: manipulating a Lupan response to Streikern aggression. Given the martial noises JP had been making, that came in one step shy of collusion with the enemy. Made it a very bad sign, indeed, that he'd got Octavian listening. Octavian couldn't care less who controlled Rogue – his merchants dealt in finished goods, not raw ore. Which meant there was more behind this than just control of Rogue. The implications tightened every muscle in Jezekiah's body.

He kept the angry flush out of his face, angled to track JP's pacing. No point in glancing at Mother. Nothing ever looked as guilty as innocence. "Am I to understand, Uncle, you are blaming us because Strongarm did *not* attack you? In which case, much as it grieves me to admit it, I fear you have severely overestimated our influence." He folded his arms, forced a smile. "Unless, of course, you are simply trying to dodge the fact that a Lupan outwitted you."

"That's not the issue!" JP reached the end of his self-allotted track and turned back. "The issue is that your damned dog oversaw the re-buy of his goods in person."

"I fail to see the point." Mother's tone was sharp enough to bring even JP up short. "Given that the man was re-purchasing an entire fleet, it's hardly surprising Strongarm would direct the transaction himself. Speaking personally, I should think you'd be grateful that's all he did."

"Ah, but the point, Muriel dear, is the 'personal'." Octavian shifted position in a jeweled ripple. "Strongarm bought his cargo back on one of my ships. In person."

"Forgive me if I fail to find that tidbit enlightening."

JP snapped around at the far end of his track. "He means the dogs have a long jump drive!"

Oh, damn. Octavian would never support the treaty if he believed Earth was cutting Pandar out of a profit pool the size a long jump drive represented. Jezekiah put his smile on lock down, pretended to discover a fascination with the feathery pink centerpiece occupying Octavian's table. "Aren't you jumping to conclusions? As my own recent travels proved, a superb holo can imitate human touch." He strolled into Octavian's holo to run his hand across the centerpiece's swaying fronds. He half-expected, half-feared an answering tickle on his palm. The lack of it let him breathe a bit easier. "I can assure you, if *we* can manage the tech, the Lupans can as well."

"Particularly if you gift it to them." JP clipped back across the floor. The discrepancy between his clipped march and silent footsteps jarred. "That likelihood, however, is irrelevant. We held the sale in free world space. At Khayyam jump point."

"Considerate of you. At least you allowed the competition the appearance of a fair deal." Jezekiah shut it at Mother's scowl.

A red light flashed on Mother's comm board. She scowled at it, then turned the scowl on JP. "Either make your point or leave, Uncle. I've neither time nor patience to endure accusations of imaginary transgressions. Particularly not from Streiker."

Octavian picked up while JP was still trying to unclench his teeth. "Alas, the point, my dear, is that Khayyam is – or should be – a three jump journey from Den Lupus. That means three weeks, real time. As you can imagine, Johann Petrovich was understandably reluctant to pay storage fees for an entire fleet-" JP *humphed* assent in passing – "so the disposal sale was held as soon as the impounded ships could be docked at Khayyam."

"Yet Strongarm turned up in person." JP paced through Jezekiah.

Behind his working smile, Jezekiah gritted teeth. "Or tangible holo."

"I assure you my ops have learned to distinguish flesh from illusion." JP's tone sent a shiver down Jezekiah's spine. "The dog was there. In less than one week, real time. Which means he used a long jump ship."

"All right, he was there. Implication being Lupans have better tech than we've credited them for." Mother leaned back to stare JP down along the length of her nose. "It seems to me, then, that if you truly believe us to be responsible for Strongarm's actions, you should both be immensely grateful."

She angled her nose toward Octavian. "You know as well as I that seizure of that fleet was intended to drive a wedge between Den Lupus and Earth at best. Or to provoke Strongarm into attacking Streiker at worst."

"Ideally, both." That one earned Jezekiah her sharp blue glare. He shut up and rocked on his heels in sublime innocence.

"If the Lupans' battle ships can jump past Streiker's defenses, then no world in the Commonwealth is safe." On Mother's comm, the red flash brightened to a steady glare. She glanced at it, lifted her chin as her eyebrows came down. "Following Johann Petrovich's accusation, then, it would appear Earth has managed to save the Commonwealth. In which case, I should expect that we have definitely proven the value of the trade treaty Jezekiah has worked out. And that we can expect your full support"

"No!"

"I wasn't asking you, Uncle." This time, Mother made a point of staring at the throbbing red tell-tale. "I'm waiting, Octavian."

"I'm thinking." Octavian rested his hands palm down on his table. The centerpiece unfurled a pink tendril at once. It brushed his finger and he tickled its underside absently, eyes flickering a thoughtful white-blue. The tendril looped around his finger in seeming ecstasy. Then abruptly snapped taut, catching Octavian's finger in a python grip. Octavian jerked his hand free with a sharp twist of his wrist, sending the tendril snapping back into the body of the plant. Red streaked his ebony skin where the tendril had been. He shook it, splattering the table with droplets of blood. A host of slender pink strands sucked the drops dry as he sat back.

Octavian yanked a gossamer handkerchief from a breast pocket. "I keep old Hubert here because he is so very man-ish. Always ready to bite the hand that feeds him. A reminder, if you will, of the penalty for trusting my own kind." He wrapped the handkerchief around his bloodied hand with short, sharp motions. "By contrast, I am reminded of a saying from an old Home World philosopher: 'If you take a starving dog and make him prosperous, he will not bite you. That is the difference between a dog and a man.'"

"Make your point, Nephew." JP had stopped pacing, but only to tap boot-toes impatiently.

"There is some debate among the true-human worlds as to whether the Lupans are men or dogs. Speaking for Pandar, we do not much care, so long as their currency holds good. However, it has been my observation that dogs or not, Lupans understand *quid pro quo* ever so well. It strikes me, therefore, that it is extremely unlikely a young, *unmarried* Lupan war lord should have come up with so … creative a response on his own."

"Excellent." JP stopped beside Jezekiah to fold arms in satisfaction. "Then I shall call a Council session to hear the formal charge of collusion."

"Not just yet, if you please." There was no flicker across Octavian's eyes now, just a Van Buren's clear, cold blue. "I believe you will find the rest of the Council shares my lack of enthusiasm for a Lupan war, Uncle. Trade or otherwise." He flashed JP a brilliant smile that said he'd guarantee it.

"Why? Worried about your profits?"

"Oh, I'm quite sure Pandar can manage a bit of war profiteering. It's simply that we should very much prefer the lower overhead of profiting from peace."

On Mother's comm, the red light intensified to a throbbing insistence. "Gentlemen, I should not have to remind you I have other matters demanding my attention! Now either make the charge or allow me to attend my duties!"

"Quite right." Octavian settled back comfortably. "I think we can avert JP's charge."

With a *humph*, JP's holo winked out.

"Good." Mother was already reaching for her comm. She stop, hand hovering, when Octavian remained. "Name it, Octavian."

"Oh, it's quite simple." Octavian smiled at the empty space JP's holo had occupied. "I should simply like a token of innocence from Home World. Shall we say the tech specs for a long jump drive?"

"You realize that means I shall have to head back out to the rim." Jezekiah's pulse spiked at the opportunity. He'd be off Earth by morning. And this time, he'd have Keiko Yakamoto with him. He made sure the hope didn't touch his voice. "That's a good twelve week journey to Khayyam Station from Earth. Three more to Den Lupus. Assuming Strongarm's willing-"

"Oh, I shouldn't worry about packing and all that, old chap." Octavian shook back a jeweled sleeve, rested fingers on the gem-crusted controls embedded in his table. "Unless I miss my guess, our good Lord Strongarm is about to visit *you*. I don't think we need to worry JP about it just yet, though, do you?" His smile turned positively beatific. "I do so look forward to seeing those tech specs soon."

His holo vanished, leaving the after-image of his smile lingering in the air. Mother slapped her comm to life. "Report."

Madam Protector Admiral Yakamoto came through on audio only. Even his voice sounded taut. *A Lupan ship has dropped into system. I have scrambled the Samurai.*

XIV

Home World. The white-swirled blue world filled the screens wrapping the gray sweep of *Khali*'s bridge. Myra's Cub, battle-named Strongarm, lifted his ears to the collective gasp from his bridge crew. He held silence himself, command habit, though the sight of Earth triggered a thrill that shivered every fiber in his body. He yanked his eyes away from the fulfillment of his dreams to sweep his gaze around the bridge. To a man, crew sat droop-eared, eyes fixed on the forward screens while ship's systems chattered on behind them.

Thank the Makers' God they hadn't dropped into an ambush or they'd already be dead. Strongarm *uhfed* softly and crew snapped back to their duties. Around *Khali*'s domed bridge, the staccato tap of talon tips on controls replaced the awed silence. Satisfied, Strongarm finally allowed himself to dwell on the sight.

He recognized the paired land masses of the Americas. Only the America of the Histories wasn't there anymore. The land bridge linking the northern and southern continents was too thin. The narrow strip where Panama should be had shrunk to a slender strip barely broader than the great gash of its namesake canal. To the north, Florida's isthmus was nothing more than a stick finger jutting down into the Atlantic. The great Mississippi river had swallowed the delta where New Orleans should have been. Lightning played across the ocean-built spires of New York. On the western shore of the continent the cities of Los Angeles and San Diego had merged into a single concrete mass. Only Denver, where the ancient American gene techs had first created LupanType, was still recognizable on its mile-high plateau. Habit kept his ears upright. But somehow the changes felt like a betrayal.

A telltale flashed on his comm panel, underscoring the whiff of musk his headset's silver nosepiece fed him. "What is it, Kait?"

"Planet side defenses have finally picked us up," his brother-in-law's voice drawled. No 'sir', of course; with Kaitin ibn Bengal, the fact he *was* reporting spoke for itself. "We have in-coming."

Strongarm *uhfed* in satisfaction. "That will be the reception committee."

"Thou were always an optimist." It was scent, not sound, that told him Kait was laughing. "Thy guests flash StelFleet IDs. Samurai division."

Suicide fighters, then. Helluva sorry excuse for a welcoming committee. Strongarm's ears tried to flatten. He held them upright with effort. Jezekiah Van Buren knew he was coming. Whole damned trip was the Van Buren's idea. But, then, even Jezekiah was still an onlie. Which meant it was still possible the man had lied. "How long to contact?"

"Fourteen minutes and counting. Assuming they drop out of Jump firing."

"Are their weapons boards active?"

"Not yet. It is their speed that bespeaks the hunt." A hint of challenge touched Kait's scent. "Allow this one to teach the flat teeth not to charge their betters."

"Hold fire. Rig shields, but hold fire." Strongarm drummed talon tips against the command seat armrest, decided to rely on trust a few minutes longer. His life was already forfeit if this didn't work. But he'd be damned if he'd let a flock of onlies scar his ship, Makers or not. "Hail Earth, Kait. I want to hear the explanation from Van Buren himself."

"On it." The Bengali's scent bespoke his opinion more thoroughly than mere words.

"Put it through to my quarters. Then meet me down there."

"Done."

If Van Buren *had* lied, he wanted to keep it private. If Home World's story was in for an ugly end, at least Kait would know the truth. Damned cat would tell it, too. Small comfort. If it came to a shooting war, destroying Home World would be his own, final claim to infamy.

Strongarm pushed himself out of the command chair. Around *Khali's* bridge ears swiveled attentively, noses testing his scent for danger as he stalked off the bridge. He willed the threat out of mind, kept his scent to business-as-usual and they turned back to their duties.

Commander's quarters were an armored deck below and five battle shields behind alpha bridge. Most of what space he had was given to comm and nav equipment. He could drive *Khali* from here, if he had to. His table was plain deck-weld, just big enough to seat his officers; his bunk barely big enough for himself. It was his walls that demonstrated his wealth. It'd cost him a small fortune to haul his book collection up to *Khali*, a larger one to have them encased in blast proof stasis pods. Worth it, though. His books dated back to the old NorthAm empire, one or two even older. He'd had stasis shields put on their crumbling pages, and installed ID and comm capacity on the pods themselves. Even if *Khali* herself bought it, the books would survive.

He heard Kaitin's scratch while he finished up in the john. He called 'enter' and started to step out. This time, though, his sidelong reflection caught his attention. He perked ears at himself in the mirror, wondering for the first time what he looked like to onlie eyes. His face was human enough even by onlie standards. He had the high cheekbones and coppery skin of his apache ancestors. His forehead was high, the nose broad and straight beneath the eagle's scowl of his brows. Only his eyes were amber, his nose bone rather than cartilage. His chin was strong and square and clean-shaven, though muscle bulged where an onlie's ears would be. Made his neck look like it merged with the corded muscle of his shoulders. Still, the fine silvery hair on his chest *was* hair, not fur. And his sister Hellas claimed he had fine, sensitive lips. He wondered whether the Van Buren sister would mind that those fine lips covered a carnivore's fangs.

He smelled his brother-in-law's presence before the Bengali stepped into his field of vision. "Allow this one to guess," Kaitin drawled from the doorway. "Thou found a zit."

"Fuck off." Strongarm splashed water across his face and reached for the towel. Only now he caught himself searching his chin for an angry red spot. Wasn't one, of course. Maker's balls, damned cat did it to him every time.

Kaitin knew it, too. He rested a shoulder against the john door, lifted a lip in feline superiority to reveal the teardrop ruby embedded in the tip of one fang.

Strongarm shook water off his face wondering yet again how onlies ever managed to claim all Lupans looked alike. Damned flatteeth couldn't see the difference between wolf-bred and tiger any better than they could smell it. He wiped his talons dry, manfully resisting the urge to flick water at his brother-in-law, and slung the towel over his shoulder. "Got Van Buren?"

"Patched in." Kaitin stepped aside to let Strongarm shoulder out of the john. He was taller than Strongarm's own six-three, and leaner, with a Bengali's characteristic black-on-orange striped mane and a prince's unshakable arrogance. "Holo coming up–" He clicked talons and the air above the table pearlesced. "Now."

The image that formed of Jezekiah looked debonair as always. He stood beside an elegant desk in a tall-windowed, day lit office elegant enough to make even Kaitin gasp. And yet... if that man had had ears, they'd be at half-mast. Instinct twitched Strongarm's nose, testing for scent clues. Beside him, Kaitin swore softly, sign he'd picked up the Van Buren's discomfort as well.

"Congratulations, Brother-in-Law," Kaitin murmured sidelong, amber eyes target-locked on the Van Buren. "Thou hast dodged a wedding and run into a war."

"Not if I can help it." Strongarm faced up to the holo. "Friend Jezekiah, want to tell me what kind of traveling orders that reception committee's of yours is carrying?"

He'd opted to keep his grin friendly. Said a lot for Van Buren that he grinned back. Except he wasn't the one who answered.

"I had rather expected, *Lord* Strongarm, to ask you that question." The tall backed chair behind the desk swiveled to let its occupant lock an unnerving blue scowl on him. Even seated, the woman radiated power.

"Makers." That was Kaitin, gone droop-eared and slack-jawed.

The Protector of Home World dismissed the Bengali with a glance. She lifted her chin to him, though with her it was a sign of authority. Strongarm felt his balls curl into a tight little knot. Kaitin, he noted, discreetly slipped around behind his own broad back. Strongarm forced his ears up to a polite angle, clasped hands behind his back. "Madam Van Buren."

"Admiral Yakamoto reports we have two minutes to contact." Damn, if the Van Buren mother didn't manage to look down her nose at him. "Be so good as to explain what kind of contact you intend it to be."

"Friendly." Strongarm realized his ears had sunk again and snapped them up. Inched his chin up with them, acknowledging her dominance in her own territory. "I'm here on invitation." He lifted an ear at Jezekiah for reinforcement.

"It seems my memory fails me." Van Buren's mother swiveled her chair to target Jezekiah.

"I did indeed invite Lord Strongarm to visit us, Mother." Jezekiah arched those Bengali red brows of his at Strongarm. "However, I expected time to allow you to prepare. He wasn't scheduled to arrive for several weeks yet."

"Timing only matters on the battlefield. Among *friends*, doors are always open." A draft of air wafted him the worrisome scent of Kaitin's satisfaction. No way to tell without a scent track what Jezekiah really felt. "Seems to me the question is whether we're still friends."

Sixty seconds to contact, DefComm murmured through his headset. Behind him, Kaitin's scent sharpened. Strongarm flicked an ear in approval, listened to Kait's mutter as he brought *Khali's* weapons boards up.

Mother Van Buren flicked a glance at Kaitin. No question she recognized the threat. She simply opted to treat it with disdain. "I must ask your pardon, Lord Strongarm. I see now we are both the victims of a miscommunication. Please consider our Samurai as your honor guard." Keeping her eyes on him, she tapped her comm. "Admiral Yakamoto: hold your fire. Repeat, hold your fire."

Fighters have dropped out of Jump, DefComm reported. Strongarm leveled an ear at Kaitin. The Bengali hissed, but muttered the command to hold fire.

Samurai breaking formation, DefComm announced. *They are waggling wings.*

"Disengage." Strongarm salaamed to the Van Buren mother onlie style. Didn't melt the blue ice in those eyes, but he caught the faintest hint of a smile in the twitch of her lips.

When she spoke, it was to her comm. "Admiral Yakamoto, Lord Strongarm is our invited guest. You will escort the Lupan battleship into orbit. Then provide our guest an honor guard down to Niihau port." Only then did she return his salaam. "Welcome to Earth, Lord Strongarm."

Strongarm tracked DefComm reports long enough to make sure the Samurai really were lining up peacefully, then lowered himself into a chair. For once, Kaitin was keeping his thoughts to himself. But his scent was troubled. "What is it, Kait?"

The Bengali lowered himself into a squat on a facing chair. Typical Bengali, he made sure his emerald bloomers draped becomingly before he spoke his piece. "Turn back now, while thou still can. Jezekiah lied-"

"Not necessarily. We're a month early. I can see where he'd want time to convince his sister to accept a Lupan husband."

"His mother did not even know thou were coming. Can think his sister was told?" Kaitin ran a red-haired hand across white mustaches. "He plans no marriage. Not in truth. The Van Buren wants thy battle fleet, not thyself."

Maker's balls, he did not want to re-fight this battle now. Tension tightened the muscles around his eyes, trying to trigger hunting vision. Strongarm shook himself to clear it. He bought himself an extra minute's calming time by hooking an empty chair into position with a booted toe. "We've been over this track enough. Jezekiah had nothing to do with Streiker hijacking my caravan. He's out to stop his uncle's war, not fight it. That suits me just fine." He propped his feet up on the chair, willed his ears upright. "I didn't dodge out of my mother's house just to re-fight the Schism." Even so, warning tinged his scent.

"Then this one grieves for thee, Brother-in-law." A brocaded pant leg kinked; he paused to shake it loose. "Among the women of Parliament the question is now asked: How many more times will thou redeem thy honor with money?"

Strongarm shot upright, fangs baring on instinct. From anyone else he'd have answered that question in blood. But then, no one else had as much right to complain as Kaitin ibn Bengal del Lobo. Knowing that, Kaitin only locked talons around his chair and let the sorrow in his scent speak for him.

"I'll take care of Streiker if I have to." Strongarm managed to cover fangs. Kait knew enough to ignore the growl. "But I'm not going to fire the first shot. End of story."

"Thy words carry wisdom as always, Brother-in-law." Kaitin sheathed talons. He swiped his tongue across fingertips and raked them through his mane to smooth it down. "This one advises thee to suit action to them. There is time yet; turn back. Complete thy Impression among thy own kind. Give thyself the chance to smell the onlies' treaty with a clear nose."

Hunter vision tried to trigger again. Strongarm shook himself till it cleared. This time the action raised enough hair shed to make them both sneeze. Just as well, too. Nothing broke tension like hair up your nose. "Can't, Kait."

"The position is still open."

"Drop it. The chemistry was wrong."

"The chemistry was fine. Thou held thy breath."

Ah, shit. He kept his ears up, but the guilt registered in his scent. Kaitin twitched his nose to prove it. Strongarm ran a hand across the table, bringing up a holo of the Hawaiian Islands. "When did you figure it out?"

"At the time." Kaitin lifted a lip enough to let light strike fire off the tear drop ruby. "There was no other explanation. This one conducted the strip search -"

"Don't remind me." Strongarm's rectum puckered at the memory.

"Thou had no hidden nose filters or scent vials. Plus, thou had thy nose between the most beautiful pair of legs on Den Lupus, so attraction was not the issue. Which left only breath control."

"If you figured it out, why didn't you just hold me in place? That would've finished the job."

"The thought occurred. Yet the stronger question was 'why?'"

"You mean why wouldn't I want to bind myself as fourth husband to your sister? Spend the rest of my life playing step and fetch for three senior Bengalis?" Damn, that sounded insulting. Their marriages had been intended to complete an inter-clan treaty. Traditional son swap, each clan marrying its alpha prince to the other's alpha daughter. Kaitin had accepted his fate, fourth husband to sister Hellas. It was himself who had ruined the plan. Strongarm lifted his chin, offering apology.

"Accepted." Kaitin folded hands atop his knees and rested his chin atop his knuckles.

"So why let me go?"

"Because-" Kaitin straightened fluidly, wafted emerald brocade into place. "This one still hoped Jezekiah Van Buren had told thee the truth. A marriage treaty with Home World offered greater advantage for all." The ruby flashed. "As this one quickly explained to our joint mothers. Did think thee would have lived to reach *Khali* otherwise?"

"And here I thought I just ran too fast." Strongarm salaamed with sincerity. "Owe you, Kait.

Kaitin kissed fingers to himself smugly. "Never allow it to be said the onlies have a lock on subtlety."

"Agreed. So – why the change in heart? Why push me to turn back now?"

"Because now this one smells a trap. For all his pretty talk, Jezekiah Van Buren has not obtained his mother's consent to the marriage alliance. And it is his mother who holds power." The fluffy white ears lowered. "One fears he has lured thee into a waiting game. One he intends to end in thy death."

"I don't believe it." The image of the Van Buren sister hot and willing in his arms formed unbidden behind his eyes. He felt his loins stir, willed the surge of desire down.

"Thy need grows daily, Brother-in-Law." Kaitin's own scent bespoke his worry. "Take *Khali* back now. Finish thy Impression with thine own kind. This one can sign the onlies treaty for thee."

"I didn't dent fortune and honor both buying Streiker off just to turn tail now." He *uhfed* softly. "I'd never make it home anyway. I may have staved off the finish, but your sister sure as hell got the hormones flowing. I either bind myself to a woman soon or I'm dead."

"*Khali* can make it."

"Not in time. Even long jumping, we're eight days away from home." He exhaled, keeping the Bengali's worry at bay. "I haven't got that long."

Kaitin pulled himself tighter on the chair, breath taking on a thoughtful purr. Under the circumstances, it wasn't a happy sound. "We need thee, Brother-in-Law. There will be no avoiding war; the Streikern Van Buren is determined to provoke it. Even if the free worlds support us, Den Lupus cannot survive: the onlies outnumber us, twelve planets to one. They can keep their supply lines safe within their Commonwealth borders. We, on the other hand, will be trapped on the defensive. That is what Streiker intends."

Strongarm upped image of the islands' holo, traced the outline of Oahu with a fingertip to give himself something else to focus on. Not in time to hide it from Kaitin. "Unless we acquire a second base. One from which our long jump fighters can strike the Commonwealth worlds."

"Home World, in other words. This one suspected such was thy intent." Kaitin stroked his mustaches, eyes drooping. From a Bengali, it was a surprising display of affection. The worry in his scent underscored it. "Yet if the Van Buren blocks thy marriage, we remain trapped. The Streiker Van Buren would know this. The risk is that Jezekiah is in truth playing thee for his uncle's fool."

"I don't see it that way. From Jezekiah's perspective I could simply blast in and grab his sister anyway." The very mention of grabbing a woman was enough to make Strongarm shift uncomfortably. He'd be soaking in ice if Kaitin kept up this line of chat very long.

"Even if the sister survived the mating, she would have but to scream rape. The penalty is death. Jezekiah knows that. It would serve Streiker's purpose as well."

Strongarm offed the holo, lifted nose to the warning in Kaitin's scent. "I'm not crossing that bridge until I reach it. Until then, we're assuming Jezekiah's been honest. We're going planetside."

For once, the Bengali took time choosing his words. "Were it not better this one remains on *Khali?* Thou will need a senior officer in Beta command."

"Our seconds can handle anything the onlies can throw at them." He pulled in a long, calming breath. "I'm not a total idiot, Kait. I'm too Impressionable. I'm going to need a level head at hand."

"And away from the weapons board, yes?" Kaitin twitched his nose, Bengali equivalent to a wry ear.

"That, too. Don't want you ending life on Earth while I'm on it."

"And if the flat teeth manage to kill thee?"

"There'll be a damned sight fewer of them for the effort." He grinned, though Kaitin would recognize the worry in his scent beneath it. "I've already logged the orders. If anything happens to me planetside, you're to get your red-haired ass up here double-time. *Khali* will fall to your command."

"Do not demand mercy of this one in such case, Brother-in-Law."

"I'm not." His ears drooped. This time he let them. "Jezekiah will only betray me if he is indeed in league with Streiker. In which case, there will be no avoiding the war."

"This one hears." There was a bit too much sincerity in Kaitin's scent when he pursed lips.

"Done, then." Strongarm rose, Kaitin following suit. "Get your dress gear together. We're going to have to make an impression."

"One nobly declines comment on such a pun." Kaitin lifted chin, then flowed out the door.

Strongarm waited till the door slid shut behind the Bengali before he sank back into his chair. He rubbed the base of his palms against his forehead, wishing he could rub the throb out of them. It was arrogance unspeakable that a Lupan should presume to address the God of his Makers. He could face his own death with nothing more than regret. But behind his hands he prayed to the God that Jezekiah Van Buren had promised true. The prayer was for Earth, for Home World. If Jezekiah had lied, then Home World would die with him.

XV

The Samurai escort brought Strongarm's landing barge into atmosphere just west of the North American land mass. Viz picked up a thousand mile stretch of diamond light lining the continent's coast that ShipMind identified as the twin megalopoli of LosanDiego and SanCouver. After that, the Samurai set an approach only a few thousand feet above sea level. Left viz nothing to see but the steel gray Pacific rolling on endlessly beneath them.

"If these flat teeth intend to disappear us, they have chosen a clear path." In the copilot seat beside him Kaitin sounded snarky as ever. His scent gave it the lie.

Strongarm grinned at the worry in the Bengali's scent. Kaitin would face death with bared fangs; it was the thought of wet feet that scared him.

Kaitin caught his grin and sniffed. "The histories say the Hawaiian Islands are the most isolated habitable bits of land on Earth. There will be neither bodies nor wreckage left if the Samurai choose to cause us an 'accident' here."

"They're in for a surprise if they try." Mere landing barge she might be, but *Kutak* packed better battle shields and armament than most onlie warships. An uncomfortable fact the Samurai's weapons boards had undoubtedly noticed. Their escort had had them on target lock since making atmosphere.

"Not likely. My guess is they're trying to create a good impression themselves." He looked out at the vast emptiness and *uhfed*. "By the time we get there, even a chunk of rock's going to look good."

"Truth. Or perhaps they intend to bore us to death." Kaitin yawned, patted it down daintily. "And so, Brother-in-Law, this one shall take a nap." And he was out, just like that, chin on chest, his breath rumbling softly above the purr of the engines.

Cats. Strongarm *uhfed* philosophically. But, then, Kaitin's napping gave him time to savor the approach. The jagged silhouette of the Hawaiian islands broke the horizon just as the sun shot sparkles across the waves beneath his wings. Strongarm's pulse leaped so hard at the sight he half-expected Kaitin to hear it.

The lead Samurai banked north and he followed, feeling his blood settle into a steady throb in his ears as the islands slipped past. At the southernmost tip of the chain he recognized the Big Island, Hawaii herself, by the volcanoes' red-orange glow against the lightening sky. Human-only eyes would see nothing but vague shadows at this range. Strongarm drank in the ragged details of the lava fields, traced the blackened fields inland to the green plains beyond.

Then they were past, following the sea channels northward. The names of the next few islands escaped him. He recognized Oahu by the glimpse of Diamond Head jutting out on the far southern shore. Impossible to miss the Van Buren Manor high in the hills between Diamond Head and Pearl Harbor. Nestled within the faint aura of its weather shields, it glowed like some mystic, golden orb. Odd, though, that the jungled shoreline of Waikiki beyond it should look so desolate.

And then Niihau. In the distance, he could make out the chevron shaped cone of the dead volcano that was Home World's deep space port. A ring of caves pockmarked the gray-brown inside curve of the mountain. A secondary ring of docking platforms jutted out over the broad central bay. Tiny flashes of white light flitted across the water, working craft momentarily transformed into bits of glory by the rising sun. Strongarm's nose twitched as scent track fed him the aromas of Home World. For some reason, he hadn't expected *this* seascape to smell of engine heat and dead fish.

Final approach, Niihau, the lead Samurai announced through his headset. *Off shields*. The tone was painfully polite. The target lock that accompanied it was not.

"Main shields down." *Kutak* shuddered as he overrode its defenses.

Two of the Samurai fighters formed up to land with him, Strongarm noted. He murphy-checked backup shields, noted the other four members of the escort remained aloft. They hovered in a gleaming crescent above the bay, guns still on target lock.

"These flat teeth lack manners." Kaitin had only one golden eye open, but he managed a glare nonetheless.

"True." Strongarm felt his ears drop, shook himself to set them straight. On any other world he'd have taken those four out just as an object lesson. Here... "Think we'd best remember their perspective. Home World's last memories of Lupans are not happy ones."

He settled the barge into its designated nest on the dock, offed all but backup systems to show good will. Then held his breath with Kaitin until the Samurai broke target lock. They did, finally, and Strongarm elbowed his bulk out of the pilot's seat to *Kutak*'s hatch.

The Samurai had settled them well out on the curving tip of the dock. The port caves swept away in a dotted line, following the inside of sweep of the volcanic cone. Viz showed a group of onlies in full-dress finery filing out of the nearest cave. He spotted a pair of unmistakably flame-colored mops in its midst. So Jezekiah had brought his sister with him. His manhood lurched at thought.

"One sees Van Buren has brought Sec as well." Kaitin's tone wavered between annoyance and contempt. SecTypes were dangerous folk, as onlies went.

"Probably just protocol. That's the Protector' daughter out there."

"Yet the dark one backs Jezekiah."

"*Magawm*, then – status sign. Sons mean more to onlies." Strongarm sharpened focus on the dark bulk of the graying SecType at Jezekiah's back. Definitely protecting Jezekiah, not the sister.

Whatever the reason was, he'd find out later. The welcoming committee had apparently reached its mark. The pack stopped well clear of the barge, the fidgeting dignitaries' bright brocades flashing glitter in the sunlight. Only Jezekiah stepped forward, motioning the SecType to stay back. He lifted a red-gold eyebrow at the hatch. And grinned.

Strongarm lifted his head, testing. Noted with relief that Jezekiah tested honest, his scent bespeaking genuine happiness underscored by worry.

"Time to say hello." Strongarm tapped the panel that opened the barge's doors and extended its landing ramp.

A blast of sea air shot through the opening, washing them in sneeze-strength scents of salt and onlie nervousness. The full impact of Home World hit him, then. The place *smelled* right. No, it was more than that – it *felt* right. All the way to his bones, it felt right in a way he'd never realized Den Lupus did not. Beside him, Kaitin's breath took on a deep purr. Sign enough he'd felt it, too. Felt the claim Earth had on his soul. The call of *home*.

Strongarm shook the awe out of his ears, then stepped into the hatchway, hands on hips where everyone could see them, chin up to acknowledge their dominance here. Except for Jezekiah, the onlies didn't seem to appreciate the courtesy. On the tarmac below Jezekiah had nudged forward a group of onlie girls in peek-a-boo skirts. The girls were apparently supposed to form an honor guard to flank the ramp – an honor guard of *women*, no less. Clearly Jezekiah had intended an honor. Equally clearly, the plan wasn't going to work. The girls were backpedalling, wide-eyed, holding their long wreaths of flowers out in front of them like talismans. The scent of their fear overrode even the perfume in the air streaming through the doorway.

"Pity," Kaitin murmured beside him. "Thou did ever have an unfortunate effect on onlie women."

Strongarm *uhfed* him silent. Wouldn't have mattered, had the Van Buren sister also not been trying desperately to backpedal. That big graying SecType had stepped over behind her, he noted. No need to question why, either: had the SecType not held her discreetly in place, she'd be half way back down the mountain by now.

Jezekiah turned to smile and hold a hand out to his sister. He looked sweet as an onlie pastry. But Strongarm's ears tried to flatten at the threat in his scent. The sister must have picked it up, too. She stopped trying to claw through the SecType's chest.

Beside him, Kaitin stroked his mustaches. "At least thou can now be certain Jezekiah has told his sister of the wedding plans."

A disturbance in the throng below saved Strongarm from having to think up a retort. Behind Jezekiah, glittering dignitaries stumbled aside in sequence as some invisible force shoved past them. Jezekiah's grin vanished as a tiny young woman in a faded red wrap and a garden's worth of flowers around her neck elbowed into sight. Jezekiah reached for her arm as she stalked past. Her scent carried only a mix of exasperation and pity, but the sidelong look she shot him made Jezekiah jerk his hand back quickly.

"Ow!" Strongarm jerked around, rubbing at the sting in his ear tip.

"Down, boy." Safely out of sight beside the hatch Kaitin resheathed talons. "Thy fate is the one trying to flee thee." He peered past the hatch and his own ears drooped. "Though one commends thy taste. That one wields a power unto herself."

"You think maybe she's a Maker?" No point even trying to hide the awe in his tone.

That earned him an out and out snort. "Let not thy balls lead thee into a deeper trap, Brother-in-Law. The Makers bred themselves out of existence centuries ago. These Type-coded onlies are no more human than ourselves. Less so, in this one's eyes."

"It's still possible, though, on Earth."

Maker or not, Jezekiah's overlaid scents of shock and worry and desire said that little woman had already claimed him. Surprise short-circuited an upswell of jealousy. *Her* scent – Strongarm tried to uhf, realized his mouth had gone dry. He'd gritted teeth for a year watching Jezekiah send women into heat across the rim. Yet this little female's scent betrayed – he twitched his nose, dismay overriding shock. Her scent carried no answering desire at all. Just anger. And a deep, burning resentment.

She marched past the terrified honor guard, yanking flower wreaths out of hands as she passed. Even Kaitin, safe in the shadows beside him, stroked mustaches nervously. "Thank the God of thy Makers that one is not angered at thee."

"Pray, is more like it." Strongarm had to lower his head to keep her in his line of sight. No perfume on her, praise the Makers' God. No fear in her, either. Made him hope for a second the terrified flower girls backing away from the ramp were afraid of her rather than himself.

He swallowed – or tried to – and stepped forward to meet her in open air with a polite grin. At the bottom of the ramp, three of the honor girls dropped their flowers and ran. Despite his better intentions, he watched them run. A wind shift carried him the pungent proof they'd shit themselves first.

"Oh." A woman's sound, spoken somewhere south of his chest.

Makers balls. Strongarm squelched the grin. Bracing himself he glanced down at Jezekiah's little woman – and found himself absorbed in a pair of lilting dark eyes. She answered him with a scent gone glorious in wonder, the chain of flowers dangling forgotten.

It was the rasp of a man's voice from the throng below that made him realize he was grinning like some drunken miner.

"Bet those ears ain't the only damn thing just snapped to attention on that fool." The wind carried him the speaker's voice on a scent reeking disapproval.

Strongarm *uhfed* sense back into his mind, tracked the voice to the big SecType holding the Van Buren sister in place. The man started as Strongarm's gaze found him. To his credit, the fellow cocked his head, bringing the silver crescent of a comm implant to bear, and held his ground. Which was more than could be said for the Van Buren girl. She'd gone back to trying to claw her way through the man's chest.

That did not bode well for sealing the treaty. He heard Kaitin's sniffed contempt, knew he'd spotted the bride's reaction.

"Ahem." South of his chin, the young woman cleared her throat pointedly.

He glanced down, bracing himself. Only Jezekiah's little woman answered him with a searching concern that erased dismay.

"Are you all right, Lord Strongarm?" Her voice was deeper than he'd expected, with a nuzzly feel that tingled his balls.

"Aside from being an utter fool, he is fine." Kaitin poked a discreet talon tip into Strongarm's ribs for emphasis. He slid out of the shadows to salaam gracefully. "This one regrets his brother-in-law's awkwardness. One fears he is unaccustomed to public graces."

"Oh." She turned those lilting eyes on Kaitin and her scent went wondering afresh. "I'm sorry – Admiral never said you'd be beautiful."

The shocked perk in Kaitin's ears didn't stop him from preening. Strongarm lifted a lip at the Bengali sidelong. "Ignore him. He's married."

"Oh. Oh!" To Strongarm's satisfaction she refocused on him, sending his ears drooping to a silly angle. Belatedly, she remembered to offer him the flowers she carried. "Aloha!"

At full reach, she could only lift the wreath up to his chin. No threat in her scent, but hunter vision tried to trigger anyway.

Beside him Kaitin stopped preening. "A trap wreathed in flowers and woman-scent," he murmured in Lobish. "The Van Buren intends to make thee bow obeisance to his woman."

"She's not his woman." Looking over the girl's flowers, Strongarm locked hunter gaze on Jezekiah. The man's expression didn't change, but his scent had gone pure worry. The big SecType clearly picked up on it. He released the sister, fell into back up position behind him. The sister, Strongarm noted, simply fell.

"Please don't be upset. There's no trick. It's a tradition. We always welcome guests with leis." Jezekiah's woman was still holding the flower chain up to him. Her expression still bespoke concern. But with a start, Strongarm realized her scent had gone neutral. She'd shifted stance, too. Gone onto the balls of her feet, warrior style. He *uhfed*, shook the danger out of his sight. "Apologies, little one. It would be wiser if you just hand the flowers to me. Our customs are designed for taller folk."

That got him a narrow-eyed purse of the lips that dipped his ears. But she gave him the flowers when he held his hands out, palms up, talons sheathed. She hesitated, then pulled a number of flowered chains off her own neck and handed the lot to Kaitin. "Aloha," she said again, and smiled. "Welcome to Hawaii."

With a quick prayer to the Makers' God Strongarm slipped the *leis* over his head. Because in the last instant before the flowers' fragrance drowned out everything else, he caught a fresh shift in the man-scents below. Jezekiah had just gone jealous.

XVI

Massive mistake, to expect Letticia to carry off her end of the formalities. Jezekiah put his smile on lock-down, used his heel to try to lock Letticia in place by the toes. She only wiggled out of her shoe and backpedaled. Nothing but Kip's solid bulk prevented her from backing straight off the dock. Jezekiah answered Kip's questioning grunt with the hint of a nod. The wind whistling across Niihau's dock ensured even the dignitaries crowding Jezekiah's shoulders did not hear the hiss of the tranquilizer hypo Kip pressed into Letticia's wrist. Their bright fluttering robes disguised Letticia's sudden sag.

Or would have, had Kip not suddenly picked up some threat that made him let Letticia go to slide back into covering position behind Jezekiah. There was no disguising Lush's straight-down drop. A couple of Mother's senior aides had her on her feet again in an instant, but the damage was done. Strongarm had seen her fall. Jezekiah felt his own heart clench at the dismayed droop of the man's ears. Felt his teeth clench after it as Keiko Yakamoto said something that brought those ears back up again. Whatever it was, it turned the man's grin positively foolish.

He ought, Jezekiah thought sourly, to be grateful that Keiko Yakamoto didn't let personal grudges interfere with duty. He'd thought adding her to Kip's Sec team would give him a discrete chance to explain his intervention on her Type coding. All he'd got for the effort was a heartful of pain. Odds were she'd have made that a full body hurt, if Kip hadn't been there. Now, he could only watch in rueful admiration as she drew Strongarm's attention off Letticia's antics and led the man docilely down the ramp. At least it was rueful admiration until Keiko grabbed Strongarm by the wrist. At that point admiration morphed into an utterly unwarranted and distinctly unjustified jealousy. Did not help at all that the way Strongarm's nose twitched in his direction said the Lupan had caught it. So, then. One more level added to the damage control he was going to have to do.

He made sure the admin op got Letticia off the dock before Strongarm and

Kaitin reached the welcoming committee. The Lupans took her absence well – Jezekiah refused to let himself dwell on how much of that was due to Keiko's presence – so he got them through the truncated dockside courtesies without intensifying the disaster. Even so, he felt the hurt droop in Strongarm's ears in his heart.

The debacle on the dock ensured the trip down to the Manor was more subdued than it should have been. Good chance he could have offset that by inviting Keiko to join them on Mother's shuttle. He would have, too, despite Kip's warning scowl. Only there was a little too much hope in the way Strongarm's ears swiveled to track the girl after she bowed herself away from them on the dock. And too much regret in the way himself had craned for a last glimpse of Keiko's retreating back.

Strongarm's ears stayed at a sorry half-mast on the trip down to Oahu. Jezekiah did what he could to ease the man's misery, but his concerns lay with Kaitin ibn Bengal del Lobo. That 'del Lobo' meant the man was married into Lobo Clan; the fact he was *here* could only mean he was married to Strongarm's sister. Wherein lay a whole new worry. Clan Bengal hadn't been an issue when he'd worked out the treaty terms with Strongarm. Having him turn up now as an in-law – and a hostile one at that – unpleasantly re-arranged Jezekiah's priorities. The man's sneering attitude also forced him to acknowledge Grandfather Ho had told that much of the truth: Kaitin ibn Bengal was no friend to a Home World-Lupan alliance. He was going to have find out why in a hurry.

Fortunately even Kaitin brightened a bit when they reached their suite in the Manor's guest wing. Jezekiah ushered the two Lupans in with a sweeping bow. "I hope you find the accommodations satisfactory." They'd damned well better. He didn't dare allow himself to think what the cost of the revamp had done to Mother's operating budget. He'd overseen the work on the suite himself. The walls were now covered in variegated shades of wood, the floors covered in a carpet of living grass. The combination added hard world depth to the holo of timber stands stretching out to far horizons. Fat, rounded couches clustered like family knots around low tables set with vases of native flowers. A matched set of sync chairs were set near the doors to each of the suite's twin bedrooms, allowing for privacy. He'd made sure their major domo set the air filters to neutral, too, so the breeze through the weather screens carried the smells of sweet oleander and ocean from the open balcony lining the suite.

Strongarm simply lifted ears in acknowledgement and ambled past Jezekiah to check out the balcony. But then, it wasn't Strongarm who concerned him; the man would make himself comfortable on a dung heap if that was all a friend had to offer. The challenge was satisfying the feline vanity of Kaitin ibn Bengal. Kaitin would be looking for a slight.

The Bengali stalked past Jezekiah in a swirl of crimson robes, ears flat, nose twitching. True to form, he headed for the living room bathroom first. Jezekiah stepped in to let the door close behind him. He kept his expression neutral while Kaitin stalked back out, kept the smugness out of mind and scent alike at sight of the reluctant satisfaction in the Bengali's ears. Praise whatever gods watched over errant Van Burens that he'd thought to expand the mirrors in the bathrooms and soften the light to flattery.

"I think you'll recognize your bedroom without difficulty." Jezekiah motioned Kaitin toward the far side bedroom with a sweep of the hand. He'd put particular care into that room just in case Strongarm's sister tagged along with him. In contrast to the comfortable functionality of Strongarm's sleeping quarters, Kaitin ibn Bengal's bedroom bespoke the decadent opulence of a sultan's seraglio. Gauzy curtains screened the massive four poster bed. Sheer green drapes trimmed in gold – pure luck he'd used clan Bengal colors – looped gracefully across the arched balcony entrance. The room itself was laid out in a series of interlocking nooks holo'd to create the image of jungled pathways just begging to be explored. Strips of sandalwood embedded in the walls lent the air a gentle woody fragrance. Judging from the sniff Kaitin gave him, the Bengali approved the arrangements, at least conditionally. He stalked back past Jezekiah to join Strongarm in their shared living room, leaving Jezekiah to follow.

Servobots were already filing in with the luggage. Most of the spidery conga line veered toward Kaitin's bedroom, exotically embossed bags held aloft on silvery arms. A single silver spider carried Strongarm's lone duffle bag. Three more trundled along under a set of something precious enough to warrant stasis packs. Strongarm ambled in from the balcony to supervise the distribution of the stasis packs.

Jezekiah felt the dread of what that something might be weigh on his shoulders. He forced the dread out of mind and scent, lifted a brow at Strongarm. "Wedding gifts?"

"No, I've got something bigger in mind for that." Strongarm shook himself, adding a fine silver mist to the sunlight flooding the balcony. "These are just entertainments."

"Entertainments? I assure you we can manage-"

"One's brother-in-law finds the *movies* of the old NorthAm Empire more satisfying than the current generation of onlie entertainments. This one must confess to sharing the preference." Kaitin twitched mustaches at a couch. He decided it was satisfactory and settled himself into a dainty crouch. The daintiness did not extend to his ruby-tipped sneer. "But, then, perhaps the human-only heir to Home World finds that surprising?"

No need for a Lupan's sense of smell to recognize the challenge in the question. "Not at all. I enjoy them quite a bit myself." At least he'd enjoyed the ones

Strongarm had shown him on Den Lupus. "They make an excellent reminder of our shared origins, wouldn't you say?"

"This one would not." Kaitin pursed lips in a Bengali's hunting smile. "This one would say the Makers did not *share* with their Lupan children. The Makers saw us as nothing more than cannon fodder, slaves engineered to kill and die in their wars. Until the Schism taught the flat-teeth how it felt to die."

"Maker's balls, let it go, Kait." Strongarm ensured the Bengali did by wrapping an arm around Jezekiah's shoulders and swinging him around bodily.

"Still, I see his point." Jezekiah would have liked to see Kaitin's face, too, but Strongarm was hauling him in the opposite direction. Nothing for it but to try and blow fine silver hair away from his nose and take a blind shot. "I wonder, however, whether friend Kaitin speaks for himself. Or whether he speaks for Clan Bengal."

"Kait's Lobo Clan now. His opinions are his own." Strongarm loosened his grip enough to let Jezekiah rub his itching nose.

"At least so far as thy sister allows." Kaitin added a disgruntled sniff, but the hostility in his tone mellowed.

"Speaking of sisters–" Strongarm dropped Jezekiah into a chair, dropped himself into its mate. His shoulders were too wide to let him stretch his arms across its back. He hooked arms behind it and rested his head against the cushions to fix ears and eyes on Jezekiah. "I'm not much of a diplomat, but off hand I'd say your sister objects to the treaty terms. Thought you were going to clue her in when you got home."

"I was working on it. I just expected to have more time to manage it." Jezekiah fought down the urge to rub feeling back into his arms. "Thought we'd agreed you would give me a couple of months to set everything up. Why the sudden rush?"

"It was a matter of motivation." Kaitin turned the ruby smile on Jezekiah. "He was running from a wife. *My* sister."

"A son swap? You dodged a son swap?" Jezekiah felt his jaw sag. He snapped it shut, felt the shock evaporate in a rush of dismay.

"He did. Shamed his mother, Speaker for Parliament, in front of the royal women of Clan Bengal." Kaitin pursed lips, his breath taking on a dangerous rasp. "Made his life forfeit. All on the strength of a flat-tooth promise."

Made his life forfeit. Jezekiah's little voice nearly sang with satisfaction. Properly played – Jezekiah shook the quick-calcs off, forced himself to *feel* the enormity of the risk. Let the horror of it show when he looked up to face Strongarm's twitching nose. "I'm sorry. My friend, I am truly sorry."

"Wasn't your fault. Timing was bad." Strongarm shrugged. "I have to live long enough for her to kill me first." He added an *uhf*, comment on some thought he wasn't voicing.

"Then for what it's worth, it sounds like our luck is still running parallel." To his own surprise, Jezekiah found himself grinning in real amusement. "Turns out I'm under just as much of a death sentence as you."

That lifted two pair of Lupan ears and set two noses to twitching, testing his scent for honesty. "It seems my uncle Johann Petrovich regards the treaty as a threat to Streikern interests. He's filing charges of treason against my mother and me. Given that Streiker's the Commonwealth bulwark against your folk-" He salaamed Strongarm with feeling – "my relatives on the Commonwealth Council regard a threat to Streiker as a threat to the Commonwealth itself. So they'll be inclined to listen."

"So, of course, you will disclaim the treaty. Sacrifice the silly, trusting dog to your own profit."

Strongarm angled a warning ear toward his brother-in-law. "Told you to leave it, Kait. There's no time now to follow that track again."

"*Hai*, leave thee to seek thy manhood in sorrow." Kaitin kept his golden eyes on Jezekiah, nose wrinkled back from his fangs. "Leave this flat-tooth to spring the trap he baited with his sister. She proved this morning that Van Buren means to make thee a slave rather than a husband."

No mistaking the threat in that snarl. So, then. Grandfather Ho had been only half right. Kaitin ibn Bengal wasn't an enemy; he was Strongarm's friend, the kind neither Grandfather Ho nor any ruling member of the Great Family Van Buren could afford: a real one.

Jezekiah squelched the flash of jealousy. Even so the chair's sensors picked up the change in his chem signals. Its servo-unit slid a glass of cold water into his hand, offering what comfort it could. Jezekiah lifted the dewy glass to Kaitin, trying not to think that he had only a machine to worry about him. "You do me a disservice, Friend Kaitin. If you will not trust my honor, at least trust in my sense of self-preservation. If we fail to seal this treaty, I shall be just as dead as our friend here. Only I will take my mother with me." He let himself feel the fullness of that bitter thought and watched their noses catch it.

"Doesn't matter who itches, I'm the one who has to scratch. So tell me what it'll take to convince your sister to accept me, Jezekiah. Because I don't have a choice about getting married." Strongarm's ears drooped, seeming to pull his eyes down with them. He looked tired suddenly. Not mere physical exhaustion. Rather the kind of deep tired that weights the body and crushes the soul.

Abruptly, little nagging details clicked home. There were shadows under his eyes, too, and a quickness to his breath that hadn't been there on Den Lupus. There was the real reason Strongarm was here ahead of schedule. The man was already into Impression mode.

Jezekiah sipped his water, kept his focus on the cool glass, kept his scent and face neutral. If he played this right, Letticia's behavior would cease to be an obstacle. Strongarm's body would respond to her even if his mind objected. Habit automatically lined up means of arranging it – Jezekiah cut the calcs off so hard he felt the mental snap. Damn it, Strongarm was here because he was a *friend*. He deserved the truth, no spin, no edits.

Jezekiah dropped the glass back in the servo-unit's slot. He leaned forward, let his working mask drop as well. Let all the old anger and sorrow show. "Listen, I can't apologize for Letticia's behavior on the dock. But at least I can try to explain it." He pulled in a breath, bracing himself against the memories. "Our father was holding Letticia when he was assassinated. He shoved her behind him, took the bomb blast face on-" Even with his eyes open, the red memories rekindled, closing his throat.

"Honor to him, then." Strongarm reached across to rest a hand on Jezekiah's hunched shoulder. "A good death, saving a daughter. Your mother must sing his memory on moonlit nights."

"I suppose we do, in our own way." He did not dare allow himself to even form the image of Mother baying at the moon.

"This one also offers condolences." Kaitin shifted knees, took a moment to re-arrange his bloomers becomingly. "Though one wonders at the purpose of the story at so late a date."

"It matters because it's the only way to understand Letticia." Damn, it was harder than he'd expected to go on. Jezekiah felt an ache in his hands, realized his knuckles were whitening on his knees. He loosened them, shook himself to loosen the tension in his shoulders. "You see, Mother never had an abundance of time for us – the Protectorship doesn't leave a ruling Protector time for a personal life. So Letticia attached herself to her nurse. Loved that woman more than she did Mother herself. And it was the nurse who threw the bomb."

He knew the anguish showed. He didn't care, didn't even care whether the display had a useful effect. "Grandfather Ho knew he'd never get a bomb past the Manor's scanners. So he had one planted on the grounds where his op could pick it up. Letticia happened to be reaching toward her nurse when the woman threw it. She saw the hatred face on. She thought her nurse wanted to kill her." He rubbed hands across his face, wishing the way he'd been wishing for fifteen years he could rub the memories out. "She hasn't trusted anyone since. She's just scared. Scared of everyone and everything."

"Really? One would never have noticed." Kaitin pursed lips at Strongarm. "She controls it so well."

"I believe she'll learn." Damn, his throat was dry. Jezekiah rapped the arm rest and the servo-unit handed him a fresh glass of water. "At least you give her a chance. Impression bonds both souls, after all. She'll know she's safe."

Damned if Kaitin didn't *purr*. "The challenge will be getting her to stand still long enough for the Touch to work."

Strongarm silenced him with the flip of an ear. "Convincing women to stand still is what marriage presents are for." He swiveled both ears toward Jezekiah. "I figured I'd offer your sister Rogue. Think that'll change her mind?"

Good thing the water glass was cold. Gave him an excuse for the shudder he could not hide. Jezekiah made a show of cradling the glass in both hands while he pried his tongue off the roof of his mouth. "Much as I hate to say it, I would not recommend handing Letticia the power that goes with that kind of wealth just yet." Or ever, most likely. "I think it would be wiser to let her adjust to married life first."

Strongarm shrugged, unhappy. "What, then? You have a better idea, let's hear it."

"Give her the specs for your long jump drive." Jezekiah held up a hand before Kaitin could add talons to the snarl. "The treaty terms already give Earth access, so you're not giving anything away. Also, you can turn the specs over to Mother for safe keeping until the Impression ceremony's completed."

"Thus granting Home World all the advantages of the treaty with none of the obligations." Kaitin settled back on the cushions, stroking his long white mustaches above that ruby-tipped fang. "Allow this one to suggest that there is yet an alternative. This great fool-" he perked an ear at Strongarm – "desires to reclaim our peoples' right of return to Home World."

"Agreed." Jezekiah felt the muscles along his shoulders tighten in anticipation. He willed his working mask back into place to cover the tension. "That's in the treaty."

"One suggests, therefore, that there is no need to force your sister into marriage. It would be more appropriate to seal the treaty with a Maker."

"That could work." Strongarm sat up, befanged grin going eager. "Even our mothers will forgive me if I find a Maker to accept me."

"Only problem is that there are no Makers left, despite the legend. Even on Earth, our naturals are just mixed-Types, not truly original species." He shut out the image of Grandfather Ho embodying the lie.

"What about that little woman on the dock?" The grin widened to terrifying proportions. "Strikes me it would take a Maker to put your balls in a vise the way she did."

"So this one thought." Kaitin pursed lips at Strongarm. "At least she will not flee screaming from thee on thy wedding night."

"She's mine." Odd that the lie should feel so true. Which was a very good thing given the way Strongarm's nose twitched. He focused on feeling the dream, keeping his scent wistful. "Only my mother opposes the match. So I can't marry the girl on Earth. Not while I'm the Heir. That's why I'm so eager to get back out to the rim." He wanted it to be true, he realized. Wanted it enough for the half-lie to pass even Kaitin's sniff test.

"Still, it is the woman who chooses." Kaitin's eyes lidded, ears going thoughtful. "If one does not mis-read, then that little woman has not yet chosen you, Van Buren."

Damn and damn again. "The reason my mother objects to the girl-" Jezekiah let the annoyance show. With luck, it would cover the spike of fear in his pulse. "Is because she is affiliated with Ho Tong."

"Yet you allowed her to greet the Protector's guests?"

"Leave it, Kait." Strongarm shook himself, making silver dance in the air. "Think we all need a nap."

"Wise idea." Jezekiah dropped the glass back in the servo-unit slot and rose. "You will want to be refreshed for the welcome reception tonight."

He salaamed gracefully, made it out the door faster than courtesy really permitted. He strode all the way back to his own quarters before he allowed himself to feel the fullness of the lies he'd told. Or the nagging fear that Letticia would betray Strongarm more thoroughly than even Kaitin feared.

XVII

With a hideous rip, the last bolt of Letticia's sync chair came lose. Miniature fireworks spouted where the synapses had been severed. The tiny energy bursts dropped the dying embers of her hope into the pile of her clothes Yakamoto's borrowed SecTypes had dumped on the floor. Slumped helplessly across her bed, Letticia felt every hiss, every tiny pop in her veins. She wished without hope that one of the sparks would start a fire. That would get her out of here at least, one way or the other.

"Mistress Van Buren." Admiral Yakamoto's boot tops stepped into her field of vision. He dropped to one knee so she could see him, since she couldn't move. He was still holding the neural wand he'd used to disable her, rapping it steadily against his hand. It clicked on his palm like metal tapping granite. "It is to be regretted that you should choose to flee your duty. You will understand, then, that you will henceforward be kept under surveillance."

She couldn't even roll her eyes up at him, but she tried to *will* him to see her hate. Maybe he felt it. He touched the neural wand to her neck. Life radiated outward from the point of contact, flooded back into her arms, her hands, her body. She wiggled her fingers, lifted a foot to be sure. Then launched herself at him, fingers clawing for his eyes.

He didn't even bother to duck. He knocked her hands aside with a backhand, trapped her wrists on the down swing. He didn't seem to use any effort at all, but the motion yanked Letticia butt over head off the bed. She landed on her rump, wrists still trapped in his. She set her jaw at him in defiance. "Let go of me. My hands are going numb."

"A word of advice first, if the young mistress will permit." He paused for effect. The serpentine chill in his expression said just how much he cared about her permission. "Your lady mother has ordered you to attend Lord Strongarm. It is strongly recommended that you not attempt to run again. You are to obey the order. Promptly. And with courtesy."

"How stupid can you get? She doesn't want me to attend him, damn it! She wants me to *gob* him!"

"Duty is to be obeyed, not enjoyed. You will follow your lady mother's order."

"It's not Mother's order!" Memory of the shaggy, hulking brute lent Letticia fresh strength. "You don't understand! It's all Jezekiah's idea! He wants me dead!"

"On the contrary. Milord Jezekiah is the only reason you are still alive." He yanked her hands up, his grip tightening until it hurt. For an insane instant Letticia actually expected to see a forked tongue flick out between his clenched teeth.

A dark presence broke the instant. Yakamoto looked up at the waiting SecType, asked his question with an eyebrow.

The fellow held out a yellow silk dress. "Found this in her pocket, sir." He twisted her skirt pocket inside out to reveal the gray metallic patch of a portable sync link.

"Leave that alone!" Letticia struggled to jerk free. "You have no authority to rifle my property!"

Yakamoto yanked her back down. "Remove it. Then check the rest of her clothing as well."

"You can't!"

He leaned forward, shoved his hand into the pocket of the slacks she wore. His expression tightened at the feel of the sync link she'd had sewn in. She tried to roll away, but he tore it lose anyway, then shoved her away and rose. He dropped the delicate link to the floor and ground it beneath his boot heel.

She launched herself off the bed at the ripping sounds coming from her closet. Yakamoto caught her wrist, shoved her back down onto the foot of her bed and held her there. She could only sob through clenched lips at the thump of her links being ground under the SecTypes' boots. By the time they finished, she couldn't even cry any more. The loss was too deep. It felt as if they'd gouged out her very heart. She didn't even realize Yakamoto was talking until he shook her.

"You will find your garments undamaged, except for the removal of these insidious links." Yakamoto let her go, took a sharp step back, like he was on some silly parade ground. Gave her distance enough to see the disgusted set of his lips. "Perhaps without the distraction of sync, you will find it possible to fulfill your duty."

"I am not gobbing a dog!"

"You will do as your lady mother orders." Yakamoto caught her hands before she'd managed to throw herself at him. He held her in place, looked over her head to address the implacable red eye of her major domo. "Prepare the young mistress for the Lupans' reception. See to it she attends. It is the Protector' order."

"You will *not!*" Letticia twisted in his grip to glare up at the watching eye. She couldn't even *think* of looking at those creatures close up. And Jezekiah would let that Strongarm thing *touch* her. She just knew he would. She turned the glare on Yakamoto. He would see her fear, but she didn't care anymore. "I'm not going. You can't make me."

"It is to be hoped, Mistress, that you will not force me to prove otherwise." His grip on her hands tightened ever so slightly, but it shot fire up her arms. He waited, pressed just a bit more. Her arms felt like he'd shot acid up her veins.

"All right! I'll go!" Anything to stop the pain.

"A wise decision, Mistress." Yakamoto shoved her hands away as if she were something slimy. "You will be permitted your Aryan escort. Be advised, however, that your Aryans will be subordinate to Sec." He waited till his silence forced her to glare up at him. "Be advised also that there is to be no unpleasantry at tonight's reception. For your own benefit, it is ardently to be wished that you understand this."

"Oh, I understand." Letticia rubbed her arms, not even trying to hide the bitterness. Yakamoto was too gobbing brain dead to recognize it anyway. "I've *always* understood. *Nothing* gets in Jezekiah's way. *I'm* only supposed to stand there and help him show off."

"It is not necessary that you understand your duty. Only that you perform it." The SecTypes had finished vandalizing her clothes. Yakamoto nodded them out the door, then turned on his heel. "Your Aryans will arrive to escort you in one hour. It is recommended that you be ready when they arrive." With that he strode out. The door swished shut behind him.

She waited till she was sure the door wouldn't open again before she slid off the bed. Gob him! Gob him and Jezekiah and all of them! She'd get them back one day. *Then* they'd see who got hurt!

Her knees threatened to buckle when she tried to stand. Stupid, useless body! She sat again, pounded on her legs until the pain strengthened them, then dragged herself to the bathroom. Fortunately, her major domo knew her well enough to have the bath already hot.

She had finished dressing when Teufelsman showed up with her escort. She told them to wait anyway. Gobbing Yakamoto had only said to be ready when the escort arrived; he didn't say she actually had to *leave*. The Aryans could just cool their heels on her doorstep for a few hours. If she was lucky, by the time she showed up the dogs would have slunk off to whatever kennel Mother had found for them.

She fidgeted away an hour. It was *hard*. Without sync, she had nothing to *do*. She almost didn't mind when her major domo lost patience. Invisible hands of compressed air brushed the wrinkles out of her red-gold gown, checked the rope of those big, gold pearls she'd had woven crown-like around her head, then firmly shoved her out the door and into the Aryans' waiting arms.

Teufelsman, at least, had the good grace to welcome her. The Aryan gave her a full body salaam, allowing his expression to show appreciation of her outfit. He also quietly flipped open his dress jacket when he straightened, letting her see the empty holster under his arm. Letting her know he was as unhappy about the situation as she was.

Teufelsman's white blond ops formed a wedge around her, keeping the *hoi polloi* at bay on the march to the reception hall. Teufelsman himself fell in behind her. He was trying to make her feel safe, she knew, but it didn't help. *Nothing* could help, tonight. She'd have to face all Mother's courtiers tonight. They'd be waiting for her tonight, all those lying, smiling sycophants. Waiting to see her grovel to Jezekiah's damned dog. Waiting with their eyes on Jezekiah, waiting to see if he wanted them to laugh at her. Stupid, store-bought Types! They'd all show her their snide, lying smiles, then laugh at her behind her back. None of them cared about her. *Nobody* cared about her.

Behind her, Teufelsman coughed gently, letting her know they'd reached the reception hall doors. She answered the major domo's scan with her own blue glare. Maybe she could just make sure Mother saw her and then sneak out again. Then maybe she could talk Mother into giving her back her links. The thought lent her courage. She could smile at even a dog if it would get her back into sync. Besides, nobody ever paid her any mind anyway. Lifting her skirts elegantly, Letticia breathed deep and stepped through the doorway.

"Mistress Letticia Van Buren!"

The unexpected boom of Mother's major domo nearly sent her skipping right back out again. She would have made it, too, if Teufelsman's toes hadn't got in her way.

Music flared inside the wide circle of the hall and the chattering idiots inside shut up to gawk at her. Hiding panic under a regal sneer, Letticia ran her gaze across them. Just once, she'd like to see a friendly face, just once meet a pair of eyes smiling at *her*. For once she did. One bright, wide-eyed face so full of joy that it lit a warm feeling in her stomach. Letticia started to smile back – until she recognized that nasty little doppelganger Jezekiah had used to humiliate her at the dock.

Of all the dirty, vile – Well, she could do something about *him*. She smiled back, working out her revenge. She'd have Teufelsman burn it to her node, too, so she could enjoy it at leisure. The thought made her feel a bit better. Keeping her back straight and her head high, Letticia allowed Teufelsman to lead her off the entrance platform. Not that anybody noticed. As soon as she stepped off the platform they all forgot about her. Rendered her invisible again. Almost.

Automatically her fingers sought her pocket, reaching for her stolen sync link. She swallowed a whimper at the ragged hole where the link had been. And the horrible, hideous realization that she was stuck inside her body, utterly, inescapably, *here*.

Teufelsman and his Aryans parted the *hoi polloi* for her. For a single hopeful second she thought he was leading her to her favorite corner near the kitchen. Without her sync link, the kitchen offered the only possibility of escape. Which she was going to need, if those two-legged dogs decided to make an issue of this morning. Only then Teufelsman stepped aside, bowing.

And left her face-to-face with Jezekiah. Jezekiah in full Heir's mode: no jewelry, no frills, just a loose silk blouse and slacks with only the tiniest orchid crest sewn into the trim. He should have looked silly, so underdressed. Instead he seemed taller, stronger, as if he could crush the universe in one hand. Just like Mother. And smiling that same dangerous little half-smile at her.

"Letticia." He captured her hand, pulled her in beside him.

Letticia threw a frantic glance over her shoulder. Her Aryans had fallen back leaving that bastard Marsden at Jezekiah's back. Making the arm-lock look affectionate, he force-marched her toward one of the arching balconies.

"Smile, Lush." He bestowed his own on the fawning pazzis melting out of their way. "And tell me you *did* do your homework."

"What homework?" Letticia flashed a sickly grin at the nearest pazzi. She knew it would be a wasted effort. The fellow didn't look appreciative at all.

"On the Lupans." From the corner of her eye she saw Jezekiah nod and the stupid pazzi's expression went silly. His own did not. "Don't try to tell me you didn't have the chance, either. Not after that wake-up call you sent me."

"I found out everything I need to know, all right?" Which was nothing. As if she *cared* what some stupid dog thought was polite. She had worries enough of her own right now.

Beyond the pazzis she could see the balcony jutting out into the vast darkness of the night. She tried to dig heels in, but her shoes only slid. "You are *not* taking me out there!"

"Guess again." He slipped an arm behind her back, pushed her along.

"It's dark!" And it would be chill. And damp. *Like it was when Daddy* – the old terror lit in her gut. She felt the tremble hit her hands, work downward toward her knees.

Jezekiah stopped, swung her around to face him. He wrapped her hand in both of his. Held them as if he could press out her fear.

The way he'd used to, back before – For a moment, she was back in one of her hidey holes, peering up at a younger Jess enticing her out with a piece of forbidden chocolate. For a moment, she remembered how she'd loved him. Trusted him...

He looked like he'd remembered, too. That little half-smile softened, went almost wistful. "I won't let anything happen to you, Lush. You're safe."

"Not in the dark!" She couldn't stop the terrified glance toward the balcony.

Jezekiah slipped a finger under her chin, made her look up at him. Even at this range, even knowing him for a sneaking, manipulative liar, he looked so earnest she *wanted* to believe him. "No one is going to hurt you, little sister. But you do have to meet Strongarm. You promised, remember?"

"Then turn the lights on!" She tried to break free. Hopeless. And that bastard Marsden sidled around to make sure none of the gawping pazzi would see her struggle.

"You know why Mother ordered the balcony lights outed. We're trying not to offer that assassin a free target." Jezekiah's tone hardened, though fortunately his grip did not. "You do remember your assassin, don't you?"

"I thought we were past that." But the reminder helped calm her. Gave her a hope to cling to. She felt the trembling stop.

Jezekiah felt it, too. He eased his tone, patted her hand soothingly. Though he kept his grip, she noticed. "Give Strongarm a chance, Lush. He's a good man. He'll love you heart and soul if you let him. He's probably the only man alive who has a chance to make you happy."

She saw the implied insult, even if he thought she was too stupid to catch on. "Why? Because I'm such a bitch?"

He gave her one of Mother's sighs, then swung her back around and started hauling her toward the balcony again. "If you refuse to see the man, then at least remember his money. Strongarm's the only man in the known universe as rich as Octavian. So far, he's willing to overlook the way you behaved on the dock this morning. If you can't return the favor for Earth's sake, then I strongly recommend you return it for your own."

Beyond the arched doorway, something moved, a flash of moonlight on silver fur. Letticia whimpered. She felt Jezekiah's hand jerk at the sound and tensed in fear.

Instead he slowed the pace a bit, leaned closer to her ear. "If you pull this off nicely, I'll get your sync back for you."

Behind them, Marsden sounded like he'd just choked on something. "Uh, your lordship-"

"I know." Jezekiah nodded the looming SecType back into place. "It will be my responsibility."

"Will you, really?" The very thought evaporated her fear-aches. She could face anything for sync. Even a dog in the dark.

They stepped out into the terrible emptiness of the night. Beyond the pale gleam of the marble balustrade, the world just dropped away. Far down to the left Waikiki curved darkly away toward Diamond Head. Moonlight turned the waves silver-white along the shore, raised ghostly gray lights among the dark trees where it touched the ruins along the beach. Dark, dark, all dark. Oh, God, it was like the darkness that just *fell* the morning they killed Daddy. Like death itself. She jerked back on instinct. Felt Jezekiah's warning pinch and forced a foot forward instead. She'd have sync again. She just had to get through this.

Jezekiah actually patted her hand before leading her away from the light of the arch. "Lord Strongarm." He clamped fingers hard on her arm. "Allow me to introduce your betrothed. My little sister, Letticia."

And in the shadows beside the doorway, a pair of yellow eyes blinked down at her.

If Marsden hadn't been blocking her back, Letticia would have run, even if it had cost her arm. Instead, she could only – "Ouch!"

"Oh, so sorry," Jezekiah sounded so honest she would've thought he meant it. If he'd taken his foot off her toes.

"My dearest little sister." He had her arm so tight now her fingers were going numb. "Allow me to properly introduce our friend and ally. Myrra's Cub, son of the Speaker for Parliament, the alpha war lord of the Lupan Dominion. Better known by his battle-name, Strongarm. Your betrothed."

The Lupan stepped out of the shadows enough to let her see him. He looked like an overgrown cross between a wolf and a mountain gorilla. What little part of him wasn't fur was fang, and what wasn't fang was muscle. He was showing enough of it, too: not even a shirt, for heaven's sake, just a crisscross harness of dark leather over the silvery hair of his chest and matching leather trousers. He had a scroll-worked silver torque around his neck with matching arm bands that must have weighed a couple of kilos each.

"Forgive me for frightening you yet again, Mistress Letticia."

"Oh, God, it talks."

"Even wisely, upon occasion." A second Lupan stepped up to join Strongarm. Even through the shadows Letticia could make out the fine black lines striping his orange mane above round white ears. Well, of course, she thought numbly, there'd have to be a cat to go with the dog.

The tigerish Lupan was taller than Strongarm and lean where Strongarm was bulk muscle. He was *dressed*, too: flowing emerald robes brocaded with what gleamed like real gold. He stroked a fine white mustache with an orange-furred finger, studying her through narrowed golden eyes.

"Since one's brother-in-law has forgot his manners, this one shall introduce himself." He didn't even bother with a salaam. "Kaitin ibn Bengal del Lobo, alpha prince of Clan Bengal, *mayo quadrato* to Hellas del Lobo." He lifted a lip at Strongarm, though somehow it didn't look like a sneer. A huge tear drop ruby glittered at the tip of one fang. "Brother-in-law and battle-mate to this great fool."

He reached out to brush Strongarm's ears up with a fingertip. The great brute *uhfed* like the dog he was, then shook himself. And remembered to smile.

Letticia wished he hadn't. She tried to back away, only Jezekiah's grip turned positively bruising. And he still had his foot on her toes.

"Why don't we move into the light?" Jezekiah nudged Letticia toward the balustrade with the words, drawing the Lupans out of the shadows. From inside the ballroom she heard the collective gasp of the snooping pazzis clustered inside the arched window. That lot found someplace else to be quickly at Jezekiah and Strongarm's combined scowls.

"I'm afraid my sister spends too much time in sync. She has yet to grow accustomed to being much in company." Jezekiah leaned on her toes, hinting she was supposed to say something. Only there wasn't anything she could think of *to* say.

"Letticia is the family's financial wizard." Jezekiah patted her hand with patently false pride when she stayed silent. He also crunched her toes, reminding her again.

"I tried looking you up." There, that was safe. She could talk money all day. "NetMind doesn't list non-Commonwealth assets. Just what do you think you're worth?"

"That's a question can only be answered in blood, Mistress Van Buren." Strongarm said it politely enough, but for some reason those fangs suddenly looked a lot bigger.

Wasn't her imagination, either. Behind her, even Marsden sucked in his breath. Beside her, Jezekiah just went still.

"My sister meant no offense. She was speaking only of money." Jezekiah kept his tone smooth, but he turned enough to make sure the Lupans wouldn't see the way his eyes sharpened in warning. "Weren't you, Lush?"

For once Letticia didn't need to fake the puzzlement. "For heaven's sake, what else is there?"

"Just minor things." That Kaitin creature apparently thought no one could hear him. "Honor, self-respect, loyalty... nothing one would expect a flat tooth to understand."

"Oh, well, then–" Maybe she should have paid some attention to those stupid histories Jezekiah had sent her after all. Then she wouldn't have to scrounge memory for – oh! *There* was something she needed to know. "Say, aren't you supposed to sniff my crotch or something like that?"

Obviously not the right question. The dog's smile froze.

"My sister also has an unfortunate sense of humor." Jezekiah's fingers tightened on her arm enough to make her wiggle.

"Is that what the flat teeth call it?" This time the tiger did sneer. "We Bengali have other terms."

"Leave it, Kait. We all make mistakes." The dog – no, its name was *Strongarm*, she had to remember that – sounded like he'd just *growled*. As if *he* had cause to complain! "Allow me to set your mind at ease, Mistress Van Buren. Crotch sniffing-" That Kaitin made strangling noises and he paused to glare the creature to silence – "is not a part of our standard greeting."

"For which this one, at least, has cause to be grateful."

This time Letticia glared at Kaitin in her own right. "At least humans don't gang-rape their wives!"

Oh, my, that was definitely not the right thing to say. Both animals bared fangs. Behind her, she felt the movement as Marsden reached for the gun he hid under his jacket. The fear came crashing back down on her. She didn't need Jezekiah to hold her in place. She grabbed his hand and clung. "But they *do*, don't they? I saw it in those vids!" She didn't even care they'd all hear the quaver in her voice.

Maybe that was a good thing. At least the two Lupans seemed to relax a bit. Though it did set their noses to twitching. Made her think of a pair of fanged rabbits.

"For what it's worth, Mistress Van Buren." She realized Strongarm's ears were flat only when she watched him raise them again. "On Den Lupus the penalty for rape is a slow and degrading death. I can assure you we do not practice gang rape. Strongarm shook himself in doggy fashion again. The movement sent a silver ripple down his mane, streaked light across the torque at his throat. "Might be wiser if we pursue introductions in the morning. It's getting late and we're all tired."

He kissed fingers to her, lifted his chin oddly at Jezekiah. Then with his golden cat in tow, he turned and stalked back through the ballroom scattering pazzis ahead of him.

It was only after the ballroom doors closed behind them that Jezekiah let her go. To her shock, he slid back into the shadows to slump against the balustrade. Marsden just slumped forward, hands on knees. Letticia massaged her arm and scowled at them in annoyance. "Now what was that all about?"

"Aside from the fact you just mortally insulted the one man standing between us and a Lupan war?" Jezekiah shook himself. She couldn't tell whether he realized he was copying Strongarm or not.

"Don't be stupid. All I did- "

"Don't. Far as Strongarm's concerned, you've done quite enough for now." He straightened, did a ten-count she could see even in the dim light. "You're on your own for the rest of the evening. I've got to get out there and neutralize the rumor mongers."

He lifted a brow at Marsden. The SecType had straightened. He rolled his shoulders like they were stiff or something, cocked his head while he listened to his Net feed. The sight made Letticia grind her teeth in jealousy. "Well, do I at least get my sync back?"

"No."

"What do you mean 'no'?" Her stomach went cold. "You put me through all this for nothing?" She caught Jezekiah's arm before he could brush past her.

"I put you through nothing. You vaporized the chance before it ever got off the ground." He shook her off and strode past. In the two steps it took him to reach the doorway, he'd dropped all sign of the tension she'd seen. He looked like he was having the time of his life. Marsden, stalking his footsteps, just looked like an overgrown shadow.

"Liar!" But the wall absorbed her shriek. Alone in the terrible dark, Letticia collapsed against the cold stone of the balustrade and sobbed.

XVIII

They reached their quarters before Strongarm managed to get his ears back up. Kaitin's mustaches were still quivering. The lights came up as they entered, shut off again at their joint growls. Their suite had its own balcony; without the false sunshine, the plump couches and polished tables of their living area took on the silvery tone of the moon light beyond. Instinct twitched Strongarm's nose, testing the air for danger. All he got was a nose full of flower strong enough to make him sneeze.

"One wonders at the flatteeth obsession with their flowers." Typically, Kaitin folded his gold-trimmed vest over a chair then curled atop the nearest cushion. "They could hide a platoon under such a stink."

"They just can't smell." Strongarm picked up the biggest flower arrangement, carried it at arm's length to the balcony. The fragrance probably would have been subtly pleasant to an onlie nose; it was rapidly giving him a headache.

The outside railing was too narrow to support the vase's fat base. He tucked the massive arrangement into the corner of the balcony instead and moved as far away from it as the railing allowed. Didn't help all that much. The buzz of the onlie weather screens still annoyed him. Not that he needed help on that score. He let his head droop, feeling the crush of his failure on his shoulders. He could endure that. It was the shattering of his dreams that crushed his heart. At least the weather screens let a soft breeze through. He lifted his face to it, welcoming the taste of salty air on his tongue. And the unexpected scent of something else -

"There is yet time to go back." The breeze carried Kaitin's scent away from him but there was understanding in the Bengali's voice.

Strongarm turned, rested his weight against the balustrade. "We've been over that one, Kait."

"We could put thee in stasis." Kaitin nestled deeper into the cushion, eyes and ears drooping in Bengali contentment, though his mind would be working at hunter speed. "This one can pilot *Khali* home for thee."

"And blow off the treaty. Make it all for nothing."

"The Home World flatteeth do not require this marriage to seal the treaty. Thou may yet honorably withdraw." Kaitin licked fingers, ran them through his mane. "Fourth husband in Clan Bengal were yet kinder to thee than life with that Van Buren bitch."

"Except the women of Parliament would never accept it." Especially not after the way he'd left Mother Myrra to explain his ducking his half of the son swap she'd arranged. "No, I've dealt enough grief to everyone else. Time I took a dose of my own." He shook his ears to an easier angle, then strode for the door.

His backwashed scent disturbed Kaitin enough to make the Bengali twist around on his cushions. "Thou would not seek out the sister -"

"Not till I can't avoid it." He flicked an ear up for reassurance. "Just going to walk off some of this misery. Be back before you finish your nap."

Uniformed SecTypes guarded the Manor's broad entrance, politely but firmly scanning IDs on their fellow onlies. The sheer number of scanners in the area raised an insect buzz that made Strongarm's ears twitch in time to his nose. Broad as the Manor's entrance hall was, the combined fragrances of a hundred full-dress onlies had his temples throbbing. Strongarm paused long enough to let the guards do their duty. The guest-courtesy was unnecessary. The guards just swallowed audibly and waved him through.

Outside, the Manor's weather screens brunted the wind. The artificial calm allowed clusters of glittering dignitaries to enjoy a stroll without putting either their elaborate hair dos or perfumes at risk. He recognized the way murmured conversations ended at sight of him, recognized the smell of fear and hope that made it through even that cloud of perfume. In true onlie fashion, they'd wait till they thought he was out of earshot before sharpening their verbal claws on his back.

Strongarm dodged past the automated cars hovering at the far end of the plaza's transit stop. Across the transit lanes a holo flashed notice of the weather screens' end. Strongarm bulled past the holo, felt the screens' hum on his skin. In the unfiltered air beyond the breeze turned to wind. Cloying perfume evaporated in the rich scents of ocean salt and wet grass and fresh earth. The aches in his neck and temples evaporated with it.

He followed a faint moonlit trail up into alien trees that still managed to feel familiar. The scent he found led him around the Manor to a spot overlooking the guest wing. He traced it to a tree wide enough to qualify as a minor jungle in itself. It took some concentration to find her among the dangling maze of air roots and branches. Worth the effort, though, when he found the tiny brown woman Jezekiah wanted for his own.

She was waiting for him to spot her. "Save yourself the eye strain. I'm coming down." Bark dust showered him as she undraped herself from the branch and scrambled down the trunk.

She was high enough up to give him time to rub the sneeze out of his nose. Her scent eased some of the weight off his shoulders: there was none of the Van Buren sister's fear in it, nor her contempt. This one smelled *happy* about finding him here. He *uhfed* softly, trying to keep his imagination polite while he watched her slide down a trailing air root.

He had ears and manhood under control by the time she neared ground level. She did a straight drop off the last branch, surprised him by landing silently as any Bengali. Surprised him again by the sudden suspicion in her scent. "You aren't out scouting the Manor's defenses by any chance, are you?"

Maker's balls, she was a direct one. Praise the Makers she was wearing loose khaki shorts and shirt. Would've been impossible to keep his eyes respectful if she'd still been in that wispy wrap. Maybe that was how this little woman had claimed Jezekiah. The thought set his ears straight. Whatever the reason, she already had Jezekiah in her pocket. He was *not* going to add himself to her pack. He folded arms and grinned down at her, full Lupan grin. "I was wondering if you were spying on us. Saw you in the tree from our balcony."

"Shaka. You really can see in the dark." She surprised him again by matching him grin for grin, eyes and lips and scent all going happy together. The combination wiped his resolution along with the suspicion. "Admiral himself couldn't've spotted me in that tree."

A whiff of amusement in her scent said her Admiral must have had cause to try. Strongarm set ears and stuck to his point. "So were you?"

"Was I what?"

"Spying."

"No." She slapped dust off her shorts, slapped hands on hips, left the challenge to her scent. "And you?"

"If I wanted to scout defenses I wouldn't call you down to talk about it."

"Then why'd you leave your own party?" She folded arms, matched him stance for stance.

"Needed..." The question drained the good feeling out of him. He needed his dream back. Needed to reconcile himself to the kind of bitter marriage the Van Buren sister promised. He pulled in a breath, shook himself. "Needed some fresh air. You know how stuffy official parties are."

"No." Her scent went wistful for an instant, then neutral. Had she been a man, he would have thought the change bespoke a warrior's discipline. Yet she accepted his word, the way a warrior would. The challenge left her scent.

"You'd best stay down on the plaza, then. SecTypes going go *lolo* they bump into you in the dark."

"Then perhaps you should walk with me, Mistress- forgive me, I do not know your name."

"Yakamoto. Keiko."

"There is a StelFleet Admiral-"

"Yuh-huh. My father." Her scent warned him not to pry farther.

That explained her warrior attitude. Even on the rim, the name of StelFleet's Admiral Yakamoto inspired shivers. "Will you walk with me, then, Mistress Yakamoto?"

"Just Keiko. I don't rank formalities." He caught of sniff of deep anger that vanished even as he identified it. "Feel free to walk along. Long as you don't mind just circling the Manor. I'm supposed to have gone home a couple of hours ago." She raked dust out of her hair, eyeing him with a doubt that made him stand straighter. "Warn you: you're in for a scratching. Bougainvillea bushes up here got some monstrous thorns."

"I think I can handle a scratch or two. We Lupans have thick hides." Physically, anyway. He was starting to feel downright dainty internally.

She stepped around the tree without a backward glance when he salaamed at her to lead the way. There was no overt enticement in the sway of her buttocks, but the sight stirred his manhood anyway. Strongarm lengthened stride to walk by her side. Proved to himself quickly she'd told the truth about the bogan-whatever-they-were bushes. Damned things really did have monstrous thorns.

She must have caught him taking a lick at one bloody scratch because she angled them up onto a higher, fern-lined path. It was a narrow track, rich in earth-scent and wild air. Tall trees broke the moonlight into slivers, casting a silvery stained glass pattern on the man-height ferns. Above them, nesting birds chittered complaint at their passing. Strongarm had to bull through the fronds that Keiko walked under. But at least the ferns caressed instead of gouging. He put his appreciation into his scent. Remembered with embarrassment that she couldn't read it and hunted for something to say instead. "Why aren't you at the party?"

"I'm not allowed in the Manor." Keiko stepped out from under one fern to grin up at him, then vanished again beneath the fronds of the next. "Why're you playing hooky?"

"Got my nose rubbed in just what kind of marriage I've walked myself into."

"You're going to marry Letticia Van Buren, eh?" She popped into sight between fronds, vanished again. "That puts you about one step below the gods. What's so bad about that?"

"Aside from the fact-" He bit off the rest of the sentence. He was *not* sharing so personal a shame. Not even with Jezekiah's *maya*.

He was sure she couldn't read his scent. Yet her own bespoke understanding when she stepped out from the ferns. Silver flecks of moonlight raised bright reflections on her hair. She put a hand on his arm, inadvertently tingling every nerve in his body. "Look on the bright side, eh? If it doesn't work, you get a divorce."

He *uhfed*, keeping the despair out of it.

She took his hand between her own, her expression going gentle as her scent. "Doesn't have to be the end of the world. Whole thing's just politics anyway, isn't it? So you live on your world, she stays on Earth, everybody's happy. From what the Admiral says, the proper Types do it all the time."

"Can't. Lupan men mate for life." The despair settled back onto his shoulders. He shook it off. Shook her hand off with it. Realized too late she'd misunderstand.

"Forgive me, Lord Strongarm." She stepped away, suddenly stiffly apologetic. "I forgot my place. Please accept my apologies." She was out of sight before he could catch her arm.

Just as well, maybe. He dug talon tips into his side until their bite shriveled the thrill she'd raised in his groin. Wiser just to get back to quarters anyway. Jezekiah was already her man. If he let himself bind to her now he'd be only a *mayo secundo*, a second husband. The women of Parliament would never approve the treaty on such terms. He licked blood off his talon tips, shook himself hard enough to wiggle some sense back between his legs. And stepped out after her.

She'd reached the section of the forest bordering the Manor's loading dock by the time he caught up. He spotted her up another tree – a tall, leaning palm this time – studying the dock. Strongarm peered around a fern tree to watch a train of automated delivery trucks going about their business. A trio of uniformed SecTypes monitored the trucks, checking each truck against the scanners mounted on their helmets. Strongarm noted with interest that the power lights on their laser rifles showed green. They were paying attention to the duty, too: the wind carried him the nervousness in their scents, the tinge of worry.

The worry-scent sharpened. As one, the SecTypes turned the laser rifles toward him.

"So, *lack* you!" Keiko scooted down the tree. She dropped the last couple of meters, bare feet barely rustling the forest's leafy ground, paused only to throw him a ball-shriveling glare over her shoulder. "Follow me."

She pushed through the undergrowth, hands up and out. Ears and hands up, Strongarm followed. Noted with amusement that she kept herself between him and the SecTypes' rifles. Then *uhfed* in surprise as one of the SecTypes shifted aim to cover her.

"No hu-hu, eh?" Keiko stepped carefully into the greenbelt between road and forest.

"What're you up to, Yakamoto?" The SecType covering her did not lift his rifle.

"Lord Strongarm wanted to take a stroll. I'm escorting him."

"Sent the monkey to walk the dog," one of the other SecTypes muttered. Typical onlie. He thought he was out of earshot.

"Through the *woods*?" The lead SecType hissed his partner to silence.

"Yes." Strongarm stepped forward and all three rifles snapped around to bear on him. He let his ears go flat, added a battle grin for good measure. "You want to make a problem of it?"

"We're just taking a stroll." Keiko kept her tone level. The annoyance in her scent hinted she would have kicked him had she been close enough to connect.

Below, the lead SecType checked something in scan, then lifted his rifle. He nodded his partners back to duty, then motioned Keiko to move on with a jerk of the rifle. Still keeping her hands out, she backtracked into the trees. Strongarm waited till she was safely out of the line of fire before following.

Keiko had already stalked off, anger trailing her wake. Strongarm recognized the humiliation beneath it and hesitated. Courtesy demanded he leave her in peace. Curiosity demanded otherwise. He strode after her.

She heard him coming. "You better head back to your quarters." She spoke over her shoulder, trusting him to hear. "SecTypes are bad enough. If any *Aryans* spot you, all hell's going to break loose."

"In a minute. Those SecTypes couldn't see you in scan. Why not?"

She stopped so fast he had to skip aside to avoid running her over. "Because I'm a monkey, all right? Now why don't you just go home?"

Shame washed her scent and knotted his gut. "I'm sorry. I didn't realize you heard that fool's remark."

"What remark – oh." She guessed its essence for herself and shrugged. "Didn't have to. I knew what they'd say. Not the first time somebody's called me a monkey. You get used to it."

The anger tingeing her scent said otherwise. "How about dog?"

"Well, now, that's a new one. Never been called a dog before." She blinked up at him, eyes and scent going puzzled.

He could have hugged her for it. He wiggled ears instead. "It's what the onlies call Lupans when they think we can't hear them. I've never yet got used to it." The words recalled memory of the Van Buren sister's fear-scent. He felt the weight of her contempt settle back on his shoulders, dragging his ears down. "Maybe because it's too close to the truth."

"How?" She reached up, startled him with the brush of fingers against his cheek. "You don't look a dog. You look-" she clasped his chin, turned his face side to side, studying him, her scent earnest. "You look kind of Samoan to me."

"Apache." He felt his ears lift at the way her eyes fluttered while she tried to place the name. He told himself it was only her grip on his chin that kept him talking. "The NorthAm gene techs who designed my Type spliced the Lupan gene pack into Apache volunteers." Personally, he suspected his ancestors hadn't known they were volunteering.

"That makes sense." She cocked her head, pursed lips Bengali style, released his chin to trace fingertips up his cheek. His ears lifted with them. "Explains where you got those high cheekbones." Her fingers worked higher to stroke the boney scowl of his brow. Strongarm bent a bit to encourage her fingers to linger. "They did a nice job on the eyes, too. I think you look downright noble."

Her scent bespoke only wonder. Had she wanted, she could have had him on his knees just now. He settled for capturing her hand between his. The feel of her knuckles startled him afresh. Her skin felt like sandpaper, the knuckles sharp and hard against his palms.

She recognized his surprise and yanked her hand free. "Now you'd better get going."

She jerked her chin toward the Manor for a hint.

He couldn't let her go, not yet. He searched desperately for something, anything to say that would keep her here. Remembered with relief that he'd left a very important question hanging. "Those SecTypes couldn't see you in scan because you don't have a Type code. No Type gene pack."

"Yeah. That's why they call us naturals." She dropped her hand and stepped back, her expression and scent going dangerously neutral. "When they're feeling polite."

"But you're a Home World natural." The very thought sent goosebumps up his arms.

"Sur*prise*." Shame was morphing into anger in her scent. "Now are you leaving, or do I have to get ugly?"

"Not just yet, if you'll permit." The implications were starting to sink in. "You have no Type coding at all."

She shrugged, but betrayal registered in her scent. The realization she felt *he* had betrayed her hit him in the gut.

"Forgive me. I meant only that you're a -" He had to force himself to swallow. His tongue had gone dry. "A Maker."

"Maker, monkey, it's all the same." Her expression closed.

An onlie would never have caught the bitterness in her scent. Strongarm bared his throat. He realized belatedly she would not recognize the apology. Maker's balls, he'd found a Home World woman – a Maker, even, maybe

– who accepted him as a man and everything he said insulted her. God of his Makers, he needed a husband's guidance on this one. His ears drooped helplessly while he shuffled feet and scrounged memory for something a *Maker* man would have said. Something that would get her up to Kait – "Would you like to see a movie?"

"A *what?*" Her scent went suspicious. Makers *balls*, what'd he said wrong now?

"A *movie*. A moving picture show. An entertainment. From the old NorthAm empire. I have some recordings with me."

"In your *quarters*, right?" Maker's balls, he hadn't thought her suspicion could deepen any further.

"What's wrong with – oh." Oh, balls of the Makers' *God*, he'd stepped in it with that one. He threw hands up in exasperation, lifted chin and drooped ears for safety's sake. "It's all right. Kaitin will chaperone."

"Yuh-huh." If he'd been onlie, it was a good bet she'd have hit him. He backed a step out of range in case she decided to try for his chin anyway. Still, he'd got her interest; her scent went curious as a Bengali. But she only shook herself. "Thanks, but no go. Monkeys aren't allowed in the Manor."

Yet there was wistfulness in her scent and her gaze slid past him to the moonlit bulk of the building. So she knew how it felt to dream when hope was beyond reach. His ears perked in answer to the sudden sense of kinship. He looked past her, studied the Manor from an attack perspective and felt a grin grow. "Bet I can get you in there. If you're game to try."

They were both giggling like a pair of tickled cubs by the time they dodged the last Sec team and scooted through the doors to the guest quarters.

Kaitin was not tickled.

Their quarters were made for lounging. As he should have remembered before hauling a woman in unannounced.

Kaitin was naked, in all his orange-maned glory, and enjoying a Bengali ball-lick on the best of the couches when the door swished open. He took one startled sniff in Strongarm's direction and cleared the couch with a roar that sent the suite's damned major domo unit into a screaming panic attack. The alarms were considerably quieter than Kaitin's full-throated outline of his ancestry. Even hiding behind the bathroom door he managed a volume that vibrated the walls.

Strongarm felt more than heard armored feet pounding around the far end of the corridor even before he let Keiko Yakamoto wriggle free of the protective shelter of his midriff. The only saving factor was that for once she looked positively delighted.

His sister's husbands were right. There was no understanding women.

She peered under his elbow, then up at him with a grin that was happily conspiratorial and said something even he couldn't hear over the combined ruckus of Kaitin and the major domo.

"QUIET!" His battlefield voice shivered the walls. It also shut both Kaitin and the major domo up.

And sent Keiko Yakamoto into a helpless fit of giggles.

He was damned if he knew what she thought was so funny, but somehow he was perfectly happy that she did. "Now just what did you say?"

"I said you better hide me." The giggle ended in a hiccup.

Outside in the corridor the armored feet thudded to a halt. Strongarm swatted the door patch before it could slide open. All that got him was a surprisingly solid thud of an armored fist on the other side. Praise the Makers these doors weren't as dainty as they looked.

"Open up, Lord Strongarm! You all right in there?" He recognized the deep husky voice of the Van Buren's alpha Sec chief.

"Fine, Captain -" Oh, Maker's balls, the door was going to open anyway. Strongarm drove talons into one panel and held it closed by brute strength. He peered under his elbow to warn Keiko Yakamoto to scamper.

She already had.

Scan prickled the hairs of his under-mane. Good man, that Sec chief; he was taking no chances. With a prayer to the God of his Makers, Strongarm released talons and stepped back to let the door slide open.

The name 'Marsden' glowed silver on the breast plate of the graying SecType who thudded into the room, matching the silver comm implant that curved from the man's temple around his ear to the base of his skull. He was still in full dress uniform, but he carried a cannon-caliber laser rifle, its power light raising a green sheen within the crook of his elbow. A whole damned squad of armored SecTypes fanned out into the room behind him, all carrying rifles at the ready. All of them scanning everything in sight. The electric tingle of the combined scan bottled Strongarm's mane.

"What's the problem, Lord Strongarm?" Marsden cocked his head. Listening to field reports through that comm implant, most likely. Checking stories, most certainly.

"Nothing." Strongarm tried for a smile an onlie could take for innocent. "Just a family discussion, is all."

"Yuh-huh." His onlie aftershave masked hid Marsden's scent, but the way his eyes narrowed proclaimed his suspicion loud enough.

At his nod one of the SecTypes tracked her scan into the bedroom. Strongarm's ears drooped in dread. But she came back shaking her head and looking disappointed. The rest of the squad ambled back from the various corners of the suite with equally glum expressions. They filed out with the reluctant relief of young warriors everywhere at Marsden's gesture. It was only Marsden himself who looked unconvinced. He left, finally, but the hunter-vision image of his narrow-eyed suspicion lingered.

Strongarm pulled in a breath, rapped knuckles on the bathroom door. "You can come out now."

Predictably Kaitin ignored him. It was a giggle from under the bed that answered.

He gave up on the bathroom door, followed his nose into the bedroom to watch Keiko Yakamoto worm her way out from under the mattress. She could have managed it easier if she hadn't been laughing so hard.

He lifted her out the last few inches. Didn't help his peace of mind any when she wrapped her arms around his waist and laughed into his middle. The jiggle of her breasts against his middle when the laughter burbled into hiccups shivered down his body straight into his groin.

"So what's this *movie* thing you were talking about?" She gasped between hiccups.

"Show you in a minute." Reluctantly, he planted her on the arm of a chair then stalked back to Kaitin's bedroom to lift a set of amber silk pantaloons and vest off the bed. He carried the slippery rig to the bathroom, leaned against the wall beside it and held the silks out at snatching height. Spoke in Lobish for the sake of any eavesdropping onlies and the treaty. "Hey, Kait – remember that little woman who shrank Van Buren's balls at the dock?" He paused for effect, knowing Kaitin remembered her only too well at the moment. "I think she really is a Maker. I've decided I'm going to take her instead of the Van Buren sister."

Now that got him an answer. Fortunately the snarl was in Lobish, too. The door opened enough to let him drape the silks across an orange-furred arm. Arm and silks vanished in a stream of Bengali invective. A minute later – record time for Kaitin – the Bengali himself stalked out. Chin down and mane bottled. "Thou cannot be serious."

"Only about wanting to get you out of the bathroom." Strongarm gave Kaitin a grin that flattened the Bengali's ears. He skipped back out of talon range with alacrity, only partly to avoid a swipe. More so to distract himself from the distressing realization that the idea of switching women had clicked home within his heart.

He might have managed to ignore the warming thought even so had Keiko Yakamoto not ducked under his guard to take Kaitin's hands in hers. Between the two of them she looked delicate as one of those tiny bright birds he'd seen buzzing the flowers around here. She didn't even say anything. Yet she lay her ridged hands on Kaitin's arm without fear, turned those tilted dark eyes up at him. She put enough contrition into her scent to soothe even a prince's wounded pride. And a warning itch along the inside of his own palm.

Scent going thoughtful, Kaitin patted her hand and murmured something polite over it. Over her head he pointed an ear at the storage case that housed their personal entertainment unit. Strongarm let Kaitin escort her to a couch – one that would hold all three of them, he noted – while he massaged his itching palms and shuffled through the unit's *movie* tracks for the one he had in mind. It was a truly ancient story of pre-Lupan tragedy, one that ought to show well on the wall they used for a projection screen.

"*The Werewolf of London?* Are thou mad or merely stupid?" Kaitin slapped the *movie* off before the title faded. "This one will select a story fit for thy foolishness. Thou find us something to eat." Shoving Strongarm out of the way, he crouched by the unit and took over the rummaging himself.

So much for good intentions. Still – Strongarm lifted a hopeful ear at Keiko Yakamoto. "Do the Van Buren stock popcorn you think?"

"What's popcorn?"

"Don't know, but the ancients doted on it. The histories always link movies to it."

"Sorry." She thought, then brightened. "Bet you can order up some tarot chips and poi, though. Get some wasabi, too, you want some spice."

Kaitin had the movie ready by the time Strongarm had relayed the order to the suite's major domo. Damn cat made a point of settling his own married butt next to Keiko Yakamoto. One glance at the white-on-gray name of the *movie* that told him the kind of lecture he was in for later on.

"What does *Casablanca* mean?" To Strongarm's immense satisfaction Keiko Yakamoto peered over Kaitin's upraised knee to ask him.

"It was a place of nominal neutrality during one of Home World's pre-Schism wars. A place where–" The ancient music swelled. The *movie's* flickering gray light ran like water across her dark hair. Strongarm forgot what he'd intended to say in the sudden urge to stroke the silken highlights.

"It is a story of love against honor." Kaitin lifted Strongarm's hand away from Keiko Yakamoto's head with a talon tip. "The story of a man who must learn not to attach himself to another man's woman." His scent filled in the warning. "Now, will the two of ye kindly allow this one to watch the *movie*?"

They were all three pretending not to snuffle by the time Bogart and Raines vanished into the fog of their beautiful friendship. It was only then, when he couldn't find a box of tissues where he wanted it that Strongarm realized the chips and sauces hadn't arrived. He was about to ask the major domo when a fist thudded against the door and a man's muffled voice called room service.

"Oh, *shaka!*" Keiko Yakamoto started like a wounded bird. She'd have bolted for the bedroom had the entrance door not opened too fast.

"You just hold it right there, Mote." The Sec captain Marsden thudded in. He had shed the bemedalled tunic jacket, but not the attitude: through the fading aftershave his scent reeked of a father's suspicion. He shoved the gleaming silver tray chip'n dip tray he carried at Strongarm, stalked past to target Keiko Yakamoto with a scowl that made even Kaitin wince in sympathy.

Strongarm trailed after him, trying to sniff out the identity of the treats on the tray. One of the sauces was a quite enticing shade of lavender yet had no aroma at all that he could detect. He dipped a curious finger in it, licked eagerly. Felt his ears droop in disappointment. For some reason the stuff made him think of wallpaper paste. Still, the dark purple chips were nice and salty. He caught Kaitin's warning scent, swallowed a second chip whole and decided to try the lump of green whatever it was later.

"It was that great fool's fault," Kaitin told Marsden. He lifted an ear, questioning the merits of the treats. Relaxed it at Strongarm's shrug.

"Yuh-huh. You dragged the Mote in here kicking and screaming. I can tell by the blood on the walls." Marsden lifted Keiko Yakamoto by the shirt collar like an errant cub. To Strongarm's surprise she didn't even try to wiggle free. "Next time you want to hide out with *haoles*, don't tell them to order poi."

"Yessir. I'm sorry, Captain." She would have done better at it if she hadn't giggled. "But we didn't do anything wrong. Really. We just wen watch a *movie*, that's all."

"Yuh-huh. Not even going to try counting the number of laws you three just broke." He marched her toward the door, turned the scowl on Strongarm over a shoulder. "Try the wasabi, Lord Strongarm. Made it for you myself. Call it the Tutu Pele special."

Interesting. Marsden smelled almost happy. It was Keiko Yakamoto's scent went horrified. Whatever had scared her, Marsden hauled her outside too fast for her to say.

God of his Makers, his palms were itching. Strongarm lifted his hands. The skin of his palms rippled. Beneath it he made out the first tiny cilia beginning to work up through the skin. First sign of the Touch. His heart sank even as his ears lifted. He could only hope Letticia Van Buren improved on acquaintance. Otherwise, he would indeed have to steal Jezekiah's woman.

In which case, he would almost certainly have to kill Jezekiah.

XIX

Praise Tutu Pele, Captain Marsden was more worried about her than angry. He covered for her so well that for once the Admiral let her sleep in next morning. That was clear when Keiko finally got both eyes open and realized the sun was full up. For one terrorized second she thought the Admiral was testing her. She reached out with *ki*. Got nothing. Her *ki* was quiet as the house. She jammed into shirt and shorts and tiptoed down the hall before she allowed herself a prayer of thanks to *Tutu* Pele. No test. No intention of kindness, either. The Admiral just wasn't there.

Better than that, he hadn't even left the usual duty list on the kitchen table. Keiko carried her cup of kona down to the Admiral's study and checked his desk in case he was testing her thoroughness. Nothing. Didn't mean she had no chores, but at least she had an excuse to bunk off punishment detail for the day. Rejoicing, she took the kona out to the living room to indulge in just *being*.

This was her room, in a way even her quarters were not. The Admiral had let her choose the haiku he'd had embroidered in pale silk thread on the red silk wall hangings. It was still early enough the weather screens hadn't triggered. The unfiltered light made the haiku's silken threads shimmer in the morning sun. The ebony tables she kept polished to military shine reflected the characters, red silk on black wood, breaking the white glare. Keiko dropped onto a pale couch, content to just breathe.

Fresh bunches of gardenia and scarlet ginger were clustered around the room, white and red flowers bright against the ivory walls. Not her idea, this time. The Admiral must have put them out. She wondered about that while she drank in their spicy-sweet scent. Red-on-white... Van Buren colors. He must have intended them to welcome her into the Van Buren fold. Only Van Buren himself had had other ideas...

The memory ruined her good mood. All she'd ever wanted was to be a person. Van Buren knew that. She'd told him so herself. So what had she done wrong? She sipped coffee, scowling at the rustling foliage in the garden just beyond the windows while she tried to puzzle it out. He must have it in for her *nui* big – yet why hadn't she picked up any danger-sense from him? Why'd he seemed so... nice? Maybe Grandfather was right; you could never trust a haole.

Outside, the bamboo lining the garden wall shook hard enough to scoot a ruby-throated hummingbird out of its nest. The tiny bird hovered just beyond the tree line; even through the screens Keiko could hear its outraged chitter. She finished her coffee in a gulp, carried the cup back out to the kitchen. She dumped it in the sink for a later wash, strode down the hall to the Admiral's study. So much for the down time. *Somebody* was sneaking through those bushes. Wasn't triggering battle sense, whoever it was. But, then, Teufelsman and his damned Aryans thought gang rape was just entertainment.

She pulled the Admiral's twin swords down from the wall, lifted his tanto throwing knife off its desk mount and tucked it in her belt. She whirled the swords, re-acquainting herself with their balance. If Teufelsman thought he was going to take advantage of the Admiral's absence, he was in for an unhappy surprise. Even the Admiral's display blades were live.

She slipped out of the house through the kitchen door, circled around through the side garden. Found the intruder lurking in the gap where she expected, hiding between wall and bamboo. He was still trying to shush the hummingbird. Silent, she crept up behind him. Drove him and the bird out of the bushes by poking a sword tip to his butt.

With a shocked bellow, Kamehameha No-Name leaped clear through the bamboo. He landed on his feet facing her, a brown, barrel-chested mountain, rubbing frantically at his rump and looking hurt. "Heia! You wen go lolo?"

Keiko slid out of the bamboo to grin up at him. "Thought you might be Teufelsman." She rested the swords on her shoulders, wicked blades up. She wished now she'd left the Admiral's swords alone; she had no place to sheathe them. "What're you doing here, anyway?"

"Come say aloha, is all."

"Good-bye?" Keiko reached to check his wound but Kameh snapped away, one hand on his butt in protective modesty. Hiding a smile she nodded Kameh toward the kitchen door. "Where you go?"

"Niihau." Kameh trudged after her, his bulk blocking the sun from her back. "Grandfather wen send me off world."

"Shaka! Lucky you." Keiko whirled to hug him. Regretted the swords again when he jackknifed around a blade. She shrugged apology, pushed the kitchen door open with her butt. "Come stay. I put these back." She skipped down the hallway to the Admiral's study, twirling the swords and fighting jealousy.

Kameh was still lurking in the doorway when Keiko returned. Keiko tapped a chair, hinting. "Come sit. Make you some kona."

"No can." He shuffled feet unhappily. "Got one shuttle waiting up Kahuku way."

There was no budging Kameh when he didn't want to move, so Keiko poured a cup of kona and wrapped his hands around it. The thrill of his escape was already dulling. The sense of his loss engulfed her, threatened to mist her eyes. Keiko shoved it down firmly. She ought to be happy for him, not sorry for herself. Self-pity never do either of them any good. "Think happy, brah. You going like it out on the rim. Strongarm says our folk got some kinda special status-"

"You like him, gul?" His hands tightened on hers, his eyes going narrow.

"Who? Strongarm?" Keiko blinked up at him, puzzling at the sudden spike of battle sense at the back of her neck. "Yeah, I guess. He's-" she had to search for the old word. "He's a *gentleman*."

"Good." He lifted the cup to blow on the coffee, his expression going bitter as the dark liquid. The black studs in his jaw and temple misted over in the rising steam.

Something in him was sending the back of her neck into jumpdrive. "Hey, brah, you okay?" She rested worried hands on his arms.

"Yeah, shaka." To Keiko's amazement, he glanced over his shoulder. He started to say something, changed his mind and drained the coffee in a gulp instead. He shoved the cup back into her hands, clasped his own around hers locking her fingers around the cup.

With a shock, she realized he was trembling. Maybe he felt whatever it was buzzing her battle sense. "What's wrong, Kameh? You don't want to go, tell Grandfather. He'll listen."

"Yeah, he listen. Only he don't care. Grandfather only care what Grandfather want. Don't matter what it cost anybody else." His expression tightened. Her *ki* thrilled at the surge of hatred in his. "Listen, gul, I got wiki it, eh? Grandfather think I no got time come say aloha-" He cut it off with a shudder.

Battle sense flared. Had it been anyone but Kameh, Keiko would have flung herself clear. Only his hatred wasn't directed at her. She tossed the cup in the sink. Reached up to cup his face in her hands. Slowly, battle sense eased until Kameh finally smiled down at her. He took her hands, planted an unexpected kiss on her knuckles. "Hey, you don't listen me, eh? Sometime I get one guano mouth, you know?"

"Yuh-huh. Just you remember tell me rim world stories, you get out there, eh?" She stroked his cheek, then stepped back. "You better wiki it if Grandfather's got a shuttle waiting."

"No hu-hu. Got one Seed truck pick me up."

She wrapped an arm around his waist, hugged him sideways while she walked with him out the garden gate. She kept her knees steady until he vanished into the scrubby brush lining the base of Diamond Head's cone. It was only when she was sure he couldn't see her that she let herself surrender to the emptiness he'd left in her heart. She dropped to her knees in the dirt, covered her dry eyes with her hands.

She remembered, finally, to *think*. She couldn't imagine why Grandfather would send Kameh away. Not unless he was trying to get Kameh out of the Aryan's reach. Even so, a registree's was still fair game anywhere in the Commonwealth. But for once maybe she could do something. For once she could really help. She'd promised Grandfather to set up a meeting with Strongarm – that might make him happy enough to ease up on Kameh's banishment.

Even if he didn't, she had a back-up. Jezekiah Van Buren had friends out on the rim. He'd know somebody who could offset a registree sentence. And Tutu Pele knew Jezekiah Van Buren owed her one helluva big favor.

XX

Someone was whispering. Jezekiah started to roll over in bed, pillow wrapped around his ears, when memory of Letticia cut in. He fired the pillow at the whisperer, shot off the bed. He hit the floor trapped in a silk cocoon of sheets.

"Sorry to startle you, your lordship." Kip Marsden regarded him from the far side of the bed with the kind of exaggerated solemnity that bespoke a suffocated grin. He was in civvies this morning, though still in Van Buren colors: a loose cream jacket and slacks over scarlet shirt. The jacket was not thick enough to hide the dark outline of the laser pistol beneath. "Only your Lady Mother wants you and Lord Strongarm in her office. Now."

Jezekiah gave the sheets a final, disgusted kick. "You could have used the major domo."

"Keepin' things outta Net till we got that assassin sorted out, you know what I mean. 'Sides, I was tryin' not to scare you." Temptation won; Kip let the grin show.

Jezekiah kicked the last of the sheets off, rose. "What's Mother want?"

"Dunno, your lordship. Her summons just said '*now*'. Didn't stop to ask reasons."

"Have you told Strongarm yet?" His major domo had clearly been listening; he could hear the shower running. Jezekiah hopped out of his pajama bottoms on his way to it.

"I'm lettin' his kitty cat bud do the honors. We'll pick 'em up on the way." Kip followed him far enough to lean a broad shoulder against the bathroom door jamb. "Say, your lordship? That Strongarm got some kind of allergy to peppers?"

"Peppers? Where'd that come from?" Jezekiah surrendered the pajama bottoms to a determined servobot. He paused, one foot in the shower to consider Kip's ceiling-searching innocence.

"Yeah, well, I kinda fed 'im some a' my special wasabi last night." He shrugged at the ceiling, carefully avoiding Jezekiah's unspoken question. "And now this mornin' maintenance says the sonuvabitch's droppin' hair like mangoes in August."

Damn. Jezekiah stepped the rest of the way into the shower. He caught a stinging dose of soap, quick-calc'd probabilities while the major domo *tsked* him through the rinse. So, then. Strongarm was deeper in Impression-mode than he'd let on. Explained why the man had turned up so far ahead of schedule. Jezekiah hurried through the shower, ran projections while the major domo buffed him dry. Meant the danger of an unanticipated mating was an imminent risk: if Strongarm didn't complete his Impression and mate, he would be dead in a matter of days. It was a testament to the man's will power that he wasn't groveling at Letticia's feet.

Still, a shorter time line was a good thing, actually. Jezekiah tracked options while the major domo slipped him into shirt and slacks. At very least it minimized the chance Letticia would manage to force Mother to execute her before she had Strongarm Impressed. He'd just have to make sure it was Letticia who was *there* when Strongarm reached the do-or-die point. And pray, his little voice murmured, that Strongarm had not already found Letticia repulsive enough to start hunting an alternative.

He had his action plan worked out by the time Kip ushered him down the hall to the guest wing to pick up the pair of Lupans.

Strongarm looked lost in thought. He stood head down, massive arms folded across massive chest. He'd left off the heavy silver torque and arm bands. He wore only what were obviously favorite trousers, their scratched blue leather worn to a comfortable fit. His mane looked unbrushed. Deliberate, most likely; odds were the man was disguising bald patches. It was Kaitin who paced. Gold bangles jingled amid emerald robes as he reached his turn and jerked around to pace toward them. Fortunately, the lip he lifted above that ruby fang was aimed at Kip.

So, then. Trouble there as well. Kip clearly expected it, too, judging from the sudden tilt of his head. He pended the observation for future exploration; right now they all had to stretch it.

Even with Mother's summons on file, it took Kip's direct intervention to convince Mother's major domo to swing the massive tiki wood doors open for the two Lupans. Within, sunlit shafts of dancing mites almost obscured the view of Pearl Harbor through the tall arched windows. Silken threads woven into the Persian carpets twirled reflected sunlight across the floor. Faint columns of jeweled lights sprang up along the walls, twinkling merrily. The sight stopped Jezekiah's breath for an instant. Neither of the Lupans would walk out of this room alive if this meeting went sour; Kip Marsden had just sync'd into the office Sec system. He willed his pulse steady before Strongarm caught the fear spike.

Mother stood staring out one of those windows, hands clasped behind her back. Even with her back turned Jezekiah knew a single curl would be dangling loose above one eye.

Odd, that it should only now strike him how much Letticia resembled her physically. The idea conjured an image of what Letticia could have been. Of what his baby sister could yet *be*, if she'd give Strongarm a chance. The thought triggered a pang of regret so powerful it drew questioning glances from Strongarm and Kip alike.

Mother apparently sensed it also. She turned, regarded them unsmiling. She'd been there all night, from the looks of it; her working shirt and slacks looked rumpled, the red-gold curl dangling above the arch of her brow had gone limp. The shadows beneath her eyes had deepened. She welcomed Jezekiah with her eyes, acknowledged Marsden with the barest nod. Proved she'd done her homework on Lupan manners by lowering her chin a bit to Strongarm and Kaitin in turn.

"I regret the need to rouse you so early, milords. Unfortunately, we are all bound to the needs of duty."

"Our honor, Ma'am." Strongarm and Kaitin salaamed in unison. "Most honored if this is a war council."

"Not yet. Ideally, not at all. We are all here precisely to avoid a war, are we not?" Mother lifted a red-gold eyebrow at Strongarm as if he were simply an errant Admin op. "Despite the determined efforts of yourself and Johann Petrovich to provoke one."

"Ma'am." Strongarm accepted the rebuke with a lift of his chin that bared his throat.

Kaitin settled for stroking his mustaches. "Then one must wonder the cause for urgency, yes?"

"Perhaps I can answer that," Admiral Yakamoto's voice said behind them. The man strode past Jezekiah to take up position beside Mother's desk. In his plain dark uniform he looked almost thread-like against Kip's powerful frame. Except for the matched swords at his side he carried no visible weapons. Yet he radiated a danger that brought Strongarm's head down and flared the manes on both Lupans.

"Matsuo." Mother welcomed Yakamoto with a half-smile. "Now we can indeed begin." She stepped away from the window to pace thoughtfully.

"May I ask the reason for the summons?" Jezekiah watched Yakamoto station himself between Mother and Strongarm. Saw Strongarm note it as well.

"Johann Petrovich has called an emergency session of the Commonwealth Council."

"So we are to hold war council after all." Strongarm sounded worrisomely satisfied about it.

"I almost wish it were." Mother paced past a window. Sunlight spun fire off the Ring bright enough to leave its afterimage on Jezekiah's eyes when she passed into the next shadow. "It would be easier to dispute."

"Which means?"

"Which means I have only been summoned myself. No reason given."

JP's work, then. Jezekiah clenched hands behind his back, fighting the cold despair that tried to take hold in his gut.

Mother paced back in a crest of light. She reached her desk, stepped behind it to include all five men in the gaze she swept over them. "Given the timing, I must assume we are all involved, directly or otherwise. This is the reason I asked you all here, gentlemen. I shall not allow Streiker or any other of my ruling cousins to sow suspicion among us."

The Council has convened, Madam, the major domo announced. At Mother's gesture, the air in the center of the office clouded. Jezekiah automatically stepped closer to Mother's desk so he could face the ruling members of his family as their sync'd figures coalesced in front of him. Strongarm and Kaitin followed suit, a pair of looming presences just behind his right shoulder. Kip and Yakamoto, he noted, flanked Mother.

Around them, the office vanished in a patchwork of eleven other rooms unharmoniously stitched together in sync. As always, Pandar held the center.

One hundred twenty thousand light years from Earth, Octavian Pandar-eh Van Buren, Lord High Protector of Pandar, lifted a crystal decanter from its wall niche as his holo took shape. Behind him, the captain's suite of his Jumpship swept away into blue shimmer – night dark, by Pandaran standards though still bright for eyes not designed to withstand Pandar's searing blue-white sun. Decanter in hand, Octavian turned to bow greetings.

Around him eleven pairs of impossibly blue eyes scowled at them beneath eleven red-gold heads of hair. Streiker's military allies clearly expected a war: those two were in their war rooms. Judging from their assortment of offices, yachts, or bedrooms the rest of the Family's ruling members had been caught on the fly. Cousin Omar, out on the playground world Derakht, balanced his elfin form on a tiny hoverboard, silvery golf club lining up on an iridescent ball. He took his shot, waited till the ball pinged into the cup embedded in a skyscraping trunk before turning his attention to the Council. Or as much of his attention as setting up his next shot allowed.

Jezekiah swallowed a grin. Stroke of luck JP had timed his summons as he had. Omar normally followed JP's lead simply as the path of least resistance. But forcing a Derakhti nobleman to interrupt a golf game was as hostile an act as that world's serious gamesters recognized. If he played this right, there was a chance now Omar would back Earth out of spite.

The patchwork images wavered, realigned as a final figure took shape.

Johann Petrovich von Streiker wore a black uniform this time, with the silver thread of a comm feed wound round his head from throat to temple. He had his head cocked, listening to some report as his image solidified. He snapped erect as his line of sight found Strongarm. "I had not expected you to make this so easy, Muriel." He swept his gaze across the Council, swept an accusing hand toward Mother. "See for yourselves. Earth is masterminding the dogs' transgressions. The proof stands before you."

"Really, JP." Mother cut him off with a dismissive gesture, then salaamed to the rest of the Council. She got only a dozen cold, blue scowls in return. "If this is to be an inquiry, then be advised, all of you, that our invitation to Lord Strongarm was extended well before the current dispute over Rogue developed. Given recent developments, I would suggest that his visit offers us a serendipitous opportunity to pursue a sensible resolution to Streiker's on-going provocations."

"An excellent suggestion, my dear Muriel. Unfortunately -" Light flared as Octavian set a crystal decanter on his table- "A Lupan battle fleet seems to have gone missing. Afraid that does rather lend weight to JP's worries, what?"

It was only training that kept Jezekiah's jaw from sagging. That was most definitely not part of their agreement. He locked his expression on 'innocent' and joined Mother in lifting brows at Strongarm.

If either of the Lupans cared, he hid it well. Kaitin lifted a lip to expose that ruby-tipped fang. Strongarm bared his fangs in a massive grin at JP. "Be grateful my fleet's not in orbit around Streiker. For which you should offer thanks to Home World."

"Collusion! He admits it!"

"Collusion in *what*?" Mother slammed a fist on her desk hard enough to make Omar foul his swing. The little Derakhti took one look at Mother's expression and opted not to protest. "I can assure you, Uncle, that there is no Lupan battle fleet orbiting Earth, either!"

For one dread second Jezekiah feared she would ask Strongarm to take a seat to prove it. But she settled for silence. Left Strongarm the opening.

Nose twitching, the Lupan stepped into it. "Lucky for you, Streiker, I'm under guest-geas here. So I tell you this once, blood free: my fleet is not orbiting Home World. I'm here to seal a trade treaty. Period." His smile shrank, lips tightening to show only the barest hint of fang. Somehow, the effect was scarier than the full battle grin. "I give you my word. If you want my blood on it, name your champions and call me out like a man."

"That can be-"

"Uncle!" Jezekiah stepped into the illusory space between the two men. He kept his hands out, palms up in peace sign. "Before anyone gets carried away, allow me to put Johann Petrovich's concerns in context." He gave that a beat, made sure he had Octavian's attention before continuing. "First: as has just been pointed out, *I* invited Lord Strongarm here for the well-documented purpose of sealing a trade treaty between our worlds. Second: in purely logistical terms, bear in mind Earth is on the opposite side of the Commonwealth from Den Lupus. Given that we no longer have vast resources to offer, there is no advantage to Den Lupus to stationing a fleet here. Third-"

He paused, hardening his expression. "Third: I remind you all that Earth is the only world to have endured a Lupan war. It cost us five point seven billion casualties in the war itself. One billion more in the sectarian wars that followed. Rendered eighty-seven percent of our land mass uninhabitable. Six hundred years later, we are still putting the pieces back together."

Sidelong, Jezekiah noted that Mother relaxed a bit. On his other side, Strongarm *uhfed* agreement. "Conclusion: self-evidently, any 'collusion' between Earth and Den Lupus is necessarily aimed at enhancing trade for the very simple reason that trade is all we have to offer. An offer which, incidentally, ensures peace and profit for *all* of us."

"Excellent! Explanation delivered, job done." Omar wove his tiny hoverboard through the forest's green gloom, caught up to his iridescent ball and took his shot. "Derakht will host the celebrations, discount on the fees. Now let's all get back to business."

There was a murmur of agreement around the patchwork. It ended when Octavian raised an elegant finger. "You've painted quite a convincing picture, dear boy. Except for one minor omission." He swept his white-blue flicker across the others to rest on Jezekiah. "The Lupans' long jump drive."

That tidbit made Omar skid to a halt. He took a wild shot anyway but the iridescent ball arced wildly, making the Protectors in the next two holos duck. "Dammit, Pandar! Piss on your surprises! I've lost my damned ball!"

"Only one?" Octavian asked sweetly. He turned back to Jezekiah, his smile a brilliant white slash in his ebony face. "Allow me to rephrase your conclusion in a long jump context, cousin. First: Earth and Den Lupus are on opposite sides of the Commonwealth. With a long jump driven battle fleet, that means Den Lupus and Earth flank the Commonwealth.

"Second, unlike the rest of us, your two worlds have only the intergalactic void at your backs. Thus, utilizing long jump capability, you can keep your long supply lines safely out of our attack range. Lastly, Lupans seal treaties with marriage. Need I remind any of you that the estimable Lord Strongarm is famously in need of a wife? Or that Muriel has a notoriously talented and eminently unmarried daughter?"

He flickered eyes at the rest of the Council. "Conclusion: with the Lupans in control of a long jump drive, and Earth in control of the Lupans' alpha war lord, Home World will have the rest of us caught in a pincer."

"To what purpose?" This time it was Mother whose thunder made Omar foul a shot. Nearly sobbing, the Derakhti Protector snapped his club over a knee. Mother ignored him, focused her glare on Octavian. "We can trade speculation till eternity, Octavian. It means nothing. Now if you have a charge to make, then make it. Otherwise I shall file a demand for reimbursement for my wasted time with your embassy."

JP answered her sneer for scowl. "The charge is this: that you, Muriel Van Buren, and your whelp Jezekiah have betrayed Streikern miltech secrets to the dogs. That you intend to seal the betrayal with a marriage alliance to the very dog now threatening our borders. The charge-" JP leaned across his podium to stab a finger at Jezekiah — "is treason!"

Silence. The assembled Protectors simply waited. Watching Mother and himself for the telltale glance or start that would betray guilt. Watching in the kind of silence that said they already believed the charge. Damn and damn again. He could win the treaty and still lose it all unless he stopped JP now. Unless he betrayed a friend. He tried not to let himself feel the sickened lurch in his gut.

"This one speaks." Kaitin's purr rasped in the silence. He swept into the space between desk and holos in a swirl of emerald robes. Golden eyes drooped as he surveyed the assembled rulers, narrowed to slits when he rested them on JP. "Greed makes you quick to call death on your friends, flat tooth. There is yet more than one way to avoid this war you seek." Gold bracelets jingled while he stroked his long white mustaches. "If any of ye has courage, send a marriage candidate of your own to Den Lupus. Make treaty offers of your own. Let the women of Parliament decide which marriage to pursue."

To Jezekiah's surprise, Strongarm rumbled agreement. "You wanted to talk two-prong attacks, Pandar. Here's your shot." Ears lifting, he turned a full-fanged grin on the Council. "In the mean time you will stop attacking my mining colonies on Rogue." Strongarm locked eyes on JP and his ears went flat. "Be warned, Streiker: attack my people again and I will answer in kind."

"Oh, I say!" Octavian flickered his blue-white gaze at the Council. "Do let's give peace a chance, shall we? I, for one, find our Bengali friend's idea quite fetching." He lifted his glass to Jezekiah in a gesture both salute and challenge. "Pandar votes to pend the charge of treason against Earth. Until we have had time to present our own ambassadors to the Lupan Parliament."

Around the Council Protectors murmured assent. With a final salaam, Octavian's holo winked out. The rest of the Council followed suit. Sunlight swelled in behind them. Light flared off Kip's silver comm implant as he cocked his head, already intent on his Sec feed. Mother sank back in her chair, finger massaging her nose. Behind her, the Admiral shifted stance marginally to focus on the Lupans.

It was Strongarm who dropped forward and braced hands on knees. Kaitin growled at him about it in Lobish, but Strongarm shrugged it off. Even that slight motion shed silver into the sunlit stream.

Jezekiah rested a comforting hand on Strongarm's shoulder. His worry was real enough. He let himself *feel* it, let the other two pick it up in his scent. No need to tell them the worry wasn't for Strongarm. It didn't matter anyway. Not now. Everything was falling into place perfectly now. All he needed was Mother's consent.

He kept his hand on Strongarm as the Lupan straightened making sure he had Mother's attention. "If Octavian manages a marriage bond first, we will be the ones caught in a pincer. We don't have time to arrange a suitable alternative. We need to seal the treaty. Now."

Mother pulled in a breath, held it for a long, unhappy moment. "Agreed. You had best inform Letticia to make herself ready." She lifted her chin, found a smile for Strongarm. "It seems we must dispense with the usual bells and whistles, Lord Strongarm. Allow me to welcome you to the family."

Strongarm lifted ears. But his chin came down. "You honor me, Ma'am. But there's no need for emergency measures just yet. I can manage a day or two more."

Jezekiah's mouth went dry. "Why? The longer you wait-"

"Because I have actually met a Maker, Jezekiah Van Buren. In which case-" Strongarm clamped a matching hand on Jezekiah's shoulder. Friendly gesture, yet the impact threatened to buckle Jezekiah's knees. "I may need to rewrite some of our treaty."

With that, the Lupans salaamed in unison, then turned and strode out.

Jezekiah caught the sudden tension in the Admiral's posture. So he'd figured who Strongarm's Maker was, too. Jezekiah salaamed to Mother, waited for her dismissal. Once into the corridor outside he broke into a near run.

He had damned well better find Keiko Yakamoto before her father did. Or, worse, Strongarm.

XXI

Quick as he was, it took Jezekiah all the way to the Manor's public wing to catch up with the Lupans. At that, they might have succeeded in dodging him altogether. Certainly none of Mother' admin ops were about to try chatting the two Lupans up. Trigger-tempered as Strongarm was getting Jezekiah wouldn't have risked annoying the man himself had he not needed so desperately to keep him away from Keiko.

Fortunately, a familiar Sprite with a SecType escort lacked a sense of self-preservation. The Sprite had clearly asked Strongarm and Kaitin for autographs. Predictably, Strongarm had wanted to brush past; he stood with chin pulled in and ears down. Equally predictably, Kaitin had stopped to preen.

The sight eased his spirits. Coming up on Strongarm's side, Jezekiah gave his doppelganger a grin. The boy had gone positively radiant in the past couple of days. Somebody had spent serious money kiting the Sprite out: his ruffled shirt was pure silk; his trousers were tapered to perfection. The way the SecType smiled at him said who the someone had been.

Kaitin passed the Sprite's pad to Strongarm, who nearly shorted it with a taloned signature. "You want to round out the collection?" Strongarm jammed it into Jezekiah's hands with enough force to knock him back a pace.

"Sorry for the bother, milord." That was the SecType. The doppelganger had gone suddenly shy. The SecType wrapped a protective arm around the boy's shoulder. "But orders say to-"

"Give my friend here the deluxe tour. I know." Jezekiah bestowed a friendly smile on his doppelganger. Fair bet what those orders were, and the tour had nothing to do with it. He touched finger to pad, allowing its filament of NetMind to certify the encounter and handed it back. Noted without surprise the faint thud of footsteps jogging up the corridor behind them.

The SecType dropped his hand and straightened to attention as footsteps jogged up to join them.

"Thanks for keepin' 'em for me, Frank." Kip pointedly did not greet Jezekiah.

"Yessir." The SecType Frank hauled his charge out of sight with alacrity.

"You weren't plannin' on leaving the Manor unescorted, were you your Lordship?"

"I wasn't planning on leaving the Manor at all, as a matter of fact." A lifetime's training let him make the lie sound true. Keeping his scent honest took effort. "I only wished to arrange a sight-seeing tour for our guests."

"Yuh-huh. And you just thought you'd tag along, huh?"

"Actually, I was going to send -"

"Keiko Yakamoto!" Strongarm perked ears with entirely too much enthusiasm.

"No!" Spoken in three voices with equal finality. Jezekiah clamped a hand on Kip's shoulder before the SecType could elucidate, nodded gratitude to Kaitin. "Keiko is not available." He let warning touch his scent. "Whereas you and Letticia have not had a fair chance to get to know each other."

"Had chance enough – no point torturing your sister any further."

"She's the key to the treaty."

"Agreed." That was Kaitin, turning to bare a rubied fang tip at Strongarm. "Thy fate is of thine own making, brother-in-law. Forget Keiko Yakamoto. She has no status."

"Tell you, she's a Maker."

That stopped whatever objection Kaitin had intended. The Bengali stroked his mustaches instead and purred thoughtfully.

Damn and damn again. They could still lose everything if Kaitin backed the Maker idea.

"Listen, you two." Beneath Jezekiah's fingers, Kip's shoulders tightened. "Mote may be a natural, but that don't make her a joy toy. That child is not on the make. Not for nobody."

"I can assure you my friend Strongarm meant no insult." Jezekiah tried to squeeze sense into Kip before he managed to sour whatever goodwill Strongarm still felt.

Kip ignored him. "Yuh-huh, then what was he doing sneaking her in up to his quarters last night? You all want to make bet on what would'a happened if Mote hadn't told 'em to send down for chips'n poi?"

"I take it you added the napalm sauce yourself." Strongarm's head came down, ears suddenly fixed on Kip.

Well, at least that explained the pepper question. A part of Jezekiah's mind winced in sympathy.

"Mind, this one does not complain." Kaitin poked Strongarm, pursed lips at Kip. "One had always wondered how the onlies' hell would feel. Though one's ass may never forgive you."

Amazing these two weren't still soaking their butts in ice water if Kip had inflicted that habanero-wasabi sauce of his on them. Still, the exchange had broken the tension. Jezekiah dropped his hand, turned the warning he'd intended for Kip on Strongarm. "Let me set both your hearts at ease. There are no Makers any more. It's a myth."

"The original species is no myth." Surprisingly, it was Kaitin who answered. "If Makers still exist, it can only be here on Earth. If so, it is a chance worth pursuing. A treaty sealed by a Maker, a true child of the one God, would be inviolate on Den Lupus. None of thy relatives could match such a mating. Thy profit and this great fool's would be ensured."

"Yuh-huh." Kip noted Jezekiah's warning cough, lightened the tone. "Don't get me wrong, your lordships, but you're sounding like Grandfather Ho. That 'true human' business is a Ho Tong claim."

Kaitin pursed lips, golden eyes narrowing. "Then one hopes such a Maker owes allegiance to thy family, Van Buren. And not to Ho Tong."

Jezekiah did what he could to keep the sudden icy thrill out of his scent, but the hairs rose all the way up the back of his neck. Stupid, deadly mistake. He knew the Lupan myth well enough. But he'd failed to work out its implications. Or connect it to Keiko Yakamoto.

Fighting fear-sweat he quick-calc'd odds on Lupan-Tong collusion. Stifled a sigh of relief when those came up null. So, then. He still had a chance. "I'm afraid you've been mis-led, my friend. Keiko is not a Maker. She is a mixed-Type natural, pure and simple. Same as you would find on any world in the Commonwealth." He smiled with dry lips. "For which you should be grateful. Considering what Impression by a Ho Tong operative would mean."

He dared not let himself dwell on it. *Damn* and damn again! No wonder Grandfather Ho had been so determined to keep Keiko a natural. A Lupan who married a Maker would have a direct connect to divinity. That would unite the whole damned Lupan branch of humanity behind him and half the free worlds to boot. With Grandfather Ho in control of it all.

"Ho Tong?" Strongarm's chin and ears came down together. Beside him, Kaitin's purr turned to a hiss. "Keiko Yakamoto cannot be a Ho Tong operative-"

"I am sorry to distress you, my friend, but there is a good chance that is the case. At very least, she is a Ho Tong tool." Jezekiah risked resting hands on Strongarm's shoulders. The Lupan started but didn't shake him off. "I urge you to re-consider. Think what Venus Seed does to your people. Think what a Ho Tong Impression would mean."

He gave Strongarm's shoulders a squeeze then stepped back, giving the man thinking room. "My sister may be difficult, but she will respond to love. Give her a chance. Give yourself a chance. Most importantly, give your people a chance. Then ask yourself how much chance Grandfather Ho would give you."

"Point seen and scented." Strongarm let out a breath that pulled his ears down with it. For one terrifying moment, he looked like he was ready to risk it all anyway. But he shook himself, clapped an answering hand on Jezekiah's shoulder. Friendly as that grip was, Jezekiah felt it in his bones. "I will bind myself to your sister. I give you my blood on it." He let Jezekiah go, flicked a talon tip across his palm. Blood spritzed across Jezekiah's cheek.

"Good. Then let's have you two meet properly. If you'll wait a bit, I'll arrange to have Letticia show you the sights."

Jezekiah saw the two Lupans settled comfortably in a shady corner of the Manor's grounds while they waited for Letticia – the orders he had Kip relay ensured it would be a short wait.

He took his leave while Kip was still managing the logistics. Waited till he was well out of sight before wiping Strongarm's blood off his face. Stared at the darkening red on his fingertips in satisfaction. Blood oath. Strongarm was bound by word and life now. Striding toward the transit hub exit, Jezekiah allowed himself a smile. So, then. So, then indeed. One trigger locked. Left only the background check he'd been postponing. If his suspicions proved out, Grandfather Ho was in for a surprise of his own.

XXII

Her palms were sweating. She wasn't even inside Mother's office yet, and her palms were already sweating. Biting her lip, Letticia started to wipe the sweat off on her satin skirt and thought better of it. She couldn't risk facing Mother with wet stains bracketing her skirt. But she felt so *naked*. She hadn't even dared risk a tiny bit of jewelry; Mother hated jewelry. But then, Mother had the Ring; anything else was a distraction. All *she* needed, Letticia thought, was her sync link. Needed it enough she was ready to fall on hands and knees at Mother's feet and beg.

She caught the evil red gleam of the office's major domo's eye tracking her – spying on her – as always. She wiped her hands down the fragrant sandalwood wall covering instead. Let it stain the wood, leave her mark right where the damned chip had to look at it forever and ever. That'd serve it right! Maybe the major domo felt the same way. The scan it ran on her bit so deep it burned.

Was it her imagination or was the damned thing actually sneering at her? *Damn*, she wished she could sync in! Then she'd know for sure. It was horrible having to rely on her stupid body, having to guess at everything. And now she was going to have to guess at pleasing Mother. Letticia swiped fresh sweat off on the door frame, then squared her shoulders and marched into Mother's office.

She wished at once she'd waited; Mother's cold blue stare dried up every pore in her body. Mother would never understand how it felt to *need* someone. She was the *Protector*. She wasn't weak. She didn't need anything or anyone – everyone else needed *her*. She'd never understand how it felt to be all alone and whimpering in the dark.

Letticia stopped two steps short of the scan chairs to drop her curtsy, remembered to keep her back straight, her head up. For once, Mother signaled her to rise before her knees shook. Maybe she'd done it right this time. Her tongue moistened at the flicker of hope.

Mother stayed behind her desk, staying cold and distant as always. She toyed with that damned crystal paperweight making confetti light dance across the walls. But her eyes bored blue lasers into Letticia's soul. "What is it that couldn't wait?"

Oh, *gob* it, that wasn't a good start. "I-I was wondering if you'd had the chance to see my duty repot."

"Why don't you tell me about it instead?" Mother slapped the paperweight down, clasped her hands behind her back and paced away. Sunlight exploded against the Ring each time she passed a tall window, replacing the confetti light with pops of broken rainbows.

"I did my meet'n greet with the free world's tourist board reps."

"Do tell me they were still interested in touring Earth when you finished."

"Of course they – " Oh, that wasn't fair at all! Letticia bit back the retort. "Yes, Mother." Spoken like a good little girl, without even a hint of the sarcasm it deserved.

"Did you also attend Admin's morning update?"

"Yes, Mother." And managed to keep both eyes open for it, too, which was the real accomplishment.

Mother reached the last window and turned. Sunlight blazed off the creamy silk of her blouse, hazing the red-gold glints in her hair. It was like looking at a goddess. The swell of awe took her breath away.

But awe did nothing to dim the diamond hard edge of Mother's glare. "So you've attended to your basic duties. Why do you feel the need to tell me about it in person?"

"Because-" oh, *Pleasepleaseplease – please let this work!* "Because I can't sync in to report properly." Letticia kept the *need* out of her expression. "If you could let me use one of the public links even-"

"No." Sun glare made Letticia flinch as Mother ran the fingers of her Ring hand along the bridge of her nose. "It will take far more than the most miniscule attention to your most minor duties to earn the right to sync access again. You have been guilty of treason, Letticia, do you understand that?"

Why did Mother always have to harp on her mistakes? "Oh, for heaven's sake! I never did any such thing and you know it. All I did was let one silly Transitliner dock near my precious brother's shuttle. That's hardly treason."

"What you did was infiltrate the Protector's node. You usurped my identity: not merely to permit that 'silly Transitliner' to dock, but to smuggle your assassin onto Earth."

"Well, what was I supposed to do? The idiot kept missing!" Oh, *wrong*. Mother's eyes went dangerously narrow. Suddenly Letticia's tongue felt like sandpaper. "I mean, that's what I was *supposed* to do, isn't it? I'm supposed to see if I can't take the stupid Ring away from Jess. He's supposed to stop me. That's the way the game's played."

"Not on Earth." Mother lifted her head, creating a red-gold ripple within the halo. "Most certainly not with a Ta'an."

It took a good two seconds for the awful implication to sink in. Took two more to get her voice working again when it did. "You think I was after *you*?" She took a step forward, reaching out. "I'd never do anything to hurt you, Mother! Never! Besides, we can't even *afford* a Ta'an! You know that!"

But Mother only glanced at those gobbing chairs. Chill fear-sweat dribbled down her ribs. And evaporated under the heat of her rising fury. "Jezekiah told you that, didn't he? He'll say anything to make you hate me. He wants me dead!"

"He wants you married to Strongarm. He is also, incidentally, the only reason you are still alive."

Oh, for heaven's sake, why did everybody have to keep harping on that? "But I've already said I'll gob the damned dog! What more do you want?"

"I want you to turn in that assassin." Mother didn't even sound angry. Just cold and distant as a dream. She folded her arms across her chest, gaze so sharp it felt like she was boring a hole in Letticia's heart.

"But I don't know where he is!" She'd have told if she did. Told anything to change that absolute, utter verdict of worthlessness in Mother's eyes. Frantic, she threw herself into a chair, clenched fingers on the arm rest. "Test me! You'll see! I really don't know!"

Expression unchanged, Mother strode back to her desk, slapped a hand on the comm panel. Letticia didn't even try to stop the shriek as its probes sank into her nerves. *Let* Mother see her suffer! Maybe she'd believe her then. Maybe, if it hurt bad enough, this time she'd *care*.

The agony faded eventually. Letticia slumped over the arm rest, listening to herself pant.

"You really don't know." Mother just sounded tired.

"Surprise." She never would, either, if she didn't get back in Net. She didn't dare let herself think about what could happen if somebody else found the fool first. "So do you believe me now?"

"No." Something like the shadow of a smile crossed Mother's face. "Though that is perhaps a less thorough 'no' than it was." Hugging herself she paced away from her desk. "Are you truly interested in redeeming yourself?"

"I just proved it, didn't I?" Letticia barely managed to push herself upright. Even that bit of movement made her nerves scream. "Just tell me what you want me to do."

"Prove I am not your target."

"*How?* I don't know where that assassin is! You have to let me sync if you want me to find him."

"'How' is your concern. Mine is to learn whether you can be trusted to manage the kind of power marrying Strongarm would give you." Mother touched a patch, frowned at whatever the feed showed her.

Oh, gob it all. Letticia sank back in the chair, not caring that its damned sensors would pick up her despair. But then – gobbing was indeed the answer, wasn't it? She'd never thought of the *power* Strongarm controlled. Lines of probability fell into place. Oh, yes. Yes, indeedy. All she had to do was gob Strongarm and nothing else would matter. Even Mother wouldn't dare threaten her then. Letticia snapped her hands into her lap before the sensors picked up the satisfaction in her readings.

Mother lifted the frown to Letticia. "You have two days."

"Yes, Mother. Thank you, Mother." She managed not to let it sound sarcastic. Simply pushed herself out of the chair, curtsied and turned for the door.

"Letticia."

She paused enough to peer back over her shoulder at the – what was it, danger? Sorrow? – in Mother's tone.

"Be forewarned: you are no longer the only candidate Strongarm is considering. During that time I shall be weighing the alternative."

"Of course, Mother. You do what you have to." As would she.

....

For some reason Teufelsman was waiting outside the door to her quarters. Man looked like a skinny white rabbit. An impatient rabbit at that, shifting from foot to foot as if he were bursting with secrets. He started to tell her something, but Letticia shoved past him before her major domo even had the door fully open.

She had to get Strongarm gobbed before Mother used that 'alternative'. Or found that fool of a Ta'an. Her fingertips burned. Letticia frowned down at them and she realized she was clawing the synclink. Nothing! The whole gobbing *universe* at her fingertips and she was trapped *here*, helpless, in this useless, stupid body. She had to find a way back into Net, she had to! There'd be no hiding anything otherwise. As soon as that assassin passed a scanner – a doorway, transport, anything – he would trigger *her* ID. Which was exactly what that sonuvabitch Marsden was watching for.

She snatched up the first thing that came to hand – a vase of some sort – and fired it at the hulking totem in the far corner. The vase shattered in a watery spray, leaving stalks of red flowers clinging to the dark wood. And Teufelsman swiping ceramic chips off his white jacket. He pulled one of those inevitable porta-scans out of a jacket pocket, checked it for water damage. The swell of jealousy didn't make her feel any better. But it did give her an idea.

She had to be careful; that bastard Marsden would have a spyline sync'd into her major domo. She looked around for something else to throw. Found a nice pot of fragrant oil some idiot had thought would improve her moods. She snatched it up and fired it at her major domo's treacherous red eye. The pot shattered the unit's lens. She'd half expected it to shriek. But it only sent a swarm of spidery servobots scuttling up the wall to attend their master. Choking back glee, Letticia yanked award plaques off their wall mounts. Fired them at the walls where Marsden's other spy eyes would be embedded.

Being an Aryan, Teufelsman caught on quickly. He ran his porta-scan across the walls. Red winkled across its display, sign he'd neutralized the watchers she'd missed. Puffing from the effort, Letticia turned to smile appreciation.

"Lieutenant." She said it nice. But the gobbing ass jumped as if she'd thrown something at *him*. She hid the annoyance and circled back to him. "Whatever are you doing?"

"I am assigned to escort you, Mistress. You seemed to want me to follow you. So I did." He pocketed the porta-scanner, clamped an arm over its pocket. "Captain Marsden's spy eyes will not remain neutralized for very long."

"Long enough, perhaps, for a mutually useful conversation."

"May I remind you, Mistress, that I am under loyalty oath to the Protector?" Being an Aryan, he made it sound like that could be changed.

"Oh, I'd never dream of doing anything to subvert your loyalty. I just want to ask for your help." Letticia circled him, forced herself to run a fingertip along his shoulder line.

"How?" Vile bastard positively ducked away from her. Useless. Gobbing idiot must like boys.

Letticia sighed and strolled over to throw herself in her defiled sync chair. "Help me get back into Net."

"I take it your lady mother still has you locked out of Net?"

"If she didn't I wouldn't need your help, would I?" Her fingertips hurt. Letticia realized she was clawing the remnants of the synclink again. She sucked on her bleeding flesh and tried not to glare at him.

"I should not think that was such a difficulty." He massaged his jaw, as if he were really thinking about it. He only succeeded in looking like he was trying to wipe off something greasy. "Not for a syncmeister of your renown."

"Just what is that supposed to mean? Gob it, I don't have to take zit from some gobbing Aryan!" She looked around for something really slimy to throw at him.

"Forgive me, Mistress. I was merely stating a known truth. Your command of NetMind is the standard against which all other syncmeisters are measured."

"And they all hate me for it, too. *Everybody* hates me." Except maybe Strongarm – he just wanted to gob her. She didn't want to think about that, either. The reality – the unavoidable *physicality* – of what she had to do was finally sinking home. She sucked harder on her fingers to stop herself form heaving the remnants of her breakfast up on the floor.

"Perhaps you should make your point, Mistress." Teufelsman swept an arm toward the servobots swarming the major domo's eye. "The privacy won't last long."

"I don't need long. You have Net access second only to dear Captain Marsden."

"So? That does not mean I can override your lady mother's orders." But he was definitely listening. His smile sent chills down her spine.

"You don't need to. You just need to be... yourself."

"I confess I am flattered. Though for one so well versed in..." – he made a show of searching for a word – "creative sync-management, I should think a syncmeister of Marsden's caliber would be better suited to your purpose."

"Well, of course he would. Only Marsden belongs to Jezekiah, doesn't he?" She reached for the chair's link automatically. Got nothing but dead metal. Her gut wrenched with the loss. She slammed her fist against the link in frustration and glared up at Teufelsman. "You're the only person with the access level I need. And you're an Aryan. Everybody expects you to pop up in places where you don't belong."

"I shall take that as a compliment, Mistress." Teufelsman salaamed, managing to make even the courtesy seem sinister. "Now, if I may: I am here as your escort. It seems your doggy guests wish to tour the island. Milord Jezekiah wishes you to act as tour guide." He started for the door. Paused, and pulled out the scanner. He made a show of adjusting a setting, then pointed it at the wall. "The animals are already waiting for you."

For once Jezekiah was handing her precisely the opportunity she wanted. If only – "Wait!"

Teufelsman lowered the scanner, lifted one silky white brow. 'Rabbit' was the wrong animal for him, Letticia decided. The fellow was a snake. "You don't have to do anything! I just need your ID."

"Indeed." He re-pocketed the scanner, folded arms across his chest. "How?"

"Build me a sync glove. Like the one Marsden built for Admiral Yakamoto." She realized she'd been plucking at a loose thread in her sleeve. Quite a few of them, actually. Lousy tailor. Letticia pushed herself out of the chair, bit her lips to stop herself from pleading. "You can arrange that."

"That would actually be doing quite a bit, Mistress. It would also be most dangerous. I'd have to find a way around Captain Marsden's node guards –"

"Don't try to sawyer me. You've been spying on Marsden for years. I pegged your spiders often enough." She gave him back one of his serpentine smiles.

"That does not make such an undertaking any less dangerous."

Gobbing, *miserable* son of a bitch! He was playing with her, she could feel it. "I'll make it worth your while. Name your price, Teufelsman. You want money? Get me back in sync and I can make you richer than you ever dreamed."

"Your lady mother pays a fair and honorable wage, Mistress. I have quite enough money, thank you."

"Then what?" She glanced at her bed, swallowed revulsion. Might as well lose it to a human; that dog Strongarm wasn't likely to care. "You want to gob me?" She yanked open her neckline, bared her breasts. "Get me that glove and it's all yours."

"Thank you, but allow me to decline the honor." Vile bastard didn't even *look*. He kept those watery blue eyes on her *face*.

Tears of pent-up rage and frustration burned down her cheeks. She didn't even care that he'd see them. "*Then what do you want?*"

"Why, to serve your lady mother." Teufelsman pulled out the porta-scanner. "And to avoid a personal appointment with Admiral Yakamoto's swords." He touched his thumb to its screen. This time green flickered across its surface. Rendering Marsden's spy eyes active again.

Letticia threw herself at him, clawing for his eyes. Teufelsman simply skipped out of range. He let her fall. She managed to avoid mashing her nose, but she felt her nipples shrink against the cold granite of the floor.

Teufelsman didn't even bother to offer her a hand up. She heard his comm link buzz. Pushed herself up, yanking her bodice closed while he slid fingers into his pocket link. She looked around, looking for anything to take her mind off the thought of sync. Saw that the servo bots had finished repairing her major domo. A fresh red eye stared down at her from the wall. Somehow, the unit's stare seemed absolutely hostile.

"If I may make a suggestion, Mistress-" Cloth rustled as Teufelsman re-pocketed his link. "It would be a good idea to hurry. It seems your dogs have already left."

Keeping her curses to herself, Letticia hauled herself into her bathroom and told the major domo to start her bath.

It wasn't hard to track the Lupans down. Letticia suspected Teufelsman could have tracked them just by word of mouth even if they hadn't sported such glaring sync-Ds. Wasn't hard to spot Mother's guest car, either, when Teufelsman finally caught up with them. It gleamed like a fat, pearly egg on the broken gray tarmac marking Punchbowl.

Gobbing dogs just *had* to pick Punchbowl. There'd been a cemetery up here once, some ancient relic of some NorthAm war. Jungle had long since reclaimed most of it, leaving only a wide green circle in the jutting gray ruins around it. Greenery and ruins alike ended where the hillside dropped away. Beyond there was nothing but open air clear out to Honolulu Harbor and Sand Island below. If she strained her eyes, she could see Pearl Harbor to the west. Even from here she recognized the faint thuds of the harbor's massive loading cranes through the wind. Why couldn't the stupid dog have chosen Pearl Harbor? Someplace *flat*. Someplace safe.

She *hated* hillsides, hated the way the open space left her defenseless. Left her listening for the *zing* of laser fire, waiting for the blast. She closed her eyes, fought down the urge to tell Teufelsman to take her back. She *had* to gob that damned dog. It was her only chance. Either that or Jezekiah would make sure she had her own personal appointment with Admiral Yakamoto and his swords.

Her palms were sweating again. Letticia started to wipe them on her skirt, remembered in time that she'd chosen the pink velvet. She wiped them on the buttery leather of the seats instead; Mother would forgive her for staining the seat as long as she brought Strongarm in. She breathed deep, ran through a calming finance calc. Reminded herself that she looked good: a full skirted dress in pink velvet with just a sprinkling of jewels – pearl ear clasps, a ruby collar, a couple of ruby and pearl rings, nothing overwhelming. She felt for the sync link in her skirt pocket, found her fingers wiggling through the hole where her link had been and suppressed a whimper. Oh, they'd pay for that theft, all of them! Once she owned Strongarm.

Teufelsman told their car to settle beside Mother's on the remnants of the ancient parking lot. That kept them well back from the brink of the hill. Maybe Strongarm would know enough to come meet her at the car. Likely not. But at least it let her postpone the inevitable for another minute or two.

A blast of salted air hit her as the car swung open Teufelsman's door. The Aryan bulled into it. He ambled around the car, made her an exaggerated offer of his pale hand. He reminded her, suddenly, of a great, white maggot with his white-blond hair whipping around his pale face above that pure white suit. Letticia accepted his proffered hand, but his touch gave her shudders. Fortunately, he was too stupid to think her shudder belonged to anything more than the wind. Which wasn't all that wrong, actually. The damned air tried to snap her skirt up around her waist the second she stepped clear of the car. But she saw the advantage despite the wind's evil intent. Couldn't hurt to let Strongarm get a glimpse of what he wanted.

Except the stupid dog wasn't looking.

Strongarm and that vile Kaitin-whatever-his-name had wandered straight to the edge of the cliff where the crumbling skeletons of old buildings edged Punchbowl's green. Strongarm stood head down, arms folded across his chest, the wind rippling silver through the mane along his back and shoulders. Staring out at toward Pearl Harbor in the distance.

Actually, he didn't look half bad, at least not from a distance. His whole body proclaimed raw animal power. She tried to imagine letting him touch her, *enter* her. Surprisingly, her body answered the image with prickles in all sorts of interesting places.

He felt her presence, too, she was sure of it. He cocked an ear in her direction, then turned to follow the ear. The afternoon sun lit his amber eyes for a moment as he swung around to face her. Gave them a feral gleam, gave the hair dusting his body a silver sheen to match the massive torque round his neck. Odd. The little patch of hair between her legs tingled at the sense of his brute strength. Definitely an intriguing sensation. Might even be pleasant to explore it.

Only the great brute lacked the manners to come to her. That nasty Kaitin creature wandered over instead, enough gold work hemming his emerald robes to fund a bank. Letticia tried to will one of the circling sea gulls to make a deposit on him. *That* would wipe the sneer off his face!

Kaitin stopped well short of arm's length. He at least had the decency to salaam. Somehow he even managed to turn the billow of green chiffon into a part of the gesture. "One rejoices you have seen fit to join us."

She might have believed him if he hadn't lifted a lip to expose that ruby-tipped fang. Or jammed hands on hips, elbows out, so all she could see was emerald chiffon billowing inward on the golden frame of his robe. She made a mental note to make sure she got a lock on the design schematic for the material; Octavian would trade his nictating membranes for chiffon that could hold such weight. Once she owned Strongarm. For now ... With a sniff, Letticia moved to step around the overgrown cat.

She found herself staring at a gem-encrusted chest. She blinked up, struggling to keep her temper down. "Just what do you think you're doing? You are blocking my way."

"Indeed. This one had not noticed." Kaitin did not move.

Letticia glanced back furtively for Teufelsman's protective presence. He was there, all right. Well and safely behind her and sneaking a peek at his scanner. Useless Aryan. She hid a moue of disgust, lifted her chin regally to the cat. Tall as she was, she still had to look up at him. "I have orders to show Strong- my *betrothed* around the island. You are interfering with the Protector's orders."

"One regrets the inconvenience." He stroked a long white mustache but didn't move otherwise. "Apologies will be made. But perhaps you will allow us to reschedule, yes?"

"Allow me to suggest you listen, Mistress." She'd forgotten Teufelsman.

The unexpected feel of his breath on her ear made her cringe. "Scan shows live weapons in the ruins. But no Type codes. It's a Tong trap."

Tong – the thought dried Letticia's tongue, raised a fresh wetness on her palms. Memory welled up, the slam-punch of the blast, Daddy's warm blood spattering all over her face... She couldn't take that again! She lifted a foot to step back. And remembered the sneer on Yakamoto's face. The kill-lust in his eyes. He'd get his kill if she failed, wouldn't he? Jezekiah would see to that. Gobbing Strongarm was her only chance. Once she had the dog bedded she would handle Jezekiah and Ho Tong both.

She set her shoulders, shook the terror off. "Ho Tong wouldn't dare harm *me.*" She shoved past Kaitin, strode toward the cliff edge to meet Strongarm. Behind her, she heard Teufelsman muttering as he scrambled to catch up. She sensed rather than saw Kaitin swirl his robes around an arm and circle back to match her.

She ignored it, concentrated on the way her pulse jumped as she approached Strongarm. "Lord Strongarm." She held her hands out, fingers dangling so he could kiss them.

"Mistress Van Buren. You honor us with your presence." Even with the wind slapping her ears, Letticia felt Strongarm's voice in her bones. Only the silly dog salaamed instead, leaving her hands hanging awkwardly.

She dropped them quickly and waited for him to say something. He didn't. Just stood there, looking awkward, like a puppy dog trying to hide a puddle. She'd just have to work around him, obviously. "You can't see anything useful from up here, you know. Wouldn't you rather see Pearl Harbor?"

"Not just yet." He added what she hoped was a smile. "I fear it would wrench my heart."

Yes, well, the view past his elbow was wrenching her stomach. "Oh, you don't have to actually go out onto the water. There's nothing of interest out there anyway."

"I would have said the most important part was on the water. Or under it, rather. For some reason, I thought I'd be able to see the *Arizona* monument from here."

Whatever the hell that was. Odd, though, the way he glanced back over his shoulder. Maybe he'd spotted the guns Teufelsman was talking about, too. Oh, if only she had a link!

Strongarm looked like he'd already forgot her. He had his head down, angled over his shoulder. Almost like he was listening to something.

Oh, well; she didn't need a link to talk about shipping stats. "*Do* let me show you around. Pearl is the islands' main deep water port. At full capacity we can offload, process, and transship seven hundred thousand tons per day. We-"

"*We*, on the other hand, are men." Kaitin's purr made her jump. "Allow this one to suggest you save your tour for Pandar's traders. The onlie merchants may find fodder tonnage of interest." The Bengali ran orange-furred fingers through his white mustaches, then stretched in a ripple of gold-rimmed green.

"Oh, really?" Letticia realized her fists had balled. Oh, she'd teach him to get on her nerves. Later. She realigned her smile for Strongarm. "I'm sure we can find plenty of other ...*occupations* to interest you." She let the hint dangle, fluttered lashes until Strongarm recognized it. He rewarded her with a gaze so intent she felt it in her gut. Ah, now that was more like it! Letticia closed in to lay her hand on his arm –

And the stupid dog *ducked*. "I fear I must postpone the pleasure, Mistress. A question has come up that I really must answer first." He definitely looked over his shoulder this time. Or rather he lifted an elbow and looked under it. Perked ears downward until a barefoot islander girl in a faded red sarong finally edged into sight.

Silly little monkey didn't even know enough to curtsy. She simply scuffed a brown toe against the tarmac then visibly remembered to bow. Even that looked absent-minded. She was far more interested in eyeing the roof tops of the adjacent ruins.

Behind Letticia, Teufelsman hissed. She glanced a question at him, gave it up. Useless. He had that glazed look of someone who'd just been shot between the eyes. She poked him with an elbow to snap him awake. She asked the obvious question with the lift of a brow.

"Yakamoto!" Teufelsman's hiss was serpentine enough to make Letticia half-expect to see a forked tongue slip out between his lips.

"Who? Oh!" So that was why the girl looked familiar! She was the Admiral's daughter. The connection clicked home and Letticia hissed herself. This was the little bitch Jezekiah had used to upstage her on the dock. Jezekiah's tool.

And now she was interfering again. The rest of the implications fell into place. Letticia felt the muscles in her neck clench. So dear Jezekiah was hedging his bets. Giving her competition. Giving Strongarm an *alternative*. Letticia nudged Teufelsman harder.

"Get rid of her!" She kept her smile on lock down, kept the command to a sidelong whisper.

"Yes, Mistress. With pleasure, Mistress." The way Teufelsman licked his lips it was actually surprising his tongue *wasn't* forked.

The Aryan stepped past Letticia, spreading his hands out from his sides. That was a standard peace gesture. But for some reason all three of those animals came on guard. Teufelsman stopped, hands out, looking lost.

"Now, really!" Letticia took a pace forward. "Lord Strongarm, surely you're aware that you're supposed to be interested in *me*. I'm the one you need to go- ah, marry in order to seal your treaty." She wiggled fingers dismissively at the Yakamoto monkey. "Not some whoring little monkey."

Oh, Jezekiah's little bitch didn't like *that*, now, did she? For a moment, she looked like she was ready to make a fight of it. Teufelsman certainly thought so: he made a show of sliding between herself and the monkey, one hand slipping into his jacket pocket. But the Yakamoto girl bowed, finally, and started to walk away.

It was Strongarm who stopped her. He dropped a hand on the girl's shoulder, pointed those wolf's ears at Letticia over Teufelsman's head. "Mistress Yakamoto is here in response to my request. If you will be so kind as to allow us half an hour, we shall be at your disposal."

"Half an hour! What for?" Then she remembered the Yakamoto girl was Jezekiah's tool and a fresh terror rose in her throat. "I'm the one you're supposed to gob, not her!"

"That's *not* what he meant, Mistress." Heavens, the little monkey answered for herself. "Lord Strongarm asked me to check something out for him. I'm getting him his answer. That's *all* I'm doing." Impertinent little bitch was snippy about it, too.

Letticia opened her mouth to retort. Nothing came out. The terror was blocking her throat.

Damn Jezekiah! Damnhimdamnhimdamnhimdamnhim… He'd set her up. *Used* her, and lied about it. It was his bed wench he wanted to Impress Strongarm, not her! Oh, it was starting to make sense, now! *He'd* control the Lupans, if his monkey controlled Strongarm. He'd be Mother's shining boy all over again. And she'd be dead.

Letticia swallowed the terror. She *couldn't* let him get away with it, not this time. She took a rolling step forward, elbowing Teufelsman aside. Forced her lips into a smile for Strongarm. "Did your little joy toy tell you she's Jezekiah's bed wench? Or that there are snipers on the roof tops up there?"

"That's a lie!" If it hadn't been for Strongarm's restraining paw, the monkey would have leaped at her.

"Is it?" Teufelsman slid forward. He held his scanner out, nearly shoved it into Kaitin's paw.

The overdressed cat hissed, but checked the reading. Growling, he nodded to Strongarm then shoved the instrument back at Teufelsman hard enough to make the Aryan stagger.

"You see, milords? Live weapons – but no living bodies. That is Ho Tong's signature." Teufelsman made a point of looking up to follow the monkey's line of sight toward the crumbling old buildings up slope. "Perhaps you should wonder just whose orders she is following. She is, after all, a known Tong operative."

"So lack you, Teufelsman!" The little monkey remembered she had a voice. Amazingly, she ducked out from under Strongarm's grip and started forward, hands up. "Captain Marsden's told you often enough. I'm working with Sec, not Ho Tong."

"Indeed." Teufelsman slipped the scanner back into its holder. "Then why bring the Van Burens' off world guests *here*? So far from the Manor – and the protection of Van Buren Sec?"

"Because this's where Grand-" Yakamoto cut the word off.

"Because this is where Grandfather Ho told you to come." Teufelsman finished for her. He spread his hands to the dogs, looking satisfied. "You see, Milords? The monkey is not to be trusted. Allow me to remove her." He reached to take Yakamoto's arm.

To Letticia's surprise, it was Kaitin who blocked him. "You have made your point, flat tooth. Now allow us to proceed. We have yet questions to which we seek answers."

"Oh, for heaven's sake! If your silly questions are that important, then just sync in!" *They* still could. Letticia's fists clenched with jealousy at the thought. Jealousy – and the makings of a beautiful idea.

She settled hands on hips, made sure the sunlight glinted off her jewels as she strolled past the Yakamoto girl in that cheap sarong. "My *dear* Strongarm, there's no question I can't answer – in Net. Maybe we can serve both purposes at once." The idiot didn't take the hint. Heavens, even a dog couldn't be stupid enough to bypass a Van Buren for a second-hand monkey! "I hear Lupan males establish a psychic connection when they mate. Why don't we see if we can establish a joint link? Together, I bet we could re-write the manual on sex." She rolled her hips provocatively, the way they did in every porn vid she'd ever seen. "Let's go back to the Manor and test the theory out, shall we?"

"The answer I seek is one that cannot be found in your NetMind, Mistress." Had the stupid dog been human, Letticia would have thought he'd shuddered. "I ask only half an hour's grace. Be so good as to grant the request."

"Why? So you can gob Jezekiah's little bitch instead of me?" The wind turned all that hair he'd shed into a stinging mist. Letticia batted at it. She wished she could bat *him*.

"I am well aware of the pledge I have made to your brother and yourself." The very air seemed to rumble of a sudden. Letticia realized with a jolt that Strongarm was growling.

"One suggests you go now." That Kaitin creature pursed lips at her, golden eyes bright above the ruby fang. "We will join you when we have our answer."

"But I'm supposed to be the one you want!" Fear made Letticia hurl herself at Strongarm.

She found herself staring at the Yakamoto girl instead. "Think you better take the hint, Mistress."

"My, my." Teufelsman stepped past Letticia. He looked as if he were beginning to enjoy himself. "The monkey attacked Mistress Van Buren! You all witnessed it!"

"Hell I did, Teufelsman! I just didn't get out of her way." Small as the monkey was, the death stare she gave Teufelsman stopped him mid-step.

"That is for the Protector to decide. Now come along quietly, girl."

"Told you before, snowball. I kill myself before I let you touch me."

"Oh, I don't think that will be necessary." Teufelsman reached into his pocket, pulled out a slender black neural rod.

"The young lady is here at my specific request. That makes me responsible for her well-being." Strongarm stepped up to join the Yakamoto monkey before Letticia could protest. He reached to place one massive paw on Yakamoto's shoulder. And got it slapped aside.

"I fight my own battles." Yakamoto sidled away to face down Teufelsman. "You know damned good and well I'm not going with you, snowball. You got a charge to make, make it to Madam Van Buren. Milords here will tell her the truth. I'm just keeping a promise."

Oh, the little bitch was going to ruin everything! "Get her *out* of here," Letticia screamed at Teufelsman. "*Now!*"

"Yes'm." Teufelsman flicked the neural rod so it gleamed darkly in the sun. "Don't make me hurt you, girl. Come along quietly."

"No." Yakamoto's hands came up, circling.

It was like watching a pair of snakes dance. Teufelsman edged sideways, wand tracing dainty figure eights in front of him. Yakamoto sidestepped when Teufelsman lunged. Her backhand sounded like a whip's snap. And left blood on Teufelsman's cheek.

Teufelsman touched the cut on his cheek. He blinked down at the blood on his fingers almost in wonder. The wonder turned to rage when he looked up. He feinted at her face, then ducked low, swinging the rod at her stomach.

Yakamoto jackknifed around the wand. With a snort of triumph, Teufelsman lunged in to finish the job. Yakamoto twirled aside to kick him behind the knee. Teufelsman dropped. He was up instantly. Wand out, he sprang at her, teeth bared.

Yakamoto kicked Teufelsman's feet out from under him as he passed. She kicked his wand hand as he fell, making Letticia skip frantically as the wand skittered across the grass toward her toes. Damp grass streaked Teufelsman's white linen suit with green as he rolled. He came up in a roar of rage to launch himself at the girl.

And snapped backward as Yakamoto's kick caught him on the chin. She snapped him forward again with a kick in the stomach. He dropped to his knees, doubled over and retching.

"Get up!" Mortified, Letticia tried to will Teufelsman to his feet.

The Aryan just huddled, gagging helplessly in the grass. Shaming her.

Beside her, that nasty Kaitin stroked his mustaches, eyes on the ruins. "If you are through toying, kill him and be done. One suspects your grandfather and these birds alike are losing patience."

"I'm not a killer." Yakamoto sidled around Teufelsman to face up to Kaitin.

"This one needs killing, though." Strongarm put in. "You've bested him in front of women and warriors." He ambled closer to Teufelsman, who was doing his retching best to crawl away. "There will be no making peace with him after this."

"Maybe. He ought to have the chance anyway."

"Your heart is greater than your experience, little one. I fear for you if this one lives. He will not forgive you today."

Odd – Letticia couldn't quite place what changed. But suddenly Strongarm scared her.

Yakamoto didn't move. "Milord, this *mahe's* been trouble for me since I was sixteen. I think maybe now he'll learn to keep his hands to himself."

Heavens, the little monkey was *protecting* Teufelsman. *Her* Aryan, *her* champion! Making her look small! *Damn* Teufelsman! How could he do this to her? Letticia swept past Kaitin, grabbed Strongarm's wrist and yanked.

The great brute snapped around – ears flat, mane haloed, those yellow eyes narrowed above bared fangs …. She couldn't even shriek. If Kaitin hadn't been in her way, she'd have taken her chances on the hillside. Instead she could only try to hide within the emerald curtain of the Bengali's wind-whipped robes.

Strongarm's nose twitched. He shook himself. Head only, first, then bent hands on knees to shake his whole body doggy fashion. The animal gleam was gone when he straightened.

"Forgive me." Strongarm salaamed, a bit too off-hand for Letticia's taste. "I had not meant to scare you."

"Oh, you don't scare *me*." Letticia felt more than heard Kaitin's grunt. She almost elbowed him for it, decided it might not be wise. She forced herself to smile at Strongarm instead. "If you want to kill him, by all means do. Consider him my gift." Heavens knew he wasn't much of one.

Teufelsman whimpered, but Strongarm only shrugged. "His life is not mine to claim either way, Mistress Van Buren. If you want him dead, it seems you must kill him yourself."

Oh, yes, and explain *that* to Mother! Oh, she'd get even with Teufelsman. But she needed to deliver this damned dog first. Bracing herself, Letticia sauntered out of the shelter of Kaitin's robes. "Then why don't we just forget this whole silly incident? Let's go find a nice, private place to explore what *you* want." She added a simper. Even managed to make herself run a fingertip along the great beast's forearm. Amazing – his arm just *throbbed* with raw animal power. The sensation triggered an answering throb in the hairy thatch between her legs. She saw Strongarm's nose twitch. Felt his gaze intensify the way it had last night. She was close enough to hear his breath go ragged.

He slipped a finger beneath hers. Lifted her hand as if it weighed a thousand pounds. Letticia found her lips parting in anticipation. "Half an hour, Mistress." He picked her up and set her aside with intense care. Then jerked his head at the other two animals and stalked toward the ruins. Walked off with that *monkey* in tow.

Heart still pounding Letticia could only gape after him. He'd walked away from her. He'd caught her interest; she knew it. He knew she wanted him and he still walked away from her. *With Jezekiah's monkey.* Her mind couldn't even form words, couldn't *think* at all. Her whole being was absorbed in the horror of such absolute, utter betrayal. And there was nothing she could do about it. She had no hope, no defense without Net.

"Mistress–" Teufelsman had recovered enough to get his backside on the ground. He sat clutching his knees, gasping.

The useless piece of shit. Letticia kicked him in the ribs, good and hard. Left a dusty footprint on his jacket as a memento.

Teufelsman wheezed. For a moment Letticia thought he was going to puke. But he only rolled onto his knees, clutched at her hand. "Mistress, I can help you."

"It's too late for that now, isn't it?" She kicked at him again, but the Aryan was recovered enough to dodge, leaving her hopping to regain balance.

"Not yet." Clutching his side, Teufelsman lurched to his feet. "I'll get you that sync glove. Get you all the access you want." He gripped her arm and his expression went ugly. "But the monkey's mine."

His palm was sweaty. Letticia shook him off, wiped his sweat off on his jacket shoulder. "Then in that case, let's go. We have work to do."

XXIII

Pearl City had been a busy town once, back before the Schism. Up here the wind off the ocean carried the faint booms of Pearl Harbor's port equipment along with the sweet scent of the oleander bushes lining the hillside below. The jungle had pretty much reclaimed the remains of the apartment buildings the ancients had stacked up the hillside. Wasn't much of them left now except empty windows in skeleton walls held together by wisteria vines and ivy. One or two green walls still sported curly glass tubes that Grandfather said used to be happy colored *neon* signs. All that was left now were glass tubes all broken and bleached to gray. Still, must have been a fancy area once: even down here at ground level the hillside offered a heart-stopper view clear out to Pearl Harbor.

Keiko reminded herself to keep calm while Strongarm picked his way across the broken tarmac of an ancient parking lot. He and Grandfather both wanted a meeting, so everybody would be happy once Grandfather showed up. More importantly, Grandfather would be happy with *her*. Happy enough, she hoped, to ease up on Kameh when she asked.

Strongarm had stopped just shy of the low concrete wall marking the edge of the cliff. He folded his arms and braced his feet apart to stare out toward Pearl Harbor like some modern king surveying his realm with the ocean wind whipping his mane into silver waves.

Keiko worked her way past the wedges of old tarmac to join him. "You're still looking for the *Arizona*."

"Been looking for it all my life." He *uhfed* softly. "Should have known-"

"It's still there, you know. Can't see it from way up here, but the battleship's still there."

"I'm surprised you know. Most onlie histories cover only the Unity Wars."

"Oh, I know all about that old attack on Pearl Harbor. Story of my life: my father's people dropped the bombs and my mother's ran for cover." Keiko snorted in disgust, not all of it due to the Admiral's brass-assed teaching; the wind was doing its damnedest to flap her sarong open. She inched closer to

Strongarm, hoping she could put him between herself and the wind without getting caught. "The place is still sacred to the people. Legend says she went down with a thousand of her crew."

"It's not legend."

"Really?" Suspicion set in. "How'd you know? LupanType didn't even exist back then."

"Because I'm human, too, in case you forgot." He turned those amber eyes her way, lifted an ear the way Jezekiah Van Buren would an eyebrow. "It so happens one of the men entombed there was named Worth Lightfoot." His chin came down, challenging her. "He was my many times great-grandfather."

"Oh. Sorry."

A snoopy seagull snuck down to see if Strongarm's ears were edible. Strongarm clipped fingers against its beak without looking. Insulted, the gull backed wings and flapped off.

Strongarm watched the bird retreat thoughtfully. "We have no birds on Den Lupus. I think I shall have to import some." He grinned down at her, looking mischievous. "It will remind me of you."

He certainly looked cheerful. So why was her battle sense acting up? Keiko rolled her neck, ran a quick eyeball on the rooftops above them while she tucked a wind-blown fold of her sarong back into place. Must be some *nui* danger – Sweet Madam Pele, even her *arm* was prickling.

Wasn't a warning prickle, either. A tingly kind of warmth ran up her arm, mushroomed into a flood when it reached her chest. It cascaded downward to trigger a throb between her legs, a physical need so strong it quickened her breath. She locked knees together, frowned down at her arm. Realized with a shock that Strongarm had his hand on it.

"My, my. How fast the children forget." Kaitin reached a green and gold swathed arm past her, removed Strongarm's hand from her arm with black talon tips. Didn't look like he was any too gentle about it, either: blood dewed Strongarm's wrist where his talons touched.

Praise Tutu Pele Kaitin wasn't angry at *her*. He was downright careful the way he shifted her bodily out of Strongarm's reach. "Has it occurred to none else that we were called to this place for ambush? There is cover enough for a flat tooth battalion up there. One suggests there are better places and ways to die."

"Been trying to avoid that line of thought myself." Strongarm shook himself, rubbing his palms on his arms hard enough to dust the wind with silver hair. He perked those wonderful silky ears down at Keiko, part question, part challenge.

"Grandfather Ho only wants to say aloha." It was the truth. Only – Keiko rubbed a hand across the back of her tingling neck, feeling her gut tighten. For once she welcomed battle sense. Gave her something to worry about beside the sudden wetness between her legs. Gave her a reason to pretend her knock-kneed wiggle was due to the wind. She focused on the worry with determination. Grimly, she forced herself to hold faith in Grandfather's promise. He'd never lied to her before, so far as she knew. She remembered Kameh's aborted warning and dismissed it. He'd just been upset was all.

Only Kaitin was right: the place *was* an ambush. Grandfather had shooters up there; she could feel the death threat. If he'd left orders, they'd all be dead and disposed of before any Sec team thought to come looking. Admiral would die of mortification if she screwed up that bad. "Maybe Grandfather got sidetracked somewhere. Why don't I see you two home? We can set up a meet some other time." And some other, happier place. She refused to let herself think what the delay might cost Kameh.

Strongarm only *uhfed*. "If I can't defend myself against a pack of flat teeth then I deserve to die." He started to pat her arm. Changed his mind when Kaitin growled. He rubbed palms together instead. "Let's give your grandfather a few minutes longer. I have the feeling we're being tested."

"A wise thought, Lord Strongarm."

Grandfather Ho stepped out of the down slope undergrowth, making Keiko's heart try to leap and sink at the same time. He swung one bare leg over the railing, rested himself atop it. The wind ruffled his fine white hair, flapped his loose red and yellow shorts around his knobby knees. Sunlight sparked silver off the band of throwing stars strung around his neck. He held his hands out, palms up in peace sign and the dragon tattoo gleamed where it coiled up his arm. He settled himself down to wait, looking contented as a cat in a fishery.

So why was her neck pounding? Sidelong, she noted how Strongarm had angled to keep ears targeted on the rooftops beyond. She checked Kaitin, felt her mouth go dry. The Bengali shrugged his vest out. He let it billow out in a gold-tinged emerald cloud, then whirled it gracefully around one arm. The motion transformed its gold border into a metal arm guard. Keiko's heart wrenched as he sidled wide of Strongarm, his red and black striped mane bottled. Giving them fighting room.

And Grandfather just sat there, smiling that cat-smile, while battle sense screamed down her neck. Oh, sweet *Tutu* Pele, why did men always have to be so lolo? Arms wide, Keiko skipped backward, putting herself between Grandfather and the Lupans. "Lord Strongarm, Lord Kaitin, this is Grandfather Ho."

"So one assumed." Gold bangles jingled as Kaitin salaamed Grandfather with his free hand. "On the rim the name Ho is synonymous with Tong. And Venus Seed. One hopes the name enjoys greater scope here."

"Greater scope indeed. Yet still synonymous." If Grandfather recognized the danger in the Lupans' matched growls, he didn't show it.

"Your head is worth a respectable princedom on Den Lupus. One wonders the price it carries on Home World." Kaitin stroked black talons across his white mustaches.

"I fear this old head has little value here. As the saying goes, a prophet is without honor in his own land."

"Ho Tong's not known for honor in any other land, either." Strongarm shook himself with an *uhf*. "I know what answers I want, old man. Question is, what are you after?"

"Perhaps to talk trade. Or perhaps merely to talk story."

"One suggests it might almost be worth doing the flat teeth a favor to kill you now." The teardrop ruby sparked red on Kaitin's bared fangs.

Behind Grandfather the brush rustled and Keiko's battle sense flared. She tried to scoot clear of the old man, tried to get a clear focus on the threat hiding in those bushes before some overly eager *mahe* got trigger happy.

Strongarm must have thought the same; whatever he said to Kaitin made the Bengali back off.

"A wise move, Lord Strongarm." Grandfather clamped fingers harder on Keiko's shoulder to hold her in place. "Otherwise we would all die with our questions unanswered, would we not?"

"*Uhf.*" Strongarm twitched his nose. "Still can. Unless you call off your pack."

Grandfather rolled his head. He made it look like he was only stretching, but he managed to sweep those old dark eyes across the roof tops. The pounding behind Keiko's neck eased back to a dull throb. "It delights me to find we understand each other so well, O Lords of Den Lupus. Let us then sit and talk story, as we say in the islands."

"So talk." Strongarm edged away from the railing, nose twitching as he put himself downwind of Grandfather.

Grandfather tapped Keiko's outstretched arm. "Come. Sit with me, *keiki*. Allow these old eyes to feast upon our honored guests." He patted her on the shoulder when she backed to his side. Kept the hand there, gently pulling her down to kneel beside him. "My *keiki* tells me you wish to know whether there are still true humans left on Home World."

"Your bird spoke true."

"Though one would ask the price before the answer." Kaitin lifted a round white ear at Strongarm, got an *uhf* of agreement.

"A wise precaution, but unnecessary. It is a question that concerns all of us. Be so good as to consider the answer my gift. A sign of good will, so to speak."

Sweet Madam Pele, none of this was making sense. Grandfather *said* he meant good will – so why was the air above his dragon arm shimmering? He had to be *nui* angry to set the dragon off. Better, then, that he should take it out on her. At least a beating would take her mind off the shameful, insistent throbbing between her legs.

Keiko twisted free, though it was going to cost her a bruise. "Grandfather, forgive me for interrupting. But Kameh came to see me-"

Oh, that distracted him, all right! For one dreadful moment, he looked so much like the Admiral she braced for a blow. Only Grandfather wasn't like the Admiral; Grandfather just breathed deep and sat back. "Such a visit was not among his instructions."

"I know, Grandfather. But I'm glad he did. He told me you're shipping him out to the rim." She laid a hand on his un-tattooed arm. For the first time, the touch made her want to shudder. She dismissed the unworthy reaction, turned pleading eyes up at him. "You know he doesn't belong out there. Can't you help him? Bring him home?"

Behind her Keiko heard Strongarm *uhf*. "An honorable plea. Are you capable of love enough to honor it?" There was contempt enough in the man's tone to make Grandfather's muscles tense beneath her fingertips.

"The young man my granddaughter champions is a registered killer." Grandfather turned to smile softly down at Keiko. "He has attracted too much attention from the Van Burens' Aryans too often to be safe here in the islands. But I will most certainly not send him off world."

"*Mahalo, Tutukane.* Thank you, Grandfather." Keiko pressed his knuckles to her forehead. Wherever else she'd failed, at least she'd helped Kameh. At least she'd been good for *something* for once.

"One rejoices to learn that even the master of Ho Tong is capable of compassion."

"You think too poorly of me, Lord Kaitin ibn Bengal."

"Good. We're all happy." Strongarm underscored his point by scanning the rooftops beyond. "Now maybe you'll answer the question. Are there still true humans on Earth – yes or no."

"Your legends are true." Grandfather ran a hand across her hair. His touch was easy. But she felt the heat from his dragon arm.

"Pity. One had begun to hope otherwise." In the sudden silence following Kaitin's words, she could hear his pantaloons snapping in the wind.

"It's enough." With a soft *uhf*, Strongarm shook himself and flicked an ear toward their skimmer. "Appreciate the gift, old man. Tell your assassins up there we're leaving in peace."

Keiko tried to rise to go with him, but Grandfather pulled her back. "Ah, but you have not yet heard the story. That is the true gift."

Grandfather never took his eyes off Strongarm, but Keiko's battle sense pulsed. She didn't need to look for the reason. The sudden cant of the Lupans' ears was proof enough the rooftop shadows had shifted into firing position. The way Strongarm and Kaitin bared fangs would've sent anybody else diving over the cliff for safety. Grandfather just smiled.

"I am glad to see you have decided to remain. Let us talk story, then." He swept a hand toward the wall opposite.

Up on the roofs, shadows slipped out of sight. Strongarm noted it with a grunt. His ears relaxed and he backed toward the wall, keeping his hands out. Kaitin opted to stay put, tear drop ruby glittering. Keiko held her breath, but Grandfather chose to ignore the implied threat.

"As you guessed, Lord Strongarm, we of the Tong are the last of the original species. We are the last true humans. The only gene coding we carry was designed by divinity, not some NorthAm gene tech. That is why the Van Burens outlawed us. That was why we rebelled."

Strongarm lifted a lip, baring a massive fang. "Rim folk still talk about that rebellion of yours. Only they claim Ho Tong started it. Because the Van Burens outlawed Venus Seed."

"The Home World Van Burens were hardly likely to outlaw Venus Seed. They need their portion of the profits too much." His hand on Keiko's shoulder clenched, relaxed. "No, our Rebellion was not about profit, or even power. It was about survival. The survival of humanity itself."

Kaitin shook out an emerald fold of in a jangle of gold. "Or perhaps some old Tong lord no longer wished to share the lucre."

Grandfather half rose, making Keiko's heart drop. But he sat back down, salaamed to Kaitin. "Forgive this old man a bit of temper. After all these years, the truth still pains me." He sank back, addressed Strongarm. "You see, it was not greed or power lust that made us finally rise up against our Van Buren war lords. It was a simple story of love betrayed. It is, you see, my *keiki's* story."

"*Heia*, wait a minute!" The injustice of it yanked Keiko's mind off the dewy feeling in her groin. "Don't blame me! I wasn't even born yet!"

"Of course it is not. But your birth is the heart of the story."

"I don't understand–"

"Yet." Grandfather cut Keiko's question off with a gentle pat, though he kept his eyes on Strongarm. "Surely among your legends you have heard that natural women are more alluring than their Typed sisters?"

Sweet Tutu Pele, whatever caused her gut to jump like that? Whatever it was, it bared Strongarm's fangs. "Make your point, old man."

"The point is simple." Grandfather was still smiling, but it sent a shudder down Keiko's spine. "When the people rose up against their oppressors, the Van Burens sent in their Admiral Yakamoto. His Samurai killed our wives, our mothers. Killed our children, in their bright and beautiful innocence. In their thousands, our children died at the hands of the Butcher Yakamoto."

At the hands of her father. Oh, why did he have to bring that up to Strongarm? The shame of it hurt worse than any beating. She saw Strongarm's nose twitch and realized he'd caught the shame in her scent. The muscles around her eyes tightened in answer, tried to squeeze out tears. Keiko shook the burn out and squeezed Grandfather's arm in silent plea.

"Shhh, *keiki*. The story is almost over."

Strongarm *uhfed*, though there was a growl beneath it. "Best end it quick, then. I'll have no part in torturing the poor little bird."

"Control your gallantry a while longer, if you will. Allow me to speak instead of my own daughter, my Lily." Grandfather stroked Keiko's hair softly, almost thoughtfully. "Her true name was Liliuokelani Kaahumana Ho. She was descended through her mother from Kaahumana, favored Queen of King Kamehameha, himself the favored son of the goddess Pele herself. It was she – my daughter, my Lily – who stopped the Butcher Yakamoto's slaughter of our towns."

That didn't sound right. Keiko frowned up at Grandfather. "But you always said your daughter died in the Battle for the Manor."

"So she did. But long before that -" Grandfather pulled in a breath, eyelids drooping. "Lily went to the Butcher. She begged him to convince his Van Buren masters to end the genocide. Begged him to see reason."

Keiko felt his muscles tighten under the skin. She knew how it felt to have to hide the pain, what it took to pretend there were no tears. She fought tears of her own when he lifted her face up.

"But she triggered only lust in the Butcher's heart. So my Lily made a trade: herself for the peace of her people." Grandfather's dark old eyes searched her face, as if he were looking for something he'd lost. "And for a while, the killing did stop. For a year the Samurai and their Van Buren masters talked of peace. They talked long enough and loud enough that even I started to believe them. I even rejoiced when she told me she was carrying Yakamoto's child."

He smiled down at Keiko, one hand stroking her hair. "It wasn't your fault, *keiki*. I regret only that you never knew her." He *looked* simply sorrowful. But something in him made her battle sense tingle. "It is time to correct the omission."

Grandfather rose, lifting Keiko up by the elbow with him. "Lords of Den Lupus, allow me to introduce my true granddaughter: Kaahumana Ho. Daughter of the House of King Kamehameha. Not merely a true human, but a true descendant of the living goddess Pele herself."

It took a second for the fullness of his words to worm past the horror, shape the impossible into a conscious thought. His words shook the walls of her soul. Yet the idea she'd had a real mother – old dreams sparked deep in her heart. Keiko pulled in a breath, held it. She couldn't afford those dreams now any more than she could as a child. Even less, now.

She pulled herself up straighter, forced the truth out between her teeth. "I'm sorry, Grandfather. That's a good story, but it's wrong. You've got me mixed up with somebody else." Her throat was too tight. She gulped air, pushing the tears back out of sight. "My mother wasn't brave or heroic, or... or romantic. She was just-" *Oh, sweet Madam Pele, why did he make her have to say it here?* "Admiral says she was just a tramp."

She feared she'd anger him. But Grandfather didn't seem at all upset. He just smiled his odd little smile and stroked her hair. "That is your father's lie, *keiki*. All these years the Butcher has denied you your true heritage, as he has denied his own."

"Admiral's not a liar, Grandfather." Anger blossomed beneath the hurt, overriding all other feelings. "He's hard and he's mean, but he doesn't lie. If he was lying, then why didn't you tell me?"

"Silence was the only protection I could offer you, *keiki*." There was no anger in Grandfather's expression, only sorrow. Only truth.

The truth that her life was a lie. The truth that he'd betrayed her. Anger welled up hot and red as fresh lava. "You let me think she was no good! You let me think she was a tramp! That I was a tramp! What kind of protection was that?" She tried to jerk free, tried to outrun the pain and shame.

But Grandfather held her in place. "Have you never wondered, *keiki*, why I have always accepted you among the people? You, the daughter of the Butcher Yakamoto?"

"Because-" The question sank shot its point through her heart. *Oh, Tutu Pele, why couldn't she just die? It would have hurt so much less.* "Because I thought you loved me."

The air rumbled, so deep she felt it in her chest. For a moment she thought maybe *Tutu* Pele was really answering. It was only when Grandfather raised his smile that she realized Strongarm was growling.

"Haven't you hurt the little bird enough, old man? Is this what you gift your granddaughter? Sorrow and shame? Or do you torture your girl children for your own amusement?" Keiko lifted her head to see Strongarm step forward, ears flat in a bottled mane, lips peeled back from gleaming fangs.

Odd. She felt his anger as if it were her own. Felt his growl vibrate her chest. Felt something else, too: a sense that she was *protected*. She shook Grandfather's hand off this time. Rose and stepped forward to lift hands to Strongarm in wonder. Saw him – felt him – reach out in answer.

She felt Grandfather's hands hard on her shoulders. And the world spun.

For one insane moment, Keiko thought Grandfather had thrown her over the cliff. She felt her feet leave the ground, felt herself airborne. Then suddenly she was looking out at the world from the emerald cocoon of Kaitin's robes, her shoulders snugged against the downy white hair of his chest, her heart pounding to the rasping purr of his breath. She clung to Kaitin in helplessness, her whole sense of being a dizzying swirl of longing and shame and sorrow.

Through the green mist of his robes she saw Strongarm doubled over, gasping, hands on knees, and realized he felt the dizzy swirl, too. Keiko tried to wriggle free. Tried to reach him, comfort him. Only Kaitin wouldn't let her move. He locked her into an orange-furred grip against his side, blocked her sight of Strongarm with his body. His talon tips raised tandem stings along her shoulders. The sting helped clear her head. She peered up through the emerald haze to see Kaitin bare fangs at Grandfather.

"One salutes your ambition, old man. But the great fool has already chosen his fate. Be grateful it does not include your blood."

Grandfather answered with a snarl that showed yellow teeth. "Why interfere? She will make him a better wife than the Van Buren chit!"

"She would make me your slave." Breathing hard, Strongarm got his head up though his ears stayed flat. "I honor Keiko Yakamoto. But by your own words she is no Maker. She is just a Samurai-natural mix, like a thousand other such on the rim." Somehow, Keiko felt the despair ...the *loss* deep beneath his anger.

Somewhere in the distance a look-out whistled warning, shrill and sharp as the gulls. Grandfather snapped around, turned an almost feral snarl on the rooftop. "It seems I must leave. We have guests in-coming." He swung one brown leg over the railing, paused, then stretched a hand out to Keiko, palm up. Asking forgiveness.

Maybe he did still love her. Maybe all the lies really weren't his fault. Keiko wriggled and this time Kaitin let her go. She was at Grandfather's side in a step. She dropped to her knees beside him, took his hand between hers, touched his ridged knuckles to her forehead in respect.

She felt the heat of the dragon as he passed his free hand across her bowed head. "I have given you sorrow today when I meant only to bring you joy. Allow me, then, to give you some small gift at least."

"You don't need-" Keiko looked up and felt her jaw drop.

Between his fingers, Grandfather held out the band of throwing stars. "Accept this gift, *keiki*. Accept it as proof of who you are."

She tried to swallow. Got nothing – her mouth had gone dry. Admiral would kill her himself, if she got caught with Tong stars. But they were Grandfather's own – *her* Grandfather's gift. Trembling, she lifted the band from his hands and draped it around her neck.

When she looked up Grandfather was gone. Leaving her with his deadly stars dangling from her neck and an aching need in her gut.

And Jezekiah Van Buren striding hellbent for leather across the tarmac toward them with Captain Marsden right behind him.

XXIV

It took Jezekiah an hour longer than he'd anticipated to finish the background check on Keiko Yakamoto. The results frightened him into a summons to Kip and a none-too-formal announcement to the Admiral. He was en route to the Manor's transit dock with a grumbling Kip in tow when the first fleeing Admin op warned him of Letticia's debacle.

Kip cocked his head, scan tracking the waddling op. "You might want to check on your sister first, your lordship. She's got Teufelsman with her. And they both scannin' nasty. I'll look the Mote up for you."

Yes, and quietly stash Keiko well out of Van Buren reach. Hide the girl the way he'd quietly hidden her secrets. Jezekiah quelched the flash of anger. There was no collusion in what Kip had done, just simple human decency. Had his findings been less frightening Jezekiah would have taken him up on the offer. As it was – "No. Just let me know when Strongarm and Kaitin turn up here. The conversation I need to have with the Admiral needs to be private." No need to add that privacy automatically eliminated sync.

Predictably, Keiko was not home when they reached Admiral Yakamoto's house. Even so he felt her presence in the way the scarlet ginger and yellow plumeria flower arrangements reflected the red and gold Samurai crest woven into the silken tapestries draping the walls. Recognized the alternative meaning, too: red and yellow – Ho Tong colors mocking the Family's red and gold banners. The realization wrenched his stomach even as it tightened his heart.

Just as well Keiko wasn't home: none of them were happy by the time the Admiral finished answering Jezekiah's questions. He traded a silent agreement with Kip to waylay Keiko before she could return. She was too important to his plans now to risk having the Admiral force her into a Samurai apology. Which possibility morphed into likelihood when Kip muttered that the Lupans hadn't turned up at the Manor. It was the dread certainty of just where Keiko was – who had sent her there – that sent Jezekiah racing Kip for their skimmer.

They were airborne in an instant. Kip didn't bother with the approved traffic lanes. He arced the skimmer high over Waikiki, rocketed almost straight down toward Punchbowl Crater. Jezekiah spotted the red sliver of Keiko's sarong even before Kip confirmed the Lupans' presence. Along with live weapons readings among the broken rooftops overlooking the rim. Live weapons where scan showed no sign of human life.

Damn and damn again! Damn Strongarm and Lupans and Letticia's syncpsych! Damn *himself* for being an egotistical fool! He could only pray to whatever gods would listen that Grandfather Ho hadn't yet managed to get Keiko into Strongarm's hands. Otherwise the treaty on which he'd staked his freedom and Earth's future went for nothing. He was not going to let that happen. If it wasn't already too late.

Jezekiah closed his eyes, quick-calc'd alternatives while Kip ordered the skimmer to settle on the ancient blue-gray asphalt beside the fat pearl of Mother's guest car. He was out of the skimmer the instant ShipMind slid the door back.

Kip yanked him back. "Goddammit, your lordship! You *tryin'* to get yourself killed? Take a look up there – Old man Ho got himself a whole goddamned army up there."

Jezekiah tracked Kip's finger to the shadowy snipers on the rooftops of the derelict buildings beyond the lot. The sight triggered an instant of pure terror before cold logic kicked in.

It was too soon, yet, for Grandfather Ho to realize Jezekiah had dug up his secrets. He pulled in a calming breath then grinned at the big SecType over his shoulder. Wasn't much else he could do, given the grip Kip had on it. The grip buzzed his shoulder: Kip had his shield up. "Leave it. Grandfather Ho's not after me. Not yet."

"Don't matter who they was aimin' at if you the one gets hit." The shield lent Kip's voice a mechanical buzz.

"They won't shoot. No Tong killer is going to risk disobeying Grandfather's orders. It's not worth that kind of death."

"They might not. That damned assassin would."

"At that range? Even close up he only managed to wing me." Jezekiah tugged at his arm pointedly.

"Yuh-huh. Too bad." Kip relaxed his grip, though only to pop open the storage bin between their seats. He pulled out a shield belt, shoved it into Jezekiah's hand. He cocked his head, listening to scan while Jezekiah slipped it around his waist and punched it on. Whatever Kip picked up, his frown said he didn't like it. "You better hear this, your lordship."

"Tell me on the stride." Jezekiah shoved himself out of the skimmer. He felt the wind buffet him, caught himself missing the scents of ocean and grass the shield filtered out. Just as well the broken tarmac made footing treacherous. Forced him to a diplomatic pace. And gave Kip time to report.

"Got a bud out in Commonwealth Sec just repaid a favor. Your cousin Octavian got an ambassador of his own cleared to planetfall on Den Lupus."

"A woman, of course." He didn't need Kip's affirming grunt to know that.

"Report says she's a SpriteType. With all the bells and whistles." Kip's expression went wistful.

Woman probably came out of Octavian's own harem. Which meant she would be as smart as she was enticing. Good thing the seagulls nosing in to check for handouts made so damned much noise; they kept Strongarm from hearing him swear. She'd have a trade contract in hand, too – and be conditioned to find Lupans sexually exciting, if Octavian held true to form. "What's her ETA?"

"Thirty hours to planetfall, Earth time local." Kip swiveled away enough to sweep his targeting his gaze across the rooftops.

So, then. Octavian already had somebody ready to nibble at his bait – Bengali, most likely. Fair bet the Lupan Parliament would be clued as well. Give Octavian's ambassador a couple of hours to meet'n greet. Another for her to ID her targets and present her case. After that – he could kiss his future and Earth's good-bye. Jezekiah lengthened his stride, footing be damned. Right now, he had a more immediate threat to defuse.

The immediate threat stood barely five feet tall and wore a faded red sarong he remembered only too well. Keiko Yakamoto had her back to Strongarm. The wind off the ocean whipped her hair into dark curls around her face, made the folds of her sarong snap like small arms fire. Even from across the tarmac he felt the yearning in the gaze Strongarm fixed on her back. The protectiveness in her stance said she felt it, too.

Only Kaitin ibn Bengal stood between Strongarm and a Tong end to the treaty. His ears were laid back, his robe wrapped around his arm in shielding green and gold bands. He stroked his long white mustaches while he watched Jezekiah approach. All too clearly running calcs of his own.

Maybe, just maybe, those calcs meant he had an ally – at least until Kaitin ibn Bengal heard about the Pandari option. Jezekiah felt his smile relax. Even temporary cooperation would do as long as it let him get Strongarm away from Keiko.

A Sec skimmer whined overhead scattering seagulls in its wake. Jezekiah lifted a brow at Kip, got a nod of confirmation.

"Called 'im in soon's I spotted those snipers." Kip cocked his head, listened, then snorted. "Nobody in sight now."

"It seems your allies have deserted you," Kaitin said by way of greeting. "Or have you cause to fear us?" He pointed one furry white ear at Keiko.

"Friends have no reason to fear each other." No need to follow Kaitin's ear. He could feel Strongarm's growl rumbling his bones.

"Then one wonders the need for a sec shield,"

"I agree." Jezekiah reached for his belt control.

"Not so fast, your lordship." Kip dragged his hand back. "Just 'cause we can't see 'em don't mean old man's Ho's snipers gone home. Just means they ain't where we can spot 'em."

"Good point." Jezekiah added a touch of concern to his expression. "Why don't we all leave? Unless you intend to rewrite our treaty with Ho Tong?" He shot an insinuating glance at Keiko, let Kaitin ibn Bengal track the implication for himself.

"A question first." Kaitin's sneer was worthy of JP. "We have had a most interesting conversation with your Grandfather Ho. Was this an arrangement of your making?"

"No." Jezekiah waited while Kaitin tested the honesty of his scent. "I wouldn't be here if I wanted Strongarm subordinate to Ho Tong."

Hearing his name must have finally forced Strongarm out of his fog. He lumbered up to join them. It cost him a visible struggle to keep his eyes off Keiko.

Jezekiah caught a red movement at the edge of his vision. Instinctively, he reached out block Keiko from joining Strongarm, noted that Kaitin mirrored the motion. Kip solved the problem by wrapping her in a fatherly arm lock. She wriggled impatiently. Jezekiah saw Strongarm's ears snap up, eyes narrowing. No mistaking the implication there. He held his breath, gut clenched, trying to will Keiko not to make an issue of it.

She decided, finally, to stay put. He heard a rasping sigh and realized Kaitin had been holding his breath, too. So, then. They'd come even closer to handing Grandfather Ho a victory than he'd feared.

"Leave it." Strongarm clamped a hand on Kaitin's shoulder. He leaned on it hard enough to make the Bengali shift balance to support his weight. "Van Buren didn't set me up for this, any more than my little Bird did. I did it to myself." He straightened, amber eyes targeting Jezekiah. His ears stayed on Keiko. "My word is good, Van Buren."

"Then complete your Impression tonight. Letticia's waiting for you at the Manor." That was at least half true.

"Agreed." Strongarm shook himself, dusting them all with silver-tipped hair.

The Sec skimmer whined back into sight. It kept enough of a distance to avoid raising dust clouds. Even so the machine's heavy repulse field throbbed the ground, sent tiny black bits of asphalt jittering across the tarmac. Gave him as good an excuse to get them all out of here as he could hope for.

"Good. Kip and his team will escort you back." Jezekiah ignored Kip's humphed objection, guided the Lupans toward their skimmer. Predictably Kaitin and Kip flanked him, keeping Keiko as far out of Strongarm's reach as possible. Under other circumstances the image would have been comic.

Jezekiah waited till Kaitin had Strongarm settled in the back, then pried Keiko out of Kip's grip and nudged the SecType into the master's seat. "I'll join you in a bit. After I take Mistress Yakamoto home."

After she was safely seduced.

XXV

Mother's private dock at Kalaeloa Harbor was only twenty klicks up Oahu's western coast from Pearl. Here, *ewa*-side of the island, the Waianae mountains sloped gently down to the ocean. The long, flat expanse of sea-smoothed lava rocks and tidal plains made for a full-sky view of the islands' spectacular sunsets. Jezekiah dawdled the skimmer along the coast so the reddening sun filled the cabin with romantic ambience.

He couldn't tell whether Keiko noticed it. Absorbed in some private dream, she hadn't so much as glanced at him, simply watched the jungled shore slide past without seeing it. The amber light softened the angular lines of her profile. It sheened her skin to bronze, deepened the shadow between her breasts. Made her look sweet as she was innocent. Made her look vulnerable. He wished she didn't, just as he wished he didn't want her so much. Better for them both if he could keep it merely physical.

The physical part would be easy enough. There was no mistaking the need behind the way Keiko crossed and re-crossed her legs. That was part one of his problem. The very intensity of her physical arousal only confirmed the suspicion he'd formed back at Punchbowl: Strongarm had used the Touch, implanted in Keiko his own driving need to mate. If it hadn't been for Kaitin ibn Bengal, they'd all be bowing to Grandfather Ho right now. Just as the old man had planned it. The horror in the realization triggered a chill powerful enough to earn him a health check scan.

Are you well, Milord? ShipMind put the question on audio. It sounded like a tinny version of Mother's major domo.

"I'm fine. Thank you." Jezekiah willed himself calm and the scan tingle faded.

"You may be fine, but you wen got lost." Keiko squeezed one knee over the other, folded her arms across her chest for good measure. "Thought you said you were going to take me home."

"So I did."

"Yuh-huh. Admiral's house's the other way."

He grinned over at her, intending to keep it innocent. Only the mix of doubt and challenge in Keiko's scowl made the grin slide straight into silliness.

At least the silliness seemed to allay her immediate suspicions. Keiko's scowl eased back to a frown. He would have found that encouraging, had she not continued to stroke her arm where Strongarm had Touched her.

"Say, Van Buren?" She rested her cheek against the seat back so the sunlight caressed her profile. "You know Strongarm pretty well, don't you?"

"Rather too well, at the moment."

Fortunately, Keiko took his answer at face value. "You think Lord Strongarm could ever care about me? I mean *really* care, not just-" She cut the question off with a shrug. But her eyes searched his in hope.

"I thought it was my intentions you were worried about." He lifted a brow at her, keeping his expression light. All it got him was a dismissive snort.

"*Yours* I know. But Strongarm's different. You think I'd have a chance?"

"Why? You like him that much?" That came out entirely too sharp.

"Yeah. He's a – a gentleman. He *understands*, you know?" Her hand rested on her arm, her expression going dreamy.

It was, Jezekiah thought sourly, precisely the expression he'd caught in the mirror when he allowed himself to dream about her. He knew what she felt. Knew only too well that she didn't feel it for him. He found an imaginary problem with the skimmer's master panel to cover the jealous flush he felt burning up his face. "Understands what?"

"Everything." The sudden urgency in the way she focused on him made him forget fiddling. "I can make him happy, Van Buren. I don't know how I know it, I just do. I can *feel* it. I never wanted anybody-" She cut herself off and discovered a fascination with her knees, trying to hide her own blush.

Jezekiah closed his eyes, felt the burn behind his eyelids. Why Keiko? Why couldn't it be Letticia – but it never would be Letticia, and he knew it. He ran desperate calcs, trying to find a defensible reason to turn the skimmer around and take Keiko to Strongarm. That was where she belonged. That was what was so obviously *right*.

Except it wasn't right. Not for Earth. Not for himself. Strongarm had promised the Lupan Parliament a marriage alliance with the Home World Van Burens. That stuck them both with Letticia. Worked out even worse for himself: matching Strongarm to anybody except Letticia left him stuck with the Ring, condemned to the Protectorship – assuming JP didn't manage to get him executed for treason. Left him with a choice that was no choice: either he betrayed the one man he knew for a true friend or he betrayed himself. So much, his little voice whispered, for friendship.

Jezekiah straightened his expression out, pretended to focus on the jungled coast rolling past beneath the skimmer's wings. They'd rounded the curve of Oahu's southern shore. A few klicks ahead the long, bright line of Kalaeloa pier arrowed out above the waves. The reddening sun limned the tall support pylons beneath the pier in brilliance. Along the pier itself arabesque railings turned sunlight to bronze and swirled it into fairy rings. Above the vast horizon the sun struck ruby-edged gold off a thousand miles of clouds.

Glory did not impress Keiko. Her dreaminess sharpened back to a scowl. "Okay, Van Buren. Do or die time. Admiral's house is Diamond Head way."

"I know."

"So that's on the other side of the island. You going turn this thing around or you planning on doing a full island circle?" But she settled for simply clamping her arms tighter across her chest.

If it weren't for Strongarm's Touch, she would have tried to turn the skimmer around herself. Or jumped for it. Jezekiah kept the truth out of his smile, let her see only wounded innocence. "I know. I merely thought you might enjoy a stroll along the pier first. Kalaeloa Harbor's a beautiful sight at sunset."

Ignoring ShipMind's complaints, Jezekiah took over the controls. Weaving the skimmer down between Kalaeloa's massive pylons he settled it on a flat dry expanse in the triangle shelter between the water line and pier flooring. "Shall we?" He popped the doors open and motioned Keiko to climb out with him.

She slid out, stepped around the hood. But only far enough to lean against it, arms still folded, and glare out at the harbor. It eased neither his body nor soul that she obviously failed to realize how enticingly the gesture pushed up her breasts.

"Are you all right, Keik?" A risk, using her nickname. But safer than attempting to touch her just now.

"Why am I here?" From any other woman the question would have been a coy invitation, a prelude to the evening's pleasure. From Keiko it was a cry of anguish.

"To watch the sunset, what else?" The sound of her pain dried the usual repartee on his tongue.

"That's *your* excuse – you and every other fool 'tween here and Hilo. But I know better. So why am *I* still here?" She rubbed at her arm, unwittingly answering her own question.

He could not let himself dwell on the despair in her voice. The sound of it triggered an anger that clenched his fists, angry at himself, at Strongarm, at the whole damned Van Buren Commonwealth. Jezekiah settled for leaning against the skimmer, hiding his clenched fists from her behind his back. He only wished he could hide from himself the loathing at what he had to do. "I will take you home, if that's what you really want." The lie left his mouth tasting rancid.

For answer she jerked away and stalked toward the rocks littering the shore beyond the pier. There was no grace in her movement. Rather she looked as if some hidden puppet master were tugging her across the rocks by invisible strings.

Which was, in a way, exactly the truth. It was Strongarm's need pulling her across those rocks. Strongarm who'd lit a need in her great enough to breach her defenses. Jezekiah tried to shut the knowledge out of mind. That was the worst of it, the knowing. She wanted what she'd felt in Strongarm's Touch: a mating that joined souls along with bodies, a once and forever love. She wanted it because it was the only kind of love she knew how to give. The kind he'd started dreaming of himself. The kind no Van Buren could afford. Safe behind her back, he ran a hand across his face, ran desperate quick calcs trying to find an alternative. The answers came up null. If he did not divert Keiko's affections *now*, the Touch would draw her back to Strongarm before the night was out. And then even Kaitin would not be able to stop her.

So, then. He started after her, jerked to a halt himself at the skimmer's tinny voice.

You are supposed to remain within my precincts, Milord. Captain Marsden's orders are to keep you safe.

"I'm quite safe here. You-" he caught himself before he said anything unspinnably suicidal. "You just stay put and keep your eyes open. If you see anything dangerous, yell for help."

The skimmer grumbled but shut up.

Jezekiah repeated the 'stay put', then strolled across the rocks to join Keiko. He caught up to her on a flat rock just above the wave line. He locked the self-loathing into the dark little attic of his mind, locked hands behind his back. Very carefully, he did not touch her. It would have dirtied what he felt for her, turned what had to be a seduction into the cheapest rut. He would not dishonor either of them so. Not when his own dreams centered on finding the very kind of once and forever love she offered. Instead he simply stood beside her, content to watch the wavelets lick the sand.

"It's okay, Van Buren. You can off the shield."

Her voice startled him. "What?"

"I said you can off the shield." Tracking the angle of her chin, he recognized the soft nimbus surrounding his body where the shield reflected the gilded light. "It's all right." She added a wry moue to underscore the assurance. "Really. I promise not to hurt you."

He only wished he could promise her the same. He used the regret to make his smile look foolish. "Just don't tell Kip I turned it off." He found the tab, thumbed it to neutral. Considered logistics and took the belt off altogether. He tossed it back into the skimmer.

"Don't worry. Admiral kill me himself I let anything happen to you." She smiled, but it looked bitter. "Now you want to watch the sunset, let's walk."

She stepped surely across the flat lava rocks littering the shore, leaving him to follow or not. Across the horizon the amber sun sank behind crimson clouds. The backlight shot pale radiance across the darkening sky and rippled red-gold glory across the sea. Water pocked-rocks tumbled reflected glories across the shore. And limned Keiko's red sarong in molten gold.

Damn and damn again! He wished he didn't want her so. Wished he dared allow himself to dwell in the warmth she lit in his heart. Wished he could afford to give her the lifetime of love he had hidden in the deep recesses of his soul. That was what she deserved, not – Jezekiah cut the longing off before the despair behind them turned treasonous. He had no honor to offer her, plain and simple. He knew too much about her now – more, even, than she knew of herself. Knew, too, that if Mother suspected he'd allowed himself to fall in love with Keiko she would solve the problem her own way, with a quiet order to the Admiral – he could not even make himself complete the thought.

"You coming, Van Buren?"

"You sure you want to stay down here?" Absorbed in his thoughts he stepped off the rocks onto hard sand. A wavelet promptly soaked his shoes.

"Don't want to run into traffic." She made a point of not laughing while he tried to shake water out of his shoe.

Which, of course, made him feel even more like a fool. He gave up on the shoe and followed her. His socks squished water between his toes with each step. "What traffic? Mother doesn't have any guests scheduled in." He'd made sure to check that before heading up here.

"You think your haole the only folk use this dock?" Keiko grinned at him over one bare shoulder. Barefoot as she was, her footing was surer than his own. "Kalaeloa's Grandfather's private dock, too."

"Nonsense. Sec keeps a permanent eye on–" He shut up as the implications sank in.

"Yuh-huh." She sounded like Kip Marsden. "Sec needs a NetMind entry to track anything, remember? So they can't see mech-only ships any more than Sec can see naturals. That's why the Captain lets me work for him. Takes one to spot one." Her expression went hurt. She looked away from him, hugging herself. "So why me, Van Buren? You got your pick of any woman in your Commonwealth. Why'm I the one you got down here?"

"You don't have to stay, you know." He locked hands behind his back again, wishing he could lock out the lie. But it was too late to let her go. And too soon to risk touching her.

"That's not what I'm asking." Amber light glistened at the corners of her eyes, sign of how much she feared what she felt. "Why *me*, Van Buren?" She lifted her arms, dropped them helplessly. "What's going on?"

He wished he dared tell her the truth. Only the truth would send her running flat out back to Strongarm. And Earth to hell. He chose a wry smile instead, folded his arms across his chest to mirror her. "Unless I miss my guess, Yakamoto, your body is answering that question for you."

"But that's not *me*!" She could not even know how true that was.

"I only see one of you." He couldn't risk saying more at the moment. Too likely he'd cry with her. He stepped closer instead, reached out at last to stroke her shoulder with a fingertip.

Keiko jerked back as if he'd hit her. Though not in time to hide the way her body rose in answer to his touch. "Can't you understand? You don't know what it's like, everybody always telling you what you are-"

"As a matter of fact, I do. I know it rather too well." Damn, he was *angry*. Wrong reaction, on all counts. Yet for some reason he'd expected Keiko to understand.

She didn't. "Yeah? Tell you what – you're special, born to rule, the future Protector- "

"The future slave to the damned Ring." He snapped his hand up and the Heir's Ring left a yellow arc in the air behind it. "*This* is who I'm supposed to be. This is my future – to never be anything or anybody for myself. To never be *me*."

"Aww..." Her hands dropped to her hips, answering his anger with her own. "Poor little princeling. What you want to be free from? Your fine house and fine clothes and fancy cars and giving folk orders?"

The taunt shot past his guard, shattered the lock on the dungeon at the back of his mind. "Just what would you know about it? What do you know about living with lies and betrayal and having to pretend you're somebody you're not? About having to betray the only friend you ever had?"

"I got news for you, Van Buren. You never *have* to betray a friend. You *choose* to-"

"I don't have a choice!" This time the anger sounded in his own voice.

"You always got a choice! You just don't like the option is all. You want the easy way out."

"There's never an easy way out. Not for a Protector." He was angry enough he didn't even care she would hear the bitterness. "You do what's right for your world, not yourself."

"So? You want to tell me about hard choices? I'm Samurai trained, remember? Would have *been* Samurai now, if it weren't for you." Her fists came up to match her chin. "Or was that another choice you didn't have?"

"No." He was the one to wrench away this time. Her words drove home the enormity of the wrongs he'd already done her, drained the anger out of his body. "No. That was just my own very stupid mistake."

"Then you can fix it." The hope in her voice only made it worse.

"I can't." He spoke over his shoulder, unable to look higher than the white foam swirling around the rock beneath her feet. "At least not yet." Not until he could break the bond Strongarm had forged with her. Prove to Mother Keiko was no longer a viable alternative to Letticia.

"What do you mean, 'can't'?" Keiko skipped sure-footed across the sun-pocked rocks to force herself back into his line of sight. "You have any idea what your blocking my Type code means to me, Van Buren? You got any clue at all what kind misery you cost me?"

"I've explained the situation to your father." Damn, she'd have him bawling like a newborn in a minute. He couldn't face her, most certainly could not meet her eyes.

"I don't care what you explained! Admiral never thought I was any good anyway!" She forced herself back into his range of vision, denying him escape. "You wen got the Samurai Council thinking I couldn't make it through Type trial. You got them thinking I'm your bed wench. That's the kind of rumor spreads fast, Van Buren. You know how that feels? To have every man you meet look at you and wonder when he going get his turn?"

"Yes!"

"Yeah? Who?"

"A whole damned crew of miners!"

The shock in her expression only mirrored his own. But the flood gates were broken. The memories welled up, washing him afresh in shame so powerful he doubled over it.

"Heia, what's wrong?" Keiko had an arm around him instantly. There was no anger in her voice, only concern.

"Nothing." He choked the word out, trying to choke off the memories of those long, ugly nights. Of gray walls and cold metal floors shivering with under the thrust of the Miner ship's drive engines as he shivered –

Keiko shook him back to the present. "Don't you 'nothing' me, Van Buren. You got a problem, you better out it now."

Startled, Jezekiah blinked down at her. Odds were she was only trying to distract herself from the desire Strongarm's Touch had wakened. Yet she didn't rub her arm when she let him go, didn't lock her knees together. She was offering him a friend's support, simple and honest. Offering him everything he'd come to dream of. The realization shook the locks on his soul. He bit his lips to stop them from trembling as well. "My apologies, Keiko. That particular problem has nothing to do with you."

"Yuh-huh. You been making me trouble since the minute you stepped foot back in the islands. You want I give you one itemized list how much it's got to do with me?"

The soft golden sheen of the sun on her cheeks leeched the chill out of his soul. He ran a finger along her cheek, tracing the sun-glow in simple wonder. "You sure you want to know, Keik?"

"Can't tell till you do." She captured his hand, tugged him across the rocks to a sheltered sandy spot between a pair of boulders safely above the water line. It was an offer of understanding, not seduction. It made him conscious of how soft his skin was against the calloused hardness of hers. How soft her heart was against the bitter shell of his own.

"Now, tell." She shoved him down onto the sand then dropped beside him to rest her back against the boulder, knees drawn up at a demure angle. "What's this Miner crew business?"

And suddenly he needed to tell it all. Needed her to know. "Mother sent me out to the rim to develop new trade lines for Earth. That's how I got the idea to build trade ties with the Lupans. Only the Lupans don't allow Commonwealth ships into their space. I couldn't afford to let JP – that's Johann Petrovich, the Streikern Protector – suspect my plans. So I signed on to a miner crew."

"How? Miner crews are all clan folk. Even I know that."

"True." He leaned back against the boulder, squeezing his eyes shut against the memories. "So I found a captain willing to adopt me into his ship's clan. Fool that I was, I never checked out his crew initiation rites. Or that the crew was all male."

"At least you fought!"

"No, I didn't!" He pulled in a breath, felt the dirt and self-revulsion twist his stomach again. This time, he let it show. "Oh, I tried, the first time. Not that it did much good against a pack of miners. After that-" Shame welled up afresh. He didn't try to hide it. Didn't need to, not with Keiko. He kept his eyes open and on hers. "After that, I made friends."

"*Friends?*" Keiko stared at him as if he'd sprouted fangs. "You should have killed yourself, then!"

"I couldn't afford to. I had a *duty*, Keik."

"What kind duty says you got to whore yourself?" Outrage drove her up on her knees.

"The Protectorship. You do what your world needs and find a way to live with it afterward." Jezekiah lifted his hand to stroke the fire out of her eyes. The Ring's golden glare only made her duck away to scowl at it. He dropped his hand with a sigh. "So I earned myself a place in that crew. I learned to scrub decks, shove ore, even to read stellar nav charts. And it paid off. That miner captain is the one who got me the intro to Strongarm."

"Sounds to me like you paid more'n you got."

"Only personally. As long as I bring that treaty in it doesn't matter."

"Damn. You're worse'n the damned Samurai." She sank down beside him, though he couldn't be sure whether she was offering him comfort or seeking it for herself. The move brought her into the sliver of light between the paired boulders. Amber sun raised a golden sparkle off the suppressed tears brimming in her eyes.

Jezekiah brushed the tears away with a fingertip. He hadn't expected the tears. Hadn't expected her to understand the heartache. Most certainly had not expected his heart to open in response. "Keik, will you promise me something?"

"What?" The quick flash of suspicion made him want to hug her to him.

"Stay away from Strongarm." He cupped her cheek in his palm, his body thrilling to the warmth of her skin. "Just for a few days. Just until after he marries Letticia."

She sat back, frowning, rubbing her arm where Strongarm had Touched her. Jezekiah nearly whimpered when she pulled away. He focused on the horizon. Across the sea the darkening light faded the golden glitter on the flat lava rocks as the sun melted into the sea. Odd. He couldn't say why, but his heart seemed to echo it. As if something had lit inside him and was melting a shell he'd spent a lifetime building.

"Why?" Keiko's voice startled him back to reality.

"Because Earth needs you to." He hadn't expected the sudden certainty that *he* needed her to. "Because if he doesn't marry Letticia the whole treaty falls apart. And then Earth loses the only hope we have of averting another Lupan war."

"But I like him, Van Buren. I like him a lot. He likes me, too. Not just for an easy tumble, but really and truly. I know it." Keiko pulled her knees up, wrapped her arms around them. Jezekiah's lips tightened with the wish she'd wrapped them around him. "I was thinking maybe he'd help me get off Earth. Always heard naturals have it easier out on the rim."

"We could try heading out together." The idea surprised himself as much as her. But his heart clutched at the idea like a drowning man. He reached out to take both her hands in his. This time she let him hold them. "I don't want the Ring, Keik. I built an out for myself into that treaty. In exchange for marrying Strongarm, I'm forfeiting the Protectorship to Letticia."

"Then what about you?"

"I'll be disinherited." He felt the excitement, the hope stir again. For once he didn't care it showed. "I'll have to get off Earth. Out of the Commonwealth, for that matter – the Family does not approve of Heirs running away from their responsibilities. But it gives me a chance to find out what I can do. On my own. With nobody to tell me who or what I am."

"Yuh-huh. And where you fitting me into all these fine plans?" She tried to sound suspicious still, but he felt her fingers grip his, felt her pulse of hope.

"I don't know." It was the first time he could remember he'd spoken the simple truth, no spin, no quick calc'd odds. It felt like all the locks on his soul had burst. "I can't promise you happily ever after. I can't even promise you we have a future together. I can only promise you my best effort. And that I damned sure want to try."

She pulled a hand free to rub her arm. This time the gesture seemed almost reflective.

It seemed so natural to slip his arm around her shoulder, to snuggle her into the crook of his arm. They leaned back together and he saw with new wonder that the Milky Way was spilling diamond dust across the sky. Keiko tracked his line of sight, her curls dark against the creamy linen of his sleeve, and together they watched the stars rise out of the sea.

Far out on the horizon, one bright star lingered on the sea line. Jezekiah studied it contentedly. Just a cargo ship, most likely, making for Pearl's deep sea port to the south. But for the moment it was something beautiful, something that reflected his own bright, lightened spirit. Without even thinking he pulled Keiko closer and kissed her.

It felt utterly natural to let the kiss deepen, let his hand slip under the sarong to cup the soft curve of her breast. He recognized the frisson of fear beneath the pleasure in her gasp. Held himself back, used skills acquired on a dozen worlds to introduce her to ecstasy before entering her. Even so she tensed when he moved over her. Jezekiah rolled onto his back, lifted Keiko onto his hips. He guided her gently until she took him into herself. He pulled her hips forward, showed her how to find her pleasure on him. Guided her until they roared together and she collapsed, panting, against his chest.

It took him some minutes to recognize the wet trickle among the fine hair of his chest. Keiko still tried to hide the tears when he lifted her face. The sight tightened his own throat. Jezekiah kissed her eyes, her temples, trying to convince himself he could kiss the truth away with her tears. "What's wrong, *ku'u ipo?*"

She hadn't expected him to call her his darling, certainly not in the Hawaiian phrase. She buried her face against his chest, shoulders shaking. "Two guesses. Second one doesn't count."

He knew all the right answers, knew what words would soothe her fears. He just couldn't make himself speak any of the pretty lies. Not now. He felt *clean*, for the first time since he'd accepted jump in on that miner crew. He rolled them onto their sides instead so their legs intertwined and her head rested against his shoulder where he could kiss her temple and stroke her hair.

Above the horizon the rising moon brushed silver across a sky full of pale gray clouds. "Still worried?"

A nod, face hidden. "Admiral kill me he find out." His shoulder muffled her voice, not the shame in it.

"Hell he will." Jezekiah couldn't have hidden the rush of anger even if he'd wanted to try. He pushed himself up on an elbow, making Keiko lift her head. The misery in her expression cut him worse than Strongarm's talons. He clutched her to him, rocked with her in shared sorrow. "Nobody's going to hurt you, Keik. Nobody, ever again. I'll kill anyone-"

"No, you won't." Her nipples brushed hard and tight against his own making him struggle to will down his body's eager answer. "Wasn't your fault anyway. I knew what you were up to when you set down here. Should've struck out for the Admiral's house right off. Should've-"

"Should have pretended you didn't care." Jezekiah closed his eyes, feeling the dirt of his memories well up.

"Yeah. Got a lot of practice at it." She shook herself, pushed away, though not out of his arms.

"We both have. It's not always enough."

He pulled her close again, felt the pulse in his groin as his body responded to the brush of her skin. He ran a hand down her hip, following the moonlit gleam of the synskin bandage streaking her thigh. Sword wound, judging from the length of it. Girl looked like she'd just come off a battlefield – It struck him, then, just what he'd done to her. The impact of it collapsed his rising interest. "Keik, about the Type trial – I'm sorry. I truly am."

"Yuh-huh. So why-"

Out to sea a ship's horn boomed. White flashed beyond the pier: ship's lights, no mistaking them for a star now. Well over the horizon, now, and heading in.

"Shuttle," Keiko squinted down his line of sight.

"Can't be. Mother-"

"Grandfather's." Keiko was already wrapping her sarong around her. "She's haulin' too fast to be haole."

Jezekiah found his clothes by touch, found he'd worked sand into various delicate parts of his anatomy as he slipped them on. He was working on getting his water-shrunk shoes back on when he realized Keiko was still watching the ship's light.

The sweet innocence he'd held a few moments before had vanished. She was all Samurai now. She backed toward him, keeping her eyes on the sea. "We better get you out of here, Van Buren."

"Jess. People I love call me Jess." Bad timing, he knew, but he needed to tell her.

"Jess." She flashed him an absent-minded smile, eyes still on the sea. "I don't like the feel of this. They're – down!"

Keiko slammed him face down in the sand between the paired boulders. A search light, its glare bright enough to darken the night around it, swept past the pier and across the rocks toward them.

Jezekiah felt the pressure of her body tingle down the length of his own even as the search light passed over them. The beam moved on, making individual rocks leap into and out of sight with surreal intensity. Jezekiah shifted enough to slide an arm around Keiko's shoulder and snuggle her closer. Allow himself the illusion, for a moment, that he was protecting her. Foolish as it was he was utterly content simply to hold her, to feel her face against his heart.

Keiko ended the illusion with a jab in the ribs. He lifted his head to object. She jammed him down as the searchlight lit their rock again on its back sweep. Not fast enough: whoever was behind the light had spotted the movement. The beam dibbeted back. This time Keiko held him down. The beam explored the crevices around them slowly, hunting now. Jezekiah's heart thudded hard enough to make him expect the hunters would find them by the sound alone.

The beam moved on finally to search the rocks closer to the waterline. Keiko yanked him upright and pushed him toward the pylons beneath the pier. She wedged him into a dark, wet hollow between a pylon base and a cluster of lava rocks. Then crushed against him as the search beam cut across the shoreline where they'd been. He clutched her hips to his. Knew she'd felt his body throb against hers when she poked him for it. Seaward, the roar of repulse engines added a thudding counter point to the whoosh of the waves.

"Why stay?" Jezekiah kept his voice as soft as the engine roar allowed. "My skimmer's right here. We can be airborne before they off load."

"And they can shoot us out of the sky, too, eh?" She poked him harder, then wiggled free to eye the pier above. "Now, listen. They saw movement down here. Better they see a reason for it, eh? I go make one diversion. You *stay* till I come back. You got that?"

"Keik-" He grabbed her arm but she broke his hold with a shrug.

"No hu-hu." She rolled her head as if her neck hurt. "Tong folk all know me. I can dodge anybody else."

Feeling a coward he watched her jog up toward the road. Seaward, the shuttle slid into its berth. Its running lights glared off the water where the ship's repulse fields flattened the waves beneath it. The harsh light stretched Keiko's shadow out long and thin across the blue-gray sand.

On the dock above, the noise of the shuttle's engines eased. A single passenger's shadow stretched out across the rocks, glided leisurely toward the road. Something in the shadow's fluid grace touched Jezekiah's memory. He watched the shadow engulf Keiko in its shade, merge itself into hers. And suddenly the way it moved became terrifyingly familiar.

Leave it, his little voice urged. The assassin was focused on Keiko. She didn't want his help, much less need it. Odds were Keiko could outrun him without even breaking a sweat. The logic was undeniable. Except – he couldn't leave it. Keeping an eye on Keiko, Jezekiah edged up the rocks, keeping the pier between the killer and himself.

At the pier's sea end, the shuttle's door clanged shut. Releasing grips, the ship backed away from the dock. The sudden thrust of its repulse field churned the waves to mist around it. Its push-off sent a set of waves rolling up the shore to soak Jezekiah to his knees. He stumbled, swore, and scrambled back up onto the rocks.

Keiko had reached the road. She ambled along it, looking nowhere, doing a fine imitation of a tired joy toy headed home. Above Jezekiah the assassin leaned on the pier railing, watching her walk past like any other healthy male. There was light enough by the road to let Jezekiah register the man's details. The assassin looked more slender than Jezekiah remembered. Even in repose his build bespoke a supple grace. His skin was a black so pure it blended precisely into his sable mane. His clothes were snagged and dirty, an odd contrast to their exquisite cut. Clearly, wherever he'd been hiding out it hadn't been comfortable. The thought would have provided a greater satisfaction had the man been watching Keiko with less intent.

On the road, Keiko passed the pier entrance. Jezekiah lost sight of her. For a moment he thought the assassin had lost interest in her as well. He held his breath, hoping. Then the killer slapped the railing. He stalked toward the road. Eyes tracking Keiko's path. Hunting.

Jezekiah scrambled up the shore. The assassin was already gaining on Keiko's back when Jezekiah made the road. He saw her roll her head, saw the movement of the assassin's arm as he reached lazily for a hidden needler. Knowing himself for a fool, Jezekiah threw himself at the killer's back.

The assassin turned. Something hard and hot skimmed Jezekiah's shoulder. He realized he'd fallen when his cheek hit tarmac. He rolled. Not fast enough. Fire raked across his throat. Jezekiah kicked up, felt his toe connect -

And the assassin roared.

A bare foot hit the tarmac inches from his face, peppered him with pebbles as Keiko leaped clear. He heard the thud of flesh on bone, heard the assassin's snarl. Jezekiah felt more than heard the heavier thud of a body hitting the ground. He scrambled to his feet. For some reason the ground didn't seem to feel quite solid -

Then all the sirens of hell broke loose.

An armored skimmer butted its blunt nose across Jezekiah's field of vision.

He tried to skip around it, found himself skidding down its nose instead. Hands yanked him back before he slid off the hood. Jezekiah aimed a punch at the hands' owner. He hit armor and swore.

"Medic!" Kip Marsden's voice bellowed. "Siddown, your Lordship." He added a downward shove that ensured Jezekiah obeyed.

"Let me go." Jezekiah's voice sounded drunken. "Have to find Keik." Using Kip's grip for an anchor, he leaned past the big man's bulk to search the dock for her through the Sec field lights flooding the doc.

"What you got to do is siddown and shuddup. You pret' near got your goddamn fool throat cut." Then, at a roar, "I want a medic here! *Now!*"

"*Here*, dammit!" The nasal voiced medic who jogged up was a standard NumbersType, medium build, medium brown hair, medium brown eyes. She motioned to Kip to ease him down against the side of the Sec skimmer while she snapped fingers for her medi-kit to catch up.

"Where's Keik?" Jezekiah lost the rest in a pained cough as she pushed his head to one side to examine his throat.

"Rammer was aiming for the carotid artery." She yanked the surgi-tools her kit proffered one-handed, explored Jezekiah's throat with the other. "Looks like he missed his grip. Centimeter deeper and he'd already be dead." She jerked her chin at Jezekiah's shoulder while she lasered the gashes.

"Got a needler burn, too," Kip put in.

"Yeah, get those next."

Jezekiah bit back a yip as she smeared synskin over the laser seals. *Damn*, that hurt. But the pain helped clear his head. He craned upward at Kip, winced at the pull of the synskin. "Where's Keik?"

"Here." Keiko limped up. She gave him enough of a smile to make his heart leap, though she looked wan.

"You better fix these up, too." Kip pulled Keiko around single handed. Jezekiah's relief evaporated at sight of the bloody trail running down her arm to drip off her fingers.

"Get a vet." The medic rose, her kit snapping shut and rising to leave with her. "I don't touch monkeys."

"Then you get your paws off me." Jezekiah jerked to his feet fast enough to make the medic jump back. The sudden motion made his head swim but he was too angry to worry it.

"Eh, no hu-hu. I wen get worse in training, eh?" The wobble in Keiko's voice betrayed the strength in the words.

"That was before." He got his eyes to focus, narrowed them at on the medic. Recognized the fear in the way the woman's own widened. "Now I suggest you do your job if you want to keep it."

Keiko started to duck away. Jezekiah reached for her. Found his hand blocked by Kip's armored one. Furious, he started to push Kip's arm away. Past it he glimpsed the way Keiko's eyes lit, recognized pride. Realized she was proud of *him*. His fury evaporated leaving a fool's grin in its wake.

"Yuh-huh." The sudden fatherly scowl said Kip had caught the look, too. His arm stayed in place while the medic swabbed down Keiko's wounds.

With her free hand Keiko stopped the medic before she could slap on synskin bandages. "Eh, you wait one sec, huh? Want to show the captain something." She steadied herself against Kip's arm, then twisted to show him her back. Cleared of the blood a matched set of oozing gashes slashed across her shoulder blades to curve down her arm. "Four of 'em, Captain. Give you any ideas?"

"Shit." Kip cocked his head, checking scan.

"What?" Whatever it was, Jezekiah was missing it.

"Those're Ta'an trademarks. That's a Ta'an assassin you got tracking you." Keiko was leaning too heavily against Kip's shoulder for Jezekiah's comfort. It should have been his shoulder supporting her. He tried to reach past Kip, pull Keiko into his own arms. The effort only got him yanked back. Hard.

Kip was still scowling at the scan report when he looked down to Jezekiah. "Bastard's gone, your Lordship. No footprints, no biopat signal, no nothin'. Search teams can't find any Net entry showing he was even here." The scowl turned worried as he turned it on Keiko. "You see where he went, Mote?"

"No-"

"Why don't you ask her how the assassin got here instead?" Jezekiah recognized Teufelsman's nasal sneer behind Kip's broad shoulders.

"I will, when I get to it." Kip pulled Keiko a protective step closer, fixed a targeting scowl on the Aryan. "Till then, why don't you just fuck a duck and leave Sec work alone? You're out of your pond, snowball."

"Ah, but anything that threatens the Heir is my 'pond' as you put it." Teufelsman ambled past Kip's armored bulk, making Jezekiah squint at the glare off his white linen suit. "Since Sec is otherwise engaged, I have been inspecting the scene. It has yielded some most interesting evidence." He angled his gaze to Keiko. Had he been alone, Jezekiah thought, he would have licked his lips. "I would like to ask the monkey how the killer got here. And just how *she* happened to be here."

"*Mistress* Yakamoto happened to be passing by on a Samurai training run," Jezekiah answered before Keik could stick her foot in it. "As for the assassin – he came in on a shuttle,"

"My lord is astute, as always." Teufelsman dropped Jezekiah an acknowledging bow, but his eyes never left Keiko. "Perhaps Captain Marsden would be kind enough to tell us whether the Protector had any shuttle scheduled in here?"

"I will ask my lady mother if she did or not." He would, too. When hell froze over.

"As you wish, Milord. However, I think you will find she did not." Teufelsman held up a hand. A Tong star shone between his fingers. "I found this on the dock, not far from where the monkey lay." He rotated the star so that the field lights caught the dark stain along its edges. "Allow me to suggest, Milord, that this little item belongs to your pet monkey."

"What if?" Kip gave Teufelsman a scowl dark enough to make the medic duck out of the space between them.

"What if she was here to greet that Tong shuttle? What if you, Milord, inadvertently disrupted her plan? The obvious conclusion is that had not Captain Marsden intervened – conveniently late I notice – she would surely have used this Tong star on you."

"So lack you, snowball." Keiko was leaning too hard on Kip's arm. "That was a Ta'an Assassin wen attack him, not me."

"Indeed. Ta'an Type carries a red-code ID. Its very presence on any Van Buren shuttle would set off alarms across Sec. Yet there has been no such alarm."

"For the record, Lieutenant, Mistress Yakamoto saved my life. At great and obvious risk to her own."

"Again," Keiko added.

"Perhaps. Or perhaps she struck you herself. A trained Samurai can strike faster than the eye can follow."

"Teufelsman, you're either drunk or crazy." Kip swung his targeting gaze down the Aryan's body. He also, Jezekiah noticed, slipped a supporting hand under Keiko's elbow. "Scan says you're sober, so that leaves crazy. So why don't you go check yourself into a WellNet ward and leave Mote here alone?"

"All I suggest, Milord, is that you allow me to interrogate the monkey. If she is indeed innocent, she will go free." This time he did lick his lips.

"I kill myself before I let you touch me." There was a spark of fire in her voice, but Keiko had to blink for focus.

"Keik, are you quite sure you're okay?"

"Yeah, fine." The way she gripped Kip's armored forearm bespoke the lie. "That *mahe* attack you before?"

"Several times." In front of Teufelsman, he decided not to add that the fellow was a miserable shot.

"Bet he didn't miss you altogether, though. Bet you that first miss came close. Second time you got grazed. Third time it hurt." She paused to catch her breath. "Left you one nice scar, too, eh?"

Which she had certainly seen well enough tonight. Something else he was not about to admit in front of Teufelsman. He salaamed to her with what grace the wooziness permitted. But a sudden cold knot twisted the pit of his stomach.

"See, Captain? That's a classic Ta'an pattern." Keiko rested her head against Kip's armored shoulder a moment. She stopped Jezekiah from dislocating his own trying to reach her with a wry smile. "That assassin wasn't 'missing' you, Van Buren. He was playing with you."

"Doesn't make sense, Mote." There was worry in Kip's voice, hard as he tried to hide it. He tilted Keiko's head up to his carefully. "Ta'an would've finished the job 'fore he got to Earth. He's too visible on Earth – got no place to hide."

"Want bet?" Her eyes rolled up. Kip let Jezekiah go to catch her as she folded.

"Keik!" Jezekiah ducked past him, shoved the medic aside to pull Keiko out of Kip's arms. It was like holding a hummingbird. She felt so tiny, suddenly, so fragile. So inexpressibly precious. He crushed her to his heart, murmured desperate sweetnesses in the old tongue.

"Out of the way, Milord." Looking disgusted the medic elbowed him aside. She lifted Keiko's eyelid with a fingertip and grunted. "Just shock. She'll come out of it in a minute."

"Are you sure?" Jezekiah stroked Keiko's face. "She's not wounded elsewhere?"

"Easy enough to find out. Lay her out here and I'll take a look."

In his arms, Keiko stirred. She shook her head, tried to lift a hand and failed.

"*Ku'u ipo.*" Jezekiah kissed her forehead. She rewarded him with a glow of trust that melted the knot in his gut. He knelt, lowered her gently.

The medic started to tug Keiko's sarong open. And yelped, even before Jezekiah's knuckles smacked into her wrist.

Swearing, the medic jerked her hand away. A silver Tong star protruded from her finger, one gleaming tip embedded in her flesh.

Around Jezekiah, sounds leaped into stark clarity. He heard the metallic whir as Kip knelt beside him. Field lights flared off the silver crescent in his skull as he reached past Jezekiah to put his hand palm up to Keiko. Grimacing, she pulled a series of Tong stars out of the folds of her sarong clinked them into a glittering pile in his armored palm. With each star, the pain in Kip's scowl deepened.

"Perhaps Milord will allow me to conduct a proper interrogation, now." Teufelsman didn't even try to suppress the satisfaction in his tone.

It was the perfect solution, his little voice whispered. Quick-calcs flashed him the outcome: suicide would eliminate Keiko as a distraction to Strongarm; the Lupan would kill Teufelsman once he heard of it. That would eliminate

Letticia's key henchman, along with whatever sync link he was providing. The Admiral would simply accept the inevitable. Yes, that was definitely the best option.

"You touch her and I will kill you." Jezekiah clutched Keiko closer. It was only force of will that kept his eyes focused on an imaginary spot beside the Aryan's head. Had he actually looked at the man, he would have hit him.

Be a cold day in hell before he let any other man lay a hand on Keiko Yakamoto. Because while he had breath left in his body he was never letting her go.

XXVI

Something was wrong with this sync. Something, somewhere within it was *clicking*. Oh, gob it all, why had she ever trusted Teufelsman? The stupid son of a bitch had given her a bad link! Swearing, Letticia ran a quick check on her outgoing spider threads. Embedded as she was within the shell of Teufelsman's sync-D, she didn't dare tap into her personal threads. That bastard Marsden would be watching those, just waiting for her to try something stupid. Instead she was stuck *here*, pretending to be Teufelsman, while some stupid gobbing glitch drove her mad with its clicking!

Her spiders reported no problems with her threads. Yet the clicking continued. So it had to be within NetMind itself. Why did these things always happen to *her*? Heavens, if that fool Teufelsman had let Marsden track him – Letticia forced down a swell of panic. No, couldn't be. That bastard Marsden wouldn't waste time just clicking at her. He'd have made the link do a crash'n burn. More likely that steady *click-click-click* grating on her sync'd nerves was a mech flaw in the portable link Teufelsman had brought her.

Which was just a crash'n burn waiting to happen. Oh, gob Teufelsman! Why hadn't he run diags before he turned the silly link over? She certainly couldn't take time to run them now! He could have done it before he backed out of the link! This first time she'd needed the Aryan's physical presence to enter his node without Marsden catching her. She'd actually had to let him cap his hand over hers in order to sync in through his ID. The memory of his damp palm clapped atop hers made her stomach rise. She shut the physical reaction down. No time for that, either! With renewed urgency, she finished embedding her own DNA code within Teufelsman's sync-D, then began the delicate work of designing an access code.

There, done! Now all Teufelsman had to do was have one of the Aryan's techs transfer 'his' ID to a sync glove and she'd be set. She'd be able to sync in from anywhere. And even Marsden would see only Teufelsman's sync-D. Oh, gods, it felt *so* good to be back in Net! She didn't want to ever un-sync!

Click-click-click ... oh, gob it all, the clicks were coming faster! She absolutely could not risk having the link fail now. And she still had to test the set up! Ignoring the panicked thud of her heart beat she ran a brazen scan of her own sync node. *Let* Marsden see it – if she'd set it up right, even his sync-guards would only spot Teufelsman being his usual nosey Aryan self. Even through sync she felt her body's temples pound while the cells guarding her node challenged Teufelsman's probe – and passed it! The pounding eased and she realized her body had let its breath out. She scanned her node exactly the way Teufelsman would have – gods knew she'd caught at it often enough to know! Only *she* knew precisely the variation within her node that would betray the location of that fool assassin. She spotted the cell cluster she needed, scanned it and moved on before the sync guards got curious. Or that damned clicking could start up again.

Gob it all, even when she did everything right it still came out wrong! That assassin still didn't show! Finding him should have been a grokker – she'd embedded his ID in a dupe of her own. Yet the idiot was gone. Nulled. Zeroed. Which was answer enough, actually. A syncmeister of Marsden's caliber could have spotted the dupe for what it was. But not even Marsden was good enough to erase it. Which meant her Ta'an was someplace NetMind simply couldn't see. And that narrowed the possibilities to one.

Well, she couldn't take time to go chasing down a link to Grandfather Ho, either, not right now. She didn't dare risk having the stupid link die on her while she was in Net. Still, she should be safe there. Grandfather Ho owed her too much to risk using that assassin on his own.

Ever so gently, Letticia recalled her spiders, coiled her data-dewed threads back into the confines of Teufelsman's sync, then pulled her hand out of the link. It took all her willpower not to shriek at the feeling of her *self* dwindling back into the smelly, nasty shell of her body.

Letticia rubbed her eyes with a shaking hand, blinked sticky eyelids until her quarters came back into focus. Even that effort was too much for her strength. She dropped back in the chair and let her eyelids drift closed.

Click-click-click... It was *here*!

Terror conjured the dark image of Admiral Yakamoto clipping across the floor toward her. Heart hammering, Letticia bolted upright, cast a frantic glance at the door. Nothing. Just the same old dull beige walls studded with those stupid old award plaques. And Teufelsman. He had his back to her, white hands clenched behind his wrinkled white jacket while he pretended to study the hulking totem guarding the far wall. Against the totem's ebony wood he looked even more like a maggot than usual.

He turned as she glared and strolled back. His heels raised a steady *click-click-click* on the granite floor. He must have seen her jaw drop as she recognized the sound. He certainly recognized the danger, because he stopped a good foot short of kicking range.

"Do you realize you nearly bollixed my entire set up with all that noise?" She put her disgust into her glare.

"My apologies." He made sure his tone let her know he didn't mean it. "I trust you have been careful, Mistress?"

"I'm always careful!"

"If you were, neither of us would be here." He lifted his nose so he could look down it at her.

Miserable son of a bitch. Acted like he was still mad. And just because she'd offered to let Strongarm kill him. "Well, I was! Even Marsden couldn't back track me to your node."

"Good. Then we can move on." Without even asking permission he stepped around to her side and reached for the portable link embedded in the chair's link slot.

Letticia clamped her hand across the slot and glared up at him. "I'm not finished yet! You distracted me!"

"You completed your sync-D set up, no?"

"Of course I did! I'm not a total idiot!"

"Then it is time to move on." He reached to pry her hand off the link slot.

As if he were Admiral Yakamoto! Clenching her knuckles together Letticia slapped his hand hard enough to make him back away. She fixed him with her most baleful glare. "Not yet it isn't! I didn't get my questions answered!"

He folded arms and sneered down at her. "If you truly wish to attract Captain Marsden's attention, by all means sync back in. I doubt you will enjoy the experience."

Oh, gob it all, he was right. Defeated, Letticia fell back into the chair and let him pull the porta-link free. Teufelsman slipped the porta-link into a pocket and sauntered toward the door. He made a show of pausing before he turned around to smile at her. "Incidentally, just what questions were you seeking answers for?"

Whyever did his smile always remind her of a ferret? "Why do you care?"

"It is my duty to care, Mistress. As it is my duty to stay informed."

Gobbing Aryans and their word games! Still, he had a point. She'd been so focused on getting back into sync she'd forgotten the man was a snoop born and raised. He really just might know. "I want to know if JP is still storing all that Venus Seed Grandfather Ho's been sending him."

"I may be able to tell you that." Though the way Teufelsman started it certainly wasn't the question he'd expected. He recovered quickly, widened his smile enough to show even white teeth. "It depends."

"On *what*?" There was a lamp on the table near her chair. Letticia longed to throw it at him. She would have, if she'd dared risk the noise. "I've already agreed to give you that little Yakamoto monkey."

"The monkey is a private matter."

"What else, then? Money? You said you had enough money." Which was most certainly a lie. Nobody ever had enough money. Except maybe Octavian. Or Strongarm.

The thought of Strongarm tingled all the way down her body. She'd extrapolated the value of the Lupan's holdings by hand this afternoon while she was waiting for Teufelsman to bring her the porta-link. Just remembering the size of the numbers she'd calc'd out moistened her tongue. Stupid dog *was* richer than Octavian. And it would all be hers –

Toes tapped impatiently. Teufelsman was talking. "What?"

"I just told you what I want, Mistress." Teufelsman's jaw clenched so hard he looked like he was chewing the words. "Now. One more time. I want to know why."

"Why what?" Instinctive response. She was going to have to change that. She had to start paying the hard world some attention.

"Why do you care what Johann Petrovich does with his stockpile of Venus Seed? Your uncle's personal investments should be no concern of yours."

Letticia felt his gaze sharpen with suspicion. Heavens, could he have somehow found out she'd been JP's conduit to Grandfather Ho? Fear pricked her heart, sped up her pulse. *Then it struck her: he didn't gobbing know anything!* It was just a trick – a tactic to make her panic, make her reveal too much.

Laughter bubbled up her throat, carrying with it the most wonderfully satisfying sense of power. Well, his trick worked better than he knew. For once she wasn't panicking. She finally had something she wanted now, something she wanted almost as much as she wanted Net itself. She'd have Strongarm. Have him and Net both. Then she'd be safe. Always and forever.

"Why I want to know is not your concern. *You* just need to provide the answer. If you can." She let her new-found confidence touch her smile when she looked up to meet the Aryan's eyes.

And Teufelsman flinched. "According to my sources, your uncle's cruiser destroyed a number of Lupan miner ships over the past year–"

"That's old history," Letticia snapped. "Tell me something I don't know." She lifted her chin and waited him out.

"What you don't–" He softened his tone. "What you may not have discovered is that your uncle has retained the hulks of those Lupan ships. He has had the hulls gutted, then locked together–"

"To form a single interlocking storage unit. Located at the Jump point midway between Bogue Dast Station and Streiker. The Jump point lines up with Rogue's trajectory. Easy strike range of Strongarm's mining colony there. I know that." Heavens, she was the one who'd suggested it! Only she hadn't understood, then, that Rogue could be hers. "The question is what has he done with the Seed he was storing there?"

"Meaning, has he yet attacked Rogue?" Teufelsman didn't even bother to hide the smirk. He looked disappointed when she didn't return it.

"Do you know or don't you?"

Teufelsman wet his lips. "If I may point out, Mistress-"

"So you don't know." Letticia snorted in disgust. She leaned back, rested her hands on the chair's arm rest, one finger absently stroking the useless sync link.

"Allow me to point out, Mistress, that any attempt to interfere with Streiker's plans-"

"Will have Johann Petrovich screaming treason again. I know." She could already visualize JP's puce-faced rage. Letticia traced her fingers up her arm. The fine hairs shimmered red-gold where they caught the light. It was kind of pretty, actually. Nothing to compete with Net, but certainly good enough for – heavens, what *was* that smell? She sniffed at the crook of her arm, got a whiff of something sharp and nasty. Oh, gob it! Her damned body needed washing again.

She realized belatedly Teufelsman was talking. She swallowed a *tsk* of disgust and lifted her nose out of stink range to let him know he'd have to repeat himself.

"I said, Mistress, you would be wise to make sure you can bring Strongarm under control in time for it to matter."

"What's that supposed to mean?" Letticia pushed herself higher in the chair. Noted with satisfaction that Teufelsman slipped back a pace.

"Surely you're aware that Pandar has its own ambassador en route to Den Lupus. A high grade SpriteType woman – quite an appealing one, my sources tell me – with a Pandari trade treaty in hand." He smiled that weasely smile. "Need I remind you that Strongarm is not Den Lupus' only unmarried war lord?"

"So what? None of the others matter. Strongarm's the one who controls Rogue. And Rogue is where the money is."

"It will matter a great deal if Strongarm dies before he mates."

"For heaven's sake, I'm not going to kill the fool, I'm going to gob him!" At least until she had Rogue.

"You don't have to kill him. He's managing it for himself." Teufelsman rocked back on his heels looking insufferably superior. "Have you not noticed the deterioration in Strongarm's health, Mistress? I had MedNet begin monitoring his biopat when I noticed how he was shedding. His initial chemsignals were already dangerously out of balance. Now-" Teufelsman shrugged expressively. "Strongarm *must* mate in the next day or so. Or he will die."

"That still gives me plenty of time to gob the silly son of a bitch."

"Indeed? Forgive the observation, Mistress, but he does not seem to be overly eager to bed you." Teufelsman considered a nail, eyed her above it. "Need I calculate for you the odds of you surviving should your cousin Octavian gain control of the Lupan market?"

"No." No, she could calc those odds out herself well enough. Gobbing, treacherous Octavian! Always smiling, always so *terribly* polite! And all that time just waiting his chance to cut her throat!

She felt anger burn up her throat, felt the anger kindle to rage. She turned the rage on Teufelsman. "I want that sync glove."

"Certainly, Mistress. In a couple of days-"

"Tonight!" Letticia pushed herself out of the chair, saw with satisfaction the first touch of fear in the Aryan's expression. "Get out and get busy. I want you back here in under three hours. With that glove ready. Because I've got work to do."

She laughed at the way he scurried out, then ordered her major domo to draw her a bath. She wanted to smell her best when she claimed her dog. In the interim – she would work out a lesson for dear cousin Octavian and his pretty ambassador.

XXVII

Keiko Yakamoto leaned back against the red stone pillar of a tourist shop atop the stairs leading into the Old World Bazaar. The stairs put her high enough to peer through the wind shields of the haole cars that flitted down Kalakaua Avenue. Let her catch a glimpse of the proper Types heading out for a night of dancing and flirting and… whatever else it was proper Types did for entertainment. This evening her imagination painted herself into one of those dainty cars, saw herself in a fancy silk dress, lifting her hand for Jezekiah Van Buren to help her step out. Her pulse fluttered at the way he smiled down at her, leaped when he bent to kiss her.

She leaped in earnest when a solid hand landed on her shoulder. She came up on guard three steps down, hands up, trying not to pant.

"Wake up, Mote." Captain Marsden held his hands out, palms upward. He was still in civ clothes, rumpled now. A gust of wind twirled her a tangy whiff of lingering aftershave. "Didn't mean to scare you. You okay?"

"Fine." Now that her heart had stopped cracking her ribs. She didn't bother trying to scowl him down. He had his head cocked, old habit, listening to comm scan even when he was talking. But the trouble clouding his face was aimed at her. "That medic of yours patched me up just fine." Though somehow she didn't think that was what bothered him.

"Good. Then walk with me a ways, Mote. Got some stuff I need to ask you." He motioned her down the steps, a towering dark presence even in his loose islander jacket and pants. Wasn't just the homies on the street who gave him wide birth. The haole tourists took one glance at that comm implant and found something else to look at real quick, too.

He didn't say anything for the better part of a block. Keiko locked hands behind her back and matched his pace. *Makai* way, ocean side of Kalakaua, the blackened ruins of Waikiki stuck up through the palms like guardian totems behind the little junk shops lining the street. A wind gust carried her the smell of rain coming in over the Koolau mountains and made the captain clamp an elbow over his jacket. If he thought he was hiding the bulge of that pistol of his, he was lolo. The people-noise on the street still went quiet at his approach. Nice, in a way. The people silence let her hear the waves whooshing in along Waikiki.

The shops petered out as Kalakaua angled south toward the shore. The captain stopped, finally, near the half-melted bronze statue to some pre-Schism demi-god. Keiko pulled in a long breath, bracing herself. "So what you want to ask, Captain?"

"Your father know about those Tong stars?" Hands behind his back, eyes on her, the comm crescent a cold silver gleam amid his graying curls.

"Huh. If he did, I wouldn't be here to say so." She hung her head, embarrassed. "Thanks for not telling him, Captain. Didn't mean to put you in a bad spot."

"No hu-hu. It's you I'm worried about." His dark face clouded again. This time there was real sorrow in it. "So how'd you get your hands on a Tong star, Mote?"

"Grandfather gave them to me. They were a *present*, Captain." She shrugged, knowing how silly that sounded. But the Captain knew. He understood.

"One goddamned nasty, mean present, you ask me."

"Only if the Admiral finds out-"

"No, dammit!" He yelled loud enough to make her jump.

"Those things put you in trouble with the *law*, Mote! They put you in trouble with *me*." He clasped her shoulders, making her look up at him. She started at the tremble in his hands. She tried to wiggle closer, wanting to hug his pain out. But he held her in place, his grip hard. "Listen and listen good, Mote. Possession of Tong stars is a Registration level crime. There is no appeal, you understand that? Only reason you're not havin' this conversation with Teufelsman right now is 'cause his lordship –

"*Jess?*" She felt her expression go silly. She lost the happy thought, the Captain shook her so hard.

"Listen to me, dammit! I don't know what old man Ho is up to, but right now he's put you in serious danger. You got *no* wiggle room, Mote, not any more. Old man Ho knows that. What scares me is he's using you, same way he used your parents. So you know anything about what Grandfather Ho's up to, you tell me. Now." He shut up, waiting, holding her hard and fast at arm's length, with sorrow in his face and mist in his eyes.

Keiko felt her throat tighten. She groped for words, searching, wishing for anything to tell him, anything that would put the smile back in his face. But she could only shake her head, helpless. "I don't know, Captain. Honest. You want, I'll ask him for you-"

He let her go so abruptly she stumbled. He turned his shoulder to her, blocking his face. There was such a miserable tension to his shoulders she was afraid to even touch his sleeve. She wouldn't have blamed him if he hit her – *Tutu* Pele knew he had cause – but she couldn't bear it if she'd made him cry.

Instead, he just straightened and cocked his head again. He rubbed a hand across his eyes before he turned to look down at her. His voice, when he spoke, was quiet and hard. "Got to go, Mote. Got other folk to worry about, too." He took a step away, stopped. "Listen, child: stay clear of Grandfather Ho, you hear me? That sonuvabitch Teufelsman saw those stars. If he ever finds a way to prove a connection between you and old man Ho, there ain't one goddamned thing I can do to protect you. So you just keep clear of him, you got that?"

"But Captain-"

"No buts, Mote. Do it."

"Yessir. But Captain, everybody *knows* I know Grandfather-"

"What everybody 'knows' is hearsay. Hard evidence is proof. So you stay clear of him, hear?"

"Yessir. Do my best, sir."

"It better be a Samurai best, Mote." He nodded and stumped back down Kalakaua toward the Manor.

"Say, Captain?" She jogged after him to make sure he'd hear. "What'd you mean Grandfather used my parents? How?"

"Means I talk too much is what it means." He glanced down at her looking sorrier than she'd ever seen him, but he didn't even break stride. "T'ain't my place to say. You gotta ask the Admiral that one."

He ruffled her hair and strode off, leaving her to think on her own. Just as well, probably. She already had a list of questions for the Admiral anyway.

XXVIII

Teufelsman strolled back through the sec screen guarding her door in just under the three hour deadline. The wilt of his linen suit looked like he'd sweated through the entire time, but he dangled the sync glove in front of her with an air of skinny white triumph. Letticia yanked the glove from his grip, jammed it onto her hand, and slid the mesh fingers into her link.

Glory! She made sure NetMind could not spot *her* buried within Teufelsman's sync-D before she waved him off to go spy on somebody else. Waited again until she saw the sec shield on her door ripple into place behind him. Then slowly, sweetly, she gave herself to the glittering vastness of NetMind.

She felt her body's pulse sync to NetMind's rhythm, felt her *self* spring back to life. Every fleeting synapse spark felt like a welcome. Every gleaming, ethereal thread of the data stream sang of universes yet undiscovered, worlds yet unexplored. Oh, *God* how she wanted to stay here! Just get away from everything. But she didn't dare linger too long in Net. Not yet. Not until she owned Strongarm. And she'd never own him at all if Octavian's silly ambassador got to Den Lupus first.

She recognized the red tinge seeping outward along her spider strands. She sucked the rage back, watched her outbound strands go clear. Step by step. She'd worked out her plans while she waited for Teufelsman. Now she had to take them step by step. JP was step one.

With soul-wrenching effort, Letticia tore her mind away from glory. She found the outbound Jumpline of the Streikern ambassador, attached a spider to its message thread. Then allowed herself a few moments' glory while she waited for the spider to infiltrate JP's personal node.

Lord Johann Petrovich Van Buren her major domo intoned. JP's holo pearlesced before the words faded.

JP was clearly planning for trouble. She'd caught him in his war room: the star charts and grids forming the walls around him couldn't be anything else. He was in battle uniform, too, a fat silver comm thread spiraling around his head to his mouth. Against his black uniform, his red hair looked amazingly like a lit match stick. He barely bothered to look up from the panel of comm displays in front of him to sneer at her. "If you are going to beg for a ride off Earth again, I shall petition your mother for permission to execute you myself."

Like she was some damned dog... well, she'd let him enjoy himself. For now. "Not at all, Uncle. I'm quite content to stay here now. I simply came to help you. A purely friendly gesture." Letticia settled more comfortably into her chair and smiled beatifically up at him. "You're going to need help if you manage to provoke a war with the Lupans."

JP didn't even glance up from his displays. "I assume you did not hijack my ambassador's Jump line again merely to announce you've found a way back into Net."

"Hardly. But I do have an ambassador to discuss with you."

She just sat back and waited. It was her game now. As he was about to find out.

JP muttered something into his mouthpiece, then crossed arms to glare at her. "Whose?"

"You do know that Octavian has his own ambassador en route to Den Lupus, don't you?"

"Spare me your obsession with the obvious." JP tsked in disgust and glanced back at his display panel. "Personally, I find the idea of a Pandari-Lupan mating infinitely preferable to yourself."

"I'm only obsessed with survival. As you should be."

Oh, now that got his attention! JP stopped with his hand frozen above his comm to turn those icy blue eyes on her. "Do you presume to tell me what to do, Niece?"

"I'm not presuming anything, Uncle. I'm merely wondering why you haven't intercepted Octavian's ambassador." Letticia turned her smile beatific. "Unless, of course, you're *trying* to commit suicide."

Amazing. She'd never thought JP had enough color to lose, yet he managed to go whiter. "I wonder that your mother has not executed you simply to eliminate the annoyance." He tapped his comm display to break the connection. It didn't break, of course. JP swore and slapped it outright.

Letticia leaned her head back against the chair and allowed herself an instant to *feel* the satisfaction. "You can punch your fist right through your panel if you want, JP. It won't work. Not until I decide it will."

JP went quiet. She would have to learn that trick, Letticia thought. The effect was more terrifying than his rages. Or would have been. If she hadn't been in control. "So. Are you quite ready to chat?"

"The only thing I have to discuss with Home World is your execution.

Now release this link. Before you force me to inform your mother that you have been acting as Ho Tong's facilitator for its Commonwealth distribution of Venus Seed."

"Go ahead and try, JP. See how far it gets you. Mother won't hurt me." Mother loved her. Mother kept her *safe*. But JP would never understand such a thing. Letticia turned her smile pitying. "What you should be worrying about it what happens to Streiker if Octavian's ambassador hands him control of the Lupans before I finish Impressing Strongarm."

JP dismissed the threat with a snort. "That's Home World's worry, not mine."

"Oh, really? Then tell me: what purpose does Streiker serve? Why was that nasty ice ball you call a planet even colonized?"

"I do not need you to teach me history-"

"I think you do, Uncle. Because the Commonwealth only supports Streiker as a buffer against the Lupans. You can't survive a year without your Commonwealth subsidies. Your very expensive subsidies." She gave him a whole second to think that through. "So what do you think happens to your subsidies if Octavian controls Den Lupus?"

"Irrelevant. I will control Rogue. There's enough mineral wealth in those mines to render Commonwealth support unnecessary."

"Oh, for heaven's sake. Do you really believe Octavian's going to just *gift* you a treasure world like Rogue?" Letticia allowed herself a chuckle. She hadn't a clue, actually, what Octavian's plans were. But she'd made sure his personal node's records said what she needed them to before she hijacked the Jump line. Just in case JP's syncmeisters found a way to check. "So tell me, JP, just how do you plan on feeding your world with neither Rogue nor Venus Seed to fund you?"

"I will not be blackmailed, Niece." JP gripped the edge of his comm panel with both hands. "I will take care of Octavian's ambassador – as a trade. In exchange-" He looked like he was trying to smile, only habit turned it into a sneer. "Your brother is supposed obtain the Lupans' long jump drive specs for Octavian in exchange for Pandar's support when the Council convenes to hear his treason case. You will obtain the specs for me, instead."

"Certainly, Uncle." After she had those specs safely in hand and under production on Home World. "Once I finish Impressing Strongarm."

"No. You will provide them within the next twenty-four hours." JP straightened, leaving the ridged imprints of his fingers denting the edge of the panel. "From what my sources tell me, it's unlikely you will ever manage to Impress Strongarm. Apparently you have proven to be as repugnant to Strongarm as you are to everyone else."

"That's not true! He wants me!"

"Perhaps he did before he met you. Now-" JP paused long enough to lift a lip. "Your precious Grandfather Ho has ensured the dog has found a more appealing alternative."

"If you mean that stupid little Yakamoto monkey-"

"I hardly think stupid is the right word." JP folded his arms and rocked back on his heels. "I shall take care of Octavian's ambassador in my own way. I suggest you find a way into Strongarm's bed quickly. Before Grandfather Ho does."

He glanced at his comm panel, lifted a brow. With a tsk of annoyance, Letticia released her lock. The holo evaporated, leaving her alone. She wrenched the sync glove out of the chair's link before she screamed in rage at this latest betrayal.

The rage faded, hardened into determination. Letticia drummed her free fingers on the arm rest. She couldn't afford hysterics, not now. She had too much to do. So Grandfather Ho thought his little monkey could trump her, did he? Letticia threw her head back and laughed out loud. Oh, she'd show that vile old man just what it meant to be a Van Buren! Slowly, sweetly, she slipped her gloved hand back into the sync link. She'd see how much Strongarm liked his pet monkey.

If there was anything left of Keiko Yakamoto *to* like by the time she got through.

XXIX

He shouldn't be here. With a grunt Strongarm picked up a flat, black pebble, fired it at the moon rising behind Diamond Head's dark slopes. He was supposed to be at the Manor getting ready for the Impression ceremony, not shuffling along Waikiki. He was *supposed* to be panting in anticipation, not kicking at the dust of his dreams. Well, he had the panting part down, anyway. He was just panting after the wrong woman.

Keiko Yakamoto was a Ho Tong tool. Giving himself to her meant death to the treaty, and likely Den Lupus to boot. Logic, history, and Kaitin all told him so. Didn't help. His soul simply refused to believe it. Because his body still tingled with the memory of the *oneness* he'd felt when he touched his little Bird. Because he'd felt, now, what a soul-match could be. Because no matter what he'd promised Jezekiah, his heart was still hunting Keiko Yakamoto. Strongarm lifted his head to the sky wide clouds and bayed his heartbreak at the moon.

He shuffled around Waikiki's broad curve, past the shattered skeletons of ancient hotels whose names the onlies themselves had forgotten. Fitting, somehow, that he remembered their names. He'd dreamed of wandering this shore since he'd first woken to the realization he was a man. Spent a thousand hours pouring over the Histories, memorizing the mystical names of Paradise. Now he was probably the only man in all of humankind who recognized the old Hilton Hawaiian in the rainbow tower down the beach. Or who mourned the rubble – faded pink still showing in the crevices – that had been the Princess Kaiulani.

This was what he was trading his soul for – a dream that was shattered even before Den Lupus was ever settled. Strongarm found another pebble and fired it at the waves. But it was still Home World. At least he'd accomplished that much. His treaty would give his people *aliya*, at least. Whatever misery Letticia Van Buren inflicted on him, it wouldn't be totally in vain. His people would have the right of return, the right to *feel* their humanity again. Maybe, together, they could even rebuild, make Home World whole again.

Only he'd wanted so much more. He'd wanted the whole Makers-be-damned fairy tale: wanted a man's name, and a one-man woman to go with it. And so he skulked out here instead of dressing for Impression. He didn't even want to think what touching that Van Buren bitch was going to feel like. Damned girl didn't just not like him, she found him downright repulsive. Made sure he knew it, too. Strongarm shut the thought out. He filled his ears instead with the soft *whoosh* of waves on sand, the tentative chitter as night insects decided he wasn't a threat. Filled his lungs with the scents of sweet flowers and salt air. Not smart. It was too easy by far to imagine his little Bird here. Made his nose play tricks. He could even imagine her scent.

"Heia." Her voice filled his ears.

"Bird!" Strongarm whirled, ears and jaw drooping in unison.

"Thought I heard you down here." If Keiko Yakamoto noted his embarrassment she had the grace to pretend otherwise. She stepped out from the shelter of a flowering bush to smile up at him. She was still wearing that faded wrap-dress, was still bare-foot, still smelled of – antiseptic. The worry in that jarring scent drew him closer. "Bird? Are you all right?"

"Yeah, fine." She picked her way down to the water's edge. Stopped to watch her toes tickle the wavelets washing the shore, wrapped in woman-thoughts. "Just came down to do some thinking. Got to talk some story with the Admiral tonight. Figured I'd better have my arguments lined up first."

She looked paler than the moonlight warranted. He lifted ears, remembered she wouldn't recognize the gesture. "You're hurt. What happened?"

"Nothing. Tangled with that damned assassin that's been chasing Jezekiah is all." Her expression brightened. "Did you know that's a *Ta'an* he's been dodging?"

Under the antiseptic her scent took on a wistfulness that perked his ears. It was only the lingering antiseptic smell that stopped the rest of him from perking to match. That and – "You took on a *Ta'an*? Why?"

"It was me or Jess. Jezekiah. He said I could call him..." Her lips curled into a dreamy half-smile. She caught herself at it, tried to hide it with a shrug.

"*Uhf.* I'd thought higher of Van Buren than that." The thought of his little Bird facing a Ta'an's claws – Strongarm felt the growl in his throat, shook himself before it turned into a snarl. "What kind of man lets a woman fight his battles for him?"

"A smart one in this case." She straightened, hands going to hips, scent to challenge. "I'm Samurai trained, in case you'd forgotten. Only thing I know is how to die. Or kill." The challenge faded from her scent, leaving behind a bitterness she tried to cover by kicking at the wavelets foaming around her ankles.

"But he let you get *hurt*, Bird." Common sense forgotten, Strongarm waded into the water after her.

"So? Life hurts." She meant it, too. There was joy in the way she looked up. It was one of the things that stopped him from reaching for her.

So she'd made her choice. He tried to tell himself it was the wise one. But his gut knew better. Bird was just another woman to Jezekiah. Another in the long line of women he'd watched Van Buren enchant and use across the rim. Another woman to be politely set aside and forgotten once she'd served her purpose. Once she'd been got out of his sister's way. He'd used her for a pawn, nothing more. And it was *wrong*. "Do you really think Jezekiah Van Buren would die for you, Bird? The way a proper man should?"

"Don't be silly. Van Burens don't die for people. People die for Van Burens." She laughed at him for even asking. Laughed with her eyes, warrior-style.

"You think he's worth dying for?"

Her scent answered for her. Strongarm felt her bliss in his pulse, his soul, his groin. God of his Makers, he knew that feeling. Knew its finality. Recognized, finally, that Jezekiah had won again.

He told himself that was a good thing. That giving himself to her could only bring death to them all. He still had to dig talons into his arms to could lock himself in place. The scent of his own blood cut through the feral urge to grab her, use the Touch wipe Jezekiah Van Buren out of her soul. Blood-scent tightened the muscles around his eyes to hunting focus. Gave him strength to take her loss like a man. "Then I offer you my congratulations, Bird. I hope you will invite me to your wedding."

"Huh?" A larger wave rolled across her knees. She wobbled, winced as she threw her arms out for balance. "How so?"

"Onlies celebrate weddings, no? When you marry Van Buren-" Even his own blood scent couldn't make him finish the sentence. Praise the Makers she couldn't hear the whimper it cost him to say even that much.

"Oh, Jess would never marry me."

"Hell he won't. You're a *Maker*. He knows what that means."

"Yeah, it means I'm a nobody." She shuffled, dropped her gaze a moment to scuff a toe through the white-tipped water lapping her feet. "Far as the Van Burens are concerned, all I can ever be is a bed-wench." The bitterness in her scent overrode even the antiseptic smell, triggered a twice-dangerous urge to nuzzle her hair.

"Then why-"

"Because Jess loves me!" She drew herself up tall enough to bring her challenging scowl to bear on his chin.

Hope lifted Strongarm's ears. He shouldn't give into it, should just bow and leave. Only his feet wouldn't move. "Did he tell you so?"

"Not exactly. But he called me *ku'u ipo*. That's the old language for 'my darling'." His heart tightened at the way her scent went dreamy. "And he said I could call him Jess. Said the people *he loves* all call him Jess." Her chin stayed up, still challenging. "For a monkey, that's about as good as it ever gets."

"You're not a monkey, Bird. You're a Maker."

"No, I'm not, dammit! I'm just a mixed-Type natural, same's half the other islanders. I'm a nothing and a nobody. Only person ever loved me was Grandfather Ho."

That name finally cold-cocked sense into him. Maker's balls, he'd nearly done it in blood this time. Been ready to sacrifice all of Den Lupus to his own fool need. Strongarm lifted his hands, dropped them again helplessly and shuffled toward the shore. At least the feel of grainy sand working its way between his toes gave him something to feel other than his own profound stupidity.

"Sorry, eh?" Bird's voice, at his elbow, Bird's scent mingling with antiseptic and ocean.

"No need." She was too close by half. Strongarm lengthened his stride to put safe distance between them. He only succeeded in throwing himself off-balance as the waves' backwash shifted the sand beneath his feet. An incoming wave slapped him face first into silvery foam and Strongarm found himself chewing salted sand. He spat it out, tongue curling around the skin-cracking intensity of the salt water, and pushed himself to his knees. Makers be praised Bird didn't understand Lobish.

He ignored the hand she automatically extended to help him and pushed himself up on his own. Had to – his fingertips tingled, Touch-need writhing just from her standing so close, with her scent bespeaking love and laughter. He'd have lost it all and forever if he'd taken her hand. Lost honor and treaty together, and gifted it all to Ho Tong.

"Friends, eh? You're not mad at me, are you?"

Strongarm sensed rather than saw Bird reach for his arm when he didn't take her hand. He nearly leaped aside. The effort it took to avoid her doubled him over. A wave drove salt water up his nose. At least it gave him an excuse for the wrenching whimper.

Only Bird followed, worry strong now in her scent. "You okay? No hu-hu?"

"No. Not mad." He managed to straighten, though he couldn't risk looking at her. Not with the worry still strong in her scent. "Still friends."

"Good. So prove it."

"I said so–" No, he had no reason to snap at her. His misery was not her fault. "How?"

"Jess gave me his family's name for him. So you give me yours. What do the people who love you call you?"

"Nothing I can repeat here." He perked ears at her. And wished he hadn't. Moonlight ran like liquid silver down her hair, raised a heavenly glow on her bare skin.

She tracked his gaze. Folded arms in response and added a smile to the challenge. "Yuh-huh. Friends always have nicknames for each other. People I love call me Keik." A wave whooshed too close to the sarong and she waded up the sand. The wind blew her scent away from him, leaving him with that half-blind feel of sight only. Though truth be told, the sight of her butt swaying in rhythm to the push-pull of the water was – he cut that thought off with an *uhf* and waded up to join her, relieved she couldn't see his hopping attempt to shake the sand out from between his toes.

She almost caught him at it at that. She turned around when she reached the jungle's edge. Jammed hands on hips, challenged him with her eyes. "So? You not mad, then you got to tell me your friendly name."

"Strongarm." His tongue was too dry to get anything more out.

"Wrong. That's your battle name."

"Sorry. It's the only one I've got." At least it was until Letticia Van Buren gave him one. Bitch the Van Buren girl was, he'd be damned lucky to get off with 'Fido'.

"Okay, that's how you want to play it, I'll give you one myself." She gave him a smile that was pure mischief. "I'm going to call you Alex."

"But-" Strongarm swallowed, hard. She didn't know what that meant. Didn't understand – He turned his nose to the ocean, drank in the wild, free scent of its vastness. Tried to concentrate on the feel of the wind exploring the under hairs of his mane. Anything to keep his writhing fingertips clenched at his sides. Anything to keep himself from forgetting she hadn't intended to accept him. She wasn't his, didn't want to be.

Scent blind as she was, she misread his reaction. "Eh, no offense, huh?"

He *felt* her worry. Felt it in his gut, behind his eyes, exactly as she felt it. Felt her reach out to him and knew the gesture for a friend's worry, not a lover's. And decided he didn't care.

Strongarm turned to take her hands, palms down where she wouldn't see the Touch writhing along the fleshy pads of his fingers.

Light flashed – And he found himself nose to nose with Kaitin ibn Bengal.

Fangs bared, Strongarm struck with a roar. It was a decapitating blow. Some still functioning part of Strongarm's mind registered that even as he struck. Not in time. Not before the horror of the killing drove ice through his veins, turned the roar of rage into a howl of despair.

Peace, Brother-in-law.

It took Strongarm gasping seconds for the fact of the words to register. Shaking, he clenched talons into thighs to brace himself before he could look up, apologize with his scent. Words would not come.

Kaitin bared chin in response, the tear-drop ruby glittering above the gold lining his emerald robes. He said nothing. No need to. The holo's scent track spoke for him.

Slowly the rage-tinged sorrow in the Bengali's scent filtered through the shock. Slowly, man-thought crept back in, bringing logic with it.

Scent-track – the Van Burens' holos carried no scent; no onlie holo did. So Kaitin had to be patching in through *Khali*... Strongarm shook his ears back up, pushed himself erect. "What is it?"

A gift, Brother-in-law. Delivered to thy vassals on Gerard. From thy onlie friends. Kaitin flicked an ear toward Bird.

"Hey, no hu-hu." Bird was already backing away toward the Diamond Head's slope. "Got to talk to the Admiral anyway."

Strongarm opened his mouth to call after her. All he got was a tongue full of sandy wind and an eye full of Kaitin's warning snarl. Just as well that way, maybe. Had to be. There was no hope, no future at all if he bound himself to Ho Tong. That was almost certainly why Van Buren had seduced Bird tonight.

But she'd given him a name. Despite himself his ears perked. His Bird had given him a *Maker's* name. No matter what that Van Buren bitch did to him, he would have that. He stared down Bird's path long after she'd disappeared, feeling the shape of his name with his tongue, feeling it settle in his heart.

He was still staring after her when Kaitin swatted a holo'd hand through his head. "We have more important troubles, Brother-in-law."

"Well, let's get to grapple, then." He turned, lowered his chin at Kaitin. "But the name is Alex."

XXX

Even reaching a ride up Diamond Head Road on a homie's gardening truck, it was well past moonrise before Keiko let herself through the garden gate. She found an 'ohelo berry bush by touch, offered a few of its sweet berries to *Tutu* Pele in thanks. Without that ride, she'd probably be pancaked helplessly on the roadside now. As it was, her knees felt watery, her arms leaden.

She spotted the soft yellow light from the Admiral's study when she shouldered open the garden gate. The sight triggered a shiver of old dread and new anger. He'd be working on his memoirs, and fuming because she wasn't there to make his tea. Keiko clung to a trailing honey flower vine a moment, feeling the anger kindle. Well, tonight that was just too damned bad Tonight she was going to get answers.

She let herself in through the kitchen. Odd, the living room lights were still on. That was worse than odd; that looked like company. Keiko's knees nearly gave out on the thought. Sweet Tutu Pele, if she'd been late for *company* – She held her breath, braced herself to peek around the kitchen door.

Nobody. Just an old house light reflecting off the polished tables and shimmering the red silk wallhangings above the couch. Still smelled good, too. The bunches of gardenia and scarlet ginger she'd stationed around the room this morning had saturated the air by now.

Keiko let her breath out with a sigh. Well, whoever it'd been, they were gone. Admiral must just have forgotten to turn the lights off. Despite her anger, Keiko shuddered. *Nobody* visited the Admiral, not for friendly. Somebody was in *nui* trouble. Pity whoever it was when the Admiral showed up.

She put the tea water on to boil, used the minutes while the water boiled to jam through a shower and yank on her khakis before she slapped a travel kit together. Odds were too strong the Admiral would throw her out. If he did, he wouldn't give her time to pack once he gave the order. She yanked the kit closed, tossed it out her bedroom window where she could sneak back to pick it up later. She almost packed Grandfather's band of throwing stars, then re-thought it. Might need those tonight. She put them on, tucked them carefully out of sight beneath her blouse.

She opted for the Admiral's favorite tea set tonight. Cups were nearly a thousand years old; minimized the chances she'd have to duck one. She worked out tactics while she carried the tray up the hall to his study. For once she was not going to just blurt out her feelings, anger him right off. Tonight she was going to work up to the question diplomatically. She knelt beside his door, put the tea tray on the floor and breathed a prayer to Tutu Pele before she knocked.

"Enter." Damn, she could hear the stink-eye in his voice.

Keiko slid the door back, shot a sidelong glance at the desk as she scooted herself and the tray through. The Admiral was seated, *haiku* quill in one hand, the other holding open a long scroll, its paper bright against the deep blue of his kimono-style shirt. She knew without seeing that he'd have on sharp-creased, white cotton pants. Knew, too, that he wouldn't write another character on the scroll till his tea was poured.

Keiko heard the Admiral grunt, giving her his opinion of the khakis she wore. She'd known that would be a glitch; she was supposed to wear a traditional kimono at home. But the rig wouldn't fit over the khakis and she was too likely to get thrown out tonight to risk it. Not tonight of all nights. Tong folk wouldn't be the only ones hating Samurai tonight.

Wouldn't be the only ones hating here, either. Battle sense flared at the back of Keiko's neck. She locked hands on the tray to stop herself from hurtling aside. Not an appropriate response, not here. Not with the Admiral.

She took an instant to make sure the throwing stars didn't show under her blouse. Safe there, so it was something else. She did a quick-check the study, trying to see what might have set the Admiral off. Weather screens formed its outer wall so the fairy-lights scattered among the plumeria and pale stones of the courtyard beyond lent the room some sparkle despite the *gusto* suit of ancient Samurai armor hulking beside the screens. Thing gave her the shudders. That and the Samurai's great swords – the meter-long *katana* and barely smaller *wakizashi* – mounted on the wall behind the Admiral's chair. It was the scrolls of his own *haiku* flanking the swords that always seemed out of place. *Love* poems, of all the things in the world.

Love poems ... she'd never even thought to wonder about that before. He must have written them long before she was ever born. Maybe even... The full depth of the betrayal buried in the possibility triggered a swell of rage that darkened her vision. Keiko heard the cups rattle, heard the creak in the tray where her grip crushed the handles.

"You are angry." It was a statement, not a question.

"Yessir." So much for the stealth approach. Keiko willed her hands steady, willed the rage down while she knelt before his desk and whisked tea into his cup.

"Why?" No inflection, no hint of his intentions. Only the battle sense throbbing the back of Keiko's neck warned of the danger behind his calm.

The comm on his desk chimed. Keiko jumped but the Admiral ignored it. "Why?"

The comm chimed again, insistently. He shut it down with the flick of a finger. He lifted the tea cup, cradled it in his palm. Watching her.

"Because I found out who my mother is."

The tea cup shattered in the Admiral's grip. He did not move at all beyond that. Just sat. Eyes gone laser sharp, with the dark tea glistening his hand and trailing across his desk to blur the ink on the scroll he'd been writing.

By habit Keiko grabbed the tea towel from the tray to blot up the spreading stain.

The Admiral slapped her hand away, spraying tea from the shattered cup still clutched in his fist. "Who told you?"

"Grandfather Ho." Spoken with her head up, eye to eye.

He caught her hand in his fist at the name. Had she not been Samurai trained, his grip would have crushed her bones. But she clenched her knuckles and answered ice with fire.

He shoved her hand free, finally. "He lied to you."

"You're the liar!" Keiko heard the forbidden sob in her voice, didn't even try to shut it down. "You've been lying to me all my life. Made me ashamed, made me believe my mother was no good. Made me believe *I* was no good because of her!"

The lump in her throat nearly blocked her breath. Keiko swallowed a sob, blinked back tears, needing him to *understand*.

"You don't know what it's like, Admiral. You're Samurai by *Type*. You've never needed somebody to hold you. You never needed to have somebody care whether you lived or died. But I do. You can't train that out of me."

"So your mother's blood tells after all."

"*Nui* right it tells!" The lump in Keiko's throat stopped her from raging the way she wanted. This time her voice came out quiet as his own. "Only she wasn't a whore. She was a somebody!"

"A traitor and a whore!"

"She's Liliuokelani Kaahumana *Ho*! She's Grandfather Ho's daughter! And she was your wife."

The words hit him like a death blow. Keiko watched the rage drain from his face, watched white fury drain to a terrible ashen gray. "Who told you?"

"Grandfather Ho."

The Admiral shot to his feet. His backhand would have shattered her cheek had Keiko not rolled clear. "Get out!"

"Not yet." Keiko came to her feet in a fighting crouch. "Oh, I get, okay. Don't you go worry that. But not till you answer the question. Why did my mother leave you?"

"She was a traitor and a whore!"

"Stop lying! You want to talk blood – she carried the blood of the ancient *ali'i*, of Hawaiian royalty. You want to talk treason – her only crime was loving *you*!"

And the Admiral just…*shrank*. Just stood there, facing her but staring at something a thousand yards off. Left her to rage at his silence.

Only she couldn't even rage. Her voice came out barely above a whisper. "Why couldn't you tell me? Why'd you make up those awful stories?"

He slumped over onto his knuckles. "Because it was better than the truth."

"Sweet Madam Pele, *how*? What could be better than the truth?"

"Anything!" For a moment, she thought he was going to strike. But this time the fire faded. He leaned onto his knuckles amid the sharp, white shards of the tea pot. Hung his head, shoulders hunched in a misery deeper even than her own.

"What? Because you'd done something so wrong she ran away from you? Because you made her hate you the way everybody else does? Because-"

"Because I killed her!"

His rage crumpled in pieces. Like a mirror cracking outward from an impact hole the tremble worked up his face from his lips. He seemed to collapse inward, as if he were curling around a wound. When he finally spoke it was to some memory she would never share. "You want the truth, then hear it. And may the ancestors forgive me for inflicting it on you."

For a few moments the Admiral just stood there, knuckles grinding the tea cup shards to powder. When he lifted his head he looked and sounded calm. But the effort it took left him shaking. "I grew up with Lily Ho. Throughout our childhood she was my soul, my dreams. I endured Type trial to prove myself worthy of her. Clawed my way up the StelFleet ranks to claim her hand. Everything I ever did was for her."

"So you loved her, too." The thought should have pleased her. Somehow it only felt like a betrayal.

"Yes." For a moment, the Admiral seemed almost happy. Then his lips settled into the familiar hard line. "Yes, fool that I was." He pulled in a breath, let it out in a sigh. "When Grandfather Ho agreed to our marriage I thought we would save the world. And when Lily told me she was pregnant with our child-" He shivered, his breath rasping. "Fool that I was, I begged the Protector to allow me to retire from StelFleet. I convinced her I could negotiate an end to the rebellion."

"Then why didn't you? Grandfather would have-"

"You think I didn't try?" The Admiral raised trembling fists, held them tight to his chest, ridged knuckles starkly white against his blue shirt. "Oh, Grandfather Ho talked. For months he dragged the talks out. For months – while Lily Ho worked her charms on the Protector and her consort. Until she had them almost as much in love with her as I was. Until she worked her way into their very family. While we watched you grow in Lily's womb."

Whatever it was he saw in that thousand yard stare, it made him angry enough to trigger her own battle sense. Instinct as much as training screamed at Keiko to dive out of range. She held her place by force of will. "What happened, Admiral?"

He didn't answer at once. Even when he spoke his eyes stayed locked on the past. "It was all a lie, all of it. Our marriage was nothing more than a ploy, a way to let Grandfather Ho get an assassin access to the Protector. But the plan failed."

"You stopped it." Keiko tried to find pride in the thought and failed. At least it would explain –

"No." The Admiral crunched his shoulders, eyes closing. "No, to my shame. I was so besotted I did not even recognize there was a plot. Not until – not until the explosion itself. It was Marsden who saved us. All of us he could."

"Except my mother." The tightness in her shoulders evaporated. Keiko nearly folded over her knees from the relief. "Then her death wasn't your fault."

"She didn't die in the explosion!"

"Then what happened?"

"The shock sent Lily into premature labor. We took her to the Manor, Marsden and I. To give birth to you."

"Sweet Madam Pele – she died because of *me*?"

"No. I wish she had." The Admiral's face had gone gray. He looked *stretched*, somehow, as if the effort it took to pull the words out were dragging his heart out of his body with them. "Madam issued the order while Lily was in labor. As soon as you were born I dragged Lily out of the Manor."

Keiko shot to her feet to face him with fists clenched, eyes stinging dry. "No! I don't want to hear it!"

"You asked for it, damn you, now listen!" He gulped air, as if he were drowning beneath the memories. "As soon as you were born, I dragged Lily Ho from her birthing bed. I dragged her to the garbage dump behind the Manor. And I cut off her head. After that, I showed Grandfather Ho what it meant to be Samurai."

The truth of it blossomed slowly, horror opening onto horror. "But she was innocent!"

The Admiral slammed knuckles into the desk. The tea set jumped, ancient cups jingling. "She was an-" His lips formed a word, bit it off. He rammed knuckles into the desk top so hard Keiko saw the wood dimple beneath the blow. But his voice came out barely above a whisper. "She was a traitor!"

"It doesn't matter! You said you loved her! How could you -"

"It was my duty, damn you!" This time the tea set bounced off the edge of the desk. The aged porcelain splattered white shards and dark tea across the pale wood of the floor.

"Is that why you raised me? Your *duty*?" Keiko's voice failed. She felt as if her whole body had been dried out, her blood turned to sand. "Or did Madam Van Buren have to order you to raise me, too?"

"I raised you the only way I could. To protect you."

"That's a lie!" She was sobbing outright but she didn't even care. "It's all a lie! It's all only ever been a lie!"

The desk comm chimed again. Wasn't just a chime this time, either. It was the Protector' own code. A summons.

The Admiral snapped a fist up. For a moment Keiko thought he would smash the comm. Her heart rose in the hope he would, that he'd turn his back on the woman who'd made him kill her mother. He shook with the effort but lowered his fist slowly and answered.

Keiko was down the hall to her bedroom. She was gone into the night before her father ended the call.

XXXI

Using a strand of DemoNet Letticia wove a fresh data thread around her personal spider hole. She'd been locked out of her own node long enough for Marsden's own spiders to weave new code across the strands of her web. It took her far too long to worm the DemoNet strand through the new code. Longer still to pry open the bubble inside the hole where she'd stored the Ta'an's sync-D. Too long – one of Marsden's viral guards swooped in to investigate and she felt her body's heart thump in fear.

Gob Grandfather Ho! Miserable, treacherous son of a bitch! He'd *used* her! Used her – used her *trust* – to make his worthless monkey look appealing! It was only the fear of what Marsden's attack viruses would do to her that let her keep the rage burn under control. But she'd built her hidey hole well. Even Marsden's guards couldn't find anything out of place. Letticia waited till the guard cells moved on. Then she ripped through the last enveloping code strings till she found the dupe ID she'd created for that stupid assassin. Carefully, she lifted out the bubble containing the Ta'an's code and merged it into Teufelsman's sync-D.

Once she had the Ta'an's code re-absorbed she took care to wrap an extra thread around it. She had a project for that idiot Ta'an, a tiny bit of belated revenge. She intended to deliver the project instructions personally so she had to be extra cautious. No matter how careful she was people tended to scream when she dropped her spider into their minds. And she wasn't in any mood to be gentle about it just now.

Good thing she'd done the extra wrap, too. Stupid Ta'an screamed so hard he generated an energy spike hot enough to alert SecNet. She lost whole seconds calming the fool assassin down enough to get her instructions through. Her outliers were throbbing by the time she let the Ta'an go, sign that Marsden's advance scouts were already backtracking the energy flash. Gob it all, she wasn't finished yet! Forcing herself to calm, Letticia hooked a passing MedNet thread. She scuttled free barely a nanosecond before Marsden's guards could spot her.

She rode the MedNet thread to a DemoNet junction. She split a strand off there, used her new DemoNet host to track down Strongarm. Good! The dog and his kitty cat were in with Mother. They must be prepping for the Impression ceremony. Oh, gob it – that meant she needed to get her stupid body ready, too. The thought made her stomach lurch – anticipation as much as dread this time. Be worth it to let the dog thump her body. She could almost *feel* all Strongarm's money pouring into her account. But first she had to finish up *here*. Hooking a fresh neuron stream Letticia scuttled toward the golden orb of Jezekiah's node.

Careful...careful.... Jezekiah's node guards knew her too well. She'd spent a marvelous amount of time with them while Jess was out on the Rim. Wasn't any other way to pull off that trick with the holo feedback. Letticia shut down the happy memory of Mother forcing Marsden to allow her access before her chuckle rippled outward through Net. Well, she'd covered for Jezekiah like a good little girl. She'd also laid spider eggs around the borders of Jezekiah's node. Marsden suspected her, of course, but he couldn't prove it. She'd wrapped her eggs in code so ancient even his virals took it for flotsam. But Marsden still kept a personal tab on Jezekiah's node. Paranoid son of a bitch.

Letticia checked her outliers – nothing. Marsden's viral guards seemed satisfied her spider eggs were indeed the dead-code flotsam they pretended to be. Good. Next step. Letticia anchored herself to an ancillary node, spat a data thread across Jezekiah's orb to a second node opposite, then another and another until she'd spun herself a nice little circlet from which she could hatch her eggs. *No* room for error here: that bastard Marsden wove the guards around her precious brother's ID himself. Amazingly, the outer shields looked familiar. Old code! Letticia squelched a throb of joy. Of course – Marsden thought she was locked out of Net. He thought his golden boy was *safe*. Oh, was he in for a surprise!

Ever so carefully Letticia hatched an egg. She embedded instructions in her newborn spider and sent it burrowing deep into Jezekiah's node. It was certain the Yakamoto monkey would seek Jezekiah's protection when she found herself trapped. Less certain, but possible Jess might actually stand up for the girl. They were both in for a surprise now.

Something pulsed the far end of her data thread. Odd, there shouldn't be anything down there. Gently, Letticia extruded a probe –

And screamed. Code mutated at her touch. Viral cells sank acid fangs into her probe, shot up it toward herself.

Letticia sprang onto a passing data stream. The guards followed. They'd never done that before. Frantic, she leaped off it to piggyback on a FunNet cell, hid herself in a nano-pixel of Pandaran sex headed for the ambassador's link. She fled the cell an instant shy of delivery, hooked a neuron. Even through the stream she felt the needle prick of Marsden's guard cells. Still tracking her. Fighting terror, Letticia burrowed into the stream itself, merged her blip into its very essence. She rode the stream deep into NetMind's core, to the safety of her spider trap.

Damn Marsden! He'd snooped even here! A blanket of new cells was trying to penetrate her spider hole's firewalls. No choice, though, not now. Already her outlier strands shivered in warning. Delicately she spun a data droplet off a neighboring thread. Squeezed her energy blip under it. The droplet fell back into place a millisecond before the virals caught up. Letticia blended herself into the data bed while the guard cells sank needle probes into the strands of her hidey hole.

It took almost an entire *minute* for the guards to satisfy themselves. She felt the outer cells of her defenses relax as the guards' probes withdrew. Even so, Letticia waited another eternal minute before she began reintegrating her data feeds. She wove new defenses, then eased out a tentative probe. Good. The guards had skittered off. Chasing a chimera of Teufelsman's ID –

Oh, for heaven's sake! Teufelsman must have sync'd in! Letticia forced down panic. The idiot! She'd told him she was going to test the sync glove! She hadn't thought she'd need to warn him to stay out of Net while she did it. Now Marsden's guards would be chasing his *real* ID.

She had to get out! No, wait, wait – she had to *think*. The glove already tapped Teufelsman's sync-D, but it still showed in NetMind as a separate entity; if they sync'd in at the same time, Net would show Teufelsman in sync in two different locations. But if she cross-linked the glove's ID to Teufelsman's node... That would work. It'd look like he'd been sync'd in all along. It was a dangerous option. Once she laid a cross-link, Teufelsman would be able to backtrack to her spider trap if he tried. But useful – with a cross-link she could implant her instructions directly in his node. If things went wrong, Teufelsman himself wouldn't be able to prove the instructions weren't his own idea.

She hooked a tentacle into the energy blip that was Teufelsman's sync'd essence and burrowed into the Aryan's ID. Hideous experience. She nearly lost her connection altogether under the impact of the Aryan's mental shriek when she dropped into his consciousness. The quivering fool actually tried to break contact! Well she had no time to coddle him now. That shriek would draw every Net guard in the lobe.

She held him in Net by force while she cross-linked the glove's ID and imprinted her instructions directly into his node. She grabbed an exiting feed-line and shot out of Teufelsman's node right through the incoming swarm of SecNet guards. *They* couldn't spot her, of course. SecNet's standard guards were designed to search out little people crimes like thievery and murder.

The beauty of it was that the sheer mass of the swarm hid her presence from *Marsden's* virals.

She backtracked to her hidey hole. Ran a last check on her defenses, then forced herself to yank her hand free of the sync glove. She nearly howled at the loss as she shrank back into the constraints of bone and breath and bodice. No time to mourn, though. Mother would be sending an escort for her any time now. She had to be ready when it arrived.

She pinched the fleshy underpart of her arm savagely. *Ewwww* – vile sensation! She'd forgotten she was still wearing the pink velvet dress from that debacle at Punch Bowl this morning. Touching the sweaty velvet made her shudder with disgust. But it forced focus. Clutching the sync glove Letticia shoved herself out of the chair and wobbled into the bathroom. She'd had her major domo build a little cubbyhole behind the toilet when she was still a child. It had been her hard world hidey hole, a place to hide a child's purloined treasures. It'd been there so long, even the Admiral had never thought to check it.

She dropped to her knees beside the toilet, holding the glove out from her side while she clawed open the loose tile behind the toilet tank.

Admiral Yakamoto is here, Mistress, her major domo announced.

Old habit made Letticia jump. She banged her head on the toilet tank, blinked desperately through the lights popping across her vision for the Admiral's terrifying presence.

No one.

Letticia gulped air, felt her heart start up again. "He is not! Just what was that all about?"

At your door, Mistress. Maybe it was her imagination but she could have sworn the damned thing was sneering.

Her heart tried to stop again. This time she forced herself to stay calm. It couldn't be anything serious. The Admiral wouldn't have waited outside if he knew she'd been tampering with Jezekiah's node. Most likely Mother must have sent him to be her escort. "Well, he can stay outside. Tell him I'm getting dressed."

She threw the glove into the hidey hole and jammed the tile back in place. No time to clean up now. She'd just have to pretend she'd been getting ready all along. Letticia ripped off the suffocating velvet, then pushed herself up by the toilet seat. She splashed water on her face. She threw some talcum under her arms to dry the sweat while she rifled her closet for something cooler. She found a strapless red-gold sheath of some sheer Pandaran brocade that fitted itself to her slender figure and wriggled into it. There – that ought to make Strongarm happy!

Admiral Yakamoto was standing at his usual stiff ease when she strolled out. He certainly wasn't dressed for a wedding. He wore just a plain black uniform. Even those archaic twin swords dangling at his sides were sheathed in black. For some reason the outfit looked familiar in some unpleasant way. Letticia puzzled the discomfort for a moment then shrugged it off. Most likely, he was just mourning her success. Well, she couldn't let it annoy her now. She'd get her own back once she finished Impressing Strongarm. She concentrated on the satisfaction in the thought and met the Admiral's glare with a regal sneer. "Are you ready, Admiral?"

"One is always ready, Mistress." No smile, no frown, no reaction at all. His very lack of expression sent shudders down her spine. "It is to be hoped you are, also. In case the Impression fails."

Spoil sport. Letticia merely sniffed in disdain and marched off, leaving the Admiral to follow. She was almost to the end of the corridor before she remembered, finally, where she'd seen him wear that outfit before.

It was his executioner's uniform.

XXXII

Keiko caught a ride up to the North Shore in the back of an empty flatbed hauler. Admiral would've gone lolo if he knew just how easy it was to reach Grandfather from home. The Admiral's house overlooked Waialae Bay so there was always a hauler of some sort trucking up Pali Highway, and all the truck drivers were Tong folk. There were plenty of trucks tonight. They were all heading north, too. For Memory Night.

She wondered if Kameh had a fire lit tonight, then *tsked* at herself for the silly idea. Not likely, not on a Jump ship bound for the Commonwealth rim. Still, he was on a Tong ship so they'd be honoring the memories. Maybe he'd be remembering her – Keiko scrunched her eyes closed, willed down the forbidden tears. She rested her hands on the flatbed's rough wooden slats and concentrated on the crooked shape of Mokoli'i Island – the one the haole called "Chinaman's Hat" – slipping past a few klicks off shore. Beyond the islet, the ocean rumbled like some great, slumbering beast. The wind of its breath smelled of flowers and fish. Island smells, reminding her afresh of Kameh with holiday leis round his neck and a fine mahi mahi fish under one arm. *Sweet Tutu Pele, make Grandfather bring Kameh home.* Let her succeed in that much. The gods knew she needed a friend.

The wind turned harder as the truck lifted over the pali ridge. Keiko stretched out on the remnants of a burlap sack, let the lazy thrum of the engines ease some of the itches out of the synskin salve on her back and thigh. Far above, the Milky Way stretched out forever, a silver mist of stars against the glistening sea. The truck bounced over an air pocket, making her grab a slat to avoid bouncing out.

She felt the twitch in her fingers against the wood that said she'd picked up a splinter. Wedging herself into the corner behind the driver's cab, she felt along her callused palm for the bit of wood till she found the splinter and bit it out.

The flatbed switched its running lights to yellow and red soon as it climbed above the Koolau Ho Tong colors shining proudly over Ho Tong turf. Local folk talked about the small towns used to dot the coastline. That was before the Rebellion. Before the Admiral and his Samurai exterminated them. There were no lights along Oahu's coast any more. Just the dead roads.

The truck bucked as it crested the mountains and hit the wild North Shore winds. Sliding madly, Keiko grabbed a wooden slat and hauled herself upright. They were high enough to see all the way out to Kahuku Point at the northernmost tip of Oahu. Hear it, too. Even from here the thunder of the North Shore breakers added a bass rumble to the wind. A bit inland, she saw the orange speckle of the camp fires that marked Grandfather's party. Keiko rapped on the back of the driver's cab, pointing, and the homie nodded. He dropped her off on the shoreline then took off again, headed for wherever his *ohana* honored their dead.

Keiko clambered past the rocks and spindly *kiawe* trees till she found the tarmac surface of the dead road. The road was as much pebble as tarmac, but it was easy walking – if you knew how to find it. She followed it up hill, tracking her course by the jagged black border where the Koolau Mountains' pushed up against the Milky Way. She felt the eyes watching her from the dark long before she reached the outer circle of watch fires.

There was no death-intent in the those hidden eyes, not this time, but she recognized that cold *ki* just the same. Good thing that killer was working for Grandfather Ho – *Sweet Tutu Pele!* Lifting her hands slowly out from her sides, Keiko angled to face the killer's location. She might not know his name, but she knew his *ki*. Knew it from Type trial and Punchbowl and Kalaeloa. She could only hope, here, that the Ta'an did not have orders to kill her as well.

The Ta'an's *ki* dwindled. Still, it'd been a warning. Keiko stayed where she was and waited. Eventually a small, unsmiling boy stepped out of the darkness. He waved her forward, pointing the way with the barrel of a laser rifle nearly as long as himself. Keiko ruffled his hair as she passed, and he forgot the rifle in grinning up at her.

The dead road ended in a village-sized clearing a quarter klick later. Rows of broad, concrete slabs broke the tangle of fern trees and underbrush, the remnants of Kahuku town. Bonfires flickered on maybe half the slabs, adding the scent of wood fire to the fragrance of night-blooming jasmine in the underbrush and the plumeria of the leis piled on the fireless slabs. There'd be fires like this on all the islands tonight. This was memory night.

Ki lingered here, ghost-*ki* of the women and children the Admiral and his Samurai had slaughtered in their homes. The ghosts were all that was left of Grandfather's home town, now. Elderly men tended the bonfires on the slabs. Gray-haired aunties knelt on the dark ones, rocking slowly as they chanted over the leis, singing to the spirits of their lost.

Keiko wished she dared kneel with the women. She didn't dare. Not yet. Other days, the people could accept her for herself. Tonight – tonight she was the daughter of the Butcher Yakamoto. Even in passing the undercurrent of hate prickled the back of her neck.

At the shadowed border of the *kuleana* young women laid out the shells and grass skirts they'd use later for the hula. Their brothers and male cousins squatted around the *imu* tending the fire pit. A shift in the breeze brought Keiko the aroma of roast pig and her stomach rumbled. Hunger triggered the unworthy but fervent hope that Grandfather would let her eat even if he didn't accept her.

She found Grandfather Ho, finally, where she'd expected, beside the bonfire of his dead house, where the Samurai had killed his wife and sons. The old man was seated cross-legged beside the central bonfire. He was bare chested as always, in a pair of baggy red and yellow cut-offs, Tong colors on proud display here among his own, a silvery band of throwing stars slung across one bare shoulder. He held a star between his fingers, turning it end over end so the firelight gleamed red along its razored edges.

A line of aunties in loose muumuus inched along the slab of his house. Each woman carried a gourd bowl. Keiko knelt near the back of Grandfather's slab as the next woman in line knelt in front of Grandfather. A drop of dark liquid sloshed over the rim of the bowl as she held it out to him. It trailed down her bare arm to mingle with the other thin ribbons of blood there.

Grandfather stretched his hand across the rim. Firelight rippled redly along the rows of dark drops dewing his forearm. He touched the tip of the Tong star to his wrist, starting a new row. A single drop of blood caught the firelight as it fell, joining the pool of blood already in the bowl. He took the bowl from her then, holding the star out between gnarled fingers as he sipped.

The woman pressed the bowl to her forehead when he returned it, and rose. She stepped past Keiko without a glance. Behind her, the next woman knelt to offer her bowl to Grandfather.

The last woman in the line stepped away finally. Keiko's eyes lingered on her back, wishing. Felt Grandfather's eyes on her and looked up to see the flash of hope in his eyes. Felt her lips tremble at the way it died.

"*Ke ha pilikia?*" He wiped the star carefully between his fingers, then slipped it into its sheath, watching her. "What's the trouble? It is not to be hoped you are here with your father's consent."

"No, sir." Keiko ducked her head in apology and shrugged.

"I ran, Grandfather. I asked the Admiral about what you said. And he said – he said – " The tears came burning up. She curled around them, pounded her fist on the concrete to keep them down.

"He said he killed her, did he not?"

"He said she was a traitor!" Keiko felt his gnarled finger beneath her chin. Gentle though his touch felt, it broke her resistance, lifted her chin against her will to make her meet his eyes. "He said he loved her." Somehow, that hurt worst of all. That most perfect of betrayals.

Grandfather let her chin go while he slid into cross-legs on the raised platform beside her. "Do you believe him?"

"I don't want to. Only the Admiral's never been much of a liar." She leaned her forehead against his bent knee. "He couldn't love her and kill her both. How can you kill somebody you love – somebody who loves *you*? Not unless she was really guilty."

Grandfather rested a hand on her cheek. It felt like her own hands: too big for his body, too hard to be skin and flesh. He wrapped an arm around her shoulders, let her nestle against his side feeling safe. Feeling *loved*. It made her feel like singing and crying together. "Sometimes a man finds it easier to believe a lie, *keiki*. Your mother was a wild and beautiful girl, but she was no traitor."

"Then why'd he kill her? Admiral's mean, but he's not crazy."

"No. He is Samurai." He stroked her hair softly, yet even so the rough edges of his hands snagged strands of hair loose. "When he accepted SamuraiType code he gave up himself. Accepted the slavery of obedience. To the Van Burens."

"Then she was guilty."

"Is it treason to defend your family? Your people?" A thrill of hatred rippled his *ki* so hard Keiko tried to jerk free. Grandfather held her in place, though he did it gently. "This is the something you must decide. Where your loyalty lies. For now-"

Somewhere in the dark, a hollow log drum clacked. Another answered it, then a third, setting up a throbbing, dangerous rhythm. In the shadows beyond the central bonfire smaller hula drums took up the rhythm, added their own. Slowly, softly, elderly women stepped down from their *kuleanas* to form a central circle. The thud of their feet on the earth answered the drums as they began their *hula*. Began dancing the story of Kahuku Town's death. Relived in hand gesture and dance the murders of their husbands, their sisters, their children.

"These are your people, keiki." Grandfather nodded at the dancers. He still held his hand against her face. The drums echoed in his pulse. "Look at what your father did to us. And ask yourself who is the traitor." He looked down at her, and she shivered with the effort to ignore the battle sense pounding her neck. "Then tell me: have you come home at last?"

It was the invitation she'd been hoping for. So why was it so hard to answer? "I don't know." She felt his hand clench. She caught his fingers between her own when he started to pull away. "*E 'olu'olu – Please*, Grandfather -"

He pulled his hand free leaving Keiko to hang her head, still feeling the drums throb in her pulse. "*E kala mai ia'u, Tutukane*. Forgive me, Grandfather. I want come home. I want to *belong*. I really do. But- " She couldn't find words to say what she meant. All she could do was shrug helplessly.

"But in your heart you wish also to be Samurai." There was no hatred in the look he gave her. Just a slow, cold anger that chilled Keiko to the very bone. "You still long for the Van Burens' slavery."

"Oh, but Jess isn't like that! He's -" Keiko felt the joy die stillborn. Battle sense shrieked down her neck even before she recognized the fury in Grandfather's face. She couldn't even dive clear. His grip on her hands felt like a steel trap. The dragon tattoo coiling up his arm caught the silver gleam of the throwing stars and turned it red.

"So you have already sold yourself to the Van Burens."

"It wasn't like that! It wasn't like that at all! Jess is sweet, and kind, and – and gentle." Keiko tried to pull away. Grandfather only tightened his grip. The injustice of it all kindled an answering fury in her. She felt her jaw set, clenched her knuckles against his. "I never sell myself to anybody, Grandfather. Jezekiah Van Buren loves me. He told me so."

"Ah, yes. Love. The most insidious weapon." For a moment Keiko thought he would strike. But he only relaxed his grip so her hands fell free. The battle sense faded to a dull ache at the back of her neck. "Perhaps you are less your mother's daughter than your father's after all. My Lily was made of stronger stuff."

"I'm strong as I need to be, Grandfather." The sting in the voice made him start. At the moment she was too angry to care. "Enough at least so I don't betray somebody who loves me. There aren't that many of them."

"I have lost one daughter to the Van Burens. It seems, I must lose another."

"No, you don't have to. I'm still *me*. You still love me." But his expression went neutral, the way the Admiral's did. He didn't speak. It was the answer in his silence that scared the anger out of her. "Don't you?"

"Love is not the cure-all youth wants it to be." Grandfather lifted her chin with a fingertip. "But it is a powerful tool in the hands of a master manipulator like Jezekiah Van Buren. I am forced now to wonder how long it will take him to turn you against me, *keiki*."

"I'll never turn against you, Grandfather!" She nestled her face against his knee, felt the hot wetness build up on her cheek, the tears trapped against the hard muscle under his wrinkled skin. "Please don't hate me!"

"Shhh, *keiki*. Save your tears for the sorrows you've yet to meet. Even if they make you Samurai, I will always love you." He pulled her close to his side, ran a hand across her hair, his touch gentle again. "But I must send you away even so."

"Why?"

"Because you still do not know yourself."

"But I can help-"

"In time you will. Only that time is not yet." He patted her head and shifted onto one knee. "I fear it will take a bitter lesson before you understand. When you do, then you may come back."

She could only stare up at him, fear and anger melding into a terrible, terrible emptiness. "Then do one thing for me, Grandfather? Last thing, I promise." He looked grim but he waited, gave her the chance. "Up on Punchbowl – you said you'd help Kameh. Please bring him home. He never did anything wrong, you know that."

"Do you now doubt my promise, Keiko Kaahumana Yakamoto Ho?"

"Never doubt you, *Tutukane*." Though she did, now, even if she couldn't say why. By habit she reached to touch his knee. This time he twitched back from her fingers and she dropped her hand. Felt her heart drop with it. "Just asking you to keep your promise. Please bring him back. It won't be so bad for him here anymore. I can get Jezekiah to help him."

He recoiled as if she'd hit him. It was only an instant. But for that moment even the shadows could not hide the way his face contorted in hate.

Keiko dropped to one knee, head down hands up in submission. Too late she remembered it was a *Samurai* gesture. Stifling a sob she could only wait for Grandfather to kick her.

Only the blow didn't come. Keiko lifted her head, felt new tears burn her eyes at sight of Grandfather's expression. The hate was gone. What was left was… just empty. He studied her…like he wasn't really looking at her at all. When he spoke he sounded almost like the Admiral, criticizing the way she'd handled a blade. "I fear it no longer matters, in any case. I kept my promise, *keiki*. I contacted the ship's captain. Told him to send Kamehhmeha No-Name back."

Keiko shot to her feet, joy erasing doubt and fear and loss. "Then he's on his way! When'll he be back?"

"He won't. It pains me to tell you, but he didn't want to come back." Grandfather shrugged, closing the subject and herself off together. "Can you blame him, *keiki*? After all, it was his own idea to go. Why should he want to return?"

This time Keiko's knees did collapse. It wasn't right. Grandfather must have misunderstood. Or maybe the messages got garbled. But Kameh would have come back. If he'd had the chance. She felt Grandfather's hand on her hair and looked up, hoping.

"I fear there is something I must demand of you, Keiko Yakamoto." The warmth she'd always known in him was gone. His voice was colder, scarier than even the Admiral's. "I gifted you a band of throwing stars. Those are not an appropriate gift for a Samurai. I fear I must ask you to return them. At least until you choose to claim them for yourself."

She could only bow her head. With numb fingers, Keiko lifted the silvery band from beneath her blouse, pulled it off over her head. The loss cut deeper than the stars' blades when she felt Grandfather lift the band from her fingers. "*E kala mai ia'u, Tutukane.* Forgive me, Grandfather -"

She looked up, but Grandfather Ho was already gone.

Slowly, painfully, Keiko pushed herself up and stumbled off toward the dead road and highway beyond. To Jezekiah.

XXXIII

Rudyard Kipling Marsden grunted as he dropped into the rec chair. Except for himself, the Manor's Sec rec was empty, so the room's fake sunlight was wasted on the munchie dispensers and clustered sync chairs. Place already had a hollow, weehours feel to it, though it was only twenty-hundred outside. Suite him; the atmosphere fit his mood. He was feeling pretty damned hollow himself about now.

He ought to be heading home. He was off-duty, and hanging out at the Manor was just tempting fate to find him a problem. At home he could pour himself a cold one, sit out on the lanai and watch the Milky Way. 'Cept that was about all he could do at home, unless he wanted to tackle his repair list. And he could ignore the house work just fine right here.

Marsden worked his butt deeper into the rec chair's shell, sighed contentedly as its cushions molded themselves to his form. The entertainment unit in the headrest automatically fed subliminal trailers into his synclink, FunNet trying futilely to override the voiceless litany of SecNet notices. Off-duty or not, there was no turning off his comm implant. Habit made him check a murder alert; SecNet said the corpse was up on one of the dead roads along the Pali coast above Chinaman's Hat. Tong settling one of their own, most likely, up there. Shit. Second one today. Old Man Ho must be feeling the need to make one *nui* big point. The boy Marsden'd got stuck identifying off the north shore coast this morning bore all the hallmarks of a Tong object lesson. He was not up to facing another one. He set his filters on high, added the alert to his auto-settings to be forwarded to his second. Lepper could handle that one.

He muttered an order for coffee. The FunNet scanners took a final poke at him, scanning for the biochem blip that would signal interest and trigger a full display. Marsden ignored them. The unit decided finally to leave him alone and just get the coffee.

Which was fine by him, Marsden thought. He was feeling his age tonight. Felt it in his joints, in the irritating rub of his uniform pants on his knees, in the slow burning frustration at himself for failing to dig up that damned Ta'an. Sonuvabitch'd come into Oahu on a *Tong* shuttle, his lordship and Mote'd both said. Right into Madam's personal dock! A Ta'an on a Tong shuttle at a *Van Buren* dock – hell, that ought to have scrambled the goddamned Samurai. Yet the only one who'd showed was Teufelsman.

Now what the hell was Teufelsman doing at Kalaeloa? Damned snowball was attached to Letticia – Marsden sat up so fast the chair yelped. Shit on a shell, he shoulda thought of that sooner. Dry-mouthed, he replayed the Kalaeloa time sequence, backtracking all the players' biopats. Yeah, Teufelsman was there, ID sitting pretty in a skimmer up above the road a bit. There was his lordship, too, just hanging loose on the rocks by the pier.

No real surprises, there. With Letticia confined to the Manor, Teufelsman would be her spy on Jezekiah. Explained why the Aryan was there. Raised another question he shoulda asked, though. His lordship sure as hell hadn't been there to meet that Ta'an. Shit. Wasn't but one reason Jezekiah Van Buren ever hung loose at Kalaeloa. Only this time, the reason was Mote.

Praying he was wrong Marsden took scan down to heart beat level. Came up with a population the size of old New York and realized he'd picked up the goddamned gobbing fish. He narrowed params to human only and swore again. Yeah, there it was: a human heart beat, damned near merged with Jezekiah's own. Right where every other girl his lordship took up there wound up.

Marsden sank forward, elbows on knees, a father's sorrow crushing his heart. Damn, he'd thought better of his lordship. Boy knew the kind of pain he was letting Mote in for even if she didn't. Sure as hell he knew Mote wasn't joy toy material; he'd said so himself. Worst of it was there wasn't a damned thing he could do about it now. Except stick to the job. And resist the temptation to give that Ta'an a clear shot next time.

A cup of steaming coffee slid up into his hand from the arm rest dispenser. Marsden slid back into the chair's shell and took a sip, willing the sorrow and anger down with the bitter liquid burning his throat. Okay, take it from the top: that Ta'an was here on Oahu. Sonuvabitch had to've crossed a doorway, got into a car, gone *somewhere*. Hell, Ta'an Type was red-alert coded; he'd set off alarms the second he even walked *past* a doorway. Couldn't just blend into the homie crowd, either; that black panther coloring stood out like blackheads on a snowball. Yet both SecNet scanners and hard world telltales came up null.

So maybe Teufelsman wasn't there for something worse than spying on his lordship. Goddamned snowball had his own skimmer parked right above the road. Ta'an could've hopped in there and hidden –

Only Marsden'd scanned that skimmer himself and come up blank. Even when he left, biopat'd shown Teufelsman was solitaire. Fuzzy, but solitaire.

Marsden snorted in disgust. 'Course the goddamned paranoid snowball could've been running a block – Marsden tried to swallow and nearly choked on coffee. Except an ID block wouldn't read fuzzy. But a sync merge would. Marsden pulled Letticia Van Buren's dot, ran full scale cross check. Every lobe in NetMind insisted she was still locked out.

Hot coffee sloshed across his fingers. Swearing, Marsden drained his cup, then grabbed the wipe the chair offered. The coffee burn didn't even touch the chill growing in his gut. He mopped his hand, felt the tremble strengthen as the connections snapped into place. Teufelsman wasn't enough of a syncmeister to merge an ID. Hell, aside from himself, there was exactly one other person on Earth with the know-how and clearance to manage it. Which meant that somehow, Letticia Van Buren had wormed her way back into Net.

Terror flashed. Sweating and shivering together, Marsden ran diags. Checked for spider tracks like he'd never checked in his life. He could hear himself panting by the time he decided the little bitch hadn't infiltrated his link. At least not yet, though it felt like he had spiders running up his arms. Marsden blinked the rec room back into focus. Goddamn, felt like he really *did* have spiders running up his arms. He shot out of the chair, swatting at his arms. Got a distinct sniff of annoyance and realized it was through sync. Damned if the chair's bioscan hadn't been running diags on *him*.

Marsden rubbed a calloused hand across his eyes, thought out the sequence that triggered a murphy check on his personal node guards. No surprise there, praise all the gods of the islands: the viral cells were mutating happily, formatted by now into sequences even he couldn't predict. He probed a guard just to play safe, got an immediate and searing response. Good, so she hadn't found a way to neutralize the guards. Yet -

Sorry to bother you, sir.

Marsden jumped so hard he nearly fell back into the damned chair. But sync only fed him the image of his second's broken-nosed face. *Dammit, Lepper, I'm off duty. What you got can't wait till tomorrow?*

Checked that sniffer up on the Pali. Sync viz showed Lepper glance over her shoulder. Dark as it was, her complexion had a definite green tinge to it when she faced back. *Think you better come see this one yourself.*

Damn it, that floater off Kahena Point was enough for one day. Marsden refused to let the image of the burly shark-ravaged body take hold. His stomach was unhappy enough already. At least the sharks hadn't touched the young fella's registree's studs. Took the worry out of ID'ing the body. Saved him from having to notify kin, too. Old Man Ho was all the kin that boy had ever had. And a death like that meant old man Ho already knew more about it than Sec was likely to find out.

Yessir. Still think you wanna see this one. Damn, something was really wrong with this. Lepper wasn't even swearing. Woman was just about hopping nervous, too. Shit. By instinct Marsden ran a murphy check: the Van Burens all came up safe. He cross-checked the two Lupans, found them wandering the Manor grounds. Probably looking for trees to piss on. No worries there – if that Ta'an was fool enough to tackle those two he deserved what he got. He just wished he could say the same for Mote. *Why?*

Lepper hesitated, chewing a lip. *Looks political.*

Swearing, Marsden broke sync and headed for the Pali coast.

SecNet co-ords put the body ten klicks north of Chinaman's Hat. Marsden's skimmer followed the old Kalanianaole Highway up the coast. Out on the horizon, a blazing orange moon trailed pale reflections across Hanauma Bay like some magic ball rising out of the sea. Pity Mote wasn't here to see it. Child was still innocent enough to see magic in the world. Or had been. The thought tightened the muscles at the back of his neck. Innocence hadn't been enough to save her from Jess Van Buren's wenching.

He wrenched his mind back to Lepper's report before his thoughts took a seriously treasonous turn. Political... evil as the old man was Grandfather Ho didn't butt into Van Buren politics any more than Van Buren Sec butted into what he did to his own folk. Likeliest connection there put the stress right back in his neck. Dear God almighty, if that was Mote up there…. He closed his eyes, trying to shut out the images of what Grandfather Ho did to his victims before he let them die. The memories twisted his insides hard enough to earn himself a MedNet scan.

He held his breath, reminded himself Mote was most likely still learning the facts of life from his lordship. He clung to the hope. At least it got his heart rate down enough to make MedNet leave him alone. Let him calm down enough to put his mind on neutral, let the data flow stream past him. Below the skimmer's stubby wings grass and palm trees gave way to saltbushes and scrawny *kiawe* trees. The skimmer found the opening of a dead road and followed it inland, its repulse field raising a thudding echo off the ground. Yeah, Ho Tong territory all right. And no Tong challenge. Not good. Not good at all.

Marsden filed that uncommon tidbit away for further consideration as ShipMind settled the skimmer onto the concrete platform of a vanished house in the center of a vanished town.

The breeze carried Marsden a whiff of shit stink as soon as the skimmer door popped open. He pushed himself out of the car, feeling the coffee burn its way back up his throat. He followed the stink down the remnants of the main street, past the fire-blackened *kuleanas*. No mistaking the pattern: this was a Memory Night site. He noted the size of the circle where hula dancers' feet had flattened the earth. The gatherings were getting bigger, too. He added the note to Grandfather's SecNet file. Meant the old man was pulling more youngsters into his fairy tale version of the rebellion. Filling their heads with his stories of lost glory. Wily old bastard never mentioned the twenty-four/seven terror. Or the way the screams echoed in your sleep forever.

Or the stink – shit on a shell, this was getting uglier by the breath. If this really was a political killing, it was *deep* shit. The thought added to the acid nibble in his gut. Still didn't fit, though. Wasn't like old man Ho to give Sec a heads up. Not unless he'd got hold of a Samurai -

Please dear God, don't let that be Mote up there – Marsden picked up his pace, trying to out run the sudden image of Matsuo Yakamoto's face that horrible morning, dragging those damned swords of his, trailing Lily Ho's blood in a long, dribbly red string behind him.

The stink was choking strong by the time he passed the last *kuleana*. About a hundred klicks beyond, Lepper and her Sec team were squared off against a pair of body baggers eager to collect the sniffer. A few yards past all of them the corpse dangled from the bottom branch of a banyan tree, so low its toes almost brushed the earth.

Praise God. Least there was enough left to show it was a man. Or had been. Marsden jerked to a halt, his pulse dropping so fast he swayed on his feet. Not all due to the stench, either. He took in the remnants of the human being and extended thanks to *Tutu* Pele and all the other Hawaiian gods that it wasn't somebody he recognized. Not even a shark should die that way. He pulled in a breath, regretted it instantly and upped shields.

Whoever'd killed the poor sot was out to make an announcement. They'd broken the victims arms instead of tying him up before they hanged him. Probably broken his legs second, just before they castrated him. The shredded ends of his testicles dangled from his mouth, smearing what was left of an expensive shirt with worse than blood. Marsden took a moment to say a prayer that he'd still been in shock when they cut his guts out and wrapped them around his throat. 'Cause judging from the amount of blood spatter, he'd sure as hell still been alive when they did it.

Marsden's stomach tried to contribute his dinner to the stink. *Damned* if he was making that mistake with screens up. Shields held nasty stuff in just as effectively as they kept it out. He clenched lips, hunted up Lepper. She'd held her place, keeping the body baggers at bay, though she was jiggling with worry. The trouble that was waddling out to meet him was the pudgy woman in charge of bagging.

In the circle of field lights she had the red hair and freckle-face of a Celtic gene-pack tacked onto the nondescript features and no-nonsense attitude of a low-cost NumbersType. She also had her chins up, looking for hu-hu.

"Listen, Captain-" She didn't even wait till she'd drawn up. "I no got time admire Tong handiwork. What I do got is a floater to bag down on the Big Island, two dead-ass medics to update, and my kid's birthday party. All waitin' on da kine here." She jabbed a thumb at the gently swaying corpse. "Your folk've already scanned that sniffer from here to doomsday, so you mind I just bag it and get going?"

"Yeah, I mind."

"Aw, c'mon, Captain!" The pudgy body bagger poked Marsden's shoulder for emphasis, swore as his shield bit her fingers. "Only reason Ho Tong go kill this way is punish rape. You wanta be sorry for a rapist, do it on your own time. Me, I got a birthday party waiting."

"Yuh-huh. 'Cept old man Ho usually leaves that kind of lesson out where his folks can learn from it." Rape wasn't the only reason old man Ho killed ugly, but Marsden wasn't about to trade notions. Or start rumors.

He swung around the bagger, trudged up to Lepper's side. Behind the sergeant the Sec team was lined up shoulder to armored shoulder in a metallic wall. Story, there, but he'd get to it later. Wishing he had a gas mask Marsden bit his lips closed and paced the kill zone around the sniffer.

He'd been a young man judging from the smoothness of the skin. Damn sure couldn't tell from the face: whoever'd killed him had gouged a parallel series of ragged gashes from the hair line to jaw. Something about that niggled at the back of Marsden's mind. Fellow'd been an off-worlder, though, that was sure. His matted hair was that near colorless blond you saw on the Streikern with skin the fish-belly white of the deep space mining clans. Body type was pure Sprite: lithe and willowy. Somebody's joy toy, most likely: those clothes'd been expensive. That somebody'd been taking good care of him, too, to keep skin that white from frying in the Hawaiian sun. Maybe that somebody had a nastier streak than this kid could have imagined: SecNet sure as hell had no missing persons report that matched this joy toy's description.

Marsden came back up at Lepper's side. Breeze shifted, and they fell back in unison a few paces ahead of the stink. "Yeah, looks like Tong work all right." Like Lepper he kept the worrisome question to sync. *So what makes you think it's political?*

Frank over there. Lepper nodded sidelong toward the armored wall of her team. Behind their sheltering backs scan showed Marsden a uniformed SecType kneeling on the grass, sobbing with gut-wrenching intensity into the shoulder of a team mate. *He's been doing tour duty, remember? You wanna guess who for?*

"God dammit to hell!" Marsden bulled past her. He stepped up to the corpse, yanked the genitalia out of its mouth. The bloody contents sizzled against his shielded hand before he tossed them aside. Willing his stomach down, he offed his shield. Then used his palms to smooth the victim's face back to a semblance of repose. He made himself look past the red rows of gashes. And wished to God he hadn't. The face staring blindly back at him belonged to his lordship's doppelganger.

Marsden backed away from the boy's dead eyes. His own eyes were burning suddenly. God damn it all to hell, he'd promised the kid he'd be safe. Promised him a *good time*, dammit. Promised him in person. He lifted a hand to rub his eyes, smelled the boy's death on them. "Goddamned gobbin' shit ass suckin' old man -"

The chief bagger waddled closer, chins belligerent. Lepper stepped up to block the woman. She snatched a steri-wipe from the bagger's coverall breast pocket, turned to hold it out at fingertip length to Marsden. "See what I mean, Captain?" Then, in sync, *You might want to be careful on the audio, Captain. Little baggers got big ears.*

"Yuh-huh." Marsden grunted thanks and put the wipe to use. He only wished he could wipe hard enough to clean his soul.

"Hey, c'mon, Captain. You done got you nose full, now let me bag 'im. I got places to be."

Marsden realized he'd reduced the wipe to shreds. He gave his hands the sniff test, got a nose-twitching dose of antiseptic and decided they'd pass. "Okay, all yours." He shoved the used wipe into the bagger's hand as she waddled past. He nodded for Lepper to follow and strode away before the bagger realized what she had and shoved it back. "So how'd you find him, anyway? Nobody's reported him missing."

"Frank. The toy didn't show up home when Frank got there."

"Why didn't he report it straight off? He knew this was a Van Buren thing."

Lepper glanced past the line of SecTypes expression tightening. "My fault, Captain. I been tellin' 'em all to keep shit outta Net. So he was just tryin' to keep it quiet."

"Yuh-huh. So how'd Frank find him?" The more he thought about it, the better the pattern that'd been forming fit. And the less he liked it.

"Got a tip." The worry in Lepper's tone said she'd figured the implications for herself. "One of the Aryans dropped a hint there was 'something interesting' up here."

"A homie. Shit." Marsden's heart dropped. Yeah , that fit all right. Just like the fuzz he'd spotted in Teufelsman's feed. "Need you to do some checking for me. Want you to put techs on every filter in every lobe of NetMind. Tell 'em to check for blank spots, gaps, fuzzy links. Especially fuzzy links. I want to know every – you got that? *Every* – anomaly they find. I want to know it yesterday. And I want those reports going to you. Hard world only, you got that?"

"Hard world?" Lepper's jaw sagged. She pulled it up, set it stubborn. *"How?* What they gonna do, write 'em out by hand?"

"Your call. Just keep the answers out of Net."

"Shi... Uh, sir-?" Lepper glanced back to check on the baggers. Lowered her voice anyway. "Think you better look at these first, Captain. Found 'em beneath the body." Putting her back to the baggers, she pulled a plasti pack from her collection pouch. She reached in, pulled out a bloodied, silvery band of throwing stars. "Found 'em beneath the body. Murder weapon, Captain."

"Hell they are. Tong stars didn't make those wounds." Marsden scowled past Lepper to where the bagger team was wrestling the doppelganger's remains into a body bag. Took claws to make those ragged gashes. Wasn't the Lupans – talons like those two had would've sheared through the bone. The claws that'd ripped that poor boy up had been Ta'an.

"Maybe not." Lepper shuffled an armored foot, breaking loose a clod of dirt. In the field light glare even the earth was red. "Ran pats on 'em. Blood belongs to the body. But the biopat came up null."

"Yuh-huh." Figured. That little bitch Letticia had her Ta'an's records scoured clean. "You didn't happen to find Teufelsman's biopat on 'em did you?"

"Wasn't that lucky."

"Yeah, well, wouldn't'a believed it if you had – sonuvabitch'd wear gloves." Marsden started to run a hand across his eyes. Remembered where the hand'd been and dropped it. "Listen, Lep. You wiki it back to the Manor. Got a job I need you to do. Out of Net." He ran Lepper through the steps, made her repeat it twice for safety's sake before he dismissed her.

Only Lepper didn't move. She started a sentence, re-thought it. Settled for kicking up another patch of grass with an armored toe.

Something in the way she did it made Marsden's gut go cold. "Okay, spill. What's the hu-hu?"

She shrugged, looking helpless and not liking it. "Figured the killer for a homie, anyway, given the method. So I cross-scanned for straight DNA signature. Didn't get nothin' there, either. So I scanned simple finger prints." She found a sudden fascination with her feet. "Came up with Keiko Yakamoto."

XXXIV

Jezekiah and the two Lupans were already waiting when the Admiral ushered Letticia into Mother's office. Except for Mother they were all dressed up, too. Well, at least Jezekiah and that nasty Kaitin were. Jezekiah had on a creamy ruffled blouse with lacy cuffs and matching slacks in heavy silk. That Kaitin was wearing mega-thou credits worth of gold trim on his emerald chiffon robe and pantaloons. But Strongarm – He looked worse, if anything. He was still wearing the same blue leather trousers he'd had on this morning, only they were water-stained. Looked like the silly fool had gone wading in them.

Oh, something was definitely wrong. Letticia hesitated, trying to buy time to reason it all out. Strongarm wasn't sucking up to Jezekiah the way he usually did, either. Instead, he and his kitty cat were standing off to the side, leaving Mother and Jezekiah facing them across Mother's desk. The whole gobbing lot of them looked like they'd come for a funeral gathering instead of her wedding. She almost laughed aloud as the realization sank home. Of course it was a funeral! She'd told JP exactly what he could do with that Pandari ambassador. But heavens, JP must have moved fast to get his hands on the woman so quick.

"Mistress Letticia, Madam." The Admiral shoved her forward on the announcement.

And Mother turned a scowl of pure blue murder on her.

Oh, God, what could have gone wrong? Had Uncle JP sawyered her? If he'd told Mother about their little agreement – Sheer terror locked Letticia's smile in place. If the gobbing Admiral hadn't blocked the door, she would have backed right out again. As it was, she couldn't even stay put. The nasty old man kept pushing her forward.

For once she was grateful Mother was such a stickler for protocol. The Admiral had to let her pause two feet shy of Mother's damned chairs, had to give her time to curtsey. For once Letticia held the pose as long as she possibly could without her knees giving way. It didn't matter if JP had betrayed her or not. Mother would forgive her – *had* to forgive her! – for it as long as she Impressed Strongarm. After that, JP wouldn't matter at all.

Letticia straightened, focused her smile on Strongarm. He really wasn't all that repulsive, she decided, if one allowed for the fur and fangs. He'd lost quite a bit of the fur over the past few days; it served to put that magnificent animal musculature on full display. Had he been truly human, he could have passed for a god no trouble at all. That odd little spot between her legs tingled at the thought. Maybe, just maybe, gobbing him wouldn't be all that bad.

Keeping her smile on lock-down Letticia took a step toward him before the Admiral nudged her at Mother again. She held her hand out for Strongarm to kiss anyway, fluttered lashes at him above it. "I'm *so* glad we're finally going to mate. Shall we get started?"

"Mistress Van Buren." Strongarm bowed slightly, but ignored her hand. His amber gaze slid past her, settled somewhere in the distance beyond. For a dreadful moment he actually reminded her of Admiral Yakamoto. Except the Admiral didn't have doggy ears to go flat.

It was that Kaitin who actually spoke. Whatever was going on here, his ears were flat, too. And there was a rasp to his voice that sounded for all the world like a growl. "It seems some of your relatives have already sent-" he hesitated, then jerked his head sideways at Strongarm – "your betrothed a marriage gift."

"Oooh, a gift? I love gifts!" It took Letticia a moment to realize the silly cat was being sarcastic. It took a long second after that to recognize that Mother and Jezekiah had just let their breath out together. Letticia locked her knees straight before they buckled. She'd never, ever, ever turn her nose up at another present. Never, not as long as she lived! Because she knew even before she faced Mother that her reaction had just saved her life. "What kind of gift?" She made *damned* sure she sounded innocent.

"It seems Grerrar has been attacked." Jezekiah answered for Mother.

"Grerrar? What's – Oh! That Lupan mining colony on Rogue." Oh, indeed! Letticia turned back to Strongarm – quickly, before Jezekiah spotted the way her eyes widened. "See? I've been doing my homework on your – in your – interests. Why don't you tell me all about it? After we finish with your Impression." She reached for Strongarm's hand.

The stupid dog jumped back like she was a snake or something. "Just what is this all about?" Letticia didn't even have to fake the annoyance.

"This one would not honor onlies' subterfuge with the term 'attack'." Kaitin whirled about thirty pounds of gold-weighted emerald chiffon around his forearm as he stepped between them.

"Whatever are you talking about?" Oh, please, *please* don't let JP have done anything stupid.

"A Pandari merchant docked at Grerrar last night, planet time local."

Mother spoke at last. Letticia didn't even dare turn around to look at her. Not while there was death in her voice.

"Oh, for heaven's sake – *Pandari?*" How on earth had JP got himself a Pandari ship? Letticia let her breath out in a gust of annoyance. Probably his troops had just killed the crew and stolen it. Not that she was about to share that little tidbit here. "If it's just Octavian trying to cheat some silly miners then I can deal with him later. Let's get on with the Impression. Before-"

"Why the sudden rush, Letticia? You haven't even heard the story yet." That was Jezekiah. Heavens, he sounded almost as cold as Mother.

Oh, this was bad. Letticia sidled toward Strongarm. She clipped her nose on gold filigree for the effort.

Kaitin shook her face off his arm as if she were some kind of bug. "Records show the cowards docked under kin-claim. They claimed they were carrying a gift from Home World. A gift from Lord Strongarm's *betrothed.*" He stroked his mustaches, the rasp in his breath intensifying. "Once the air locks opened they flooded the dens with Venus Seed dust."

Strongarm's head snapped up. Above the bared fangs his face looked ashen. "There were no survivors. Not the women. Not even the babies."

Gob it, she'd never dreamed JP would move so fast! Or *could* – miserable son of a bitch must have had his crews stringing jumps to make it to Rogue that quick! The truth clicked home, then: those crews were already en route to Rogue when she'd had her chat with JP. Only, why should he blame her? Even so – "But it was only Venus Seed!"

"So it was you." Jezekiah wasn't even pretending to smile any more.

"I-" The awful implications sank in at last. "It most certainly was not! What good are a bunch of dead miners to me? Besides, Venus Seed never killed anybody! So let's just get on with the Impression! We can figure out what really happened afterward."

"No, we can't." Heavens, Strongarm really, truly actually *growled*. He lifted a hand, flexed it. Black, evilly sharp talons snapped up from his fingers, arc'd over the back of his hand. "Understand this, Letticia Van Buren: the Makers designed LupanType for combat, not love. Even with the Touch we have to be careful. Without it…"

He jerked away, dusting the air with silver and leaving Kaitin to pick up.

"Without the Touch, a Lupan man will almost certainly cut his *maya* to shreds." The Bengali ran an orange-furred hand across his mustaches, golden eyes narrowing. "If your Pandari operatives-"

"They weren't mine!" Letticia shrieked.

Kaitin's nose twitched. He lifted an ear at Strongarm, got a shrug in return and continued. "If your *kinsmen*, then, had infected only the men, their wives could have barred the dens, waited till the Venus Seed effect wore off. If they'd affected only the women-" He lifted hands in a golden shimmer. Lifted a lip to bare that ruby fang. "But your kinsmen flooded the dens. Then watched while the men shredded their wives. And raped their own babies to death."

"Well, at least they died happy!" Letticia jammed her hands on her hips in disgust. "Whatever are you so upset about?"

With a roar, Kaitin snapped his arm up -

Suddenly the world around her spun. Letticia hit the floor on her side and skidded. She gaped up to see Admiral Yakamoto facing Kaitin, swords drawn. Both Lupans faced him, crouched, snarling. Across the desk she saw Jezekiah push Mother behind him. None of it mattered now. Because along the walls columns of ruby lights had winked to life.

Holding her breath, Letticia tracked the ruby rows around the office. They looked so pretty, like holiday fairy lights. At least they'd be pretty until the SecDef lasers behind those lights let go. As soon as either of the Lupans jumped, those SecDef lasers would fire. They wouldn't leave survivors, either, not even Family members. Just Mother. And, of course, *dear* Jezekiah. Ever so cautiously, Letticia began inching her butt across the floor toward the door.

"Enough!" Mother elbowed Jezekiah out of her way. She waited till Strongarm backed off, then motioned the Admiral to stand down and ran a hand over her console. The ruby lights vanished.

"Now, then." If she was scared Mother didn't show it. But then, she didn't need to be scared. She hadn't just bumped *her* back into the Admiral's bony knees.

Letticia didn't have time to wonder how the Admiral had even got around behind her so fast. The cold, blue gaze Mother fixed on her was more terrifying than even Admiral Yakamoto.

"We will accept that you were not personally responsible for such a slaughter of innocents. Nonetheless, the question Lord Strongarm has raised suggests another concern: just how did a Pandari trader manage to obtain so large a load of Venus Seed? The export limits we impose on Ho Tong should render it impossible."

"Not to mention why a Pandari merchanter would risk running JP's blockade to deliver a goodwill gift to Rogue." That was Jezekiah. "Particularly to deliver a gift supposedly from you." He'd dropped the pretty boy mask. What showed now was just as cold and scary as Mother. More so, even. "Octavian has no profit in pulling a stunt like that."

"I don't know!" Thank heavens she was already on her butt; her legs would have given out otherwise. Just as well the stupid tight skirt made it near impossible to get up, too. Having to wriggle upright bought her a moment to try to think. Maybe, just maybe she had a way out.

Letticia rolled onto her knees, made sure she came up facing the Lupans. "Lord Strongarm, I really, truly don't know anything about what they're asking. You said Impression creates a bond between man and woman. If you'll just finish our Impression, you'll see for yourself that I'm – we're – innocent." She stretched her arms out to him, for once truly and sincerely imploring.

He looked… tired. Almost really human, somehow. For a terrible moment she thought the great brute was going to ignore her. Then he shrugged and bent down to her. She'd have felt better about his proffered hand, though, if his ears hadn't been flat above it. He shook them up, shaking a cloud of silvery hair into a flickering halo.

Letticia literally fell into Strongarm's hands. She felt his palm stroke her neck. Waited for the lust rush –

Nothing.

"Well?" Letticia blinked up at him. She couldn't move enough to do anything else. "Is that it? Are we married?"

"No."

"Well, why not?" She felt Strongarm ease his grip. She didn't *care*. Frantic, she grabbed Strongarm's hand, jammed it against her neck. His fingers felt hard as a hangman's noose.

"I am afraid it's beyond my control, Mistress Van Buren." He pulled free, leaving Letticia's heart pounding in fresh terror.

"Then do it again! It has to work!" Letticia threw herself on his chest, rubbed herself against him in desperate haste.

Strongarm didn't even seem to notice. He stared down into his upturned palm, then lifted it as if he were taking some kind of oath. It was just a plain palm, nothing special. But the sight of it drew a collective sigh from the others.

"We still have time." It took Letticia a moment to realize it was Jezekiah who'd spoken. He gave Letticia the barest sidelong glance, but it was enough to give her shudders. "If we move quickly, we can still find an alternative."

Alternative? Give all that money to someone *else*? It was only her grip on Strongarm's paw that kept Letticia from collapsing at the dog's feet. She couldn't talk, couldn't even think past the horror of Jezekiah's betrayal. He'd sawyered her again. All Jezekiah's talk about finding riches and safety – all this time he'd had some little bitch as his back-up plan. Just waiting. Hoping his sister – his own sister! – would fail. But she *couldn't* fail! Not now! Frantic, Letticia jammed Strongarm's paw between her breasts. She felt no sensation at all beyond the velvety steel of his talons. Fighting sobs of terror she shook his paw with both hands. "Gob you, do it! You promised!"

"I'm sorry, Mistress Van Buren." Using fingertips Strongarm pried his hand free. With gentle finality he pushed her into Jezekiah's unwilling arms. "Sorry for all of us, Jezekiah. I fear it comes to challenge after all."

"Challenge over what?" Letticia tried to shake Jezekiah's hands off her arms.

He didn't even look at her. Only clamped down harder. "Challenge won't convince your Parliament to accept the treaty. We can still find an acceptable alternative."

"There's only Bird." Strongarm grunted, shook his massive head. "She's the one who triggered Impression mode, Van Buren. I bond with her or I die. I don't have any alternatives."

"Bird? What bird?" Letticia twisted to frown her question at Jezekiah. He ignored it.

"Keiko Yakamoto." If Strongarm recognized the Admiral's hiss, he didn't seem to care. "I am sorry for you, Jezekiah, but if you will not step aside, then accept my challenge."

Jezekiah folded Letticia's hand over his arm. "We can still-"

"The women of Clan Bengal will not seal this treaty on another flat tooth trick." Kaitin blocked whatever Strongarm had intended to say with an emerald-clad shoulder. "This one can convince them to accept a Maker to seal our treaty. But they will not allow you to substitute some functionary's brat."

The Heir's Ring throbbed a dull white against the bronzed skin of his hand where Jezekiah crushed her fingers beneath his own. In profile she saw the line of muscles along his neck tighten. "The women of your Parliament will not accept a Ho Tong operative, either. Which is almost certainly what Keiko Yakamoto is."

"No!" The Admiral's shout rattled Letticia's bones.

Or so she thought until she heard Jezekiah's breath hiss between his teeth. Letticia yipped in pain as his hand clenched tighter around her wrist.

The Admiral didn't seem to notice any of it. The nasty old man looked as if he didn't even remember he still had his swords up. He stared at Mother between the twin slivers of steel, his lips forming words Letticia was quite sure he didn't even realize he was speaking. "It cannot be. Not again."

"It's not. Stand easy, Matsuo." Obediently, the Admiral sheathed his swords. For a terrible moment, Mother just slumped, head down, shoulders hunched. When she straightened, she looked like someone had torn her heart out.

Letticia whimpered in recognition. Oh, she *knew* that feeling! Knew it as none of the others ever could. Mother looked like she'd lost *Net*. She clawed at Jezekiah's hand, trying to free herself, trying to reach Mother. To tell her she could make it better, she could fix everything -

Then Mother looked at her. No, not at her, Letticia realized. *Through* her. Reducing her to nothingness again. Letticia opened her lips. She tried to scream, to force Mother to see her, to love her. But no scream came out. Just a stupid, keening, helpless whimper.

When Mother finally spoke it was to Strongarm. "It seems, then, that Keiko Yakamoto has completed our treaty terms for us."

"Madam, it won't work!" Jezekiah dragged Letticia forward a step with him.

"Stop it!" Even without the command, Mother's hard-eyed glare would have frozen a squad of Samurai. Jezekiah stopped so fast Letticia lurched into his shoulder.

Mother ignored them both. "I fear Jezekiah is allowing his feelings to interfere with his duty," she told Strongarm. "Do I have your word, Lord Strongarm, that you will still honor your commitment to the treaty?"

"Give you my blood on it." Strongarm drew talon tips across his throat, flicked red droplets across Mother's desk.

"Aren't you forgetting something?" Jezekiah pulled Letticia with him as if he'd forgotten he held her wrist captive. "You gave me blood oath, too, remember?" He wrenched Letticia's wrist up, the Heir's Ring pulsing yellow fire above it. "Both of us."

"I never forget a promise. I've honored it, too, heart and soul. It's my body that's betrayed us." Strongarm lifted his chin to display the bloody streaks running down his neck. "You have the right to call challenge, Jezekiah. But if you want your treaty signed, you'll have to let Bird accept me first."

"There's been enough bloodshed already. It's time we ended it all for good." Mother dismissed Jezekiah with a glance, turned her attention to the Admiral. "Matsuo, your daughter passed her Samurai Type trial a day or so ago, if I'm not mistaken." She waited till the Admiral jerked his head in a nod. "I instructed my son to correct the error that… delayed her Type coding. Has he done so?"

The room went so quiet Letticia could hear Jezekiah's shirt rustle against his skin with his breath. The Admiral shook his head, finally. Somehow, that simple gesture made Mother go even colder.

"Then I shall manage the correction myself. Bring Keiko here. We shall administer the Samurai oath together. After which-" She grimaced at Strongarm, though she probably thought she was smiling. "We shall reconvene to conclude a proper Impression ceremony."

"Agreed." Strongarm bowed, head up. "In the interim, we will withdraw to make our own arrangements." He lifted his chin at Jezekiah then turned and strode out of the office. That vile Kaitin paused only long enough to flip them off a sort of salaam before he swept out after him.

For long seconds after the doors closed behind them, Mother kept her hand on the comm patch of her desk, tracking the Lupans' departure. When she finally lifted her eyes, it was only to the Admiral. "Matsuo, I suggest you get Keiko up here double time. That Pandari ambassador has dropped out of sight.

She may well have already reached Den Lupus. We must have that treaty signed before she has the chance to Impress another warlord. Otherwise we will have to face the Council and JP's charges empty-handed."

Letticia hadn't even realized the Admiral had moved until she felt his dark presence looming at her shoulder. She shrieked in terror when the Admiral clamped a hand around her arm.

"Madam?" The horrid old man didn't even bat an eyelash when Letticia clawed at his fingers. Just held her at arm's length. And locked eyes on Mother. Waiting for the kill command.

"Not yet. I shall deal with my children after we have properly settled yours." Mother didn't even look up. She just fixed her gaze on some invisible speck on her desk. "May whatever gods still exist grant your Keiko the happiness denied the rest of us."

"As you will, Madam."

"Mother, you can't! You need me!" Terror pushed Letticia forward.

The Admiral yanked her back. His fingers bit into the hollow of her neck, cutting off her words as he pulled her toward the door. Letticia tried to dig her heels into the carpet against him. Useless. In mortal desperation, she stretched a pleading arm out to Jezekiah.

For a moment, the chill in his eyes sent shivers of terror down her spine. Then he smiled, that familiar, sneaky, crooked smile. He lifted a hand – and the Admiral stopped. The smile vanished before Jezekiah eased around the desk to face Mother. "You might want to reconsider."

"It's too late for that now." Mother turned, finally, to look at Letticia. There was a haunted sorrow in her face that scared Letticia worse than any of Jezekiah's veiled threats. "Strongarm was our last hope."

"Lush could still be useful, you know."

"Do not presume to tell me who or what remains useful. I cannot afford your emotions to wreak any further havoc."

"I'm not trying to disrupt anything." Jezekiah stepped away to rest his back against the wall behind Mother's desk. "I'm thinking of ways to stave off JP's treason charge."

"I shall make sure Keiko Yakamoto takes the Samurai loyalty oath before she Impresses Strongarm. After that, I should think the Lupans' battle fleet would be enough to give even JP pause."

"Not if he's got Venus Seed stockpiled."

For once Mother didn't even glance at him. Just stood there hugging herself. Staring at Letticia, with horror slowly dawning in her expression.

"It wasn't my fault!" Letticia tried to pull away from the Admiral. He yanked her back.

"You see?" Jezekiah locked those blue eyes on Letticia, his smile gone predatory beneath them. "With the proper inducement, I'm sure we can convince Letticia to share the details of her arrangements with us. We're going to need every piece of incriminating evidence against JP she can provide."

"Agreed." Mother spoke over her shoulder, not looking anywhere in particular. "Take her back to her quarters, Admiral. We will take the matter up later. After I've spoken with Kip Marsden."

"Yes, Madam." The Admiral dragged Letticia sobbing out of the office. The doors hissed shut behind them.

Letticia was too numb to scream while he dragged back to her rooms. She didn't even resist when he shoved her through the door, not even when she heard the screen-lock buzz to life. The sobs didn't start until she threw herself on the floor.

How could it all go so wrong? *How?* She hadn't told JP to do *anything* to Rogue! He was supposed to take care of that stupid ambassador! She started to imagine the horror of an interrogation by Marsden and the sobs turned to shrieks. Something thumped on the floor near her head. Letticia jammed arms over her head and scooted onto her butt, half-expecting to see the Admiral's polished boots strut past. She found nothing but a box of tissues her major domo had dumped on the floor beside her.

The sobs caught on a hiccup. She pushed herself up, held her breath till the hiccups stopped. She had to think. They'd all lied to her, all *used* her to get what they wanted – Jezekiah and JP and Grandfather Ho. All of them except Mother. Only Mother kept her safe. She just had to make Mother see none of this was her fault. Mother would understand. Mother would protect her.

Yes, that was it. She wasn't helpless yet. Oh, yes indeed, they'd see just how much Venus Seed JP had stored. And just where he'd got it. All she had to do was erase her own tracks…

Slowly, Letticia climbed to her feet. She staggered toward the bathroom and that precious tile behind the toilet. Lines of probabilities were starting to take shape now. It made her feel so much better. Then she remembered the surprise she'd arranged for Strongarm's precious little Yakamoto monkey and her mood turned jubilant. Oh, yes. Mother was going to have a fine time mating Strongarm to Keiko Yakamoto now.

XXXV

The moon was full up by the time Keiko reached the Manor's grounds. Would've been faster to use the old Kuhio road: Manor was barely a five mile run along the straight route. She'd opted to follow the jungle track instead. No chance the Admiral would come after her – not with the Protector calling – but both Sec and the Aryans were out in force tonight. And she just didn't have what it took to face either Captain Marsden or Teufelsman right now.

Keiko paused beneath the fronds of a fern tree to rub the throb out of her neck. The run had help soothe the ache in her heart. Let her block out the horror of what her father had done. Wasn't much of a block; she could still feel the shiver at the edge of her mind. But she wasn't choking back sobs any more. It would hold until Jess Van Buren took her in his arms again, until he smoothed all the hurt and dirt and shame out of her soul. Right now, though, something out here was making her battle sense act up.

Twigs snapped a couple of feet away. Keiko dropped to a crouch, twisted to follow as a SecType crunched past. *Nui* strange. Woman was in full combat gear. Against the jungle shadows the battle shield raised a mystic glow above her armor that shone green where it reflected the ready light on her laser rifle. The SecType walked with the full body swing that said she was running scan sweep. Yet she triggered no spike in Keiko's battle sense. Keiko let herself relax a bit. Whatever trouble Sec was hunting tonight must be haole. Captain Marsden knew better than to waste scan on Grandfather's people.

She waited till the SecType was out of earshot, then slipped out of the ferns. She'd taken only a step when battle sense flared.

Neck pounding, Keiko leaped onto a leaning palm tree. She scrambled up it islander style, bare feet silent against the bark, to hide among the coconut clusters in its canopy. At that, she was almost too late. The Aryan paused beneath her tree, white-blond head bent as he swept the scanner across the spot she'd just occupied. Praise Tutu Pele those old scanners gave line-of-sight readings only. It couldn't pick her up unless the Aryan pointed it in her direction. Clinging to the bole of the tree with fingers and toes Keiko willed her *ki* to neutral and melded herself into the palm's leaves. She didn't dare even *think* about the Aryan looking up. If he did, she was in for it. Because that old scanner didn't read Type codes. It hunted heart beats.

The Aryan grunted, finally, and moved on. The throb of Keiko's battle sense eased. She thought for a moment about warning the SecType that she had company, decided against it. Odds were Sec and the Aryans were working together. Keiko stifled a snort of disappointment. She'd thought Captain Marsden was better than that. Either way, she'd tell Jess. He would know what to do about it.

Keiko waited till the Aryan was out of scanner range, then slid down the tree and worked her way through the jungle. She dodged another patrol – Aryan only, this time – before she managed to reach the banyan tree overlooking Jess' quarters. Whatever was going on, looked like it had everybody up and about. Jess' lights were off. She hoped that was a good sign. She really hoped he was *alone* tonight. Keiko reminded herself sternly she had no right to think he had damned well better be. Even so, the thought he might not be alone triggered a hot stab of jealousy.

Battle sense throbbed again as she clambered up the banyan tree opposite Jess' balcony. Keiko crouched among the branches till the Aryans turned the corner at the far end of the Manor. Her neck still tingled, but with the snowballs out in such force the warning was probably not going away. Besides, she'd be safe once she reached Jess' room.

The banyan's trailing air roots had been cut off so the branches formed a shady green canopy over the path behind the Manor. Precaution, probably, from a haole point of view – made sure nobody could climb up the roots from the walkway. Only like every other haole, the gardeners had figured the intruder defenses in the weather screens would keep anything else out. They'd just never figured on a monkey.

Silently, she edged through the tangle of dangling branches until she reached the end of the outlying branch. Keiko focused her mind on 'cloud', felt her body go light. Spreading her arms wide, she dropped off the branch.

Too late, she remembered that Captain Marsden had re-set the screens' defenses. She braced herself for agony as she landed spread-eagled on the screen. Only – nothing. For a moment, she felt nothing more than the usual stinging bite of the screens. Then the stun bolt hit her and the world went white.

Numbly, Keiko realized she was sliding. The screens raised a sandpaper scrape down the length of her body where she tried, uselessly, to cling to it. She got nothing; her body couldn't move. She slid downward, felt the slide turn into free fall as she passed the shield's outward curve about twenty feet above the stone path. Nothing for it after that but hope whoever'd shot her would let her die quick.

She hit the ground feet first and hard. It was more of a thump than the bone-shattering crash she'd expected so she only folded over on her knees like an old Seed sack. Still, it wasn't Captain Marsden behind that shot. Couldn't be- 'cause whoever was watching her slide was triggering battle sense. Frantically she struggled to shake off the deadening numbness trapping her body. Knowing, even before he kicked her onto her back, that the watcher was Teufelsman.

"Mistress Yakamoto." Teufelsman made the courtesy sound insulting enough to clench her throat. And earn a round of snickers from his companions.

Keiko couldn't even turn her head to see how many Aryans Teufelsman had backing him up. Four, maybe, judging from the shuffle of feet on gravel. And none of them up to any good. Even through frozen muscles her battle sense screamed warning.

Teufelsman squatted beside her, smiling, close enough for Keiko to smell the cloying sweetness of his aftershave. "I see your talents exceed even your father's. Perhaps you would like to tell me who just who taught you to climb weather screens. And why."

He ran a pale finger along her cheek and down the side of her throat to her shoulder. He kept the finger in bounds, barely, but his touch still felt like he'd dragged slime across her skin. Instinctively Keiko tried to kick him away. Her frozen muscles refused to move. All she could do was try not to pant.

Teufelsman locked a hand in her hair, pulled her up to rest her head against his knee. When he spoke his voice was soft enough to blend with the crickets and other night sounds. "You know we've been looking for you, don't you? You know what happens to monkeys who commit murder." His fingers trailed across her chest, came to rest in the hollow between her breasts. The stun was wearing off. Keiko tried to wrench free and failed. At least it was enough to let Teufelsman feel her shudder.

The Aryan seemed to find satisfaction in it. He pulled her closer, dropped his voice to a near whisper. "I'm still willing to offer you an alternative, you know. Monkeys like you need a protector. Somebody to give them pretty little things. Warm them up in bed. Keep the law at bay." He ran his hand back up her body to stroke her temple. "Otherwise-" He snapped fingers against her temple and jaw, marking the spots of a registree's studs.

This time her muscles obeyed. Keiko snapped a knee up, caught Teufelsman in the cheek. The blow sent the Aryan tumbling off the shield cushion. Keiko back-flipped off it. Mistake. The sudden movement made her head spin. Cost her one precious second too many. She whirled to block Teufelsman's charge. But she was too late. His neural wand caught her on the arm.

The wand's touch spasmed the nerves in her arm. It felt like her flesh was being torn from the bone. Too slow she swung knuckles up to block the next blow. This time Teufelsman only feinted. It was another Aryan who jabbed the wand into her side. Its disruptive field arched Keiko backward over it. Teufelsman slapped his wand across her chest and the field snapped her into fetal position. She hit the ground on her knees, tumbled in a curl onto her side.

She was too pain-blind to see. It was the whiff of cloying sweetness told her Teufelsman had knelt beside her. Then her body spasmed again as he ran the wand down the side of her face. Keiko bit back the shriek, but the effort left a coppery tang of blood on her tongue.

He bent close enough to let her hear him *tsk* softly. "As you can see, monkey, that wasn't the right answer. Now-"

Then somewhere above him the air roared.

XXXVI

Mother's office felt hollow for a number of reasons after the others left. Jezekiah leaned against the back of a leather chair, trying to track Mother's line of reasoning. She stood as she'd been standing since the others left them: with her back to him, staring out the tall arched windows. Over her shoulder he watched silver moon light dance across Pearl Harbor in the distance. Judging from the tension in Mother's back, she didn't even see the view. Her hands were clenched behind her back, the Ring throbbing bright and hot against the wrinkled cotton of her shirt. Jezekiah felt the despair in her silence, the crushing fear that it'd all been for nothing. All the loss, the discipline, the sacrifice – all wasted. All her life a failure. His own soul echoed it. Because with Keiko now promised to Strongarm, he'd lost it all, too. The difference between them was, it was all his fault.

He dropped into one of the leather scan chairs, too desolate to care whether the chair liked him or not. His dreams didn't even matter anymore. Not his dreams, not his hopes, not the hubris he'd mistaken for honor. He could not afford to dwell on the hole gaping in the center of his being. All that mattered now was saving Earth from the folly he'd brought on them. Without that, there was no future for any of them. He rubbed a hand across his eyes, repeated the question Mother had been ignoring. "So, then. Which way do you think Octavian will jump on the treason vote?"

"With Strongarm mated to Keiko Yakamoto instead of Letticia?" Mother spoke over her shoulder, almost absently. "That arrangement removes the last of our bargaining chips. Unless-" She turned enough to lift a tired brow at him over a shoulder. "Have you managed to obtain the Lupans' long jump specs?"

"Afraid not. There was no point in it. Not while we had any hope of Letticia." Another failure. The thought of it added to the weight on Jezekiah's shoulders. "Even so, Octavian won't want to eliminate us until he has his own tie to the Lupans locked down. We may be able to at least get him to postpone the vote."

"The end result will be the same. With Strongarm attached to Keiko

Yakamoto, control of any Lupan treaty passes out of our hands. Octavian will see that as clearly as you should."

"Aren't you forgetting something? Keiko will be under loyalty oath to you. No Samurai has ever broken the oath. Ever. Add in Strongarm's wealth -" He bit his tongue. He did not dare let himself think about the other things Strongarm offered: love and truth and loyalty. The things his dreams were made of.

"Pray finish enlightening me. What am I forgetting?"

Jezekiah rubbed his hand across his eyes, buying an extra instant to shoved his dreams back into the dungeons of his mind. With a start he realized that the calluses didn't scratch any more. Appropriate, he thought bitterly. His palm had softened since he'd been home. It was his soul that had hardened. "Simply that there's no bribe even Octavian could offer that could subvert Keiko Yakamoto."

"Octavian won't have to. The fact remains the girl is *not* SamuraiType. The Type code she earned is a courtesy ID only. It won't hard-code her for loyalty. Worse, she will be on Den Lupus, freed of the Admiral's influence. The oath will become less and less pertinent with every passing year."

"Great gods, Mother-" Jezekiah saw Mother tense and smoothed his tone. "That's a future 'maybe!' Let's focus on our immediate defense-"

"Without control of that treaty we have no defense!" Mother whirled, Ring hand raised. She was white-tired, making the shadows under her eyes even darker. But had he been close enough, she would certainly have hit him. "We are not defending ourselves, Jezekiah. We are defending Earth herself. Now, tomorrow, forever." She let her hand drop. Even so, the Ring shone hot enough to make him wince away from its glare. "Tomorrow, JP will call the vote. Thanks to my children, we will be found guilty of treason." She pulled in a shaking breath. "That is my failure."

"It's not a failure yet." Jezekiah leaned forward, resting forearms on knees. He could not afford to let the chair's sensors pick up any hint of the jealous fury he felt. Could not afford to let himself dwell on it, either. He'd done them all enough damage that way. "We can still attach ourselves to Octavian's coattails."

"Why should Octavian bring us in? He quite likely has his own treaty in front of the Lupan Parliament by now."

"That doesn't mean they'll accept it. Strongarm said it'd take a Maker or a Van Buren princess to get the women of his Parliament to approve a treaty. Octavian has no daughters, and Pandar sure as hell hasn't got any original species humans in residence. So Octavian just might have hit a snag he can't overcome. Witness the fact he's keeping his ambassador's efforts hush-hush. Even Kip hasn't spotted any news of her progress."

Mother was still staring out of the window. Judging from the way she massaged the bridge of her nose, she didn't see the vista beyond. "Perhaps you should have asked Letticia instead."

"Maybe I should." Several lines of probability clicked into place on the words. The implications in them sent a cold shiver down his spine. "That's not a bad idea, you know. Shall we call her together?"

"No. At least, not yet. It would only compound the charges against her if she knows." Mother rubbed the bridge of her nose with a slender finger. She dropped her hand, her expression haunted. She jerked away from him and paced away. Sensors in the walls lit up at her approach, casting her in a soft golden halo that faded again as she passed. "I'd rather not give either of us cause for false hope."

"Why not? Every damned thing we've done has been nothing more than a false hope."

"Careful, Jess." She spoke over her shoulder, almost absently. "That reeks of bitterness."

"Forgive me." This time he let the bitterness show. "I've just had to give up the one woman I ever dared hope would love me for myself. I think a little bitterness is in order."

Mother whirled to face him. She held her working mask in place, but the effort showed in the taut lines around her eyes, in the hard, bitter set of her lips. "Do you presume to preach to me about sacrifice, Jezekiah? Or love? Or loss? I suggest you rethink it if you do. Because I've had a gut full of them all."

"No, Ma'am, not at all. I'm sorry." He meant it, too. "It's just-" He shrugged, trying to shake off the spreading chill. Quick calcs had triggered, weaving probabilities into a terrible pattern. The answers that came up spread the chill from his spine into the pit of his stomach. He wiped suddenly sweaty palms on his knees. "If Octavian's keeping his ambassador quiet on his own, then that implies the woman's hit a problem he didn't anticipate. I really think we'd better ask Letticia. Or at least warn Octavian."

He watched Mother work her way back to her desk. His stomach knotted a bit tighter at her every step. She pressed fingers to the bridge of her nose, Ring pulsing so bright it flung its own shadows across the walls. Those shadows haunted Mother's voice when she finally spoke. Mother ran her fingers across her comm unit. The room's soft light bounded off the Ring to splash rainbows across her throat. "Warn Octavian of what, Jezekiah?"

Madam. The sonorous baritone of Mother's major domo made them both start. *We have-*

Mother's office wavered, vanished. Then exploded in a blast of searing light that even the major domo couldn't dim. The light blast dimmed, but its aftermath left Jezekiah squinting into a green-black haze.

My, my. How utterly unsurprising to find you two together, Octavian's voice drawled through the haze. Jezekiah's eyes cleared enough to make out an elegant ship's interior – Octavian's personal Jumpship, judging from the subtle engine hum underlying the image. The Pandari Protector sounded diffident as ever. Yet there was an underlying danger in Octavian's tone.

That tone brought Mother's chin up. "We're facing a treason charge in two days. Surely you didn't think we'd forgotten."

Oh, I'm quite certain you haven't forgotten. I've proof of it, as a matter of fact. The blue eyes flickered white, cleared again.

"I take it, then, that the Lupan Parliament didn't respond favorably to your ambassador." It was a tribute to Mother's skill that neither her voice nor expression hinted at relief.

Possible. Had they ever met her. But then, that was a possibility Home World could not afford, what?

Jezekiah caught Mother's eye, got a brow lift of permission and said a mental prayer to every god in the islands that his fears were wrong. "If your ambassador had a problem getting cleared to Den Lupus, that's nothing to do with us. However, I should think it might work out for the better. Having two warlords Impressed to Commonwealth worlds would only be a recipe for a Lupan civil war. This way-" Jezekiah let his shrug bespeak invitation as well as sympathy. "The Lupan Parliament will back Strongarm, Strongarm will back our treaty, and Pandar profits along with Earth. Once we're cleared of treason, that is."

Of course. Such a simple answer to qui bono. *So simple, in fact, I think I shall allow my ambassador to answer it for me.*

Octavian smiled with his lips. The danger lay in the cold blue glitter of his eyes. *If you can convince her to see the profit in your suggestion, then you have my support as well. Otherwise* – Octavian fluttered graceful fingers at a control. *I fear I shall have to cast my vote with JP.* His image faded with the words.

The holo'd image shifted, refocused on a single elegant table bearing a matched set of transparent stasis cubes. The central cube contained the still beautiful face of the Pandari ambassador. The woman's dead eyes stared back at him, her dead lips parted in some last plea for mercy. Someone had taken the time to quarter her arms and torso, so one arm and a half torso occupied the cubes on either side of her head. The next cubes out held her legs, equally distributed.

Jezekiah clenched lips shut to hold his stomach down. Across the desk Mother sank into her chair. She'd gone white with shock, one hand clasped over her mouth.

Even when Mother found her voice again, she could only manage a cracked whisper. "Find Keiko Yakamoto. Get Kip Marsden to help you, but find her. Now. Before your sister does." She sank back, arms clutching her shoulders. "I will deal with Letticia."

XXXVII

The moon had set by the time Marsden gave up hope. He squatted on haunches on the dead remnants of a kuleana, beside the dead ashes of some homie's Memory Night fire. He ran fingers through his curls, grunted at the sharp pinch where they hit a snarl, and tried to focus his bleary mind on Net. Wasn't any *physical* evidence at the kill site other'n that Tong star. He'd known there wouldn't be, though he'd done a Murphy search anyway. Took a pro to kill the way that boy had been done and Ta'an were real careful to clean up after themselves. But that little bitch Letticia tended to get careless...

Just not this time. Carefully, Marsden unwound his sync bots from their search patterns. He'd poked around Letticia's node enough to satisfy any spiders she had watching him. He could only hope – he didn't dare let himself even finish the thought. Letticia Van Buren might get careless, but she was the best goddamned syncmeister the Commonwealth'd ever seen. And he'd seen enough to know she was tracking *him*. Marsden thought out the mental sequence that took him off active duty in SecNet's register. He could only hope he'd held Letticia's attention long enough to let Lepper finish the job he'd given her. With any luck at all, the little bitch wouldn't think to cross-check a subordinate node.

The babbled litany behind his eyes evaporated, leaving his thoughts to spill into the vacuum it left behind. He rested his aching head in his hands, listened to the night whisper memories of its own. Shit on a shell, why the *hell* did they have to kill his lordship's doppelganger here? Why'd they have to add more heartache to the memories? Weariness let his guard down. The wind blew images he'd held at bay for half a lifetime in on a waft of night-blooming jasmine. Suddenly he could see them all again, as if the last quarter century'd never happened: young Matt Yakamoto chasing Lily Ho through the trees, two of them laughing themselves into hiccups. He saw this house again, bright and clean and alive with children. Saw Lily Ho sitting cross-legged by the doorway, singing a dreamy song while she wove her wedding leis. Before Grandfather Ho got his claws into her. Before -

To hell with it. Groaning, Marsden pushed himself up. Wasn't anything he could do for Mote here. Wasn't anything he'd be good for at all if he didn't get some sleep. He trudged back to his skimmer, told it to take him home. He dozed while the little machine flew back across Oahu's southern tip to old Pearl City. Didn't wake up until it'd settled on the landing pad beside his bungalow with a waking thump. Feeling his age, Marsden dragged himself out of the car. He noted for the thousandth or so time that the house needed paint, bad enough to show it even in the gray shadows of the night. For the thousandth or so time he tacked the job back on the bottom of the to-do list and hauled leaden feet up the steps.

The bungalow door slid open as soon as it recognized him, let him into the loneliness of a house that'd never felt like home. He must be tireder than he'd realized; place felt colder than usual tonight. Quieter -

The *thoroughness* of the silence registered then. Marsden leaned his hand on the weathered door jamb. He rested his head against it and let the chill dawn wind flap his shirt against his ribs while he listened to the utter silence running through his mind. Listened for the first time he could remember to nothing more than the sound of his own pulse thudding in his ears.

He realized numbly that his body'd gone cold. He called up the mental command that re-activated his Sec feed. Nothing. Just silence. Even then, it took almost a minute for the truth to fully register: he was locked out of Net.

He kept the hand on the door jamb for balance as he staggered into the deeper shadows within. He stopped abruptly, knuckles tightening on the door frame. Within the living room, one of the shadows was smiling. And the smile had fangs.

XXXVIII

It was the sound of crunching bone that cleared his hunter vision. Strongarm shook the corpse of a skinny Aryan off his talons and roared a final challenge at Teufelsman's fleeing back.

"One begins to think that Aryan has nine lives." Kaitin gave the Aryan whose spine he'd crushed a final sniff. He decided the fellow was dead enough and tossed the body aside. "Or perhaps the onlies' devil does not want him, either."

"We'll find out how many lives he has when I see him next. If he's -" Strongarm could not even finish the thought. Not with Keiko Yakamoto spasming on the gravel by his feet.

Warrior spirit that she was, she was struggling to rise. Strongarm eased as close to her as he dared. Praise the Makers Bird's body did not carry sex-scent, nor any signs of the trauma onlie men inflicted on the women they raped. Still, her eyes were glazed with pain and her scent carried terror beneath the rage. His body shook with the need to pull her close, hold her safe.

"Not yet." Kaitin hauled him back with talon tips in his shoulder.

Strongarm ripped his shoulder free, though the Bengali's talons ripped bloody trails across his flesh. He whirled to face Kaitin with fangs bared.

Kaitin bared his throat in submission. Gold jangled as he lifted his arms out from his sides. A breeze heavy with ocean salt and fresh grass billowed the emerald chiffon of his robes around his body. He waited till Strongarm sheathed talons before he risked speech. "This one begs forgiveness, Brother-in-Law. But if thee Touch her now, thee will thyself be guilty of rape."

It was true. Strongarm sagged forward. He would have dropped completely if Kaitin hadn't caught him. The Bengali clasped him tight, his scent bespeaking his sorrow, until Strongarm found the strength to stand alone. He nuzzled Kaitin's neck in thanks, forced himself to back away. "Bird? Can you stand?" He dug talons into his arms to hold himself in place.

"Alex?" Joy flared in her scent. She was still pain-blind but she twisted toward his voice. "Alex? Is that Jess with you?"

She wanted Jezekiah. Talons in his throat would have felt kinder. A breeze washed her scent over him, driving the feel of her hope into his bones. And the knowledge that her love was already given to Van Buren into his heart.

Then he forgot it all as Bird's eyes rolled back. She crumpled to the ground in a heap.

Kaitin shouldered Strongarm out of the way. He scooped Keiko up while Strongarm danced at his elbow like a hungry cub.

"She is hurt. Think thee she could survive thy loving now?" Kaitin swung Bird out of Strongarm's reach, blocked him with a green-clad shoulder.

It was the desperation in Kaitin's scent that finally drove sanity home. The man was right. Strongarm dug talons deeper into his arms, focused on the smell of his own blood until he had the Impression-need under control again. He gulped air, felt his shaking knees steady.

The soft brush Kaitin's nose against his ear surprised him. But it was the love in his scent that brought his ears up and stung his eyes. "It need not be much longer, Brother-in-" He caught himself, twitched mustaches. "Alex. This one will take thy Bird to a medic. Hie thee back to *Kutak*. This one will bring thy Bird as soon as she is fit to travel."

"Not yet." Strongarm let his scent bespeak his gratitude while he scratched sense back into his brain.

"Be not a fool!" Kaitin shifted Bird to his other arm, rested his freed hand on Strongarm's shoulder. "Thee can marry with proper honors when we reach *Khali*."

"Bird wouldn't accept me. Not yet. Not until Jezekiah Van Buren sets her free." He gulped air. The smell of his own blood helped clear his head. "First we get Bird to a medic. Then I'm going to find Van Buren."

The broad stone plaza fronting the Manor was deserted when they reached the building's entrance.

"Trap." Kaitin lifted his nose to the breeze, long white mustaches quivering, and shrugged Bird higher on his shoulder. "That Aryan must have sounded a warning."

"P-p-put me d-d-d-down. I c-can t-take c-care of myself." Bird tried to push herself free of Kaitin's arms. She succeeded only in setting off a fresh round of spasms. Her scent came alive with shame.

"Breathe easy, little one. Thy clansmen guard thee." Kaitin nosed Bird's temple, adding emphasis to the reassurance in his purr.

Clansmen. The word stopped Strongarm as hard as if Kaitin had struck him. Which was, clearly, what the Bengali had intended.

Kaitin turned the purr on Strongarm, added a ruby-tipped sniff. "One finds no objection to the girl herself." He said it in Lobish, keeping it private. "It is her choice of relatives that gives concern."

"Bird'll give up old man Ho once she sees what his Venus Seed did to our people on Rogue. It's Van Buren's lock on her heart that worries me." Strongarm lifted his nose toward the Manor's great doors, testing the air for warning. He got nothing but sea smells and well-oiled hinges. Yet everything about the emptiness of the place bespoke trap.

"Think thee they have marksmen in the windows above?" Kaitin pursed lips in a hunting grin, eyes and ears targeting the upper floors.

Strongarm shook his head, focused on the plaza beyond. "Not likely. Jezekiah's life depends on the treaty. He'll make the trade."

"J-jess?" Bird couldn't track the conversation, but the sound of Van Buren's name made her wriggle upright, giving Kaitin a challenge to keep his talons clear of her arm. "Have to find him. He'll know–"

"Rest easy, Bird." It was the burst of eagerness in her scent that challenged Strongarm's self-control. "I'll find him for you." Good thing her eyes drooped. She wouldn't see how the thought of handing her over to Van Buren bared his fangs. He snarled up at the windows. "If I'm wrong, we're going to find out right quick."

They almost reached the broad glass doors to the Manor's great entrance hall before they got an answer. Through the doors, the hall showed uncommonly empty. One or two harried admin ops scuttled across the brilliant Van Buren orchid mosaic covering the floor. But even those cast nervous glances their shoulders. There was no visible threat: sunlight bounded off the ivory petals of the red-tongued orchid mosaic covering the floor, raised ruby reflections from the twinkling red lights embedded in the petals' outline. It was the subtle vibration of the ground itself that gave warning.

"T-trouble coming." Bird squinted blearily past Strongarm toward the Manor. She tried to wriggle.

The sound behind the vibration was almost audible to onlie ears now. Strongarm lifted an ear toward the thud of armored feet echoing up from the Manor's interior.

Inside the Manor a squad of SecTypes thudded into the entrance hall. The bulk of the squad formed up just within the Manor's broad doors. The squad's alpha trooper stepped outside alone, hands spread wide in peace sign. The nametag on the SecType's armor read Lepper.

Kaitin's mustaches quivered in disapproval. "A woman. After Rogue do they still think she would be safe?"

"More likely she's trusting to the armor." Strongarm *uhfed* thoughtfully. Even from this distance worry dominated the woman's scent. Worry, yet not fear. Either this onlie had never encountered Lupan warriors, or she had a problem deeper than merely staying alive. "Find out soon enough. I'll take point."

"Got it." Behind him, Strongarm heard the swish as Kaitin swirled his robes around his free arm and lined up.

Good. His broad back would shelter Bird. Strongarm strode forward, hands out, talons retracted, matching Lepper peace sign for peace sign.

"Hold it right there, Lord Strongarm." To her credit, Lepper jittered but held her ground. It was her pack mates safely inside who touched the comm links at their throats. Calling in reinforcements, most likely. She upped her visor to reveal vaguely familiar sea-green eyes in a broken-nosed face.

"We need a medic, Lieutenant." Strongarm pointed an ear back at Bird, shivering in Kaitin's arms. "Your Captain Marsden will clear us."

"Captain Marsden's not here." The worry in her scent spiked. "Real sorry, Milord, but I got orders to arrest the mon-uh, Mistress Yakamoto."

"Arrest me for what?" That was Bird herself, outrage giving her voice a strength her body lacked.

"For murder." Lepper said it hard enough. But her scent bespoke doubt.

"Murdered who?" Behind Strongarm the soft *ching* of gold scraping gold said Bird was trying to escape Kaitin's grip. Her *oof* said how that'd ended.

"On whose orders?" Strongarm forced himself to keep the grin minimum, keep his talons sheathed. "If you mean those two Aryans out back, that was us. We will be more than happy to explain the reasons to your Captain Marsden."

"Yeah, well, I wish you could." Marsden's name triggered a surge of hope in Lepper's scent. Hope underscored by fear. "You guys seen the Captain?"

"Your captain is not our concern. It is a medic we seek." Gold swirls glinted against emerald along his free arm as Kaitin rolled his shoulders. Loosening muscles in anticipation of a fight.

Lepper recognized the danger in the gesture. She covered well enough to fool an onlie, but her scent had gone scared. Oddly, Kaitin's unspoken threat didn't seem to be what she feared. "Listen, you two, if I could find Captain Marsden, he'd be down here. But I can't. All's I got's those goddamned fuckin' Aryans." She touched the comm at her throat, frowning at some report. "Or had."

Lepper threw an involuntary glance over her shoulder. She snapped back to face him, scent-worry deepening afresh. "Listen, if I had the authority to let your girl go I would. But I can't. What I got is a warrant for Mistress Yakamoto's arrest."

"So *lack* you!" This time the scuffle behind Strongarm ended with a Bengali curse. Bird stumbled up beside him, Kaitin in muttering tow. "Arrest me for what?"

"For the murder of a joytoy under his lordship's personal protection."

Strongarm's heart lurched as Bird swayed. She steadied caught herself without grabbing him, straightened her stance into pure challenge. "Says who?"

"Says Jezekiah Van Buren."

"That's a lie! Jess never gave you that order." Bird stepped forward. She wobbled, but her fists clenched at her sides. "You ask Captain Marsden. He'll tell you!"

"Like I said-" Lepper bit the sentence off. For a moment anger challenged doubt in her scent. The doubt won and she shrugged. "Okay, guess you got the right." She lifted one hand – carefully – to touch a stud embedded in the armor above her wrist.

The air between them coalesced. For once Strongarm was grateful onlie holos didn't carry scent tracks. The figure dangling by his guts from the branch of a fat tree would have a stink he could live happy without. At that, the image alone was enough to make Bird clamp both hands over her mouth. Her scent went cold in horror.

The hideous image wavered, reformed. When it solidified, Jezekiah Van Buren faced them. His holo angled down a bit, making it seem he was speaking to Bird directly. *A young man in our employ has been most foully murdered.* He held up a silvery Tong star, turned it slowly down his fingers, those impossible blue eyes on Bird. *We have incontrovertible proof that the murderer is Keiko Yakamoto.*

Only a Lupan could have heard Bird's whimper. Or caught the betrayal in her scent. Both evaporated in a rush of anger. Her chin came up, hands clenching to fists on her hips. She was barely chin high to Lepper but she still managed to make the SecType shift nervously. "That's not Jess. He wouldn't ever say that. He doesn't even talk that way."

"Yeah? Well, that's not what NetMind says-" Lepper seemed to forget the sentence. Her jaw sagged, her scent going cold with fear. She swallowed, hard, then tapped the comm at her throat to 'off'. "Listen." She bit her lip at Bird, looking almost apologetic. "Maybe you do want to talk to the Heir direct. Whyn't you follow me and we'll see him together?"

"Yeah, why don't we just do that?" Bird started for the doors. She made it two whole steps before her knees buckled.

Kaitin body-blocked Strongarm's leap. He grabbed Lepper's arm in passing, shoved her into Strongarm. He scooped Bird into his arms as the SecType bounced off Strongarm's chest. Lepper hit the ground on her armored butt. The Manor's broad wings caught the clang of armor on stone and turned it into a ringing echo.

Within the Manor alarms honked in answer. Past Lepper, Strongarm saw the SecType squad spread out, shooing stray admin ops out of the way. The ready lights on their laser rifles shrank to green pinpricks as they brought their weapons to bear.

"Get us to your sick bay!" Strongarm bellowed over the din. He yanked Lepper to her feet and shoved her toward the door.

"God damn it to hell, listen-" Lepper staggered around to face him. The sudden stop brought her face first into Kaitin's ruby-tipped grin.

"We will listen later. Mistress Yakamoto needs a medic now." Kaitin settled Bird's twitching form higher on his shoulder and strode for the doors, fangs bared in a hunting grin.

Within the doors he heard the clicks as her pack mates brought laser rifles to life. Strongarm grabbed Lepper's armored shoulder, spun her to face her pack.

"Stand down!" Lepper raised her free arm. Within the Manor doors guns lifted. But the buzz of live lasers remained. "You got somethin' you wanna say, Lord Strongarm?"

"Just this- "

Strongarm slammed past the entrance scanners. He charged the Sec pack talons out, fangs bared. Alarms shrieked in warning. Outside on the plaza he heard Lepper shout something. The SecTypes scattered.

Across the great hall, a couple of Admin ops who'd wandered in from side corridors stopped to gape. They turned and fled as the SecType pack pounded past them. Kaitin leaped after them in a flutter of green film, golden eyes targeting the pack.

"Leave it! Aim for the door!"

Snarling, Kaitin jerked to a halt atop a sunlit petal of the great orchid mosaic, ruby droplet glittering in the sunlight. Mustaches quivering he lifted his nose to the sun to test the air, round white ears drooping in puzzlement.

The sunlight dimmed. Growling, Strongarm backed across the orchid mosaic, listening to the subtle buzz of the battle screens blocking the entrance. "All I want is the damned sick bay!" he roared at the ceiling. Then roared in earnest at the heat singeing his feet.

So that was why the SecTypes fled. The very floor was a trap. Across the broad orchid mosaic twinkling lights outlining the petals bloomed into a hot orange glow. Around the entrance hall the rising heat wavered the air. Strongarm glanced back at the entrance doors. Outside, Lepper had backed away, was snarling something into her comm. The view hazed in answer. Beneath Strongarm's feet the floor buzzed. Ended any doubt he had: the entrance doors were now shielded.

"Alex, tell him to let me go." Bird tried to wriggle free of Kaitin's grip. "It's me they want, not you two."

"Shush, little one." Kaitin tightened his grip on Bird's butt enough to make sure she did. "We are not onlies to abandon our women folk." Already his delicate pantaloons were crinkling in the heat. He hopped to the other foot and switched to Lobish. "Let us not stand here all day. These robes were thy sister's groom-gift. One does not wish to risk their ruin."

Strongarm lifted ears, felt a telltale tickle along their edges. The way Kaitin's nose twitched said he'd caught the sign, too. Somewhere at the far end of the hall was an opening. He jerked an ear at Kaitin. "Head for the back."

"Done." Kaitin was already skipping past him, tracking the angle of the draft.

Strongarm pulled in a breath and followed suit. His leather trousers trapped the heat. He could feel his sweat turning to steam against his skin. Maker's be praised the source of the draft wasn't far. It came from a camouflaged service door tucked into a curve of the wall. Ahead he saw Kaitin leap off the last petal toward the door – and bounce. The Bengali hit the ground on a shoulder. Strongarm caught a whiff of burnt hair as he rolled to his feet.

The impact broke his grip on Bird. She scrambled clear as Kaitin rolled. She was still woozy, but she managed to skip out of reach before Strongarm could grab her. She headed toward the main doors, hands above her head. Barefoot as she was she didn't seem to even notice the blistering heat. "Stop it! I surrender!"

On the other side of the door Lepper touched the comm at her throat. Strongarm could hear her profanity even through the buzz of the doors' shields. Instantly the shield haze cleared. Beneath his feet Strongarm felt the heat begin to fade.

"Now you all get your goddamn asses out here!" Lepper shouted through the doors. "And keep those hands up where I can see 'em!"

For answer Strongarm bared fangs in battle grin and roared challenge.

"No!" The desperation in Bird's voice brought him up faster than Kaitin's talons in his shoulder. "You can't! Not here!"

"I'm not turning you over, Bird."

"You try to fight and they'll kill us all." She slowed enough to plead with him over her shoulder. "I'll be fine, don't worry. Jess will set this all straight. You'll see."

The doors opened as she reached them. The rush of cool air nearly knocked her over. She wobbled, but straightened on her own before Lepper reached her side. "You two get going. I'll be fine."

"She's right. Attack them now and we die for nothing." Kaitin dug talons into Strongarm's shoulder to hold him in place. Together they watched while Lepper led Bird away. The rest of the squad backed along behind the two women, laser rifles at the ready. At that, it was only the fact Lepper did not try to put restraining rings on Bird that kept Strongarm from diving for their throats anyway. But it was the backwashed fear in Lepper's scent that sent him looking for Jezekiah Van Buren.

XXXIX

Oh, that was just utterly delicious! Curled around the sync glove, Letticia barely even felt the cool tile of the bathroom floor against her naked body or heard the gurgle of the water running in her tub. Thank *heavens* the damned Admiral was too stodgy to take her up on her invitation to watch her take her bath. He'd taken up position outside her quarters instead, standing there straight and stupid and scaring Mother's admin ops. She giggled to herself at the thought of how he'd look if he could have seen her dig Teufelsman's sync glove out of its hidey hole behind the toilet. Oh, that would be *such* a sight! Because she was going to make that little monkey daughter of his sorry she'd ever been born.

Slowly, Letticia slipped the metallic glove over her hand, slipped her mind out of her disgusting body and into the glory of Net and her true Self. She jammed the thrill down savagely. She couldn't afford excitement. Not yet. She still had enemies, even here. Ever so carefully Letticia wound her immaterial Self around Mother's node. Good – the spider holes she'd planted in Mother's defenses on her earlier forays still held. She ran a quick check on Mother's whereabouts, noted with a private chuckle that she was still in her office. Oh, and with *dear* Jezekiah parked in one of those dreadful chairs. On impulse, Letticia pulsed the chair's feedback system, heard her body giggle at the way Jezekiah jumped.

It would have been *so* nice to give him a real taste of the chair! But she didn't dare, not with Mother there. Didn't have time, either, not just now. Letticia listened in only long enough to be sure Jezekiah wasn't talking about her. She backed out of Mother's node, tested her neural strands again, just to be sure the node guards hadn't rewoven defenses behind her. She couldn't afford to leave any traces at all, not here. Besides, she had work to do.

She caught a hyperstrand of NetMind, found the Streikern ambassador's ID and added an addendum of her own to the ambassador's report telling JP just what she thought of his ruining her chances with Strongarm. Stupid man – did he think she'd got him that Seed shipment just for *his* ends? Heavens!

Still, she had no time to linger on JP's idiocy, either. Letticia dropped out of hyperlink onto a passing data stream. She hopped streams until she found Marsden's link. Careful indeed, here. Viral guards spat even before she even brushed past. It was a whole new type of virus, too, a code type she'd never broken. Letticia let the stream sweep her on past. Oh, for heaven's sake! When was she supposed to find time to sawyer another set of defenses? Why *did* Marsden always have to be so paranoid?

Still, the main byte she needed was already logged into SecNet. Letticia found the report on the doppelganger's death, stored a copy away in her own hidey hole for future entertainment. Pity she hadn't thought to tell Grandfather Ho to have the Ta'an record the killing. She'd have enjoyed watching the little monster pay for the way he'd humiliated her. What mattered at the moment was that the fool Ta'an had left the evidence right where she'd told him.

So... all she needed to do now was set the play in motion. Flinging her Self onto an outward bound strand Letticia backtracked to Teufelsman's node. No need to tell him what to do; he seemed to have his own reasons for tracking the Yakamoto monkey. But she needed his access for the next step. Mother would never punish her dear Admiral Yakamoto's brat the way she ought. Mother didn't care enough about her own daughter to put that vile little monkey in her place. So she'd just have to do it herself. Grimly Letticia slipped inside Teufelsman's node. And slowly, delicately began the deadly process of capturing Mother's ID.

XL

There! She was in! Ever so carefully, Letticia wormed her Net essence deeper into Mother's node. She hatched a swarm of spiders, sent them skittering up her anchor strands to serve as a rear guard. The fact Mother's node guards hadn't re-woven defenses behind her didn't mean they wouldn't. And she absolutely did *not* want to get caught poking around in the Protector's node now! She gave her lines a final check. They came up clear and she heard her body sigh with relief.

She settled into one of the spider holes she'd dug on her earlier forays and got to work re-setting NetMind's records. This was the easy part, fortunately. She'd been in here often enough for even Mother's node to consider her presence semi-normal. Moving swiftly, Letticia switched out the records' biopats. When she finished the records showed that Jezekiah had been diverting Seed shipments to JP himself. There! Just *let* him try to blame her for that Rogue business now! Mother's own node would testify against him. And Marsden wouldn't be there to prove she'd tampered. Now all she had to do was watch the Family vote his execution. After that, even the Admiral wouldn't dare bother her. Because Mother would *need* her then. Mother would love *her*, then.

One of her outlier strands flashed warning. She checked DemoNet and the alarm intensified. Mother had left her office. She was headed for the family's wing, her biopat reading dark and grim. She half-expected to find the Admiral's biopat standing guard. Remembered belatedly that Mother had sent him to find his stupid daughter. Letticia heard her body chuckle. Oh, he'd be a long time searching for his little monkey now!

Odd, though: thought of the Admiral triggered a telltale within Mother's personal files. A *secret* file, too, secured with Mother's own biopat. She really shouldn't take the time – but the draw was too strong. Setting her outliers to red alert, Letticia morphed her ID into Mother's and opened the file.

Oh, how utterly perfect! The nasty old man had secrets even Jezekiah didn't know about! Just wait till she – an outlier shrieked warning. Mother was coming! Sync itself shivered until Letticia managed to will her body's hand from shaking the link. No time for caution now. Quickly Letticia backed out of Mother's node, erasing her neural trail behind her. Good thing she didn't have to worry about Marsden anymore; she hadn't time now to be any more careful than simple survival required.

She caught a strand of SecNet, rode it straight into the Manor's core defense code. Not much to do there: Marsden had done an excellent job on the Manor's room-by-room defenses. Almost a pity she'd had to remove him. Though not as much of a pity as the fact she'd have to miss out on watching him die.

She wove her personal instructions into the code, then fled SecNet. No time to even wipe her trail this time. But then, it didn't really matter. Not now. She was ready for anything now.

Bracing herself, Letticia yanked her hand out of the sync glove. The bathroom whirled back into focus, its tiled walls echoing the ragged whisper of her breath. Think, *think*! She had to think! More than anything else, she had to keep the glove with her. She ran a hand down the tight line of her dress. Not in this rig! Knees trembling, Letticia pushed herself off the cold floor. Tucking the sync glove beneath her chin she ripped the dress off and kicked it behind the toilet then slipped the glove between her teeth to ransack her closet.

She found a yellow day dress with a pocket big enough to hold it and a skirt full enough to hide the bulge. At least the glove wouldn't fall through the hole Marsden's gobbing ops had left when they'd ripped out her own link. She wrenched the dress on, nearly ripped the pocket further jamming the glove in. She was still fumbling the buttons closed when the door to her quarter hissed open.

"Letticia." Mother's voice, from her living room. Mother's *working* voice, cold and clear and emotionless.

"Here, Mother." Letticia fumbled the last button closed and forced her shaking feet to carry her out.

She'd expected to see Mother standing in the middle of her living room, tall and bright like a pillar of sunlight holding back the night. She'd meant to face Mother's anger with her head up and an answering sneer. What she hadn't expected was for Mother to look so ... empty.

Had Mother been angry, or sad, or – or *any*thing Letticia could have managed dignity. Only Mother had wiped all expression out of her face, put her working mask on. It was that awful nothingness in Mother's expression, the *finality* of it, that drained the strength out of Letticia's knees. Her legs collapsed and she dropped in a flare of yellow skirt.

"Get up, Letticia." Mother's lips trembled but her voice was cold and calm. The very nothingness in her tone re-woke terror.

Letticia tried to obey but her knees refused to work. "It's not my fault! I've been good! You know I have!"

But Mother only backed away from her touch. "Letticia Van Buren." Mother intoned her name ritually, fixed her eyes on some spot on the wall over Letticia's head. "You have been proven guilty of two offenses: first, you have imported a Ta'an assassin to Earth. Worse, upon discovery, you have refused to turn this assassin over to Sec."

"But I told Jess! I don't know where the silly fool is!" Oh, why couldn't Mother *see*?

But Mother just droned on. "Second, you have infiltrated the Protector's node and usurped the Protector's authority to your own ends. Either of these is a capital crime."

"But you *told* me to!"

That finally made Mother look at her. Letticia wished instantly she hadn't. It felt like looking up at death itself.

"I granted you permission to use Jezekiah's node to the extent necessary to protect him from Streiker's assassins while he was on the rim." There was no anger in Mother's voice. She sounded cold and toneless as death, too. "Not to use his node as a jump-off point to invade the Protector's node."

"But I didn't!"

"I saw you, Letticia."

"But you couldn't-" The sheer, absolute, utter impossibility of it stopped her.

"I am the Protector, Letticia. No aspect of NetMind on Earth is closed to me."

Mother's working mask flickered. For a moment Letticia thought she would hit her. Right now she would have welcomed the blow. But the flicker steadied, leaving Mother's expression neutral again. The effect was more terrifying than any amount of rage.

"Then ask NetMind! It'll tell you! You locked me out of Net, remember? I couldn't sawyer anything, even if I wanted!" Oh, thank *heavens* she'd covered her tracks!

Stepping past her, Mother slid her hand into the sync chair link. The sight made Letticia lick dry lips in yearning. Still, she could afford to wait a bit longer for sync. She knew exactly what questions Mother would ask. And precisely what answers NetMind would give. Everything would be all right now.

"It is only fair that you see this." The air in the center of the room swirled as Mother put the Netmind feed on viz.

Letticia had to hide a sneer of triumph as the little scene she'd created coalesced in the space before them. She kept her expression neutral while viz showed Jezekiah using his Heir's authority to leapfrog Mother's NetMind defenses and open the Protector's node. She managed not to fidget while viz showed Jezekiah ordering SecNet to ignore the biopat of that Ta'an assassin. It was a triumph in itself that she actually managed to look *sad* by the time viz finished the heart-rending image of Jezekiah laying out his plans to use the Ta'an to assassinate Mother.

The holo vanished, leaving Letticia blinking up at Mother, still standing beside the sync chair. She'd gone white as Letticia had expected. Yet it didn't seem to be the white anger she'd expected. Instead she just looked... tired.

"How much of the NetMind recording we have just witnessed is your doing?"

"Mother! How could it be? I'm locked out of Net!"

"You had no part in either smuggling that Ta'an onto Earth, nor in any plot to assassinate your reigning Protector?"

"Of course not! You just saw for yourself."

For a moment Mother looked doubtful. Then her eyes drooped closed with that inward look as if she were absorbed in sync. Oh, thanks heavens! It'd worked.

And then Mother raised her hand. Suddenly the Ring flared so bright it wiped Letticia's vision. "NetMind: Protector's override. Verify last sync display."

Blinking through green after-glare, Letticia felt her heart jerk in terror at the sonorous baritone of Mother's own major domo.

Verification denied. Data inaccurate.

Still Mother kept that inward focus. "Confirm: did Jezekiah Van Buren infiltrate the Protector's node?"

No, Protector.

"Confirm: did Jezekiah Van Buren neutralize the biopat of a Ta'an assassin for the purpose of bringing that assassin onto Earth?"

No, Protector.

"Confirm: has the Protector's node been infiltrated?"

Yes, Protector.

"By whom and for what purpose?"

"No!" Letticia surged against the chair, tried to drown the treacherous voice with her shriek. Useless.

Infiltrator: Letticia Van Buren. Frequency: multiple. Initial incursion to assess capabilities. Subsequent incursion to create personal identity site within the Protector's node–

"Liar!" Mother didn't even look at her. Her eyes locked on some point a thousand yards beyond the office's walls. When she spoke it was almost to herself. "Let the record show that our daughter Letticia is proven guilty of high treason. Judgment is rendered accordingly." Her working mask crumpled, leaving her face scrunched up, like she hurt too much to even cry. The way she'd looked the day they killed Daddy.

Oh, God, she knew how that felt! She *understood* that kind of loss! "Oh, Mommy, I'm *sorry*!" Sobbing, Letticia threw herself at Mother wanting to hug all the pain and sorrow and loss away.

Mother's backhand caught her by surprise. The blow sent Letticia sprawling face first on to the chill tile. She climbed back to her knees, hand to her throbbing cheek, to gape up at Mother through the blur of tears. "But, Mommy – why?"

"Damn it, why *now*?" Mother made the question sound like a cry of anguish. Why couldn't you believe me before-" Her body shook so hard she locked her hands around her waist. It looked like she was somehow holding herself together. The Ring's pulsing glare flash-drained all color from the room, left nothing but blinding white. And the sound of Mother sobbing.

"Mommy?" Even to herself Letticia sounded plaintive. For once she didn't care. "Mommy? Let me help. Please."

"Enough." Through the Ring glare she heard the sobs stop. "Major Domo. Record judgment." Mother's voice sounded like ashes. "The sentence is death. To be executed immediately." Her voice caught, went on. "Summon Admiral Yakamoto."

"You can't!" With a shriek Letticia threw herself at Mother's knees. "You don't mean it! Say you don't mean it!"

Mother stumbled away from her. She backed toward the door, hunched, hugging herself. "Why couldn't you listen?"

"You never loved me!" Letticia put all her rage and terror into the scream. "You never cared about me! Only about Jezekiah!"

"I warned you, Letticia. I tried to ignore it all-"

Through the shimmer of tears Letticia saw the doors open. "No, Mommy, listen-"

But the doors swished shut. The sec screen buzzed to life. Letticia threw herself at them anyway, but she only bounced off the screens. Landed once more face down to beat her fists in helplessly on the cold tile floor. Even Mother! Even Mother had betrayed her! Mother'd never loved her. She wouldn't keep her safe – She didn't even *care*! She was going to turn her over to that damned, nasty old Admiral – the full, awful *finality* of it clicked home at last. Letticia shot upright, horror draining the warmth from her body. Oh, God...ohgodohgodohgod...Mother was going to kill her! Really, truly kill her! Nothing could save her –

Nothing except Net. Letticia gulped air, felt warmth seep slowly back into her veins. Teufelsman's sync glove. She still had Teufelsman's sync glove. She was still safe. She fumbled the sync glove out of her pocket, slipped it on and dove back into the wondrous reality of Net.

Thank heavens Mother hadn't thought to ask her Major Domo whether she was *really* locked out of Net! Traitorous thing would have zit her out. The realization triggered a burn in her feed. It took Letticia a frantic moment to recognize the burn as tear sting – her body was crying. Well, she'd fix the major domo, too. Once she was sure she'd be safe. But for now -

She checked Mother's progress as soon as she reached her spider hole. Good – Mother was headed back to her office exactly as she'd expected. That gave her seven, maybe ten minutes – whole *minutes* – to set up her own defenses. Moving swiftly, Letticia wove her way into Sec's node. She hooked a strand of secured data, rode it into the SecDef site for the Protector's office. No need to worry about covering her trail now. Once she was done nobody would care where she'd been. But she still had to be careful – one slip here and she could kill everyone in the Manor, her personal body included.

She invested nearly a whole minute in modifying SecDef's commands. Now… Letticia opened her back-up cells within Mother's node – oh, thank *heavens* she'd thought to take this precaution! – and morphed her ID into Mother's. A second thought, and 'Mother' was facing a grim Admiral Yakamoto.

"Madam." He snapped to attention in a clink of swords as Letticia formed Mother's image in his sync. "I am on my way."

No need, Admiral. Letticia made sure she sounded like Mother, too. *I'm glad I reached you in time. I've issued a stay of execution. Your services won't be needed.*

"Again?" If possible the nasty old man went grimmer. "Madam-"

One does not question, one obeys. Safely invisible behind Mother's image Letticia's Net-essence nearly giggled with delight. Oh, she'd been *dying* to throw that one at him!

"Yes, Madam." He looked like he'd just swallowed a worm. "Anything else, Madam?"

Just one. Have you found your daughter yet? Ah, that made him squirm!

"Not yet, Madam. I regret she was not at home." He had sense enough to look worried about it.

Well, keep looking. Strongarm won't wait forever, you know. With that, Letticia cut the link off. Oh, just wait till he found out where his precious monkey was!

Listening to her body hum, Letticia opened the thread that linked her to the Protector's dais within the Manor's Hall of Justice.

XLI

"You sure you can walk?" The armored hand Lepper slid beneath Keiko's elbow bespoke her concern more than her tone.

"Yeah." No lie, either. The effects of Teufelsman's neural wand were nearly gone. Enough so that Keiko couldn't puzzle out why battle sense was burning the back of her neck.

Wasn't anybody in the Manor corridor to threaten her. Sgt. Lepper'd turned out to be downright nice once Alex and Kaitin left. She'd sent her team mates back to Sec HQ so it was just the two of them. The Manor's haole staff folk must have headed for home when those sirens went off, because there sure wasn't anybody around now. Even the air smelled better than she'd expected – more like salt water than the dead, piped in air you usually got in haole buildings. The wall holos created the illusion they were strolling along the black sand beach at Punalu'u down on the Big Island. The image conjured memory of her Type trial, of killing the biomech that bore her father's face. Maybe that was what was bothering her so.

"Listen up." Lepper's voice yanked Keiko's attention back to the SecType. "Here's the drill. I'ma take you to the Manor's clinic. I want you to *stay* there, hear?"

"But I'm okay, now. Really." Keiko rolled her head again. Sweet Tutu Pele, whatever the trouble was it was *bad*. Definitely not just memories. Sgt. Lepper looked like she expected trouble, too. She had her face plate up, but she'd slung a borrowed laser rifle across her shoulder. And its power light shone green.

"Yuh-huh." Lepper sounded so much like the Captain Keiko's heart jumped. "Maybe you are. Maybe you're innocent, too. I just wanna find –ask– the Captain somethin' 'fore this goes any farther."

"Why not just call him? You got a link."

"He's not answerin'."

"*The Captain*? But he always -" Then they turned into the next corridor and Keiko's battle sense flared.

Lt. Teufelsman lifted his shoulder off the holo'd image of a coconut palm. The effect was like watching a tall white python uncoil. Behind him, a trio of Aryans spread out to block the corridor. Teufelsman's own hands were empty. But each of the Aryans around him held a laser rifle. And each of those rifles was pointed at Lepper.

"Thank you, Sergeant." Smiling that slimy smile, Teufelsman stepped into the center of the corridor to block them. "I shall take charge of the prisoner now."

"You're in my way, Teufelsman. Get out of it." Facing those rifles, Lepper couldn't unlimber her own. But Keiko noted gratefully that she let go of her elbow and sidled away. Giving her fighting room.

"Really, now, Sergeant. Surely you would not disobey the Protector's orders?"

"Madam ain't given *you* any orders, either, Teufelsman. Sec handles arrests around here."

"Except in political matters." Teufelsman oozed forward. He was looking at Lepper rather than herself, but Keiko felt the touch of his *ki* against her battle sense. Even his psychic essence felt dirty. "I caught Mistress Yakamoto attempting to break into the Heir's quarters. I was in the process of arresting her when those Lupan animals attacked me."

"Liar!" Keiko surged forward, hit Lepper's armored forearm. "You were trying to-"

"I have the Protector's summons to trial right here." Keeping one hand out, he reached into his jacket pocket and pulled out a portable sync link.

The holo'd image of Madam Van Buren coalesced in the space between them when he thumbed its message tab.. She looked like she always did, regal and cold. And yet somehow she looked... mean. *Lt. Teufelsman.* The way the holo spoke made even the name sound like a sneer. *The human monkey known as Keiko Yakamoto has been charged with the murder of an off-world visitor. You are hereby authorized to use any means necessary to bring her to trial.*

Teufelsman thumbed the holo off and re-pocketed the link. He reached behind his back. When his hand re-appeared, a set of restraining rings dangled from his fingers. "And now, Sgt. Lepper, you will turn your prisoner over to me." He slithered closer, eyes on Keiko. "Unless you propose to disobey a direct command from the Protector?" Behind him, the other three Aryans brought their rifles to bear.

"T'ain't right." Keiko heard Lepper add something obscene under her breath.

"You don't have a choice." It took all the will she had for Keiko to step forward and let Teufelsman lock the rings around her neck and wrists. It would be all right, she told herself. The Protector would know the truth when she heard it. Especially when she heard it from Jess.

The corridors filled up again as Teufelsman led Keiko deeper into the Manor. She kept her head up as much as the restraining rings allowed, building a mental map of the corridors leading to the Hall of Justice. She'd never even dreamed of getting inside the Manor. Probably wouldn't get another chance, either, not the way Madam Van Buren felt about naturals. Even Jess hadn't included it among all the sweet dreams he'd whispered in her arms.

Most of the corridors they passed apparently led off to lesser courts. All those bustled with haoles. Pinched-faced advos in fancy suits strolled by in pairs, trading secrets for favors. The advos never noticed her. But Keiko recognized a couple of the uniformed SecTypes hauling haole prisoners to or from trial. Helped to see how those two shouldered their prisoners into the advos to open a path for her. The thought that somebody here, at least, knew she was innocent helped ease the shame. Helped her walk just a bit straighter.

The crowds thinned as the last corridor blossomed into the atrium fronting the Hall of Justice. Skylights in the roof let sunlit shafts streak the open space like pale columns. The sunlight blazed the creamy petals of the Van Buren orchid mosaic set in the floor. Its brilliant red stamen pointed the way to the great carved doors of the Hall. For some reason the orchid's fiery tendrils reminded her of the flaming tongue of Grandfather Ho's dragon tattoo.

The guards flanking the Hall entrance were Samurai. The trademark twin swords gleamed at their sides, but they cradled laser rifles in their arms. Keiko felt their contempt. A week ago, she would have slunk away in shame. Now she could answer contempt with defiance. They'd hear the truth from Jess himself soon enough. The great doors of the Hall swung outward and Teufelsman jerked her to a halt. He nearly pulled Keiko off her feet but she barely noticed. Because the doors opened on to – absolute nothing.

Within the Hall there seemed to be no walls, no floor, no ceiling. Just the black, vast emptiness of space. A single broad strip of burnished gold arrowed across the black emptiness, a gleaming lifeline to the solid floor of the atrium. The far end of the arrow vanished into infinity beyond. Common sense told her it was only a holo, but primal instinct refused to believe.

Teufelsman shoved Keiko onto the band ahead him. He kept her leash short, so the move yanked the restraint rings binding her wrists up, driving the rings' biting sec shield into her chin. But she caught the shiver in the leash and recognized the fear behind it. She found satisfaction in that. Not waiting for Teufelsman to shove her again Keiko tapped a toe on the emptiness bordering the golden band. Solid, cold floor clicked under her foot. Pulling in a breath, Keiko stepped off into the nothingness, hauling Teufelsman with her.

Teufelsman's trembling hand shoved her forward down the golden band.

Around the encircling space, the twelve suns of the Van Buren Commonwealth orbited the central orb of Earth's sun. Pandar's blue-white star commanded the three o'clock position. Its cold glare dimmed the gentler yellows and reds of the lesser suns on its flanks and cancelled out the sun's warmth. The crushing vastness pushed down on her, drove her insignificance deeper into her bones.

The golden arrow ended at a link rostrum in the center of the Hall. Teufelsman reeled her in when they reached the defendant's rostrum. His Sec contact lenses filtered the glare, so he could look directly into the sun. Keiko squinted up, trying to track his gaze against the sun's brilliance. She made out the shadow of a looming dais with a throne-like sync chair centered on it. The hazy shade of a tall woman stood in front of the chair.

"Protector Van Buren." Teufelsman bowed short and sharp toward the dais, then slipped a hand into the link. The podium contained a second link, but Keiko's rigging rendered that useless even if she'd been able to sync in. "I present the prisoner Yakamoto for your examination." He yanked Keiko's leash downward, pulling her into a bow with her hands to her throat.

"Set your link to viz, Lieutenant. The prisoner has the right to witness the charges."

The sneer in the Protector' voice shocked Keiko more effectively than the feedback bite in the restraints. She blinked into the glare, trying to place it. Lost the sense of familiarity when Teufelsman jerked her upright again.

A speck of mist formed in the void between the podium and the dais. It ballooned into a cloud, solidified into an elegant oval room lined by tall arched windows. Keiko realized with a start that she could see through the windows, clear out to Pearl Harbor in the distance. There was no mistaking the resemblance to Jess in the red-headed woman facing her from behind the desk. Keiko's mouth went dry at the realization she was staring into the Protector' own office.

The Protector lifted her head to look down her nose at Keiko. "Name the charges, Lieutenant."

Maybe it was just the way Teufelsman set the controls, but the Protector' voice sounded almost whiney. Against the unspoken power of the office, it sounded out of place. Not what she'd expected Jess' mother to sound like at all. Not the *feel* she expected, either. She certainly hadn't expected sight of the Protector to send a twinge of battle sense shivering down her neck. Belatedly she realized Teufelsman was talking.

"The charges against the prisoner are as follows: First, that the accused has utilized forbidden Tong weaponry, in defiance of Van Buren law.

"Second, that the accused has used such a weapon to commit the most foul murder of a Commonwealth citizen, a young man under the personal protection of the Heir himself.

"*What?*" Keiko tried to whack the Aryan with the restraining ring, but Teufelsman only slammed her into the podium base.

"Lastly." Teufelsman looked down to meet her eyes for this one. Keiko swallowed a shiver at his cold, pleased smile. "That the accused has assisted Ho Tong to smuggle a Ta'an assassin onto Earth for the purpose of assassinating yourself. In defiance of the laws of the Protectorate, the Commonwealth, and all common morality."

"That's crazy and you know it!" Keiko lunged, driving the rings' shield into Teufelsman's ribs. "You know damned good and well I've been working Sec! You get Captain Marsden in here! He'll tell you!"

"Alas, Captain Marsden is not available."

It was the satisfaction in the Protector' voice that stopped Keiko more than the words themselves. That and the spike in her battle sense. "Then ask Jezekiah, Ma'am." Her mouth was so dry suddenly the words tried to stick to her tongue. "He'll tell you. I saved him from that Ta'an out there on Niihau dock." She swung the restraining rings around to poke at Teufelsman. "Me and Captain Marsden."

"Silence!" Teufelsman pressed a stud on the leash.

The restraints tightened to strangling strength. Keiko fought for breath until the world swirled. She felt her knees hit the floor before the fire in her lungs eased.

"Really, now, Lieutenant." The Protector waved a lazy hand and Teufelsman eased up on Keiko's leash. "The law does not forbid the accused to speak for herself. Let us hear what our dear Mistress Yakamoto has to say for herself."

Sweet madam Pele, she'd never thought Jess' mother would be as bitchy as his sister. Still, it was Jess who mattered. Even mother Van Buren would listen to Jess. Head swirling, Keiko forced herself onto one knee. "Ask Jezekiah. He'll tell you the truth."

"Indeed. Well, then, in the interests of justice, do let's hear what my dear ... Jezekiah has to say." The Protector touched a comm patch on her panel. "We call the Heir, Jezekiah Van Buren, to witness."

A second patch of mist appeared within the vast emptiness of space. The mist coalesced in a holo of Jezekiah. He was lounging in somebody's sync chair, those long legs of his stuck out before him. Only the glint in those bright blue eyes warned of danger. The sight made Keiko's heart jump. He should be angry! He must have been listening to all these lies. He'd tell them where to go!

"Jezekiah." The Protector swiveled her chair to face Jezekiah's holo'd image. "A Ta'an assassin followed you here to Earth. Do you know how that happened?"

Keiko had thought his eyes would seek hers, the way she was drawn to him

Yet Jezekiah only lifted his head enough to target some point in the space between them. "Ho Tong arranged the Ta'an's passage on a TransitLine ship."

"And how do you know this?"

"Keiko Yakamoto told me." Maybe it was just as well he didn't look at her. She would never have been able to keep her feet if he had.

The Protector wasn't finished yet. "We have a Sec report from Captain Marsden that you were also attacked by that same assassin on our very own dock two days ago. Is this true?"

"No." Jezekiah actually *stretched*, as if the whole process, the balance of her life, bored him. "It was Keiko Yakamoto who attacked me. If Sec hadn't intervened I'm quite sure she would have killed me."

"So *lack* you!" Keiko leaped for Jezekiah's holo'd figure. She was fast enough to make it past Teufelsman. Just not past the restraining rings.

Teufelsman yanked her leash. She sprawled face up on the cold stone floor. She lay there, her soul savaged, staring up into the infinite universe, wishing she could meld into the darkness. Anything to escape the absolute, utter indifference in Jezekiah's voice. She barely noticed the bite of the rings when Teufelsman hauled her back to her feet. Her heart hurt too much to feel physical pain.

"I have researched the Yakamoto girl's connections to Ho Tong." The holo'd Jezekiah sounded as bored as he looked, like the lie didn't even matter. Like she didn't matter. Like the love they'd shared had never happened. "She is Grandfather Ho's own granddaughter. A fact both her father and Captain Kip Marsden have conspired to disguise." He snapped a hand up, flipped his palm aside like he'd caught something and thrown it back. Like he'd just brushed the whole incident, her whole life, off with a shrug.

"Lieutenant?" On the dais above, light shifted with the Protector's movement. "What has the prosecution to say?"

Teufelsman slipped his free hand into a jacket pocket and pulled out something bright and shiny. Dully, Keiko recognized a pair of Tong stars. "These two stars were removed last night from the body of an off-world natural boy. A boy murdered in a most cruel, heinous manner. A manner, incidentally, that is characteristic of Ho Tong."

"Why should this court care whether the accused murdered another natural?"

"Because the murdered boy was under the direct protection of Milord Jezekiah himself. The prosecution contends that the boy's killing was intended as a deliberate Tong challenge to the authority of the Great Family Van Buren."

"How does the accused explain this?" The Protector's tone implied she'd already decided the answer.

Teufelsman yanked Keiko's head up by the leash. "The Protector asked you a question, monkey!"

"What's it matter?" The ache in her soul left no room for feelings.

"Then does the defendant plead guilty?"

"Doesn't matter," Keiko muttered.

"Very well, then." Madam Van Buren's tone went prim. "Keiko Yakamoto, we have listened to the charges and evidence brought against you. As Protector of these Islands, I therefore rule that you shall be judged guilty as charged on all counts. You are hereby sentenced to Registration. Sentence to be executed immediately."

XLII

Six stories below the Manor proper Jezekiah stepped off Mother's private elevator into Sec HQ. The complex was a fortified rabbit warren of corridors hollowed out of the black volcanic rock. In the early years of the Protectorate, this had *been* the Manor. The first Van Buren war lords needed a home base that could survive the kind of attack that had flattened old Honolulu. So Sec ran its own generators, drew its power directly from the island's geothermal heart. The lava rock walls were reinforced by carbon-threaded ceramics, lit solely by organic phosphorescents. Even the air filters and elevators were strictly mech. The result was depressing, but effective. In a pinch, Sec HQ could even work without NetMind. Which was why he expected Kip to be down here. He certainly hoped so: he hadn't a prayer of finding Keiko before Strongarm did otherwise.

A few feet down the corridor and he began wondering if even Kip could help him. *Something* was wrong. He felt it in the way the SecTypes he passed waited to watch him down the corridor. Felt their suspicion between his shoulder blades. The sense of invisible watchers gave him the hideous feeling that Letticia was peering over his shoulder.

White light flared beyond the corridor's curve. Jezekiah dropped for cover as the boom of heavy fire rolled over him. He lifted his head enough to see the pair of SecTypes he'd passed crouched nearby, guns drawn. His question died with the realization those guns were aimed at him. He rose slowly, taking care to keep his hands out from his sides, Ring up and glaring. The SecTypes rose with him, guns tracking his movements. Keeping his tone neutral, he raised a brow. "Mind if I ask just what this is about?"

A second explosion – this one of stunning female profanity – answered for them. No mistaking that voice. Even out on the rim he'd never heard anyone swear with the enthusiasm of Sgt. Lepper. Kip's second in command. And somebody in Sec HQ was shooting at her.

For an instant his mind simply refused to accept the thought. Then training took over, imposing logic. Whatever was going on, couldn't be Lupan work, at least not yet. Considering the alternatives quick calcs flashed him, he almost wished it was.

Without waiting for the SecTypes' order, Jezekiah backed toward Lepper's voice. A gray haze hung in the air around the corridor bend. The air here carried the ozone smell of laser fire. The filters hadn't yet absorbed the dust from the explosion, leaving a haze that stung his nose and made his eyes water. Glancing over his shoulder Jezekiah saw Lepper fifty feet farther down the corridor. She was in full armor but she'd lifted her visor to meet a major domo's red eye glare-to-glare. A pair of laser cannon muzzles protruded from slots on either side of the eye.

Looked like the stinging dust didn't bother Lepper at all. That privilege went to the slender plumes of smoke curling up from the floor just beyond each of her elbows. Even in profile her expression threatened pain to all and sundry.

She paused the tirade but only to draw enough breath to reach parade ground volume. "You know goddamn good'n well who I am, you goddamned cock-sucking son of a bitch!"

"Sorry, Sarge." The disembodied voice behind the watching red eye sounded torn between embarrassment and fear. "Captain's orders. Nobody gets in here without full body scan. You gotta take the armor off. Either that or gimme your scan-D code."

"I ain't strippin' for a snot-nose like you." Her volume intensified. "And you know goddamn good'n well I ain't never hadda look up my ID code in my whole goddam motherfucking life."

Keeping his hands ups, Jezekiah turned to face Lepper and the watching red eye. "I believe I can resolve this, if you'll allow me?"

"Fuck off." Lepper didn't waste so much as glance at him. The red eye ignored him, too.

"Name, rank, or sync-D code." the watcher's voice sounded genuinely regretful. "State it or I gotta shoot again. And you know I gotta take you out second time."

"Name's *Lepper*, you goddamnedcocksuckinmotherfuckin*shit*asssuckin-sonuvabitch'n a bastard." She jammed hands on hips with a metallic *clunk*. "It's still *Sergeant* Lepper to you till I get my hands 'round your goddamncocksuckinmothuhfuckin neck. An' I'ma tellin' you here'n now you take another goddamn pot shot at me an' I'ma look my goddamnedmotherfuckincocksuckin*shit*asssuckinsonuvabitchin' sync-D up and carve it in you ass!"

"Sure sounds like Lepper to me," one of the SecTypes behind Jezekiah muttered.

The comment drew Lepper's attention. Drew the major domo's attention, too. The unit's red eye and cannon swiveled to cover them. Behind him, Jezekiah heard the suddenly nervous shuffle of the men's feet. He drew breath to speak. He inhaled a noseful of rock dust instead. The burn up his nose triggered a sneeze loud enough to draw Lepper's attention away from the major domo's red eye.

"What the hell *you* doin' here?" She reduced the volume, fractionally.

"Thought maybe he was another ghost, Sarge," the nearer SecType said.

"Wasn't askin' you, fool." Lepper turned enough to focus her sea-green glare on Jezekiah. "What do you want? Milord." She made the title sound dirty.

The attitude called for an arrogant response. Jezekiah could only answer between sneezes. "I'm looking for Kip Marsden."

"Yeah?" Her tone did not improve.

"We ran scan on him, Sarge," the talkative SecType put in.

"That don't prove nothin'. Every goddamned ghost we've seen scans clean." Lepper clumped over to Jezekiah. Above her back the cannon in the wall swiveled to track her.

At least the sneezes were dying. "If you'll allow me-" He lost the sentence in a yip as Lepper's armored fingers clenched around his testicles. The pain curled him into a knot.

"Yeah, he's real." Lepper whacked Jezekiah on the back in false compassion. "Sorry, Milord. Hadda be sure."

The impact nearly drove him to his knees. It also made him angry enough to ignore the pain. He jerked upright, jaw clenched, and let the anger show. "About what?"

"'Bout you." Lepper didn't even try to sound apologetic. She stopped just short of sneering. "No offense, but your sister's got real good at makin' holos feel like warm bods. As if you didn't know."

The fact she was angry enough to face him down hinted at troubles deeper than he'd anticipated. "Just how does that justify a frontal assault on my person? If Letticia was faking my holo, it would still *feel* real to you."

"Yeah, but it wouldn't've felt real to *you*. Little bitch hasn't figured out two-way feeds. Yet."

The stars were fading from his vision, leaving a growing urgency. "Then it sounds like we both need to see Kip."

"Yeah, maybe." She tilted her head, let him see her test the truth in his words.

Sec doubting his word – Jezekiah tried to swallow and realized his mouth had gone dry.

But Lepper pivoted to glare up at the watching red eye in the wall. "You goddamned sons of bitches gonna let me in now?"

The voice behind the watching red eye sounded almost embarrassed. So, then. Whatever was making Lepper so suspicious, it wasn't common Sec knowledge. The thought was not comforting. "Still need you to give me your sync-D," the watcher told her. "Those are the orders."

"Listen, you goddamned-"

Jezekiah forestalled the rest of Lepper's tirade with a hand on her arm. "The fact Sgt. Lepper does not know her sync-D code is the best proof you could have. Any holo my sister created would have recited the code instantly." He turned his hand so the Ring faced the watching eye. The glare of the Ring flashed yellow pulses across the walls. "In addition to which, I can assure you she is most certainly physically present."

Silence. Jezekiah waited for the familiar tingle of scan. Nothing. He lifted a questioning brow at Lepper, got only a scowl in return. Easy guess that the SecTypes behind the watching red eye were holding an impromptu conference. Easier guess what their response would be if they decided they didn't trust his word. Jezekiah locked his eyes on the wall to keep them away from the still-smoking holes in the floor beyond Lepper. No point trying to gauge the distance to the elevators. If the watchers decided against him, he wouldn't make it that far anyway. Then the doors whooshed open. Interestingly, Lepper's sigh of relief matched his own.

Beyond the doors the dark corridor blossomed into a spacer's dream of paradise. Holoscreens lined the circular walls, giving the post a three-sixty view of the Manor and environs. Above the ring of gray consoles a rising moon silvered the vast Pacific. Overhead the Milky Way swept across the blackened skeletons lining Waikiki, starlight glimmering the waves that washed the shore beneath them. The satin light traced the jungle's climb toward Oahu's broad central plain. The effect was so powerful Jezekiah instinctively expected the salty caress of an ocean breeze. He got stale air and a mix of aftershaves in dubious tastes instead.

Kip's station was a shielded console tucked into the rock wall to the left of the door. The position gave Sec command full view of the center. It also ensured no attacker could take Sec command out in a rear assault. Only Kip wasn't there.

What *was* there was a team of armored SecTypes scattered across the post, all with laser rifles trained on himself. Lepper, he noticed, had her hands up now, too. Damn and damn again! This was getting him nowhere. Jaw set, he stepped forward. The Ring's pulse looked even brighter here. "If you're waiting for me to reveal some secret birthmark, I'm afraid we are doomed to disappointment. If not, then I suggest we all get on with our respective duties." He nodded toward Lepper, turned the tone innocent. "Unless any of you want to try patting Sgt. Lepper down."

"Or die tryin'." Lepper's tone made it sound like a promise.

But the exchange broke the tension as Jezekiah had expected. The lead SecType lifted his visor and nodded. Around the post, rifles lowered and the SecType sitting station started breathing again. Jezekiah let his hands drop when Lepper poked his ribs.

The poke was hard enough to hurt. But Lepper was already stalking around Kip's console. He decided to believe it was only because of the armor and followed her. "I thought you expected to find Captain Marsden here."

"Was more hopin' than expectin'." She didn't bother to look up. To Jezekiah's surprise, the console's shields hummed to life. "Okay, *Milord*, ain't nobody gonna hear us now. So you wanna tell me what the hell you're really after?"

The worry in her voice set off a new, scarier, round of quick calcs. "Exactly as I told you: I'm looking for Kip Marsden."

"Yeah?"

"Yeah. I expected you would know where he is." Lines of probability were fitting into place. He waited her out, dreading the confirmation.

"NetMind says he's home." She touched a spot on the console, and a holo'd image of Kip's bungalow materialized above her hand, Kip's image within it. "Only I had a team do a warm bod check. And he ain't there."

"And?" Jezekiah urged.

Lepper chewed her lip while she weighed a lie of some sort. Fortunately for them both, she decided against it. "He ain't in Net, either."

It took a long moment for the implications to fully register. "At all?"

"At all. No blip, no biopat, no nothin'. It's like he's gone natural or somethin'."

"Then how can NetMind say he's home?"

"Depends which lobe you ask. You do a standard DemoNet check, he's home. But you go lookin' direct for his biopats-" She folded arms, trying to disguise her fear. "You happen to know anything about it? Milord."

"Only the obvious implication that Letticia is involved." His shared ignorance should have eased her hostility. It didn't. "You mind telling me what you're mad at?"

"Nothin' that matters. Just figure even naturals got a right to be treated fair."

"Agreed. Only right now I need to find Kip Marsden." This was not a topic he needed to pursue just now. Yet something in her attitude sent a shiver of foreboding up his spine.

"Yeah." Lepper turned her hostility on the console. The board thrummed where she slapped armored fingers against it. "Guess you got your reasons for turnin' the Yakamoto girl over to Teufelsman-"

"What?"

Lepper kept her eyes on the console. "You're the one filed the murder charge against her. Milord. You tellin' me now you didn't think I'd arrest her? Shit, man, those two Lupans 'bout took the Manor-"

"*What charges?*" Jezekiah wrenched Lepper around by the arm. Watched her sneer morph to doubt.

"Somebody chopped up that spacer boy you had us watchin'. Captain was gonna keep it quiet till he got some questions answered. Only after he left we got your holo sayin'-" Lepper let the sentence trail off. Beneath her tan, the color drained from her face.

"What is it?"

"Ghosts."

"Talk sense." He gripped Lepper's armored bicep so hard his fingers were going numb.

"Fuzzed biopats. Dupes. Here, take a look." She shook his hand off with the jerk of an elbow, tapped control patches in earnest. A holo'd galaxy materialized above the console. Hollow circles filled the display like star systems, each circle filled with moving pricks of light. The circles remained stationary but the pinpricks wove slowly around each other like rogue planets in search of a home star. Other bright pinpricks flitted between circles. "That's the raw feed on DemoNet for Oahu. You stay in this job long enough, you learn to read it." She favored him with a sidelong grimace. "So you can see who's where without sync'ing in."

"Meaning even Letticia can't tell you're watching."

"You got it. Now this here-" Lepper tapped one red-orange circle in the lower left of the display. Instantly the red-orange circle jumped to front and center, pinpricks swelling to glowing orbs. "This's the Manor. See those?" She tapped again and the magnification swelled enough to let Jezekiah see three red-orange lights within the Manor's encompassing circle. "That's you three: yourself, the Protector, and your goddamned little sister." Another tap and the orbs swelled to let him see that each tiny bright orb was actually a sync-D code. Two of the red-orange sync-Ds had sharp, clearly defined codes. The third looked softly blurry. "These two-" Lepper poked the sharp-edged orbs in sequence – "are the Protector and you."

"Why-"

"I'm getting there. Look at this." She swept a finger across the neighboring sync-Ds.

The lights were sharp enough that he could actually see their code imprints. Except for one. Lepper tapped the orb with softly amorphous edges. "That's Teufelsman's biopat. See how fuzzy the edges on his pat are? Now look-"

She brought up a second holo'd galaxy. This one looked empty as intergalactic space. Only a smattering of sync-Ds lit its dark field. "This here's North Shore."

"That's Tong territory."

"Sur-*prise*." Lepper shot him a look of profound disgust. "Why you think it's so empty? Goddamned monkeys got no sync-Ds. Only thing we can see up there are the goddamned tourists. Except-" She lined the two displays up, poked a finger at one of the few sync-Ds in the second. "What you make of that?"

"It's fuzzy." Jezekiah peered closer. "That's Teufelsman's sync-D-" His mouth went dry as the implications sank in.

"Yeah." Lepper pulled up the matching sync-D in the Manor display. "So either that snowball's in two places at one time, or we got us a ghost." She swept the finger across the Manor's neighboring sync-Ds. "Now you want to guess just who's -"

Her hand froze above the three red-orange orbs within the Manor. Tracking Lepper's finger Jezekiah saw a second of those had gone fuzzy as well.

She offed the displays instantly, tapped another patch and the sec shield evaporated. "C'mon, Milord. We're getting' you outta here." She grabbed Jezekiah's arm and tugged.

This time he tugged back. "Fine. Once I find Keiko."

An expression akin to sorrow flitted across Lepper's face. It hardened to grim determination. "Forget her, Milord. You can't help her now. Only thing you can do is try to stay alive." She glanced at the display, lips pursing in calculation. "Gonna have to move fast, too." She jerked her head toward the exit. "Now, c'mon."

He held his ground, fury overcoming sense. "I said, first I find Keiko. Then I leave."

"Well, then, guess we're both gonna be sorry."

She slammed her armored fist into Jezekiah's jaw. The world went black.

XLIII

Suspended from an anchor thread within her spider hole, Letticia allowed herself a nanosecond to enjoy her victory over the Yakamoto monkey. It was a small thing, only a test step to ensure she could control Mother's node. But it worked perfectly. Now she had only to finish the job. Slowly, carefully, Letticia pushed the borders of her spider hole within Mother's node outward. Her outlying strands bored into the chains of code comprising Mother's node, her threads enveloping Mother's, tapping at last directly into the stream of data and connections and authority that was the Protector's node. She felt the power surge thrum her essence. Oh, wonders beyond dreams! *This* was what Mother wanted to hide from her! Oh, it made perfect sense, now! Of *course* Mother wanted to keep such glory for herself! She didn't blame her at all. Pity was, Mother didn't know what to do with it. Well, she was about to change that.

It didn't take long – minutes, hard world time; eons for NetMind – before Mother sync'd in. This time Letticia was waiting for her.

Looking for Admiral Yakamoto, Mother?

Letticia expected Mother to scream and try to break sync when she dropped into her mind. Surprised, yes – Mother's reaction struck like a shock wave, nearly knocking Letticia loose from her anchor thread. But the shock vanished almost instantly. Something else filled its place, something warm and bright and...and *welcoming*.

Letticia. She felt Mother's voice, felt the sorrow behind it through every strand of her feed, all the way into her body's bones. *I've wondered when I would find you here.*

Letticia scrambled to regain her anchor, close her lock on the Protector's node. Only Mother was wrapping her in something wonderful. She found memories welling up suddenly, of childhood fever and Mother's soothing hand on her forehead... of Mother's kiss on a scraped elbow... felt again the wonderful feeling of utter safety as Mother embraced her, felt the thrill of power as Mother's sync'd essence enveloped hers, hugged her close.

Yet…something wasn't right. Slowly she realized Mother's embrace was *too* close. With rising horror she recognized the tendrils that sprouted from Mother's sync-D. Nullifiers! The code-eating tendrils coiled around Letticia's threads like sucking vines. Her own code evaporated beneath the nullifiers' touch. Each lost byte left a break in her spider hole. The tendrils sank searing probes through each break, shattering Letticia's interloper codes wherever they touched. Each probe hooked anchor codes into her threads, each anchor agonizing as a dagger slicing into her veins.

Each reconnected tendril twined into the last, building an interlocking chain. Each link in the chain blossomed into new tendrils that fanned out around Letticia's spider hole. Forming a seal. Spinning a cocoon around her, one spider preying on another. Sealing her into a living death to wait, helpless until Mother was ready. Until Mother had time to backtrack her entries – Until Mother called the Admiral back in. And told him what she'd done with the Yakamoto monkey. Oh, god …ohgodohgodohgod… she'd seen what the Admiral could do with those swords before he let his victim die…

And Mother would let him! She *felt* that now, felt Mother's dread determination as if it were her own. Letticia heard her body's shriek.

Data streams exploded like sunbursts where the tendrils connected to NetMind's core. They were hooking Mother back in! Inexorably reclaiming the Protector's ID. Letticia's horror blossomed into terror. Frantically she called in her spiders, sent them scuttling across Mother's tendrils, gnawing away the outer layers of Mother's data streams. But Mother's tendrils simply reformed behind the spiders. Viral code morphed instantly into brilliant red sequences in her spiders' wake. The red viruses leap-frogged her spiders, spread out ahead of them like a lava flow. And sank, inexorably, onto the outer shell of her spider hole.

Oh, god, she *felt* the heat! Felt it sear down the length of her body's nerves! Pain so brutal it left no room to think. Left *nothing* except itself, consuming her mind, her essence, her life, beckoning her toward sweet unconsciousness. Toward the darkness – No! Not the dark! Not again! Terror drove her past the pain, gave her an anchor against panic. She slapped new code on the walls of spider hole. The nullifiers absorbed her patches, but they bought her time. She spun a set of spiders into a whirlpool against a single data byte within a single nullifier cell. The disruption turned the nullifier back on itself and the cell's own cannibalistic code forced a self-destruct. Gave Letticia a single micro-second to launch one last spider. But it enough.

That spider triggered her defenses. The overrides she'd set on Mother's office defenses reversed the air flow in the office. Wall and window seals locked into place, made the room air tight. Then the filters reversed flow. Sucked every last atom of air out of the room.

For another fifteen agonizing, terrifying seconds Mother clung to sync. The pain intensified, drove the darkness closer, deeper, wider. Her nullifiers were eating into Letticia's last cell wall before Mother's link went dead. Sobbing in relief Letticia could only dangle, panting, from her anchor thread. She spent an eternal two minutes running damage controls, plugging critical gaps in her code strings. She made sure she was *safe* before she plugged herself back into the office viz.

Mother had collapsed across her desk. She was still twitching, still had her hand in her sync link. But her face had gone a terrible purple-blue, her brilliant eyes protruding above her open, gasping mouth. The Ring's flare dimmed as Letticia watched to a sullen white pulse.

It wasn't supposed to be like that! She'd never thought Mother could *suffer*! She'd never intended that! Anguished, Letticia wove herself into the fabric of Mother's sync, locked into Mother's fading presence. Even now, Mother recognized her. NetMind itself quivered under the impact of Mother's love. Letticia forgot danger, darkness, forgot even death. Desperate for that welcoming embrace she wove a sync field around Mother, fed air into it. Felt Mother's grim determination as her own as Mother gasped in the air. Felt her own heart swell with Mother's breath. She reached immaterial hands to stroke Mother's face, to clutch at the safety of Mother's all-powerful embrace. Welcomed the way Mother grasped the life line Letticia brought her to sink her essence into Letticia's being.

Only the swell of Mother's love vanished. Left her *nothing*, nothing at all but the hideous, searing void of Mother's grief. And the desolate, driving need to drag her daughter down into death.

Shrieking, Letticia tore herself free. She neutered the air flow, sucked the last air out of Mother's lungs herself. Hovered in sync long enough to make sure, this time, that Mother was dead.

Only the horror of Mother's dead face lingered. *Oh, mommy, I'm so sorry! I didn't mean it! I really didn't!*

She hadn't wanted this! She'd never wanted to hurt Mother. Never thought anything *could* hurt Mother. She wanted to shake Mother, make her understand that there'd been no choice, no options. It hadn't even been her fault, not really. Marsden was the one who'd designed that vacuum seal. She never would have even looked at it if Jezekiah had just left her alone. It wasn't her fault! Not this! It couldn't be!

Somewhere, something was screaming. Letticia opened a scan feed by instinct. Realized with a shock it was her body screaming at the sync'd image of Mother's dead face. Letticia tore her hand out of the sync glove so hard she ripped the pocket slit open. Even that small motion knocked her body over. She landed on her side, face against the cold-damp porcelain of the toilet. For once, she welcomed the hard world feel of the skin of her face. She felt hollow, as if the universe had gone empty. She managed to stop her body's screaming. Thought perhaps tears would follow, but they didn't. She was just numb, inside and out.

It couldn't be her fault. The words ran on in an endless loop, circled her mind like a hazy, empty cloud waiting for code. Gradually need hardened the mantra to certainty, certainty flooded the cloud, gave it shape and meaning. It *wasn't* her fault! She was only Jezekiah's instrument! His pawn, like everyone else! He'd pushed her into killing Mother, as surely as he'd done it himself! She was innocent! It was Jezekiah's fault. It had to be.

Oh, yes, that was the answer. That had to be true. It had to be. She couldn't bear it any other way. And she'd make Jezekiah pay for it, oh, yes, she would. Surely, now, Letticia sync'd back in, ran checks on her spider threads, made sure her defenses had blocked all the outbound feeds from Mother's office. She rewrote the viz feed, too, triple-checked the override on Mother's major domo. She really ought to burn the unit out. Traitorous thing would back-stab her first chance it got. But she couldn't do it just yet. She was going to need its viz records to prove Jezekiah's guilt. She added a last layer to the viz locks on the major domo's memory, then took another minute to run full system overview. Yar, all yar. Far as NetMind was concerned, Mother was simply very tired and napping at her desk.

Letticia leaned back against the wall, drew in long sweet breaths. Teufelsman would make sure the physical cleanup was handled discreetly. It was all going exactly right at last. She'd make Jezekiah pay for what he'd done. She'd make sure of it.

She was in control, now.

XLIV

The Van Burens' Registration center was in Hilo town on the Big Island. Keiko thought vaguely that Teufelsman would try something on the flight down to Hawaii. He set her up for it sure enough, locked her restraining rings into a holding loop in the side of the Aryan shuttle. She wished he would. The rings held her hands, but left her legs free. She could kill him just as well with her feet. Better that way, all around: the other snowballs would kill her for sure when they saw their headman dead. Save everybody trouble all around. She set her mind to killing, emptied her soul of feeling. Gave herself to death. And realized, bitterly, that she'd finally learned how to feel Samurai.

Only Teufelsman spent the hour-long ride down to the Big Island up front with the shuttle guide. Never even looked back her way till the shuttle set down on the black lava field surrounding the registrar's facility. He lounged against the guide's cabin door, touched a spot on the rings' control. Numbness spilled down Keiko's arms. Teufelsman waited till her knees buckled under her before he ambled into kicking range to pull her off the wall and hook the rings back into the leash.

The registrar's people took no chances, either. They left the neural block on while they sampled her blood and tissue, ran brain and bio scans. A pair of Aryans took charge of her leash while the medics fed the DNA samples they'd collected into DemoNet for Registree coding. Some distant part of her mind recalled Captain Marsden describing how DemoNet coordinated with SecNet and Admin and Transit and every other lobe of NetMind. Took everything – and matched it, finally, to a pair of tiny implant chips.

The memory triggered a shiver of rage. Of all the people on the planet, the captain was the one she'd never thought would betray her. He knew what Registration meant. He'd warned her – The rush of terror brought her alive. Her knees threatened to buckle again. She let them go this time, let her weight drag the Aryan off-balance. She kicked up as the man lurched. Her foot caught him in the chin. She heard the bone crack, but he clung to her leash. The second Aryan grabbed for her. She kicked again. Felt his shin bone give beneath her foot. She used momentum to slam her captor into his partner. The men went down in a groaning pile. Keiko jerked the leash out of her captor's hands and ran for the door.

Teufelsman's neural block dropped her mid-stride. She heard his lazy footsteps come up the corridor. They stopped over her prone body, making her heart pound with fear. He lifted her head by the leash, forcing her to stare into his serpentine smile. "You don't get to die that easy, monkey. You only get to die when I decide to let you."

At his order a team of Aryan medics dragged her to the fitting table. They forced a vise around her head for the chip fitting. The Aryan in charge anchored her leash to the fitting table and gave her the back of his fist for good measure. Then a medic pressed the implant gun to a spot just above her left temple and pulled the trigger.

Training blocked Keiko's scream. But her body bucked of its own accord. She thrashed until heavy hands imposed stillness by force and held her down while the second chip was driven into her upper jaw.

Keiko knew dimly after that that Teufelsman was pulling her through Admin offices. The Aryan shoved her into a linkchair, jerked the restraints off. Her numbed arms dropped, and blood raged back. She almost whimpered when Teufelsman jammed her knotting fingers into the sync link. Then images, words, sounds exploded behind her eyes as the link opened NetMind to her. She tried to grasp some kind of sense through the pounding ache in her head, find a focus in the chaos. She got only flash. Not that it mattered. NetMind acknowledged her existence straight off bioscan. And labeled her unfit for human contact, no questions asked.

Teufelsman jerked her out of the link. Keiko jerked back. She found herself on the floor, looking helplessly up at the dark, tear drop control in his hand. He squatted beside her, licked his lips as he ran his eyes down her body, bouncing the tear drop gently in his palm. The registree's studs sparked agony at every soft bounce. He held her eyes, smiling. "And now, monkey, you're mine."

Using the tear drop, Teufelsman lifted Keiko to her feet. In horror, she found herself trapped, her body slaved to the tear drop's command like a puppet in some homie children's show. Her mind threw itself against the walls of her skull, but her body dragged itself into the Aryan's skimmer, lay quietly on the throbbing metal floor letting Teufelsman use her hip for a footstool.

The skimmer set down on an old *pahoehoe* lava field on the Big Island's south shore. She shrieked silently as her body followed Teufelsman out onto the rolling black coils. Her eyes traced waves foaming over the ends of the rocky black fingers. She tried to will herself to dash for the final safety of the deep water beyond. Her body simply hung, limp and waiting, in the tear drop's grip.

She heard a second skimmer buzz up. Felt the thud as it settled beside Teufelsman's. Keiko heard the thud of boots as the Aryan squad stepped out of their machine in unison. Their footsteps approached in unhurried, even rhythm to halt beside her. A younger version of Teufelsman stepped past her to hand Teufelsman a sealed packet.

At Teufelsman's nod an Aryan captain ripped Keiko's sarong off with matteroffact economy. Her mind screamed the actions that would block him. Her muscles did not even twitch. Her body did nothing while the captain finished stripping her, not even when Teufelsman ran one hand over her breasts his breath turning heavy. "You should have listened to me, monkey." Hand tracing a terrifying line across her body, Teufelsman circled Keiko slowly, the packet dangling from his fingers. "You could have been private property. Been kept in style. Now-" He stopped in front of her. His lips smiled but his eyes were cold as a snake's. "Now, you're public. And you're going to be happy about it."

He ripped the packet open. She could not even resist when he slapped the venus seed powder over her mouth and nose. Then touched a control that released the neural block.

It was dark again before they finished with her. Only hours, though it felt like centuries. A boot nudged Keiko's ribs, flipping her onto her stomach. She recognized the sandpale features of the Aryan who knelt beside her. His collar bars marked him as a captain, though she had no name to go with the face. She would recognize all their faces, she knew. And remember what she had done with each. Seed destroyed the soul but it left memory intact.

They took her always in order of rank, each more brutal than the last and Teufelsman worst of the lot. She could ignore the physical agony; a lifetime's training saw to that. But she could not escape the horror of the venus seed. She should have fought them. Should have tried to save some shred of honor. But the seed washed out training, honor, respect. Left nothing but irresistible desire. She *wanted* what they did. Wanted and cooperated in every disgusting, shameful act. And tried not to listen to the bets they traded above her head, though they used Commonwealth Standard to make sure she would understand. She knew which of them it was who knelt behind her, ground her face into the dirt. The big one. The one who liked to go last.

Keiko heard her body moan, knowing what was coming. And wanting it, too, through the battered agony. The big Aryan crouched behind her, pawed her breasts before her clamped hands on her bruised hips. She bit her lips closed hard enough to taste blood, smelled the blood running down her thighs and smearing her buttocks. She could not deny them her body; the venus seed saw to that. But she could at least deny them the sound of the seed-lust. She could lock the rage and shame deep in her soul with each vicious, thudding thrust.

The Aryans left her lying crumpled in the sand when they finally finished. Keiko did not know how long she lay, nor how many times she tried and failed to climb to her knees. She found her sarong by touch at last and struggled into it. She would not die naked, give the haole another excuse to mock her.

Already the horrible memories were starting to replay. She closed her mind to them, shut out all feeling. It didn't matter. Nothing mattered now. Except finding the strength to crawl to the edge of the lava field. The ocean would wash away the dirt with her life.

A half-moon had risen by the time she reached the edge of the lava field. Silver light danced across white foam, traced glitter down the rivulets running between the lava's black fingers. Against the cold light the ocean's rumble seemed to echo up through the stone. Keiko dragged herself along one pale gleaming finger. Her body stung where the salt water washed over it. Keiko forced her head up, sighting on the white foam ahead. Blinked, refocused. A shadow stood between her and the water's salvation.

Not again. Somewhere an animal shrieked. In horror Keiko realized the voice was her own. She made it to her feet somehow, launched herself at the shadow. Her knees gave out with the first step. She fell on her face at its feet.

The surf rumble drowned any sound of the shadow's movements. She heard nothing until rough hands trapped her arms at her sides. She kicked back, but her heel only brushed muscled thigh.

"*Malama pono, keiki.* Take care, child." She recognized that familiar old voice, heard the sorrow in it.

She twisted up to see Grandfather's worried face.

XLV

The clouds along the infinite expanse of western sky had taken on the first faint cherry tinge of sunset. Far below Strongarm's balcony warm sun sparkled the waves rolling into Waikiki, turned the deeper water beyond the perfect blue of the history vids. The perfect image of paradise. Alex Strongarm yanked his gaze away from the bitter, beautiful irony of the approaching sunset and stalked back into his bedroom. Felt too much like Home World's sun was setting on his life. Makers knew, if he didn't find Bird and convince her to accept him, it was likely the last sunset he would ever see.

He strode back to his trunk and shoved the last of his *movie* vids in. God of his Makers *damn* Jezekiah Van Buren and his vicious little sister and his mother and the whole Makers-be-damned lot of them! Could they really be so stupid as to think Home World would survive a war? Of all the flat teeth in the universe, Jezekiah knew they were balancing on a powder keg. He knew how strong the anti-onlie sentiment had grown on Den Lupus. Could Jezekiah really be willing to lose it all just to keep one woman? He wouldn't have wasted breath asking the question of a Lupan. Trouble was, he'd never expected Jezekiah to make the Lupan choice.

Strongarm slammed the trunk closed. A trail of shed hair that lingered in the air like tracer bullets along the arc of the motion. The light pouring into his bedroom from the balcony struck cherry glitter off the hair, made it look like some kind of magic dust. Fitting image. Makers knew dust was all that was left of his dreams.

He felt a tug on his arm, looked down to find one of those bug-like little servobots running a slender metal vacuum tube down his arm, sucking up loose hair. With a roar, Strongarm swatted the damned thing across the room. It hit the wall, bounced, and scuttled for its wall niche. He could hear it chittering mechanical imprecations at him even after the niche closed up behind it. Good thing his trunk sealed itself; he'd likely have put it through the wall after the damned thing if he had to fiddle with locks just now.

The sound of a ripped hem followed by a Bengali oath told him Kaitin wasn't in any better mood. "You ready over there, Kait?" He asked in Lobish, keeping it as private as anything in this spy nest could be. At least, so he hoped.

"This one was ready before we arrived." Something that sounded like it'd been delicate shattered against a wall. The invective that followed said it'd likely been expensive as well. Strongarm cocked an ear, waiting. A moment later something else hit the wall with a mechanical yip. Strongarm found a shameful amount of consolation in the thought the servobot hadn't fared any better under Kaitin.

The Bengali himself stalked through Strongarm's door a moment later, ears flat and mane bottled. His mustaches twitched at Strongarm's scent and he shook his mane back down. Kaitin, Strongarm noticed sourly, did not shed. "Why all this show of packing, Brother-in-Law? Let us just go. Leave the flat teeth to the fate of their making."

"Not leaving without Bird."

"One took that as a given. We can pick her up from the sick bay on our way out. These vile bots can load our gear."

"I'm not slinking out of here like a whipped cur." Strongarm rubbed his hands across his ears. Only made him feel worse; even that touch tingled the cilia lining his palms. "We'll pick Bird up and leave, all right. But I won't be the one to break my word."

Kaitin's scent deepened, sorrow mingling with anger. "It no longer matters, Alex. Thy treaty is dead. The women of Parliament will not accept thy Bird as bond for a marriage alliance."

"She's a Maker, Kait."

"Be thee not a fool, Brother-in-law! One shares thy sorrow, but thy Bird is no more than a mixed-Type natural-"

"It's mothers who matter. Her mother was a Maker!"

"And her father is SamuraiType. There are a thousand such across the rim. Worse, she is the granddaughter of Ho Tong's own lord. Think for a second what Ho Tong's Venus Seed has done to thine own vassals. Thine own kinsmen will challenge thee out of vengeance when they learn who she is." Kaitin stepped up to rest a hand on Strongarm's shoulder. The misery in his scent nearly matched Strongarm's own. "This one will stand champion for thee, Brother-in-law. Together we will save thy Bird. But thy treaty is dead. And Home World with it. There will be no averting the war now."

"Still got to give it one last try. The Van Buren mother should listen to sense, even if Jezekiah won't." Strongarm forced a smile. Even that much ached. The ache reached down to his heart when he answered Kaitin's gesture in kind and felt the other man's muscles tremble beneath his touch.

"*Phah!* Bloody, beloved idiot -" Kaitin broke away, licked his palm and ran it across his mane in a futile effort to cover the embarrassment in his scent.

If they'd been home Strongarm would have nuzzled the Bengali. He put his love into his scent instead and lifted an ear to the ever-watchful red eye of the suite's major domo unit. "Get me a line to Madam Van Buren. Put it on viz in here."

Oddly, the unit actually hesitated before it acknowledged the order. *Yes, Milord. If she's* – again, that odd pause – *available, Milord.*

Strongarm perked an ear at Kaitin in question, got a puzzled sniff for answer. Made the speed with which Madam Van Buren's image coalesced beside the sync chair all the more surprising.

The Protector looked the same as always. She wore the familiar pale slacks and shirt. Her hair was pulled up in a twist, with a curl dangling loose above one eye. Yet *something* about her was wrong. Strongarm tested the air for a clue, swore under his breath at the holo's lack of a scent track. A disgusted sniff from Kaitin's direction said the Bengali had tried the same. Still, she'd come and that was what mattered. Strongarm shook his ears up to a courteous angle and salaamed.

"You asked to see me, Lord Strongarm. How may I help you?" Madam Van Buren pre-empted the rest of his greeting.

"I'd like to talk with you about the treaty, Madam."

"Why? Haven't you done enough damage yet?" She ended the question with a sniff. "You've already rejected my daughter. What more do you want?" The sniff slid into a sneer. "Or are you perhaps more interested in my son?"

Strongarm felt his ears go flat. He heard the rumble of Kaitin's growl. The sound triggered hunter vision, made the man-part of his mind shriek protest. Not here. He would not be the one to break his word. He shook his ears back up, dug talons into Kaitin's arm in warning. He held his breath, let Madam Van Buren fidget until the blood-lust pound faded from his temples. "I wanted you to know I am still willing to honor the treaty, Madam." Even the best intentions could not keep the warning rasp out of his voice. The Van Buren mother did not seem to recognize the danger in the sound. Or maybe she just didn't care. "I regret I could not complete Impression with your daughter. Nonetheless, I have found my *maya*. If Keiko Yakamoto accepts me, I will consider the treaty sealed."

"And this one will defend his choice on Den Lupus." It was only Kaitin's scent that betrayed what that promise cost him.

Had they been in private, Strongarm would have nuzzled the man in thanks. In front of the Van Buren mother's new attitude he could only lay a grateful hand on Kaitin's arm and let his scent speak for him. He kept his eyes on Madam Van Buren. "I only want to ensure that you will also accept Keiko Yakamoto to seal the treaty."

"Well, it's a little late for that now, isn't it?" *What* was wrong with the woman? She actually smirked.

"I don't follow-" His heart and gut lurched together. "Your own Sgt. Lepper was taking Bird to your sick bay. What happened?"

"On Earth, Murder charges pre-empt sick bay visits, Lord Strongarm. I'm afraid your Keiko Yakamoto has been tried and found guilty of murder."

"Impossible!" Good thing for the Van Buren mother she was in holo. Strongarm would have had her up against the wall by the throat otherwise. "Bird never-"

"I'm afraid she did." Madam Van Buren strolled away to run fingertips across the back of the nearest sync chair. Makers balls, the woman looked like she was enjoying herself! "It seems she killed some little off-world joy toy. Unfortunately, the boy was under Jezekiah's personal protection, so I could hardly overlook the infraction."

"It doesn't matter." He was growling full out now. "I will pay any blood money the boy's clan demands. All I need is your agreement to bind the treaty."

Madam traced the curve of the chair's arm. Her eyes and fingers both lingered where they reached the sync link. The image made it seem as if she was talking to the chair. "You rejected the treaty when you rejected my daughter. Why don't you just finish packing and leave now? That might be more convenient for all of us, don't you think?"

"You won't find it convenient once the war starts." God of his Makers *damn* these onlie holos! Something was horribly wrong with the woman, but without a scent track to guide him he couldn't guess what it was.

"Allow this one an observation." Kaitin stepped forward, mane bottled above the seared ruin of his emerald robes. "The treaty your son and one's brother-in-law devised protects you more than Den Lupus. Without it, Johann Petrovich of Streiker will succeed in pressing his charge of treason against you. You will die at your cousins' hands. What profit do you see in death, Madam?"

"Nonsense. Unc- JP only wanted to kill me because he thought we were in collusion with *you*. That's obviously not going to happen now." She waved a hand airily. "So the threat leaves with you."

"So you will help Streiker start the war they seek." Kaitin grated, voice reflecting the anger in his scent. "Then this one makes you a promise, Madam. When war comes, this one will lead Den Lupus' fleet. And Home World will be the first to die."

"Oh, for heaven's sake." The Van Buren mother waggled fingers at him impatiently. "Why don't you just go ahead and leave? I think you've done quite enough damage as it is."

This time Strongarm would have lunged for her throat if Kaitin hadn't body-blocked him. "Not leaving without Bird," he said through bared fangs. "Now, where is she?"

The Van Buren mother studied him as if he were some kind of bug. It sank home, finally, that to her he probably was. "I turned her over to her father the Admiral about half an hour ago."

"*Where*, Madam?" Damn these onlie holos! It had to be a lie. If she'd been on Lupan viz, he'd have known for sure.

"I expect he'll kill her at his own house." She paused, looking inward, the way onlies did when they were listening to a Net feed though she wore no comm thread Strongarm could see. Whatever she heard seemed to please her. "Jezekiah certainly thinks so. TransitNet tells me he's just left for the Admiral's house himself."

"Then you do not need to bother yourself with us any further." But she was gone before Strongarm finished the sentence.

Even Kaitin didn't take long to finish packing after that. Fifteen minutes later Strongarm watched a straggly line of servobots load their luggage into a pearly skimmer at the Manor's transit platform. The public suggestion he didn't trust his host would have been a blood insult on Den Lupus. It was no compliment among onlies, either, but Strongarm no longer cared. Not that there was anyone around to note the offense. The admin ops who usually crowded the entrance had instantly found themselves other places to be the second he and Kaitin stepped onto the plaza. Only witnesses left were a trio of Aryans lounging against the outside walls. The ocean breeze carried Strongarm the acid reek of their contempt.

Beside him Kaitin purred thoughtfully. "One wonders whether perhaps a few trophy heads would not make a fitting apology." He swept the frizzled ruin of his robe across one shoulder, scent sharpening dangerously.

Strongarm broke the Bengali's burgeoning blood lust with a talon tip on his shoulder. "Not now. There'll be blood drawn soon enough."

"But no heads left for trophies."

"Too bad." He motioned Kaitin forward with the flick of an ear. They reached the nearest skimmer in two strides. The doors opened and Strongarm stalked around to the master's seat. The car wobbled as Kaitin slid in and settled his robes to his satisfaction.

Where would you like to go? The damned sensors built into the skimmer must have picked up on his woman-need. ShipMind's sync suggested pleasures that made his balls ache to even hear.

"Niihau."

The skimmer lifted smoothly. Once clear of the Manor's screens it banked, angling north. Moments later the Manor's looming bulk vanished behind the jungle's green canopy. Strongarm waited till they were well past the traffic swarming the Manor's vicinity to pry open the tool box beside the master's seat. He found the patch that triggered manual override and punched it. To his relief the dash lit in the red-orange-yellow override sequence.

Dash controls reached yellow and the override joystick lifted up from the floor. The angle forced Strongarm's knees apart. He squirmed down the image its motion raised in his manhood. The dash engagement light finally showed green. Then he reached under the dash. He found the power patch for the skimmer's Net link. Cabin lights fluttered as he drove a talon tip through the patch.

"Is one allowed to wonder?" Kaitin shook a kink out of a smoke-smudged hem, folded it into a smoother drape along his shoulder.

"Don't want this thing dumping us in the nearest joy shack. Or spying on us for the Van Buren mother." Strongarm pulled back on the stick and the skimmer engine hummed as it lifted away from the platform.

"Still north?" Kaitin lifted ears, scent questioning. "The Admiral's house lies southward, by Diamond Head." He purred thoughtfully, scent going relieved. "May one hope thee has found thy senses? Thee can stay in stasis once we reach *Khali*. This one will smooth thy path with our womenfolk on the journey back. Thy mating den will be ready when we make Den Lupus."

"*We* are not leaving."

Kaitin said nothing for once. Just stroked his mustaches and drew his own conclusions. From the smell of it, they weren't any happier than Strongarm's own.

Strongarm let the question simmer till they were well out of Manor air space. He stayed on course till he was sure they hadn't acquired a tracker then banked inland. South east, toward Diamond Head.

"Into Ho Tong territory?" True Bengali – Kaitin's scent carried as much curiosity as surprise.

"Yep. From what Jezekiah's said, Ho Tong's got some kind of block on Sec's scanners. I'm hoping they'll block our signal for a bit, too." Strongarm throttled back on the speed. He held the joy stick steady his knees while he pulled his duffel bag up and open. He pulled out a small, translucent holo case and rolled it into Kaitin's palm. "Careful with it; it's secured to your thumbprint."

"One has handled holo cases before." Kaitin balanced the delicate orb within his palm, sniffed it cautiously. "Purpose?"

"It's a self-portrait. I set it up on *Khali* before we made planetfall. Thought maybe it'd help ease the introduction to the Van Buren sister." Strongarm's ears dipped in embarrassment at the memory.

"So one may assume the holo carries scent and biopat tracks?" Kaitin stroked his mustaches with his free hand, scent bespoke the calculations going on behind it.

Strongarm nodded. "Ought to make these onlie scanners think I'm still in here with you."

"Thy biopat will still show here. Even the flat teeth should have sense enough to investigate a duplicate."

"They'd have to have the brains to look, first. From what we just saw of the Van Buren mother, I doubt they will." Strongarm *uhfed* in disgust. "It's a chance I have to take, in any case. Once you get to Niihau, make a show of having all our luggage stored, keep them guessing till you're ready to lift. Once you're up, I want you making Jump speed second you clear atmosphere."

"And then?" Golden eyes narrowed, hinting at hunter thoughts.

"Tell *Khali* to send down my working gear. I'll wait for it at Bird's house."

"She may already be dead, Alex."

"No." Strongarm had to hold his breath to block the mixed sorrow and worry in Kaitin's scent. "She's in pain, Kait. I can feel it. But she's not dead." He shook himself. He'd lost so much hair it barely raised a shed. "Track me from *Khali*. If Bird accepts me, I'm going to do what I can to salvage the treaty."

"Despite-"

"Gave my word, Kait." He put warning enough in his scent to make even Kaitin shut up. "There are going to be a lot of dead worlds if it goes to war. I will not be the one to start it."

"And if she rejects you?"

"Then I'm dead anyway. Just get her off Home World first."

"Done." Kaitin shifted the holo case to his other palm, used his free hand to pull Strongarm close and nuzzle. The love and misery in his scent nearly made Strongarm whimper.

He took the joy stick back and angled them south again, back toward Diamond Head. Toward Bird and the fate of the Commonwealth.

XLVI

Jezekiah came awake to a throbbing ache in his jaw and the thrum of engines beneath his seat. He almost shot upright. Rethought it quickly, and not just because the very idea of moving made his skull hurt. Lepper must have tranked him, though given the ache in his jaw she probably hadn't needed much of a dose.

Shamming unconsciousness, he tested his arms gently. No restraints. So he wasn't captive. Wasn't *home*, either. Felt like he was on a skimmer of some sort. He opened his eyes and found himself staring at the gray metal interior of a Sec skimmer. Somebody had draped him neatly into the master's seat, even taken the time to rig him a safety harness. That somebody had also activated the skimmer's armored panels, so he had no view of the outside. Not that he had much to see inside: the skimmer was running only the barest red emergency light. If it hadn't been for the yellow brilliance of the Heir's Ring – he frowned down, puzzling at the Ring's pulsing intensity. Must just be the dim surroundings; damned thing looked far too bright. Something else to worry about later. Right now he was grateful for the light. "ShipMind. What's our course?"

No answer. ShipMind was live: the dashboard's Net link patch glowed a soft green. It just wasn't talking. Which meant somebody – Lepper, most likely – had logged in a manual course and told it to stay shut en route. Jezekiah willed down a surge of fear at the dread possibilities. Odds were in his favor Lepper was trying to send him someplace safe. Only he wasn't trusting the odds just now. Right now he had to find a way to reach Keiko.

Wriggling out of the harness, Jezekiah explored the panels lining the center aisle. Sec built its skimmer controls with multiple redundancies. There ought to be at least two back up brains within reach of the master's seat. He found a flip latch where he expected, snapped it open and smiled in satisfaction at sight of the soft, green glow of a brain box. "ShipMind. Lower the panels."

He waited, expectantly. Nothing. Not even a 'no'.

So, then. Lepper had been thinking ahead. He'd have to talk to Kip about promoting that woman. If he didn't throttle her first. Fortunately, Sec systems always included a last-ditch manual back-up. Unfortunately, the handle on this one felt like it hadn't been oiled since installation. Sweat made his shirt cling to his back by the time he managed to winch the armored panels down.

The view outside was worth it, though. A glance at the scenery below the skimmer wing showed him the skimmer was barely above tree-top level, low enough to puff the flowers off a cluster of sunshine trees. Coils of yellow blossoms twirled in the ship's backwash. The sun was still up, though the trees cast long shadows across the green haze below. Below the wings strands of coconut palms nodded lazily. The skimmer's backwash spun golden petals into airy pirouettes around their dark leaves.

Good – he hadn't been out too long: it was still light enough for him to recognize Oahu's broad central valley rising in shadowed steps toward the Koolau mountains beyond. So, then. He was headed north. That suggested two possibilities. Either Lepper was trying to get him to Niihau port. Or she was gifting him to Grandfather Ho.

Either way, it was the wrong course. Using the Ring's light Jezekiah found the emergency sync link and slid his hand into it.

Ah, there you are, dearest. I've been looking for you. Mother's image materialized behind his eyes. She wore the same simple shirt and slacks she'd worn last time he saw her. Had her hair swept up in her usual twist, with that one errant curl dangling loose. She twisted the curl around one long finger, studied him through hooded eyes, her smile predatory.

"*Letticia?*" He recoiled so hard the link image wobbled.

Her smirk vanished in disappointment. *How did you know it was me?*

"Lucky guess." Auto-response: he was too numb for anything else. Quick calcs tried to shove alarms through the shock. Jezekiah shut them down. He couldn't afford the distraction just now. "Get out of there, you little idiot! If you scramble, you just might make it to Niihau before the Admiral gets there."

Oh, Mother won't execute me, brother dear. Mother would never hurt me.

"She was summoning the Admiral when I left, damn it."

Oh, that. Letticia/Mother's sync'd image held her Ring hand out, fingers up so she could admire the rainbow play of light across the Ring. *That's all yar now. I – we – sent the Admiral home.* She pouted at him above her fingertips. *We wanted to tell you sooner, only some nasty person put a sync block on your skimmer. You wouldn't happen to know who that was, would you?*

"Haven't a clue. I just came to, myself." Training kept his pulse from betraying the lie to any bioscanners she had watching him. He shut out the alarms flashing at the back of his mind. He couldn't afford to think about what Letticia could do if she'd gained control of Mother's node. Not now. All he could do now was try to stay alive long enough to alert Mother. "Seems like congratulations are in order. Just how did you manage to avoid execution this time, little sister?"

The chance to crow distracted her as he'd expected. Letticia prattled on, her story making less and less sense as it progressed. The fact she was making up a story – that she knew she had *time* to spin out a fantasy – scared him worse than the story itself. But it bought him the chance he needed. Mimicking interest, Jezekiah worked his free hand along the door side of the master's seat, searching for a secondary back up box. His probing fingers found the latch. He flipped it up, found the long tube of the joy stick by touch.

In sync, Letticia finally ran out of imagination. She inclined, imitating Mother, waiting for the effect.

"Brilliant." Jezekiah made it sound sincere. Quick calcs tried to flash terrible probabilities at him. He shut them down, willed his body to *feel* happy. Wouldn't have fooled Mother for an instant, but the bioscanners only looked at chem signals. "So what's next, Lush? How are you going to save us from JP's treason charge?"

Oh, I'm not. You are. Her voice rippled with mirth that had a mad edge to it.

"Really? How?" Quietly, he pried the joy stick out of its holder, began the maddening process of trying to work its stem into its power socket by touch alone.

You're going to prove to the Council that you've been helping Grandfather Ho supply JP with the Venus Seed he used on that dog colony on Rogue. Then the Council can just convict you of treason and JP of war-mongering and leave Mother and me off the hook.

Damn, the joy stick's base only skittered around the edges of its socket. He inched the stick higher, brought it down straight. This time he felt it click home. He locked it in place with a twist, heard the hum as the backup system started its engagement diags. "Mind telling me how I managed it? I'm going to have to know if you expect me to confess."

Oh, we know better than to trust you with words, silly. The skimmer rocked sideways, pendulum-style, like a little girl swinging her skirt.

"You'll still need to come up with a story. Even JP couldn't get a ship from here to Rogue that fast." The thought of Lush could do in Mother's node rocked his stomach worse than the ship.

He didn't have to. JP's been stockpiling Seed out on the Rim for just ages. You know that.

Damn, how long did those diags take? Cold sweat trickled down behind his ear while the backup unit tsked itself through the engagement sequence. All he could do was keep her talking. "By the way, did I happen to take out Octavian's ambassador, too? I expect they'll ask."

Sync rippled with her delight. *What a wonderful idea! I'd forgot all about that. But now that you mention it, I suppose you must have, didn't you?*

"How? We got confirmation she was cleared through to Den Lupus." *Damn, how many cycles did that unit have?*

Don't be stupid! You think I can't sawyer a silly little thing like a port clearance? Letticia hid a giggle behind fingertips. *She certainly thought she was cleared. So she walked right onto one of JP's raiders without even questioning it.* She smirked in satisfaction. On Mother's face the expression made Jezekiah sick. *That joy toy wasn't half so pretty when those Streikern got through with her. Or maybe she was four times as pretty. Depends on how you look at it.*

"JP wouldn't murder an ambassador. Especially not Octavian's. No one on the Council is going to believe that line." Diags finally showed green. Jezekiah willed down a swell of relief. Keeping his sync hand steady, he pulled the safety harness back into place.

They don't have to. According to NetMind you're *the one who sawyered their orders. JP will like that.*

He nudged the joy stick delicately, felt the skimmer's wing tip up in answer. "On second thought, Lush, I don't think I like the idea at all." Two years working crew had taught Jezekiah a thing or two about handling manual controls. He jerked his hand out of sync and leaned back on the joy stick. The skimmer rolled smoothly and banked east.

Ah, well. I suppose I should have known better than to expect you to cooperate. Letticia's voice filled the cabin. She was using the audio, direct feed through TransitNet. *So we'll just have to do this the hard way, won't we?*

The skimmer bucked so hard it nearly jerked the joy stick out of his hand. Ship's audio hissed and crackled, giving voice to ShipMind's battle for self-control. It leveled off high enough up for Jezekiah to make out the spiny ridges of both the Koolau and Waianae mountain ranges. For a moment, Jezekiah thought he'd won control. Then, ignoring the joy stick, the ship flipped onto its back, putting its belly to the sky. Jezekiah found himself staring straight down at darkening green fields rolling past a thousand feet below.

Damn and damn again! Somehow Letticia had managed to bypass the manual override. Bracing himself against the harness Jezekiah slammed his heel into the green orb that was ShipMind's 'face'. The dash spat hot bright sparks where the viz panel cracked. He kicked it again and the cabin went dark as even the emergency lights winked out. An instant later he cracked his head against the seat as the skimmer flipped upright and leveled off. Free of Net, it answered the stick with grace. Jezekiah righted his stomach and checked the landscape for bearings. Far off to the west the sky flamed orange and purple above the Waianae mountains.

To the south, he glimpsed reddening sunlight streaking the ocean beyond

Waikiki. So, then. Craning his neck he could make out Diamond Head's dark shape in the distance. If Letticia had indeed convinced the Admiral to stay home... He leveled the little ship out and banked for the coast. Toward Diamond Head. And his only hope of finding Keiko.

The Milky Way was rising by the time Jezekiah set the skimmer down on the landing pad inside the Yakamoto's garden wall. The night brights had already activated. Tiny pinpricks of light floated across the yard like curious pixies. Good thing, too: he was running without lights. The dancing pixie brights let him put down beside the Admiral's skimmer. The Admiral wouldn't be home; his shuttle was gone. Now, that was interesting: the Admiral had taken his shuttle rather than the skimmer. Made no sense. The shuttle was actually a StelFleet scout ship. It was designed for space; in atmosphere, it would wallow like a drunken pig. For a simple flight to the Manor – or anywhere else on Earth, for that matter – the choice made no sense at all.

Another question he could only pend for later. Right now, he could only hope Keiko had come home. And that she was alone. Strongarm would most certainly be on her scent. If he had got here first – Jezekiah felt his stomach muscles tighten on the thought.

The breeze washed him in the sweet fragrance of plumeria as soon as he winched the skimmer's door open. A trio of night brights bobbed over. Their dancing light cast sinister shadows across the skimmer's interior, but at least they gave him light enough to locate the mech lever that lowered the stairs. A gentle breeze rippled his shirt as he stepped clear of the skimmer's bulk. It wavered the tops of the tall bamboo bordering the garden, too. Gave him the dread sense that unseen eyes were tracking him across the courtyard.

Odder and odder: the Admiral had never installed a major domo unit since NetMind couldn't see Keiko anyway. Yet the door opened at Jezekiah's touch. The spicy-sweet scent of gardenias hit him as soon as he stepped inside. House lights were on, too, though at minimum. Even that soft light was enough to raise reflective gleams on the polished tables. Red silk hangings shimmered on the walls, softened the stark lines of the functional couches. All of it, even the bowls of gardenias – wilted now – stationed around the room spoke of Keiko's touch.

"Anybody home?" He stayed just inside the door, polite distance. A Van Buren would be safe from whatever defenses the Admiral had installed in his house. But he had no desire to catch Keiko unaware. Or Strongarm, for that matter. Especially not if they were together.

No answer. Jealousy kindled, sent him striding down the hallway to check the bedrooms. All empty. Still, he recognized Keiko's room without difficulty; the odds were against the Admiral leaving a red sarong in his closet. Her room was as tidy as he'd expected. Her bed was still made, which was a relief. Only thing out of order was a scrap of rolled parchment atop the wood block that passed for a pillow among the Samurai. He lifted it, unfurled it carefully. Nothing helpful there: the characters trailing down the paper looked like one of the Admiral's incomprehensible haiku. Yet he'd clearly intended it as a note for Keiko. A note written in haste, too, judging from the uncharacteristic ink blots staining the page.

So, then. The Admiral had seen through Letticia's impersonation as well. Certainly explained the Admiral's absence. Odds were, the man was already en route to the Manor, those vicious swords in hand. Jezekiah heard himself sigh in relief. He couldn't argue against the necessity any more. Lush had left them no options this time. Made the sorrow he felt all the more bitter.

Nothing he could do about it now. Jezekiah rolled the parchment back up and tucked it into a breast pocket. He'd give it to Keiko when he found her. The question now was where she'd likely gone.

He found his answer in the Admiral's study. The sliding paper panels to the study were still open. Jezekiah glanced through them. Then glanced again, curiosity morphing to cold fear. A dull stain ruined the polish of the Admiral's desk, left a drying puddle on the floor where dark liquid had cascaded off the desktop. A lazy droplet glittered at the edge of the desk. It dropped like a falling star into the puddle below. Jezekiah watched it fall traced its course back to the shards of a shattered cup. Tracked the scattered white pieces of porcelain to the broken remains of a tea pot.

Certainly not Strongarm's kind of damage. Whatever the trouble was, it had been between the Admiral and Keiko. The air itself felt taut with the psychic aftermath of that confrontation. Damn and damn again! Keiko would have tried to come to him after a fight like that. He felt the muscles along his shoulders tighten with his gut. If she'd reached the Manor after he left –

He rounded the desk, reached for the sync link. Jerked his hand back an instant shy of contact. The thought of letting Letticia get her claws into him again sent ice seeping down his spine. No options, now. He had to get back to the Manor.

He made it three steps past the front door before he saw the Aryans.

They were waiting for him. Five of them stationed between himself and the landing pad. Five white linen suits gleaming in the garden's pixie lights, five sets of white teeth grinning at him in white faces beneath white-blond hair, all exuding insolence. Beyond them, he made out the faint pearly gleam of one of Mother's skimmers on the far side of the courtyard gate.

Their leader stepped forward to sweep Jezekiah a mocking bow. Against his pale skin the silvery thread of the comm unit winding across his head to his mouth just looked dirty. His white-blond thugs fanned out, closing a circle around Jezekiah.

"What a welcome surprise–" Jezekiah lifted a brow at the Aryans' leader, inviting a name. He got only silence, and an serpentine Aryan smile. So, then. These were Letticia's tools. Feigning nonchalance, he offered the leader a salaam, using the gesture to cover a glance at the Sec skimmer.

Damn. Another pair of Aryans lounged on either side of its door. Odd. Something about their lopsided posture didn't look quite right. No time to puzzle it now, though. He'd worry about those two when he got there. Right now, he needed to bluff the leader into obedience.

"I take it my lady mother sent you to escort me back to the Manor." He started toward the landing pad, nodding at the Aryan to follow. "Well, then. Let's not waste time."

The Aryan merely touched the silver thread of his comm. He murmured into it, cocked his head in a travesty of Kip Marsden while he listened to the answer. There was real pleasure in his expression when he tapped the unit off and straightened. "The Lady Letticia does indeed wish us to escort you. However, she has graciously allowed me to decide how we entertain you en route."

Smile widening, he reached into his jacket's breast pocket, pulled out a neural wand. Cloth rustled as the other four thugs followed suit. They sidled inward, tightening the circle. Blocking any hope Jezekiah had of ducking back into the house.

Jezekiah dodged the leader's neural wand jab at his shoulder. He grabbed its holder and jerked him into the path of the next Aryan's wand. The Aryan screamed as his partner's wand caught him in the throat. Jezekiah yanked the wand out of the Aryan's hand, then shoved the man into his fellows. He parried the next wand jab. Kicked its owner aside, buying himself an opening to his skimmer. A third Aryan lunged for him. Jezekiah slammed a boot heel into the man's face, felt the nose give way. He kicked clear – and bellowed as the leader's wand caught him at the base of his skull.

Agony turned the world black. Jezekiah's knees gave way. He barely felt the gut-punch that drove breath out of his body. He knew, vaguely, that the Aryans were kicking him. But the seared agony of the wand overrode all other sensations. It took every ounce of control he could summon to bite his lips closed, take the punishment with the stoicism expected of a Van Buren. He could only curl around the pain, take the Aryans' blows on his back.

And hope with what part of his mind could still hope, that the screams he heard were not his own.

XLVII

The screams were fading into a watery gurgle. Or maybe it was just his imagination, inspired by the dulling throb in his skull. Jezekiah forced his mind through the pounding ache to logic. The screams couldn't be his; his throat was too constricted to scream. The gurgle – he pulled in a breath, decided with relief it wasn't his own. He pried his eyes open. Didn't help. He couldn't see anything beyond the knuckles of his hand. At the moment, he hurt too much to even be sure his hand was still connected to his body. But he managed to recognize the gurgle – it came from the garden's water fountain. And the smell. The grass near his face stank of fresh blood and worse. The smell cleared his head, got him thinking again. Someplace beyond his feet heavy thumps punctuated screams that were dwindling to whimpers. Maybe the Admiral had come back? Sounded like a squad of Samurai was giving the Aryans a taste of their own.

He took comfort in the thought. Then hands yanked him up. His captor locked a steel-tipped hand around his neck and shook him hard enough to rattle his brain.

Jezekiah slammed an elbow backward into his captor's chest. The impact shot white agony up his arm.

"Don't give me any more reasons to kill you, Van Buren."

"Strongarm?" The flash of hope died with the rest of the sentence as the Lupan lifted Jezekiah by the throat. Pinpoints of pain dug into his throat beneath the man's talons.

Strongarm twisted Jezekiah around so he dangled face to face in the Lupan's grip. Arm's length, yet, Jezekiah could smell the blood on the Lupan's breath. A set of fairy brights wandered over. Their dainty light danced across the blood and worse matting the patches of silver hair on Strongarm's chest and mane.

"Where's Bird, Van Buren?" Strongarm relaxed his grip enough to allow Jezekiah to speak without tearing his adam's apple out.

"If I knew, I'd be there."

"Don't push me. Not now." Strongarm jerked him closer, fangs bared. But his nose twitched, testing. He *uhfed*, finally, in disgust and tossed Jezekiah aside.

The move bounced Jezekiah off the Sec skimmer's hull. Wand-bruised nerves shrieked at the impact, left him pain-blind again. He tripped over a lump and fell face first onto something that was not grass. The stink of voided bowels told him even before he blinked sight back that he'd landed on a corpse. He recognized the dead face staring back at him as one of the Aryan guards he'd seen lounging here by the skimmer.

Explained why the two skimmer guards had looked wrong: the Aryan's head was bent at right angles. He scrambled away from it, used the skimmer wall to push himself upright. Still, the stink helped clear his head, get his mind working again. Raised questions, too. "When did you get here?"

"About the same time as these cowards." Strongarm stepped across another body and strode for the garden fountain.

"You mean you *watched* them?"

"With satisfaction." Strongarm perked an unapologetic ear back at him. "Thought maybe they'd find out where Bird is." He shrugged, swiveled his ears toward the sky, listening.

Whatever he heard, it wasn't audible to human-only ears. Jezekiah picked his way across the corpses toward the Lupan. He slipped in a puddle, gagged at the reeking warm steam that wafted up. His stomach tried to rebel. He bit his lips closed to hold his dinner in place. Pain bit back where crusted blood dissolved against his teeth, left the taste of blood on his tongue. He pulled in a careful breath, winced at the ring of fire that shot around his ribs. The reminder of what additional delights the Aryans had planned for him helped. His stomach decided not to rebel after all. "We'd best get back to the Manor. There'll be a squad out looking for this lot before long."

"I don't think Bird's still there. Lost her track back of the place." Strongarm's ears went flat. "Lost it under the spoor of that bitch-son Teufelsman."

The very air seemed to go cold. If Teufelsman had Keik – he forced the horror down, ran a suddenly hopeful glance across the remnants of men strewn across the yard. "Pity you didn't save one of these for questioning."

"I'm not a total fool." Strongarm clapped a massive hand on Jezekiah's shoulder in a bone-creaking grip. He hauled him across the shattered corpses toward the garden gate.

The Aryan leader sprawled face down near the gate, neural wand still clutched in his hand. He'd fallen in running position, the wand under one knee. The cloth of his trousers protected him from the wand's neural disruption. Not that the man likely realized it. Not given the way bones protruded from z-shaped breaks in his arms and legs. It was a tribute to Aryan determination that the fellow was still conscious. And levering himself slowly toward the gate by his chin. The Aryan shrieked as Strongarm flipped him over with a toe tip.

Strongarm squatted beside the Aryan, bracing himself on the taloned knuckles of one hand. For a moment his head drooped, giving Jezekiah a glimpse of the bald patches in his mane, silent testimony to the strain he was under. Any other sign of exhaustion vanished in a hunter's grin when the Lupan looked up. "Waste of time questioning a real man. But you can usually get answers out of a flat tooth."

The Aryan's eyes found Strongarm's grin and went round in horror. The horror morphed into groveling hope when his gaze found Jezekiah. "Milord! Save me!"

"Why?" Jezekiah resisted the urge to give the fellow a kick in the ribs himself.

"I can help you!"

"You already had that chance. I'm going to need a better reason than that now."

"Where is Keiko Yakamoto?" Strongarm punctuated each word with the tap of a talon tip on the Aryan's chin. Glistening red dots sprang up on the pale skin.

"B-but..." The Aryan wrenched terrified eyes back to Jezekiah. "Milord, you don't understand! The dog has betrayed you! He has a battle fleet in bound."

"Don't make me repeat the question." Strongarm extruded a talon, ran it down the Aryan's sleeve. The cloth fell open behind it. Beneath, the man's skin was white as the linen.

The Aryan's body spasmed in terror. "Teufelsman arrested her! She's being Registered!"

"For *what?*" Jezekiah yanked the Aryan up by the shirt front, making him spasm again.

"For treason! Milady ordered it!"

"That's not even a good lie. Mother would never issue such an order."

"Not the late Protector-"

Jezekiah yanked the man up. Mistake. The Aryan spasmed. Blood flooded over his chin and he arched back, quivering.

"Dead." Strongarm *uhfed* and rose. "Better get going, then. Don't want to be caught landlocked when these fools' pack mates show up."

Jezekiah knew he should follow suit. Get up, get moving. He couldn't even unclench his fist. Dimly, he heard Strongarm's surprised grunt, felt Strongarm slap the dead man's shirt out of his grip. He knew, physically, that Strongarm was shaking him, but he couldn't respond to it. Couldn't feel or think at all, couldn't see anything past the pulsing diamond prison that was now the Protector's Ring. Couldn't think or feel anything beyond its terrible truth.

The late Protector. Lines of probability clicked into certainty. The certainty punched the breath out of his body. All the puzzle pieces he'd refused to consider clicked home. That was why Letticia felt safe enough to usurp Mother's node.

Mother was dead.

XLVIII

"Out with it, Van Buren." Strongarm hauled him upright. He wasn't particularly gentle about it. "What's the problem?"

"Mother's dead." It took every ounce of willpower he had to say it. And it still felt like a lie.

"How?"

He wanted to say he didn't know. Wanted to believe there'd been an accident. But the time for lies was past. At least for lying to himself. He doubled over Strongarm's wrist, heard his strangled breath gurgle in his throat. "Letticia. Can't be anyone else."

"So that was the reason." The Lupan let his breath out in a hiss. "I owe your mother's memory an apology, then."

"For what?" Jezekiah straightened to see the Lupan's ears flatten. Their silvery tips were ragged, but the great amber eyes were sharp.

"Thought it was your mother who invited us to leave. Should have known better." Strongarm's nose twitched thoughtfully. "You sister's usurped your mother's identity, hasn't she?"

"Mother's image, at least." He needed to *think*. But his mind, his whole body, was numb.

"Looks like she intends you to be next." Strongarm pushed Jezekiah out to arm's length. "Unless, of course, this was all your own plan. You are Home World's Protector now."

The implication burned through the numb haze, ignited a spark of crystal rage. Jezekiah launched himself at Strongarm, fury erasing sorrow and self-preservation together. He hit the Lupan shoulder first, drove a vicious undercut into the man's gut. Pounded Strongarm's body with every fiber of his being in every blow. Pounded until he collapsed, breath sobbing, in the Lupan's arms.

"I sorrow for your grief." Jezekiah felt the rumble of Strongarm's voice through the man's chest. "Best to get it out, now, while you can. A man should not die with his grief unassuaged."

He realized, finally, that Strongarm was holding him like a child, one hand gently stroking the back of his neck. He should be grateful for the friendship in that gesture. Only quick calcs sprang to life, profit potentials suggesting alternatives even uglier. Jezekiah pushed himself upright, though he could not shake Strongarm's hand off his neck. "That Aryan said you've got a battle fleet in-bound. That's exactly the move the rest of the Council fears. It's enough to convict me of treason against the Commonwealth by itself."

Common sense and survival instinct screamed at him to shut up. But the dregs of his fury drove him on. "*Why*, Lord Strongarm? Why break our treaty terms now, unless you see an advantage neither Mother nor I could offer you? Unless you and Letticia-"

The grip on Jezekiah's neck took on a steel edge. Drove home the realization of just how fast he could die in the Lupan's embrace. So much the better. Any death would be faster than the slow torment of the Ring. He lifted his chin as much as Strongarm's grip allowed and met the Lupan's snarl with defiance.

He felt the cold trickle of blood down his throat and braced himself for the final, crushing clench of Strongarm's talons.

Instead, Strongarm turned on his heel. He dragged Jezekiah across the Aryans' shattered bodies to the tiered fountain. In the silence, even the rustle of the wisteria blossoms lining the wall behind the fountain seemed sinister, the water's gurgle deafening. "Your grief speaks louder than your sense, Van Buren." Jezekiah felt Strongarm's voice rumble through his neck. "Think you'd best clear your head." With that, he jammed Jezekiah head first into the fountain bowl.

Strongarm held him under until Jezekiah kicked for air. He let him go, finally, and Jezekiah dropped to his knees, spitting water. "That answer your question?" Strongarm leaned back against the house wall, arms folded across his chest. His ears were still flat but his nose twitched, questioning.

"Well enough." Jezekiah gagged the last water out of his throat and pulled himself up by the fountain's rim. The fact he was still alive was proof he wasn't in collusion with Letticia. Careless as she was, Lush would never have made the mistake of leaving him alive now. He started to offer thanks. The sight of the Lupan's face stopped him.

Strongarm had leaned back against the vine covering the wall. The Lupan's eyes were closed, his massive shoulders slumped. Clusters of wisteria formed a lilac crest around his matted mane. Pixie brights winked in and out among the flower blossoms. In their dainty light Strongarm's face showed haggard.

Might be only a matter of hours, now, Jezekiah's little voice murmured. If Strongarm didn't complete his Impression soon, the man was dead. Without Strongarm the treaty was dead. As Earth would be, with Strongarm's battle fleet in-bound. Because there could be no doubt that Kaitin ibn Bengal would be in charge of it.

Unless – Jezekiah felt a grim smile form. Desperate as he was now, Strongarm could be Impressed by the first female *anything*. Which meant it was only a matter of making sure he controlled just who – or what – that anything was. He hid the budding idea behind his working mask and reached out to tap Strongarm awake. "I'm done. You want to wash up?"

Strongarm opened his eyes with visible effort. He dragged fingers across his chest, winced as talon tips snagged on clumps of drying gore. "Yeah, I'd better. I need to get the smell of blood out of my nose. Otherwise, I'm too likely to add yours to the rest of this shit." He shook himself, triggering a shower that coated his mane with purple blossoms and drove an iridescent hummingbird out of some hidden nest to buzz challenge. The Lupan chased it off with a puff of breath. He lifted the top tier of the fountain, drained its contents over his head.

Jezekiah rested his own back against the wall while Strongarm rubbed the filth off. He pretended not to notice how much silver hair came loose with the gore. "Sooner we get out of here the better, don't you think?"

"We'll give it another minute or two." He raked flowers out of his mane, then lifted the second tier and repeated the process. Glistening lilac droplets blossomed across the wall when he shook himself dry.

"Listen. The next squad won't have to hunt for us. Letticia will have them tracking our biopats."

"We've still got fifteen, twenty minutes maybe." Strongarm shook water out of his mane. He lifted his head, ears targeting, nose twitching. "It'll take these bitch-sons' pack mates that long to realize this lot's not coming back."

Jezekiah shuddered at the image of just how much more damage Letticia *could* do before she got around to killing them. "If we're caught on the ground-"

Lightning whined past overhead. Jezekiah dove for cover. The missile hit the far side of the garden wall. The yard beneath his body shuddered under the impact, waking fresh protests from his bruised ribs. He felt the shock wave roll over him. He could only pray any shrapnel spray would pass overhead, too.

"*Now* we can go." From the sound of it, Strongarm was still standing.

Clearly, the Lupan did not share his worries. Jezekiah rolled over enough to see Strongarm striding for the smoking ruin of the garden wall. Fine gray concrete powder swirled around his broad form. The dust cloud closed in behind him. Tiny granules of concrete drifted into Jezekiah's nose. He coughed them out, wished instantly he hadn't. Ignoring his aching muscles Jezekiah shoved himself to his feet and trudged after Strongarm.

The dust around the wall was too thick to for him to see what had hit it, but he heard metal screech, punctuated by a Lupan curse. He twisted his ankle stumbling over the broken concrete and added a curse of his own. Then he was through the worst of the dust and staring at Strongarm's powerful back.

The Lupan was bent over the open maw of a Lupan stasis canister. As Jezekiah watched, Strongarm backed away from the metal tube. He held up a man-length battle axe. A massive laser pistol dangled from a pair of bandoliers he'd tucked under one arm. "Told Kait to send down my working gear."

"Were you planning to take on the Aryans and Sec single handed?" Considering the state of mind Strongarm was in, that was a distinct possibility.

"Not unless I have to." Strongarm slung the bandoliers crisscross over his shoulders. His ears swiveled, targeting the sky behind Jezekiah. "That skimmer of yours armed by any chance?"

"It's one of Sec's. What do you think?"

"Good." Strongarm snapped the pistol belt around his hips, swung the axe across his shoulder and started for the skimmer. "Because we've got in-coming."

Jezekiah forced protesting muscles to jog past the shattered bodies. He made it to the skimmer a couple of steps ahead of Strongarm and nodded the Lupan toward the passenger's door.

Strongarm ignored him. He shouldered Jezekiah aside to slide into the master's seat.

"We don't have time to argue!" Jezekiah tried to push the Lupan over. "This is a Van Buren skimmer-"

"You ever fly combat?"

"No, but -"

"Then shut up and get in. I'm driving."

Strongarm had the skimmer powered up before Jezekiah could dive into the passenger's seat. He locked the axe down beneath the master's seat while Jezekiah snagged the safety harness into place. A moment later, the little ship shot off the landing pad. Hugging the tree tops Strongarm swung it northeast toward the pali coast.

Jezekiah peered through the sliver of screen visible past Strongarm's shoulder. In the distance, sunlight flashed on skimmer wings coming from the direction of the Manor. They were definitely headed for Diamond Head. "Looks like there's three of them."

"Not bad." Beneath them, green-brown coast gave way to steel-blue ocean. Strongarm dropped over the cliff edge to skim the waves. Headed north.

"How are you planning to get back to the Manor this way? Swing around the entire island?" Jezekiah kept his tone level. He only hoped he'd managed to keep the suspicion out of his scent.

"Not going to the Manor. "I'm tracking Bird. She's up ahead somewhere. I can feel it." Strongarm ran talon tips across the dashboard. "Maker's balls, Van Buren, what did you do to this thing?"

"Kicked it. Had to get it out of Net."

Strongarm grunted in disgust. He reached under the dash, probing. He grunted again, this time in satisfaction. The air took on a buzz as the skimmer's battle shields went live. Strongarm straightened, pulling a mech arm out from under the dash by a talon tip. The back-up weapons board sat atop it.

"Strongarm -"

"Name's Alex." Strongarm's talons flicked across the colored patches of the board's surface.

"Alex, then." He didn't dare let himself think through the implications in the name. "We don't have a choice, Alex. We've got to stop Letticia."

"Wrong, onlie. *You've* got to stop your sister. I've got to find Bird."

He bit his lip, barely noticed the coppery tang of blood it raised. "Letticia was the one behind the attack on your Rogue miners." He could keep his voice from betraying the shame and sorrow the admission cost him. But no amount of self-control could keep it out of his scent.

"Glad you smell innocent." Strongarm turned enough to bring those great amber eyes to bear. "I thank you for your sorrow, Van Buren. But it doesn't change anything."

"Damn it, man! Letticia's going to start the war! If we don't stop her now, Den Lupus and the whole damned Commonwealth are going to die!"

"What you want me to do about it? If I don't find Bird now, I'll already be dead. So shut up and let me drive."

Damn. In the distance ahead, Jezekiah spotted the crooked tip of Chinaman's Hat off shore. He checked the rearview scanners, tightened focus to the shoreline. Behind them the Aryans cleared Diamond Head and banked northward, tracking them. "Don't you think we ought to gain some height? They're going to have the drop on us."

"You want to live, Van Buren?"

"That was the general idea."

"Then shut up." Strongarm had the weapons board up, but his talon tips only skittered across its surface. He swore, retracted them. And flipped the skimmer up onto a wingtip.

Laser bolts boiled the ocean where her nose had been. The Aryans shot past in formation. Strongarm danced the skimmer above the waves on its wing. The Aryans overshot and he brought the skimmer up behind them. He tapped the fire patch.

Nothing.

"Maker's balls! Thought you said this thing is armed!"

"It is!" Jezekiah tried to swallow. His throat refused to cooperate. "Must have shorted out when I kicked the dash." His Ring flared, reflecting the spike in his pulse. "Got an idea. Even the back-up board ought to have sync capacity. Give me that."

Strongarm shoved the board into his hands. Jezekiah ran his hand along the board's underside. His fingers found the smooth round ball of a secondary link to ShipMind. Breathing a prayer, he laid the Ring against it and willed the board to activate. An instant later lights rippled color across its surface. "Thought so. A Protector's Ring overrides anything in Net. We're live now."

"Then you better shoot like you talk." Strongarm shoved the board toward him. Ahead, the Aryans had peeled out of formation. They arced back in unison. Into kill position.

Strongarm slammed the brakes so hard Jezekiah doubled over the board despite the harness. Ship lights flickered as a trail of laser bolts blossomed across the upper shields. The Aryans flashed by overhead. White lines of steaming geysers erupted along the waves under their fire.

The skimmer's targeting arrow lit at Jezekiah's touch. He got target lock. Narrowed his lasers to a pinprick beam and fired – one, two, three bursts locked into a single point on the Aryan's shield. A tiny sun bloomed on the leader's tail where a microspot on the shields failed. He held lock, fired again. The lasers found the engines. Man and metal exploded within the gleaming sphere of the Aryan's shield. Then the shield collapsed in on itself. The blackened shards within glowed red.

"Nice trick." Strongarm snapped the skimmer away an instant before the Aryan's imploding shields went nova.

Shielding his eyes against the glare, Jezekiah saw the other two Aryans split up. Circling back on their flanks for another shot.

Strongarm stood the skimmer on its tail. They shot skyward, arced over portside. Beneath them the world turned green again as they crossed the sheer pali cliffs. Strongarm came up behind the inland Aryan.

And suddenly the skimmer bucked as if it were trying to throw them off. Snarling, Strongarm fought it back under control.

The weapons board still showed clear. Stomach clenching, Jezekiah tested it anyway. He knew before it failed what the results would be.

"Dead." Jezekiah punched in the backup system code again anyway. No response.

Strongarm managed to right the ship by brute strength. "You people want to fight a war with catshit like this?" He whipped the skimmer around in a tight curve, staying on the Aryan's tail. Beneath them, the ground dropped away again. Far below the sea foamed against rocky walls. "We didn't pull that much fire."

"Letticia. Has to be."

"How –"

Ship lights went out as the Aryan's partner fired. Laser bursts traced tiny suns along down the skimmer's flank shields.

The lead Aryan shot past. Strongarm flipped the ship into an on-going barrel roll. Jezekiah caught the metallic glint of the hunter's wing tip off starboard. The third hunter had sights on them.

Through the roll, he caught sporadic glimpses of Chinaman's Hat ahead. Strongarm leveled off, picked up speed till the island's rocky peak filled their forward screens. He shot under the belly of the lead Aryan. Stood the skimmer on its tail in front of the Aryan's nose to arc over its canopy. They were so close Jezekiah caught a glimpse of the woman pilot's white face.

She was a millisecond late pulling up. The outcropped tip of the island's 'hat' clipped her wing tip. The impact whipped her ship around, slammed it into the sharp rocks. The explosion raised a halo of white hot shrapnel around the peak. Through the screens Jezekiah watched the Aryan's remnants skitter across the waves below. He bit his lips closed to stop his stomach from joining it.

Strongarm was still flying them upside down. Jezekiah nearly choked as some invisible hand slapped the skimmer downward, sending the sea rushing up toward his face. Twin lines of white fire spat across their belly shields. Each burst bounced them onto the water until he could see the lacy currents crisscrossing the waves. Another burst of fire hit close enough to spit boiling water across the shields over his head. Then the hunter was past, rocketing skyward for another round.

Snarling in Lupan, Strongarm righted the skimmer. Good thing, too: the faint gleam of the shields flickered, died. He wrestled the little ship up and over a cresting wave, giving Jezekiah a dolphin's view of the surge. Then they were clear, and banking back toward Chinaman's Hat in pursuit.

For a moment, the island hid the last hunter. Strongarm nosed the skimmer's belly skyward. He kept it belly up while he closed in on the Aryan. Keeping eyes on the ship ahead, he leaned over and unsnapped his battle axe.

In seconds the hunter was beneath them. Strongarm lined up on the Aryan's cockpit. Jezekiah yanked his harness out of the way as the Lupan lifted the long pole of the axe. He tucked the gleaming blade beneath his arm, sank talon tips into pinprick triggers on the handle. The savage blade of the axe glowed hot blue. Bracing the joy stick between his knees Strongarm locked knees around his seat and popped off the skimmer's canopy. He roared challenge as the wind rippled silver lightning across his mane.

Beneath them the canopy bounced off the hunter's shields. It did no damage. But it was enough to make the pilot duck. And buy Strongarm an instant to ram the axe blade straight down.

Shields spat. Then the blue blade sliced through. Blood and gray matter spattered the inside of the hunter's cockpit.

Strongarm yanked the axe up, used his knees to swing the skimmer free. Beneath them, the pilotless hunter dropped away. The ship wobbled, then settled as its ShipMind took over. It shot off *ewa* way. Toward the Manor, and home.

Strongarm bellowed, but let it go. The blue glow of the axe blade vanished when he sheathed talons. He snapped the battle axe back into place, snapped the skimmer right side up.

"Thank you," Jezekiah breathed.

"What?" Strongarm cocked one ear in his direction.

"Nothing." Jezekiah leaned against his harness, content for a moment to simply be breathing. Off to port, the gray cliffs of the pali rose sharply. They passed the sparkling froth of a waterfall dropping a thousand sheer feet out of the jungle into the ocean.

Off to *port* – they were still headed north, away from Waikiki and the Manor.

Into Ho Tong territory.

XLIX

Suspended deep within the very nexus of NetMind, Letticia felt her immaterial *self* swell into the whole vast, jeweled universe of the Protector's node. Heavens, it felt so *good*. She dedicated whole seconds to simply reveling in the unbridled power. No need to sawyer Mother's Net guards any more. No more *fear*. Oh, just *let* JP try to boss her around now! She'd show him just what real power was. She was finally, really truly, completely *safe*.

Of course, there were still a few anomalies. SecNet traffic was down a good eighty-seven percent, for one. The Lupans were another: Strongarm was heading home. She'd checked biopat readings on his outbound shuttle herself to make sure. Odd, though, that it showed fuzzy – well, it didn't matter. Likely he was already dead and that vile Kaitin was just stuck hauling his corpse home. So that was one off her list. Which left only Jezekiah. And she'd sent an Aryan to tell Grandfather Ho that it had been *dear* Jezekiah who turned Teufelsman and his squad loose on the little Yakamoto bitch. Would have been better to tell him herself, but the silly old man couldn't sync in and she couldn't very well go to him. Still, the Aryan had come back alive so the old man must have believed the story. Letticia heard her body sigh. Pity she wouldn't be able to watch Jezekiah die. Grandfather Ho could think up some wonderfully creative modes of execution.

Ah, Mistress? The urgency code in Mother's senior Admin op's reading was high enough to override even her personal filters.

What? Can't you see? I'm busy. Mourning.

We have messages coming in, Mistress Van Buren.

Well, answer *them, idiot. That's what Mother – I – pay you for, isn't it? Now go away.* As the dithering idiot ought to have sense to realize. Heavens, CommNet was just livid with messages. Surely he didn't expect her to monitor them all. Well, actually, she *could*. She just didn't feel like it. For a nanosecond, Letticia considered feeding crash'n burn feedback into the fool's synapses. That'd teach him to interrupt her!

Yes, Mistress. But –

A ripple in sync made her stomach lurch. Through the distortion she caught the whimper that said Admin op had felt it too. Then her feedline steadied. And Letticia found herself facing a pair of black and white scowls.

Leave us, JP snapped.

The admin op vanished. Habit almost drove Letticia to pull her hand out of sync as well. It was only the certainty that *she* was all-powerful here that kept her from breaking sync. That, and the sure knowledge JP would follow her in holo if she fled.

JP looked the same as always, same red-gold mohawk above the same pinched white face above the same boring black uniform. Only difference was the silver spiral of a comm mic he wrapped around his head. Its braided band was so fine it looked as if it were spun from the silver strands in his hair. But there was a fresh danger in his biopat. His feed read almost black as his uniform. *Deep* anger there, even for JP.

Heavens, had Streiker's spies breached her lobe? Fighting panic Letticia sent a spider brood scuttling back along her anchor lines. The answers came back clear. Every world in the Commonwealth had probed her defenses. They'd all failed. The edit she'd done on Mother's major domo's record held.

So she was safe. Letticia felt her body shiver in relief. *She* was Protector of Earth, now. She pulled her sync'd image up to face them down. Regally. Like Mother. *To what do owe the honor of this visit, Uncle?* Hope suggested the answer. She squashed the spike in her pulse before sync betrayed it. *Have you come to arrange the passing of the Protector's Ring?*

Hardly. JP lifted a colorless lip in a sneer and paced off.

Well, then what do you want?

Merely a courtesy call, Cousin. That was Octavian. Impossible even in sync to ever tell what Octavian felt. Line of sight was worse: the feathery brightness of the pink centerpiece on his table blocked any clear viz. He seemed to be wearing Pandari mourning, though. His high-collared robe glittered darkly with garnet trimmings. If it hadn't been for the white-blue flicker of his eyes, he'd have blended into the cushions around him. Worse, his biopat was in Pandari business-mode: totally neutral. Well, that showed how much *he* cared! And here she'd always thought Octavian rather liked Mother.

Well, she could play games, too, now. *That's so sweet of you, Cousin.* Letticia allowed her sync'd image to smile sweetly. *Condolences accepted. So, if there's nothing else?*

It was too much to hope that JP would take the hint. Vile old man reached the end of his box and turned to sneer at her face on. *Be advised that the Council session remains on schedule. Prepare yourself to appear at nine, Earth time local.*

Whatever for? The trial was for Mother and Jezekiah! Letticia shut down the shiver of re-awakened terror before it reached her hyperlink feed. Ought to impossible, but – Letticia risked a frantic microsecond to confirm the major domo's notices read right. All yar – the miserable gobbers really were summoning her. But why? *I wasn't part of their stupid treaty, remember?* She didn't even have to fake her puzzlement.

Oh, we remember quite well. Octavian sat back, flickering those white-blue eyes at her. And smiling a feline little smile that really should have had fangs. *The problem, you see, is that the Lupans seem to have some rather strong objections to the loss of Jezekiah's treaty. Not to mention the mass murder of their colony on Rogue.*

So? Heavens, what was the man up to? *You were going to try Mother and Jezekiah for treason because of that stupid treaty. You should be happy it's dead.*

Oh, not me, my dear. Octavian twisted around to select a crystal goblet from the display above his seat. He placed it on the table, turned to choose a decanter. Behind his back, a feathery pink frond shot out to explore the goblet's rim hungrily. *Lamentable as Jezekiah's treaty was from Streiker's perspective, it was quite interesting from Pandar's. Which was why I granted Jezekiah and your late, much lamented mother, time to solidify it before the Council met.*

Some kind of emotion surged Octavian's biopat as he turned back to set the decanter beside the goblet. He squashed it so quick Letticia couldn't even be sure what it was. Thwarted greed, most likely. Nothing unusual there. What scared her was JP. The old man just kept pacing, looking for all the world like he was listening to comm and not Octavian. Heavens, had JP betrayed her? Letticia felt her body try to swallow. Felt like she was swallowing sand.

A tingle in her veins warned her Octavian was running scan on *her*. Of all the nerve! Letticia made sure her biopat readings were correct then locked her sync'd gaze on the Pandari. *All that still has nothing to do with me! So why are you bothering me with it? I'm trying to mourn!*

As are we all. Liquid sparkled as Octavian poured some of the decanter's contents into the goblet. A serpentine pink tendril tracked the glittering stream hopefully. He flicked clear liquid from the decanter across the table. The frond snatched the droplets out of the air, then coiled attentively.

Heavens, why didn't JP say anything? He certainly knew what had happened on Rogue! He was supposed to be her ally! But he just paced off. Letticia refused to give him the satisfaction of twisting around to track him. Only the sense of having him at her back was sending prickles down her back. *If you want me to sign Jezekiah's treaty, just say so. We can always find another Lupan for the marriage pact. It's no big deal.*

It is a very great big deal! JP stormed back to shake a fist at her. Sync quelled his thunder but Letticia felt it through her anchor lines anyway. *It takes a reigning Protector to seal a treaty! A Protector Earth no longer has!*

Oh, for heaven's sake, Uncle! I'm the Protector now!

Not yet you're not! Not while Jezekiah is alive. JP marched back to glare down at her. There was enough threat in his stance to make Letticia's body cringe back in its chair.

Nonsense! Jezekiah's disqualified! He killed Mother. You saw her major domo's report yourself!

We saw it. Octavian sat back to flutter lashes at her, Pandari equivalent to an arched brow. *The question, of course, is whether it's true.*

The horror of Mother's dead face tried to rise up again. Letticia heard her body whimper. She jammed the image down. She *hated* that memory! Hated it! But they'd never understand. *So just what more proof do you want?*

We want to hear it from Jezekiah himself. On the opposite side of her viz field, Octavian took a moment to scratch the underside of a curious pink tendril. Above it, his eyes flickered white-blue. *You should hope he confesses. Because I have volunteered to personally oversee the execution of the murderer.* The tendril curled over his finger, probed it daintily. Then wrapped itself around his finger and sank needle sharp suckers into his ebony skin. Bright red droplets sprang up and vanished instantly. Above the needles the tendril's color deepened from pink to rose.

Octavian snapped his hand free. He splashed liquid from the goblet across the table. The pink fronds shot after it. *It may interest you to know that Pandar grows its own executioners. Old Hubert here is a sample.* He wrapped a gleaming white handkerchief around his finger, watching her thoughtfully. *One of my ships will fetch your mother's killer to Pandar. We'll see how much the murderer enjoys a stroll in our afternoon sun. Who knows? Perhaps the radiation will kill you – or him – before Hubert's cousins find you.*

JP glanced at some chron outside the viz field's scope. *Be prepared, girl. We will not have time to dither with you any further.*

Quite so. Octavian lifted his crystal glass in salute and touched a patch on his table. His image vanished.

Letticia realized with a start that JP had disappeared as well. Oh, God. She needed to concentrate, settle all her infinite strands. She needed to contact Grandfather Ho. Needed to find Jezekiah.

For once, she hoped Jezekiah would still be alive when she reached him.

L

The skimmer's nav panel died as they passed Kaaawa, leaving Strongarm to navigate by light of the great yellow moon rising over the sea. Amber moonlight glazed the shadows beneath their wings, gilded the rivulet they were tracking across the Koolau. It was a gift to appreciate, given that they were running without lights.

Pity the moonlight couldn't brighten the darkness that had seeped into his soul. Without Mother – Jezekiah squeezed his eyes closed, shutting down the tears if not the sorrow. He'd lost Mother, probably lost Kip. Would lose Strongarm, too, before much longer. All that was left of his dreams was the nightmare of the Ring. And Keiko…

The Ring pulsed in answer to his misery. Strongarm cocked at ear at him. In the glow of the Ring his nose twitched suspiciously. "What are you plotting, Van Buren?"

"Can't think straight enough to plot." Which was distressingly true. He was too numb to even calc out how to spin Grandfather Ho's likely reaction to their appearance.

"Good thing my nose still works. Because if I were a flat tooth, I'd say you were lying." Strongarm flashed a befanged grin at him over his shoulder. He left the threat behind it unsaid.

"Right now I don't care enough to think up a lie." It was just the truth for once. He couldn't *think* at all. Couldn't even really feel the grief and rage Mother's assassination deserved. It was all crushed beneath the infinite weight of the Ring. Jezekiah tucked his Ring hand under his leg, leaned his cheek against the strap of the safety harness wishing he could lean the weight of his duty on the straps.

Beside him he heard Strongarm grunt. "You want to crawl back to the Manor, Van Buren, I can drop you off on the downslope."

"What for? So I can help Letticia finish us all off?" Even those few words took herculean effort.

"So you can stop trying my patience." Strongarm twitched his nose at Jezekiah for emphasis. "I know self-pity when I smell it."

"It's not self-pity. It's despair." Which was true enough. The thought only deepened the dark well that had swallowed his dreams. "She's won, Strongarm. When she killed Mother she killed the last hope we had of proving our innocence. Letticia hasn't the wit to understand just how much the treaty means. The Council will convene in the morning. She'll feed them the story I killed Mother and NetMind will confirm it. After which, no one in the Family will support the treaty. There'll be nothing to stop JP from pushing our worlds into war."

"You underestimate your clansmen." Strongarm clamped a steel-tipped hand on Jezekiah's shoulder. "And the name is Alex. Don't make me tell you again."

"Alex, then. Sorry." There was another loss behind that name. It was a sign Keiko had felt the pull of Strongarm's Touch and answered it with her heart. Yet the name conjured images of Keiko. Of hope. A flash of possibilities cracked the darkness in his mind.

"Getting closer." Beneath the skimmer's wings a fine haze dimmed the gilded thread of the river. Strongarm eased over a bit, ears angled forward in concentration. He swiveled a ragged ear in Jezekiah's direction. "Smells like you're getting ideas, Van Buren. Sure you don't want me to put you down? Just as soon not have you underfoot when I find Bird."

"Why? Afraid of the competition?"

Strongarm snorted. "Afraid I'll have to kill you if you call challenge is all."

"You won't, though. Not unless Keiko tells you to." He said it automatically. But the words triggered another spark of hope. Pinpricks of possibility linked up behind his conscious mind; links connected, formed lines of probabilities. Yes, he did indeed still have something to fight for.

Maybe there was still hope after all. To hell with the Ring and duty and obligation. Let Letticia have the damned Ring. Wasn't worth his life, much less Mother's death. There were plenty of nubile young women in Ho Tong; all he needed was to get one of them close enough to Strongarm to force an Impression. The man was far enough gone now he could probably respond to a rock. After that, Jezekiah would have no trouble buying Keiko and himself a way off Earth. Despite himself, Jezekiah realized he was grinning.

Good thing Alex Strongarm could only read scents and not minds. Because had the Lupan caught scent of the idea Jezekiah was forming he would most certainly have killed him on the spot.

LI

They crested the Koolau just north of Puu Konahuanui peak. Strongarm followed the mountains northward. The rivulet blossomed into thundering glory beneath them as it tumbled off the mountain side. Strongarm shot the skimmer over the ledge with a roar that sounded like pure joy. He raced the waterfall nine hundred meters straight down, leveled them off barely above the misted rocks at the fall's base. "Feel that?" He pulled the skimmer's nose up to hover just above the cloud of pale mist and perked ears at Jezekiah.

"Feel what?" Jezekiah unpuckered his buttocks and wiggled experimentally. To his great relief his pants felt dry.

"That thump under your butt."

"It's my stomach, dammit!"

"Cat shit. That thump's a battle shield. You can feel the throb in your bones. We must be right on top of Tong's HQ."

"Damn." Quick-calcs ran probabilities on how Grandfather Ho managed to acquire battle shields. Especially shields so sufficiently stealthconfigured that SecNet had never spotted them. The fact the shields were there didn't scare him nearly as much as the implications behind them. It was only too likely SecNet *did* register those shields – and Letticia had hidden their signal.

The elements had carved a clearing out of the Koolau around the misted pool at the base of the well. Strongarm pulled the skimmer around in a tight bank within the fall's broad well and the stars vanished in a haze of mist and thunder. He settled the skimmer into a moon-shadowed grove of umbrella plants on the far side of the well. The machine's repulse field twisted the mist into spectral whorls, making the meterwide umbrella leaves nod like gossiping old women.

Strongarm offed the skimmer's engines. Silvering moonlight raised a soft halo on the patches of his mane. Moonlight gleamed, too, within the fern forest, cool light on cold metal. Strongarm's ears ran target sweep across the rest of the clearing. The ears drooped when he dropped back in his seat. "Listen,

Van Buren…" He breathed deep. It sounded tired and unhappy. "I know my odds. If Bird chooses you–" He shrugged. "Kaitin has instructions. If Bird chooses you, he'll get you both off Earth."

"Why?"

"Because without that treaty, Den Lupus is going to need a secondary base." His eyes gleamed a feral yellow in the moonlight. "Makers balls, man, why do you think I brought a whole damned battle fleet with me? Those ships are sitting out on the far side of Sol, at the edge of the void."

"Just waiting for the attack command." Jezekiah unlatched the safety harness slowly, giving himself a moment to extrapolate the implications.

"Not waiting." One ear flopped forward, hinting at the depth of Strongarm's exhaustion. He must have felt it because he snapped the ear up again. "Kaitin'll have made *Khali* by now. He's got his orders. Fleet will be in-bound."

"How long do we have, then?" Jezekiah couldn't even feel. His very heart seemed to have gone numb.

"Twelve hours, give or take a stray minute. They'll come in firing, too, if my biopat drops off Kaitin's screens."

"In other words, if I don't get out of your way Earth dies. That it?"

"If I had it that easy, Van Buren, you'd already be dead." Strongarm cocked an ear, listening to something outside. "Like I said, it's Bird's choice. She needs us both there to make it. I'm not spending my life loving a woman in love with a dead man." He *uhfed*, popped the master's door open. "Now get out. Reception committee's here."

In the darkness beyond the skimmer wings moonlight gleamed on a rifle barrel. The gleam shifted and a skinny, dark-eyed boy stepped out of the fern trees' shadows. The rifle he carried was as long as his body, but its ready light glowed green and finger he kept on its trigger looked confident. Even so, his eyes went wide in boyish wonder when Strongarm climbed out of the master's seat. The boy let out a sigh of audible relief when Jezekiah stepped around the skimmer's nose to join the Lupan.

Using the rifle barrel for a guide he motioned them toward the waterfall. Jezekiah made out the deeper shadows of a cave mouth behind the fall's mist. The cave was the entrance to a lava tube, most likely. Some ancient lava flow must have flowed underground here instead of pushing upward to erupt out of the caldera. The molten rock would have followed the downslope till it drained finally into the Pacific, leaving hollow tubes heat-seared in the mountain in its wake.

The thinking must have slowed him down. The boy jabbed his rifle muzzle into Jezekiah's aching ribs, encouraging him to move faster. He did not, Jezekiah noticed, risk poking Strongarm. His skin prickled as they passed the entrance. The shock of it nearly made him stumble. Bioscan. They'd just been bioscanned.

Beside him, Strongarm growled softly. "Thought you people kept Ho Tong out of Net."

"So did I. Looks like I was wrong."

Their guide ended the conversation by poking his rifle muzzle into Jezekiah's kidneys. Still, another piece of the puzzle had fallen into place. The implications tightened muscles already bruised by the Aryans' beating.

Rippling moonlight shimmered the cave opening behind the falls. Loose rocks had been allowed to accumulate on the floor, giving the tunnel an untouched, natural look. Made the footing naturally treacherous, too, and Jezekiah twisted an ankle when a rock slipped under his feet. Worth the fresh ache, though. Their guide couldn't question his limp. Gave him an excuse to force them to a slower pace. Buy himself some thinking time.

There was nothing natural at all about the way the lava tube curved sharply a dozen or so meters deeper into the mountain. Around the curve the upper arch of the tunnel had been polished to a near mirror finish. The black rock reflected the yellow gleam of the phosphorescents embedded in the stone just below the arch. No question they were in Grandfather's HQ, now: around the curve, the tunnel was busy as any of the Manor's admin wings. Bare-chested men in shorts ambled by at islander speed. Most of them carried admin type tablets, but others balanced baskets of pineapples and mangoes against their hips. The yellow gleam leached all true color out of their bodies, gave the green and gold fruit in the baskets a sulfurous sheen. Not a woman in sight, Jezekiah noted. Clearly, the old man wasn't risking an impromptu Impression. Proof, there, if he'd needed it, that Grandfather Ho had plans of his own for Strongarm's Impression.

Jezekiah caught his shoulders slumping. He forced them back, forced his mind back to the implications in that bioscan. The fury the conclusions inspired set Strongarm's nose to twitching, earned him an inquiring ear. He didn't try to answer; Grandfather Ho would prove soon enough what a fool the Van Buren Heir was.

Maybe it was a mercy Mother'd died – at least she'd been spared the disappointment of learning both her children were unworthy of her trust. If ever he'd needed proof he wasn't fit to wear the Ring, he'd certainly provided it now. The treaty was dead. Even if Strongarm's battle fleet somehow left anyone alive, the spin JP and Octavian would give it would make Earth a pariah even to the Free Worlds. That would end even the new tourist deals he'd worked out. After which Earth would just die a slower death.

They rounded another curve with Strongarm a pace or two in the lead. They were definitely nearing a power hub. Jezekiah felt the buzz of shield generators through the tunnel floor. The number of ops passing them increased. All men, still. Not a woman in sight, not even an old auntie. No sign of tech, either, aside from the sound of the shields. The men they passed all wore the unmistakable preoccupied frowns of admin ops. Yet their chart pads were strictly the ancient scratch type, and they ran their numbers on abacuses. The click of abacus beads nearly drowned out the shields' buzz. One gray-haired homie in a yellow sarong was too intent on his abacus to notice them until he heard Strongarm's warning *uhf*. The man flattened himself against the wall with yip.

Jezekiah watched the homie tuck his abacus under his arm as he scuttled off. A Ho Tong op using an *abacus* – in a battle-shielded compound. That was what Grandfather Ho wanted for his people – to send them back to the dark ages, keep them ignorant enough to believe there were re-creating some imaginary past glory. Only Letticia would make sure he had access to Net. Make sure he could still ship out his Venus Seed. She could manage it, now Mother was gone. Venus Seed's profits would fund any other ambitions Grandfather Ho had. At least they would until JP or Octavian decided to take over the trade. Without the protection of Strongarm's battle fleet Earth would be defenseless –

Unless Keiko Impressed Strongarm. The full scope of the old man's plan clicked home so hard the impact of it put a glitch in Jezekiah's stride. That earned him another poke from the boy's rifle, but he barely noticed the pain. It all fit. Grandfather Ho had no more intention of leaving Earth defenseless than he had of relying on Letticia. If Keiko Impressed Strongarm, Grandfather Ho would have a whole damned Lupan battle fleet at his disposal. After that – the old man wouldn't stop at controlling Home World. With Strongarm behind him, he'd turn the whole damned Commonwealth into a Ho Tong satrap. And arrogant, ego-blind fool that he was, Jezekiah had let the old man gull him into making it all possible.

The sudden finality of it punched the breath out of him. Jezekiah would have doubled over if Strongarm hadn't caught him. The mental barriers Mother had trained into him triggered even as he nodded thanks. He was beginning to understand the need for those barriers now. They let him hide the loathing of what he had to do from himself. But they couldn't make the necessity pleasant. He tried desperately to think up an alternative. He came up blank. Either he betrayed the one true friend he'd ever known, or he betrayed every other living soul in the Commonwealth. There were no other options: he had to find a way to kill Strongarm before Keiko finished the Impression.

He locked the last, lingering trace of decency and honor into the dungeon at the back of his mind and fell back into step at Strongarm's side. Yet even Mother's training could not stop his little voice from noting that betraying Strongarm eliminated his only competition for Keiko.

Their tiny guide stopped them at a polished stone door. The child motioned them aside with a swipe of the rifle. He scraped fingers through his hair, clearly gathering his courage, then touched a spot on the wall. Silently Grandfather's door slid back into its stony niche.

"*E komo mai, e ka'u kamali'i,*" Grandfather's voice said from within.

"He say 'come in, my children'." The boy motioned them through with a jerk of his chin. He closed the stone door behind them with a touch to a wall patch then disappeared into a second room that opened off to the right of the entrance.

Grandfather Ho's quarters betrayed none of the riches the lord of Ho Tong controlled. The walls were rough stone, the furniture nothing more than plump, worn pillows clustered around an ancient Chinese table. The old man himself was seated cross-legged on one of those pillows behind the table. He held a chipped tea bowl in both hands, watching them over its rim as he sipped. All simplicity itself – the mark of true power. Bitter thought: it reminded Jezekiah of Mother. The old man did not so much as lift a finger off his tea bowl. Yet Jezekiah was suddenly, profoundly and guiltily grateful for the solid feel of Strongarm's presence.

Strongarm must have picked up the sense of threat as well. The Lupan *uhfed* softly. His head came up, nose twitching, ears swiveling in his own personal scan. A suite of caves opened off the living area where Grandfather sat. Heavy curtains draped one opening – sleeping quarters, presumably. Opposite the curtain a second cave served as the suite's kitchen. A fireplace of sorts had been carved out of the rock; a blackened kettle was hung above a small wood fire within it. The charred wood filled the room with mesquite aroma. The stone wall hid the rest of the kitchen-cave, but pots were clinking inside, hinting at refreshments in progress. Jezekiah's stomach growled in response, reminder he hadn't eaten since – he couldn't even remember when. He ignored the hunger pangs and focused on learning the room. There'd be one other opening, too, if Grandfather Ho held true to form – a camouflaged one hiding larger guards than the boy who's brought them in.

"The scion of the Great Family Van Buren honors this humble abode. As does the great Lupan warlord." Grandfather lifted the cup to Jezekiah and Strongarm in turn.

Jezekiah stepped into the empty space fronting the table to salaam Grandfather Ho. "Allow us to thank you for your hospitality." It was his own private testament to Mother that he sounded sincere.

Grandfather swept a hand toward the pillows facing his table. The position would put their backs to the blank wall. Well, at least he knew now just where Grandfather's assassins were hidden. Jezekiah bowed acknowledgement of the unspoken challenge. He was sliding down onto a pillow when he realized Strongarm had backed away.

"I'll stand." The Lupan angled his back toward the kitchen. He folded his arms across his chest, feet apart, nose twitching. And ears locked on the kitchen cave.

"Surely the great Lupan war lord does not fear one poor, foolish old man?" Grandfather Ho put the cup down, folded his hands primly. He smiled benignly up at Strongarm over them. The gesture reminded Jezekiah of a cobra contemplating a mongoose.

"It's your granddaughter I'm here for, old man, not you." Strongarm only flicked an ear in Grandfather Ho's direction. His nose and eyes were locked on the kitchen.

"Ah. Age tends to forget the needs of youth." Grandfather sipped, turned the cobra smile on Jezekiah. "What, then, does the great Jezekiah Van Buren need from this poor old man? A ride off Home World, perhaps?"

Jezekiah answered him smile for smile. Political smile, as false as the old man's hospitality. "Not just yet, if you don't mind. I've no desire to be part of a Venus Seed shipment to another Lupan colony."

That brought Strongarm's ears around, as Jezekiah had intended. "The Rogue massacre was Streiker's doing."

"True." Jezekiah kept his tone neutral. Too soon, still, to push Strongarm into a charge. "But it would take Grandfather Ho's connections to get that much Venus Seed out to a Streikern pick up point." For a moment Jezekiah feared Strongarm would charge then anyway. But the Lupan's ears only swiveled back to track the kitchen noises. He did not dare let himself dwell on the reason for the man's fixation. "Which makes me wonder-" he lifted a brow at Grandfather Ho. "Did my cousin Octavian by any chance lend you one of his ships?"

"Not to his knowledge."

So, then. At least Octavian hadn't been in on the attack on Rogue. But the fact confirmed that Letticia had been. The Pandari ship would have screamed for help when JP's troops hijacked it. It would take Letticia's skills to block the SOS.

He couldn't even make himself pretend Letticia was too foolish to realize she was helping to murder an entire tribe of innocents. Murdered because *he'd* interfered. Because he wanted to be free. The thought triggered a flash of shame so powerful it shivered the locks on his mental dungeon. Jezekiah pulled in a breath, held it till he'd shoved the dirt into its dark hollow.

In the kitchen dishes clattered. Grandfather let the noise dictate a pause.

He sat back, cradled his tea bowl within the cusp of his dragon hand. Within his palm the base of the bowl glowed red. The sight raised the hairs on the back of Jezekiah's neck. His muscles tensed, expecting a strike. But Grandfather only lifted the cup in salute. And waited.

"Bird!"

Keiko stepped out of the kitchen carrying a tray bearing a ceramic tea set that looked older than Grandfather Ho. Jezekiah could only see her profile but her face looked swollen. Still, Grandfather had clearly taken some care for her. She was dressed in a fresh red cotton sarong trimmed in yellow. Her black curls had been brushed to a silken gleam. Strongarm reached out for her as she passed, but she dodged him without a glance. Instead, she walked with an almost drunken fixation on Grandfather.

Behind him, Strongarm growled. Jezekiah saw the reason when Keiko dropped to one knee at the old man's side. She looked up to face him as she placed the tray on the table. Let him see the twin black studs embedded in her temple and upper jaw. He searched Keiko's face for a hint of any emotion at all. Got nothing except the killer's emptiness in her eyes.

"God damn you-" it was Jezekiah who lunged across the table at Grandfather. He found himself staring down the needler that appeared in Keiko's hand. The sight drove a cold line of sanity through his rage. Jezekiah sat back, put both hands on the table with care. "What have you done?"

"I? Perhaps you forget that Registration is uniquely a Van Buren sentence." Grandfather Ho placed his unmarked hand on Keiko's shoulder. It was a light touch, yet she flinched at it. "Are you not pleased with your handiwork, Jezekiah Van Buren? Are these studs not a lasting token of your regard? A guarantee of your control over my *keiki*?"

Strongarm's roar cut Jezekiah's answer off. Steel-corded claws ripped Jezekiah off the pillow by the throat. He grabbed at the Lupan's talons. But he knew, even as he kicked up it was too late –

"No!" Keiko shot to her feet. Some red and gold light flashed along the edge of Jezekiah's vision. Strongarm's grip on his throat eased. "Let him go! He's mine!"

Growling, the Lupan flung him aside. The gesture bounced Jezekiah off a rock wall. Lucky for his aching ribs he landed on one of the floor pillows. He stumbled to his feet, ignoring the sudden cold wetness along his neck and palms. Forced himself to face Keiko. And the horror of the gleaming, red-gold dragon coiling down her outstretched arm. "What happened, Keik?"

"Exactly what you intended to happen, Van Buren." She rounded the table to face him directly. Within her palm, the dragon's fiery breath glowed like real fire. This close, he could feel its heat. "Question I have is before I kill you is 'why'?"

He wrenched his gaze away from her. Felt hatred burn up his throat as he met the satisfaction in Grandfather Ho's eyes. "You better ask Grandfather that one."

"Liar!" But the cry drained the killer stare out of her eyes, left her heart on naked display.

Even now there was no hatred in her. Just the raw, honest belief he'd betrayed her. "*Why*, Van Buren?"

The knowledge of it branded his soul with sorrow as thoroughly as if she'd used the acids in the dragon's breath. "I don't know, Keik. You'll have to tell me."

"Tell you what? You owe me a 'why', Van Buren! Why'd you lie at that sawyered trial your sister ran? I saved your *life*, you lying son of a bitch! You know I did!"

"What trial? I never testified at – "

Her backhand cut the rest of his sentence off. "What trial you think, haole?"

"Let me end this, Bird."

Jezekiah caught the flicker of motion beside him. He jerked away. Too late. Strongarm locked a hand on Jezekiah's shoulder. Jezekiah held his breath to block the gasp at the knifing pain of Strongarm's talons. "Keik, listen! You want proof? Here it is!" He held up his Ring hand, though the movement drove Strongarm's talons deeper into his flesh. Shards of golden light spattered across the stone walls, pretty counterpoint to the warm, wet feel of blood running down his chest.

"So what?" Keiko ran the back of her hand across her face. The dragon's breath left a glowing trail in the air behind it.

"This is a *Protector's* Ring, Keik."

"So?"

"It means Mother's dead."

"You want me to feel sorry, you're too late." But she gestured to Strongarm to let him go.

"It means Letticia killed her." Just saying it still threatened to numb his mind. Maybe that was a good thing just now; it eased the feel of Strongarm's talons sliding out of his shoulder. "It means she was using you to get at me–"

"It was Teufelsman and your Aryans who used me!" Keiko kicked him this time, a gut-level blow that dropped him gagging to his knees. "They used Seed on me, Van Buren. Did you have them record that in Net, too? Give yourself a chance to watch the monkey beg for it? A souvenir for you and your haole friends to laugh at?" Her voice caught, sign of the shame behind her bitterness. "I'm a nothing, now. A Registree, a whore to anybody with a neural wand, any time they decide to make me."

She could have kicked him again. He wouldn't have cared. Wouldn't even have felt it – the pain in her words curled him into a knot at her feet had nothing to do with the physical blow. He heard her back away instead. And the cold calculating little voice at the back of his mind noted her reluctance with satisfaction.

The satisfaction ended with Strongarm's knee in his ribs. Scrambling for balance, Jezekiah saw the Lupan extend his hand to Keiko.

"No flat tooth will ever touch you again, Bird. Together we will hunt down the animals who raped you. I will bathe you in their blood before they die. Take my hand. You'll know I speak truth."

"Keik, wait!" Jezekiah lunged sideways into Strongarm's knees. It was a sign of how weak the Lupan had become that he managed to knock the man off balance. Jezekiah lurched to his feet before Strongarm recovered, careful to keep what distance he could between himself and the Lupan's talons. "I have a message for you. From your father." Slowly, he reached into his breast pocket, pulled out the note he'd lifted from the Admiral's desk and held it out.

"Admiral's got nothing to say to me." There was bitterness in her voice. But she reached for the scrap of paper.

Grandfather was faster. He snatched the note from Jezekiah's fingers, flicked it open. The dragon breath flared in his palm when he looked up. "What does this say, Van Buren?"

"Don't know. I can't read Samurai script." Jezekiah kept his hands up, grateful he did not need to fake the ignorance. The risk in that note left Jezekiah's mouth dry. He said a fervent prayer to every deity he could name that the Admiral had not ordered her to commit suicide.

"Let me see it, Grandfather?" The hand she held out was steady. Only the tremor in Keiko's voice betrayed the effort it took for her to ask.

Eyes still locked on Jezekiah, Grandfather handed her the note.

"It's just a haiku." Keiko studied the words, a frown forming as her fingers traced down the characters.

"Which says?" No threat in Grandfather's tone. It was his scowl that promised Jezekiah a slow death. "Translate for us, *keiki*. What did the great Admiral Yakamoto say?"

"Absolutely nothing." Keiko's laugh was short and bitter. "It's not even one of his own. This one's been around for centuries." She held the paper up, tracked the words with a fingertip as she translated.

A sign of blessing
The snow on the quilt
From the Pure Land

"Well, that's helpful." Strongarm snorted in disgust.

"The Samurai specialize in pretty poison." Grandfather turned the snake eyes on Keiko. "Does it have a meaning among those butchers, *keiki*?"

"Yeah. It means snow's pretty. And the Admiral's even crazier than I thought."

Keiko folded the paper back up and held it out to Grandfather. She sounded only contemptuous. But a lifetime's training let Jezekiah read the subtle tightening in the muscles around her eyes. She was lying.

She'd handed him an opening. He shot a sidelong glance at Strongarm, saw the Lupan's nose twitch. So, then. The Lupan had caught scent of the lie, too. Jezekiah edged forward, quickly, to cut Strongarm off. "Maybe, Keiko, your father was trying to tell you there's always hope. Maybe he wanted to remind you there's still beauty in the world. No matter how hopeless we feel."

She didn't even look at him. "Gob yourself, Van Buren."

"There are other worlds, Bird." Strongarm clutched his ribs. In profile his face looked as gray as his mane.

Yet something in his voice finally brought Keiko's head up, finally gave her eyes the first flicker of life through the killer's stare. "He could be right, Grandfather. You told me before Kameh didn't want to come back. And he's Registered."

She'd touched some kind of sore spot there. Grandfather Ho took the slip of paper she held out easy enough. But he made a show of searching his worn shorts for a hip pocket. The move let him hide his expression. But Jezekiah read the angry tension in the old man's shoulders. So, then. There was some ugly piece of this Kameh's story Grandfather Ho was hiding from Keiko. Long shot, but it was a chance to distract her from Strongarm. "She's got a point, Grandfather Ho. The free worlds pride themselves on not following Van Buren rules. Even a registree gets a fair chance out there." Jezekiah arched a brow at Grandfather. He made sure it looked innocent. "Why not set up a line to Kameh? Let him tell Keiko himself?"

"That is hardly necessary." Grandfather had his expression under control again when he looked up. Even so, Jezekiah felt the kill-lust in the old man's gaze. Grandfather lifted Keiko's hand in his so the twin dragons merged into a single gleaming figure. "My granddaughter needs no other world. Her place is here, among her own people, as the future *zhu* of Ho Tong."

"Why? So she can carry the weight of your crimes, old man?" Strongarm clutched his ribs with one hand. He held the other palm up, taloned fingers curled in misery.

It was Keiko who whimpered. She closed her eyes, shoulders hunching. Good. That eased some of the jealous knot in Jezekiah's chest – she was still fighting the call of Strongarm's need. But she certainly felt it. Her dragon hand curled in unconscious mimicry of Strongarm's.

Strongarm knew it, too. His mane flared, ears and eyes locking on Keiko.

"Den Lupus is yours, if you want it, Bird. You want Home World, too, just speak the word."

In horror Jezekiah watched her expression waver. Watched in jealous wonder as her eyes widened with hope, saw the trust that had fueled his dreams reawaken in her expression. He was losing her. He felt the loss close around him like black water. Felt himself drowning in it even as he watched Strongarm's psychic pull bring her soul back to life.

It was a rebirth that meant death for them all. Yet it wasn't the threat to the treaty or even Earth that made Jezekiah launch himself at Strongarm when Keiko stretched her arms out to the Lupan. It was blind, desperate jealousy. A jealousy that Strongarm should be the one to rekindle the spark in Keiko's eyes and not himself. He succeeded only in bouncing off the Lupan's forearm. But he'd bought Grandfather Ho the instant he needed.

"Not quite so fast, I think." Grandfather Ho snatched Keiko back. She collapsed against him like a puppet whose strings had been cut.

He'd managed to cut the psychic bond Strongarm had on her, too. The loss of it folded Strongarm over his knees, left the Lupan huddled in a wretched ball, massive shoulders shaking behind taloned fists. It made their situation more dire, yet it still shot a thrill of jealous joy through Jezekiah's veins.

Grandfather slipped a hand around Keiko's ribs to hold her up. He waited till Strongarm managed to lift his head, then twined his hand around hers. He jerked her hand up with his so their twin dragons spit fire across their matched palms. It was the fire that shone in Keiko's palm that kept Strongarm on his knees, not Grandfather Ho's – the acid proof that she was Ho Tong now.

Within Grandfather's grip, Keiko stirred. She shook her head, tried to shove clear. The effort made her whole body shake. She would have fallen if the old man let go. She had to struggle for focus. Jezekiah's surge of joy darkened again. She managed to get her eyes focused – yet the focus she sought was Strongarm. Broken bond or not, it needed no Heir's training to realize she felt Strongarm's misery.

No question Grandfather Ho recognized it, too. He pulled her closer, made her rest her head against his boney shoulder. Her fingers groped at the hip of her sarong. She found the pocket she wanted, slipped her fingers inside.

"Let her go, old man," Strongarm rasped through bared fangs. "Or I will give her your black heart on a stick to go with her Empress' crown."

"Oh, I will certainly let my *keiki* come to you, Lupan." Above her head, Grandfather Ho answered Strongarm's snarl with his serpentine smile. "But there is a small matter of allegiances to arrange first, no? You see the proof of my *keiki's* loyalty. The question is, will you also swear fealty to Ho Tong?"

"Alex, you can't!" Jezekiah jumped into the space between them. Jumped right back again before Strongarm's backhand swipe could cut him in two.

The move put his back to Grandfather Ho and the muscles along his spine clenched in anticipation of a needler shot. "*Think*, damn it! If you give in, he'll bring down the whole Commonwealth. You know that."

"Ask me how much I care." Strongarm elbowed him aside to extend his hand to Keiko. Cilia writhed within Strongarm's outstretched palm.

Keiko answered with her eyes. Within Grandfather's grip, she pulled something from her pocket, twisted to press her free hand against the arm Grandfather held.

At the moment, the loss embedded in that gesture was more frightening than the very likely end it meant to his life. He grabbed Strongarm's wrist, desperation overriding survival instinct. Strongarm snapped him off by reflex. The move sent him tumbling into Grandfather Ho. Jezekiah grunted as the old man's ridged knuckles caught him in the back. But the impact broke Grandfather's grip on Keiko. Bought him the moment he needed to grab her by the arms, shake her attention back to himself. "Keik, listen! Grandfather's using you, same way he used your mother."

Beneath his fingers Jezekiah felt her trembling stop. She knocked his hands off and stepped back, steady again. She flipped aside the reason contemptuously. Jezekiah recognized the silvery tube of a hypo vial. So that was what she'd been reaching for in that pocket: she'd given herself a stim shot.

Keiko rolled her head. Her eyes cleared, found focus. *Saw* him finally. He didn't care if she killed him or not. Ignoring the matched growls of the two other men, Jezekiah cupped her chin in his palms. Spoke for once straight and pure from his heart. "*Ku'u ipo*, listen to me. Grandfather is out to start another war. You know that. He's been talking about it all your life. Only there won't be any survivors this time. Is that what you want? To kill your own people?"

And she listened. His soul thrummed as her eyes locked on his. Some infinite sadness flickered in her expression. He promised himself by all the gods of her ancestors he'd make sure she never knew such sadness again. What mattered was that she didn't knock his hands away, didn't dash past him for Strongarm.

"Bird-" Strongarm's voice was barely more than a whisper, yet the agony in it made Keiko jerk as if she'd been shot.

Jezekiah tried to clutch her tighter, stop her from throwing herself at Strongarm before Grandfather Ho could pull her away from him. But she only lifted his fingers from her face almost mechanically, held onto his hand when she stepped back. His little voice warned there was something *wrong* in the way she smiled up at him, that the infinite sadness in her face masked something deeper.

"Keiki-"

She'd managed, Jezekiah realized, to put Strongarm between themselves and Grandfather Ho. Explained why Grandfather Ho hadn't intervened. He shut out the warning alarms at the back of his mind. Nothing he could do about them right now anyway. Whatever Keiko planned, his best bet was to stay out of her way.

"Do not draw this out, *keiki*." Grandfather Ho clearly wasn't willing to risk stepping into Strongarm's strike range. But there was no mistaking the danger in the old man's tone.

"I know, Grandfather." She let go of Jezekiah's hand. She reached into her pocket again as she stepped back and turned to face Strongarm. In profile, he saw her lips quiver, saw the sadness give way to a despair that matched the Lupan's, the bond between them almost palpable.

Jezekiah reached for her. She batted his hand aside mechanically, but the gesture brought her back to face him. She pulled her hand out of her pocket with effort. Only this time the slender bit of silver she pulled out was a needler. She lifted the gun as if its weight were too great for her strength. Then in one serpentine motion she whirled, dropped to one knee and fired. A tiny sun blossomed between Strongarm's eyes.

"*Keiki*, no!" Grandfather Ho struck at her gun hand. Keiko danced aside and shot again before Grandfather's kick sent her spinning.

Smoke drifted up from the tiny black spot in the Lupan's forehead. Eyes still locked on Keiko, Strongarm pitched face first onto the floor.

Grandfather Ho's explosive curse was the only sound to break the numbed silence. Instinctively, Jezekiah waited for Strongarm to rise, to bare fangs at his tormentors. But the man only lay there, taloned hands bracketing his head as if in some final obeisance. Odd, Jezekiah thought. He should feel relieved. Should feel at least some small sense of satisfaction. The sharp edge of his grief surprised him. Jezekiah shut it out. He couldn't afford grief, not now. He focused instead on Keiko. On calc'ing out ways to play the choice she'd made.

The cost of that choice showed in the way Keiko dropped to her knees beside Strongarm's body. She lifted the Lupan's head, rested her unscarred cheek against the silver-tipped ears to stroke the patchy mane. A wisp of gray smoke from the needler burn curled up between her breasts. Even now, Jezekiah felt a flash of jealousy at the sight.

"That was not the correct choice, *keiki*." Grandfather Ho's voice shook with barely controlled rage. "The dog was ours. Why kill him?"

"He was lying, Grandfather." The unshed tears in her voice ripped at Jezekiah's throat. "He never meant to obey you. I could feel it."

"Keik-"

"Shut up, Van Buren." She didn't even look at him. She had eyes only for Strongarm. She laid Strongarm down gently, ran a final mournful stroke across his head, then rose. And went to stand beside Grandfather Ho. Her expression was even harder than the old man's. The killer stare was back.

The alarms at the back of Jezekiah's mind intensified. "I'm sorry you were forced to such a choice, Keik. Let's not waste Strongarm's life. We still have a Lupan battle fleet in-bound. If I don't get back to the Manor, then we all die."

"Oh, we'll get to the Manor, all right." Keiko answered him with a cobra's smile that mirrored Grandfather's. The sight sent a chill down Jezekiah's back.

"You won't get in. Not without me." He lifted his Ring hand.

Grandfather's smile slid into a sneer. "Unfortunately for you we already have an operative at your Manor. A far more malleable operative. And one whose command of your *haole* NetMind will provide us all the protection we need."

Letticia. Only a lifetime's training kept Jezekiah's expression from revealing the blow. Not that it mattered. Grandfather Ho knew the value of what he said. He focused on Keiko instead, keeping the desperation out of his voice. "You can't trust Letticia. Look what she's done to you-"

"Your sister's just the same bitch she's always been, Van Buren. But she's still useful." Keiko lifted the needler. "You, on the other hand, are replaceable. Same as Alex was."

"Then why-"

"Didn't I kill you just now?" Keiko slid around Grandfather. She stopped in front of Jezekiah, smiled Grandfather's own serpentine smile at him. "Because I'm going to kill you the way you planned on killing me. Slowly."

She kicked up so fast he barely saw the blur of her motion. Then her heel slammed into the Jezekiah's temple. And the world went black.

LII

It was cold when Jezekiah came to. He lifted a cautious eyelid. Got nothing but ghost pain whispering behind his eyes and a darkness black as the grave. The chill draft on his face was musty…dank as the grave, too. The horror in that thought popped his eyes full open. Still nothing. He tried to rub away the sudden cold sweat stinging his eyes. Metal bit his wrist. A quick tug told him the reason: he was manacled to a wall, hands locked above his head.

At least that answered the 'where' question. He would be in a Tong dungeon somewhere beneath Grandfather's headquarters. Odd, though, that the Ring didn't provide light. He could feel its insistent pulse against the barrier of his will. He wiggled fingers of his Ring hand, recognized the feel of leather. So, then. Someone had taken time to put a leather pouch over his hand before binding him to the wall. Obviously Grandfather wanted him to enjoy the full impact of total darkness. Which meant Grandfather Ho still needed him alive. Which meant in turn he still had a chance to get Keiko and get off Earth before Kaitin and his battle fleet arrived. Assuming, of course, Grandfather Ho hadn't simply left him here to die slowly.

Beside him, feet shuffled in the darkness. "Keik?" Foolish question. More foolish wish.

"Hate to disappoint you, your lordship. It's just me."

"Kip?" Hope flared, faded beneath the instant warning at the back of his mind. Grandfather wouldn't put him in with Kip just for company. There would be ears in these walls. Very attentive ears. So much for doing any real catch up. He'd have to keep the conversation public. "What happened to you? Are you all right?"

"What happened was that goddamned Ta'an caught me at my place." Cloth whispered against stone as Kip shrugged. "Far as all right goes – Guess I'm 'bout as right as can be, considerin' I'm chained to this goddamned wall." He shifted his weight and metal clinked. "Uh, pardon the observation, your lordship, but *damn* you stink!"

Jezekiah rubbed his head against his chained arm, realized hair and arm alike were sticky with blood. He tried to scratch some of the stink out of his scalp on the rough stone of the wall. The effort revealed, painfully, a number of bruises he hadn't known he'd acquired. "Look on the bright side: at least it proves you're still alive."

"You don't mind, your lordship, that ain't sayin' much." In the darkness Kip sneezed. "Don't suppose you got any miracles up your sleeve?"

"At this point I barely have the sleeve. I take it you're out of Net?"

"Huh. Think I'd still be here if I was sync'd?" A rattle, and Kip's breath hissed in pain. "Been Net-blind since I left the Manor. Figure the little bitch's got me blocked. Only what she don't know – ow!"

Jezekiah gave thanks through the fire in his wrists that his captors had pinned him within kicking distance. If Kip had found a way around Letticia's block, he emphatically did not want Grandfather Ho to know. Fortunately, Kip caught on fast. The SecType was already swearing lustily at his manacles.

"You know Mother's dead?" It was hard to ask it. Harder still to make himself believe, even now.

"Shit." Kip put a world of sorrow in the word. His silence proved loudly enough that he'd figured the cause.

"Strongarm, too."

"*How?*" The disbelief in Kip's voice would have been comic under other circumstances.

"Keiko shot him."

"*Mote?*"

"I saw her. Needler. Right between the eyes."

"Needler, huh?" Kip sounded uncommonly thoughtful. "Well, hell."

"Hell is quite likely to become the operant term." He could only hope Kip caught the hint to change subjects. Whatever the big man was thinking, he didn't want to explore it here. Wiser to bore the unseen ears with banalities. With luck, maybe even keep the anguish at bay a while longer.

Somewhere in the darkness beyond, stone grated. A stone door slid back, carving a slice of gray light out of the darkness. A wash of warm air flooded in and instinct lifted Jezekiah's face to it. Past the silver sheen of Kip's comm implant he made out the hazy silhouette of Grandfather Ho.

The old man lifted an arm. The glow of the dragon's breath created a golden halo around him that pushed the shadows back. All except one.

A sliver of darkness oozed into the dragon's halo. The Ta'an stretched in answer to Grandfather's unspoken question. The movement sent a gray-gold shimmer down his ebony skin, lit a feral yellow glow in his feline eyes. "The Sec Captain has found a way around the Van Buren girl's Net block. Van

Buren thinks he has kept it secret." The killer hesitated, cat eyes narrowing. "Is it true your girl shot the Lupan? With a needler?"

"My granddaughter is disposing of his body even now." Grandfather lifted his dragon arm. Against the darkness the dragon seemed to rear its head. "Are you questioning my actions?"

"Merely to understand." The Ta'an salaamed fluidly.

"Good. Tell my granddaughter to join me when she is finished. Then take your rest. Your skills will be needed again soon enough." Grandfather turned to watch the Ta'an slink out.

"A worthy demonstration of honor among thieves." Jezekiah twisted around the bite of his shackles to watch the assassin leave.

"So speaks the scion of the robber clan Van Buren." Grandfather Ho stepped deeper into the cell, using his dragon arm to light his way. "We of the Tong are hardly thieves. Murderers, certainly. But not thieves. It is not thievery to reclaim that which is rightfully one's own."

"Earth was never yours, Grandfather. Any more than it was ours."

"Allow me to disagree. Earth is the *natural* home of humanity. Your man-made Types offend the gods." His dark eyes glittered red in the dragon's gleam. "I shall cleanse the world of your man-made abominations. Return Earth to her rightful children. The children of the gods, not man."

"You dreamin' yourself one *lolo* pipe dream, old man." Kip tugged at a manacle and grunted. "Even in Tong you ain't got enough naturals to out-breed the rest of us."

"All things in time." The serene madness in the old man's smile scared Jezekiah worse than any threat could have done. Still, it offered an opening.

"Unfortunately, time is the one thing you lack. There's a Lupan battle fleet in-bound. With Kaitin ibn Bengal at its head. Given that Keiko just killed one of the only two men who could stop it, I suggest you may wish to reconsider your methodology."

"Meaning I should spare you, of course." Grandfather stopped his hand up just short of cradling Jezekiah's cheek. "Why should I believe you, O scion of liars?"

Jezekiah winced against the heat of the dragon's breath. "Because Strongarm himself told me so. He also told me Kaitin has orders from the Lupan Parliament to make Earth an example for the Commonwealth." He answered the old man's serpentine gaze with a lifted brow. "I don't expect Kaitin intends any of us to survive the lesson."

"Ah. And how would you avert our destruction?"

"By delivering the treaty. Bad as Letticia is, we can still use her to complete the marriage contract. Kaitin will deal with me. I can buy time to find another Lupan noble to seal the treaty. You can't."

"You seem to have forgotten my own sweet *keiki*." Grandfather inched his fiery palm closer to Jezekiah's cheek.

"Strongarm was the only Lupan who'd accept Keiko and you know it. Far as they're concerned she's just another mixed-Type monkey." He kept his expression innocent, fed Grandfather the visual clues that said he believed the lie. And prayed Grandfather would put the fear-sweat he felt dewing his forehead down to the acid heat of the tattoo.

"Then they are in for a surprise. On several counts." Jezekiah swallowed a sigh of relief as the old man stepped back and lowered his hand. "I thank you for the warning. I shall alert your little sister that she will have to endure a marriage after all."

"Letticia won't listen to you." Habit kept Jezekiah's voice level. His tongue had gone stone dry.

"Quite the contrary. She has been listening to me for quite some time." The old man actually chuckled. "She is, of course, as yet unaware of the fact. But it is time to disabuse her of the illusion in any case."

Pieces of the puzzle snapped into place. The answers hurt worse than the metal biting his wrists. "So you had her bring that Ta'an in to kill Mother after all."

Odd. The statement seemed to amuse the old man. "Oh, that was very much the long-term plan. As it turned out, however, the natural course of events rendered it unnecessary."

Beyond the old man Jezekiah saw another figure ripple the gray shaft of light from the doorway. He strained against his rings, making sure he kept Grandfather's eyes on himself. "You seem to be fond of unpleasant necessities for others, old man. Did you tell Letticia to have Keiko Registered, too?"

What looked like genuine regret dimmed the old man's expression. "Alas, we are driven by necessity these days."

"What 'necessity' made you turn Keiko over to Teufelsman? What did you do, old man? Stand there and *watch* him?"

"Watch *what*?" Kip's Sec implant shone briefly as he tried to focus it on Jezekiah. Then the answer registered. "God *damn* you to hell!" He kicked out. His long legs forced Grandfather to leap back.

"There were six of them, actually." Something – regret? – touched Grandfather's expression. "It was the reason I made sure Teufelsman had Seed. My *keiki* would have forced them to kill her, otherwise."

"You set her up? For a gang rape?" Kip lashed out with both feet this time. He missed and his back hit the wall with a thud. "You goddamned, gobbing son of a bitch! She's your *granddaughter*, goddamn you!"

"And my heir."

"Why, Tutukane?" Keiko's cry echoed from the gray light of the doorway.

Grandfather Ho whirled, the dragon leaving a streak of gold in the darkness behind it. He threw only one brief, sidelong glance over his shoulder, but Jezekiah felt the hatred in it.

Still, the ruse had worked. Keiko stepped farther into the dungeon. A string of Tong stars glittered across her chest in the shaft of gray light, bright contrast to the long, dark barrel of her laser rifle. The reflected light raised blue-green-yellow sparkles from the beads of sweat glistening her forehead. Sign that stim shot she'd taken was starting to wear off.

Jezekiah twisted to face her. "You know why, Keik. Same reason he betrayed your mother. Same reason he betrayed the Admiral -"

Grandfather's knuckles cut him off. Jezekiah felt a tooth crack through the stars popping across his vision. Worth it, though. The anguish in her expression said his barb had struck home.

"It was a most unpleasant necessity, *keiki*." The dragon's acid light etched shadow scales across Grandfather Ho's sallow skin. "I have tried all your life to bind you to us with love. But an old man's love was not strong enough. It was necessary to teach you to hate."

"You didn't have to shame me to do that!"

"Yes, he did, Keik. You're too honest for his use. Too loyal. You'd never betray someone who loved you-"

This time Grandfather Ho drove his knuckles into Jezekiah's gut. Retching, Jezekiah folded over the blow. He buried his face against his arm to stop himself from vomiting. Wet warmth smeared his face where it touched his arm. At that, it didn't hurt as much as the self-loathing beneath it.

"The shame belongs to the *haole*, not you." Jezekiah couldn't straighten enough to see the old man. But he heard the subtle touch of defensiveness in Grandfather Ho's tone. "You are the last of your line, Keiko Kaahumana Ho. The last full-blooded descendent of *Tutu* Pele."

"You left out 'Yakamoto', old man." Jezekiah swallowed bile. He tried to focus on Keiko, but the stars popping across his field of vision blotted out her expression. "You left out 'Samurai'. And loyalty. And love."

Silence. He wrapped his hands around his chains to brace himself as Keiko stepped up to him. She stopped, rested her head against the raised barrel of her rifle to consider him. The power light on her heavy pacifier raised a green shimmer on her bare shoulder. "And what makes you any different, Van Buren? You going tell me now you haven't used me to get what you want? You going tell me how much you love me now?"

"Wouldn't do me any good, would it? Especially since it's true." Which it was. That was the worst of it. He barely felt her back hand, though it finished the job of breaking the tooth Grandfather Ho had cracked. It didn't hurt a fraction as much as the truth. "Not that it matters. We're all dead if we don't stop Kaitin and that battle fleet."

"Liar." She lifted his chin with a dragon-tongued finger. Surprisingly, the acid in the tattoo didn't burn as Jezekiah expected.

"Grandfather has all that worked out and you know it. Those Lupan battle ships have to start monitoring your precious NetMind long before they get here. And once they touch sync, your little sister will take control of their ships' brains."

"Shit on a shell." Beside Jezekiah Kip's chains rattled as the big man shifted his weight. "Mote, you ain't gonna-"

"Enough!" She rapped the word out sharp as any Samurai. It was the way the dragon on her arm flared to life inches from his face that shut Kip up. His silver comm implant caught the dragon's red breath and wrapped it through his matted curls.

She stepped back, held her arm so the tong stars she wore sent a serpentine reflection slithering between her breasts.

"And what will you do with these two, *keiki*?" There was satisfaction in Grandfather Ho's tone now. A gloating counterpoint to Jezekiah's despair.

"Kill them, of course." She smiled up at the old man, matching him death-stare for death-stare.

"A wise decision." Grandfather lifted his arm to let Jezekiah see his smile turn beatific. "Do not kill Van Buren just yet, though. He is quite right: we do need him to reach the Manor. His little sister seems to have acquired a desperate need to present him to the *haoles'* Commonwealth Council. But I shall certainly oblige you where the good captain is concerned."

"No, *Tutukane*. I have to kill him myself."

"Are you sure, *keiki*? It will be a bitter test for you."

"I know. But it's a test I have to take. I'll never be certain of myself otherwise. And neither will you." Once again, *something* flickered across her face. It was vanished too fast for Jezekiah to read it. Her eyes were empty again when they flicked to Kip. It was only then Jezekiah realized he'd lost her. He felt the hope die even before she laid her dragon hand in Grandfather Ho's.

LIII

Jezekiah hadn't been chained long enough for the blood to feed fire down his veins, yet he swallowed a groan when the Samoans tugged his arms down from the wall rings. It would be far worse for Kip; he didn't dare let himself imagine the kind of pain Kip was enduring. He saw proof of it enough in the way Kip's face had gone gray when the Samoans dragged them into the light of the corridor.

Keiko had the Samoans bundle Jezekiah and Kip into a set of full-body restraining rings. The rings' field drove tiny cruel needles into the bloody mementos the manacles had left circling his wrists. The Samoans threw them face down and helpless into the flat bed back of an island hopper and ambled off. Jezekiah accepted the manhandling in silence. No point getting his jaw broken now; words were the only weapon he had left. The back window of the flat bed's cab was open. Once they were air-borne he could work his way up to it, talk to Keiko. He still had a shot if he could talk.

Once they were loaded Keiko slid into the pilot's seat and lifted off. She banked southward, sending him rolling into Kip's solid bulk. He lay trapped there, wrapped in the sweaty-sweet mix of man and aftershave, listening to the rapid thud of Kip's heart. Judging from the way the wind buffeted the flat bed Jezekiah guessed she was running ocean side of the Koolau mountains down toward Diamond Head. Easy guess where she was headed. His stomach tried to rebel at the memory of what was waiting there. Interesting, though. The fastest way to the Manor would be inland, straight across Oahu's central plain.

Jezekiah rolled away from Kip when she leveled the ship out and inch-wormed his way toward the hopper's cab. It was a slow, painful process. By the time he wormed himself up the cool metal back of the cab he could see the crooked cone of Mokolii Island through the wooden slats of the flat bed's sides. An upturned wingtip flared orange near the peak, marking the Aryan's scattered wreckage. Out on the ocean horizon the first gleam of the rising sun gilded crimson clouds with molten gold. Earth's last dawn. Fitting, his little voice whispered, that it should feature Van Buren colors. *His* colors.

His fault. The Protector's Ring throbbed against his side. Reminding him of the price Mother had already paid for his egotistical stupidity. Reminding him of the price eight hundred fifty million other souls on Earth would pay for the mistake of trusting him. He had maybe three hours till the Council vote. Maybe an hour more before Kaitin ibn Bengal dropped into system with Strongarm's battle fleet and rendered the Council's vote irrelevant. Unless he could turn Keiko now.

Jezekiah chinned himself up to the cab's open back window. Keiko didn't bother turning to see him. Simply turned her dragon-blazed arm up to rest it atop the cab's seat. The dragon's breath raised a glow in her cupped palm like a red echo of the rising sun. He was close enough to feel its heat against his cheek. "You know why Grandfather Ho told put this bag over the Ring, Keik? Did he trust you enough to tell you that?"

For answer Keiko banked the hopper, hard. The motion sent Jezekiah and Kip both tumbling into the wooden slats on the downward side. Five hundred feet below first sunlight spattered cherry glitter across the waters of Kaneohe Bay. She flipped them back an instant shy of death, left them gasping in a tangled pile as she eased back toward Diamond Head.

"Your lordship?" It took Kip another few gasps to catch enough breath to go on. "Just shut up a while, wouldja? I wanna be dead before they make me shark food."

Made two of them. Only Jezekiah no longer had a choice. Above the windscreen he spotted Diamond Head in the distance. Ignoring Kip's grunted objection he wormed back to the cab window, chinned himself up to his knees. "Listen to me, Keik. Mother's dead. I'm the Protector now. I'm the only one who can stop Kaitin. Not Letticia. Not Grandfather Ho."

"That's not what Grandfather thinks." She put on a burst of speed that knocked him backward into Kip. Kept the flatbed pitched at an angle that ensured he didn't get back up, too.

Diamond Head loomed above them when Keiko brought the hopper down in a walled clearing. No question where they were. Jezekiah felt Kip shudder at his back as the mingled smells of gardenia and death registered. The stink raised memories that dewed Jezekiah's forehead with cold sweat. Keiko could not have been prepared for the carnage littering her father's yard. But if it bothered her, she had it under control by the time she lowered the flat bed gate.

"Rise'n shine, Captain." She leaned across the gate to grab Marsden by the feet. The battered truck bobbed on its repulse field as the SecType's weight slid off. Keiko dumped him face down in a clean patch of dew-damp grass, then clambered up to haul Jezekiah out.

She dropped Jezekiah face down beside the hopper. His body yearned to just lie where she left him, nose buried in the soft, cleansing scent of fresh grass. He inch-wormed to his knees before the yearning darkened to unconsciousness. He wriggled around to let his back drop against the hopper's side, grateful for the insistent bump of its idling repulse field. In the yard beyond, the fading fairy lights bobbed above the Aryans' shattered bodies. Their dancing luminance traced lacy patterns on the fly-encrusted corpses littering the garden. The flies' happy buzz drowned out even the hum of the truck's repulse field.

"Shit on a shell." Kip squirmed his way up to a semi-squat. His face was ashen, though his expression said the reason was the stench. He angled himself toward Jezekiah as much as the restraining rings allowed. "Those fools musta pissed the Admiral off one *nui* lot. Just tell me 'fore I die that these're the Aryans that got Mote."

"Don't know." In shame Jezekiah realized that he'd never thought to wonder.

"They're not." Keiko ambled out into the yard to kick flies off a loose head. She cocked her head, considering it. "That's not the Admiral's work, either. Strike angles are all wrong."

"It's Strongarm's work."

"Shut it, Van Buren!"

"We were looking for you. We just weren't fast enough."

"Told you to shut it." Keiko flipped a Tong star from its sheath, twirled it through her fingers. The star spun silver through the golden gleam in her palm. But the pain in her voice begged for hope.

"There's no time, Keik. Grandfather doesn't believe the Lupans will destroy Earth. He's too locked up in his fantasy. But *you* know they will."

"Told you to shut it." She snapped her wrist.

The Tong star thunked into the hopper beside his face. Jezekiah dodged by instinct. Bad move – he lost balance, slid sideways down the flatbed's field. He hit the grass face first, beside a thick puddle of dead Aryan. Worth it, though. She hadn't intended to hit him. She was buying herself thinking time. All he had to do now was find a way to guide her thoughts to the necessary end.

"Leave it, your lordship." Kip was still braced against the hopper's side. He lifted his head and the silver crescent of his comm implant shot a bright reflection of early sun through his matted curls. "If Mote went and killed Strongarm like you say, then old man Ho's got his hook into her too deep for her to care about folk anymore." He shifted his weight against the restraining rings with a grunt. "You wanna tell me Mote – old man Ho have you kill Kamehameha No Name, too?"

"Kameh's not dead. He's shipped off world is all. Grandfather sent him out to the rim."

"Hell he did." His expression was taut with misery when he looked up. "Shore patrol fished a registree outta the water up above Kahena Point. Called me in to ID the body." This time he did shudder. The hopper shook with him. "Sonuvabitches didn't even bother to kill the boy first. They just cut him. And dumped him in the ocean for the sharks to finish."

"Name one reason why I should believe you." But her voice was husky, a telltale of tears she would not shed.

It was a chance. Jezekiah retched filth, wormed back up onto his knees. "When'd Kip ever lie to you, Keik? When'd he ever do anything but try to keep you safe?"

"Told you to shut it!" She wasn't suppressing tears now. It was fury. Fury at the lies in which the men who claimed to love her had trapped her. Fury at herself for the decision she had to make.

"Leave it, your lordship." Kip set his jaw in a stubborn line and locked his gaze forward. "Now, you gonna kill me, Mote, you do it and get it over with. I got no use for a fool who turns on her friends. Just appreciate you make it quick. Once between the eyes, you don't mind."

"Yeah." She strode around the hopper to the driver's cab. When she returned, she had the laser rifle slung across her shoulder. She stopped in front of Kip, tapped the power on.

Desperate, Jezekiah threw himself across Kip's body. She shoved him aside with her foot. Kicked Kip face down onto the grass. She set the beam to narrow focus. Fired twice.

Kip jerked spasmodically with each shot.

It took the big man the better part of a minute before he moved. This time, the rings came loose.

He pushed himself to his knees, braced himself with one hand against the hopper and leaned there, gasping. The garden lights sparkled on the beads of sweat along his dark brow, danced across the silver crescent lining his curls. "Dammit, Mote." He paused, trying to swallow. "Ya could'a warned me."

It took Keiko only seconds to kick Jezekiah onto his face and burn the rings off. She was leaning on the rifle's muzzle by the time he wiped splotches of Aryan off his face with a sleeve and lurched to his feet. Beneath the sweat, her face was white. Beads of sweat sparkled on her forehead in the early light.

"Lean on me, Keik—" She toppled as Jezekiah slipped a hand under her elbow. For a moment, he let himself forget everything except the feel of her face against his chest, her body in his arms.

"Van Buren?"

He felt her voice in the vibration of his skin. "Hmmm?"

"Damn, you get one *nui* big stink." She sneezed emphatically and pushed herself clear. This time all Jezekiah could do was break her fall. He dropped with her, taking her weight on his arms.

Kip was beside her on the instant. He laid a palm against her cheek, his hand big enough to nearly hide her face. "Mote, you got a medi-kit in that cab?" His expression bespoke a worry he kept out of his voice.

"Under the driver's seat." Her voice was barely a whisper. She rolled her head, massaged the back of her neck with a shaking hand.

Kip stumbled around the flat bed. He returned with a tattered blue and white box in hand. He knelt beside her. His expression darkened when he popped the lid. "Dammit, Mote, you ain't got nothin' in here but stim shots."

"What you think I been going on, eh?" Keiko sounded annoyed. The tremble Jezekiah felt in her body betrayed the weakness behind it.

"Yuh-huh." Kip kept the kit out of her reach. "This stuff kill you, you stay on it too long."

"No loss. 'Sides, Grandfather kill me any way soon as he figures out I let you two go." She pushed herself higher on Jezekiah's knee, reached for one of the injection cylinders lining the kit. Her hand shook too much to manage it. "Now we got to wiki it. Give me one of those, would you, Captain? I'm good for a dose or two still."

She reached for a hypo. Jezekiah blocked her hand. "Not yet." He hated the suspicions his little voice whispered, hated himself for listening to it. "So why did you let us go?"

"Dammit, your lordship, Mote just saved our lives."

"I know." He could not permit himself to imagine, yet, what he'd have to do if her answer didn't ring true.

Kip opened his lips to object, shut it down himself. He wouldn't like the implications any more than Jezekiah. But he'd realize the question had to be asked.

"No hu-hu." Keiko shoved herself out of Jezekiah's arms. If she noticed Kip move the medi-kit out of her reach, she chose to ignore it. She swiped at the sweat, bit back a yip when her fingers brushed the swollen skin surrounding the black stud at her temple. The pain seemed to help clear her head. "You can thank the Admiral for part of it, Van Buren."

"The haiku." Well, that fit at least. "Somehow I didn't think the Admiral would leave a note just commenting on the landscape."

"You thought right. That old haiku was written by Kobayashi Issa about a thousand years ago. Samurai use it to say 'have faith'. Admiral being the Admiral, he could only mean to have faith in you."

"Huh." Kip laid a fatherly hand on her neck, massaging those of her pains he could reach.

"And the other part?"

"Kameh." She caught Kip's hand in hers, the gesture half grateful, half pleading. "They really kill him that way, Captain?"

"'Fraid so, Mote. Wish it was a lie, but it's not."

"Knew he was dead when Grandfather told me he didn't want to come back." She rested her cheek against Kip's hand, eyes drooping in sorrow. It was full dawn now and the sunlight deepened the dark lines of exhaustion under her eyes when she looked up. "Just never thought Grandfather would do him that way. Kameh never betrayed him."

"But he did, Keik. He gave you somebody else to love. Grandfather was simply eliminating the competition." Jezekiah wished he could shut out the knowledge that in Grandfather's place he would have done the same. Still, what mattered was that her answers checked. "Now we better get moving. We'll all be dead if we don't get to the Manor."

"Yeah." She reached for the medi-kit.

"No." Kip moved the box farther out of her reach. "Ain't nothin' gonna happen his lordship and me can't handle. You need to rest."

"Can't. You never make it to the Manor without me." Keiko leaned her head into the crook of Jezekiah's arm. She was still holding Kip's hand. Yet her expression went neutral. Catching Kip off guard she yanked him down.

A needler beam frizzed the air where Kip's head had been. The SecType rolled, flipping the medi-kit at Jezekiah as he dropped. Needler fire raised a string of bright, bubbling patches in the grass behind him.

Jezekiah wrapped himself around Keiko. His shoulder blades tensed in expectation but the shot didn't come. He pushed Keiko and the medi-kit against the hopper's field and scrambled to his feet.

No one. Around the garden not even a branch twitched. Keeping his hands out from his side, Jezekiah stepped away from the hopper. Only dented grass hinted where Kip had been. Kip and, he noted, Keiko's laser rifle.

"Assassin!" No need to raise his voice. The Ta'an would be listening. If he kept talking, he could cover whatever noise Kip made. He just hoped the Ta'an would not be able to resist the chance to play with his victims. "You've picked the losing side. Kill us and you'll never get off Earth alive. You must have realized that by now. Save yourself. Join us!"

"Ah, but I was not sent to kill you." The assassin's voice came from behind him. Jezekiah whirled to see a sliver of darkness separate itself from the shadows of the bushes.

"For which you should be grateful, Jezekiah Van Buren." Dainty white fangs flashed in the Ta'an's feline smile. Yellow cat eyes darted past Jezekiah. "I was sent to ensure the girl completed her task."

"She simply recognized that Grandfather Ho can't win." Keeping his hands out, Jezekiah sidled away from the hopper, hoping to draw the assassin's gaze with him. "Surely you've realized that by now."

"Unfortunately, unlike you onlies we Ta'an honor our contracts." The Ta'an somersaulted backward an instant before a laser bolt caramelized the ground where he'd stood. He dropped, swiveling to fire at the bolt's source.

"Dammit, Van Buren!" Something hard and heavy hit Jezekiah between the shoulder blades.

The impact sent him sprawling. Keiko bounced off his back, knocking out what little breath her feet had left him. A string of silver specks flashed over his head riding an arc of red-gold light. Miniature stars erupted in the air above him where needler fire caught the throwing stars. Not enough of them, though. The assassin yowled.

Jezekiah pushed his nose out of the grass to see Keiko leap into an airborne roll. She fired a last Tong star at a pool of darkness. Firefly needler pulses spat and the star evaporated in a silver burst. The Ta'an rolled an instant before Jezekiah heard the heavy thump of Kip's laser rifle. Earth sparked, bubbled where the laser bolt struck but the Ta'an was already clear. His answering shot back-tracked the bolt. Jezekiah heard Kip bellow. Bushes crashed beneath a falling body. Then silence. The Ta'an rolled to his feet, needler already targeting Keiko.

Jezekiah catapulted himself off the grass. He didn't see the Ta'an turn, just felt the hot iron bite of needler fire drill his shoulder. He hit the Ta'an in the knees, wrapped his arms around the killer's legs. He twisted so the next shot seared along his back. Fire scorched his shoulders. He answered by sinking his teeth into the back of the assassin's thigh.

Sharp claws added tracks of his own blood to the matted gore in his hair. Jezekiah bit harder, anchoring himself teeth-first against the assassin's effort to pull his head back. Claws raked his cheek, aiming for his eyes. Somewhere above the claws he heard the sickening crunch of bone. Beneath him the Ta'an bucked. The bucking dwindled to a spasm. Then the spasms faded and the killer lay still.

Jezekiah jerked spasmodically himself as new hands tugged his teeth out of the Ta'an's bloodied thigh.

"Okay, Van Buren, you can let go now." It was Keiko's voice, sounding like she was torn between amusement and the urge to hit him herself. At the moment, he wouldn't have cared if she had. He probably couldn't have felt another kick in the ribs anyway.

He dragged himself away from the Ta'an's body to see Keiko wiping gore off her foot. Morning sun raised a fevered glitter in her eyes, turned the stim-sweat dewing her forehead to diamond dust. She lifted a foot, decided it was clean, then stretched a helping hand down to him – her untattooed hand, fortunately. Pride demanded he ignore it. His body told his pride to gob itself. He let her help him rise. Then wrapped his arms around her and pulled her close. The feel of her answering embrace wiped away the aches in his body and soul. For one magical moment he allowed himself to just hold her, allowed himself one perfect moment before the demanding throb of the Protector's Ring beat its way back into his consciousness.

He kissed her hair softly. "We've got to get to the Manor. Better find Kip-" He couldn't make himself say 'body'.

"Yuh-huh. Only thing you need to find, your lordship, is a way outta here."

Jezekiah whirled, feeling fresh cuts on his lips split open under the size of his grin.

Marsden trudged around the nose of the hopper. Leaves stuck at ludicrous angles to his tight curls and a long crater darkened the silver gleam of his comm implant. But he was moving under his own power. He took in the Ta'an's body with a grunt of satisfaction, shifted the laser rifle he carried to his other shoulder. Its power light added a green trim to the comm implant. He started to cock his head, aborted the gesture with a grunt of disgust and poked the hopper with the rifle butt instead. "Don't know 'bout you, but I sure as hell don't want to go up against the kind of fire power we're gonna face around the Manor in this thing."

"No hu-hu. Admiral's skimmer is operational." Keiko pulled out of Jezekiah's embrace. She ran a hand across her eyes. Swallowed a yip when her finger tips brushed the dark swell of the stud in her temple. She closed her eyes against a rush of pain. For a moment the exhaustion showed through the artificial energy of the stim high.

Above her head, Jezekiah saw Kip's frown go grim. "You better let us take it from here, Mote. You going to crash hard when that stuff wears off."

"Don't you worry about me. I got enough stim sticks on me to make it through."

"Keik-" Jezekiah pulled her closer

She snapped her arms free, rested her plain hand against his cheek and smiled up at him. "Listen to me, Van Buren. You're Earth's *Protector*. Once this is all over, you're going to regret all this love talk."

"Like hell I will!" He grabbed her by the shoulders and shook. "Listen to me, dammit. You're all I've got left. I need you, Keik. I need you with me, now and forever."

"Least till you get to the Manor, eh?"

"If I'd wanted the Protectorship, Keik, we wouldn't be in this mess. I don't. All I want is my freedom. And you." She stayed stiff and unyielding in his hands. "I'm not asking you to believe me now. Just promise me you'll stay with me, Keik. Always."

She shrugged his hands off, refusing to meet his eyes. The evasion cut him deeper than the Ta'an's claws. "I'll stay."

"For life."

"For life, then." She still wouldn't look at him. "You want me, you've got me, for as long as you say."

"Yuh-huh. And *I* say we damned well better get our asses outta here."

It was only when Keiko peered around Jezekiah's shoulder that he realized Kip's voice had come from the landing pad section of the yard. Turning, he saw Kip squatting at the edge of the garden. The man still looked disgusted.

A wind shift drove the putrid-sweet smell of death and gardenias up Jezekiah's nose. The flies checked him out of their own accord. Motioning Keiko to follow, Jezekiah stepped around a fly-encrusted blob and trudged over to join Kip.

Ocean breeze pushed the flies and death stink away when they rounded the house. The garden broadened out into a landing pad here, giving them a worm's eye view of Diamond Head's blunt peak beyond. Tall stands of bamboo lined the garden wall creating a soft green offset to the gray concrete. The Admiral's skimmer squatted in the center of the pad. It was still in Diamond Head's shadow yet its domed gray roof and stubby wings seemed to give off a glow of their own.

Kip rose when they reached him. Swinging the rifle onto his shoulder he paced the length of the machine. He kept a good five feet away from the ship itself, only ran fingertips across the air. Even so, blue lightening marked his hand's trail. He reached the shuttle's stern, turned to fix Keiko with a disgusted scowl. "Only your father would put up a battle shield at his own house."

"No hu-hu. That skimmer's got a real Samurai attitude. You pull rank on it and it'll drop its pants for you."

"'Cept I can't sync in to pull it." He tapped the scarred remnant of his comm implant for emphasis. "Good thing the little bitch already had me locked out. Shock probably would'a killed me otherwise."

"Oh, well. Back door it is, then."

"To a battle shield?" Jezekiah pulled her closer, as if his touch could meld her soul to his. Make her forget Strongarm.

Keiko shrugged him off, wrinkled her nose for emphasis. "Samurai always got a back door, Van Buren. You just got to be willing to die to use it."

"Damn it to hell, woman! For *life*, remember?"

"Yeah, well, didn't say it'd be a long life, did I?"

Jezekiah grabbed her by the arms and shook. "You are not going to die. I love you, Keiko Kaahumana Yakamoto Ho. I am not giving you up. Not tonight, not tomorrow, not ever. *We* are going to live. We are going to put a stop to this war. Now. Together."

"Not if you want to get into that shuttle."

"Now we are gonna cut this dyin' talk." Using the rifle barrel, Kip nudged her a step farther from the shuttle.

"Not going to talk, Captain. Going to overload the shield."

"Using yourself? Hell you are." Jezekiah grabbed for her. He stopped a breath shy of an acid burn when she snapped up her dragon hand. Even against the early sun the dragon's breath filled her palm with a golden glow.

"Now listen you two. We don't have time to argue." She swung her hand over the door's control panel close enough to raise blue warning flashes. "Concentrated mass plus energy can blow one of these shields. Captain, you set your rifle to tight beam. Three shots, tandem. Right here, soon's I hit the screens. That gives us about a one second gap in the shield." She barely glanced at Jezekiah, but he felt her haunted look in his gut anyway. "Van Buren, you follow my body through the gap. Get your Ring hand onto the door's sync patch before the shields reset. That'll shut the shields down. Ring overrides everything in Net."

"If you want to suicide, you're going to have to take me with you." He held his hands out from his sides – peace sign, not trying to touch her. Just enough to bring the Ring into the sunlight. Enough to make her avert her eyes from the glare of the miniature sun the Ring spun around his finger while he edged between her and the skimmer. Then he spun and slapped the Ring against the barge's shield.

What felt like a full-body back hand kicked him off his feet. Jezekiah hit the wall back of the hover pad. He bounced off, landed face down on concrete. Someplace in the distant back of his mind his little voice groaned gratitude the Admiral had planted bamboo along the wall instead of bougainvillea.

Rough hands jerked him on to his back, lifted his head and shoulders off the ground. He recognized the soft curve of Keiko's breast against his face. Felt wonderful. Until she slapped him. Hard. "You wen gone lolo? What you think you do, eh?"

"Trying to save your fool life, that's what I was doing – Ow!" Her second slap knocked breath back into him. It also woke a litany of pains he had managed to forget he had. "Damn it, you said the Ring would give me an override!"

"You're still alive, aren't you?" At least she didn't hit him again.

"Think he's all right now, Mote." Strong hands pulled him upright. Jezekiah caught a whiff of sweat mixed with the last traces of Kip's aftershave. "Now, we gonna end this dyin' talk once and for all."

The bamboo's fine green leaves blocked Jezekiah's line of sight but he heard Kip trudge across the concrete pad. He wrapped his arms around Keiko and settled, for one precious moment, to just feel her warmth and pretend she loved him.

"You want mass?" Kip's voice called from the yard. "Well, we got mass." The big man's footsteps thudded back. He grunted and something heavy thudded on the ground near Jezekiah's feet.

A sudden upwash of death stink made Jezekiah and Keiko skip apart, gagging in unison. Half of a dead Aryan gaped up at him, mouth still open in a final scream, eyes hidden beneath a coating of black flies.

"If one little girl's got mass enough to blow that shield, then a squad of Aryans ought to do the trick even better." Kip tossed the Aryan's bottom half and legs down a moment later. "Always figured the damned snowballs'd have to be good for something."

LIV

The sun was full up by the time they lifted out of the garden and cleared Diamond Head. They'd lost time in setting up a manual override. The plan would only work with Keiko in the master's seat but the damned Samurai ShipMind was too pigheaded to grant control to a registree ID. Jezekiah willed his pulse to slow, forced panic down. The Council would be in session by now. It would take the Family time to recap the charges, work through the inevitable familial bickering. With luck, he still had maybe an hour before the actual vote.

Beneath the skimmer's wings sun streaked the waves along Waikiki, pointing a rippling golden finger toward the high bluff beyond. The golden ripple blossomed where it touched Manor, swept up into an opaline arc above the building.

"Shit on a shell. Battle shields." Kip was supposed to be playing dead on the floor of the passenger compartment. Instead he knelt behind Jezekiah, scowling over his shoulder. "You think those Lupans're already in-bound?"

"Yes." Jezekiah's stomach tried to rise in fear. He clenched muscles to force it down.

"Long range screens're clear. Somebody's spotted Grandfather's people most likely." Keiko kept her eyes fixed ahead. Exhaustion showed in her profile and Jezekiah leaned over on impulse to kiss her hair. She didn't look at him, but her lips quirked in a half-smile. He'd have felt happier if she hadn't rolled her neck.

"Thought your sister was gonna let Grandfather Ho in. Think she changed her mind?"

Jezekiah felt Kip's scowl on his back. He sat back obediently, grinning into the SecType's disapproval. "Not likely. More likely she forgot to tell Sec the plan." Which raised a possibility that broadened his grin. "Or your Sec folk decided to forget she'd told them."

"You wanna guess who did the forgettin'?" Kip clapped a hand on Jezekiah's shoulder. It was a happy gesture, but the pressure made Jezekiah wince. "Mote, take this thing round back of the Manor, will ya? I got me an idea."

"No hu-hu." She banked inland, keeping low over the trees.

"Why the delivery dock?" Jezekiah started to twist around to ask Kip directly. Bone and muscles protested together and he rethought it, quickly.

"Anybody coming at the Manor from inland's gonna come straight at the docking platform. If Grandfather's doing what I think he is, then that's where my people're gonna be." Kip nearly rubbed his hands in anticipation. "Got a hand-patch sync link back there, too. If I can sync in there, I can get us in past even the goddamned snowballs. Give that little bitch a surprise she ain't lookin' for."

"If not?"

"Then you just try to live long enough to make sure I got boy-flowers on my casket."

Far in the distance, silver bolts streaked skyward from the military base near Pearl. In the master's seat Keiko rolled her head, looking as if her neck hurt. "Well, that tells us where the Admiral went. Samurai just scrambled."

So, then. The Lupans must have already made system.

A sun burst skittered across the barge's forward shields. Jezekiah clung to his safety harness as the barge dropped a couple hundred vertical feet. Behind him, Kip's sharp curse ended in a jangle of harness straps. And a desperately determined gurgle.

An armored skimmer screamed past overhead. The glimpse Jezekiah caught of its underbelly flashed the dragon insignia of Ho Tong. "'Bout time he showed up." Keiko actually seemed to relax. "Grandfather get *nui* mad folk go running on island time."

"When did Ho Tong acquire armored vehicles?"

"Always had 'em, far as I know." Keiko threw Jezekiah a sidelong smirk. "They just don't use sync. Mech only. So all your fancy haole systems could never see 'em."

Ahead, the skimmer turned on a wingtip for a repeat run, sunlight running like liquid gold down its length.

"Only one?" Kip twisted in his seat searching for a view screen that wasn't there.

"His partner's back there." Keiko arched her neck. "I can feel him."

Beyond, the Tong skimmer swung around the Manor, headed back toward them. "Keik-"

"Shut it, Van Buren. I got to think."

She made sure he did. Jezekiah and Kip yelped together as she flipped the skimmer belly up. Flying upside down, she flipped open the master's storage bin, fished out a dainty metal filament atop a simple wooden pad and locked it into a depression atop the bin. Rapidly, she tapped fingers against the metal.

The Tong skimmer slammed past, rocking the skimmer in its wake. But it didn't fire. Instead the metal filament clacked a staccato response. Keiko answered in kind. The skimmer waggled wings and banked away seaward. An instant later its hidden partner shot past after it.

"Never thought I'd be so glad to be hungry," Kip grumbled from the back. His voice sounded queasy.

"Sorry, Captain." Keiko righted the skimmer and headed for the jungle behind the Manor. "I wen tell him we took stabilizer damage. Nobody but Ho Tong remembers that old tapper code, so I figured he'd take my word for it." She flashed Kip a tired grin over her shoulder. "Couldn't risk letting him see you."

Staccato flashes of laser fire greeted them when the barge crested the bluff above Waikiki. Bursts of firefly lights popped across the Manor's shields.

"Knew it!" Kip beat a victory rhythm on his safety harness. "Lepper's got the sonsuvbitches locked out!"

"Question now is how we get in ourselves." Jezekiah scowled at the Manor's docking platform taking shape ahead. Through the burr of the shields it looked like Kip's folk had built a makeshift barricade of storage bins. Shadows lurked behind the bins. At his shoulder Kip's exultation drained out in a long sigh. Too many of the shadows behind the hulks were not moving.

"That's not Tong work." Kip wedged shoulders into the space between the seats for a broader view of the jungle. "Those troops got nothin' that'd pierce a battle shield."

"Which means your people are fighting an inside battle."

"Snowballs." Kip spat the word. He pulled back, knelt scowling past Jezekiah's shoulder thoughtfully.

"Almost certainly." Which meant Letticia. Jezekiah felt his skin flush, realized he was letting the fury show. He tamped it down, locked his working mask in place.

"So what we do now?" Keiko glanced over from her controls. "Grandfather knows we're here. I don't land this thing quick he going to figure what happened."

"Can you get me into Lepper's line of sight? Ought to be…right about there." Kip pointed a dark finger toward the stairs leading up to the docking platform. "If she's done what she ought, then even that goddamn little bitch Letticia can't take those shields down without workin' on it." He chuckled grimly. "But I can get us in."

"Good." Jezekiah twisted as much as the safety harness and stiffened muscles allowed. Enough light from the cockpit filtered back to let him see the drying blood smeared across Kip's clothes. The man could certainly pass for a corpse at quick glance. Good thing they were all inured to the smell now; the stink in the cabin must be eye-watering. Certainly it was strong enough to ensure nobody with a nose was going to probe too close. "Keik, land us on the road as close to the dock stairs as you can get. This is what we're going to do."

LV

A milky way of star bursts popped across the barge's shields even before Keiko settled it on the roadway. The fire was all coming from the jungle side – Ho Tong fire. Above the trees, armored skimmers and battered island hoppers swooped over and around the Manor's shield dome like dragon flies. Too many of the skimmers had been rigged with laser cannon. Fat splashes of light backlit the Manor where laser blasts hit the shields on the far side.

Jezekiah's pulse spiked as one flare swept a circlet of hot light around the opaline dome. His breath caught expectantly, waited for answering fire. There was none. There was no covering fire from the SecTypes on the docking platform, either. Jezekiah studied the dock while Keiko made a show of undoing his harness. At the far end the body of a SecType officer rested upright against the wall, the shattered remnants of one hand still cupped above the sync patch. A nubbly red spray smeared the red alert lights within the patch. What was left of her head left a long red stain on the wall beyond. The back of Jezekiah's mind noted the angle of the killing shot. So, then. Her killer had been someone on the dock itself.

Which could only be Letticia's work. But *why*? Grandfather Ho knew Mother was dead. Letticia should have anticipated he'd try to take advantage of Mother's loss to storm the manor. Even if she didn't, Sec most certainly would have. Yet she had the Aryans firing at Sec's back, as if she *wanted* the old man to gain entry. He thought how close Grandfather Ho had come to managing it and shuddered.

"You ready, Van Buren?" Keiko finished rolling the harness straps into a truss around Jezekiah's wrists. "Better test that now. You won't get a second chance once we're out there." She gave him a second to make sure he could snap his wrists free from the truss then pulled him up and popped the skimmer's hatch.

The scent of gardenias and salt air rushed in as the door slid back. Somehow he'd expected to smell smoke and death stink. The air's sweet fragrance seemed out of place.

Keiko shoved Jezekiah out first, giving him an instant to orient himself. She'd set the skimmer down almost at the end of the platform. Its bulk hid the bottom of the stairs from any jungle watchers. On the platform above, he caught a glimpse of a dark face peering down at him. The face jerked back as a cluster of star bursts spattered the shield above it.

A hulking Samoan wearing the yellow-edged sarong of Ho Tong ambled up. He shoved the muzzle of his laser rifle against Jezekiah's nose by way of greeting.

"*Heia*, you go leave him be." Keiko hopped out of the barge, the other end of the makeshift leash wrapped around her free hand. "I'm delivering him to *Tutukane*." She lifted her dragon hand, palm out and the Samoan went wide-eyed. He swept the rifle back across his shoulder like a child's toy and stepped away to give her room to lead Jezekiah past him. Glancing back, Jezekiah saw the fellow lean through the hatch to check the interior. The Samoan skipped back in a hurry, rubbing his nose.

A tug on his wrists warned Jezekiah to keep eyes front. He ran a mental guesstimate of the number of troops the Tong had hidden from the number of laser rifles targeting his midriff as they crunched across the pale gravel path. From the looks of it the old man must have pulled just about every op the Tong had. Praise Kip and whoever'd had got those shields up. There would have been no survivors if this horde had made it inside.

They clambered through a break in the bougainvillea bushes to the higher ground beyond. They reached the tight circle of homies around Grandfather Ho and Keiko yanked Jezekiah into a bow. "*Heia, Tutukane.* Here he is."

Doubled over the strap Jezekiah could only see a pair of calloused brown feet. But there was no mistaking the fiery palm the old man placed beneath his chin. Or the heat radiating up from it.

"*Mai'kai no.*" The satisfied purr in Grandfather Ho's voice would have done Kaitin justice. "Well done, *keiki*. And the good captain?"

"Body's in the skimmer, Grandfather. Shot him myself."

A grunt at Jezekiah's back confirmed both the statement and the presence of the Samoan. Grandfather Ho straightened Jezekiah with a fingertip. He looked past him, nodded. Jezekiah realized the Samoan had left more from the subtle easing of tension in Keiko's profile than any sound the man made. He forced back the thought of death treading so quietly behind him, forced himself to smile at Grandfather Ho. "So, then. I see you've discovered the consequences of trusting my little sister."

"It was hardly an unexpected development." A skimmer swooped overhead low enough to make them all duck. It trailed smoke that smelled of hot metal and burnt fuel. The craft wobbled across the tree tops, dropped over the bluff and down toward Waikiki. It was out of sight in an instant. But not before

Jezekiah recognized the orchid crest of the Great Family Van Buren on its belly.

Jezekiah's heart lurched at the sight. Word of the pending Lupan attack must have made it through the diplomatic grapevine before Letticia locked down NetMind. Diplomats would be running for Niihau port as fast as their major domos could vaporize their files. Only if Letticia had control of NetMind, there wasn't much chance they'd make it. Somebody's ambassador must have tried to navigate the route on manual. Looked like the poor fool hadn't even made if off Oahu.

From below the bluff metal shrieked across rock. The boom of its impact rolled over the trees on a dusting of black smoke. Swearing in Hawaiian, Grandfather Ho waved in the direction the skimmer had taken. The Samoan who had escorted them echoed the gesture to a pair of relatives. The burly trio vanished down the jungled slope, rifles slung across their broad brown backs. Jezekiah breathed a silent prayer that the wayward ambassador had managed to die in the crash. It would be easier on him than Grandfather Ho's methods.

He put the thought of another innocent's blood out of mind and made as much of a show of dusting his pants off as the straps around his wrists allowed. He waited till Grandfather Ho's sneer found him, then arched a brow. "Now, why don't we talk about how to get you what you really want?"

"Your presence grants me that. Your sister will lower the shield once you sync in." He reached into a pocket, pulled out a portable scanner. "To her misfortune, her precious sync scan will not be able to show her that you bring company." He lifted his chin at Keiko. "Bring him."

Too soon. He had to buy Kip time. Jezekiah heaved back on his leash. Keiko landed hard against him. For a moment he thought he'd pulled her off balance. Then her knuckles found his kidney and all thought ended in vision-popping pain. Some part of him mind realized she'd managed to keep him on his feet, keep his body blocking Grandfather's line of sight. He reminded himself to feel grateful. When he'd got his stomach out of his throat.

"You disappoint me, Jezekiah Van Buren." Grandfather Ho sounded almost amused. "I expected greater creativity from one of your abilities."

"Then it's mutual." Would have sounded braver if he hadn't wheezed. "I expected you to know your own advantage. Letticia is nothing more than Streiker's tool." He lifted his hands as much as Keiko and the leash allowed. The Ring filled the space between Grandfather and himself with a hard, throbbing light.

Somewhere behind them a homie shouted. Jezekiah twisted to see Kip sprinting for the stairs to the docking platform. Laser fire boiled the ground around him, spattered across the battle shield ahead.

With a curse, Grandfather waved troops after him. Jezekiah locked his hands into a fist and swung at Grandfather's chin. He felt his knuckles crack against bone. But not hard enough.

The old man rolled with the blow. He kicked and his calloused heel caught Jezekiah in the thigh. Muscles spasming, Jezekiah dropped. He rolled by instinct. Grandfather's heel crunched gravel where his shoulder had been.

Some homie's shout preempted Grandfather's follow up blow. Like the old man, Jezekiah tracked the line of the homies' pointing fingers.

Down on the gravel path a good half dozen homies were closing in on Kip's back. On the platform itself a SecType woman was fairly dancing in dread. She yelled something, aimed what looked like a portable scanner at the stairs. Kip dove for the shield a hair's breadth ahead of the lead homie. The shield rippled when Kip hit it. An breath later blue lightning crackled as the lead homie hit. Ocean breeze scattered the black powder that had been his body across his team mates.

Snarling, Grandfather Ho swung round, bringing his dragon hand to bear on Jezekiah's face.

"Grandfather, no!" Keiko threw herself into the old man as fire spat from the dragon's mouth. She blocked his fire with fire of her own.

"So your father's blood tells at last." Grandfather Ho recoiled from her, his face contorted in a feral snarl. "He has made you as much of a traitor to your people as himself."

"Admiral's not a traitor, Grandfather. He told me what you did to him. And to my mother." Keiko kept herself between Jezekiah and Grandfather, hands weaving a golden arabesque against the dark backdrop of the jungle. Around them, the circle of men fell back in silence.

Jezekiah pushed himself to his feet to face Grandfather Ho. "Why don't you tell her the truth for once?" He knew how to project his voice, make himself heard at distance without shouting. He put all the strength he had into the effort now. He needed them all to hear him now. It was the only chance they had. "Why don't you tell your granddaughter how you betrayed her mother? Tell her how you betrayed her father! How you betrayed Kamehameha No Name."

"Listen to him!" Grandfather Ho raised dragon arm and voice together. "Listen to the liar, the scion of a house of liars!"

"Yes, listen!" A lifetime's training lifted Jezekiah's voice so it filled the jungle. He lifted his hands, too. The Ring glared so bright it cast new shadows among the trees. He made sure the Tong fighters could see it, see the symbol of the one power they knew to be greater than Ho Tong. He pitched his voice carefully, enticing belief. "Remember the stories your mothers only dared whisper. Listen to the truth at last!"

"Tell *me* the truth, Grandfather!" Keiko extended her hands to Grandfather

Ho – palms up. The dragon's breath spun the air above her hand into a tiny sun. "Tell me why you killed Kamehmeha No-Name!"

"He was dangerous!"

"He was my *friend!*" Her voice broke. "Why would you kill him?"

"Because he was a distraction!"

Around them the silence rippled outward. The gun fire died away, leaving only the snap of the wind against the tall palms. And the rustle of underbrush as brown, red-skirted men stepped out of the trees, laser rifles dangling at their sides. Green power lights twinkled amid the darker greens of the jungle.

Too late Grandfather Ho recognized the sound of people wondering. Too late he recognized the trap Jezekiah had set for him. The understanding pulled his lips back from his teeth.

"That is your truth!" Jezekiah lifted his voice to the troops rustling in through the trees. He allowed a hint of sorrow to edge his tone. "Your *zhu* cares nothing for you! You are just tools to use. And discard."

A murmur of voices rose, a human whisper within the wind brushing the trees. Jezekiah felt the pulse of that whisper. Caught it and shaped it to his needs. "Tell me! Tell me why you live in poverty. Why, when Ho Tong controls the Seed trade on a dozen worlds? Tell me! Tell me where all the treasure goes!"

Silence. Throughout the trees, bare feet shuffled underbrush. Good. So he'd got them thinking. Grandfather Ho might re-form them, but not in time to stop him. They would wonder before they fired now.

Grandfather Ho realized it, too. The old man shifted his attention to his followers. Gave Jezekiah a chance. He caught Keiko's eye, lifted a brow to alert her to run for it. With Keiko covering his back, he inched through the break in the bougainvillea bushes and down the short slope toward the Manor. He was almost even with the skimmer when something hard hit him in the shoulder. He tumbled across the skimmer's nose as something bright streaked past his eyes.

The Tong star vanished in a silver arc. "Run!" Keiko urged him to it with a shove.

From the platform Jezekiah heard Kip shout. A glance gave him his bearings. He slid off the far side of the hood. And made the mistake of looking back.

He'd been right about the homies hesitating now. A squad of them had followed him but their rifles hung at their sides, their expressions closed. Doubting. Grandfather Ho faced Keiko alone. A fresh throwing star glinted between the fingers of his upraised hand. He wove, cobra-style, seeking an opening. Keiko blocked him with her body. The Tong fighters simply formed a half-circle. Solemn men and women in red skirts and sarongs leaned on their laser rifles. Watching. Waiting to see who they would follow.

A sweep of wind carried him Keiko's voice. She spoke in the old language. Jezekiah could not follow all the words. But her tone pleaded for reason. Grandfather had no such concern. She took the next star he threw in her palm. But she never stopped talking. Whatever she was saying, it was working. Around the half-circle homies began to nod. Hands weaving, she blocked Grandfather. Took another star in her palm. Took the next in the back of her arm.

Run! his little voice hissed. She was buying him a chance. He owed it to her to use it! Only he couldn't. He could not let her buy his life with her death. He threw himself back at Keiko as Grandfather flung the last star. Knowing even as he lunged that he could not save her.

Something else did. Something round and dark shot into the star's path. The star's bright blades thudded into it. She had already slapped the thing aside by the time Jezekiah's mind recognized the object as a human head. He slid to a halt at Keiko's side before he recognized it as the head of the Samoan who'd led the hunting party after the crippled skimmer.

Beside him, he heard Keiko's sigh of relief. He back-tracked the head's trajectory. Saw the circle of men there scramble for safety, rifles forgotten. Felt the jealous burn behind his eyes even before a grinning Strongarm stalked past the tail of the barge.

Dappled sunlight deepened the burn spot between Strongarm's eyes. Almost lazily he swung the massive battle axe he carried off his shoulder. The grin peeled back into a full-fanged snarl. He snapped the axe blade up under his arm, bringing the long handle to bear. Talons clicked into triggers.

And Grandfather Ho ran. A streak of blinding blue vaporized the underbrush where he'd stood. No underbrush rustle betrayed his path. Instead a broken line of brown fingers pointed the way he'd taken. Keiko plucked the stars from her arm. She stuck reddened tips into her sarong above her breast and started after him.

Jezekiah pulled her back. "Leave him."

"He'll only come back -"

"I know. We'll deal with him then." He wrapped his arms around her. The terrified knot in his heart eased when she leaned her head against his chest, accepting the support of his strength. But he read her longing in the way she twisted to keep Strongarm in sight.

He saw her longing reflected in Strongarm's face as the Lupan stepped up to join them. His eyes drank Keiko in as if he could absorb her by vision alone. Beneath his amber eyes the skin had darkened into gray circles, the cheeks had gone hollow. Bald patches showed through his mane. Its silvery sheen gone gray as well, making him look old. He held his hand out to Keiko, palm up, the cilia in it quivering.

Jezekiah edged his body between them. "Sorry, Alex. But Keik's given me her word. She's mine as long as I want her. I'm afraid that's going to be for life."

"Bird?" He planted the blade of his battle axe on the ground and leaned on it. No mistaking, now, that he needed its support.

"Keiko's already given me her word." Jezekiah calculated his tone to trigger her Samurai training, let the Admiral's teaching stop her from thinking. From *feeling*. He wasn't her choice. He could only hope the various types of stink he'd acquired would prevent Strongarm from scenting the lie.

The knowledge it was only her father's training that kept her in his arms cut him deeper than any assassin's claws. He knew what she felt for Strongarm, knew it because it was what he felt for her. The fear he would lose her overrode all conscious thought.

"He's right, Alex. I promised him." Her voice was barely a whisper, but it shook with the effort it took her not to break free.

"She's made her choice, my friend." He spoke quickly, before she could take the hand Strongarm still offered. Before Strongarm's Touch healed the scars on Keiko's soul, before Strongarm's strength made her whole again. Before he was forced to accept that *Strongarm* was the one who'd truly won Keiko's once and forever love.

"Challenge." Strongarm no longer had the strength to roar, but the danger was back and real.

"She's already decided, Alex." Jezekiah kept his tone understanding, persuasive. He kept his grip on Keiko, too. "If you love Keik at all, sign the treaty. Otherwise we're all dead, Keik included. Is that what you want?"

"She won't die. Kaitin has his instructions. He'll get Bird off world first." He bared fangs at Jezekiah, ears flat. "You, too, Van Buren, if you're what Bird wants. No worries, either. Whatever I have is Bird's. Kaitin will make sure she's set up right."

So he could have his dream. Have it all: Keiko, freedom, riches. All he had to do was let his world die. "You know Keiko would never accept those terms. Any more than I could."

The danger drained out of Strongarm. He let his hand slip to his side. The weight of it seemed to pull his head down with it. "You should've aimed for the throat, Bird. It's not armored." He did not need to add that death would have hurt less, too.

"Wasn't trying to kill you. Just needed Grandfather to think I had." She let Jezekiah hold on to her. Only the twitch in her muscles betrayed the truth. Every fiber in her body strained toward Strongarm.

Didn't matter, Jezekiah told himself. He'd make her happy. He'd make it up to her once this was over. She'd let him, once Strongarm was dead.

She pushed away from him. Frowned up past him, one hand reaching for the back of her neck. Strongarm tracked her line of sight, ragged mane rising.

For a horrified instant Jezekiah thought he'd lost her anyway.

Then the world erupted around them.

The Lupan fighters came in ahead of their sound waves, a pack of dark wedges spitting fire.

Vision vanished in a sunburst glare as energy blasted off the Manor's shields. The answering shock wave slammed Jezekiah to the ground. Heat seared his back, triggered new explosions in the jungle beyond. He tried to gulp air. Got only vacuum until the backwash rolled over and shoved breath back into him. Then thought vanished, too, as the trailing sound wave ripped past.

"Keik!" She was face down in the gravel, dragon arm outstretched. Dragging air back into his lungs, Jezekiah lurched upright. He half scrambled, half crawled to lift Keiko. Felt his breath stop again until she shuddered awake in his arms.

"Recon." Strongarm dragged himself up to join them. Leaning on the gray metal pole of his axe he tracked the attackers' path with an approving ear. "Good thing it's only scouts. Otherwise, we'd already be dead."

"Right now that doesn't sound so bad." Keiko pushed herself clear of Jezekiah to fumble at the hip of her sarong.

"You're hurt, Bird." Strongarm's eyes followed her. He kept his hands away from her, but the axe shook with the effort.

"No hu-hu." Keiko blinked him into frowning focus. The way her lips tightened bespoke how she felt his need. Felt it, and was bound by her father's honor to deny it.

Jezekiah couldn't let himself think of that now. "We better get going before those scouts come back." He bent to help Keiko up. Backed off at her scowl. She'd hissed another stim shot into her arm before he realized what she was after.

Her eyes were too bright, her skin already flushed when she tossed the empty hypo aside.

"Damn it, woman! Are you trying to suicide?" Jezekiah grabbed at her arms.

She slapped him aside, chin setting in defiance. "That's my last shot, Van Buren. I got an hour, maybe two at the outside. After that, I'm out for the count. So if you got any ideas, you better tell 'em to me now."

Strongarm *uhfed* softly. "Ignore the fool, Bird. If he's what you want, then I will get you into the Manor." He lifted a lip at Jezekiah in contempt. "After that you're on your own."

LVI

Kip cleared the platform shield for them himself. Jezekiah heard it buzz back into life behind Keiko as soon as her bare heel cleared the bottom step of the stairs. Jezekiah swallowed the jealous flash as she turned to lift her rifle in salute to Strongarm one last time. On the grounds side of the shield Strongarm waited only long enough to make sure Keiko reached the platform before leading a squad of homies toward the Manor's main entrance.

Kip shoved Jezekiah into a crouch the instant his head topped the stairs. On the platform a few uniformed SecTypes crouched on the dock-side of the impromptu crate barrier. Far too many more were scattered, shattered, across the docking platform. Taking in the set-up Jezekiah swore softly. They were facing *inward*, toward the half-open doors of the Manor's storage bay. Oddly, the survivors knelt among mounds of piled stones.

The implications triggered quick-calcs. The calcs vanished in a flash of star-popping pain. His knees hit concrete an instant before a laser bolt spat against the shield behind him. He tried to rise. Keiko kneed him back down, leaned on him for good measure. She'd swiped a rifle from a homie on their way up. She snapped off an answering shot now. Somewhere near the entrance doors a man screamed. The laser fire stopped.

He spotted the green light of a charged laser rifle near the hip of a pair of shapely legs. The rest of what had been a woman SecType was simply gone. Jezekiah wriggled Keiko's knee off his back and stretched stomach down to grab for it.

"Hey! Ya wanna suicide, stay clear of me." At the next crate over, a green-eyed, broken-nosed SecType woman flattened backward to reach for a stone from the pile at her side.

"Clams, Lepper." Kip slid up to lay a welcoming hand on Jezekiah's shoulder. The big man had enough aches of his own to keep the touch light. "Somebody bollixed the guns, your lordship."

Jezekiah shoved the rifle back in disgust.

LVII

Two of the surviving Aryans formed up front and back of Keiko and Jezekiah. Their pale suits were blood-stained and torn. Heat aura wavered the air wavered around their rifles' muzzles. Interesting that neither of them poked those blistering muzzles into his back. An Aryan confident in his power would never have missed such an opportunity to indulge his penchant for abuse. Even more interesting was the fact neither Aryan objected to Keiko accompanying him.

Jezekiah hid his satisfaction beneath a suitably sour expression. Easy bet they'd already had a dose or two of Letticia's temper. Odds were the Aryans wanted Keiko along to serve as scapegoat in case Letticia proved more mercurial than usual. So much the better. It meant at least two of Letticia's noddies were already hedging their bets.

It was a long trek from the delivery dock to the Hall of Justice. Jezekiah felt the tingle of scan at every doorway but the corridors themselves were empty. At this hour, the hallways should be in full madcap bustle. The absence of harried Admin ops drove home again the enormity of Mother's loss. He stamped the anguish out of his mind. He would deal with that later, as he would deal with Grandfather Ho and Letticia later. Assuming he had a later. What mattered right now was that Letticia still wanted him alive.

Or *someone* in the Family did, rather. Lush had gone too far to risk keeping him alive on her own. She knew she'd lost Strongarm, too; what she'd done to Keiko proved that. He had to cut that line of thought off. The rage it engendered threatened to black out his whole string of probabilities. So, odds were it was one of the Council who wanted him alive and present. The question was why.

The doorway scans turned painfully challenging when they reached the Hall of Justice wing. Jezekiah heard Keiko's gasp beside him. A sidelong glance showed him she'd gone white and his gut lurched. Damn, he hadn't thought how painful a scan would be through a registree's studs.

One more thing he couldn't afford to think of right now. He focused instead on calc'ing out angles and probabilities. Strongarm and the homies should have no trouble reaching the Hall. Kip had sent the remaining SecTypes ahead to make sure they got through the shields. All he himself had to do was buy Kip time to reach Sec HQ and sync in. After that it was Kip against Letticia, in NetMind.

Jezekiah willed down a shudder. That was a fear he most certainly could not afford. He concentrated on the implications of the still-empty hallways to distract himself. More and more the emptiness felt wrong. The Manor was on high alert: Samurai and Sec guards should be crawling all over these corridors. Yet the whole damned building seemed deserted. Staff couldn't have fled, not with the shields up. Which meant the hundreds of admin ops who should have been on duty were instead raising terrified pandemonium in Sec HQ's underground caverns. He could only hope Kip and Lepper managed to get through before it was too late to matter.

Tellingly, the guard posts at the Hall of Justice were empty, too. Only the red eye of the Hall's major domo glared above the Hall's great carved doors as it should, signaling that the Council was in session. Jezekiah felt the scan even before the lead Aryan pressed his hand to the sync patch. The tingle faded. The doors started to swing open. They shuddered, suddenly, and shut again. Looked as if they were having second thoughts – either that, or somebody was interfering with their Net feed. Jezekiah hid a burst of hope. So, then. Maybe Kip had made it to Sec HQ already after all.

The two Aryans traded sidelong glances. Sign enough, there, that they'd reached the third thoughts stage about their choice of loyalties. So much the better. Jezekiah leaned between them. His little voice snickered at the way they skipped aside at his stink. "You two wait out here. Your services won't be required in the Hall." No need to do more than whisper. These two were already looking for an excuse to dodge.

They proved it an instant later by stepping back into guard positions when the doors finally swung open. He lifted a brow at Keiko and let her lead him through. The doors closed behind them and the floor vanished in the vast nothingness of space. Automatically, he lined up on the burnished path arrowing across the void to the defendant's podium. He noted sidelong that Keiko stayed at his side, ignoring the psychological safety of the path. The sight gave him a rush of pride.

Around the Hall the stars of each Commonwealth world were dimmed to mere watermark glows behind their respective Protectors, lending his ruling relatives a singularly inappropriate aura of saintliness. Jezekiah cast a surreptitious glance across the holo'd faces, found the telltale expression of relief where he'd hoped for it.

The defendant Jezekiah Van Buren is now present. The sonorous baritone of the Hall's major domo boomed when they reached the defendant's podium.

"Well, it took you long enough!" After the major domo's boom, Letticia's echoing whine sounded childish and petty. It took Jezekiah a moment to recognize the cause of the echo. She was using audio. Squinting past the other suns, Jezekiah made out Letticia's figure occupying Mother's sync chair on the Protector's podium. She must have loaded on every gem she owned; she managed to out-glitter even the dimmed halo of Earth's own sun. Alone among the Family, she had a guard at her side: a white-blond, white-suited Aryan, one hand ensconced in a portable link. Teufelsman.

He caught a whiff of burning cloth, saw a wisp of smoke curl past Keiko's shoulder. He shifted balance, forcing her death stare off Teufelsman. "Not yet, Keik."

He wished the death stare had softened when she turned it on him. Still, she listened. She shifted the strap of his leash to her unmarked hand, pinched out the red edges where the dragon's breath had touched the material.

No time for heartache now. Expression locked on neutral, Jezekiah offered his kinsfolk as much of a general salaam as well as his false leashed allowed. He made sure the gesture gave them all the full benefit of the Ring's yellow glare. He couldn't sync in while he was leashed so he had to read their responses in pantomime. But that was enough to tell him just how far the situation had deteriorated.

Even dimmed, Pandar's blue giant backdrop lent Octavian's holo a glare powerful enough to give the feathery pink centerpiece of his table a brilliant white edge. The glare wasn't quite strong enough, though, to hide the danger in Octavian's expression.

Johann Petrovich was in full armor, his helmet sitting ready at his elbow. Above the grim casing of his armor, the swath of silvery white hair bordering JP's mohawk had widened; gray shadows underscored the ice blue of his eyes. Sign enough, there, that Strongarm's first attack wave must have reached Streiker.

Tellingly, it was only Letticia whose eyes widened in surprise when Jezekiah tugged his hands free of the leash. Around the Hall, his reigning cousins traded comments he could not hear. Another bit of Letticia's childishness. She'd turned the audio off. Locking his working mask into place, Jezekiah saluted Streiker and Pandar in turn, then slipped his free hand into the defendant's link.

Nothing. Damn.

"Trouble?" Keiko murmured. She stood close beside him, arms folded, death stare still locked on Teufelsman.

"Sync's dead." *Damn* Letticia and her childish games! There was no hope for any of them if she could force him to silence.

"I can take her out from here," Keiko lifted an elbow enough to let him see the throwing star hidden between her fingers.

"No." The Hall's defenses would vaporize the star the second she threw it. Then vaporize both of them for good measure. No point in suiciding just yet. On the dais above, Teufelsman stepped forward. Beside him, Jezekiah felt Keiko come on guard.

"Stay where you are." He'd spoken to Keiko, but Teufelsman opted to listen, too. Jezekiah waited until the Aryan backed smoothly into place at Letticia's side, then lifted his brows at the Council.

JP snapped something at Letticia. Clearly ordering her to let him sync in. So, then. Alliances had shifted. With a moue of annoyance, Letticia wrinkled her nose at Jezekiah.

He made a show of sync'ing back in. This time the familiar falling sensation of sync link answered. Only the greeting he'd expected wasn't there.

Kip? He willed down the dread. Without Kip to run interference he had no way of knowing whether he was even hearing or seeing the same things as the Council members.

Are you quite settled, brother dear? Within sync Letticia sounded almost regal. She allowed Jezekiah a nominal moment to orient himself then shifted her attention to the Council.

Quite. So, then. He was on his own. Jezekiah shut down emotion, everything but the immediate present.

Aunts, Uncles, Cousins – Letticia paused, giving for her relatives a moment to acknowledge her. It was a child's courtesy, not a Protector's and the Family treated it as such. They ignored her.

Milords! Jezekiah felt the frisson of Letticia's hatred through sync as the Hall went quiet. *This Council was called to assess the charge of treason against my lady* – sorrow welled up. He shoved it out of mind, but not before sync washed it across the stars. *Against my late mother and myself. I submit to you my lady mother's assassination serves as de facto proof of her innocence. I therefore suggest that all charges against her be stricken from the Council records.*

Around the Hall, the stars whispered as members of the Council traded notes.

Silence! JP snapped and the star-flung whispers went quiet. *I see no reason to deny the request. I move the charges be stricken.*

A murmur of approval answered. JP nodded, then ran armored fingers across his console. *The request is granted. Let the record show all charges of treason against the late Protector Muriel Van Buren have been expunged.*

So, then. The Lupans must already have breached Streiker's outlying defenses. No wonder JP was feeling cooperative. He could never have expected the Lupans to break through Streiker's defenses so fast. Which meant he would be looking for a way to backtrack without losing face, now. Jezekiah kept the satisfaction hidden. The question was whether he could swing enough

Council members to clear both his name and the treaty before Kaitin ibn Bengal broke through the Admiral's defense forces as well. He had his working smile in place when the Streikern Protector finished. *Uncle, you charged us with treason on the claim that a Lupan-Earth trade treaty would threaten Streiker's security. You have taken drastic steps to ensure the treaty would not be signed. Even to the point of provoking a war.*

That's a lie! JP never did any such thing! On Mother's podium Letticia pounded her free fist on the chair's arm rest. *Have you all forgotten that Jezekiah's the one who started all this?*

That earned her an answering murmur of commentary. Good. Maybe they'd keep Letticia distracted. Jezekiah let the back of his mind form Kip's image, hoping.

Heavens, brother dear, are you still looking for your tame syncmeister? The answer wormed into his consciousness through the primal burrows of his mind, deep below the level of sync itself. *Surely you didn't think that pathetic old man could get past* me, *did you?*

The sync connect was so deep Jezekiah felt the wormy slither when she shifted her focus back up to standard sync level. It left the very inside of his mind feeling slimy.

Something poked Jezekiah's side sharp and hard. The pain shocked his focus back to the real world. And the realization he'd forgotten Keiko was there. He blinked down into her scowl.

"That sister of yours just pointed at me." Keiko threw Letticia a scowl. "What's she saying?"

"Nothing. She was pointing at me." He heard a whisper ripple around the Hall. Realized too late sync had broadcast the exchange.

"Oh, by all means, do let the little monkey listen in." They both jumped when Letticia's voice boomed out. On audio she sounded childish and petty. "Even a murdering Tong assassin has the right to hear the charges against her."

On the far side of the Hall Octavian leaned back deeper into the shadows of his cushions, leaving only the white-blue flicker of his eyes visible. Still, he put his sync on audio as well. "Kudos on the fair play and all that, my dear. But the question of treason remains. I submit our dear cousin Jezekiah has taken his own drastic steps to promote his treaty at our expense. As my late ambassador could attest."

On the opposite side of the Hall, JP lifted his sneer from his console. "We're here to assess treason charges, Octavian, not collateral damages."

"I'd say the proof of my innocence is banging on your front door. Unless I miss my guess, you've got your war now." Jezekiah let his smile speak innuendo to the rest of the Council. "Admit it, Uncle. The Lupans jumped right past your defenses. You cannot save yourselves much less the Commonwealth."

JP started to say something. His image wavered again. His holo went silent.

"See for yourselves." Jezekiah swept his Ring hand wide, drawing a glaring yellow trail around the assembled Council. He fixed his gaze on Octavian. "The treaty Strongarm and I worked out offered a profit to all of us. All you've got now is a war. And in case you'd forgotten, Lupans fight to annihilation."

He gave that a beat. Let the audio feed their sync links the sound of the faint rumble rolling up the corridor outside. The way the Council went silent told him they'd heard. And were drawing the correct conclusions. "I may still be able to stop JP's war from spreading," he said into their silence. "I may even be able to save Streiker. Otherwise – where's the profit in annihilation, Octavian?"

The rumble outside intensified as it grew closer. A glance at the Protector's podium showed him Teufelsman had heard it. Only Letticia, absorbed in Net, seemed deaf. Judging from the fresh sheen of sweat on her forehead she had discovered Kip wasn't as easy to get rid of as she'd anticipated.

Jezekiah tamped down a surge of joy. With luck Kip would keep her occupied long enough for him to finish this. "Johann Petrovich!" He waited till JP finished a harried sweep of orders. "Tell us: do you still believe you can protect the Commonwealth?"

Whatever JP intended to say was cut off. His holo'd image rippled, then went silent as he barked fresh orders into his headset. Whatever those orders were, they were secured enough for his sync link to block the sound.

Around the Hall holos shifted to focus on the grim sterility of the Streikern image. Now or never. Jezekiah targeted each world in turn. "Johann Petrovich accused me of treason on the grounds my treaty threatened the safety of the Commonwealth. Thanks to his efforts–" he jerked his chin at Letticia "- and those of my sister, that treaty remains no more than a dream. And what is the result? Now Streiker itself is under the very attack I sought to prevent. Worse, none of us are safe now. Not Streiker, not Pandar, not Derakht. Most especially not Home World. Because Home World will be the next to pay the price of Streiker's errors. We will be the next to die."

He balled his Ring hand into a fist, held it up. It glared hot enough to force every Protector except Octavian to shield eyes. "I asked Pandar, now I ask all of you: where is the profit in annihilation? Can any of you imagine I would betray my own world?" He gave them a moment to let the nervousness in their murmurs register. Prayed desperately that somehow Kip could manage to hold Letticia's attention just one minute longer. "Call the vote, Streiker! Decide now – where does the guilt lie? Is attempting to save the Commonwealth the act of a traitor?"

Sync itself lurched, making the illusory star field of the Hall spin. Outside, something heavy boomed against the doors. The echo rolled across the Hall.

On the podium Letticia and Teufelsman jumped in unison. The rumble coalesced into the sound of voices. Voices mingled with the spat and clatter of weapons.

The doors crashed open. The infinity of the Hall shrank to dull gray walls as a long shaft of light from the outside corridor destroyed the illusion of infinity, turned the glory of the Commonwealth Council to a series of pale moving pictures on concrete walls. Jezekiah knew by the way Keiko's eyes lit that Strongarm had stalked into the Hall.

On the Protector's dais Teufelsman slid away from Letticia's chair toward the Protector's entrance now visible behind the dais. Cold light haloed his outline when the door opened. He scrambled backward, hands out and up. Brown-skinned men in red shorts jogged past the podium behind him, laser rifles at the ready. And aimed at the podium.

Letticia grabbed at Teufelsman's arm when he bumped into the Protector's chair. He shook her off without a glance. Then turned and vaulted off the platform.

Jezekiah did not see Keiko move, but she was there to block Teufelsman when he reached the floor. Her kick caught him in the groin. He doubled over, but managed to keep his feet. Staggering back he groped in his jacket pocket, pulled a needler free. Keiko kicked it out of his hand. Bone crunched where her knuckled backhand struck his cheek. The glow of the dragon's breath gave Teufelsman's skin a golden sheen when she raised her hand again. She slapped him once, flat-palmed, and the smell of sizzling skin lent body to his terrified shriek.

Teufelsman came up in a vicious kick that forced Keiko to jackknife away. Whirling, he stumbled for the door. And directly into Strongarm's taloned backhand.

For a moment Teufelsman seemed frozen in shock. Then blood bubbled down his chin. He sank to his knees, clawing at the red mess spilling out of his torso.

Strongarm wiped his talons on the Aryan's hair, streaking the white-blond head with red. Swinging the battle axe off his shoulder Strongarm stepped up beside Jezekiah to face the Council. The stars rippled in his wake as Council members instinctively backed their holos out of range. Only his ashen pallor bespoke the toll getting this far had taken on him. "You better be done, Van Buren. We're just about out of time." The way he fixed eyes on Keiko said the rest.

"Almost." He held out his hand, summoning Keiko safely back to his side. She started to obey. Then stopped, halfway to him, eyes locked on Strongarm. He saw her shiver, *felt* what it cost her to keep her word. He willed it out of mind. He was not about to lose Keiko now. Yanking his hand out of the link,

Jezekiah stepped between them. He kept a hand on Keiko's shoulder, pulled her with him gently back to the defendant's podium with him when he sync'd in again.

Only something had gone wrong. This time sync carried no sense of falling. Rather the link shot acid waves of cold nausea through him. He willed down a rush of bile, forced himself to think through it, track the fear back to the source. Wasn't hard to find. One glance at the Protector's dais told him where that was. Sync had fed Letticia's sick terror to the entire Council. It was the final proof he needed. He should be relieved, exultant. Yet the impact of her fear simply left him heartsick. He heard it, knew they all heard it, in his voice. "Call the vote, Streiker."

"You can't!" Letticia finally collected enough of her wits to point at Jezekiah. Her mouth worked helplessly a moment before she got the words out. "You don't understand! He killed Mother!"

The stars themselves seemed to hiss at the Council members' collective intake of breath. Around the holo'd circle, a dozen Protectors focused laser blue eyes on Letticia.

"My, my. Interesting you should only bring such a charge up now, what?" Octavian stroked a probing pink tendril thoughtfully. Alone among the Council, his clear blue gaze fixed on Jezekiah. "Yet it does rather leave the treason charge open, what?"

"I can prove it!" Letticia sank back into the sync chair. Space itself seemed to ripple with her desperation. "Look!"

A cloud formed in the center of the Hall. The cloud contracted, settled into a holo of Mother's sunlit office. Mother herself stood behind her desk, looking thunderous. The familiar red-gold curl dangled lose at her brow. The sight wrenched a gasp of misery from Jezekiah before he could stop it.

The angle shifted. Jezekiah sat in one of the leather chairs facing the desk, sweat glistening his forehead. He broke sync abruptly. Face contorted in rage, he stalked around the desk, wrapped his hands around Mother's throat. And slowly squeezed her life out.

Even knowing it for a lie the sight of it froze Jezekiah's mind and soul together. He'd lost. There was no refuting those hideous images, not without Kip. And Kip must have failed. The very fact Letticia could still wind NetMind into such a travesty of the truth proved it.

He felt Keiko wriggle against his embrace. He clutched her tighter, clinging to her, to his last refuge. Looked up only when he heard Strongarm's growl at his shoulder.

The Lupan leaned on the tall handle of his battle axe. He fixed Jezekiah with a hunter's grin, managed to force words out through the growl. "Tell me you love her, Van Buren. And you had damned well better scent honest on it."

"I love her." Sync picked the admission up. Fed the Council the sure knowledge that he loved a Registered killer, a convicted Ho Tong op. He'd handed Letticia the one thing she had not thought up for herself: a motive to make her charge seem real. His link tabulated the evidence accumulating against him, fed him the Council members' re-calculated alliances.

"Done, then." Strongarm slumped against the battle axe. His ears drooped, the great amber eyes closing in exhaustion. With visible effort he pulled himself straight, turned to face the assembled Council.

"Flat teeth! Listen and learn wisdom!" Weak as he was, Strongarm's voice still raised echoes enough to shut the Family up. "Each of you wears a ring as symbol of your power. Your Ring dies with you. Is that true?"

"Really, old boy, I don't see-"

Strongarm's roar silenced even Octavian. Around the Hall, red-gold heads nodded eager assent when he swept his amber gaze over them. "Know then: If I thought Van Buren guilty of matricide I would have killed him myself. But I was with him on the far side of this island when his Ring came to life. The holo you have seen is a lie."

"Major Domo!" Letticia had finally found her voice. She'd found confidence, too. The sick fear faded out of sync. "Report: is the foregoing a true and accurate report of the Protector' murder?"

It took the major domo many seconds too long to answer. When it did, it used audio as well. "It is a true and accurate report, Mistress."

"Well, then, isn't it obvious?" Letticia leaned back in the chair, smirking. "The dog is simply doing his master's bidding."

Silence answered. Silence, while sync lit up like tiny novas as the Family re-calc'd odds and profit lines. Silence, while Kaitin ibn Bengal fought his way closer to Earth. He'd lost, utterly and finally-

Your lordship? Dammit, your lordship, wake up! Kip's voice, through sync.

Kip? The shock of the big man's voice shattered Jezekiah's brooding despair.

I can get you in, your lordship. Don't know how long I can keep you there- The sentence ended in a burst of static.

So sorry, brother dear. Looks like your precious Marsden won't be able to rescue you after all.

Fire shot through his fingers where they touched the link. The force of it knocked Jezekiah out of sync, sent him staggering back clutching his Ring hand. The link sparked. A gray plume of acrid smoke curled up from it.

No one could rescue them now. He realized, dimly, that Letticia was speaking. On audio again. "Well, then, JP. Don't you think you really ought to call the vote?"

All the fury and sorrow and loss coalesced. Jezekiah dropped his mental guards, opened his will and soul to the Ring. Let the bitter, diamond torrent of pure, raw power that was the Ring flood into his very essence. Surprising, how little time it took. When he looked up, he met the dozen cold, blue reflections of himself. He lifted his Ring hand high. The stars of the Commonwealth faded beneath the golden flare of Earth's own sun. "Major Domo!"

Nothing. The silence stretched gut-wrenchingly lone. Around the Hall, shadows shifted across a haloed stars.

"An admirable attempt," Letticia's chuckle was edged in hysteria. "I told you. No one can rescue you now, brother dear."

Out of sync he could only see Omar in pantomime, but it looked like Derakht's impish Protector had just opened a fresh round of bets. Judging from the expressions on the betting cousins, the odds were not in his favor.

Letticia raised her voice triumphantly. "Major domo! The former Heir Jezekiah Van Buren stands charged with the assassination of our Protector! Arrest him!"

Silence. Then something inside the defendant's podium burst in a shower of sparks.

"Gob that shit." Kip Marsden's voice thundered across the Hall.

"Kip!"

"The Ring did it, your lordship," Kip's disembodied voice answered. "But the little bitch has a lock on–"

"Forget it!" Jezekiah pointed at Letticia. The Ring created a light display that flicked Octavian's eyes to white and made the other Protectors shield their own. "Kip! Major Domo! Protector's override! Show us the actual events. Unedited."

"You got it, your lordship. Full viz – now!"

The cloud image of Mother's office reformed. Only this time the scene split. This time NetMind melded the feed from Letticia's own major domo side by side to those final, awful moments of Mother's death.

The cloud image flickered at last. The images ended. "No-o-o-o! "It's a lie! It's all a lie!" Letticia's shriek seemed to bounce back from the holos of the Council. She got nothing back except a dozen cold blue death stares.

So, then. Jezekiah let his hand drop. "Now. Call the vote, Johann Petrovich. Do you still think me guilty of treason?"

For a heart-shredding moment JP simply scowled. Then – "No. That will not be necessary." He filed his seal on the Council register, lifted his head to the Family. "Streiker withdraws the charge."

With a shriek, Letticia flung herself out of the chair. She hurled down the steps, arms outstretched. Running for Strongarm.

Keiko lifted her hand, stars at the ready. Jezekiah swung her aside. Mistake. Stupid, hideous, fatal mistake. He realized it even as the stars flashed harmlessly past Letticia's head. Strongarm lifted his hand, palm up, the cilia within it desperately alive.

She was too fast, too far away for Jezekiah stop her. He was still three steps too far to catch her when Letticia lunged for the Lupan's arms.

And bounced. Strongarm dropped at the last moment, took the impact of Letticia's body on his shoulder. Rebound knocked Letticia onto her buttocks, sent her skidding spraddle-legged across the floor. Keiko caught her before she could regain her feet. She hauled her upright, howling, with an arm twisted high behind her back.

Jezekiah kept Keiko clear of Strongarm with a gesture. "Why? You could've had her, had the treaty, Earth, all of it."

"Had what? That?" Strongarm flipped an ear in Letticia's direction. He sagged against the battle axe, but there was no surrender in his voice. "Better a clean death than a living nightmare."

And suddenly the world erupted around them. Beneath his knees the floor hiccupped. A thundering explosion made holo'd star fields wink out, leaving only dull gray walls where the Milky Way had been. Visuals kicked back in a moment later on a string of Kip's invective that earned a whistle of admiration from Omar.

"Kip, patch a line through–"

"Already on it, your lordship." The Milky Way vanished behind a gray mist. The mist brightened, coalesced.

Greetings from the Lupan Dominion. Kaitin ibn Bengal bared a ruby-tipped fang in a snarl that triggered Net defenses across the Commonwealth. The silken robes were gone, replaced by the polished casing of battle armor. Behind him, wolf-eared crewmen in combat suits sat station around *Khali*'s bridge. *Accept one's compliments on thy defenses, Van Buren. Thy Admiral Yakamoto even now continues to harry our flanks.*

His golden gaze slid past Jezekiah to Strongarm. His round, white ears drooped seeming to pull his chin down with them. When he spoke it was in Lobish, though sync put it on automatic translation. *One rejoices to find thee alive, Brother-in-law. There is yet time. One will send a shuttle for thee and thy Bird.*

Strongarm shook his head, though he managed a tired smile. "Wouldn't make it, Kait. Pick up Bird." He swung his great head around to lock eyes on Jezekiah. "And her chosen. Get them both off world before you blow it."

"No. That won't be necessary." Jezekiah did not believe he could speak the words even as his lips formed them. Did not believe any human heart could survive the wrenching agony of it, a psychic pain so intense it pounded at his ears, drummed out the sound of Kaitin's answer. Drowned everything except the sound of his own footsteps as he made the terrible trek across the floor. "Keiko. *Ku'u ipo.*" It was the last time he would ever dare call her his darling. Somehow he managed to smile down into her frown. Took her dragon hand

and pressed it to his lips. "I'll handle Letticia from here. Go to Strongarm. He needs you."

At first she only blinked. Then the realization sank in. He hadn't thought it was possible to hurt any worse than he did. But the joy that lit her face nearly drove him to his knees. "Go, dammit. I release you." He couldn't even speak, only whisper.

Keiko shoved Letticia into his arms hard enough to knock him back a step. Then she was gone, whooping, hurtling into Strongarm's embrace.

He had barely sense enough to keep his grip on Letticia. He barely had wit enough to hear Letticia's shrieked obscenities. He felt his dreams, his hopes, his future dribble out into nothingness when Keiko took Strongarm's hand between hers. Strongarm dropped to one knee, placed his palm gently on Keiko's throat. Jezekiah heard Keiko's joyous gasp as the Touch melded the Lupan's soul to hers. Heard the sob in his own throat as Keiko molded herself to Strongarm's embrace, as the embrace deepened in a lover's kiss.

Jezekiah closed his eyes, did what he could to shove his despair into the darkest recess of his soul before he turned to meet Kaitin's holo'd image. "Call off your attack, Kaitin. Earth has honored the marriage contract."

Alas, one fears you have sacrificed in vain, Jezekiah Van Buren. Kaitin's golden gaze found Strongarm and Keiko, turned sorrowful. *We have spoken of this before. The women of our Parliament will not bind the treaty with nothing more than a mixed-Type natural. Not even one from Home World.*

"Not even for a Maker?"

There are no Makers any more, Van Buren, as you yourself have said. Merely mixed-Type naturals.

"I lied." Jezekiah fixed eyes on Kaitin, raised his voice to the stars. "Kip. Link in the Admiral's feed. Stat."

A moment later Admiral Yakamoto's battle suited image coalesced beside Kaitin's. The viz cam focus was too tight to show his surroundings. The fact he kept his suit faceplate down said enough. Even through his face plate the snarl he aimed at Kaitin would have done justice to a Lupan.

Milord Protector. The Admiral's gaze shot past Jezekiah to Keiko and Strongarm. His lips hardened into a dangerous line.

Jezekiah cleared his throat, drawing the Admiral's attention back to himself. "It seems our friend Kaitin ibn Bengal believes the original species no longer exists. Would you care to correct that error, Admiral Yakamoto?"

Milord – The man spoke without inflection. That single word was protest enough.

One more betrayal to add to his collection. He couldn't afford to think about it, not now. Jezekiah locked his working mask in place, merely lifted a brow. "Tell them, Admiral. Tell them who you are."

"As my Protector commands." Within his armor Matsuo Yakamoto pulled himself taller. Whatever he felt, his voice betrayed nothing. "Milord Protectors: you all know that status as SamuraiType is earned, not born. The name Yakamoto was granted me upon my completion of the Samurai Type trial. My birth name was -" His eyes settled on Keiko. "Ho."

The Admiral settled into a thousand yard stare, eyes focused on his past while the Council members checked sync for significance. "I was not of Grandfather Ho's own family, merely of his clan. But I was Tong born and Tong raised, the natural son of natural parents." His voice broke, eyes closing.

"As your wife, Liliuokelani Ho was the natural daughter of Grandfather Ho." Jezekiah forced the words out through the burn in his own throat. He swept a hand back toward Keiko. He did not dare look. He was too likely to throw himself at her, try to pry her out of Strongarm's embrace. "As your daughter is the natural daughter of natural parents."

He spread his hands, encompassing Keiko and Strongarm in the Ring's golden gleam. "Lord Kaitin, allow me to present Keiko Kaahumana Yakamoto Ho. Descendent on her mother's side from the house of Kamehameha the Great. A living descendant of the goddess Pele herself. The truest of true humans." He lifted a brow, called up a wry tone from reserves of strength he hadn't known he possessed. "I think your Parliament just might find her an acceptable match."

For a long moment Kaitin stroked his mustaches, nose twitching. Then he pursed lips, clicked talons at a wolf-eared crewman. Around Khali's bridge weapons boards went dark. He lifted a lip to expose the ruby-tipped fang. "It seems, Jezekiah Van Buren, that we have a treaty."

Unshed tears blurred Jezekiah's vision. He rubbed a palm hard across his eyes. Blinked up to realize the Council members had risen. One after another, they raised their Ring hands. Acknowledging him as the new Protector of Earth. Oddly, it was JP whose sad smile told him they knew, each and every one of them, the price he'd paid for it.

He brushed the ashes of his soul into the dark little dungeon in the back of his mind, put on his working smile. Somehow, he would find a way to live with it.

THE END

CPSIA information can be obtained at www.ICGtesting.com
Printed in the USA
BVOW03s1706290414

351785BV00001B/18/P

9 781927 559246